Z
LETTER

Letter Z
Chronicles of Peace and War
A Research Novel

by Oleksandr Sambrus

Translated from Ukrainian by Svetlana Payne

Proofread by Jack Monro

OLEKSANDR SAMBRUS

LETTER Z

Chronicles of Peace and War

Translated from the Ukrainian by Svetlana Payne

GLAGOSLAV PUBLICATIONS

Contents

The first-person narration in this book conveys the point of view of the fictional protagonist. All his friends, relatives and associates are, likewise, a work of the author's imagination. Views expressed by these characters represent their personal subjective opinions.

In writing this book the author used the following materials: statements / declarations / thoughts / comments made by Ukrainian, global, Russian, and Belarusian statesmen, politicians, military and religious leaders, ambassadors, press secretaries, advisers, military experts, et al. Statements /declarations / thoughts / comments of non-Ukrainian (in particular, Russian and Belarusian) individuals have been translated into English. The author is not responsible for absolute accuracy.

To ensure continuity, consistency and clarity of the narrative, the above-mentioned materials have been slightly edited and abridged. The occasional failure to quote specific sources stems from the necessity to maintain the momentum of narration (and therefore shall constitute no grounds for appeal). On no account has the author sought to reduce the cohesiveness or intent of the pronouncements or distort their context (i.e. no wrongful or unlawful actions have been undertaken). The author particularly disclaims responsibility for possible regrettable imprecisions / errors in presenting the factual components of this work of fiction. Songs / poems / verses have been composed by the author himself, excepting works of folklore and works specifically named in the text. All rights for those compositions are reserved as are the rights for the novel in its entirety. When quoting from the novel, referencing is mandatory.

Dedicated to the 'brotherly' Russian people
who have invaded my country[1]

<hr>

[1] **Brotherly people**: a political cliché, a pupular idiom or ideological trope used in launching and managing political and ideological campaigns in imperial and post-imperial states. Today, it is still common coinage in Russia inasmuch as Russia is intent on conquering her neighbours and overpowering neighbouring nations.
This ideologeme is firmly planted even in the minds of some prominent Europeans.
On 15 April 2022, in Rome, during the Good Friday festivities, according to the script created by the Vatican, the Cross, at one of the Stations, was carried by Albina, a Russian girl, and a Ukrainian girl by the name of Irene, thus symbolising 'reconciliation' between the two peoples.

'These are two brotherly nations, and I believe that in the nearest future friendship and love between them shall be demonstrated many times over,' said the Russian girl, Albina.

'We hope that there may still be a turn towards peace, and what will change, before anything else, will be relations between our countries. We are brother nations, we are ever so close,' said Irene, the Ukrainian.

The festive procession, torches and all, returned to the ancient arena of the Coliseum, for the first time after the Covid pandemic. A thousands-strong crowd of pilgrims and tourists held up lit candles while Pope Francis, under his canopy, was seated on a raised platform from where he could survey the crowds.

A senior figure in the Ukrainian Greek-Catholic Church later commented on this initiative from the Vatican: 'Gestures symbolising reconciliation between Russia and Ukraine will only become meaningful after the war is over and those guilty of crimes against humanity have been justly condemned.'

Practically at the same time, Emmanuel Macron, the French president, referred in a TV interview to Russians and Ukrainians as 'brotherly nations' – and this notwithstanding a many-months-long full-scale war unleashed by Russia on Ukraine. All this notwithstanding the wronged nation perceiving such rhetoric as an insult.

December 2021. 'Your Country Is Cobbled Together from the Off-Cuts of the Two Empires!'

Taras and I, we were among the first to arrive – came at a gallop and scored some seats in the best row.

Right on our heels, Liubchik breezed in too. 'A starlet of local significance', according to Taras. I disagree wholeheartedly – I believe Liubchik can attain the municipal level without even trying… True, she dearly craves to be in the centre of everyone's attention – if only with the outfits she normally chooses. A somewhat boyish body type definitely helps in this uphill struggle. On the other hand, going is tough at times but Liubchik gives it her all…

She would only ever be seen in pants. Goes without saying, nothing but avant-garde would do, but today she really excelled herself… Imagine if you can – one trouser leg some funny rusty colour, the other one yellowish. Provocative, of course, but there was some funny sense of measure there, too – the colours muted, not a complete eye-sore. Then there was this belt – black and cracked from time and wear. Perhaps bequeathed to her by her dear granny? Not a thin job, either, but a broad affair, some fifteen centimetres-wide at least.

'What-ye-say, boyzzz?' she twirled in delight in front of us.

The rusty-coloured leg got extended to one side. And back. Then the yellow one – sideways. Back. Peng? *A la mode.* Stylish. Just the thing for the young ones…

'What's there to say? Freaking awesome! Quality vintage!' – I needled her slightly but hastened to sweeten the jibe: 'A knockout!'

'You'd be top of the charts in any hang-out! No doubt 'bout it!' piped in Taras.

Then, there was Liubchik's hair style… Pure avant-garde, too! Half her skull practically shaved clean, the other – festooned with tufts. And her mane – quite something as well! On the left, it curtained the entire half of her face, and her eye – the poor thing probably never saw the light of day… I tried to get a rise from her:

'Look here, gal, can you even see who you're talking to?'

'Partially...' her standard riposte. Then again, really, why bother inventing something new? 'But you, Stinger, don't you get your knickers in a twist, my other eye clocks it all, and how...'

She sat down next to us, pulled out of her cosmetics bag a little mirror and the lipstick and, concentrating on her reflection, set about laboriously applying colour to her babyish lips...

'Are you totally nuts?' Taras was appalled. 'Are the girls with lips still on the agenda? You are what, fresh from the evening Khreschatyck?'[2]

She replied, matter-of-factly:

'You all for stamping out the sprouts of modernity? Shock-horror! Last century! What's with this country – any new initiative is trampled underfoot, right in the bud!'

Oops, dear Taras... Got taken down a peg? Enjoy, it could've been worse...

Luckily just then Arkady sidled up, saved the situation. This very fact was already to his credit for he hates showing up anywhere ahead of time – 'Me? Hanging about, waiting? No way!' As for Arkady, he only wears branded clobber, no point trying to describe his get-up.

Just then Alka had arrived too. She's not the one for making a splash with her fashions. Everything about her is down-to-earth and laconic, she won't bore herself with a usual 'How's it going?' or some such crap.

'Hi!'

'Hi!'

Our Alka is more of a traditionalist, perhaps even a borderline conservative. It's beyond belief – she wears her hair pleated in a braid! True, it doesn't reach down to her waistline – as used to be the case with celebrated beauties in God knows which century. Her plait was of medium length. And here she was – a picture of concentration, leafing through her notepad, looking for something. Truth be told, Alla and I – we'd been on the 'brink' of something, then it all somehow cooled off but now things were sort of picking up again. OK, we'll live and see.

Aha, finally here they were too – Spyridon and Bolik, both out of breath, unmistakable sound of Deep Purple's 'Highway Star' blasting forth from their headphones. Must've cranked it up to some serious volume if we could hear it all too!

Spyridon's earpiece was held to his ear, while Bolik, accordingly, pressed the other one to his. Those two have a clear-cut division of labour: Spyridon chooses a hit and Bolik calibrates the volume.

....

[2]   **Khreschatyk**: the main street of Kyiv, the capital of Ukraine. (Hereinafter, unless specifically stated, notes are provided by the translator.)

'Phew! We missed much?' – both rocking to the rhythm of their record.

'Nick of time… Another minute and we'd be yielding seats to common fresh-ers, seeing as they are about to launch a proper offensive…' hissed Arkady in reply.

'Commoners,' in his mind, are first- and second-year students. We are year five[3], so, automatically, the 'nobles'.

'So, which muzak today gets more respect among the rock crowd? Classic stuff? Glam-rock? Hard stuff? Or perhaps industrial, God help me?' Arkady wasn't ready to let go.

'He-he, the *garage* type,' I joined in with a little dig of my own.

'Perhaps, a nice quote came up from some place?' Arkady kept ploughing on. 'Or you dug up something interesting?'

'Indeed, we have.' Spyridon beamed. 'From Jimmy Page, that's Led Zeppelin. He says: "I'm just looking for an angel with a broken wing"…'

'I agree here,' Bolik sprang up, happy to intercept the initiative. 'All of us… well, it's not impossible, innit? – have an angel… And then – bang – and his wing gets broken…'

'Christ Almighty! Rescue me, bros!' Arkady rolled his eyes upwards, throw-ing up his hands. 'Hold me tight or I won't survive all this drama and collapse!'

He pulled a face and turned away.

'Turn it down, though… You'll frighten the crowd,' that was Alla, trying to reason with Spyridon and Bolik. 'Especially, the commoners.'

'Let them listen,' Spyridon disengaged himself from his earpiece. 'Rock is a phenomenal thing. Not like all this tired pop crap!'

'Rock,' Bolik joined in, 'it's the nerve of our times! It holds up a mirror to our beastly reality, not like some glammed-up tosh! As such, quite good for the commoners!'

'Who's arguing?' Taras chuckled. 'It's just way too loud!'

Arkady turned back, facing them again, raising his finger, clearly, about to deliver a short speech – that's his speciality.

'Ah well… Goes without saying, blasted history is forever repeating itself… Take Roman Empire – what happened there? It kept losing its hold, little by little, till some bloody plebs – barbarians, in short – did it in, once and for all.' He turned towards Spyridon and Bolik: 'Still, esteemed rockers, do lower your volume. You are in a public place – that's for starters. And secondly, our commoners may get such a high from your music that they'll just move in and finish us off, the lot of us…'

They took the hint, and didn't just turn the volume down but killed the record entirely.

....

[3] Typically, a master's degree requires five years of study.

It's worth mentioning that Spyridon and Bolik are die-hard veteran metal rockers. Perhaps been like that from childhood. 'Our metal is from God...' – they say so themselves. Dunno, perhaps it's true. Whatever the case, their get-up is in strict compliance with whatever fashion dictates to 'metalists': short studded leather jackets on top, tattered trousers below, and boots – must be three kilos apiece. One would need some well-toned-up calves, to wear those. Massive signet rings on nearly every finger. Should there be a bust-up – which, allegedly, does happen, from time to time, in their world – these rings must come in very handy as a defence weapon. Our rector, should he ever clap his eyes on them, gets immediately crippled by a severe migraine. Still, they are quite considerate, in their own way – do their damnedest to stay out of his sight. Thing is, the rector – that's before succumbing to his migraine – can lay into them like a man possessed. What's the bloody point – now, in the final year of studies when the end is nigh – to look for grief?

As for Taras and me... Against such a colourful background we both look like some poor relatives – no quirky traits to offer, and usually kitted out in regular casuals...

Sure enough, the audience at our *alma mater*, the Institute of Cinematography, was filled to bursting point. That day, we all came because of a very important lecture – to be delivered by the Professor of Modern History Dashkevych. There were even crowds from other universities and colleges – who also got in on the act. Small wonder, though – the situation in the country was extremely tense, one couldn't relax even if one tried... For several months now Russia had been concentrating her troops on our borders. In response to all enquiries, they invariably came up with a standard excuse – those were training exercises; or sometimes even with something boorish, like: 'On our own territory we do whatever we please.'

So here we all were, sitting, waiting...

'Some nice rellies you've got, man...' Taras gave me a wink.

Oh no, he was about to set off... I could understand it, though, what with everyone being so anxious... And so Taras got onto his pet subject:

'What a mighty name they've given you – Kiril! Your surname is really cool, too – Zhalovaha![4] Boy, does it reflect your pernickety nature! 'Tis like an early warning for the unsuspecting – don't trifle with this dude! Or else prepare to be stung. You haven't got your nickname for nothing – Stinger. Come on, you must've stashed some vitriol – to aim at this well-touted lecture? After all, this invited professor is a celebrity...'

....

4   This Ukrainian surname comprises two words: '*жало*' (pronounced *zhAlo*) – stinger; and '*вага*' (pronounced '*vAha*') – weight.

'As if we didn't have our own professors!' that from a gruff Arkady.

'Guys, stop bickering,' Alla chimed in. 'The recent developments – they do call for a fresh eye.'

'Come on, let him take the piss! Stinger, do say something fun…' Liubchik gave her fringe a resolute shake, suddenly equally keen for me to offer something 'spicy'.

Crikey, the way they were laying into me… Then again, the atmosphere was electric, affecting us all, even if we'd all been on edge lately.

To tell the truth, I didn't feel like wisecracking. What if this professor would tell us something sensible? Why should I deride him in advance?

Meanwhile Taras seemingly forgot all about me, busy typing something into his mobile. Must've been a significant message to his recent love interest – I wasn't even sure what her name was. Perhaps Olga. I only knew she was from the Art Institute.

As for Spyridon and Bolik, having had an earful of rock, they now were quiet – something to be grateful for… Theirs is a somewhat weird tandem: Spyridon a real beanpole while Bolik, on the contrary, a shortie. Still, something does keep them together… Perhaps it's those scripts they are writing for the documentaries? Even if they do pepper those with insertions more appropriate to feature films. In short, their output is quite a mix.

Frankly speaking, our ability to joke had recently been on the wane. Small wonder, though, the situation was hardly conducive, quite the reverse. For several months now we'd all lived in a state of anxious presentiment: would Putin attack us or not? My lord… What had the world come to…

Americans keep repeating it, over and over again, like some mantra: get ready for an attack! They even mentioned a provisional date. The American attitude, of course, was a serious indicator, they don't use such predictions lightly. Then again, the Brits told us the same. When all is said and done, their intelligence services do rank highly in the world…

But as for our president – he insisted on the opposite. Enough, he said, of this scaremongering! We've got intelligence information from our own sources. Those rumours you disseminate bring about nothing but panic, they erode our economy. As it is, investments are already leaving our country…

So, how to work it out? Who made more sense about any of it?

'Quiet!' suddenly, the entire audience was shushing. 'He's here! He's here!'

Indeed, the professor was already making his way into the auditorium – determined, confident. In his wake – the rector, our Department Chair, and two more characters… Assistants? Interns? Who could tell, but the procession looked impressive. Quite a spectacular entrance.

The professor placed his folder on the lectern.

'Hello everybody! Today we shall talk about the most extraordinary events unfolding in our world.'

He delivered this extremely forcefully. The audience fell silent immediately.

'Let's make a brief excursion into history and recall the situation in Europe as it existed after the First World War. From the geo-political point of view, several empires – once powerful and important players on the global arena – suddenly crumbled and collapsed. Almost overnight! Several new states sprang up on the territory once belonging to the Russian and Astro-Hungarian Empires. The map of Europe went through a radical change. Whilst prior to the war there had been 23 states, now there were 34! Peoples who had been, over years and even centuries, fighting for their independence, finally achieved statehood. So, dear audience, these are facts from history.'

The professor clasped his palms together and carried on.

'Just then, from under the ruins of the two empires – Russia and Austro-Hungary – emerged an independent state of Ukraine. Worth noting, Ukraine was among the biggest in Europe – both in terms of territory and population. Let me briefly remind you: after the Provisional Government was overthrown in Petrograd by the Bolsheviks, in Kyiv in November 1917 there appeared the Ukrainian People's Republic, with Professor Hrushevsky at its head.[5] Within a year followed unification of the UPR with the West-Ukrainian Republic... The Bolsheviks, however, intervened yet again: in December 1917, they established their power in Kharkiv. Even though a mere month earlier, only 10% of the electorate had voted in their favour in the election into the Constituent Assembly, ... But what was Lenin's *modus operandi*? He pursued a very cunning policy. On the one hand – as decreed by the provisions of the Treaty of Brest-Litovsk[6] – he recognised the right of the Ukrainian people to

....

[5]   **Mykhailo Hrushevsky** (1866–1934): Ukrainian academician, politician, historian and statesman who was one of the most important figures in the Ukrainian national revival of the early 20th century, leader of the pre-revolution Ukrainian national movement, and head of the Central Rada (Ukraine's parliament in 1917–1918).

[6]   The Treaty of **Brest-Litovsk**: a separate peace treaty signed on 3 March 1918 between Soviet Russia and the Central Powers. It recorded Russia's defeat and its exit from the First World War.

Earlier, the Central Rada had appealed to Germany and Austria-Hungary with a request for military assistance against Bolshevik aggression. This treaty was signed on 9 February 2018 likewise in Brest-Litovsk. In exchange for military assistance, the Ukrainian People's Republic undertook to supply Germany and Austria-Hungary (where there was a threat of famine) with large batches of food and raw materials. Allied troops stepped into Ukraine almost immediately. On 2 March 1918 they entered Kyiv.

independence. But on the other – what are you talking about? To accept the loss of Ukraine in its entirety?'

One of the assistants clicked a button on the control, the curtains slid apart, now displaying a large map of Eastern Europe.

'The difficult times did not stop there. In early February of 1918, a treaty was signed between the UPR and the Central Powers, under which they recognised the sovereignty of the UPR and the Central Rada.[7] The UPR applied for protection against the Bolsheviks. The German and Austrian forces entered Ukraine and shortly re-established the UPR's jurisdiction on territory stretching as far as its eastern borders. For a time, order and stability were reinstated...'

'Germans... and order...' someone couldn't stop themselves, 'can't have one without the other...'

The professor made a pause. He could, of course, rebuff the arrogance, but didn't. Taras and I looked at each other – perhaps, that's what he was after: a lecture conducted as a sort of immediate exchange with the audience?

'Hmm,' the professor cleared his throat. 'Since we are on the subject of the Germans... Let me share this interesting factoid with you. The order is all well and good but survival is of primary importance... The German soldiers, starved after their experiences at the Western front, dug into the local food... And do you know what they were after most of all? You wouldn't believe it – pork fat was an absolute favourite. And all this because their metabolism had been deprived of fat during the three – or even more – years of war...'

'Ha-ha! That's truly curious!' came another voice from the amphitheatre.

'Yes, one can tell many stories about this period... Later on, the German Occupational Authority fell out with the Central Rada over their dissatisfaction with the feeble stance of those socialists. Instead, they decided to put in a hard-line dictatorship, and at the end of April in 1918 Pavlo Skoropadsky, a descendant of Hetman Ivan Skoropadsky,[8] came to power. Skoropadsky was himself pronounced Hetman at the so-called 'congress of grain growers'[9]... Let

....

[7]   The **Central Rada** (the Central Council) of Ukraine, established on 17 March 1917 as a revolutionary representative institution, decided to establish the Ukrainian People's Republic and proclaimed its independence. Subsequently, it was the state's highest legislative body.

[8]   **Hetman:** a political title used in Central and Eastern Europe, historically assigned to military commanders.

[9]   On 29 April 1928 the All-Ukrainian Congress of Grain-Growers in Kyiv (predominantly consisting of landowners and peasant landholders, about 7,000 delegates in total) taking advantage of the protracted crisis in the UPR's Central Rada and supported by the German occupational forces and the sympathetic attitude taken by affluent peasantry and Cossacks, pronounced Pavlo Skoropadsky, a former general in the Russian imperial army (who was at the same time pro-Ukrainian), Hetman.

me just say that the role played by the Germans in that brouhaha of ours was pivotal and far from straightforward. At the time, they were acting in Ukraine as sort of... "king makers". This is a separate and painful subject... However, look here. We are digressing from our main topic.'

The professor came up to the map.

'In the end, the Bolsheviks returned to Ukraine – they were forced out, yet again, while their managerial bodies were relocated to the Russian Kursk... The regimes in Ukraine kept alternating with lightning speed... So, while our politicians were sorting out their differences, Bolsheviks moved in, yet again, from the north, in January 1919. This time they did manage to proclaim Soviet power in Kharkiv. However, for some time the city was under the control of the White movement. Still, in December of that same year, 1919, the red commissars once more advanced, and this time they really came to stay. That's how Soviet power originated in Kharkiv and gradually started spreading out...'

'Hm... nice, innit?' I covered my mouth so that only our gang could hear me. 'The esteemed professor has built his lecture exclusively on the factual basis of modern history!!! Yet he could've recalled our glorious Cossack republic – the Zaporozhian Sich![10] The one that the fearful Russian Empress Ekaterina the Second got rid of...'

'Hush, Stinger!' Liubchik put me down. 'The last thing we need now is your wit.'

'W ell, when you're a professor yourself...' Alla joined the ranks, 'you'll be free to plan your lecture as you please.'

The professor went around his lectern.

'It has to be said,' he went on, 'that the Treaty of Versailles accommodated the demands put forward by the newly created states. Alas, with one exception: that of Ukraine. Its larger part – the Right and Left banks[11] – ended up, in fact, within the confines of its erstwhile colonial power which, at the time, meant Bolshevik Russia. As for its western territories, there was an idea to create a national Ukrainian entity upon the wreckage of the Austro-Hungarian Empire – perhaps, not so representative but still... Unquestionably, that would have been a step forward... Unfortunately, the Versailles meeting didn't agree, otherwise it would have meant re-carving the territories of several adjacent nations. In

....

[10] **Zaporozhian Sich:** a semi-autonomous polity and proto-state of Cossacks that existed in the 16th to 18th centuries.

[11] In 1667 Ukraine was partitioned along the Dnipro River: the west part, known as the Right Bank, reverted to Poland, while Russia was confirmed in its possession of the east, known as the Left Bank, together with Kyiv (which is actually located west of the river on the Right Bank). The arrangement was confirmed in 1686 by the Treaty of Eternal Peace between Poland and Russia.

which case all of them would have resolutely opposed the move. And that's how it came to be: Versailles, hereto dressing up in the mantle of democracy, cunningly bypassed the issue of granting the Ukrainian people – one of the largest ethnic groups in Europe – their statehood… Following all this, in July of 1919, the Entente Cordiale recognised the jurisdiction of Poland over Eastern Galicia.[12] It got worse. The Riga Treaty of 1921 ratified this decision: the territory of the Ukrainian People's Republic was divided between the USSR and Poland. [In March 1923 the Conference of Ambassadors of the Principal Allied and Associated Powers, based on the terms of the Riga Peace Treaty between the Soviet Russia and Poland, upheld the decision to make East Galicia part of Poland with the proviso that the Ukrainians be given autonomy (the Poles never implemented this decision)]. And in this fashion the division of Ukrainian territory between Poland, Czechoslovakia, Romania, and the USSR became final. Thus, Ukraine's age-old aspirations to sovereignty were doomed…

And then in 1922 the Bolsheviks announced the creation of the USSR, and therefore, Ukrainian Left- and Right Banks, already under their power, were made a constituent part under the name of the Ukrainian Soviet Socialist Republic, the UkSSR. No one, as per usual, asked for the people's opinion. And finally: in March of 1923 the Conference of Ambassadors of the Principal Allied and Associated Powers, based on the terms of the Riga Peace Treaty between the Soviet Russia and Poland, upheld the decision on making East Galicia part of Poland with a proviso of establishing autonomy for the Ukrainians (which was never implemented). And in this fashion the division of the Ukrainian territory between Poland, Czechoslovakia, Romania, and the USSR became final. The Ukrainians didn't get a chance to create an independent state of their own. However, there was one extremely important factor: the Soviet Union treaty enshrined the right of the union republics to secede!'

Taras and I exchanged impatient glances. It all sounds correct… Still, we'd like to hear something closer to home… On the other hand – how could you move forward without digging deeper into history?

The same assistant clicked his control again: the screen now showed two maps side by side – Europe before and after World War I.

'The Second World War broke out,' carried on the professor. 'Under the terms of the Molotov-Ribbentrop Pact, in 1939 the Polish segment of the Ukrainian territory became incorporated into the Soviet Ukraine. After the war the process went even further: the Soviet Ukraine received the remainder of what had been previously shared among other states. Thus, the territory was

---

[12]   The Entente Cordiale was signed in 1907 between Great Britain, France, and Russia to counter the threat posed by the Triple Alliance of Germany, Italy, and Austria-Hungary (also known as the Central states).

16

consolidated, even if in such a way. It's a different story that all of this took place within the Soviet Empire. In essence, Ukraine's new enlargement was purely a formality. Goes without saying that the civil rights for the local population were not even a subject for discussion... Meanwhile, in the forests of the Western Ukraine, members of the UIA turned to intrepid guerrilla warfare.[13] Please note that some of those units were still active in the early sixties... However, one can never win over a behemoth like the Soviet Union. Consequently, those endeavours aimed at national liberation failed. Long story short, it all ended up with us existing within this simulacrum of a state – an administrative-territorial unit called the Ukrainian Soviet Socialist Republic – all the way up to 1991. To tell the truth, all hopes for anything better were thus crushed, for what felt like forever...'

The professor made a pause and approached the map yet again.

'And then something happened that had been the subject of dreams, not hopes, not anymore. It's incredible but not a single intelligence service, not one Western analytical think tank ever could imagine the disintegration of the USSR! It's quite significant to remember that this 'colossus on the legs of clay' had been kept in existence by the 25-million-strong army of the Communist Party members! And not one among them came out into their street and cried out: what on earth is going on? Why we'd been living in such confidence and optimism for so many years and now what? Suddenly, it's all in ruins? Understandably, it's a huge subject and a separate matter, let's put it aside for now...'

The professor cleared his throat.

'And thus, the break-up happened momentarily but – note! – legitimately. After all, let's not forget that the Constitution of the Soviet Union provided for the rights of individual republics to secession! As regards Ukraine, the will of the people was further enhanced at the national referendum where 90% of those taking part voted in favour of independence, and the decree was passed by the Ukrainian parliament. So far so legal and substantiated. And that's what it felt and looked like over the course of many years. However, even now, even 30 years later, the tectonic consequences of that decomposition – the disappearance of that monster, the USSR – are still being felt. It is obvious nowadays, that the erstwhile motherland was gradually undermined by the "ulcer of imperialism" – there was no way it could reconcile itself to such a state of affairs! Naturally, for a while it mimicked democracy but eventually reverted to its filthy basics...'

The professor extended his hand towards the map.

....

[13]   The **Ukrainian Insurgent Army**: a Ukrainian paramilitary and partisan formation founded by the Organisation of Ukrainian Nationalists on 14 October 1942. It engaged in armed resistance against the Communist regime in Western Ukraine.

'And that's when barbaric things started happening… It transpired that the "rule of force',' as it existed in the times of both world wars, was still very much there. In April of 2008 the NATO summit was deliberating the issue of enabling Georgia and Ukraine to join their defence union. Yet Germany and France did their utmost to block such a decision! The culmination arrived during the in-camera session of the NATO-Russia Council. When the agenda moved to Ukraine, Putin flew into a rage. Turning to President Bush, he hissed contemptuously: "You do realise, George, what this Ukraine really amounts to? It isn't even a state! Part of its territory is, in essence, eastern Europe. While another part, and a significant one at that, has been *our gift to them*!" He then went with his transparent hints that should Ukraine be after all accepted into NATO, this so-called state will simply burst at the seams. In other words, that was a thinly veiled threat that Russia may consider annexation of Crimea and Eastern Ukraine. And then… Sort of, think of it…'

The professor stopped to draw breath and I saw my opening:

'Surely, to feel equal to "George", and also to look taller, he wears special soles inside his shoes…' I finally felt in my own element, and whispered, to our gang, what felt like a totally innocuous witticism. 'It happens to midgets… those who wear size-5 shoes but harbour Herculean ambitions…'

'Well, that's debateable,' Taras whispered back. 'Peter the Great was two metres tall but his feet were size 5 … This, by the way, is a very eloquent detail…'

'Hey, the two of you, Stinger, shut up!' Alla glowered at us. 'You, Taras, too! Some of us are trying to listen!'

'And that's how it all came to be,' the professor gave a sigh. 'And only thanks to the stance taken by several countries, primarily the Baltic states and Poland, it became possible to smooth this situation over. The summarising communiqué stated unequivocally that leaders of 26 states provided guarantees and undertook the responsibility of acceding Ukraine and Georgia into NATO!'

The professor stepped away from the map and turned to face the lectern.

'Let me reiterate: some bestial transformations are plaguing international agreements! After all, the topic under consideration was an attempt on a sovereign country, a founder and member of the UN since 1945! The country whose sovereignty and the right to secession was recognised even by the Soviet Constitution! Yet, the leaders of the main European countries continue yielding to the Russian President's blackmail! And all this on the continent tirelessly proclaiming the principles of democracy! The continent where large and small countries are allegedly enjoying equal rights, enshrined in important agreements and treaties! Finally, let's ask ourselves whether the Final Act of the Helsinki Accords of 1975 is translated into reality? It has, after all, confirmed such profound precepts as the inviolability of national frontiers in Europe. Also, equality of partner countries. And especially, human rights!'

The professor looked around the audience.

'Obviously, we all remember that Putin acted on his threat against Georgia. As for Ukraine – even more so. He keeps applying pressure in this direction and doesn't miss a single opportunity to declare that Ukraine has no historic rights to independence and sovereignty! In other words, the break-up of the Soviet Union is nonsense. An epic geopolitical catastrophe… A convoluted conflict of various political forces that has brought about creation of a 'fake state'! Allegedly, the claims put forward by Ukraine are nothing more than irresponsible political manoeuvring… Let me be absolutely frank: modern history has never seen such lawlessness!'

Professor Dashkevych grew silent but suddenly his face lit up with a mischievous smile.

'You know, Putin's evolution as regards this historical question is simply ridiculous! He even stated, once, at one of his press conferences, that Ukraine had been dreamt up by… Count Pototsky!'

The audience broke out in a murmur of indignation.

The professor carried on:

'Let me remind you. The Pototskys were the richest magnates in Ukraine. They owned hundreds of thousands of serfs. So, which one of them "dreamt up" the Ukrainians? Putin, of course, doesn't go into details, for his processing of the facts of history is… let's say, extremely arbitrary. And recently he insisted on something else… It turns out Ukraine was incidentally invented by Lenin when, in 1922, they were putting together the Soviet Union. As if Ukraine had never had a mighty – let's be more precise, powerful – movement for national liberation. As if there had never existed any other variants of the state formation! What glibness of the tongue – if that's what it's called. Nothing but a cynical shuffling of the ideas and facts of history. It's evidently as common as swindling at a gambling table. It's a pity but some people take it on trust, especially abroad where they know nothing about any of this and remember even less. However, initiating a historical discourse with the "master of the Kremlin"? Insanity. Although even school history books – if he even remembers they exist – say that a Kyivan Prince, Yuri Dolgorukiy,[14] was the founder

....

[14] **Yuri Dolgorukiy** ('Long Arm', c. 1099–1157): a prince of Rostov and Suzdal. He spent much of his life in internecine strife with other princes of Rus' for suzerainty over Kyivan Rus, which had been held by his father and his elder brother before him. Although he twice managed to hold Kyiv and ruled as 'Grand Prince of all Rus', his autocratic bearing and perceived foreign status made him unpopular with Kyivans, leading to his presumed poisoning and the expulsion of his son in 1157.

of Moscow! Let's remind ourselves that at the time when the Russian capital was only about to be built, numerous Orthodox cathedrals and trade quarters had already long since existed in ancient Kyiv. Yet, Putin the "historian" feels it's best to leave it all out, as if it's a glitch of memory…'

The professor pulled a handkerchief out of his pocket and wiped his brow.

'Meanwhile, there is no limit to Russian appetites, the whole thing is on the up and up. They are boring the world with this age-long trope: our country is allegedly cobbled together out of the off-cuts of the two erstwhile empires. Our northern neighbour is ready with a plethora of arguments. This hackneyed assertion that allegedly we are the territory 'defiled and usurped by nationalists and extremists" that must, finally, come into embrace of the "principal" nation!'

Someone cried out: 'Do they feel it's unfair that part of our population are ethnic Russians?'

'Does one feel injustice when some of your compatriots ended up in another country? Come on, each European country has its national minorities – what of it? If we were to dig deeper into this question we could end up, yet again, on a slippery slope leading to the situations that had provoked the First and the Second World Wars. After all there were agreements put in place after the most recent meat-grinding experience: enough! No more trifling with the frontiers, whatever the previous history of their creation. They are the way they are now, and that's it. Taboo! It's even worse embarking on any of this now. Makes no sense whatsoever. The world is full of possibilities… Move back to your historical motherland if you feel so aggrieved… Get integrated in the country where you live… Cultural and educational institutions, various associations, etc. So do whatever you please! It's nothing like it used to be, when everything was harshly proscribed and regulated. Nowadays we have TV channels, the internet, books, press – no one is cut off from anywhere! Make your choice! The main thing is that borders are open! One is not constrained at all! It's all ludicrous… To make such considerations a priority? It's pure insanity. To unleash a war because somebody "resides in the wrong place"? To provoke a bloodbath, send people to slaughter? Including those who "be of one blood" with you? Barbarity! Antediluvian stuff!'

The professor came up to the map. He picked up a pointer and was about to show something with it, but instead returned to the lectern.

'Yet nowadays it isn't simply some crazed drivel… A huge concentration of force is observed along our entire perimeter! We live under immediate threat of the Russian intervention – and this is not a bad dream.'

The professor heaved a deep sigh.

Taras leaned towards me, agitated: 'But why? Why is it happening like this?'

As if he could overhear, the professor picked up:

'It is the right time to ask why the great European powers are staying silent? To demonstrate their spinelessness? No, it's because *they are afraid…* They feel vulnerable against such an imperial monster! So what should we all do, given the situation? Are they at least capable to express their decisive stance?'

The audience froze in breathless silence. Suddenly there was an eruption of indignant cries:

'But it isn't only Europe in NATO! Americans are members too!'

'Let the Americans give those freaking Russians a good kicking! And call it quits! Isn't it clear who's the strongest guy here?'

'And maybe even proactively?'

'Nah, don't talk nonsense… A whack is all very well but it would destroy everyone else at the same time! No, there's got to be another way…'

'Yes! Yes! We should all unite!'

'That's it! That's the answer!' exclaimed the professor excitedly. 'We should all unite: Europe and America, Australia and Japan – the entire civilised world! And not just them: Asia, Africa, Latin America – everyone. And that would be a steely, persuasive, the one and only response!'

'Right! To come together and push forward as one! And no beating about the bush!'

'Only militarily! With such…'

'Wait! That's not what I meant, not at all!' Professor Dashkevych threw up his hands. 'Calm down! Self-control and common sense! What's really required now is a powerful counter-strategy, not something advocated by some hot-headed militants!'

'Is there any other way? To keep tickling them with sanctions?'

'Ha! That's the source of all fakes – their sanctions. These very sanctions have been in place for so many years after Crimea – and? Russia doesn't even feel the itch!'

'I mean something else,' the professor elaborated. 'I mean joint resolute and efficient measures!'

'Bah, nothing will come out of it!' Taras waved his hand in frustration. 'All like before – they'll keep going in circles… Sanctions, my elbow… Just empty talk. What good are sanctions when Russia has oil and gas? Europe must completely renounce all that stuff, stop licking the imperial backside. That would be the most effective measure!'

'True!' Arkady perked up. 'Giving up oil and gas – that's the ticket! Smack on the money! Till this happens nothing will ever move. But how could Europe do it? They are not ready to agree to this, that's the point…'

'That's enough,' piped in some guy. 'The civilised world is planning, by 2050, to walk away from the use of harmful fuels. So what, we should all wait until that happy time? When it all gets resolved by itself?'

'Resolved? No way our "neighbour" will sit on his hands until 2050! We'll get swallowed up way before!' Spyridon flared up.

'Are you all off your rocker? What are you talking about – 2050?' bristled Alla. 'We'll then be.. what? Over fifty? With hardly any appetite for life left!'

'What utter rubbish!' Liubchik gesticulated animatedly. 'Nowadays a woman is young even if she's over fifty… Seen how they look?'

'Sure, fashion, plastic surgery, the works… But there's no cancelling the laws of biology… No, by 2050 we'll lose our thirst for life…'

The bell erupted out of nowhere. The exhausted professor wiped his face with a handkerchief:

'Now, what do we conclude? All that's now happening to us may be summed up with a degree of irony: an enforced impetus for joining ranks. Have they really forgotten this proverb – love can't be forced? So what, they're trying to smother us in their embrace? Must have forgotten, looks like. Then again, we all at some stage got drunk on illusions. Such an empire collapsed! We were jubilant and got complacent, started cutting back the army and engaged in disarmament. And so on and so forth… Yet a disintegration of such a monster simply cannot take place without some latent consequences. And here it's coming back to bite us. And will be with us for quite some time…'

The professor grew silent to take breath. The audience, once again, grew resentful:

'They keep banging on about us being one people! Once he's got a bird in his claws, the predator will bear his gnashers straight away!

'Look, why are they forever miffed? It's all forever against the grain? The Baltic states are bad. Same with Poland. Moldova, Georgia – the same old story. Don't even mention Ukraine – all die-hard bastards…'

'They only like dictatorships!'

'What's there to understand? They fear NATO's extension! So, looks like NATO is our only guarantee of safety and independence!'

The professor raised his hands placatingly.

'Dear friends! Let's briefly summarise and refrain from emotions. It's not NATO they fear but democracy. That it may seep in through their concrete walls. And that it will close its steely hand over the throat of their disgusting authorities!'

'Right you are! That's it!' the audience started chanting. 'Uproot all this villainy!'

The audience was united in their vociferous resentment.

The professor started hastily packing up his belongings.

'So, it means…?'

The professor was clearly reluctant to talk about anything else. It looked, though, like he was being prevailed upon. His face reflected a conflict of emotions.

The audience fell silent, yet again.

'… war?'

The professor stayed silent for another moment, still undecided whether he should say something else.

'Well, you are perfectly aware that over the last several months Russia has been concentrating its forces along our borders…'

Silence, again. He made a resolute wave of his hand – ok, I'll be out with it! – and breathed out:

'Yes, war… However, if someone is afraid of this evil word, we could call it something else: intervention, onslaught or simply conflict…'

He was speaking softly but his voice was reaching every distant corner.

'It looks like war… is unavoidable…'

And having promptly assembled his possessions he rushed out towards the exit. The assistants removed the map, picked up the pointer off the lectern and hurriedly followed suit.

We all started raising up from our seats. Packing was also done in silence. It felt as if a bomb had just gone off here…

In the corridor there was a general rush forward, and then the agitated hubbub:

'So, what does it mean, in the end? Why has this West gone all flaccid? Russia should be really taught a good lesson for all her mischief?'

'Wallop bloody Russia! With all our might!'

'Tear those bear's claws off! Scrape the eyes out!'

'And those Kremlin towers – to hell!'

'A Kievan Prince was stupid enough to have moved northwards from his estate and – with nothing better to do! – founded this bloody Moscow, to our common grief! So, we all now must live with the consequences!'

The crowd started breaking up into small groups where heated arguments continued:

'It's weird where it concerns their Putin. Some 10 or 15 years ago he might've got away with what he's after… But now? Lots of things got clear by now, even the blind ones can see. No, all of this is… just madness, that's what it is!'

'He gnawed off Crimea and now is sharpening his teeth to bite off what? The entire Ukraine?'

'Come on, there should be a plaque dedicated to him, and what's more – somewhere very obvious. For our population has been sort of comatose up till now. Whilst he's managed, through his mean deeds, to bring everyone together. To make us one!'

'But he's just an idiot! He's cut all of us off by his criminal deeds! And this is a statesman? Laughing stock! Can someone like this even foresee the consequences?'

'Sure thing, all know by now: as a tactician he may well be a cunning fox. But as a strategist? He's a nonentity! And which is more important? So there…'

'Something else comes to mind. Allegedly, the guys from his year intake into the KGB school recalled him as something miserable, humdrum… Cagey, too. So they slapped this nickname on him – the Moth…'

'Ha! So why has this "Moth" become, thirty years later, president of the biggest country in the world? That's the incredible bit!'

'It is true. Same as the fact that out there, in Russia, they are labelling us "fascists"! And call our authorities "junta"! Even if we have free elections! And there's a true plethora of political parties!'

'That's it! Totally unlike their totalitarian pressure house!'

'Exactly! We've got the sixth president in place, unlike their "irreplaceable leader"! We're free, we speak our minds – not whisper tremulously in dark corners lest someone would nick us…'

* * *

Lectures, individual assignments – it all went on as per usual. Still, now our major problem was planning a sabbatical, given by the syllabus at mid-point of the final year. This meant conceiving and writing a script for a short film and also getting a blessing from the head of the respective creative workshop. After that, one could shoot a film, get a credit, defend your graduation thesis, snatch your much-coveted degree paper, and wave the beloved institute goodbye!

Although each graduate student is perfectly aware that possessing the degree documents does not guarantee getting a job. For all that, without such papers you could not be even considered human… Each layabout behind each counter, eager to flog you some crap for twice the price, is sure to have a managerial degree, or maybe even two…

So here we were, huddled together by the notice board, scrutinising the rector's instructions. We, the final year students, were now expected to form groups of three, comprising a script writer, director, and cameraman. Well, this bit was easy: I'd write the script, Taras Paliy would operate the camera and as for a director – we'd find someone in our year…

On the whole, nothing new, everything according to the age-old tradition of our institution: a decent writer must come up with such a script as to have it approved by the head of the workshop. The director has to formulate his vision and plan the blocking. The cameraman was expected to offer various angles and winning approaches. And all of this for the sake of a short film, some 20-25 minutes-long, for such was the allotted length. In short, you then would be expected to defend it in front of the graduation committee which represents the apotheosis of the whole undertaking.

To tell the truth, I'd never considered myself a productive script writer: barely scraped together two complete scripts in four years. Whereas the 'seasoned' ones could've scored as many as ten per person! On the other hand, not even one script out of this voluminous output was ever in demand... But it did sound good – ten pieces to your name! Not like my pathetic two...

However, even I got my portion of infrequent praise. The overall opinion was that although my scripts were nothing special as such, but they brimmed with some creative schticks...

All of this was true. Pity, though, that at that stage I didn't have a single decent idea. Not even a shred...

He's an Odd One, this Putin...

The situation around us was full of anxiety – both outside or within the country. On the external parameter Russia continued to draw in her troops. The Americans were sharing their satellite images and warning us of danger.

But as for us, the prevailing intent was to keep calm. Even if the parliament and media were more boisterous than ever. President Zelensky had been onto Medvedchuk – an openly pro-Russian leader popularly referred to as 'Mertvechuk'.[15] Nothing funny about any of this: the potential charge was treason! Even abetting terrorism! My, oh my...

The court ruled that while the hearing was going on the defendant should stay under house arrest: a bracelet on his hand enabling them to follow his movements. In short, to prevent him fleeing...

'Urgh!' grimaced Spyridon. 'I really don't like any of it. This Putin here, he knows how to bear a grudge, he'll never forgive it... He's sure to pay back in kind... Putin is Medvedchuk's daughter's godfather, so it's no trifle. They are truly connected. Putin had been placing a serious stake on him all the way until 2014. He advised Yanukovych to appoint him Prime Minister. He

....

[15] **Mertvechuk:** a play on a similarity of pronunciation. *Medvedchuk* refers to Medved (*Vedmed*, in Ukrainian), a bear; *Mertvechuk* invokes the word *smert*, death.

used to say: "So here, Vyktor Medvedchuk – who better as a Prime Minister for Ukraine"?'

'Whatever the past,' that from Taras, 'he and his beauty Oksana Marchenko are probably quite comfortable in this palace of theirs… And the bracelet is clearly not going to be in the way…'

'Just look at him – such a common mug, somewhat repulsive, even…' I put in my tiny dig, too. 'Yet he scored himself a TV presenter for a wife, pretty as a model…'

'Dough, dude… that's what rules the world…' Bolik clasped his fingers expressively. 'He may well have been repugnant to her too, that's to start with. Then he bought her, and got attractive…'

'Enough, guys,' Alla sounded indignant. 'Some connoisseurs of the woman's heart you are!'

Well, Medvedchuk – that was just to get the ball rolling. The conversation promptly moved on to the topical developments.

'Putin places his bet on provoking immediate chaos here…' Spyridon added fuel to the fire. 'Sort of, it'll all "blow up from within"! And when the situation spirals out of control, a new Maidan will flare up![16] And this time they'll be in the right place at the right time. They'll bring in their army – what else? – to liberate their "compatriots". Of whom there's probably 10-15 percent left here…'

'It's clear now, of course, why they kept pushing their insane plan forward so brazenly! One people, my ass!' Arkady was getting all steamed up. 'No, guys, the thesis of liberating compatriots is clearly wobbly. They'll need a new pretext for aggression now. We, allegedly, are "one people"? But Ukraine, as part of this integral unity, has always been presented as a captive of Bandera toadies![17] And they'll barge in to defend not just some miserable part but the whole unity…'

'Look, it's all true,' Bolik flung up his hands. 'But it's simply not possible that there aren't people in Russia opposed to those insane ideas…'

'You're talking about the so-called "good Russians"?' Liubchik was amazed. 'Do you believe that they even exist?'

....

[16] **Maidan**: the so-called 'Second **Maidan**' (or Euro-Maidan) was a wave of demonstrations and civil unrest in Ukraine which began on 21 November 2013 with large protests on Independence Square (Maidan Nezalezhnosti) in Kyiv. The protests were sparked by President Yanukovich's sudden decision not to sign the European Union-Ukraine Association Agreement, instead choosing closer ties to Russia and the Eurasian Economic Union. The First Maidan (Orange Revolution) took place in November 2004 – January 2005 in response to huge falsifications in the 2004 presidential election.

[17] **Stepan Bandera** (1909-1959): a Ukrainian political activist, revolutionary, one of the radical leading ideologists, practitioners and theoreticians of the Ukrainian nationalist movement in the 20th century. Was assassinated in 1959 in Munich by a Russian KBG agent.

'Recall, Bolik, the end of August of 2014: our forces went on the offensive near Ilovaisk, thus practically solving the problem of liberating Donbas…' Taras extended his hand towards him. 'But Russians promptly moved in: started launching missile attacks from their territory, and brought new forces into the battle zone. That was the decisive factor – our guys got trapped… During some complex talks the Russian side guaranteed the Ukrainian troops safe passage out of the encirclement. Putin personally suggested setting up a "green corridor". And then what? You know yourself: the Russian artillery shelled this celebrated "green corridor" to bits…'

'They gave "the word of an officer"!' Arkady flew into a rage. 'Better still– it was a general! The personal word of the bloody Russky president!'

'I'll tell you what,' Liubchik joined our exchange. 'Don't you know what the "good Russians" are calling the events of 2014? All of it: Crimea, Donbas, and specifically Ilovaisk? Let me remind you… They are saying it was a tiff between two peoples. Nothing more!'

'And it's the "good Russians" saying this.' Spyridon sounded really angry. 'Of which there is a minority. To say nothing about the "bad Russians" who are definitely more numerous… Goodness gracious…'

We all fell momentarily silent, it felt so painful.

'I was listening to some boffins on telly yesterday. They envisage the entire Left Bank being conquered within a week, all the way to the Dnipro… They give Kyiv no more than two or three days…'

'I heard it too. One of those talking heads says something else, though: they may well advance so far. But what will they do afterwards? We've got a short fuse, that's for sure! Besides, people got much more switched on lately. Getting in is probably possible but getting out? Even if our army won't succeed straight away, some civilians will join the partisans. They may arrange them a proper "welcome"!'

'God save us from any of it… That's totally absurd… yesterday sort of brothers but today – enemies? It's true when they say this Putin of theirs is a monster.'

'Pity no one can get inside his head… Why is it: they're armed up to their eyeballs yet militarism is blasting forth! And we should give it all a proper thought…'

'The way I see it, he's made some grievous mistakes. For example, he believes that the issue of Crimea has been closed. From his point of view, that's how it is. Pity the European Union is way too cautious: verbally it's one story, but in reality they're weaving and bobbing. Thing is, politics is all well and good but there're some serious business interests involved. And what does it all mean to the US and UK, the signatories to the Budapest Memorandum?[18] It's a different

....

[18]   The **Budapest Memorandum** of Security Assurances (in Ukrainian and Russian

deal altogether. Their reputation has taken quite a blow. Now go and try to curb any country's ambitions if they try to create nuclear weapons. And those who already have it, try and keep them from piling it up… They would answer back: "Look at what happened to Ukraine? Some serious papers got signed. And then a lot of zilch and fizzle. And we don't want anything like it to happen to us too. So let us work at our nuclear programmes. And leave us be, save your admonishments." Don't you see? After this Russian escapade, it'll be much harder to control the nuclear stuff! If at all possible…'

'So why are they dragging their feet, the US and UK?'

'They are smart. Waiting it all out. Hoping that the colossus does sit on the legs of clay, and will eventually crumble…'

'What's there to mull over? He really sucks. He's something from the last century, a product of the rotten Soviet system…'

Unexpectedly Alla raised her hand, calling us to attention.

'Look, guys… I'd like to remind you of something … Remember how our Zelensky came to power?'

'Sure. His main election promise was peace with Russia! He said: for the sake of that, I'll speak with the devil himself!'

'Me too, I remember… After he was elected, his entire team genuinely believed in the possibility of reconciliation with Russia. They were even saying that his abilities as an actor would help! A dialogue was indeed started. Zelensky made calls, met Putin in Paris, there were large-scale exchanges of prisoners of war. But… simpletons they were… Didn't they take into account the fact that the Kremlin guy is a stubborn maximalist. Who wanted everything for himself… Well, now what? Having had their chips?'

Alla raised her hand again.

'Still, I've had this idea. Perhaps, it's silly…'

We all froze for a moment.

'This here Putin…' she carried on. 'Isn't he, sort of…'

She fell silent and said nothing for a bit.

'Well? What? Do go on!'

'What idea?'

'… err, how shall I put it… could it be… that he's a Devil of some sort?'

....

texts: guarantees) was signed in Budapest, Hungary on 5 December 1994, to provide security assurances/guarantees by its signatories relating to the accession of Ukraine (as well as Belarus and Kazakhstan) to the Treaty on the Non-Proliferation of Nuclear Weapons. Under the memorandum Ukraine renounced its nuclear status; nuclear weapons were either neutralized or transferred to the Russian Federation. [The bomb was (most of all, intentionally) set in the inconsistency of these assurances/guarantees].

'Whoa! Hold your horses...' Arkady sounded worried. 'Wait a minute... Now, to cast such aspersions...'

'Put on the brakes yourself...' Taras looked taken aback. 'Perhaps... perhaps there's something there? They do say that some weird rites are practised in the Kremlin... And they also invite witch doctors...'

'Come on, who can say it for certain, apart from him personally?' Spyridon's forehead glistened with sweat. 'He may well be the Evil One ... Interesting thought though, must chew it over...'

'What's there to chew?' Bolik visibly cheered up. 'He really is a Devil! Hundred percent true!'

'Dear Christ, give me strength, 'Arkady screwed up his face. 'You are sure to drive me nuts. The mere train of thought is weird. We are supposed to be educated young people! It's 21-st century out there, not some Middle Ages, yet we are blabbering about some evil spirits. It's ludicrous!'

'Yeah... it does sound weird, that's true...' Clearly, Bolik had already made an about-face.

'I know why things like this come to head...' chuckled Spyridon. 'All it is, is some spine-shattering discrepancy. He looks one way on TV – like what we all say, cool beyond all measure, every bit a global leader. Yet his head is full of all sorts of bizarre ideas and weird stuff. It's well known that he's obsessed with his health and jumping out of his skin to fight the old age. Just imagine how many laps he puts in daily in his swimming pool! It does tell us a story...'

We all stopped dead.

'Well? For example?'

'What I'm saying is that he's not quite sane... I hear that there are some seriously funny things going on in his inner circles. So, what, then? Ok, a person's got his mentality slightly out of sync, it doesn't mean, not really, that one can ascribe all sorts of silly things to him... What you now call "Devil" invokes popular mythology, nothing else... A person displays some psychological deviations – trifles, given his age – and you are slapping all sorts of labels onto him!'

We silently tried to take it all on board.

'Hey! I've got an idea!' Taras perked up. 'It was our rector who first started it. And so it got lodged in the subconscious. Forgot the optional course he delivered at the beginning of the year on Gogol's early output?[19] How he first found fame? How he first arrived in this cold unwelcoming St Petersburg and found it revolting? And kept thinking about his native land? Ukraine... The land of luxurious gardens, young beauties, dashing lads and wonderful songs... But...

....

[19] **Nikolai Gogol** (1809-1852): a Russian novelist, short story writer, and playwright of Ukrainian origin.

Hello, dear audience of St Petersburg! In this Ukraine, there also exist forest elves, house spirits and mermaids… More than that – all kinds of evil forces! So let me inundate you with all this stuff, esteemed aristocracy! Scary tales and legends – I'll give you an earful! And so he set off, flogging this subject… He kept begging with his mother in each letter: give me, give me yet another legend! So that they'll all tremble with fear all over this Petersburg!'

'Hmm… Quite possible that it was our rector who planted this seed…' Alla was deep in thought.

'Look! I'm sick and tired of all this drivel!' Arkady, by now, was thoroughly annoyed. 'Gogol… Scary tales… legends… If you talk of Gogol, stay on what he did write about. What does a devil look in Gogol's tales? Sports little horns, a goatee, a snout of a nose and spindly legs with hooves… Is it all coming back? Meanwhile the one you are trying to label here – what does he look like? Let me refresh your memory: he prefers Italian brands, suits from Brioni, ties from Valentino or Moschino… That's it, fuck it. I've had it with you…'

'Wow, that's some angle…' Liubchik gave her fringe a shake. 'What do'ye say, Stinger? Why don't you say something?'

'What's to say?' I tried to remove myself from the fray.

Normally, I tried to stay away from political discussions. Yet now… And whether or not someone is… a Devil? Total bonkers… Although… Perhaps Spyridon had a point when he insisted that it deserved thinking over?

In short, I just waved dismissively – get lost. Stop all this nonsense. Your discussion is getting really weird…

Arkady was clearly overjoyed to find an ally in me. He, too, brought his hand down forcibly:

'All this is ancient superstitions. What evil forces? They don't even exist… And overall, we're heading in some funny direction… We've had some fun, and that's it. The subject is closed!'

And we all stopped talking. Stood around for a while and then went our separate ways…

January 2022. The 'Immortal' Soviet Realia

'A Faceted Glass from the Soviet Days'

'Hi there, man!' the following day Spyridon, this giant of a man, pulled me on the sleeve amidst the hustle and bustle in the corridor. Boleslav – the Squirt – was peeping from behind his back.

We stepped aside, better to chew the fat.

Spyridon gave my sleeve another tug and said, as if in confidence:

'You know, Stinger, I don't read fiction anymore. Still, it's a common phenomenon with all folks– to prefer serious stuff, say, history, economics, finances. In the very least, memoires and auto-biographies. Why waste time on all those things created by some author's imagination? Fiction is mostly consumed by women; it's somehow better suited to their tastes...'

'Well, I wouldn't generalise like that...' I tried to counter his arguments. 'You may sometimes find such stuff in quality literature... It's like precious utensils in which gold dust gets accumulated, speck by speck... But the most important thing about fiction is that it teaches compassion, empathy... Ah well, it's hard to summarise it just like that...'

'Oh yes, we all know you're a dreamy type...'

Bolik listened to all of this, a mischievous smile on his lips. Although specialising in documentaries, they still managed to introduce some proper fiction devices into their work, albeit stealthily, and despite being generally critical about the arts, didn't feel any particular qualms of conscience over the fact. Unlike me, a pure 'artist'...

Spyridon was going, bull-like, at his chosen topic of peculiarities of life in the Soviet Union. For all that, he was still somewhat undecided where to start, since those peculiarities were endless. Boleslav, however, was nice and clear: 'Chornobyl and the Times of the General Secretary Leonid Brezhnev's Rule.'

'Look here, bro',' he clasped the lapel of my jacket. 'Chornobyl, Brezhnev in his final deranged state, the disintegration of the USSR – these are enormous subjects which will never let you down. Long-playing ones...'

His hand let go of my jacket.

'And now also the build-up of the Russian military presence along our borders! The tension sends jolt after jolt not just at us but the whole world… It looks like an eternal, or even immortal subject in the making…'

'Ok, Kiril, dear,' Spyridon winked at me. 'You can't lose if you go with any of this. However, my sweetie-pie, all you ever wanted was to write scripts exclusively for fiction films… So, face the music now.'

Bolik evaporated in some direction and Spyridon pulled me into a corner.

'Let's step aside, I've got something to share.'

Oh boy, he was about to start bragging again. I'd noted that the pair of them, as of late, felt some funny elation when showing off with their good progress on all fronts. Bloody sadists…

We dived into some nook.

'You see, looks like I've found my way… The project will be called "The Soviet faceted glass". In other words – a *granchak*. An inalienable attribute of bloody Soviet daily life. A common object, some 200-g-capacity, but if you fill it to the brim – it could easily hold 250! And I've jumped at this idea! My little script will be about just this, the bloody faceted glass!'

'I don't quite get it, though…'

'Small wonder. Yet it's hard core! Look here, for example, what do you really know about it? Nothing, which is a shame… The Soviet *granchak* is a symbol of the entire era!'

'Ok, whatever. But how are you going to attach this bloody glass to the entire era? Squeeze it into your script?'

'What a sweet baby you are! What the fuck they've been doing all those years, teaching us the tools available to a director? Let me spell it out. Imagine a veteran of war, or labour, or whatever, sitting round in his kitchen. He's just had his dinner and reaches out to get his ciggy. His wife is washing up, casually knocks this glass over, it drops and breaks. The veteran gives a shudder. And what about his wife? She sweeps the shards aside and empties it all into the bin. Meanwhile the veteran is nearly hysterical. He sobs. She turns to him: "What's wrong? There, there, my darling…" And some such crap. "I'll go tomorrow and buy you a new one…" But he goes: "You have no idea! I've carried this *granchak* throughout the war! Peaceful times, too… We shared all: joy and hardship… children – first born, then growing up… What shall I do with this new one of yours?" Long story short, the following day she drags herself to the supermarket, to get him a new *granchak*. Nothing! She asks the assistants. And they go: "Wha' are you talking about? What *granchak*? That's some prehistoric stuff. We don't carry glasses any more. You should check in a museum…"'

Spyridon made a pause and gave me a triumphant look.

'Wha' d'you say? A gigantic subject! There's stuff to work at, Stinger, take my word for it...'

'Uhm... I'm not following, not yet...'

'You country bumpkin, you! That's why you're not getting it... Your knowledge of those times is miniscule...'

I nearly opened my mouth to admit that, true, I didn't know much about any of this, but he cut me short.

'Ha! What does the encyclopaedia say? A glass is a vessel resembling a cone with its tip cut off. Has neither handle or stem. Can be used for hot or cold drinks. A classical glass had 16 facets and cost only seven kopecks! The Soviet people at the time saw it as a symbol of the era, something that united them all... Those glasses were supplied in the machines dispensing fizzy water, right there, in the streets. Also, in canteens, kindergartens... The stuff the people used to put in those glasses: tea, fruit drink, kefir, fruit desserts...'

'If you want a full list, you must remember spirits too...'

'Look here, man, stop showing off. It's not a secret – what it could be used for. Meanwhile few are aware that the appearance of this glass was a direct result of the progress in science and technology... Its shape and composition had been developed in answer to the manufacturing requirements, not some individual designer's dreams. In short, just then the Soviet engineers had discovered a dish washer!'

'My-my, some inventors they were. The first ever dishwasher had been displayed at the Chicago World's Fair in 1893!' It just popped up in my memory from somewhere, must've read it some place. 'So, it looks they nicked it from their predecessors, the Soviets did have a reputation for that...'

'Stop splitting hairs, let me make my point. The thing is, a dishwasher would only accommodate the crockery of a certain size and shape. And this glass fitted the bill ideally. The facets made it much more robust; it could easily be dropped down onto the concrete floor and remain intact! Besides, there was a particular method for manufacturing this glass...'

'You're really overdoing it on the technical side. Who gives a toss?'

'I wouldn't be so sure but OK, here's some non-technical info. In the days of the USSR, *granchak* was indispensable for drinking *horilka*.[20] Abroad, they even called it a "Russian *horilka* glass". They saw no difference at the time between "Russian" and "Soviet". And in the blasted Soviet days consuming strong liquor for no good reason was commonly referred to as the "Holiday of *Granchak*". That was when the soul craved alcohol but there was nothing to celebrate...

....

[20] **Horilka:** a Ukrainian alcoholic beverage. The word *horilka* may also be used in a generic sense in the Ukrainian language to mean vodka or other strong spirits and etymologically is similar to the Ukrainian word for 'to burn'.

You know what I mean – it's when you shouldn't down a shot or two for no good reason but must mark an occasion of sorts…'

'Great stuff. And how do you plan to ram it all into your script?'

'Easy-peasy. I'll find myself such a "scientist", bow tie and all, who will spout out all this scientific rubbish. Also, three pissheads who will measure a bottle to share it "between the three". The result will be a sort of historical excursion into the Soviet era. The young will be curious – no one knowing a thing about any of it – it's all been thirty years ago now. Innit a good find? Super material!'

Spyridon forcibly exhaled, exhausted by his monologue.

'Promise me, not a word to a living soul about any of it!'

At this point Bolik materialised from somewhere, right on cue.

'Have you explained your idea?' he asked of Spyridon.

And then, not waiting for a reply, he urgently turned to me:

'Look here! The tragic explosion at the Chernobyl Atomic Station took place on 26 April 1986. A strong northern wind was then blowing straight towards Kyiv,' he quickly riffled through the main data. 'Microparticles of the poisoned dust carried deadly hazard for anything living. The acceptable radio-active reading in Khreschatyk went up multi-fold. Theoretically, the population should have stayed inside behind the tightly shut windows. Yet, the May Day demonstration was supposed to go forward as planned! Clearly, it was nothing short of murder… The local leaders wanted to cancel the celebrations. And then Gorbachev sent them this harsh message: "What's this indulgence? If the demonstration fails, I'll drive the lot of you out! It must take place in Khres-chatyk as per usual! And make sure young pioneers are there, too! In any case, stop this panic-mongering. This will be a way to show the whole world that nothing "untoward" has happened in our country. That everything is the way it should be!'

'Yeah, sure, that's how it was. My rellies told me about how horrified they all were…'

'There's more. On the whole, this whole Chernobyl saga is but a crime story. To start with, the authorities were categorically denying all knowledge. And only later – twenty days later! – Gorbachev admitted on the telly that there had been an accident. That was when panic started in earnest. It was horrible. The Kyiv Railway Station brought to mind the war footage. A frenzied crowd was storming carriages. Pushing each other aside, people were throwing their children into the train windows. It made not one iota of difference where those trains were heading, none whatsoever. The main thing was to send their children away from this deadly disaster. Once the children had all left Kyiv, the city looked deserted. Not a soul in the street, empty playgrounds, beaches, and parks…'

'Yeah, my Mum also told me that that was a real turning point in the hearts of Kyiv residents. '

'Exactly right! The ordinary people finally realised that trusting such grandiose institutions as the Central Committee of the Communist Party, also its Politburo and all this hellish system was mortally dangerous! The people twigged that the "state of workers and farmers, the most advanced entity in the world" was nothing but a fake, and more – a questionable, and what's worse, irresponsible historical experiment. So, who's to blame? The consequences can be felt even today, far out of the Ukrainian borders but the main recipients of all this horror were we...'

'That's it! I heard that no one was venturing into the streets, there were no mass-scale rallies. Yet, no doubt about it whatsoever, a radical change had taken place in people's minds and hearts!'

'Yeah, that's as regards our collective consciousness, after all, lots of our people had been impacted. Yet nothing of the kind was ever observed in Moscow! That's what I am planning to build it all upon: that was the sentiment here, yet over there – all was quiet as reinforced concrete, and no radical changes...'

'A formidable subject, Bolik! Bull's eye – as per usual. You're sure to have it approved...'

'Only not a peep to anyone! Not even a whisper! You do know how it is here – ideas get snatched in mid-air... We only share it with you 'cause you've got nothing to do with either *gronchak* or Chernobyl...'

'We only confide in you 'cause you're a mate, Stinger,' Spyridon leaned towards me, trust personified. 'Perhaps this info will put some useful ideas into your head, too. We are mates, after all, aren't we?'

We shook hands and parted.

So. Spyridon and Bolik somewhat opened up about their chosen topics... Didn't hold out on me which, naturally, was to their credit... Famous rockers... By the way, their love interests were also invested accordingly. Always some Teutonic types: invariably clad in black, laced-up black boots – even in the summer. The hair raven black too, to say nothing about heavy black make-up. The main thing with them, the Teutonesses, is that everything should be black, from the crown of the head and all the way down to the soles of the footwear.

One of them called herself Brunhild, the other – Greta. Both with divinely beautiful faces but all this paint... It did mess things up a bit. Ask Taras or me, not our cup of tea at all. But Spyridon and Bolik were thrilled...

Even Borsch Got Nicked![21]

Long story short, all our guys were doing fine as regards the progression of their scripts. Spyridon and Bolik, as veritable giants, were busy mulling over several ideas at once.

Alla made her own mark: she embarked on some little-known facts from the life of Mayakovsky.[22]

'You know, it all somehow falls into place... Also, the material is plentiful – photographs, the old footage... I start with what's well-known: sort of, *Mayak* became a figurehead for those craving modernity and categorically renouncing the bourgeois hypocrisy. Like all members of the avant-garde, he believed that all the old stuff should be discarded into the dustbin of history. This rebellion led him to Futurism. If everything was to be destroyed, why not start with rhymes, metre, and syntax? Away with classic iamb and trochee!

'For they are as "bourgeois" as white collars and ties... Yet here lies a paradox! What do we see as a result? A catastrophic discrepancy between the ideology and his appearance and daily life. On the one hand – his signature yellow woman's cardigan that was supposed to scandalise and hurt the common feelings of propriety. Yet, subsequently most Mayakovsky's photographs depict somebody exquisitely elegant. And all this at the time of universal ruination and chaos... Meanwhile here he is, complete with this faultless bow tie, peeping from underneath immaculate white collars... Such a direct association with the world of the old! And he doggedly kept cultivating this image of himself as an aristocratic dandy. Can you imagine?'

'True, it's interesting...'

'Let's get on. And here we come upon another paradox. The new reality rapidly started developing artistic forms and images. A rebellious iconoclast, a "loud-mouthed ringleader"[23] of the revolutionary people is getting noticeably close to the Soviet officialdom. Do you recall his glorification of the Soviet passport? Who would've thought that this document could, allegedly, put the fear of God into the hearts of all foreigners! The message is that you should

....

[21] **Borshch**: a sour soup, made with various vegetables, of which red beetroot is the main ingredient, giving the dish its distinctive red colour. Common in Eastern European countries and still considered to be predominantly a Ukrainian dish. Place of origin: Ukraine (known from the times of Kievan Rus forward). Ukrainian borsch has been included in UNESCO's Representative List of Intangible Cultural Heritage of Humanity.

[22] **Vladimir Mayakovsky** (1893-1930): a Russian and Soviet poet, playwright, artist, and actor. During his early, pre-Revolutionary, period, he was a prominent figure of the Russian Futurist movement.

[23] A quote from Mayakovsky's epic poem *At the Top of My Voice* («Vo ves golos»).

be anxious and tremble, for the global revolution was in the offing. Do you know what strikes me most? All this irreconcilable animosity towards the West doesn't stop him one bit from falling for a Parisian beauty Tatyana Yakovleva! And his turbulent affair with an American lady, Ellie Jones? His disdain towards bourgeois values somehow went perfectly hand in hand with purchasing an expensive French motor for his Russian lover – Lilya Brik… Doesn't that remind you of something?'

'You bet. Look at modern Russia… They wholeheartedly hate the West but prefer to reside not somewhere in the Russian sticks, not even in Moscow or St Petersburg but in Londons and Parises! Nothing changed, not one little bit. The kids of the elite – the very same one that spends its days needling the West – have all got entrenched over there…'

'And then I've got some real icing on the cake: Mayakovsky and Ukraine! Hardly anyone knows about it now.'

'I'm intrigued…'

'Consider this – Vladimir Mayakovsky was among very few people who dared speak about the "imperial debt"! Russia's debt to Ukraine. That's the title of his famous poem written in 1926.'

Out of her backpack Alla pulled a notebook.

'Listen to several extracts:

So, what do we know
about the countenance of Ukraine?
With such knowledge
a typical Russian
isn't awash.

What they do know:
the Ukrainian borsch.
Also, Ukrainian lard.
And the culture
got also creamed off:
apart from
two
celebrated Tarases –
Bulba[24]
and the famous Shevchenko[25] –

....

[24]   Taras Bulba: one of the main characters in Nikolai Gogol's novella *Taras Bulba.*
[25]   Taras Shevchenko: the most famous Ukrainian poet (1814-61).

nothing else to squeeze out,
try as hard as you can.

And if really pressed,
he'd mention
a couple of oddities –
anecdotes
about the Ukrainian mova.[26]
I'm telling myself:
comrade Russky,
refrain
from poking fun
at Ukraine!

...this mova –
is sublime and honest:
"Lo, the surmas start playing,
The hour of vengeance has come..."

'Tis hard
everyone
in one mixture to pound.
Stop putting
your ego on show.
Do we know much of Ukrainian nights?[27]
No,
That's not something we know.

'Well, what d'you think?' Alla was so excited that her eyes sparkled. 'Valuable stuff, innit?'

'Alka, that's wonderful!'

'You mean it?'

'Sure thing! It's top marks!'

Alla stuck out her palm, satisfied.

We shook hands.

....

[26] **Mova**: Ukrainian for 'language'.

[27] "Do you know the Ukrainian night? Oh, you don't know the Ukrainian night! Take a look at it…" A famous passage from an early work by Gogol.

There you go. I did heap praise on Alla, true, but somehow couldn't supress a gut feeling that no matter how fantastic and pro-Ukrainian the poem, one couldn't rule out that in the nearest future Vladimir Mayakovsky might become totally inappropriate…

Hmm… It looked like everyone was moving forward. Meanwhile I was stuck…

By the way, Liubchik, also, had long since made her choice: true nature of a photo model's life. She told me once:

'Know what, Stinger? I'm just like you! I need things to be modern, don't get those excursions into history… For example, what do you know about the life of photo models? That's one killer of a subject! Real treasure… It's all so complicated there… Could research it till I'm blue in the face…'

My face must've fallen but Liubchik took it in her stride.

'Making faces? Come on, Stinger, bite me! Go for it, I give you my permission!'

'Come on, don't be silly. True, a quality subject…'

'Bah, what's the point trying to explain it to you? You simply don't get it…'

Sure thing, I believed her. If she thought it was treasure, treasure it was.

What was there to say? Even Arkady was diligently scribbling away even if he, of all people, hardly felt the need. Everyone knew that script or no script, he would beautifully make it through the final stage of studies.

In other words, everyone little by little shared their creative plans with me. Taras didn't count as he saw his future as a cameraman. For all that, his plans were down to earth and consistent. Unlike me who kept skipping from one idea to the next. Taras sometimes teased me, sort of – *that's the script writers for you, it comes with the territory. Say, you dream up a sweet little piece but half an hour later it would be so raked over, one would never recognise the original!*

However, they, the cameramen – that was a different story altogether! Everything with them was foreseen, grounded, substantiated. The profession itself forbids meandering… If only because one is expected to drag around a heavy camera, hither and thither, on your shoulder. Say, one would stagger, collapse, and whack the said camera against the pavement – nothing but additional costs.

Ok… I listened to everyone politely, didn't initiate any arguments and joined no unseemly debates. Great stuff… I had to conserve my energy, so as to come up with something of my own. Kept thinking about it all around the clock. Day and night, night and day – whatever. Thing was, they all had an idea, so had a direction to follow. As for me – nothing whatsoever. So, what was I supposed to do about that script? What a bee in the bonnet!

* * *

I came home and found mum anxious.

'You know, I've been watching the telly… Christ, the things I've heard…'

'Which things, precisely?'

'They talked about our history. Only Russia shamelessly re-tailored it to suit their own narrative! She appropriated the past – that's the Kyevan principality and its people. Muskovy, in effect, is a shard of the Kyevan Rus, at the time being torn asunder by various feuds. She even made the name "Kyevan Rus" its own. To start with, the word *Russia* was spelled with one "s". The second one appeared only later. But "Rus" – that was us! For all that, Muskovy came up with another name for us – Malorossia, Small Russia. In other words, the same Russia, only a small one…'

'Sure thing. Later on, the word "okraina" appeared since we had always been an "outer land"– both for Russia and our neighbour Poland.[28] And hence our name – Ukraine.'

'Whereas it would be correct to use the name "Ukraine-Rus!" That was how our first president Hrushevsky, a prominent historian himself, used to refer to it…'

'He went further and even penned a fundamental work on the subject! "History of Ukraine-Rus" in ten volumes…'

'The main point is that the tsars were perfectly aware of all of this. One can never build a great power if you don't possess a powerful past. In effect that's how they appropriated the heritage left by the Kyevan Rus. But the worse was yet to come. They kept banging on about a triune people – Great Russians, Small Russians, and Byelorussians. With Russia, naturally, being the "big brother" across the huge expanse of territory…'

'You're right! Also, Russia has stealthily "privatised" the victory over the Nazi Germany… But every Soviet republic sent their soldiers there too, and they also were fighting and dying… And what about the Allies? Nice try! And this is becoming the narrative the world over…'

'They go round nicking whatever's available! Even heroes from the ancient folklore!'

'And the Black Sea Fleet after the collapse of the Soviet Union? Pooh!'

'Even borsch, our time-honoured heritage! They now claim it's theirs. There was this lady from Moscow, contemplating the subject… You know, a hat, fashionable glasses, gloves – a picture of sophistication: "How can you identify

------

[28] **Okraina**: translates from Russian as *fringe, border land*. Phonetically, this word is close to how the name of Ukraine is pronounced in Russian – *Ukraina.*

ethnicity of borsch? What is the ethnic origin of potatoes? Beetroots? Cabbage? It's just a type of soup, nothing more. Same for bread – what's its nationality?'

'Ah well, those sophisticated ladies, especially from Moscow… She's just a fool. For potatoes, cabbage and beets are agricultural crops whereas borsch is a dish. True, soup is soup, the world over. Yet Pho is a soup from Vietnam while żurek is Polish. Same story with bread: baguette is French while ciabatta came from Italy.'

'And wine? Seemingly it exists everywhere. It's just… wine! And yet with certain wines, their geographic provenance is in copyright.'

'And another thing…' It suddenly came to me. 'Our classical poet Taras Shevchenko is little by little referred to as…"Russian *and* Ukrainian"!'

'That's just for starters, to get the juices flowing. Very likely, in the near future, he'll become a great Russian poet, period. And "Russkies are evil people" in *Kateryna* will be simply brushed under the carpet…*29* Or let's take Gogol – which nation can claim him as its own?'

'Yeah… it's a good question, even though a painful one… This anguished duality of his… He felt Ukrainian with every fibre of his being, he was born in the area near Poltava! But the force of circumstances made him a Russian author. Say, his famous *Evenings on a Farm near Dikanka*? It's a veritable encyclopaedia of Ukrainian realia: clothes, customs, festive meals…'

'That's it!' Mum nodded in agreement. 'That's the root of a profound antagonism between Ukraine and Russia… The fault line, so to speak…'

Meanwhile I got absorbed in my own thoughts. We are constantly bombarded with arguments that Russia is allegedly a requisite 'stepping stone' for Ukrainian unity. That without Russia we won't ever make it into the big world. However, the point is not just that Ukraine has detached itself. It has broken away *irrevocably*! And the gap gets wider with each passing day. Ukraine now must mould itself through its own efforts.

* * *

Dmytro Petrovych,[30] the head of our creative workshop, decided to engage us in a series of practical classes, to demonstrate how the masters used to work in the genre of script-writing. The first in the syllabus – 'Hollywood and Henry Miller: The experience of writing a script.' He introduced his lecture thus:

....

[29]   **Kateryna**: a poem by Taras Shevchenko.

[30]   In Slavonic languages, the polite way to address or refer to a person is to use his or her name (in this case: *Dmytro*) followed by the patronymic (in this case: *Petrovych* – meaning that the character's father's name was Petro).

'Henry Miller's relationship with Hollywood was complicated. To be precise, practically not-existent. All writers of note who milled around Los Angeles in 1940-50 were involved with Hollywood, one way or another. The "golden rain" of studios commissioning scripts was never-ending. Those who got a knack for doing it, could cobble scripts together as a matter of course. Meanwhile Miller, by then a well-known author, had no invitations. He was steadily ignored, as if he'd never existed. On the other hand, he wasn't particularly enamoured with the "factory of dreams" either. Miller wrote: "The studios' doors are wide open for me (in reality, no one had any intention of opening those), but I've no desire of "walking the streets." Perhaps that was why he had no commissions – speaking his mind like that! Miller was unquestionably an outstanding artist. However, in many practical aspects he was naïve – believing that "an American writer who's made an honest attempt to share his life experiences and overcome the temptation of selling himself short, should definitely find a place somewhere in Hollywood."

'Hollywood, respectively, demonstrated its indifference towards the master… At the same time Miller couldn't earn a living – his scruples prevented him from any attempts. One "well-wisher" decided to help – enlighten him as to the secrets of success in Hollywood. Allegedly, it was all very simple: "one had to invent some *shit, wrap it all up in cellophane and season it with self-sacrifice.*" He glanced at Miller to make sure that the latter got the idea, but Miller had already clammed up: either he did get the message or was struck with an idea of his own. The well-wisher decided to check: "You got it? As for cellophane – the more the better, don't skimp on the stuff".'

Dmytro Petrovych opened his attaché case, probably to fish out his folder and tell us something interesting.

Suddenly, I felt a jolt: that was it, the coveted recipe! Sacrifice is on trend in our days, too! So go on and develop this vein! And luck would finally smile on you.

Meanwhile Dmytro Petrovych went on:

'My, how the master was insulted by the recipe that involved "shit"!'

Ha! That was Miller, and he was insulted. As for me, neither shit nor such a recipe upset me one bit!

'He just couldn't take it lying down. And what do you think happened next? He struck out with a caper of a script! To be more precise, its synopsis. Let us now listen to this synopsis – with some omissions.'

Dmytro Petrovych opened his folder and started reading:

'Starring: follows the list of the brightest stars of the day.

Genre of the fiction film: a romantic drama.

The love scenes must be reproduced in every detail, without a shade of hypocritical modesty. If the romantic lead is kissing a girl he must immediately reach underneath her skirt, then strip her of all clothing and then "give it to her". Only after that should he return to what's in the script. To follow: brief surrealistic interludes involving stars of the world of pornography – anonymous monsters, in the shape of a juvenile French telegrapher, or else whores lasciviously licking their lips in front of the camera, and other "lures". Fiery scenes in hotels, peep-shows, a train wreck in the subway… Exhibitionists who flash their "assets" whenever possible… Champaign flowing river-style. Stylistically, George Grosz plus some techniques invented by Dali and Bunuel with assistance from indefatigable de Sade. Psychoanalytical sessions. Dreams à la Walt Disney. Feasts à la Giono. In other words – one unending fiesta where they tirelessly keep eating, drinking, copulating, and killing. Directors: Marcel Duchamp and John Ford[31]".'

'That's it,' Dmytro Petrovych shut his folder. 'Over to you.'

The folk started sharing their views. All knew what 'Hollywood' stood for, and all were 'showing off' on this account. But everyone was unwittingly letting this secretly coveted leitmotif come to light: 'Oh, how I would like to hang around the very same Hollywood… Work my way upwards…' Such cosy little dreams…

I also said something convoluted – just to make my presence known.

And there it was: I suddenly knew which route to follow. That erstwhile well-wisher with his 'shit wrapped up in cellophane and seasoned with self-sacrifice' gave me a real impetus. The master himself, too, with his caustic parody. So, for me it proved a veritable boost.

I understood clearly: Dmytro Petrovych intended to discuss this script purely along the parody lines, he hardly pursued any other goals. For all that, it impacted me in a very different way. I'd finally heard an instruction to act! That's what it was – the key! What the well-wisher suggested for Henry Miller as a recipe for success may well become a recipe for me!

In essence: take, dear Kiril, some piece of 'shit', and having identified a 'heroic victim', wrap the whole thing up in glistening cellophane! What's more – don't skimp on the stuff!

Ah well, I decided to be generous. Sure thing, first I had to ram in a hefty portion of something juicy. After that – not simply an intimation of a scandal but a murmur, a roar! And it'd get me noticed, no doubt…

Ok, even if the task in hand wasn't all that straightforward, I should have confidence… I had to make do!

In a word, the approach was extremely primitive – as old as the world itself. For all that, tried and tested, and proved successful. The main thing was to be certain of the forthcoming success.

....

[31] This passage mentions prominent art and culture figures mainly from the first half of the 20th century.

My thoughts, like a swarm of bees, were all a-buzz. So – scandal and provocation! Richly seasoned not just with erotic stuff but something more profound... Yet the exact details still had to be decided upon.

Shouldn't descend, though, to overt pornography... Say what you might but it was our graduation thesis, not an adult video. Erotic stuff must be present, it had to be obvious that physiology was there but still... the result should be more subtle, more artistic...

The idea for the plot hit me in an instant. I'd always been puzzled by the phenomenon of the young idolising the Asian mega-stars – to a point of insanity at times. So quite a few factors were, so to say, obvious. But how should one form a dramatic narrative? The main thread?

I spent about a week churning it all over in my head... Aha, here was this idea... A young Asiatic cine-idol got all exhausted at the shoot, sick and tired of the whole show... He wheedled a week's leave out of his producer and scarpered to Australia, incognito. Even without his usual security – like a normal young guy. And there he was, walking up and down a park, en-joying life.

Yet somehow, he got spotted by a posse of schoolgirl fans. They got round him – gi'us an autograph! He tried to flee the clingy admirers but they caught up with him and overpowered, the whole crowd against just one man. In short, they defiled the star and gang raped him... And kept clicking their cameras all the way through...

Just the ticket. I won't hold it back – I was strutting around like Napoleon on the eve of his decisive battle. I felt good with myself, truth be told.

I showed it to our group – they just gasped. Whoa, what a script! It could well win the contest! And the film, too, could queue for a prize of some sort...

The acting department was all abuzz – everyone dying to be cast as either the protagonist or one of those lustful fans... Crushing success, full house. Brilliant prospects, in short...

But Dmytro Petrovich axed this script straightaway. With a mischievous grin he gave my folder back to me.

'Well done, Kiril! Stuffed your piece full with cellophane, didn't skimp on erotica! Up to the very brim! I am pleased that our practical classes hit home, at least with somebody...'

I turned as red as a beetroot.

'As for the subject-matter... In a nutshell, it's not at all appropriate as a graduation piece. Find another subject...'

So that was that... I told myself: take a deep breath, dear Kiril, and come down to sinful earth... Your great plan misfired... So now what? Melancholy? Something that would morph, gradually, into a state of total apathy? It was the stuff of nightmares: you are persecuted by some heavily armed criminals and you – forget running away – cannot even move a finger…

To summarise – my script hit the proverbial fan…

There is this theory that we tend to find friends among our direct opposites. Which was definitely true in the case of Taras and me. Ours was a state of interdependency. In other words, we complemented one another.

And so, he plunged straight in, offering his diagnosis:

'My, oh my! Those "creative souls", if you please. Those who develop neurosis at the mere sight of a first glitch! Remember: life is sure to kick you in the teeth more than once! Everyone thinks it's normal, even if it means feeling blue at times, who'd say otherwise? Something went tits up? No sweat, let's move on, something new is sure to appear. But the "creative" ones take it all as drama and tragedy. The world's coming to an end, an apocalypse! You simply need a nudge of some sort, something to help you come up with a normal script. And that's the whole story…'

Of course I needed a nudge, something to help me grope my way forward… Who would argue?

The Specific Date of Invasion has now been Named…

I could've continued wallowing in self-pity because of my mishap but more important things took over – I was barely able to keep on top of the news. Americans were now paying frequent visits, one after another: the Secretary of Defence, the State Secretary, and a host of other officials. And all of them kept warning us: Russia is planning an attack! They'd been saying it all along but the theories about the exact date were vague. But now they already had a specific date – February the 16th!

Still, our leaders were full of sangfroid: 'War? What are you talking about? Between our nations? It can never be! Besides, some other dates have been mentioned by now. So what? The dates came and went, and nothing happened. It will be the same on February the 16th, too! We are sure there's no danger, all you do is spread panic and inflame emotions… The drain of investments makes quite an impact on our economy, and it's going from bad to worse!'

Yet the Americans wouldn't budge. They even moved their embassy to Lviv. Then the others started following suit…

Moreover, the 16th was resolutely rejected by our side for yet another reason: the opening of the Winter Olympics in China. In addition to the original Olympic motto – *Citius – Altius – Fortius!* (that is, Faster – Higher – Stronger!), each country that acts as an Olympic host tries to come up with its own message that would reflect the principal idea of the games. The Chinese selected this: 'Together for a Shared Future!' In a word, it was impossible to ignore such a meaningful slogan.

We recalled what happened in 2014 in respect of Crimea. Russia was the host and during the games (7-23 February), nothing untoward took place. No IFOs, nothing. Russia had upheld the tradition of inventing a slogan and came up with: 'Hot. Cool. Yours.'

The Organising Committee used to brag: 'This motto is a combination of novelty and dynamism. The word "Hot" represents tensions inherent in sporting competitions, also emotions of the fans, and refers to the location chosen for the games – a southern resort, Sochi. The word "Cool" indicates the season in which the games are held, the type of the games, and also reminds everyone of the way Russia is traditionally perceived around the world. The word "Yours" invokes the idea of involvement, of bringing the past events closer; it reminds us that the Games are a large-scale multi-faceted project that enables everyone to celebrate victories, experience feelings of pride and empathy.'

Who could argue it was beautiful? Bloody marvellous…

But as soon the games were over, all hell broke loose in Crimea.

So, forget about the sixteenth! Americans may well have disposed of some super intelligence, yet they failed to make allowances for the Olympic factor.

* * *

Arkady and I stayed on in the lecture hall, everyone else had already left. He turned towards me:

'Look, why don't you take a leaf out of Spyridon and Bolik's book? Why don't you select something from the Soviet past and cobble together something uncomplicated? By the way, I've bumped into something, be happy for you to have it…'

'Why? And yourself?'

'Why should I bother? My dad'll pull some strings, I'll get my credit anyway…'

'Ok, Soviet. What exactly d'you have in mind?'

'Why not Yakov Sverdlov?[32] Lenin's closest ally. An extremely primitive archetype. Lenin practically worshipped him. Short of height, kinda puny sparrow. But as soon as he opened his gob – 'twas like a trumpet of Jerico!

....

[32] **Yakov Sverdlov** (1885-1918): a Bolshevik Party administrator and chairman of the All-Russian Central Executive Committee from 1917 to 1919. He is sometimes regarded as the first head of state of the Soviet Union, although the latter was not established until 1922, three years after his death.

He'd drop into a factory and bellow – "Com-ra-des!!" They all stop in their tracks and listen. An imposing person he was… In other words – the first Soviet president. Just to make things completely clear: Lenin was sort of Prime Minister (at the time, the top official in the entire state), with Sverdlov being sort of president. That's it – Lenin's right-hand man. Pedantic he was, and well-organised… When sharing digs with Stalin in exile, he kept thing orderly for everyone, mended his clothes himself. Also insisted that dishes be washed up – always. Although housemates, Sverdlov was Stalin's exact opposite. The latter liked poking fun at his neighbour and was quite boorish with it. Stalin later reminisced about their shared experiences in exile: "We used to go fishing… Hunting, too… I had a dog, called it Yashka. Clearly, Sverdlov wasn't best pleased – he and the dog were namesakes! Sverdlov used to do the washing up, all those plates and spoons. Me, I never did. After a meal I would place dishes on the floor – the dog licked it all clean…"

'What do you say, Kiril? Prime material, if you ask me. There's this thing, too. Their opponents called the Bolsheviks 'the 'leather lot'' – because of their clothes. This uniform, in fact, was started by Sverdlov – he was clad in leather from head to toe. That's to say – from his leather cap down to his boots. The style resonated with the times and became really popular…'

Arkady grew silent, watching my reaction.

'Do you know where Sverdlov also made a splash?'

'We-e-ll…'

'In July of 1918, Lenin and Sverdlov personally sanctioned the execution of the tsar's family, in custody at the time. They issued a direct order… Must be said, Sverdlov paid for this, and for many other things, too! In 1919 he was returning from Kharkiv to Moscow by train. Officially, he contracted fatal Spanish flu. Yet rumours started circulating – allegedly he'd been battered to death by… some workers! But this fact was brushed under the carpet – so's "not to defile the image of the revolution"!'

'Well, all this is somehow… Generally speaking, it's interesting but…'

'You're weird, that's what you are! Listen then – here's the real icing on this cake. After the Soviet Union disintegrated a certain letter surfaced in the archives. Not just any letter, but penned by none other but Yagoda,[33] the head of the NKVD! In it he was informing Stalin – that was already 1935 – that a safe belonging to Sverdlov had been discovered in the storeroom of the Kremlin's Commandant. The safe hadn't been opened for 16 years – since Sverdlov's death. What do you think they found inside? Gold coins issued by the Royal

....

[33] **Genrikh Yagoda** (1891-1938): a Soviet secret police official who served as director of the NKVD (the precursor of the KBG), the Soviet Union's security and intelligence agency.

Mint! Totalling some astronomical sum in value. Also, over seven hundred pieces of gold jewellery with precious stones. And a pile of passport blanks filled in the name of Sverdlov himself and some persons unknown. Not to mention the royal bonds, etc. Allegedly, Stalin personally inspected the safe and kept the key. Instructed total secrecy. As if to say – the revolutionary leaders – it's something sacred. They must remain infallible in popular memory, whatever the truth… This very safe may well still exist somewhere in the Kremlin cellars.'

'Bah! They all had safes like this! Make no mistake! Professional revolutionaries – where would they be without bogus passports and a gold reserve? What if one had to do a bunk? Leaders always think along these lines – then as now. Use your time in power to stash something substantial. Tables may always be turned on you… So in this case grab the most valuable of your possessions and leg it!'

'So what d'ye say? You like it?'

'You see…' I really didn't want to hurt his feelings. 'The material is classy, impressive. Yet what could one dig up there for a new angle? As a reference, it's not bad. But for a film… In a word, we'll raise the issue but will never be able to bring it to a close. Alas, all answers are in Moscow, in the cellars of the Kremlin, under lock and key. And those who have even the remotest idea have all been bound by scores of secrecy acts. One step aside and you face a firing squad. That's the only way over there…'

'Hmm… You have a point here. Perhaps when power in Russia changes, those safes will get opened…'

'No, Arkady. They will never expose such secrets. Whoever comes next…'

We parted company, me thinking: *lucky bastards*!

Each one had already made a choice! And each one was already elaborating on it. Not to put too fine a point on it – even Brunhild got inspired by that 'Soviet glass' as suggested by her Spyridon. She promised to knock together some staggering installation – uproar at the exhibition guaranteed! She said she saw this glass as something huge, at least three metres tall! It would have to be filled with something, of course. However, she wasn't yet sure how to go about physically producing a glass of such dimensions…

A Bare-Chested Putin

Whatever the events elsewhere, the life of a student follows its own course: lectures, seminars, practical classes. On Thursday the rector was delivering a specialised course – 'Situational analyses'.

Spyridon and Bolik treated it as a special occasion – pitched up clad in no-nonsense sweaters, the studded gear left back at home. No tattered trousers, and no signet rings with skulls either. Sat there, docile – no thrashing around the auditorium, no frenzied outcries, just two well-behaved house-trained kittens...

That day the rector prepared a surprise.

'Let's analyse a slightly unusual situation... Bodily nakedness as a challenge to the world community... And that brings in Putin. Or, to be precise, his penchant for stripping in public. Why does he enjoy posing for those photos without a shirt? What's more, not once or twice, unwittingly, but all the time? Although nowadays it's a somewhat different story. He's getting on a bit, plus the ailing body doesn't help. But earlier! Are you aware of any of this, by the way, or did it pass you by?'

'Sure, we're aware!' Arkady cleared his throat. 'There was period in his life – "the macho time"! Today he's on a submarine, tomorrow – on a glider, alongside the cranes, then on horseback – again, semi-naked...'

'I, too, remember it well!' Liubchik got really animated. 'Him in the saddle, riding a horse with no shirt on... I think the media were discussing nothing else...'

'It's a good thing he only bared his torso, didn't go all the way – boxers and all...' that gibe from Spyridon.

'Look here! I recall how he'd been bragging about his choice of profession...' Bolik sneered. 'Allegedly he dreamed about secret service when still a school-boy! Even approached the KGB for advice. And they went: "Apply for a degree in law, we'll definitely accept you in the end!" He also wanted to be a pilot...'

'Oh yeah, such a big mouth!' Alla started riffling through her pad. 'And lots of sexual overtones. Le'me find it... Aha, he said: "I've been asked once when I'd first had sex... Can't remember... I do, however, remember when I had it last. Down to the exact time...'

'Hmm...' The rector also took a peek into his folder. 'A funny habit – to make a note of spicy moments in one's life... May come in handy... Ah well... Let's analyse this situation. Since all of it has a meaning. He is definitely trying to communicate something. Sending a clear signal to the world... Let me offer one assumption... Perhaps, it's because he's rich? And thus, in his view of the world, a successful person? And all this comes on display as a confirmation of the fact?'

'Money?' Taras pulled a face. 'Even if he's believed to be the richest person on the planet? Yet I think that's not the main thing for him...'

'Then what... power?' I looked at the rector inquiringly. 'To position your-self above the whole world as a dominant presence? One-sixth of the world's territory is under the Russian Federation... But it's still not enough for him. He's eager to expand...'

'Aha, the centripetal aspirations are off the radar screen,' Bolik picked up on this. 'Constant activity along the entire perimeter of the Russian borders. Anyone can see – hot spots and conflicts flare up all the time...'

'All those hybrid wars and other gimmicks! Whereas in reality it's undisguised intervention!' Arkady looked hurt.

'Say what you like, it's genuine war all over!' exploded Spyridon. 'He crucified Georgia... He's at war with us since 2014... Eight years! It's shameful to admit but there are people here who are gradually getting used to this... They forgot what war is all about. The theorising goes like this: ok, somewhere there's a simmering conflict...'

'Ok, go on, on!' the rector kept prodding us.

'He wants to be perceived as a hunk...' Liubchik grimaced ironically. 'A pure case of narcissism...'

'Wait a minute. But what about the West?' Alla sounded alarmed. 'After all, the collective West has it all! Economic advantages, military, and technological ones...'

"Tis all true,' Taras gave a sigh. 'However, the collective West, alas, increasingly looks like an assemblage of myopic people. Don't they see what's going on? Christ Almighty, how is it possible not to understand this?'

'Well, back in 1938 they somehow failed to see it. Everyone had their suspicions but they all concentrated on their own agendas. The main thing was that no one wanted to get involved! Their own welfare was more important. Nobody wanted to upturn their comfortable existence...'

'Good, go on,' the rector kept urging us.

'Maybe that's not the whole story,' Arkady uttered this with authority. 'Perhaps it's all about bullying the West? Sort of, you're all steeped in your own problems... Tirelessly playing a game of democracy... Meanwhile macho guys achieve their serious aims...'

'So that's just validation of self-esteem, nothing else. To show the world one's supremacy. That's what he really believes! For from where he stands, compared to other world's leaders who get replaced every several years and disappear from the political arena, everything with him is like reinforced concrete and meant to stay!'

'That's it! They all get replaced... While he's eternal, irreplaceable, and therefore the total ace. In his view...'

'So? Your conclusions?' exclaimed the rector.

'Everything we've discussed here is true.' Arkady was summing things up. 'But looks like the most important thing is to confirm his superiority... And thus issue a signal to the leaders of the world: I'm going down my own path. And no one will send me astray. As for the lot of you – swallow it whole. Got it?'

The rector clapped his hands:

'Great stuff. Just what's needed. I'm really satisfied with our class today. All your deductions are to the point. And the conclusions are brilliant. Thus, through an image of his 'bare chest without a shirt' he made it clear that he would stop at nothing. He'll do what he sees fit. And the rest of the world will only observe, cast in the role of international extras. The ones who would only ever be capable of making a statement, or expressing concern, well, perhaps, also feel slighted...'

The rector pushed the tape recorder back into its package. He picked up his case and headed for the door.

'My God, the horror of it all...' softly exhaled Alla.

'Horror?' Liubchik locked her hands together. 'Feels like life isn't worth living, given the prospects.'

The rector didn't hear any of this, he was on his way out.

An Exercise in Linguistics

Our hangout was abuzz on account of a super-development: Liubchik pitched up sporting a new tattoo!

An itty-bitty tail of some tiny snake, first appearing on the little finger of her left hand, then running upwards towards the shoulder, transforming itself into a full coil around her neck (Liubchik deliberately shaved her nape to make it visible), and then sliding down towards her right palm where it was finally presented with its mouth agape... Gross...

'What's gross about it?' how Taras could always read my mind I'd never know. 'It's ok, man. The way it should be!'

Sure, it was ok for him, seeing that he had several tattoos of his own. Nothing as weird though, just some innocuous otherworldly creatures...

'You're not getting the trend, Stinger. Folk with tatous, soon as they spot one another, get it at once: "Aha, we belong to the same community! This guy or gal is one of us!" 'Tis a brotherhood of sorts...'

'So, I'm not one of yours?' desperately looking for an argument to take him down a peg.

He flashed his nice teeth in a smile, refusing to get upset, the bastard.

'Relax, you are one of us. Although, alas, without a tattoo...'

A couple of hours later, everyone got used to the tatou, no one was amazed anymore... We agreed to assemble after lectures by the staircase in the main entrance.

Arkady said that booze was waiting – his dad had won some ministerial tender. Most likely, the process involving a sweetener of some kind...

We all stood in silence – the fatigue had been building all day. Besides, it made sense to save the energy for libations – just one toast and we'd let our hair down and start chatting non-stop. However, Spyridon and Bolik were still missing.

Aha, here they were – speak of the devil! – sliding down the staircase, predictably in time with 'Ooh la la in L… A…! O la la in the USA…!' – confirmed fans of the band Slade.

'This thing is sort of ok…' Alla didn't lose a beat with her comment. 'Smooth. Yet the majority of the stuff, all this meowing…'

'You say, Slade? But practically every rock band uses this trick!' he hastened to explain, although still out of breath. 'Is there such a thing as rock without expressiveness? Insane dynamism, tension! No lyrical tenor would ever manage to convey any of this! Nothing will do but high-pitched and abrupt exclamations. Besides, in our complicated times, rock is the only thing that mirrors the nerve of modernity! Yes, some special features may, possibly, shock but…'

Spyridon joined in:

'Yet it can't be static, that's the whole point, its very nature! It's a must, in other words, to be whimsical, insistent, scandalous! Even shrill! There should be a real show on stage. Sparkling, memorable, often involving fancy dress… Something that blows your top!'

And added:

'Don't like it, don't listen…'

'Come on,' Arkady was in a placatory mood. 'Shall we head out? Dad must be already celebrating this tender with his mates. And I'm like, in the morning: 'What about us? Don't we count?" He couldn't do anything else but shell out. "Let your mates," he said, "share this joy".'

'All heart, your daddy.'

And so, we flocked to our usual joint…

Arkady, however, liked that things should proceed in a particular way. Not for him just some primitive carousing without a promise of some sensible return.

What did he prepare for our hangout that day? Off he went:

'Look here, guys… I've been thinking a lot about it lately… In her attempts to substantiate the historic, cultural, and linguistic unity, Russia quotes an allegedly unquestionable unity of the Russian and Ukrainian languages…'

He fished a pad out of the inner pocket of his jacket. I respected this habit of his… Even if it was a regular get-together, he was sure to come up with something curious…

'Let's take the contiguity of languages… On the surface, nothing to argue about. Yet it's illusionary. Say, German and Dutch. Languages sound very similar but at times hard to understand – both for Germans or the Dutch. In fact, quite a few words are practically identical but at the level of phrases or sentences – more often than not, it's incomprehensible. Do you know that one reputable paper calculated linguistic concurrences across the board?'

'Wow, that's really interesting!' Spyridon and Bolik were the first to react.

'Here we are. I've made some notes… Which language is the closest to Ukrainian? It's believed to be Byelorussian. In terms of vocabulary, they are only 16% different. Then what? Ukrainian diverges from Polish by 30%, from Serbian – 32%, Slovak – 34%, and Bulgarian – 36%. Yet if it's Russian or Czech – it's already 38%! By the way, the closest language to Russian is Bulgarian. There are only 27% of lexical discrepancies…'

'You don't say!' Liubchik brightened up. 'What about other European languages?'

'The least divergence is between Serbs and Croats. Also, Danes and Norwegians – a mere 5%…'

'Once we're on the subject. As regards Serbs and Croats…' Alla added. 'I've been to both countries… The language is the same, true, but the peoples are different.'

'There's data from other languages,' Arkady went on. 'Spanish and Portuguese, German and Dutch – 25%. French and Italian – 30%. German and Danish – 41%. Finnish and Estonian – 45%… Finally, German and English – 49%. In a word, such a linguistic insight.'

The folk started mulling it over.

Meanwhile, Alla leaned towards me.

'Speaking of which… What's with your choice of a subject?

…Ouch, that was hitting where it hurt…

But she was already addressing the masses:

'Can you imagine, I've recently learned that many Hollywood stars have Ukrainian roots! Who do you think is on the list? Sylvester Stallone, Milla Jovovich! And also – Dustin Hoffman, David Duchovny, Steven Spielberg, Mila Kunis… Even Leonardo de Caprio!'

'Well, I never! They must be not just of Ukrainian stock, Jewish too… If they're originally from Ukraine!'

'Here's your theme, Kiril!' cried out Arkady.

'Of course, next thing – a business trip to Hollywood! At the expense of the said Hollywood!' piped in Bolik.

He couldn't control himself, could he? How could he waste an opportunity for a dig?

We all burst out laughing. They were taking a piss, of course, bastards. I joined the merriment – what else could I possibly do?

* * *

When I returned home, the TV was on. What's more, tuned to the Russian federal channel.

Mum said:

'It's a good idea to watch your enemy's stuff from time to time, so's to be in the know… Have a listen to this panopticon of a political talk-show, just have a listen!'

'We'll rip this Ukrainian outskirt apart!' bellowed some geezer. 'They are too full of themselves! We'll tear 'em from limb to limb, there'll be enough morsels to go round. Poland shall get the entire Western bit, Slovakia – a portion of Transcarpathia, Hungary – the whole rest of Transcarpathia. Romania could pocket Bukovina… '[34]

'What's wrong with this plan? On the contrary, everyone stands to gain…' another character nods in agreement. 'Name me one country that would be against the territorial expansion?'

'Look here, that's exactly where we and the Poles don't see eye to eye, and for some time now!' at least one sensible person joined the fray.

'Who cares? The Poles have their own agenda!'

'As regards Slovaks, do they count at least a thousand in number? There was nowhere to "squeeze" that part of Ukraine, so they shared it round under the Treaty of Versailles… Aren't you aware that Versailles was reluctant to create an independent Ukraine after the collapse of Austro-Hungary? And… by the way… Hungarians account for a meagre seven percent of the population of the whole of Transcarpathia…'

'It's a provocation! Who on earth invited that nerd here? Out of the studio!'

* * *

Truth be told, every script-writer feels like that at times: a dead-beat horse, hunting around, looking for a suitable story. Those whose proposals had already been approved were in luck, say, Spyridon and Bolik – the former was to write 'A Ballad of the Soviet Faceted Glass', and the latter – 'Chernobyl and the May Day Demonstration'.

Bolik – good friend that he was – offered me a folder:

----

[34] **Bukovina:** a historical region located on the northern slopes of the central Eastern Carpathians and the adjoining plains, it is today divided between Romania and Ukraine.

'Look, man… I've written a spare script… In case Chernobyl got thwarted… In short, some stuff about the CPSU general secretary Brezhnev[35]… My title is "Brezhnev's iconostasis"…'

'??'

'Well, the older generation knows all there's to know and remember about the feeble-minded Soviet leader. Where's the young people know sweet FA. Meanwhile in his final years Brezhnev was seriously deranged. Just imagine – he accumulated nearly a hundred decorations – Soviet and foreign ones! Just the Stars of the Hero[36] – he had five of those! He even had a special tunic made, with metal strips reinforcing the front, so's to withstand the weight. Two kilos on each side – which fabric could possibly carry it? The people nicknamed this tunic "an iconostasis". I also have a couple of super-jokes about him. Will knock you sideways. Say, the one about Brezhnev and the young pioneers. Heard this one?'

'Rings a distant bell…'

'Ok, so here we go. Brezhnev and Carter once made a wager[37]– for a hundred dollars. The question was: where did people screw more often – in the USSR or the USA? So, the engineers fitted out their aircraft to carry a special device that would register each intercourse.

'So, they were flying over the United States. The device goes incessantly: "Peep… peep…"

'Then they were over the Soviet Union: "Peep… peep…" – once an hour, or even less frequently.

'Brezhnev's sitting there, gloomy as hell – after all, it means losing the wager and paying it in hard currency.

'Suddenly the device goes mad: "Peeeeeeep!" Without a slightest pause.

'Brezhnev looked through the window – they were over Artek.[38]

....

[35] **Leonid Brezhnev** (1906-1982): first secretary (1964-66), then general secretary of the Communist Party of the Soviet Union until his death in 1982 and chairman of the Presidium of the Supreme Soviet (head of state) from 1960 to 1964 and again from 1977 to 1982. His 18-year term as Communist Party leader was second in duration only to that of Joseph Stalin.

[36] The title **Hero of the Soviet Union** was the highest distinction in the Soviet Union, awarded together with the Order of Lenin, personally or collectively, for heroic feats in service to the Soviet state and society. The medal looked like a star and was made of gold.

[37] **James Earl Carter Jr**. (1924- 2024): the 39th president of the United States (1977 to 1981).

[38] **Artek**: the first, largest, and most prestigious Soviet Young Pioneer camp, located on the shore of the Black Sea in Crimea. Artek began life in 1925 as a children's sanatorium. Most of the early campers came for medical treatment. Soon, however, a trip

'He slapped himself on the knee: "Wow, young pioneers, well-done, lads! The future of the country!" Ha-ha-ha… Innit bloody hilarious?'

'Well, really…'

'Cut to the chase – I'm gifting you this idea. Do understand, it's not the joke I have in mind, it's the topic. Imagine how you could amaze everyone if you embellish it a bit… Such a theme shall be approved, no probs!'

He registered my lack of enthusiasm. But he wasn't about to give up, the cheeky devil.

'Alright, you don't like that one – there's another. This one is in direct reference to the current affairs. Do you know who first invented the "little green men"[39] The ones operational during the Crimea annexation in 2014?'

'Who?'

'Lenin! In August of 1920 he issued this written instruction: "I suggest that we invade the territory of Latvia and Estonia in the guise of the "greens".[40] Hang the wealthy peasants, priests, and landowners… That done, we'll use them as fall guys. The bonus: 100 roubles per person hanged"…'

Bolik pressed his folder into my hands.

Well, the subject was probably not too bad, but not really my kettle of fish… Still, I received the folder. Why hurt Bolik's feelings? His motives were sincere…

At this point Spyridon drifted into view from around the corner, swept Bolik up and the two of them raced off… May well be on the way to meet with their Teutonic sweethearts…

So that was that. In a couple of days, we were to break up for the winter vacations. The very same that were to be used as a sabbatical…

As for me, I was overcome with anxiety: what was to come? The Russians, after all, continued tirelessly building up their military presence on our borders… And in response to all enquiries – the same blunt bureaucratic excuse: military drill, our territory where it's our right to do what we like…

....

to Artek became a reward for Pioneers who had played an exemplary role in various ideological and Soviet propaganda campaigns. This camp was the calling card of the country's Pioneers organization.

[39]　A play on words: **little green men** is vernacular for aliens or otherworldly creatures while also alluding to the green uniform of the Russian occupational force. With no clearly identifiable insignia, the invading army looked unidentifiable.

[40]　The **Green armies**, also known as 'the Green Army' or 'Greens', were armed peasant groups which fought against all governments in the Civil War of 1917 to 1922.

The following day I was rushing down the university corridor. Time of the final credit! And thus, I flew straight into our Head of Department's open arms:

'Whoa! Off to somewhere, my lad?'

Had he been waiting for me?

'Look here, Kiril... The rector asked you to drop by... Heads of creative workshops reported on their approval of scripts... That's how you appeared in the "cross-hairs"...'

I could barely control my breath. There – the rector, too, was about to give me a proper telling off!..

The rector was waiting for me. His gaunt face melted in a grin. Grabbed me by the elbow, manoeuvred into a quiet corner.

'Let's cut to the chase. You're clearly in a tight spot. That waffle about the sexed-up fans – makes one sick... Not everything's lost, though... If the current events don't inspire, why not turn to the past, eh? Equally topical, if you ask me...'

He nudged me towards the sofa.

'I've got this great idea. I got this stuff brought to me. Just consider: unpublished diaries of one of Gogol's aunties! And here she writes that nothing about *The Dead Souls* was straightforward. Well, I'm sure you're aware of the official narrative: allegedly, Pushkin supplied the storyline and Gogol picked it up and felt eternally grateful... After all, it was Pushkin, while in Bessarabia,[41] who realised that in Bendery acts of death weren't always registered.[42] Hmm... "Not always"... The fact was that the local population was often referred to as the "immortal community"... Not a single case of death had been registered there for years! The ensuing investigation revealed that there'd been this rule – "keep the dead ones within the community" while their names were passed on to the new arrivals – peasants on the run who kept flocking towards those places from various provinces in the Russian Empire...'

My eyes must've lit up and the rector clocked it.

'Pushkin did float this idea, it's all true. Still, there's a "but"... For Gogol *had known about this beforehand*! Even better than Pushkin himself. Others knew, too – it was an open secret, those "dead souls". And so, this auntie,' the rector picked up a notebook from his desk, opened on the marked page, 'she insisted that the

[41] **Alexander Pushkin** (1799-1837): Russian poet who spent three years in exile in Bessarabia, the southern region of the Russian Empire (most of what used to be Bessarabia is now in Moldova), as a punishment for his social activism.

[42] **Bendery**: a city in what is now Moldova.

whole story originated from the writer's native Myrhorod region.[43] Just listen to this: "The idea of *The Dead Souls* came to Gogol from my uncle Pyvynsky. The latter had some 200 acres of land, 30 serfs and five children. Not enough for an affluent life, so the Pyvynskys supported themselves with a grain and fruit distillery. At the time, many land owners had those, there was no excise duty in place. But then, all of a sudden, all kinds of clerks started dropping in, collecting data about everyone in possession of distilleries. Rumours started spreading that allegedly, a right to produce your own wine or spirits could only be exercised but those owning at least 50 serfs. Which got the small holders thinking: there was no way they could make ends meet otherwise! Which was when Kharlampy Pyvynsky slapped himself on the forehead and cried out: "Wow, bet they haven't thought of that!" And off he set to Poltava and paid the per-soul tax on his dead serfs as if those had been alive. Since the number of his own "souls", even counting the dead ones, fell short of the required 50, he got himself a trap, stored up on *horilka* and went round his neighbours. He acquired those "dead souls" for the price of the said *horilka* and entered them as his property. Thus, having become, on paper, the owner of 50 serfs, he continued producing alcohol till the end of his days, and also gave Gogol who'd visited him in his native village of Fedunky, the idea. Besides, the whole Myrhorod area was aware of the Pyvynsky's "dead souls".'

The rector inhaled excitedly and slapped his pad shut.

'Can you imagine? Few people have read this journal. Or else failed to see its significance. Can you see what can be made with such material? No one, of course, belittles Pushkin's contribution, even if Gogol had been aware of the fact. Pushkin nudged him in the right direction… And that was when Gogol "switched on" the subconscious and things got awhirl!'

My jaw must have been dropping from everything I'd just heard.

'Let's sum it all up. Pushkin makes a gift of the story, unaware of the fact that Gogol had some previous knowledge of all of this. But Gogol was a well-mannered young man. He couldn't very well blurt it out: "Alexandre Sergeyevich, you've made such a gift, such a wonderful story, thank you ever so much… Yet the idea isn't exactly new to me. I've known all of it since I was a lad…" He couldn't possibly say anything like that. Never in a million years! He said "thank you" and got to work. Must've thought: "If it were successful, the legend will start making rounds all over the world. There were witnesses there, after all… Hmm… Let it be like that… The classic's contribution was significant, whatever the angle. Much as I've known about this, I've never used the idea and supressed

....

[43] **Myrhorod**: a city in Poltava Oblast, central Ukraine. Homeland of Gogol: many of his characters originate from there.

it into the "cellar of my memory". While Pushkin drew my attention to this. So, whatever, respect to him!'

What could I possibly say in response?

'Hmm… That's how it is… Can you imagine the hoo-ha it may create? Let me be open – you're a brainy one. So, I won't keep it a secret – I've a personal interest in giving this subject a proper boost…'

Well, it was common knowledge that he'd applied for membership by correspondence,[44] so was in dire need of numerous publications…

The rector must've read my mind:

'It's necessary to say something new on the subject… Better still – make a discovery. One could dig up enough material here for a proper monograph! Could be a break-through!'

I still wasn't getting it – ok, he was excited, it was understandable. What did it have to do with me?

'So that's how it is, son. What are your immediate plans? Still nothing specific? So hit the road and take yourself over to Poltava Region – Gogol's native land. Find yourself lodgings in the countryside, with some old dear, for a pittance… Get around a bit, ask around – the location itself will prompt you in the right direction. While in the Myrhorod area, talk to some local history experts, there's a local lore society there. Go to museums… Your requisite references are ready. And goes without saying, pay a visit to this legendary Pyvynsky estate. You see – I desperately need confirmation for the memoir. Much as I think it's all true, still, factual proof is what's really needed. Meanwhile we'll process this business trip of yours as an ethnographic expedition. I'll help you write a script on this basis… In the end, everyone stands to gain…'

He pulled a sizeable notepad out of his cabinet.

'Here, that's for you… This is where you'll write down everything you see or hear. All your valuable observations!'

'That's if I make any…' I was befuddled.

'Don't be silly. A script writer without ideas? There's no such thing. Yet a story that refuses to come' – he poked his finger at me – 'this does happen. But impressions, comments? It's like that well-known tale about filmmakers, you might've heard. They brought some common guy into a greenfield. It hasn't been ploughed, grass everywhere. "Describe for us," they tell him, "everything you see!" "What's there to describe? The field isn't ploughed. Nothing but grass around… And that's that." At this point a script writer arrives, quickly glanced round, plops on a tree stump and starts scribbling. By the evening, he filled his entire notebook. "What are you writing there?" they ask. "Don't ask!" he goes.

....

[44]   **Membership:** of the National Academy of Sciences.

"The ideas simply mushroomed; I barely had the time to take them down..."
Ha-ha-ha!'

The rector laughed at his own joke.

He was in great spirits but I felt close to tears...

'Oh, Serhiy Olexandrovych... What if I fail? Really wouldn't like to let you down...'

'Stop it. You'll manage just fine.'

'But still, what if?'

'Well, I've got a second option – jus for this eventuality...'

My eyebrows crept up.

'Dostoyevsky, no less!' the rector game me a wink.

My heart sank. Given the eerie situation around us...

'Do-sto-ye-vsky?!'

'You didn't expect this? Digging around in "Dostoyevskian insights" – that's not for everyone[45]. Much as everyone read the stuff, for it was mandatory...'[46]

'But you said so yourself in your lecture – Europeans have a distorted view of Russia. They judge her by such exceptional figures as Tolstoy and Dostoyevsky. Thus, towards the turn of the previous century Europe was already seeing Russia in this romantic light... despite the fact that their mysticism, their particular views on Christianity were completely alien to her educated circles...'

'Hmm... As regards romanticising – it's still there, hasn't shifted throughout the entire twentieth century. And even in this one – was firmly in place until the start of the 2014 war. It's only started crumbling now, but the process is far from linear. Listen to this!'

He picked up his memo book.

'In 1968, after the Soviet invasion of Czechoslovakia, the novelist Milan Kundera found himself out of a job. He had a friend, a theatre director, who wanted to help and offered Kundera a commission – a theatrical adaptation of Dostoyevsky's *Idiot*. Kundera reread the novel and decisively turned down the offer. "Even if have to starve, I can't possibly engage in this project. The Dostoyevsky's world, with its exalted characters, murky depths, and aggressive sentimentality, was repulsive to me," he wrote later.

On a more profound level Kundera was asserting that the Russian civilisation lacked rationality and evolved along a distinctive anti-Western trajecto-

....

[45]   A reference to "dostoevschina". This term alludes to distinctive features of Dostoevsky's works, such as psychological analysis and characters who are unbalanced and conflicted. It implies a shade of condemnation of the excessive drama and immersion into the gloomy depths of the human psyche that is found in many of Dostoevsky's characters.

[46]   Part of the school curriculum.

ry. Kundera saw the Soviet Union as an embodiment of the Russian Empire, especially where it concerned its ideas steeped in Dostoyevsky's irrationality. He admitted that he was sick and tired of the dark abysses of the Russian subconscious and ached for a straightforward, clear European rationality, similar to what characterised the novels penned by Denis Diderot.'

I raised my eyebrows questioningly, signalling my interest. Yet what could one do with all of this, how to come up with something *special*?

'Easily!' cried out the rector, as if looking into my thoughts. 'Kundera was writing more than fifty years ago. Since then, Russia moved on Georgia. And eventually – onto Ukraine, by snatching Crimea and Eastern Donbas! Irrationality reigns supreme! One could easily bring it all together with our times. Still, to my mind, something is still missing…'

He scratched his temple and added:

'In short, don't be a chicken. There should be a monograph. As for whether it will be Gogol or Dostoyevsky – that will depend on what you bring back… For all that, I believe that the subject of Gogol should come trumps. Therefore, we are left with just one choice – Mykola Vasyliovych Gogol!'

The rector's gaze landed, once more, on his memo pad.

'As soon as you're back, bring this notebook straight to me. No, keep whatever you need for your script. But bring the pad to me. After all, you won't need the whole lot…'

The rector looked at me as if trying to cheer me up.

'Those are mysterious lands, enigmatic even. Perhaps, the most overlooked place in Ukraine. It hasn't changed much since the Gogol's times. No railway ever built, no highways crossing the territory. Not a single plant or factory. In short – subsistence farming. Primeval existence! Unique identity! "An ethnographic paradise"!'

The rector squeezed my arm.

'And all of this, mind, will serve to inspire creative vibes. After all, it's the heart of Ukraine. And all Gogol's early output originates from there. Say what you like, but all this "ethno-" stuff is trendy now, as they say, and it may play right into your hand. So, think it over, but what if you bump into something that Gogol himself would've been impressed?'

He touched my shoulder lightly.

'At the same time, you'll reinforce yourself on all this organic food – who'd need a resort after that?'

"Tis all true,' I mumbled indecisively. 'But the situation in the country now is far from straightforward. What… if… something… were to flare up?'

I cast a telling glance at the TV.

'Alright… Who do you trust more? The Americans or, whatever the doubts, our own president?'

An iron-cast argument… Who was I to doubt our president's pronouncements? And I kept stum.

Whereas he was already offering me an envelope.

I was amazed.

'Come on, take it. Who knows what costs you'll run into? But this is between the two of us, of course.'

He gave me a tap on the shoulder and gently pushed me towards the door.

'And as for this chat we've just had – not a peep to a living soul. Not a peep. It's not only money that loves discretion, the same is true of science… As for the real subject matter – mum's the word. Once more, concentrate on the key issues: I need proof! For there definitely exists such a farmstead. Yet whether Pyvynsky ever owned it… Put it this way: if you do dig up something, it'll be priceless.'

* * *

Taras was probably happier than me with such a turn of events – obviously, I told him most of it. I did leave out some details (the money issue, for example).

'Wow, Poltava is really gorgeous! Not many like it left in Ukraine! The capital of a province in the erstwhile Russian Empire – not to sneeze at… Myrhorod and its environments… All Gogol's debut writings, the ones that made him a world celebrity – the roots are there. The entire St Petersburg was mad with excitement when reading it. It simply ain't possible that you wouldn't dig up something relevant. And the committee's approval in this case will be a cinch! Off you go!'

'This "ethno-" bit is somewhat suspicious…'

'What's wrong with it, Stinger? There is, after all, ethnic music, and literature with ethnic motifs. There's a plethora of ethnic scripts turned into films! Why not have one of your own? And we'll make a film out of it. And our trump card will be – against all this "ethno-" background – that we've been helped along not just by anybody but Mykola Gogol! As for your destination, let me tell you this: there's nothing more remarkable in Central Ukraine. Anyone who has any idea of the Poltava Region will agree. And there's nothing more remarkable in this land that the area around Myrhorod, Gogol's birthplace. Do you have any idea? Whichever way you turn – Gogol is everywhere.'

I was about to reply but he snatched my arm.

'You know, Stinger, what comes to mind? You gonna laugh, man, but…'

'Wha'?'

'D'ya remember how after the professor's lecture we'd been banging on about all those evil spirits? And hurriedly closed the subject? But now that's what I think. When travelling out there, don't rush to discard this way of thinking. It's Myrhorod's area, after all... If all those wicked spirits had a run of the place in Gogol's times... Moreover, he, himself, was assuring everyone who'd listen that that was where their hub was, where they all were swarming... So, this is what I find curious. Firstly. What if something like this has survived until now? Secondly. Say, Putin... ok, let's just assume it were possible, why not? If he were such a creature... Is he of the same species, or is it the two varieties of the same accursed pestilence? If only one could find out! What d'ye think of such a project? So why not get to the bottom of it when you're down there? Adopt this additional direction of research?'

I'd be damned! He could've knocked me down with a feather. The thoughts in his head!

Meanwhile Taras was forging forward:

'Why d'ya stay silent, you nincompoop? Trust me, dude, this is pure Klondike! All those demons and devils will be just the ticket for us, you dimwit! Forget the Soviet *granchaks*! Or even Sverdlov's safe with its royal gold pieces! Eventually, we could even make our mark on the international arena – with all those evil spirits, and let anyone dare throw a spanner in this ethno-express of ours! Don't you see, the entire mankind will be blown away by the rich nature of our ancient exotica!'

Phew. He blurted it all out and grew silent.

Well, well, well! The prospects in store for me – weren't they really breath-taking? Firstly, the rector's personal mission. Now Taras's idea, too: to investigate the nature of evil spirits... Both of those overlapping with the fate of Gogol – a prominent Russo-Ukrainian author! Or should it be Ukraino-Russian? Which one was more adequate? Whatever, that was not the point at this stage. The main thing was not to spill the beans to the rector – he was unlikely to approve of this parallel investigation...

I could see Taras getting anxious, clearly eager to be somewhere else. He thumped me on the shoulder:

'Go for it, Stinger! See you... Now probably not until after the vacations...'

As soon we took leave of one another, Spyridon and Bolik pitched up, like two jacks out of the same box. Little devils, the pair of them. Well, I didn't tell them any of this.

'Well, Stinger, goodbye for the vacations? It's worrying, this. Who knows, perhaps it's our last vacation ever? Have you heard? The concentration of the armed forces on our borders is off the scale? And no one can tell if they are going to invade or not. I wonder if even the Russian Head of Staff knows. It all depends *on that man.* The Department has just put out an advert on the notice board: we're all requested to stay in touch. Who knows what can happen...'

They popped out of nowhere and disappeared the same way. Accompanied, throughout, by the same well-known track by Slade: 'Ooh, la la in L.A., O, la la in the USA...'

That's when I thought – anything was possible... So that instead of Slade's 'O, la la in the USA' we soon might well have to sing something else. For example: 'You're in the army... Now...' Another cult piece, really famous... However, that was already Status Quo...

Back home, I opened a volume of *The Dead Souls*, started riffling through the pages.

I found the place where Pavlo Ivanovych Chychykov[47] first presented himself to the governor. For this appointment he chose 'a tail-coat of the sparkling red huckleberry colour'...

I then cast my eye over the introduction written by some critic, scanned the comments. It only took half an hour to restore it all in my memory, down to minutest details. Well then, *The Dead Soul*'s Chychykov had a dream: to buy 'dead souls' from various landowners, then use them as security with a Board of Trustees, obtain a loan and thus ensure himself an affluent existence and a hereditary estate. All this under the umbrella of a coveted dream – to marry the governor's daughter. To start with, all was going in his favour, splendidly so. Chychykov charmed the entire population of the provincial capital with his wondrous bows: ever so slightly askew! They'd never seen anything like it... And when the rumours started circulating that Pavlo Ivanovych was a millionaire, their love for him escalated to new heights. Meanwhile families with daughters of marriageable age completely lost their minds. But even that, Chychykov was making a perfectly satisfactory progress – his scam was gradually moving to fruition. But in the very end – and here one had to use obscenities – it all went tits up. What a troublesome life journey...

I leafed through some more pages. True, it could've all gone without a hitch. Why shouldn't I become... kinda... an explorer of *The Dead Soul*'s primary sources? Myrhorod area... Gogol's turf... Take Gogol's ethno-motives and make a leap into modern ethno-motives? And go even further – up to the point when he personally burnt his own manuscript in the fireplace?! Far from a trivial idea... Perhaps, after all, we, together with the rector – he-he! – have stumbled on something of merit?

....

[47] **Chychykov**: the main protagonist in Gogol's *The Dead Souls.*

　　　　　　　　　　　　　　　　　　　　　　OLEKSANDR SAMBRUS

I licked my lips in excitement.

* * *

I deliberately chose a 'mug's train'. Turned out, they still existed – the ones that stopped for several minutes at each lamppost. Made sense, though: why should I arrive into an unfamiliar city at three in the morning? Better to spend a night in my own berth, nodding off peacefully...

I'd been packing in a frenzy, so there was no time to check the contents of the rector's envelope. I opened it only now...

And inside was such a sum... The rector was clearly pulling out all the stops... Also, a sheet of paper. I unfolded it:

'And here, my dear Kiril, is a little question for you... Completely in keeping with the task that we've formulated jointly – the real origins of *The Dead Souls*. Once you start "prospecting" please remember that there's no way you could cover all angles. That's the first point. And secondly: tell me, had it so happened that Gogol would've never broken away from his native province and made it to Petersburg, the capital city of the Russian Empire – would he have ever managed to write *The Dead Souls*? To write *such* a book in the Myrhorod area?

PS – Somewhat discombobulated? All I'm trying to say is that when "digging around" you must listen to everyone, take onboard opinions from all sides... Good luck!'

The train crew were from Kharkiv which meant that communication would be fun, theirs being a particular form of Ukrainian. True enough, as soon as the train pulled off, the attendant addressed us on the radio:

"Lad-i-i-ies and gentlemun! Our train is now on its way. Please no soiling the toilets; plus, no filthy language in public and no sashaying around with no clothes on. Offender-rers-s shall be chucked off our train by force. Straight into a steppe somewhere...'

We exchanged glances with my neighbour, seated across the aisle. Cultured appearance, could easily be an assistant professor of some significant department somewhere.

'What do you expect? Sloboda Ukraine[48]... The historical motherland of surzhyk!'[49]

....

[48] **Sloboda Ukraine**, usually referred to locally as Slobozhanshchyna: a historical region located in northeastern Ukraine and southwestern Russia.

[49] **Surzhyk:** a Ukrainian-Russian pidgin used in certain regions of Ukraine. The term *surzhyk* is, according to some authors, generally used for 'norm-breaking, non-obedience to, or non-awareness of the rules of the standard Ukrainian and Russian languages.

I nodded in assent.

'On the whole, though…' he added, 'this is Ukraine, after all. Everyone here speaks the way they want. Or are able to…'

All I could do was to make a helpless gesture with my hands.

We were already settling for the night when the carriage attendant's radio spoke to us again:

'So's to raise your spirits during these na-e-sty times, I'll put on this immortal-le hit by the band called Rammstein – "Where are you?" It be your bedtime treat. Since you might not know the translat-tsion but I do, let me tell you this: the singer here cannot decide whether he loves someone or not. Or whether anyone ever loved him or not… Can you imagine the mess he's in? Just have a little listen…' And he switched the hit on, full blast. We could barely make out: '*liebe*'… '*dich*'… '*nicht mehr*'… '*weniger*'… '*geliebt hast*'…

Gosh, all those thumping, chopping sounds… We both gave a start of surprise and silently exchanged glances.

'You got that?' the attendant turned the volume down and addressed us again. 'That's effing life, innit? Tell me frankly, you lot, are things pukka with you? 'Tis always like that, if you ask me – "I'm in love"… "I ain't"… "I loved"… "no I didn't"… For let me tell ya this: life ain't no bed of frigging roses. They even say so in a proverb… Hard, innit, to keep a steady course in life!'

The 'assistant professor' was the first one to regain composure:

'Wow! *Liebe… nicht mehr…* Nothing like all this French molly-coddling – *Je t'aime*, say, or *mon amour…*'

'Right you are. France it ain't.'

I felt like I had to contribute something too…

'*eesh..eesh..eesh..*' the loudspeaker kept churning out this lament, delivered in sharp abrupt syllables – '*Ja-a-a… ich… liebe…dich…*' The singer was clearly complaining about his endless suffering. Over and over, the march overtones kept pouring out of the carriage loudspeaker. As if a hundred of heavy-booted soldiers clomping across a barrack square.

Finally, the immortal hit was over.

'Have you heard it all?' the attendant's voice ran out again. 'D'you like it? Sure thing, hard to say… That's not the point, though. The point is, it's a profound human tragedy! I'll be damned! Total horror… Feels like you don't want to live anymore…Ok, go to sleep, all said and done. 'Tis nearly the night time…'

The 'professor' and I didn't know what to say.

'Feels like the train's slow…' – he offered finally. Clearly, his social awareness was getting the better of him – a cultured person couldn't simply sit around, silent, for too long.

'Slow but steady,' I came back. 'I'll be in Poltava in the morning... Even if it's too early... You?'

'I'm all the way to Kharkiv...'

'What sort of a city is it? Never been there...'

'You from Kyiv?'

I nodded.

'Let me put it this way, then... It's such a city... Somewhat bitter... In comparison to Kyiv, and in a word...'

'An interesting observation...'

'It's a cross-the-border city, only 40 kilometres from Russia... And Russia is a spiteful country. The influence is clearly felt, we're getting our share of it...'

All I could say was 'Ouch...'

And that marked the end of our decorum. We wished each other good night and started settling down.

And here I was, I made it.

Poltava Region, as is well known, is a fertile area. Nothing but black soil, abundance of animals and birds in the forests, and the fish flowing in its waters are so huge that they make waters splash over, out onto the river banks...

The city of Poltava itself is remarkable. It wasn't by coincidence that it was one of the nine 'Small Russia' provincial capitals in the erstwhile Russian Empire. It's the city where Peter the Great defeated the army led by Charles XII of Sweden – an event that defined the lot of Ukraine for the two subsequent centuries. Some were jubilant, others – grieved...

I started out with the 'to do' programme. Here it was, the ensemble of Circular Square. Eight administrative buildings along its perimeter. Everything in classic style. Nice...The tsar Nicolas the First did put in an effort. Some researches maintain that the architect's idea for the ensemble of Circular Square was to become a sort of 'Little Petersburg' – a scaled-down copy of Palace Square in St Petersburg, complete with the Alexandre Column – a monument of glory as its focal point. But in the end, unlike the granite-clad Palace Square, the compositional focus of the central square in Poltava is a green park.

A few minutes on foot, and here we are in the alley lined up with Gogol's characters: Taras Bulba, Solokha, Vakula, the Nose, compositions from the *Fair at Sorochyntsi...*

I made another round. Aha, here it was – the monument to Poltavian dumpling – *halushka*! The popular belief is that you must touch each of its twelve dumplings and that'd guarantee your affluence.

And that was what I had for lunch in the nearby joint. Six ones filled with potatoes, six – with cabbage, and three with cottage cheese as dessert...

In Gogol's youth and childhood, he used to live on this diet himself. Later on, of course, he got a bit precious about his food – that was after his stint in Italy. Over there, he twigged that pasta (not the same as *halushkas*, of course) was only supposed to be *al dente*. In other words, cooked for a shorter length of time so that you could taste the inherent elasticity.

Once, when in Moscow, he invited his friends over. 'I am about to treat you,' he said, 'to the wonders of Italian cuisine. Finger-licking stuff!' He served the dishes himself, too. He popped out to the kitchen, to get something he forgot, and one of his friends – Aksakov – softly said to the others: 'It's undercooked… How can you eat this stuff? Why's he so fascinated?'

In short, that Moscow city is a veritable backwater. If you know what I mean.

Then again, why linger in Poltava?

And here I was, at the bus station, waiting for a service to Shyshaky. A sizeable distance away – some 70 kilometres.

One third of the way in – whoopsie, Dikanka! The very same as in *The Evenings on the Farm at…* – Gogol's first significant creation.

And straightaway one felt – this was special place, full of mysteries… Not clear at all whether it was well-disposed towards the visitors. I was already seeing treacherous witches and forest spirits lurking behind every tree, and behind the bushes – mire devils and mermaids…

But then – what good luck! – the bus stopped for a whole 15 minutes. I raced towards the nearby St Trinity Church… That was exactly where blacksmith Vakula once painted his godless Satan: 'on the wall, to one side from the entrance, Vakula painted a devil in hell – so repulsive it was that anyone who happened to pass by couldn't refrain from spitting at it…'

I paused momentarily by the icon of Our Lady. She gave me this astonished look… As if whispering: 'How goes it? Still fooling around? You'd better start getting prepared…' Although I never made out what I was supposed to get prepared for…

Back to the bus, and off we went. Another stop – by the Kotchubeys' oak trees.[50] The trees were over 800 years old, the trunks – way too wide to put your arms around…

Shortly before reaching Myrhorod, I got off at Shyshaky – doesn't sound much but nowadays a local capital, having snatched a good slice of territory from Myrhorod. So, I'd reached my destination and my ethnographic expedition was about to begin…

....

[50]   Dikanka: a hereditary estate of the **Kochubey** family, situated in the Myrhorod area. Several of the oak trees survive and are mentioned in songs and legends.

February 2022. An Ethnographic Paradise

I didn't take me all that long to locate the Local History Society – here, it was known to everyone. On the other hand, I simply couldn't miss this impressive building – what with the portico and columns – situated smack in the village centre. In front of it ran several rows of white cedars, and among the trees some neatly trimmed boxwood bushes. Nothing short of an English park!

'What's your business?' a buxom woman asked me, regally perched behind a solid reception desk, on top of which sat as many as four telephones! Wow – although obviously a relic of the Soviet days, it did make you feel small. An immediate signal that the place was a seat of an important bigshot.

'A matter of mutual interest,' thankfully, I did manage to get my wits together. 'Would you please announce that I'm from the capital...'

'One moment...' she dived into the office.

I pricked up my ears and heard some muffled snippets:

'An unknown individual... Says he's from the capital... could it mean an audit? But to look at him... Seems just a regular fellow... A sort of a plucked peacock... But then again, who knows? My lord, what a bother...'

'What's to be done? Ask him in...'

She floated out of the office:

'Do come in.'

I approached the massive oak door and momentarily lost my power of speech! In the centre of the door gleamed a brass plaque, and on it, for all to see, the name – scrolled in black enamel: President of Shyhaky Local History Society Anatoliy Semenovych Pyvynsky!

My word! Could he be related to the original Pyvynsky, the one from the Gogol's times?

Meanwhile the door flew open:

'Welcome, do make yourself at home, my good Sir!'

Our eyes made a fleeting contact in an attempt to size each other up. Stayed locked for a second.

The guy was – what's the word? – corpulent but not excessively so. What caught my eye was a kind of discrepancy: the face was that of a country dweller – slightly too broad. But it was in contrast with this sleek veneer of his...

The hair neatly in place, the face shaved to perfection, the gaze wary but also confident. Clad in an expensive well-cut suit. And his black shoes glowed as if they'd been attended to by at least three shoe-shiners at once.

Hmm… Curious mismatch with his surroundings, this backwater of a place…

'Christ Almighty, I'm so glad!' Pyvynsky interrupted my train of thought. 'But what a surprise!'

He grabbed me by the elbow and steered towards the sofa.

Could it be that the secretary had given him such a fright that he didn't even bother to ask for my credentials but instead rushed forward with explanations.

'A matter of local history? Let me assure you that our activities here meet the national requirements for quality!'

He leaned towards me and whispered:

'The head of district administration is a personal friend. In a word, we are doing all we can to put our Society on an impressive footing!'

And continued, somewhat more confidently:

'Thanks to the substantial support from the authorities we've been able to reach out to practically every resident: our ranks include everyone – from teenagers to those more advanced in age. Five thousand members altogether!' He raised a finger. 'But next year we plan to involve younger school children, too!'

What a charade! A real-life vignette from Gogol's *The Inspector General*! After all, I had no interest in his assurances and plans. So, I cut straight to the chase.

'Kirilo Zhalovaha,' I put out my hand. 'A graduate student of the Institute of Cinematography.'

And added, dropping my voice slightly:

'On a personal mission from our rector…' and handed over my letter of introduction – printed on the watermark paper, complete with two stamps and a rubberstamp, as if to say: take that, man! With such an introduction to my name, I was good enough the be rapidly promoted to some presidium or other!

The president started reading my papers carefully, which gave me a chance to look around.

It was obvious at first glance that the office belonged to a high-ranking official.

A bookcase stretched across the entire width of the wall behind the desk, its shelves crammed with encyclopaedias showing gilded spines. To the left and right were massive mahogany doors. One of those unquestionably led into a bathroom, complete with a fitted shower; the other – into a lounge. Sure thing, it would be furnished with a comfortable sofa, a TV screen, and a dinner table. A dream come true! On a par with an office of some minister…

The most impressive thing about Pyvynsky's office, though, was that all this opulence was unexpected. I was unlikely to see something similar ever again. A veritable museum of antiquity, no less! The solid oak desk, of vintage workmanship. Some three metres across... In a corner – a spinning wheel, perhaps a hundred-years old. In the opposite corner – a sheaf of wheat tied with a blue-and-yellow ribbon. But not of the type currently available from every street corner – clearly, something from the days of the glorious Ukrainian People's Republic, even some old medals pinned to its sides. The walls hung with a variety of pictures. In yet another corner – a fireplace, and not just any old fireplace. This one was stylised to look like an ancient Ukrainian oven...

'Ah, what an apt remark from Mr Rector in his letter...' Pyvynsky finished reading. His face was glowing with satisfaction. '"To conduct research into certain unknown facts in the history of Myrhorod Region..." True, some time ago we became an independent district... However... We look at these areas in the light of Mykola Vasyliovych Gogol's creativity... And all those areas lie in Myrhorod Region...'

It was obvious that the rector's letter made quite an impression – he started going all over it again.

'Hmm... "For the purpose of ethnographic research"...' the president pointed his finger at a line in the letter. 'Do you plan to stay just here, in Shyshaky, or have you mapped out an additional route?'

'I'd like to achieve a broad coverage...'

'That's very shrewd!'

Suddenly, he faltered.

'Would be good to process it all in the right way...'

'???'

'You wouldn't have anything against becoming a member of our Society?'

'A-a... Willingly!'

'However,' the president spread his hands bashfully. 'It involves a joining fee... I'm sorry but it's all set out here, in the rules...'

'How much?'

'Whatever you can afford. It could be a purely symbolic sum, you're a student after all...'

Oh my. It was clear as day that a lot of things depended on the president here. Perhaps my whole expedition was in his hands...

Pulled out the rector's envelope and offered him, without looking, a hundred. A substantial sum for a place somewhere in the sticks.

'All of it!' I tried to make it abundantly clear that my offering was intended for Pyvynsky himself, seeing that he was more precious to me than gold.

The president looked discombobulated.

'So, we'll summon the accountant then...'

'What for? I don't need any paper evidence – no one's expecting supporting documents from me...'

'Uh-hu,' the president gave me a timid smile, his hands indicating a degree of uncertainty. 'Well... Anyway, it will all go to society's needs...'

My hundred promptly disappeared in his pocket. Our mutual understanding was thus expediently established...

His telephone rang and while he was on the call, I carried on my careful
observation of his office. A picture on one of the walls – quite an image –
depicted eyes semi-closed by enormous eyelids. It looked horrible.

Pyvynsky registered my interest, gave me a wave as if to say – come closer
and have a proper look. I was sorry I did – it was a disgusting sight.

The president finished his call so I felt free to ask:

'Who's that, Anatoliy Semenovych?'

He came up to me, slapped me on the shoulder:

'Oh you, the young... Can't work it out by yourself? This is Gogol's *Viy*.
Have you read it?'

'But of course!'

'So, this, my dear fellow, is him. In popular myths and legends – the
spawn of hell whose gaze kills... But even he himself cannot lift those eyelids
of his, only with somebody's help ...'

I was stunned... Only now did it come to me that, true, I'd seen such an
image in the book... But that was an illustration whereas here was a proper
picture! Also, my gut told me it wasn't a copy...

'Correct. It's not a copy!'

Wow, was he reading my thoughts?

Pyvynsky was clearly enjoying the effect it made on me – his face beamed
with satisfaction.

All right! That was just the moment to ask a question about his surname.
By now the road was clear.

'I beg your pardon, Anatoliy Semenovych, but are you at all related to the
family of landowners by the name of Pyvynskys? Those who lived nearby
on their own farmstead?'

The president's smile was smug:

'But of course! I'm their direct descendent. The last one of them was
my own great-grandfather. You know, his story was as dramatic as the
lives of all members of that family. But look, you've just arrived, must be
knackered...'

So, I decided to leave any other questions for later. *All of this can wait...
Most importantly, I've happened on such a person straightaway. What pure luck!*

I could feel that the president had taken a liking to me, acting as if I were his kin.

'We'll put you up with two old dears... One of them is over eighty, the other one – over ninety. But you're sure to profit from the experience. Between the two of them they'll tell you lots of tales... They live in a real adobe house, intact since the penultimate century – that'll be your full immersion in pre-historic times... Besides, in their worldviews, the Slavs have kept a lot of heathen features. Gogol talked about it in his day. And it's evident even now. At least here, in our neck of the woods...'

The president patted me on the shoulder.

'These grannies are exotic types, but for all that – reliable. Last summer a couple of tourists from Great Britain happened to drop in on us and were very pleased with their experience. Practically trembled with excitement when it was time to leave... Couldn't even manage an entry into the visitors' book – looked like their hands wouldn't obey. Even forgot where they were supposed to go next... Someone asked them: "So now what, where're you heading next?" They just stared, numb. Gave us all a scare! I'm telling you – we've got a proper ethnographic paradise here...'

When already in the car, he asked me quietly:

'As for the capital city... What's the chat... about this intrusion?'

'Lots of opinions... Some people are certain of it, the others deny it point blank...'

'Same as here. Although, to tell the truth, there's more confidence in the position of our authorities. They hope it will all die down by itself... In a word we're waiting for the sixteenth... If they do attack us – then that's it, the war. The Americans, too, have a point... But if there's no attack – all this is fake news. I've also heard that whatever the developments, the West is prepared to sacrifice Ukraine for the sake of European welfare...'

The further away we drove, the worse was the state of the asphalt cover on the road. And the houses were getting few and far between. By now we'd left the village of Shyshaky far behind.

I poked his hand questioningly.

"Tis OK,' Pyvynsky reassured me. 'After all, they live on a farm. But it's not all that far, a mere half-a-kilometre... No distance at all.'

And a couple of minutes later:

'And here they are, the grannies – waiting for us over there... In their embroidered vests – keen to make us feel welcome. My secretary telephoned their neighbours, and they alerted the old ladies. You and I, we may not see too much of each other... From here to the centre is about three kilometres. And I'm not sure if there'll be time to visit you... Perhaps, by the end of the week... But that's not the point. The point is that no one will interfere with your questions and their answers. Ask them whatever you like, to your heart's content…'

We got out of the car, greeted each other.

The day wasn't too cold, so the hostesses let their entire feathered tribe out into the little enclosure by the porch: the chickens were clacking, the ducks quacking, and the geese gabbling and chuckling. The whole gang of them plodded around the forecourt, popping in and out of the little garden, enjoying a walk over the open ground – must've been sick and tired of sitting around in their bird-houses… One goose – looking older than the others – moved in to attack me. His neck extended, he was about to pinch me on my trousers – clearly not giving a hoot to the fact that these had set me back a whole thousand!

'Hey you, get off!' one of the grannies was quick to my rescue. 'Look at him! Proper smartie! You'll scare all guests away, silly thing. Shoo – I'm talking to you!'

We were led inside.

'We'll put you up here, in the living room, son…'

We entered the room – my, a good half-a-stadium in size…

'This room of yours… It's like a dance floor!' I even whistled softly in amazement.

'So? Might come handy, then, who's to tell?'

I started unpacking my case but quickly left it. I felt like being outside – perhaps the attraction was all those animals? I ambled up and down, looked at the forecourt from the side of the next-door house – seemingly nothing special. I walked round the adobe's windowless wall.

That was when I twigged that our hut was the last in the row, sitting on the corner. The vegetation beyond was so thick that it almost gave me creeps. I ventured a little further – and spotted something like a ravine… I looked downwards – Christ Almighty! My knees momentarily grew weak – below was a vertical drop of some good fifty metres…

It wasn't even a proper evening yet but something in those bushes was already stirring and wailing gently. I lingered for another couple of minutes – a flock of some birds whooshed out of the bushes next to me. And then like some shadow followed the flock… God help me! My, oh my, what was yet in store for the night? And what if I'd pop out of the hut for a leak? Small wonder, I trembled all over… What if some impish creature would snatch me now, force into its devilish chariot and whisk me off to hell?

Knock on wood, the things that came to mind… In the name of God, it really felt like a good plan to simply do a bunk – and the sooner the better.

As soon as I approached the porch, from somewhere came the sound of wonderful chants… And shortly after – the musical chords. My, what was that? What was it – these local exotica?

But then somebody started singing softly, their enunciation all distorted. And the title kept blinking at me from the bushes – 'On a Farm':

Hey-all, hey-now, hey-do, hey-you,
Hey, hey, hey…

Our farmstead here is truly splendid
Where life unfolds of its own accord.
And whether you cast your eyes left or right –
You'll see a complete unfettered world.

Here, in the forecourt, waddle around
The pompous geese and puddling ducks…
As for the chickens, all they know
Is how to say 'cluck-cluck-cluck-cluck.'

Meanwhile the rooster – he is bossy…
A teacher of the little birds,
Who'd spot a speckled hen and – hop on top!
Then on another one – afterwards.

He then would proudly clean his beak,
Munch on a grain he'd found somewhere.
And off again towards the specked females,
By Jove, we've got a Casanova there!

The ducks and the geese – those just keep gabbling,
As if preparing for an attack.
The boar, the sow, and the piglets –
Keep stuffing themselves, in all this muck.
The cow is suffering in its shed
Pining for lush green meadows.

Well, that's the everyday life…
But lo, something behind the hut goes – bang!
A most deep and scary ravine –
Don't go there, not on your life!

Better still, stay completely away,
So's not to court disaster.

But then again, why would you do it?
For the entire life is here.
And there's nowhere else to go,
So may the dew and water bring you luck.

Hey-all, hey-now, hey-do, hey-you,
Hey, hey, hey...

And then this rang out in the distance:

That's how it is in the country...
That's the only,
Only way
In the country...country...country...

My God, that was about me, too... For now, I was in the country. Only with me it was even worse – I was on the farmstead! Somewhere with a veritable abyss of a ravine next to it... I could feel that I wouldn't get off lightly.

Meanwhile from the same distant place, someone was drawling:

In the country, in the country...
On this very farmstead...

Delivered in a nasty scratchy voice!

Hell on wheels! Probably no one but the devil could bellow like this...

The wailing chants gradually petered out... But I wished they would've carried on, for suddenly on the other side of the hut someone started bawling, while from afar came a string of moans... Followed by such howling that my blood froze. I raced back into the hut...

The grannies, indeed, were wonderful: vivacious, perennially hustling around their household, attending to various domestic stuff. They immediately turned to me with the same burning question:

'Is it true that the Russkies want to barge in on us?'

Even here, in the back of beyond, it felt like the real crux of the matter.

'We-e-ll... No one can be certain now... really, no one...'

'Ah well. In the time it'll take them to get here we'll have at least fatten you a bit, you'll look more human. What sort of a master of the house you gonna make otherwise, when it's your time to start a family?' granny Horpyna winked at me mischievously.

I made back to my hall, found my case and the backpack, started arranging my books – I brought with me several volumes by Gogol. Pulled out the dictaphone, notepads – to use for rough and clean copies, pens, pencils. Got ready, in a word, for my 'ethnographic reconnaissance'. By now I twigged that they all were talking rapidly, so I would have to take my notes in shorthand and then decode it all and transfer to the 'clean' notebook. But should I mess up with the notes, the dictaphone was there to help me out...

Before the nightfall my grannies brought a pail into my room.

'During the night, you only ever stay inside – need a tinkle, go into here. There are shutters on the windows, we bolt them in the evening. And if someone will be scratching or calling out – don't reply! Never open windows or doors... You never know who's going to ferret around...'

The night fell. I could hear the trees swinging back and forth by the windows of our cabin, their branches thumping the walls and the roof... The wind would howl from time to time, sickeningly... Suddenly I could make a sound of hustle and bustle around the house... As if someone were scratching against the window frames... It sounded like some muted hubbub, or perhaps lowing – I was so frightened I couldn't be sure.

'... Do you know the Ukrainian night?' two hundred years previously, Gogol had been asking this mysterious question of his Petersburg readers. And the question was making their collective heart melt. Yet they knew absolutely nothing... So, they could deduce that it was something enigmatic, unknown, chimerical, and probably very scary...

And now I was asking myself the same question: did I really know what the Ukrainian night was all about? And not as a general idea but something happening here, in those mysterious and barely comprehensible thickets?

But if you dived straight into the world of Gogol's characters... Even a soft nocturnal sigh meant something mystical and inimitable. You were surrounded, on all sides, by unearthly sounds – unfamiliar birds kept chattering, the trees and bushes rustled incessantly in communication with one another...

In the morning, I started questioning my grannies. I opened my pad, switched on the dictaphone. It turned out that granny Motria's favourite subject was that of house spirits.

'They mostly live by the huts. Could be wicked. Could be kind, too. Both have a serious influence over one's household. The main thing is not to swear at them. And closer to the nighttime not to mention them at all. If a house spirit takes it against the master of the house or someone in his family, he will cause a lot of mischief: he'd nosily walk around your attic, wake babies in their cradles, or even scare the adults, interrupting the master's sleep, not to mention his wife's. Or it could snatch you at night by the throat and smother. He'd only stop when the roosters first start crowing.

'And the ones that live in the old distilleries or dilapidated mills – those often knock on doors and yell. Even throw lumps and clods at your windows. Sometimes they make the domestic life so irksome that the family is forced to move to another place…

'Yet there are good house spirits, too… If he respects the head of the family and his kin, that's real find, real treasure. He'd keep an eye on the family's horses, look after their beloved daughter, send her some good suitors. And the master himself is lucky in whatever he starts, money simply keeps pouring in… That's how it happens…'

Unexpectedly I spotted a bowl in the corner – filled with the same food I'd eaten myself for lunch the day before…

'What's with the bowl in the corner?' I asked.

'But of course! We have a house spirit too, but ours is a kind one. We feed him time to time, and he's always ready to help.'

Holy cow! Turned out I was sharing with a house spirit who ate the same food as me… I felt my skin started crawling.

'Tell me, granny Horpyna, what's the story with those mermaids?'

'O-o-oh… They are such crafty creatures… On a moon-lit night they emerge from the waters of a pond or river. Completely naked, wearing nothing but the crowns of sedge grass and various twigs. They sit down on the grass and start combing their very long tresses. After which they make a circle and start dancing… They spend their days waiting for the local girls to go to the river. And if one of them would forget a bunch of wormwood or some other protective plant, such a water-beauty may easily tickle the hapless girl to death and drag her down after herself into the river…'

'But where do they live?'

'Eh-he… Their underwater dwellings are believed to be built out of mussels. Adorned with all sorts of pearls, silver, and corals. They, the mermaids, are very beautiful: their pale faces are enchanting, they're lithe and lissom, and their braids reach even below their knees. After the sunset they are lured to the shore by the moon and the stars. That's when they come together… Usually it would be near a forgotten mill: they sit round arranging their luxurious hair, sliding down the mill house troughs, giggling, diving deep down… And all the time call one another: "cou-cou, cou-cou"…'

"'Cou-cou"? Funny...'

'Nothing funny about it. "Cou-cou" means "cou-cou".'

I refrained from arguing with granny Horpyna...

Then again, there was hardly time – I received a call from Pyvynsky. He asked me whether I liked the arrangements he'd made. Told me a couple of jokes, we shared a laugh, and by the end, he assured me that he'd take me someplace very soon.

I spent the afternoon deciphering everything I'd been told and entering it into my 'clean' notebook.

In the evening – oh, wonder! – someone was tapping again against the shut windows while a high-pitched female voice kept inviting me to go outside. There were songs, too:

My lot is bitter, here, in winter
It's just only lonely me.
If I am without my sweetheart
What's my destiny?

I kept silent – was it some girls singing? At times it felt – yes, the girls. And then it sounded like someone completely unwelcome.

At this point I heard knocks and giggles by the front door – the one leading into the entrance passage. I hastened to the owners' bedroom trying to check how the grannies were faring. Both asleep, dead to all those sounds. So, I rushed back into bed. Stuffed some cottonwool into my ears, covered my head with the blanket. Then another one. But they kept knocking and laughing. I realised that sleep was off the menu...

Pulled out my notebook, opened up Google, entered 'Best computer games featuring tanks'. World of Tanks came top of the list. Just the ticket.

If Americans were right and Russia was about to attack us, the time was right to practice my hand in resisting this aggression. Especially since it said in the guide: 'The special advantage of World of Tanks is that is employs a variety of transportation means. You'll find here over 250 types of military hardware: from primitive means of reconnaissance to the incredibly large-scale and powerful technology. Of special interest is the fact that the game involves tanks manufactured in various countries, i.e.: France, Japan, Russia, the United States, China, the USSR, and some others.'

How very lovely! We'll show 'em... I'll be on an American tank, and Russia – on something of their own creation... I worked it all quite quickly and engaged in a battle...

I was completely immersed, by now oblivious to any hammering or titters. Maybe they'd all left by then.

Got tired. To be on the safe side, popped a sleeping pill, dived under the covers, fell asleep…

In the morning, I had serious trouble waking up. Asked my grannies if it could possibly be true that some occult forces had taken residence in their quarters?

'Christ Almighty! Where would it come from? The militia has nicked the lot by now. The rest scarpered in fear…' announced granny Motria.

'Although who knows?' granny Horpyna's voice was laced with doubts 'Life today is such that one can't really be sure… Some may well still linger here, in our neck of the woods…'

'Right you are! I agree – looks like they're gone but oops – here they are, after all!' Granny Motria agreed.

Great, now go and make sense of it all. Given that grannies themselves were confused… Dark forces were not here but a moment later – sure thing, they were likely to put in an appearance!

The day, again, was spent with me listening to all sorts of their tales. Yet about the things most interesting to me, by now vitally important – nothing. Just kept banging on about the house spirits, mermaids, and all kinds of wood goblins – predominantly, harmless characters. Sure this, all this would be useful too… But when will they get onto the *main* subject – that of the accursed devils?

In the evening, I lay down, leafing through a book. Then I heard something like voices. I darted to the window – the voices got clearer. Some girls – three of them – were standing by the window and trilling:

'Tomorrow's Thursday already… But this one hasn't crossed his doorstep yet. To stick around one's house all evening – have you heard anything like this?'

'Perhaps he's sick? Not to venture out at all… Weird…'

'Maybe he's afraid that we'll take him by force? Drain his virility?'

'Don't mind if I do. That's the way we are…'

'We are the way we are…'

'Can you imagine? Such a scaredy-cat? Yet he should be having some fun with girls… The girls, they make it all good…'

'How would he know? Miserable sort, browbeaten by science, a city creature… What's to say?'

'He-he-he!'

'Ho-ho!'

'Shh… He could hear. Come on, girls, let's go to the club. What's for us here?'

'Righty-ho, let's go. No dance today, but at least a hang-out...'

Phew... Looked like they'd left. All was quiet now.

I thought it over – could it be that they were after me? The goings-on here, in this corner of the world, that was really something.

I came to the owner's bedroom door again – not a sound. The grannies, just like the day before, were blissfully asleep, unaware of anything outside.

I stuffed my ears with cottonwool and joined my computer combats with the double zeal.

When I got tired, I squeezed a sleeping pill out of the strip, washed it down with water... I definitely had to get some sleep – to prevent me flying off my rocker. Seeing that the following day, again, was to be spent in writing down all those stories...

Long story short: by now, a sort of a schedule had emerged. I slept till late morning, following which the grannies fed me a hearty breakfast. Then I was writing down their stories – one more whimsical than the next... Some even sent little chills up and down my spine.

After lunch I would go for a stroll along the Psel, but only in crowded locations – that was my grannies' stern instruction.[51] They insisted that anything was possible otherwise. Say, the mermaids could drag me down into a whirlpool and then snatch and send me to their underwater kingdom.

After which – dinner and some another hair-raising tales.

Finally – a nightfall when I always had a sense that someone was scrabbling against the window frames, eager to force them open and crawl inside. I could distinctly make out a disgusting voice, repeating it over and over again:

'Open up, open up, you hear? If you don't, you'll get it. Those Russkies will come after you...'

To distract myself, if only a bit, yet again I was engaged in computer wars, keeping my notebook going till three or four in the morning. This time our guys were giving the Russians hell. Lots of casualties – dead and wounded.

What a horror! Could it really be possible that in several days' time it would be for real?

* * *

Meanwhile the life in the country isn't like anything in a city – something unexpected could happen at the drop of a hat...

....

51   **Psel:** a river, a left tributary of the Dnipro running through Poltava region.

One morning me and Mariya Semenivna – the local secondary school teacher, my grannies' neighbour – were walking together towards the village centre.

'The local atmosphere is far from straightforward,' she admitted. 'I've lived here since a child but still wary of some localities. Imagine, we've got one distant corner here: people always get lost there, can't get their bearings, could easily spend several hours meandering… Some say it's the export gas pipeline making an impact. Yet some others still believe in the external forces. That's how it is… Here's my school, by the way, over there, on the right, and the Local History Society is further along…'

The President of the Association Pyvinsky was already waiting for me.

Answering my principal question – whether or not landowner Pyvinsky had inspired *The Dead Souls*, he grew pensive. He sat me by his desk, then out of his cupboard he pulled a carafe and two small glasses, also a vase with sweets…

'Here's to the success of your extremely important mission. Otherwise, it doesn't feel right. It isn't even *horilka*, just some humble but nice plum brandy.'

Well, if that was the way… We clinked glasses and I pulled my pad out of the backpack.

'Do you mind if I make notes of your thoughts? Historical significance, so to say, and all that. And the requisite reference to you?'

'Whyever not? I even feel flattered. Let me pour us another drink – you do want to learn about the distillery after all. I even suspect that's your principal interest?'

He did fill the glasses, and we downed them without much ado.

'Well, imagine if you can – there was a person who ensured wellbeing of his entire family with this distillery. Same as all his ancestors before him. And then in 1820, if I'm not mistaken, a decree comes out and according to this decree, unless an owner had 50 serfs, he had absolutely no right to engage in distilling!'

Almost word for word what the rector had told me.

'Yet – and it's a fact! – that very owner, at the time, owned a mere 34 souls! Goes without saying, he got extremely agitated, even took to his bed for a while…What to say? His son was in the cadet corps – can you imagine the outlay it involved? Besides, his elder daughter was of a marriageable age – a dowry had to be provided, whatever the situation. Not to mention that he and his wife had to live a regular landowners' life – go out, receive guests… And on long winter evenings, how could you not assemble in some of the neighbours' house, play a round of cards, or three. Without incident or extortion, but simply to win or lose a trifle… What else can you do here in the winter?'

I was scribbling away, barely able to keep up the speed.

'So, my esteemed ancestor Kharlampiy Pyvynsky spent a day in bed, then another one. The day after that he had an epiphany: *Why am I, such a stupid clot, spending days in bed over something so nonsensical? I should buy a handful of those souls from my neighbours, the ones who are dead already, and that will be the end of the matter! Maybe even a few more, so's that I'll own not exactly fifty but a fifty-odd, to quell any suspicions!*'

Pyvynsky came to the end of his story. Meanwhile my heart was racing but I tried to conceal my joy. What if something unforeseen was yet to come?

'Wait!' Pyvynsky collected himself and sprung out of his chair. 'Here it is, his portrait on the wall! Come!'

He clasped me by the elbow we nearly raced towards it.

The portrait was old, that much was clear without any additional comment. A blurred background, the paint faded with time… I simply couldn't take my eyes off the image.

A person staring at me from the canvas was slightly plump, perhaps over forty. It was obvious that Kharlampiy Pyvynsky was sitting for the portrait in his best clothes: a navy frock coat – as decreed by the fashion at the time, top buttons undone so as to allow a good display of the velvet waistcoat, beige in colour. A neckerchief tied high above the white shirt; its long ends fixed together by a pin, adorned with a dark-red stone.

'What a portrait!' I said, really admiring it. 'Makes quite an impression!'

'Even if he was only gentry, still he was a nobleman, so he's not wearing a common peasant's overcoat… He-he…' commented Pyvynsky proudly.

I quickly moved my gaze from the portrait to him, then back again.

'I'll be damned! A spitting image!' flashed through my mind.

'Perhaps you know…' I fumbled timidly, 'but it looks…there's … a resemblance?'

He beamed from ear to ear.

'The genes! Who would've thought that even after two hundred years it would pop up just like that?'

As for me, I just couldn't divert my gaze from the article. I felt truly transfixed. How was it conceivable? This very person was present at the very outset of *The Dead Souls*! Enough to drive you round the bend!

Still, he had a very unusual face… The hair, however, was slightly dishevelled… Also, a rakish quiff on his crown…

'As for that quiff,' my interlocutor was clearly reading my thoughts, 'that was the fashion at the time with artists… The idea was to emphasise some personal qualities. Not anyone could convey this message by simply painting the face, so they were referring to curls and quiffs instead. For all that, if you ask me, the face isn't done half bad either.'

But I still wasn't ready to leave the portrait – it was mystifying, a source of some magical influence.

'You know, at the time the fashionable youth in St Petersburg were assiduously imitating the English dandies. The waistcoats – of the brightest colours possible! They used to change them three times a day. And the buttons? Round ones, square ones, convex ones! One row or two! Shirts – of finest cambric. Take just cravats – one had to have so many, one lost count. D'ya know how many of those were supposed to be in possession of a "respectable young man"?'

'No idea.'

'At least forty!'

'Holy cow!'

'But that wasn't the main thing! Of greatest importance was the ability to tie your cravat in such a way that it looked as if tied at the last moment before going out. All of it – just like in London. For that was the only way with those aristocrats… They would agonise for hours on end to achieve just such an effect – "done at the last minute"!'

'Christ almighty. The life they lived…'

'And then, just before showing up on the promenade – douse yourself copiously with jasmine water! So that the intensity of your "fragrance" would make the on-coming pedestrians gasp for air!'

'I'll be damned! But how could they tolerate this aroma themselves?'

'How? Just got accustomed to it since they had to preen themselves like this, poor devils, every day! Only Petersburg dandies were able to bear it all.'

An ironclad argument…

'Still… Even free from those excesses of St Petersburg, some fashionable trends were making it down to our neck of the woods, too… Clearly, Kharlampiy Pyvynsky was neither a fashion victim not a dandy. First of all, it made little sense in this backwater. Secondly, he was of conservative persuasions. Well, and lastly – he was neither a courting youth, nor a metropolitan peacock but a respectable head of the family…'

He touched my elbow.

'Well, to make your day once more…'

I could see that he was in brilliant spirits. And thus, he dropped all reserve:

'OK, I'll show you my treasures… This,' he waved his hand around the room, 'is the bigger part of my office. But over there…'

He gave me a gentle push towards one of the doors behind his desk.

'Over there is the commemorative part…'

We took ourselves into a dimly-lit space. The smell inside was rather peculiar… I clocked some flashing bulbs in the corner – could be some devices? Christ on a bike, those were sensors controlling temperature and humidity! Cross my heart, the repositories in the Louvre were not a patch on any of this!

Pyvynsky switched on the lights, led me to some glass case. Pulled apart the curtains – an antique-looking document was now discernible underneath the glass.

What could it be? I bent down.

'The Statutory Declaration of the Right to Engage in Distillation Activities'... issued in the name of Kharlampiy Pyvynsky!

Say what you will, this village of Shyshaky could easily send you off your rocker!

I scanned the document – it explained in great detail who issued it, in whose benefit, the place of issue, date. Several signatures at the bottom and an impressive-looking rubberstamp.

I patted my pockets trying to locate my smartphone:

'Can I take a picture? Of the Declaration and the portrait?'

Pyvynsky's face scrunched up.

'The rector would be elated...'

'Hm... What about the flash? It's dangerous. The documents are, after all, more than two hundred years old!'

Suddenly he had a change of heart.

'Well, if it's for the esteemed Mr Rector... But only from a distance. Move further back. Some more...'

I wasn't walking back home, I was flying!

You bet! My smartphone now contained material proof – nothing less!

The rector would now have to shower me with kisses! And if I – let's assume – wouldn't be able to use it in my script, he'd sort it all out himself! My God, what a stroke of luck!

***

As my grannies carried on with their horror stories, I was barely able to keep up with my shorthand notation. The real work started later, when back in my room – translating it all into normal notes and putting into some sort of a literary frame. And the day would pass ever so quickly...

And thus came Friday. I spent the morning making cryptic notes of my hostesses' stories, the afternoon deciphering and entering my text into the 'clean' notebook. My head was spinning... I was tired...

And then it suddenly dawned on me. From some depths of my memory popped up an English proverb – *all work and no play makes Jack a dull boy*. The message was sort of clear but out of sheer curiosity I googled it. Google said: 'Working without breaks, Jack is stupefied.' And then a more literary translation: 'Endless work turns Jack into a bore.' In other words, time for work and time for fun. OK, perhaps it stood to reason…

I plopped on my bed to have a bit of rest. Reached out to pick up a Gogol volume. Eh-he, *Petersburg Tales*. Started leafing through 'Nevsky Prospect'. In this short story, Gogol tells us that a German tinsmith Schiller '…on a Sunday would normally drink two bottles of beer and a bottle of caraway vodka, the latter, however, he would invariably curse. He was drinking completely differently to an Englishman who, straight after lunch, put a latch on his door and got plastered on his own. The other way round – as a German, he always drank in company. Sometimes it was cobbler Hofman, sometimes – carpenter Kuntz, also a German and a seasoned drinker…'

And thus, on a Sunday, Schiller and his mates set off to have a few. Along comes Lieutenant Pirogov who had placed an order with Schiller for some spurs, but having fallen for Schiller's wife, started paying him impromptu visits – allegedly to check on the progress of his order but in reality – to get closer to his love interest. Aware of the master's absence, he appeared out of the blue in front of this pretty blonde.

Pirogov 'when taking his bows, openly demonstrated the obvious beauty of his lithe tightly belted waist. He told, rather successfully and affably, some jokes but the silly German, in response, was monosyllabic. Finally, having tried this and that and realising that he failed to arouse her interest, he suggested that they should dance. The German agreed at once for the German are lovers of dance… He started some type of gavotte, knowing that Germans are in favour of gradual developments. The cute little German stepped into the centre of the room and raised one pretty little leg. The situation so enchanted Pirogov that he rushed towards her so as to implant a kiss. The little German cried out which only served to enhance her attractiveness in Pirogov's eyes; he started covering her with kisses… Suddenly the door flew open! In came Schiller and Hofman, behind them carpenter Kuntz. The lot of them were completely hammered…'

Oh, so what did happen after that? It was little fun even describing it. The three of those hairy hunks – or even hogs – grabbed emaciated Pirogov by his supple waist with their enormous German hands…

Oh no, it's impossible to read about this stuff even if it's by Gogol. I pushed the book aside and lay still for a while.

My, but that was a hint, you slow wit! Dancing! What can be better? In short, why not drop into this village club and see what all this dancing was about. What a great idea!

And to give you some revs, don't forget a little bottle of brandy that you've brought along! You don't need much, anyway! You're not English after all. Or German. A couple of glugs and you'll feel top of the world.

At this point – perfect timing! – came some distant murmur. Then again: 'Dance! Dance!'

Tonight, the Youth Club will be crowded.
Friday evening and Saturday are sacred indeed –
The folk are knackered by the weekend
Since everyone has worked themselves flat.
So, let's push the boat out today –
'Tis what's really needed!

Just one thing to worry about:
How to stock up on nice beer from the store,
A bottle, then another one,
Glug the lot in one go – and why not?
For these are, fuck it, our legitimate days off!

Fetch some rhum-cola for the gals –
Oh, how they love to simply neck it.
What d'ye say? By now, praise be to God in heaven,
Life looks not too bad.
Not a teacher in sight –
Perhaps someone took them out already?
For this is the club, this is the time for dancing,
Not some boring ministrations.

Looks like we all are here now?
Make haste, off to the club,
Where our long waited-for,
Our dreamed-about dancing is about to start!
Oh, the dance!
Oh, dancing, dancing, dancing!
The hugs, the kisses, the faintings...
Till one grows weak – nothing but dancing!

The week is over,
Thank God!
And now – dancing...

Ri-i-ight… Here it was, this 'gift from above'! After all, all the young ones were over there, at this village dance. I was the only one, sitting round here like a complete moron. Shame on me!

I started getting ready. Put on my best clothes. Was about to put on my boots and thought better of it. The village was about half a kilometre from the farm, and I had to walk at night. Who knew what could happen? The place was crawling with chimeras, what if I had to do a bunk? Sneakers made much more sense.

Dressed to the nines, I was about to set off.

'Oh, where're you off to, then?' the grannies cried in unison.

'Nothing special, just to check out the club…'

'What's your business with this club? This dance?' granny Horpyna flung her arms up. 'You'll get the same thing here…'

'They're not going anywhere…' added granny Motria. 'The dance will come hopping to your doorstep. You said so yourself – yours isn't a room but a dance floor…'

'A dance floor is all very well…' I replied. 'Still, I'm starved for company…'

'No way, we won't allow it. Anatoliy Semenovych entrusted you to us personally. So, we are responsible for you!'

'That's it! Anything's possible here. Even if someone simply has one too many and gives you a fright on your way… Besides, you'll have to return in the dead of the night. What if some rogue character comes along and grabs you? And all of this just when the evil ones swarm around… You'll be overpowered…'

And both of them firmly blocked my way.

My feelings hurt, I turned round and returned to my room, this 'dance floor' of mine…

I mulled it all over some more and deduced that my grannies, probably, had a point. I could sympathise with their warnings – after all, I experienced the local goings-on at night first-hand. OK, I should admit that I wanted to chill out at this village dance… But it was true, though – the local fun was not for the outsiders. The place itself was alien to such ways of distraction.

In the morning, I acted all hurt and put-upon…

So out of their own initiative they started spelling it out for me – what could happen here if you got involved with local gals.

'Don't you make any advances to them, child – you never know what's gonna happen. They are weird here like this – they'll make it go to your head, then cast a spell and you'll stay here for all eternity. But you are a city boy! What's there for you, in the sticks? Tough it out somehow,' said granny Motria

'Oh, my child!' that from granny Horpyna. 'Don't you yearn, my sweetheart, for that club. You've got no business there! Our gals are so sprightly – they'll bewitch you in an instant, in a blink of an eye… They'll lure you in a trap, make you marry and you'll never be able to leave…'

'Uh-hu… They only stick to some old customs at Christmas. Have you ever seen how they celebrate *Koliada* here?[52] A crowd gathers in the street. The guys are carrying a *likhtar*[53] – like a moon or a star. The lantern is made of multi-coloured paper, casts its light all around as it rotates on a stick. Meanwhile, the girls approach someone's house. The door opens in response to their knock and they start singing songs, offering greetings to the master, his wife, and children. We've got a veritable wealth of those *koliadkis*! At this time our girls are so beautiful – a feast for the eyes. Yet – let me tell you – they are evil-minded…' granny Horpyna was really insistent.

'But of course, we know what a young heart desires,' interrupted granny Motria. 'If you had it off with a young married woman – that's something else. But an unmarried girl… They all are wayward. If a guy starts paying them attention, they scrutinise him carefully as if he were their promised one. Will also "check him on the giblets"…'

'Giblets? What on earth does it mean?'

'It means this. Here, they use goose's giblet for fortune telling, if you're interested in your marriage prospects. Generally, geese are slaughtered in the winter, so, normally, the fortune telling then is all about what the winter's gonna be like. But we here have our own ways. Who cares about the winter? But marriage is something else. So, if you take a liver of a well-fattened goose – do you even know how huge it is? – that's what gets scrutinised. It first should be boiled, and then every vein and fibre get examined very carefully…'

'Better still,' prompted granny Motria, 'is to stick this goose liver into a pork belly. Then you stuff it full with buckwheat, leaving a bit of spare room – so that the liver could slide here and there while cooked. Then add some finely chopped onions, salt, pepper… Baste it closed and keep cooking slowly in its own broth. And only after that analyse what happened to the liver. If it got plastered all inside the belly, that's a sign. Not simply a suitor but a wastrel. Sure

....

[52] *Koliada:* the traditional Slavic name for the period from Christmas to Epiphany or, more generally, for Slavic Christmas-related rituals, some dating to pre-Christian times. The festival includes performance of special Christmas songs, *koliadkis.*

[53] **Likhtar:** a sort of torch or lantern.

as day, he'll waste no time sowing his wild oats. But if the liver is intact – that's the best sign of all, just the baby.'

'Then there's this custom, too,' granny Horpyna hastened to embellish the story. 'A cockerel is put into a barrel…'

'Whatever for?'

'That's what for. The cockerel is lifted down into a barrel where on the bottom, a bowl of water is placed, beside it – piles of various grains: oats, rye, buckwheat… If the cockerel darts towards the grain – the beloved will be a proper master of the household. But if it's water – he'll drink like a fish…'

As if to sum it all up, granny Motria said:

'And therefore, stay well clear of those village dances, my boy. Shyshaky ain't anything like Poltava. The girls will bewilder you before you even know it. And what's here for you, in Shyshaky? You'll waste your life…'

I returned to my room to record those tales of the cockerel, the barrel, and the girls. On the whole, it wasn't working out all that bad… But for those nightly horrors, if I concentrated exclusively on my research, I could call my local life well ordered. In comes a tale, down I write it into my 'clean' pad where by now fewer and fewer pages were still remaining blank.

Afterwards I started reading some news. Something odd was going on in Belarus. The Russian troops were now concentrating along its borders with Ukraine. On satellite pictures one could even make out the military tents – of the kind used in field camps. The military equipment was also brought in, in huge numbers – even missile systems…

Aha, here was the substantiation for the stockpiling activities. Russia was allegedly bringing in her troops into Belarus as part of joint exercises – to take place between 10th and 20th of February. The training areas just happen to be in the immediate vicinity of the Ukrainian borders. The legend for the Russo-Belarusian joint exercise Union Resolve-2022 went thus:

'A coalition of "Western" countries – Niaris, Pomorie, Klopia (evidently, the Baltic countries and Poland), together with terrorist organisations under their control, are destabilising the situation in the Republic of Polessie (most likely, Belarus) and inciting an armed conflict with the Republic of Dniprovia (must be Ukraine). The "Western allies" bring in their troops under the guise of peacekeeping operations and launch a war of aggression against the Republic of Polessie, but the Northern Federation (evidently, Russia) intercedes on its behalf. Joining their efforts, they supress and repel the external aggression.'

In response to a message of concern from the United States, the Kremlin started spinning the same yarn – issuing promises not to attack Ukraine and referring to the alleged 'preparation for an act of aggression' as hysterics.

Gogol's Road to Fame – a Ukrainian at Heart Behind the Façade of Imperial Respectability...

While I was sizing up various chimeras – and the grannies did finally promise to tell me about witches and demons – the real forces of evil kept accumulating near our borders... Goes without saying, the internet in this God-forsaken place was wobbly at times. On top of that, for two days running the telephone was playing up, too. In a word, in order to get any reliable update, I had to trudge to the village centre. Then again, where else to head here but to the Society?

Half an hour later I had arrived, plodding, at my destination.

'Is the boss alone?' I asked of the buxom secretary.

'No, but do go in anyway.'

'Oh... Look who's here! Speak of the devil!' – the Society's President nodded towards another person in the room.

'Let me introduce you – my deputy, Vasyl Mykolaiovych Yanovsky...'

I felt rooted to the spot. Could it be the heir to Mykola Vasyliovuch Gogol-Yanovsky?[54] The author of *The Evenings* and *The Dead Souls*? One could easily lose one's marbles in those Shyshaky and its Local History Society!

'That is to say...' I could barely speak.

But Yanovsky here only shrugged, spread his arms, and grinned in welcome. Sort of, what's there to say? All was clear without words...

Unlike Pyvynsky, he was lean. The facial features pointy, the expression mischievous – a spitting image of Gogol! Dressed in what in Kyiv was referred to as casual, the clothes for every day.

Pyvynsky registered my gaze and added:

'Vasyl Mykolaiovych has just returned from his travels. Been to this village where some ancient icons came to the surface...'

And promptly switched the conversation over to me:

'Well, what do you think of our grannies? Fabulous, aren't they? Told you stuff?'

I nodded affirmatively.

'Satisfied?'

'Uh-hu...'

'Stands to reason.'

Pyvynsky turned towards his deputy.

'And you, Vasyl Mykolaiovych, would you like to tell something to our guest here? Perhaps, you're keeping something back?'

....

[54]   Gogol's surname at birth was Yanovsky. Twelve years later he became Gogol-Yano-vsky.

'Indeed, I do. For example, this stuff about the vampires... The grannies are probably reluctant to mention them – disgusting creatures that they are...'

'True, unparalleled ghastliness,' agreed Pyvynsky. 'So, master Kiril, get your pad ready.'

And Yanovsky got going.

'Compared to a vampire, a house spirit is quite bearable... But a vampire – it's something else entirely. They are believed to be offsprings of witches and demons. They live in a wicked solitude. In the beginning of the 18th century, they even painted over a famous oil on the wall of the Trinity Cathedral in Chernihiv. I won't quote the name of the person who was just such a vampire in disguise – it was a well-known personality. Rich he was, too... But at the same time a miser. He was supposed to be elected hetman. Prince Golitsyn,[55] a participant in the proceedings and a loyal servant to tsar's daughter Sophia Alekseyevna,[56] decided to extract a bribe from the vampire – against a promise to ensure a positive result of the hetman's elections. Well, those Muscovites are underhand like that... However, the vampire refused to pay. Mazepa – the one called Ivan Stepanovych[57] – was a savvy person. He liked his money but also knew how to use it properly. He borrowed the required sum from the vampire without giving him an explanation as to the real purpose. He brought the money to Prince Golitsyn and the man-vampire was immediately elected hetman! Meanwhile Mazepa had access to the army treasury, so he got the entire amount from there and paid the vampire back. What an operator, no two ways about it!'

I held my breath, afraid of asking a wrong question, just kept scribbling in my notebook as rapidly as I could.

'So,' continued Yanovsky, 'that vampire, that was now elevated to hetman, was reputedly a mean person. Then again, all those miserly by nature are disgusting types, everyone knows. On top of everything, this vampire was stuffing his face with meat during Lent – against the explicit instructions to the contrary. Also, he was taking wives and daughters of his serfs into his quarters. And made his villagers dress in bearskins and then set on them his

....

[55]   **Prince Golitsyn**: a Russian aristocrat and statesman of the 17th century.

[56]   **Sophia Alekseyevna** (1657-1704): a Russian princess who ruled as regent of Russia from 1682 to 1689.

[57]   **Ivan Stepanovych Mazepa:** a Ukrainian military, political, and civic leader who served as hetman of the Zaporizhian Host and Left-bank Ukraine in 1687–1709. In Russian historiography he betrayed Peter the Great, switching his allegiance to the Swedish king, Carl XII. In 1709 Carl XII and Mazepa were defeated by the Russians at the Battle of Poltava.

Medelyan dogs[58] – each one a hundred and twenty kilos, no less! Finally, he did pop his clogs and was buried at the Trinity Cathedral.'

'Are you keeping up?' Pyvynsky shot me a quick look.

'Uh-hu...'

'The following day he was seen in a carriage, drawn by six black horses, riding along a bridge! Everything was as it should be: the coachman, the postilion, be-frocked lackeys and three companions, with him, inside the carriage. And all of them were devils! The rumour spread around the entire vicinity like fire. The church damned him straight away – so that he would die again. Long story short – he did. Several days later they decided to open his grave. And here he was, inside, red-and-blue of complexion, and the eyes wide open! The popular belief is that the vampires do not rot in their graves, just lie there. But at night they leave their resting places, creep into houses, and attack the people who are asleep inside, suck their blood... Sometimes even suck them dead...

'Well, as for this fellow, they started battering him with a wooden stake, made of aspen, till the stake did go right through him, so he finally did perish. So that was the subject of the brutish oil on the cathedral wall. I did mention it – it got painted over. Otherwise, we could've paid a visit, to have a look.'

'Well, strong stuff?' asked Pyvynsky.

All I could do was try to open my mouth but no words came.

'Rightie-oh, let's not lose the momentum here,' Pyvynsky clicked his fingers and hobbled towards the door. 'Let's go to Gogoleve! Right away! Vasyl Mykolaiovych has arranged it all already with the head of the museum. We're expected.'

It was barely several kilometres from Shyshaky to Gogoleve. No time even to have a proper conversation.

Pyvynsky was already hunting for a place where better to park his car.

I could see that 'civilisation' had reached Gogoleve too! En route, we passed at least three kiosks selling shawarma and displaying a slogan, each one of them: 'All people are brothers!'

'That's the ticket,' squinted Pyvynsky. 'All those kiosks are manned by people with Central Asian faces – that's number one. I guess they all belong to the same owner – that's two. My suspicion is that they all subscribe to the "Peace with Russia" line of thought – three. Looks like propaganda has reached even these remote parts...'

....

[58] **Medelyan**: a breed of hunting and baiting dog from the time of Old Rus, now considered extinct.

'I don't' rule out that these are planted hostile agents. But still…' Yanovsky licked his lips despite himself. 'What if we have a go at this Turkish national dish – seeing as it's international by now? Please make us three double portions with veal…'

'Some nice salad on the side?' nodded the seller obsequiously towards a pile of little plastic boxes filled with cabbage.

'What are we gonna do with that? Hold in another hand and lick it off?' snapped Yanovsky. 'If we ate here, around the table, perhaps. But we're pressed for time. We are expected at the museum!'

'Can't buy it all, can't gorge it all…' Pyvynsky added, significantly, clicking his tongue.

By the time we got to the museum, the shawarma was no more.

The director was already there, by the entrance, waiting for us and grinning:

'Nothing but a headache with this name of ours. We used to be Gogoleve, Vasylivka, too. Then it became Yanovschyna. Now – it's Gogoleve again…'

'Yeah, it did go like that, it did!' confirmed Yanovsky. 'Yanovschyna – what an apt name!

Seeing as the surname "Yanovsky" was Gogol's second surname – the one he renounced when in St Petersburg – for the sake of his writing career, and so's to be invited into the houses of aristocrats. Also, so's not to sound Polish… Polish language and surnames in a Ukrainian context is one thing. But in St Petersburg, anything Polish was, to put it mildly, undesirable, treated with overt dislike. To be more precise – the Poles had been, historically, the enemies. Let's not forget the Polish unrests, and then the uprising of 1830-31…'

I was avidly drinking in my surroundings – I felt immersed into that epoch, picking up some special vibes…

'OK, imagine you're among Gogol's guests. Here it is, the hereditary estate of the Gogol-Yanovskys…' The present-day Yanovsky made an expansive gesture with his hand. 'Gogol's personal presence here is felt more acutely than anywhere else. Here, he comes across as a normal down-to-earth person. Somebody witty, and smart… but at the same time, someone whose destiny turned out to be among the most tragic in the literature of the 19th century… Gogol is a product of all this: this air, these wide roads and boundless fields, immense vistas… Ah well, what's there to say? Gogol is a universe…'

By then, we were well inside the museum.

'That's what Gogol wrote about these parts,' the director indicated the stylised inscription on the wall. *Vasylivka is something I've known since childhood, since the age when all trees looked giant, and the farmyard of my father's household was a whole world, impossible to navigate in a day. The park behind the house was an impenetrable forest, the ponds – like veritable seas…*

We continued our tour. Examined the rooms displaying personal posses-sions. Then – stepped out and saw an unusual structure – the house built of clay; its roof made of thatch.

'And here's the outhouse. Regrettably, like many other exhibits, it's a reproduction. The whole lot got destroyed during the war... Yet we've even managed to restore his personal study inside...'

'By the way,' Pyvynsky gave a light tug on my sleeve. 'Do you remember what Mr Rector said in his letter about *The Dead Souls?* So, it was right here that Gogol spent some time working on the second volume. Make a note, Kyriusha, in this file of yours. The rector is sure to want to know this!'

I returned to Shyshaky and suddenly it occurred to me. As for my script... What if I took a theme from the *Evenings on a Farm near Dikanka?*[59] Selected a specific extract and adapted it to our days? And put together a nice little plot? Given that Gogol's phantasmagorias were still quite scary for most of the readers, why couldn't I concoct two or three hair-raising horror stories? Stick them into a script, thus pulling it all off?

I started leafing through the *Evenings,* read closely an introduction by the prominent academic...

So, what did we have here? An ambitious youth from the Poltava Prov-ince, born in a family of impoverished gentry. His father was also an author of Ukrainian comedies – Vasyl Gogol-Yanovsky. Mykola worshipped his father and valued his literary work. Yet he harboured his own passionate dreams about achievements of his own, about international fame. But where could he accomplish any of this? If he was serious about furthering such a career, the only choice was to move to the far-away capital of the empire – a common decision at the time.

In those days (although what had really changed?) a talented individual could only hope for a break-through in the capital. First, get assimilated, fuse into one with the titular nation and its language. And hence, this accursed duality, a scourge of so many... Ukrainian at heart but outwardly – the façade of imperial respectability...

In comparison to sunny and colourful Ukraine, he saw Petersburg as gloomy, cold, even surreal. "Silence in it is unusual, no spirit shines among the people. All employees and officials, everybody talks about their depart-

....

[59]   ***Evenings on a Farm Near Dikanka***: a collection of short stories by Gogol, written in 1829-1832. They appeared in various magazines and were published in book form when Gogol was just 22. The collection's frame story takes place in Dikanka, a settle-ment in the Mirhorod area in Central Ukraine.

ments and collegiate bodies. Everything is suppressed, everything is mired in idle labour, in which people's lives are stuck".

Besides, he was immediately confronted with harsh reality: his modest means were totally inadequate for life in a big city. Still, Gogol's secret weapon was his strength of character. He also had a practical streak – went through several options, attempted to become an actor, then a clerk, and finally – a man of letters.

It should be noted that trends in the contemporary literary market were in his favour: Ukrainiana was fashionable. And so, Gogol turned to the cherished native land he'd left behind. His *Evenings on a Farm near Dikanka* were generously peppered with exotic details and vignettes depicting life in Ukraine. Suddenly, he was surrounded not by a grim Nevsky Prospect but a colourful and vivacious fair in the village of Sorochyntsi! The success was incredible, surpassing his boldest expectations.

So much so, that shortly after the appearance of *The Inspector General* and *The Dead Souls*, some critics started referring to Gogol as 'a founder of the Russian prose'!

And now – attention! Thus, the Russian prose was founded by… an alien? A person who reflected not only the Russian experiences, realia, and values but the Ukrainian ones, too! Who was fearlessly fusing elements of the two languages, thus departing from the established tradition pioneered, first of all, by Pushkin.

Bloody hell! The Russian reading audiences – writers, critics, and the general public alike – were amazed and impressed. Even discombobulated! But there were voices of reproach, too: why was this 'Malorus' making the contrast between his 'beautiful Ukraine' and the 'gloomy Russia' so stark?[60] He did, after all, make a mockery of the empire, never skimping on sinister or satirical notes! And more like this…

Or perhaps I should run with what Yanovsky tried to lure me with at the museum? That Gogol started avoiding his other surname, the Polish one? And eventually dropped it completely, so that not a trace of his partially Polish background would remain… This way the Russian aristocrats, in their salons, would have no reason to look at him down their noses.

But there had always been an abundance of Polish presence in Ukraine. Polish language could be heard everywhere in Kyiv. When the Kyiv Province was first formed in the beginning of the 19th century, there were huge logistical problems with finding an administrative staff to employ – there were hardly

....

[60] **Maloros**: a person originating from 'Small Russia' – the erstwhile name for Ukraine. At the time the term was common as an appellation. From the end of the 19th century it was considered derogatory by Ukrainians.

any Russian speakers around. The officialdom in St Petersburg were scandal-ised. They kept burning the night oil in the windows of the imperial quarters within the Winter Palace – the sovereign must have lost sleep over the state of affairs in that 'Okraina'…

And the famous trade-and-contract fairs?[61] Half of the landowners that attended were Poles.

In 1834 Kyiv University opened – only to run into the same problems with finding teaching staff with a more or less fluent command of Russian. They couldn't, in all honesty, agree to the tuition being conducted in Polish – this was, after all, an Imperial University.

Meanwhile the longed-for stardom failed to make Mykola Gogol happy. Worse than that, it started a painful split within him, and eventually became the cause of a grave mental illness. This duality was virtually eroding his soul. The writer spoke to his closest friends of an incessant conflict between the two constituent parts of his soul. He complained that at times he couldn't tell himself whether his was a Ukrainian or a Russian. For all that, he did hope to find a way of bringing those halves together, uniting them in harmony.

At some point he decided to leave 'this Muscovy' and return to his native Ukraine. But that didn't work either… Shortly afterwards, he made a hasty escape to the sunny Italy, leaving the glum imperial capital behind. Italy, best of all, reminded him of his motherland. His lengthy stay there culminated in some celebrated output.

Oh my, it was necessary to return to this duality of his. A conflict between the 'two souls', or in modern terms – two ethnic identities. Which only expedited the tragic course of his destiny. Those two souls simply refused to peacefully coexist inside one human being.

What else could I possibly do to make up my mind and finally choose a script?

What if I tried to write about attempts to create a federation of the three states: Poland, Ukraine, and Lithuania? What a powerful union it could have been! Surely it would have been such a strong union if only on equal terms…

Or… What else?

I felt incapable of arriving at a decision…

* * *

....

[61] **Kyiv contract fairs** (from 1797 forwards): fairs where trade was conducted and loans agreed. They played a significant role in the economic life of the Russian Empire and its South-western region, of which Ukraine at the time was a part.

In the morning, I set off towards the village centre and popped over to Pyvyn-sky's, where I found him standing by the window, a book in his hand. He shut the book immediately and waved it in front of my face.

'They are saying here that a national literature is normally based on two epic motives – travel and war. This is why, prior to sending the main character in *Dead Souls* on a journey, Gogol made the trip himself. Let me show you, I just need to make this call.'

He called the head of archives.

'Shoot off to the archives,' he steered me towards the door. 'You're about to go travelling too – to follow original sources of *The Dead Souls*... As for the war – we all are waiting, for now...'

Several minutes later I found myself in the archive where I spent several subsequent days.

That was the picture that by now started emerging. The storyline of *The Dead Souls* was suggested by Pushkin, probably in September of 1831. It was superimposed on Gogol's personal impressions from his experiences in Myrhorod area. Kharlampiy Pyvynsky... The purchase of 'dead souls' for the sake of being able to obtain a licence and thus keep a distillery – that was the writer's specific interest. For all that, this information remained dormant in his mind for four solid years...

Gogol's health was becoming more fragile. In 1833, he was even considering moving back to Kyiv, for the climate of St Petersburg did not agree with him at all: 'I'm sick and tired of Petersburg, or rather not the city itself but of its accursed climate: it really annoys me...' However, his attempts to secure a position of the head of history department at the Kyiv University came to nothing.

Yet in his mind certain patterns of his future story were already taking shape... The protagonist – the writer refers to him as a 'master' or 'buyer' (he didn't yet have a name or surname for him) came from the petty gentry. Whatever he had achieved in his life, it came at a price. After a string of failures in his line of service, he came up with an idea: what if he should buy some 'dead souls' and use them as security with the Board of Trustees? It used to be common practice at the time. True, though, the souls were perfectly alive. In other words, landowners could get access to credits against the security of their villagers that were treated as assets. The amount in cash payable was 200 Roubles per soul – good money for the times.

In May of 1835 Gogol came to visit his ancestral home, the village of Vasyliv-ka, and spent about a month there. While in Vasylivka, his health took a turn for the worse. A doctor invited from Poltava recommended a course of treatment in Saky – a town in Crimea, since the healing qualities of the muds from the local saline lake were by then firmly established.

In early June Gogol headed towards Crimea. Having left his native Poltava Province, he travelled through the neighbouring Province of Kherson. In his possession, he had an official map. The long hours spent en route gave him time to practically memorise it. His attention was suddenly captured by the river Chychyklia – a right tributary of the Southern Bug. Allegedly, a Turkish khan had once travelled by his ship along this river that, at the time, was in full flow. He stepped out onto the stern and saw that the river banks were lined with rosehips in full bloom, and mallows, and all sorts of the multi-coloured flowers of the steppe. He couldn't contain himself and cried out: 'Chychyklia!', which translates as a rose valley. And the river had been called it ever since…

That was how Gogol's protagonist got his name – Chychykov. By the river side stood a village – Pavlivka. Great stuff! The character now had a name and a patronymic – Pavlo Ivanovych. The riverside valleys were famous for their fecundity – Gogol was aware of the fact even back in his Peterburg days. At the time, the announcements detailing assignment of land plots were published in the specified section of newspapers. And thus, the Kherson Province with its internal areas – still at an early stage of attracting new population, a province where plots and allotments could be obtained for free, became the future destination for Chychykov's newly acquired souls.

Gogol continued his voyage down the river, past the ancient Turkish fortress of Chychakli, constantly admiring the river's affluence. Though barely a rivulet in the summer now, at the time it was navigable. So, Gogol made a remark in his notebook. Later, Chychykov would be insisting that 'my life is like a ship tossed around by the waves…'

During a break at a roadside inn, Gogol listened to stories about how luxurious life in the fortress had been in the days long gone – the fortress' premises had been used for printing counterfeit money. Counterfeit money – bogus money – fraud… It was all coming together.

The inn's menu was boasting a rack of lamb with a side of buckwheat porridge – Gogol noted that too. Eventually, his Chychykov, fresh from travel and newly arrived in the capital city of the province, would check into a hotel, and order this very dish.

Gogol continued tirelessly building up his character…

Before the story of the dead souls even started, Chychykov had wormed his way onto a reputable commission set up 'to manage the construction of permanent government-owned facilities.' Goes without saying, no such building project ever took off. At the same time, 'each commission member ended up owning a nice building somewhere on the outskirts of the city.' Chychykov was one of them. 'That was when he started employing a decent chef, took to wearing fine Dutch shirts, acquired a good supply of such fabric that the entire province was envious, and ever since wore nothing but clothes in shades of brown or sparkling red. He got himself a horse and carriage, and adopted a custom of wiping himself clean using a wet sponge sprinkled with eau-de-cologne. He even started buying some quite expensive soap to ensure suppleness of his skin…'

All things considered, it all was going quite well. So, whose fault was it that the erstwhile nincompoop of a governor was replaced by a new individual, appointed from above? 'An army man, a person of stern persuasions, an enemy of bribe-takers and everything that could be classified as falsehood.' Long story short, 'the nice buildings were taken over by the treasury and underwent conversion, to enable them to be used by various charitable establishments…'

Following that, our hero wriggled his way, with great difficulty, into a customs service – and that went well for him, too. However, some unpleasantness awaited him there too – he narrowly escaped criminal proceedings. It should be clear now why he had to engage in an enterprise with those dead souls…

Meanwhile Gogol continued on his way across the Kherson Province. He liked it there, undoubtedly. Once more – that was precisely to where Pavlo Ivanovych Chychykov would resettle 'his' acquired villagers. For it was there that 'land was distributed for free'! 'Off with them! To Kherson area! Let them live there!'

All was working out well with the name of the village, too. 'It could be named Chychykov settlement, or else carry his christening name – Pavlivske village.'

Eventually Gogol did reach his destination – Saky, and moved into a local hotel that consisted of 12 rooms. According to Gogol's contemporaries, the mud treatment was delivered thus: 'On the lakeshore, in places where the saline water had evaporated, they would dig some holes that would get thoroughly warmed by the sun. The healing mud would then be placed on the shore, on wooden platforms and shaped in an oval, about a human height in size. On the windward side, the bath was enclosed with some trellis covered with a blanket. The optimal hour for taking a mud bath would be announced by running up a flag. The patients would place themselves in the bath and have the mud spread all over the surface of their skin, about two inches-thick or more, nearly hermetically. The initial burning sensation would gradually be replaced by pleasant warmth spreading around the entire body – as if the skin were creeping but in a nice way. Then the patients started sweating profusely. Some forty minutes later the patient's ears would start ringing, the breath would quicken, the chest tighten, they would feel dizzy, nauseous, and weak all over. Once this stage was reached, the patient was promptly evacuated from the bath, wrapped in woollen blankets, and transferred to a tent. In there they 'd be washed and carried back to their lodgings, placed in bed and covered with warm quilts. An hour or two later, once the sweating stopped, the patient would change into dry clothes and after some rest, eat their lunch.'

That was the course of treatment undertaken by Gogol, too. Although in his case he ate no lunch but took raspberry tea, or tea with herbs and honey prepared by his servant Yakym.

After a three-week course Gogol left Crimea and, still on the road, wrote to Zhukovsky:[62] 'I've tried and experienced nearly everything… My health is better, if only because of lengthy travel. On my journey I've amassed a real abundance of stories and plans, and but for the sweltering summer I would've been using lots of paper and quills…'

In a word, Gogol was profoundly satisfied with his trip. When back in St Peterburg, he brimmed with creative energy. In the autumn of the same year – 1835 – he started writing his play *The Inspector General*.

Practically concurrently, he started *The Dead Souls*. Which meant a physically demanding and painstaking effort. He had to construe, in minutest detail, the characters of the landowners from whom Chychykov intended to buy his requisite dead souls, five of them in total: a saccharine parasite Manilov, unduly familiar and messy Nozdiov, a lickpenny haggler Korobochka, a boorish dimwit Sobakevych and a pathological miser Pliushkin.

The provincial *beau monde* required filigree treatment as well…

And thus, the story finally took off – Chychykov arrived into the capital town of a province… Effortlessly and nonchalantly, he got on excellent terms with all the local bosses. From the off, became a dear friend for all and sundry, gladly reciprocating the sentiment. The local nobility were going out of their collective way to be friendly.

A peculiar detail: when drawing up deeds of sale in the treasury chamber, the chamber head realised that the total value of the transaction was nearly a hundred thousand rubles and therefore took the matter under his personal control.

The only question he then asked was this:

'If I may ask, Pavlo Ivanovych, how come – why is it that you'd like to buy peasants without land? Unless… perhaps, for removal to southern territories?'

'For removal…' confirmed Chychykov humbly.

Yeah, where else to send his new property if not to the very same Province of Kherson? Gogol had all of it already 'covered'. Over there, the land was

....

[62] **Vasily Zhukovsky** (1783-1852): the foremost Russian poet of the 1810s and one of the leading figures in Russian literature in the first half of the 19th century.

wonderful, 'with lush grass, and a river, and even a pond.' Besides, the name of his little village had already been chosen!

The deeds were processed, registered in the ledger, and 'where it was appropriate' – for all that, 'Chychykov didn't really have to pay through the nose. Even in respect of the customs duty, the chamber head only charged him half, while the rest, nobody knew how, was debited to the account of another applicant.'

The province authorities gladly believed Chychykov's legend about 're-moval'. Although the ladies from the provincial high society, somewhat later, admittedly, came up with an alternative explanation. Allegedly, Chychykov was after amassing capital and, therefore, acquiring a more elevated status, in order to marry the governor's daughter! The fact that this very daughter made a lasting impression on him couldn't have possibly escape their attention...

Gogol continued with his story.

'Somewhat later he was served an invitation to the governor's ball – a phenomenon perfectly normal in provincial capitals. If there was a governor, there was a governor's ball. Otherwise, how to ensure appropriate love and respect from aristocracy?

'Anything irrelevant was immediately pushed aside and put on hold, and everything was now concentrated on getting ready for the ball... From the very creation of the world, hardly anyone had ever spent so much time on grooming and on attire. A full hour was dedicated exclusively to scrutinising the face in a mirror.

He tried a multitude of expressions: now serious and imposing, now respectful but slightly mischievous, now respectful without mischief; the mirror reflected him practising several types of bows, all to the accompaniment of some indistinct sounds, somewhat reminiscent of French, even if Chychykov spoke no French whatsoever. He even treated himself to several pleasant surprises: winked at his reflection, arching his eyebrow, and puckering his lips, and even doing something with his tongue; in a word, the things one did in private when feeling, both unusually attractive and also certain that no one was peeping through a hole. Eventually, he patted himself lightly on the chin and cried out: "Oh, ye cutie!" – and started dressing up. While putting on his clothes he remained in most excellent spirits: when clasping his braces or tying his cravat, he bowed and scraped his feet on the floor with particular vivacity... And although he'd never been a big dancer, he made an entrechat. This entrechat produced a miniscule innocuous effect: the chest of drawers started quaking and a brush fell from the table to the floor...'

After appearing at the governor's residence, Chychykov immediately found himself smothered in several embraces. No sooner did he free himself from the clasp of the chamber head, that he ended up being hugged by the police meister; the police meister passed him on to the medical council inspector; the inspector – to the tax collector, the tax collector– to the architect... The governor, who at that point was standing near the ladies, a sweetie wrapper in one hand and a lap-dog in the other, on seeing Chychykov dropped to the floor both the wrapper and the lap-dog. In other words, displayed extraordinary joy and gaiety.

' "Have you met my daughter yet?" asked the governor's wife. "She's fresh from the Institute for Noble Young Ladies...'

Pavlo Ivanovych's breath suddenly became ragged and his heart was aflutter...

They sat down on the chairs and Pavlo Ivanovych started talking. Shortly afterwards, the governor's daughter was already yawning. Had he been some young lieutenant – then she would've laughed uproariously at any nonsense of his.'

For all that, to start with, things at the ball were progressing quite well. But as often is the case with such complex and mutinously constructed 'undertakings', it all went to the dogs – and all because of a mere trifle! Who knew that this half-wit Nozdriov would ruin it all?

Just then Pavlo Ivanovych was enjoying the company of the governor and his family... And who should come along but this scoundrel:

'Nozdriov had already spotted Chychykov and headed straight towards him. "Ah, the landowner from Kherson, the landowner from Kherson!" boomed the latter, coming closer and rolling with laughter that made his fresh high-coloured cheeks, pink as a rose in spring, wobble. "What gives? Have you gained many dead souls? For you may be unaware, Your Excellency," he continued, hollering, and addressing the governor, "that he deals in dead souls! As God's my witness! Look here, Chychykov, much as you are my mate – and I'll tell you this as one mate to another, for we all are your friends here, and His Excellency the governor is present too, but I'd gladly make you hang! By Jove, I'd have you swing!"

Chychykov no longer knew where he was sitting.'

He felt tremendously embarrassed.

The public prosecutor, other distinguished persons, and even governor himself, were momentarily so confused that they couldn't even find the words...

It wasn't that all of them recoiled from him straight away. Nothing like it. Moreover, Nozdriov was a notorious liar with a reputation to match. However, even if the words uttered by a half-wit sounded silly, sometimes they were enough to discombobulate any community.

To make matters worse, a couple of days later, landowner Korobochka dragged herself out of her distant village – arrived in her funny carriage to make enquiries whether or not she'd lost money on the sale of her 'dead souls'.

It went from bad to worse. The following day Chychykov went to pay a visit to the governor – the servant had been told not to let him in! He scurried along to see the head of the chamber – but the latter 'was so embarrassed on seeing him that could hardly put two words together and talked such nonsense that even the two of them felt ashamed.' He hurried to see the others – the same story: 'either an instruction not to receive him or else an awkward and incomprehensible conversation…'

He got back to his hotel – Nozdriov was waiting.

"'Everyone in town is against you! They think you're faking papers… Why, however, have you scared them so much? Sure as hell, they must've gone mad with fear; dressing you up now as a brigand and a spy… And the public prosecutor died out of fright, the funeral's tomorrow… Oh yeah, Chychykov, what a risky enterprise you've hatched"…

"What risky enterprise?" asked Chychykov anxiously.

"Why, ensnare the governor's daughter! Frankly speaking, that's why I'm here: honestly, I'm prepared to help you. All right, I'll hold the wedding crown over your head, the carriage and horses will be on me. But on one condition: you lend me three thousand. I really need it badly, brother"!'

It made little sense to continue. If only to explain that the protagonist left the town in great haste – compelled to run for dear life…

That was it. Pavlo Ivanovych's journey came to an end. And the plotline of *The Dead Souls* was thus fully assembled.

And the author, Mykola Vasyliovych Gogol, set off on his own travels: to Germany, Switzerland, France, and Italy where he would continue polishing his creation. For some reason, none of it – the story about Russia and its ways – could ever take wing within Russia itself. All in all, *The Dead Souls* took six years of strenuous work.

OK, thank God, this part of my task was now completed. And my personal escapade – the trip to the archives arranged by Anatoliy Semenovych Pyvynsky, the president of the Local History Society thus also ended.

I returned to my farmstead and glued myself to the notebook – reading the news…

Hmm… By now it was seriously worrying. US intelligence reports that Russia is considering nine options for a military invasion of Ukraine. On February 11, during a conversation with NATO and EU leaders, President Biden told them that Putin had decided to launch an invasion in the next few days. He and Putin are scheduled to speak by phone tomorrow evening.

The Americans urgently recommended that their embassy staff in Kyiv should vacate the premises. The evacuation that started on the night of February 12th was envisaged to last for a week or two. The White House made an announcement according to which the US citizens had less than 12-48 hours available in which to leave the territory of Ukraine. 'Should you wish to stay on, you'll be doing so at your own risk, and waive any guarantees for an alternative option of military evacuation,' stated the United States National Security Adviser Jacob Sullivan in his address to his compatriots in Ukraine.

In response to this, the Russian ambassador to the USA retorted that with its declarations about intervention Washington was 'throwing dust in their eyes'. And Russian Foreign Minister Lavrov went even further. His reasoning was that if embassy employees are being evacuated and citizens of Anglo-Saxon countries are being urged to leave Ukraine as soon as possible, then it could be it's the Anglo-Saxons themselves who are preparing military provocation in Ukraine…

There is also disappointing news from Kyiv: at a briefing Mayor Klitschko stated that the city authorities are preparing to work in an emergency situation and have approved a plan to evacuate the population…

We-e-ell… Americans were advised to leave Kyiv. And me, what was I supposed to do? Perhaps return to Kyiv, with equal urgency?

But there was yet another announcement. Turned out our authorities weren't just sitting round, twiddling their thumbs… By way of responding to the Russo-Belarusian training exercise we were to retaliate with our own! The Armed Forces of Ukraine unfolded the nation-wide command-and-staff exercise Blizzard-22 – to perfect command and control of armed troops in the course of a military engagement. More specifically, on February 12th, President Zelensky attended the drill in Kherson. Quite a few foreign journalists were also in attendance. Answering their questions about possibility of a war, the president replied: it all was an exaggeration; things weren't like that at all; but, if need be, Ukraine was ready.

The next day, the news was even more alarming. Biden announced a new date for a possible invasion: February 16. Another shocking piece of news: from 4:00 p.m. on February 14 air traffic with Ukraine would be suspended due to the revocation of flight guarantees by insurance companies. Owners of private jets received a message that within 48 hours the insurance guarantees for their planes would be revoked and therefore the planes must leave Ukraine before the end of this period. Reporters rushed to Kyiv airports to see what was happening. But everything was calm there, and there were no crowds of people wanting to fly away. "Everything is as usual for this time of year…" said employees of both Boryspil and Zhulyany international airports. Hmm… But these were ordinary people… Whereas many politicians and oligarchs are hurriedly flying away, fearing war with Russia. Today, February 14, a real flight of business jets has begun from Ukraine. They are leaving Kyiv, Kharkiv, and Dnipro for various destinations: London, Vienna, Munich, Nice, Cyprus… These businessmen are taking with them on their planes not just their families but government officials as well. Some deputies, despite the factions' order to remain in Kyiv, are already abroad and have no intention of returning to Ukraine… Against this background, the hryvnia continues to fall…

So, a dilemma was emerging… First of all, if the Americans were conducting a speedy retreat, should I also depart? Even if I still had a lot of stuff to sort out here… On the other hand, our president was insisting on the opposite… Asking us to refrain from panic-mongering and rising to provocation…

Go figure out what to do…

How to Do No Harm to the Beijing Olympics…

I really didn't feel like dragging myself out of my cozy digs and venturing into the village centre. Yet I had to – mum had sent me some books, to be collected from the post office. Since I was in the centre anyway, I dropped by the Local History Society.

I blurted my concerns to Pyvynsky straight away:

'My neighbour says that apparently there's some fake Chinese letter making rounds of the media…'

'Indeed, there is,' Pyvynsky held out a printed-out sheet. 'I knew you'd ask…'

As I picked the sheet up my hands started to tremble.

In this secret message, the Heavenly Ruler of the Celestial Empire was allegedly addressing his opposite number – also an 'omnipotent ruler'.

'Most esteemed Volodymyr Volodymyrovych! I hope you are enjoying a good health… My sincere wish is that it may stay with you in perpetuity…

I am turning to you, however, with an urgent request and express my confidence that you will not ignore my initiative.

I implore you not to launch your intervention into Ukraine for the duration of the Olympic Games. I dare hope that you share my opinion about desirability of the news of the Olympic Games, and not an armed conflict, taking centre stage at this most important point in time. Even if such a conflict were of greatest topicality and importance for you personally.

We have spent ten years actively getting ready for the Games, and have invested billions in the process. Our principal wish at this time is to beautifully conduct the games and beautifully bring them to completion.

In the course of those entire two weeks, the people, the world over, will be following the games with bated breath; any alternative breaking news will only serve to distract attention of the global community.

Esteemed Volodymyr Volodymyrovych! Let me reiterate my hope that you would agree: no other important international news should overshadow the news from the games.

We appeal to you with a request to make allowance for these considerations and arrive at a correspondingly wise decision.

I appreciate your comprehension.

Sincerely yours...'

I scanned the letter and placed it on the desk.

'So, what's all this? Is it true or fake? And if it's not fake it means... WAR?'

'Hm...' Pyvynsky steepled his palms. 'Fake if you ask me... Still, ask somebody else and they may disagree... In a word, Christ knows...'

* * *

I was staying with my hospitable grannies for the second week now. Taking down everything conscientiously. Every day – several new tales.

Again, it was Friday. They could sense it that I was gravitating towards that dance and started harping on, yet again:

'Put that dance right out of your mind!' snapped granny Motria. 'We'd better tell you so many new tales about the evil spirits! Do you know that here, when the devil's name is mentioned out loud – it's only if you cross yourself before that. Oh, the ways he's referred to: demon, Satan, the pock-faced one, devil, deuce, the impure one... He's believed to have hooves, be goat-footed, his legs are covered in fur, and behind, he's got a tail! He frequently appears in the guise of a sheep or a ram...'

'Sure thing, but it could happen in many other ways, 'granny Horpyna joined the chat. 'He may pretend to be a goatling or a horse. Or at times, even a black or white cockerel or a raven... He can show up in a human guise, too... He could find work as a farmhand with somebody. Here he's capable of miraculous things! All of this 'cause he's up to no good, of course. He'd scythe – overnight – huge fields of wheat, wheel in and thrash entire haystacks... And his favourite abode is believed to be in the marshlands, the reeds, elderberry bushes or dry willows. He and his sidekicks adore doing harm to people, that's all they are good for... Oh, I don't even want to talk about this lot anymore, so disgusting they are...'

'Terrible! But now, what do you say, do they really exist, granny Horpina?'

'Whyever not? Why would they disappear all of a sudden?'

'By the way, if the northern enemy moves in on us – God forbid,' added granny Motria, 'so who d'ya reckon they are? None other but real demons! And that one, the one that sits in the Kremlin – who's he? He's an insidious shorty too… His gait – as if he were walking on springs. Waves one hand while the other one is lifeless… And this sullen gaze from under his brows… Gives me the creeps just to talk about him. Yuk, he's a devil, that's what I say.'

She crossed herself ardently. Granny Horpyna followed suit. Me too, non-chalantly, just to be on the safe side. What was the harm?

I pulled my pad closer.

'Well, and witches – what are they like?'

'A witch is nothing more than an ugly vicious broad… Her nose is hooked, her eyes red. Her face is fluid – most often sallow and malicious, and on it – the eyes that are ever so black. Her stare is downright repulsive. She's always spotted by her eyes, for she never looks at the bright sun. And keeps her eyes down even if inside a church. We used to have one hell of a lot of those in here once. Even now, there are some of 'em around…'

'Everything you've remembered is only true of the "born" witches. But any-one can be "trained" to be a witch – after she's been through some horrific tests. She would be taken, say, to a muddy river where there's toads, worms, gnats, and all kinds of snakes… Some evil creature would pop out of water, dance in front of her, chanting: "Come along, it'll do you good"!'

'She can also become a dog or a cat, a rat or a mouse…'

'That's right! Also, they fly around on milkmaid's yokes… They fly to this far-away mountain where they gather in a coven…'

'Sometimes they'd saddle a guy – for they love riding on people's backs! That Gogol guy was from around here, he described it all…'

'Aye! That novella of his is called *Viy*,' I prompted.

'Aha! But that was still somewhat tolerable… What's bad, though, is that they wander around at night, a bucket in their hand, and suck blood out of those who're asleep. Also, they kidnap children or "eat them up" with their eyes, thus placing a jinx. Or cast vicious spells – to bring all kinds of misfortune: sickness, death, infirmity, a money loss… Or shrinkage of the woods, or grain diseases. They steal stars from the sky, so that there's no rain, and the cockerels wouldn't crow… If this happens, they are free to roam all over at night, undeterred…'

'So how to you protect yourselves against those damned wretches? Don't tell me you can't…'

'But we can! It's been known since the times immemorial – poppies, hemp, and nettles work best of all. Then there's this particular breed of cockerels, too… Say, a witch shows up some place – such a cockerel would sense it from a distance of several households and start crowing. So, she'll never make it into that farmyard. And should this accursed creature be caught, they'll drown her. Or burn her at the stake…'

'Cripes!'

Just like it was described in *Viy*! There, too, when the cockerels started crowing all evil spirits were first transfixed and then fled.

In the afternoon I made a pause in deciphering my notation and felt like surfing on the net for a bit. And this was what I read there:

'February 14th. In order to enhance consolidation of the Ukrainian society and strengthen its fortitude in circumstances of an increased threat of a hybrid war, the president signed the Decree "On Urgent Measures to Consolidate the Ukrainian Society." February 16th is announced the Day of Unity. The emphasis is on the fact that both external and internal challenges that Ukraine is facing today demand of each citizen to be responsible and confident, capable of concrete actions.

In his address, the president underscored the following: "We are told that February 16th will be the day of attack… On that day, we'll put out national flags, pin on blue-and-yellow ribbons and demonstrate our unity to the whole world".'

There was a summary of respective measures to be undertaken in all residential areas of Ukraine. The national colours of Ukraine were to be erected atop all buildings and structures. At 10 a.m., performance of the State Anthem of Ukraine. The buildings of the Council of Ministers and Kyiv Municipal Administration were to be backlit. Foreign diplomatic establishments were to organise PR events aimed in support of Ukraine's unity. All national TV channels were to run telethons. A symbolic Train of Unity would set off from Rakhiv towards Mariupol.[63,64] The train would carry the Ukrainian flag across 12 oblasts and stop at 15 stations. The flag would then be signed by local residents.'

Well, unity meant unity. Still, what would happen if they did launch an attack against us on the sixteenth? Unity would probably still be there, but what would befall the said train? *We'll see… Not long to wait now: half-a-day today and the day tomorrow…*

Again, it was evening. The trees outside the adobe were swaying around violently, their branches whipping against the walls and the roof. The wind kept howling and some wildlife kept circling noisily around the hut. Again and

....

[63] **Rakhiv:** a small town located in Transcarpathian Oblast in Western Ukraine.

[64] **Mariupol:** a large city in Donetsk oblast, Eastern Ukraine.

again, the girls could be heard giggling in response to lewd jokes, enticing me to follow them…

Do come out, you pretty boy, or else we'll send a pack of predators after you… You'll suffer badly…

Ugh… So creepy… I filled my glass with some sedative stuff, pulled two blankets over my head. If only I could fall asleep…

The following day I asked of my landladies: what could those alien maidens possibly want with me? What were they doing, kicking around here all night long?

'Christ Almighty, what maidens are you talking about? You dreamt the whole thing up! We heard nothing like that at all! Although, who knows? Could've been some demons…'

In a word, if anything, boring the local life was not. All of a sudden, a thought flashed through my mind: *Why don't I get the hell out of here while still in one piece? Then again, this war – everyone predicts it now – is like an axe over our heads…*

Back in Kyiv we were concerned that we'd have to stick around and waste the winter vacations in the cold metropolis… But now all I could think about was how to get myself home as soon as possible. And then stick around, never leaving the place. Be what may…

Metamorphoses of a Ukrainian Farmstead

The morning sun was breathtakingly beautiful. I borrowed a sheepskin from my grannies – to stave off the cold, went outside carrying a small chair. Even me, I thought, could do with a bit of winter tan.

At this point along drove a luxurious four-by-four! The tires screeching, it came to a stop right opposite our doorstep.

'Get a move, let's go, right away!' an excited Pyvynsky hopped out of the car. 'We're heading to my neck of the woods. To the farmstead…'

He even raised his arms heavenwards, as if asking the Almighty for the blessing.

'Nah, no compote, no biscuits! There's no time to waste – we've got some important business to attend to!' He even wagged his finger at the grannies who came running out of the hut.

'This way you will've visited all the memorable places!' he announced solemnly.

OK, if we had to, we had to!

Climbing into the car, I asked him only one question:

'So, what gives with this intervention? I'm somewhat cut off from the rest of the world here…'

'Uh-hu, Americans aren't just trying to convince us, they insist categorically! You must've heard – the attack is allegedly planned to start on the sixteenth…'

'And our side?'

'Well, our side… Keep saying it's all bluff… So, we'll have to wait… Not long now to the sixteenth…'

And off we went… It had been noted a long time ago that all important problems often had a simple solution. And thus, we were on our way.

And we didn't give a hoot about any of those mud-clogged roads. Much as the grandiose construction plans hadn't yet reached this place,[65] our Mazda CX-7 was confidently carrying us forward along this obstacle course. Pitfalls? What pitfalls?

How could I not remember then Pavlo Ivanovych Chychykov, who kept cursing the roads as they had been back in the day? But we – we had no reason to curse: the wonder of Japanese engineering performed miracles of shock absorption; the only side effect perhaps was gentle rocking… Hm… Come to think of it, that was probably the way it should be when the driver was the President of the famous Local History Association, not some rank-and-file petty boss…

'I can't work it out,' it suddenly came to me, 'I've heard a lot about it but can't work it out. What's with this "bread wine"? Funny name. What does it taste like?'

'Ah… We looked into this issue at a special session of the Association's presidium… and concluded this. Most likely the drink had been invented one hell of a long time ago. As the ingredients, villagers normally used whatever was easily available – millets, barley, rye… It was then observed that if you mill your grain coarsely, place it in water and put aside for a while, this wort would start foaming, then fermenting, the final result being an alcoholic drink of sorts… There had been other alcoholic drinks around, of course, usually made of honey… That's how it was in this part of the world… In southern Europe they used grapes. Ancient Greeks and Romans considered anything stronger that wine "barbaric" – all those drinks produced by northern "grape-less" savages. So viewed by "noble" nations, people that lived here in those times were "savages"…'

Pyvynsky gave me a meaningful wink:

'Although, who knows? Perhaps we still are?'

And negated this statement immediately:

'However, that's laying it on too thick. People had to relax from time to time… There was so much suffering around… Besides, everyone you could

---

[65] **Grandiose construction**: an ambitious (mainly) road-building programme initiated by President Zelensky.

think of had tried, at one time or another, to encroach on our Ukraine… And in the winter that was a way to stay warm…'

I listened without interrupting. After all, little by little, we were getting to the point…

'That was how this "bread wine" made an appearance on the Ukrainian and Polish soil… It's believed to have happened in 14th or 15th century. The quality control – that is, control over the alcohol content – was performed in a simple time-tested way. If the amount of alcohol was sufficient, the light above it was blueish or greenish – if one put a light to the liquid. Hence the name – "burnt wine", *horilka*.[66]. The Russians have corrupted the word. They call it *gorelka*. Got it?'

I nodded affirmatively.

'So, to start with, distilleries were appearing spontaneously. Prior to that, the folk had been all after beer, that used to be a favourite drink. Breweries – they were called brewhouses then – gradually became distilleries. Those were a source of good income to their owners. For all that, people were producing moonshine for personal use all over the place: in villages, farmsteads, and settlements… Somewhere around the 17th century, the hetmans finally twigged – huge amounts of money were simply flowing through their fingers! That's when they started issuing decrees that enabled certain individuals to produce and market "bread wine". In the days of the Russian Empire, distilleries mostly belonged to landowners. Later on, the merchants got involved, too… Take my ancestor, Kharlampiy Pyvynsky – he was a member of the gentry. That's the story, Kiril… A bit of a complicated story, this…'

'Sure, sure,' I voiced my attention.

'Mostly, they used rye. But eventually, wheat, too, and potatoes. After primary distillation the alcohol content was rather low, perhaps, 20 – up to 30 percent. The name was appropriate – "common" or "basic" *horilka*. As for the taste? Like home brew, nothing else. Nothing to write home about. Yet a subsequent round would result in a product one level higher, and the alcohol content would be increased. Purification, if primitive, was nonetheless in place. That was already "double horilka" or just *horilka* – by now a noble drink. Then came the turn of various grains and his majesty the beetroot. But to tell you the truth, the raw materials could be sourced out of anything at all: some fermented liquids, grape wines, cyder, home brews, sugared cordials, and all sorts of other substances. Sweet berries, too – sour cherry, plums, mulberries. Also – beetroot molasses, potatoes, and maize. Even sawdust and mowed grass! You see, if the

....

[66] Burnt: the word for 'burnt' in Ukrainian is *horily*. Wine: here with the meaning 'alcoholic drink'.

need to have a drink or three became urgent, more often than not there was no stopping such an individual...'

We approached the farmstead – about ten huts, no more. Goes without saying, everyone came out running. But where was it, the master's estate? All I could make out were some hillocks...

'Oh, Your Excellency Anatoliy, sir! Welcome to our...' faltered somewhat, 'that's to say, to your... In a word, welcome!'

Some respectful bustle ensued.

'We are racking our brains what to entertain you with...! And this young gentleman – must be your relative?'

'Well, sort of. He's from Kyiv,' Pyvynsky's response was curt.

'Wow! All the way from the capital?' they even clapped their hands.

'Have you all paid your membership fees?' asked the president sternly.

'But of course, of course! The bookkeeper came round last week, we paid up, to the last kopeck...'

'Remember, I have my eyes on you!' said Pyvynsky even more severely.

He waived in the direction of the houses:

'What about all this? Everything in place? Loungers, chairs, sofas?'

'But of course! All furniture, everything...'

'And those... The halves of the grand piano... Are those OK?'

'Everything's the way it was! Yarema's grandson pitter-patters on the left side. And Vasyl's eldest kid pokes the right one with his finger...'

'You've had lots of time to put it all together into a proper grand piano. What are you waiting for?'

'It doesn't work, Mr Anatoliy, no matter how much we tried. Won't be pushed through into anywhere... Too cumbersome...'

'Well, alright, then. Me and the young gentleman here will take a short walk.'

They all reverentially bowed their heads, crossed themselves.

'Come on, Kiril. You've got your mobile on you? Let's go to the old mill and to this one... Somewhat derelict but... Getting my drift?'

'Christ in heaven!!! The distillery?!'

Could it be the same distillery where landowner Pyvynsky was producing his 'bread wine'? That served as inspiration for *The Dead Souls*? Incredible!!!

'Sure thing. It has survived practically intact. Take as many pictures as you like and present them all to the rector. As evidence. Then write your script... perhaps, you'll even come back one day to make a film...'

On the way back from the distiller I couldn't contain myself any longer:

'Why, Anatoliy Semenovych, do they address you so humbly – "Mister", "Your Excellency". Just short of slobbering all over you... Feels a bit weird...'

'And why wouldn't they slobber?'

Pyvynsky's face darkened.

'It's complicated. If you came here on your own, you'd have learnt nothing. They have no burning desire to talk about those times: sort of, it's all water under the bridge, who's sure any more about what did and didn't happen? True, what's there to discuss? For it was grand- and great-grandfathers of those guys with whom we spoke today that got carried away with the momentum of insurrection and committed an act of arson – set the whole estate on fire. Bolsheviks came over from Russia and incited them to a rebellion... So there. Landowner Pyvynsky was battered to death with sticks... They took pity on his wife and children – they fled to places all over the neighbourhood. And when the whole domain was ablaze, it finally dawned on them that they'd made fools of themselves. They were horrified: what are we doing, destroying such riches that now belong to all of us? So, they doused the blaze... Started pilfering whatever they could, lugging stuff to their houses. They couldn't decide what to do with the grand piano, so sawed the poor thing in two and dragged the resulting halves into separate households. The same destiny awaited the luxurious set of furniture by Gambs.[67] Loungers, chairs, elegant side tables – even if slightly damaged by fire – were rather easy to use, so no one complained. Large rugs were cut up into strips, so that there would be enough to go round. The kitchen utensils were the easiest – the kitchen in the Pyvynsky house had been well equipped... Eventually, they dragged the entire building asunder, even the bricks – to use as they saw fit in their own households: to build a house or an annex, or just a shed... The only thing they left intact was the distillery. The collective verdict was – God forbid it should ever be defiled! And decided to convert it into public property...

Pyvynsky pointed at the huts. The residents were standing still, just like before...

'So that's why they have all those loungers, chairs, and sofas in their dwellings. Even window curtains, even tablecloths. Whatever survived. What's there to say now?'

I felt my skin crawl – I clasped my hands tightly, trying to control my emotions... What a horrible, yet priceless story... I did know a bit about those troubled times but it felt like I heard it for the first time.

'Bloody hell! These people...'

'O-o-oh... The people... It's far from simple, you know... It's so complex that defies simple explanations... Let me take you on a short tour of history. How

. . . .

[67] **Heinrich Gambs** (1765-1831): a celebrated furniture craftsman from Neuwied (Prussia) who resided and had a furniture factory in St Petersburg.

114

was it prior to the October Revolution? The population divided into "society" and "people". That distinction was introduced by the wealthy and the educated. At least it sounds respectable. Unlike what happens today. Nowadays the separation runs along a different demarcation line.'

'Such as?'

'Such as the elite and the grrr...'

Pyvynsky stopped deliberately – most likely, didn't want to be the one uttering the expression. Looked at me enquiringly.

'...great unwashed?'

'Well, that's inurbane. The elite is nothing if not sophisticated. They use a tenderer term – "grey biomass".'

We approached the farmstead residents again, came to a stop.

'Sir Anatoliy, may we ask you a little question?'

'You may.'

'Tell us, Sir Anatoliy, will there be... war?'

Pyvynsky was in no hurry to reply. He gave a heavy sigh, and then:

'What can I say? D'ye remember what your grand- and great-grandads got up to in 1919? Who'd been goading them then?'

'How d'ya mean, who? Those ones, from the north, from Muscovy...'

'And where's the war expected to arrive from?'

'Yet again, from Muscovy. Oh dear! So, the evil wind is blowing from those parts?'

'There you are... You've got your answer...' said Pyvynsky.

We proceeded in silence.

'You know what? I deliberately come across all stern. Yet I nurse no grudges... Their forefathers were downtrodden... So, when the revolution had arrived from the north – agitators were yelling: ahoy, you rabble! They came here in droves, and whoosh! – all went up in flames. Even the hard-working ones, the good house-keepers felt their heads spin... Much as they'd kept all their affairs in perfect condition before all of this... They're still facing the consequences of those misdoings, even today. Feels as if it all was the work of the devil. By the way, here they believe that devils live in derelict mills and distilleries. You might've noticed that not a soul left till we got back, perhaps wanted to make sure we were OK...'

Holy mackerel...

I felt my face drop in amazement.

Pyvynsky took my hand, gave a smile of satisfaction.

'However, let me come clean – it's all just a game...'

'How d'ya men – a game?' I was stunned speechless.

'But of course… Forgive the old fool – I do like this "show", when they treat me this way. As if I really were a real master…'

I could barely breathe.

'And them?'

'They must like it too, totally. Besides, don't you disregard certain contradictory traits of our national character…'

'Which means?'

'Well, their ancestors once appropriated the Pyvynsky's property… Could you really give it all back now?'

'To whom?'

'To me, of course… Seeing that I'm a legal heir…'

I stood there, rooted to the ground.

'You see,' Pyvynsky continued confiding in me. 'Both sides have their weak points… And you know what? Us – me, and them, too – indulge those weaknesses, even with a certain degree of satisfaction…'

So, it was all just a show? A theatrical performance? My God… Where was I now? And what else was in store? Christ Almighty…

The rector would never believe me if I retold the whole saga. And when he recovered, he'd hammer out such an unrivalled monograph! Something to go down in history with…

***

In the morning granny Horpyna told me at breakfast:

'It's the fifteenth of February today. You know, my boy, it's a great holiday… Presentation of Jesus at the Temple…'

'Besides, it's been believed for ages that apart from the holiday, it's also the day for forecasting the future… So, keep your eyes open today, lad, perhaps you'll see some prompts. One shouldn't let them go unnoticed,' added granny Motria. 'Yeah, but it would be very hard to recognise those prompts…'

That was the way, eh? But what could possibly happen? What sort of prompts? My imagination was failing me…

My God, how could I forget? But the following day was the sixteenth! The day named by the Americans… The day on which our northern neighbour was supposed… to attack us? Ugh, the nonsense that crept into one's head…

Deep in thought, I retired to my quarters.

I spent the entire day processing the stuff I'd accumulated. After all, I'd collected lots of stories from my grannies – about evil spirits and such; my impressions about everything I'd seen there. Besides, Taras's parting words before my departure were to the effect that on top of my main task, I should sort out all the local occult stuff. Why not try and do it that evening?

What did Gogol have to say on the issue? I should freshen up my memory...

I pulled the book that I'd brought with me down from the shelf, riffled through its pages...

So, a devil, according to Gogol, personified evil, and deceitfulness. In his novels and stories, he portrayed him accordingly: little horns, a goatee, a snout of a nose. Spindly legs with hooves...

OK, that stuff was clear. But what should one do about a contemporary devil – assuming they did exist? Who could tell? Perhaps in our times they preferred Italian brands and wore suits by Brioni? And ties from Valentino and Moschino?!

Scared now, I pushed the book aside. I clasped my head in both hands – what horror! Gross...

Gradually I calmed down.

'Come on,' I said to myself, 'Nothing of merit will come into my head to-night... Might be a good idea to have a nap... And tomorrow I'll think about it all some more, once I've cleared my thoughts...'

Suddenly, I heard the same voices as before... But this time there were some additional refrains – 'Hoy! Hey! Hi!'

It all felt ominous... To start with – from a distance, as if from the yard; then – as if it were by my side. And then the front door – squ-e-e-ek!! – slid open. Ever so smoothly... But how was it possible? The grannies – they normally bolted it with as many as four bars... I checked it all myself, afterwards... I even stuffed a piece of cloth underneath, the one used to stop the draft. The door was properly shut! Tight as you please! My heart was summersaulting...

Next, I could make out a soft whispering, then mumbled voices. Shortly, the whispering became agitated, followed by cautious footsteps...

Ri-i-ght... If I wasn't imagining things and someone was really messing around, moreover – if they were more than one – what could I do, alone against several of them? I buried my head in the blankets – one, then another one. Lay there, all sweaty, completely freaked out... My heart kept pummelling against my chest, ready to hop out...

It got so hot that I had to slightly shift remove the blankets.

Meanwhile the door was trembling in its frame, squealing like mad. It sounded as if someone was making his way in, then out. Then another visitor... The ignominy of it all! Knocking around as if they owned the place! Wait a minute! By then it sounded as if four or five individuals had already crammed themselves into the entry corridor, pulling off their sheepskins and distributing them on the nails in the wall...

Christ alone knew what all this was about. I rapidly pulled the blanket back over my head. Left just one eye uncovered – what next?

In came three maidens and two lads. Proceeded to move around, checking every corner, scrutinising everything they could. To make things worse – also fingering everything…

Well, the maidens looked like typical girls. If you ask me – a bit on an impudent side. But the guys… Then again, were they even real lads? Didn't look like they were. Dressed weirdly, as if in fancy dress. And the faces sort of grotesque. Was it their real countenances or did they have some masks pulled over their heads? Wonder of wonders… Besides, the odour emanating from them… brought to mind… the stench of a goat. Could they really be devil's brood? Or young demons, masquerading?

By now the lads perched themselves on the bench and sat there in silence whilst the girls were busy prettifying themselves – smoothing the headkerchiefs, pulling up their boots. Must've been readying themselves for making whoopie. Then they started whispering among themselves. I could hear one of them say:

'Come on, girls, let's see what's there? Will these floorboards withstand our evening fest?'

They came to the centre of the room, made a circle.

One of the lads already had an accordion ready, the other one – a tambourine. They struck up together… But it wasn't like any music – something uproarious, phantasmagorical…

The girls clasped each other on their shoulders, started gliding around in a circle.

'All seems as it should,' cried out one of them.

'Sure thing, the boards will take it…' affirmed another.

'Bah, it's no biggie!' joined the third.

And all the while picking up speed, moving along in a circle… Suddenly, everything was just a blur, and all I could make out was their whirling skirts and sleeves… But this whirlwind didn't last. Their movements became slower, then sluggish, and lo! – finally they stopped. Conferred among themselves briefly in a whisper and then stared at my bed. I heard:

'Someone there… Looks like they lie around?'

'Eh-he, or someone's hiding under the blanket? Can't work it out right away…'

'Bah, must be the guy from the capital. What on earth is he doing in there?'

'Who's invited him? A stray from Kyiv… He's got no business here… Why not stay where he belongs, go round all those clubs and discos… Why the deuce come to our parts and create havoc?'

'Poor duckling… How would it know the things that could sometimes happen here? How, why, and what for?'

They crept closer to my bed.

'Even His Greatness Mykola Vasyloivych Gogol – you might've heard about him! – was warning all and sundry in his books: don't you dare show your ugly mugs in here! It's no go for outsiders! But they keep barging in! Can't be stopped… Can't twig it that all they do is court disaster…'

'An impudent lad… Although still wet behind the ears… Shall we teach him a lesson, gals? Give him a good shake up, send some feathers flying! Make his ass tremble? Still, I feel sorry for him… Maybe he's not such a nincompoop after all? Besides…'

'Righty-ho! We're one lad short…'

'Maybe he's a looker, too?'

'Sh-h-h… See? His eye is peeping at us from under the blanket? My gut tells me – he's nice and handsome…'

Underneath my blanket I nearly stopped breathing. Yuk…

'Hey, boyo! You alive there?'

'At least get out of this bed! For we're one guy short! We, the girls, are three but there's only two guys. We'll pair you off with one of us!'

Get out of the bed? Not likely! Seeing as I was nearly dead with freight.

'Hey there, d'ye hear? Stop lying around, lazybones, you!'

'Come here, let's have a natter! Say something at least!'

Yeah, right! My throat felt parched, a piece of clammy bread rammed into my windpipe like a real stone…

'Ah, he's not up to it, not yet! He's underage! Maybe even with a dinky stabber!'

'Good for nothing, mark my words!'

'He-he-he…'

'Ha-ha-ha…'

Christ! What next?

'You don't mince words!'

'They say this oaf here is a student at some college…'

'Well, I never! And who's he going to be?'

'How d'ya mean – who? Some manager or a finance guy – who else? They need lots of those in cities these days…'

'So, this thing under the blanket is a finance guy?!

'Well, such is his lot…'

'Ha! Come on, gals, let's pat down his trousers and pockets – what sort of finances he's hiding?'

My entire body contorted with a cramp; I could barely breathe. Fighting for air, I shifted the blanket to one side. Wheezing loudly, gasping.

'Oh! It's opened a bit of its face! Maybe it's ill? The kisser's red, must be out of breath… Still, looking closer, he's not too bad!'

'True! Not some plain little thing – quite the opposite, in fact! Not bad at all!'

'Got all the goods!'

'Super! Nice-looking fellow! Not too many like him even out there in Poltava!'

'Most likely he's tall and slender! Oh, how I like them lank! Say, when I pull such a thing closer to my bosom, it goes all aflutter like a leaf in the wind, doesn't know what to do with itself. Nearly makes me cry…'

'Well, Mania, you're in luck. Let's pour some life into this hottie! Size up his manhood! If he's all right on that front, he's yours, Mania!'

My cheeks were wet with tears. *Why? What have I done to them to be treated like this? Such misfortune, this whole trip, and this ethnographic research! What possessed me to get down to this God-forsaken backwater? Could've written about Brezhnev or Sverdlov, be smug as a bug in a rug… The rector, too, set me up with his guesses and half-witted theories… Good Lord, what should I do now?*

With all my might I pulled the blanket back and over my head.

'Oh! Hiding again!'

'No use trying to fool me! I did have a good look! He's over twenty, no doubt. Quite suitable for a boyfriend.'

'So why is he shunning us?'

'Maybe we're not to his taste?'

'Phooey! Why come here then?'

'To our bonny farmstead! Or he hasn't twigged yet who really resides here?'

"Tis them who love it here! And no one shall boss us 'round!'

'So, once he's made it to here, let 'im join us!'

Dear God, was that the end of me? Was I destined to die now? In this bed? So that they could carry me to the graveyard rolled in this blanket?

'And Mykola Vasyliovych – let His Greatness forgive me that I turn to him again – he did allude to things like that …'

'But of course! Gogol kept warning those city loafers about how things could get really sickening in here! Even when his stuff first got published in that Petersburg… The readers wouldn't ever read his books before going to bed – that is, if they wanted to sleep well. That's how scared they all were! Didn't dream of coming here, to pay us a visit – not in a million years! It's only now the folk got so silly… Anyone who's got a car, or even by bus – all sorts keep barging in… Even from abroad!'

'But we do teach them all a lesson – every now and then. Strike them numb! Make their eyes goggle! So that they'd keep well clear!'

'Ha! Books, you say. Do they even read books now, those city folk?'

'Who reads anything there anymore? No one even knows what Mykola Vasyloivych was all about and what he wrote about our Myrhorod area...'

'Tell me 'bout it! They're glued to their telephones, looking at some pictures... Gawp at them, in fact, from morning till night... Is called something like... TikTok? Heard 'bout it?'

'That's the one with spoofs and other funny stuff? There's another one... what's it? Ye Star Gran, or soming?'

'You're too much, you! In-sta-gram! There, each flaunts around their shameful bits. For all to see! Tits, ass, the thing between the legs – the lot, head to toe. Every little bloody thing!'

'Pshaw, shameless wretches!'

'That's new generation for ya! They've no time for Gogol... They're only after those cartoons, fun and spoofs...'

'But that's not all! TV ain't cool either, not anymore... Just those smartphones...'

'God knows what the world is coming to...'

'They fear neither God nor devil – everything's topsy turvy now!'

I wasn't sure I was breathing anymore... Could've been half dead by then, dunno.

And then suddenly I heard:

'Let's dance and sing for him. Perhaps at least this will bring him back to life?'

'And why not? Let's give him a nudge...'

And right away one of them struck up:

Oh-oh, who's in his bed lying?
Under his blanket, who is now hiding?
Still, he's eyeing us out of one eye.
Maybe he's egged on
By his virile drive?
But he's so... so... he's so mistrustful...
But he's so... so... he's so bashful...

Then the second voice joined in:
We've been working solidly, all day long.
But the night is ours, we've deserved some fun.
We're not the idiots – to waste away our prime!
We'd like letting go, and
Have exciting time!
That's why we came here,
To this pretty thing here...

And the third one went:
But a city boy, to us
Nothing does he say.
For some bizarre reason
He just shies away.

Then all of them together:
Oh, the woe, oh, the sorrow,
Oh, the sheer grief...
Those have-nots, ragamuffins...

The first:
Ask me, girls, I think, he just puts it on.
Maybe he was born like this,
And now just poking fun?

All together:
No, girls, that's weird –
To cut us cold like that!
Hoi-hei, he-e-e-i!
After all, in our quarters
We're as good as the tzar's daughters...
So, what is there to fear?
What is so odd here?

The third:
Let me tell the truth, girls,
He's got to our heads.
I wish he'd just tried to flee,
Wouldn't have been so bad...

The second:
The folk say – this here wonder
Came to our quarters from the city.
So that he could roam round
And record our ditties.
Now he's staying with the grannies,
Playing with our heads.
Always buried in his books,
Scribbling in his notepad.

All together:
Why, oh why he wouldn't go out?
All he does is stare.
Oh, save God us from the bother –
Could he be the Inspector General?

The third:
Me, I too heard funny things:
On the week days, those city bums
They all drag themselves to college
To listen to the learned ones.
But as soon as it's a weekend
All reserve they shed,
They race to all those discos
And paint the town red.

All girls together:
Oh, woe, oh, distress!
What else is there to say?
So, out there he's all for fun
But here he hides away?

The first:
Oh-oh, you, the silly thing,
'Tis no use to fight us.
Try as you might – we'll overpower you
And you'll dance among us!

Crikey, the shenanigans they were engaging in! And the guys were odd, too. As if not looking at me at all. But if I momentarily locked eyes with anyone of them, their eyes would devour me sullenly, as if trying to bore a hole in my head. As for the girls, there was no stopping them now.

At this point one of the girls cast me an arrogant gaze and barked an order:
Look here, boyo, stop this minute
Messing us around.
Come and join us, we'll dance,
Prance and sing aloud.

And then all girls in chorus:

As you now will be our date,
Take who you fancy in your arms.
And if you would like a kiss
You don't even need to ask.
Hey-hoy, hurry up!
Don't you know how?
Don't you dare to shy away!
For us, beauties, make a play!

The first one gave a wink:
Haven't you learnt how to get it up?
Ha-ha-ha!

Her friend:
Come along, do make haste!
Why ya hiding thus?
For we aren't gonna eat you
Why ya shunning us?

The third one:
Wonna some local folklore? Something to enter into your pad?
Kateryna danced with Grysha –
Yada, yada, yada.
And she knocked out Grysha's teeth,
Four teeth with her udder!

They all broke down guffawing.
Then the first again:
Now, girls, approach from here!
Don't you linger, don't you stall.
Let us grab him – us, together –
Grab and press against the wall!

They all roared with laughter. Were they going to abuse me now?
The second girl:

We all three will grab and press him,
Press him, squeeze, him squash...
He will cry and squirm in pain,
For it will hurt so...

The chorus:
Let him, let him cry in anguish,
Let him writhe in agony!

My, oh my! What were they up to? Press me to the wall, and then?
I tossed the blanket back for I was suffocating again…
Huff! Puff! – I was desperately gasping for air.
By now the tears were streaming down my face. Why? What had I done to deserve this? So's to hurt me? Defile me?

And then the third girl cried out:
No, girls, we won't disgrace him
For he'll be ashamed.
And if he's terrified
He may lose his mind.
And what use he'll be to us
If he's not alright?

Oh, I'm hopeful, dear friends,
Look, for what it's worth…
There's this ancient trusted way
And it always works.

The first and the second, together:
What way? Do tell!

The third one:
Here's the way:
Let's go dancing
Just the way we should!

They formed a ring, and ever so slowly started dancing…
The first girl:
What a brilliant idea!
Let him stare as we dance!
Maybe he, this poor thing,
Will even fall for one of us?

And suddenly they were awhirl, going faster and faster…
All of them together:

That's it! That's it!
Hey! Hop! Hop!
Step by step, little by little
He will be on fire,
After which... so much may happen,
Such love we'll inspire!
Hey! Hop! Hop!
That's the way, the way they are –
Local ragamuffins!

The dance was becoming increasingly more insane... More like a maelstrom of movement and hollering... The goings-on the girls were engaging in by then – with their arms, shoulders, and legs! It was like some pre-historic heathen spectacle...

They kept whirling round and round, and I lost my train of thought. Some frenzied rampage, no other way to describe it...

So, my end was nigh – they were getting ever closer to my bed. In a blink of an eye, they'd snatch me, and... Terrified, I closed my eyes...

And just then something outside the house started hooting ... Only to be quickly replaced by something like a drawn-out howling – gave me a new set of creeps... What was this whimpering? I couldn't tell... It sounded as if a chariot came to a stop. A shudder went through the coven, making them all stop at once... All I could here was this whispered exchange:

'It's him!'

'Him? Really? Our sweetheart Volodia?'

'But of course! He's made it here, sure as anything!'

'In a chariot? Borrowed it from someone, or just took without asking?'

'Why should he ask? Hopped on it and off he went! He's his own master! Uninhibited!'

'Full of vim and vigour! Although he's older than us... He's said to come to us from as far away as Muscovy! Must have some business, that's what's bringing him here.'

'So what if he's from afar? We welcome anyone, as long as they are decent!'

'I wonder how old he is?'

'Who can tell? Not that young... But not old yet, either...'

'They say he's had some things done to his face...'

'He may be as old as 70 but doesn't look it...'

'Ha! Wants to look young?'

'What if he does? Do we mind?'

'Of course we don't. 'Tis all the same... Some say he's got a heart of gold. He says so himself – we are, all of us, one family, one people, and should, thus, be together...'

'That's it! How true! We are so lucky to have bumped into him! Such a successful giant of a man!'

'They say he's spent about two months here, in our neck of the wood. Vasyl Namyipyka – heard about him?[68] A farmer from some remote place hired him as his manager. Got nothing but praise for him. So many things he's improved during this time!'

'Any job in his hands goes like clockwork!'

'Didn't even ask Vasyl for money. Vasyl is amazed... How is it possible – to work like that and charge nothing? He tried many times to force some money onto him. And he goes: "*I don't need this money of yours... I'm doing my best to promote our shared goals*"...'

'What would he want the money for? He's got a proper pile of his own! He's giving it away – hand over fist! As soon as he sees that somebody would like some – here you go! Get it! Use it!'

'True-true... I did say – a heart of gold. Everything for the people! Everything for the community!'

'Precisely! He did say yesterday, though, that he was tired and needed to rest... Bah, didn't last long in that remote spot...'

'No wonder! He's been missing us!'

'Right you are! He's sad if we're apart for too long...'

'What would he do without us? We're fun!'

'Ha-ha-ha!'

'What, then? Let's get going? Join him?'

'Straight away! Until he's popped in here and spotted this handsome boy of ours...'

'OK, on the double!'

And the whole gang just – woosh! – disappeared. To somewhere... Only the front door banged. Praised be our Lord in heaven that they hadn't passed me on to someone even more scary. Was I safe now? Saved? Phew!!!

I rushed to the front corridor. God Almighty! It was all shut on the inside! Every bar in place! As if it had always been like that! So how did they get in, then? What sort of devil's work was at play here?

I raced back to my room and – straight to the window. Peeped out through a crack... A chariot was parked to one side, the horses prancing impatiently...

....

[68] **Namyipyka**: yet another 'telling' surname. In Ukrainian it means 'one who doesn't wash his mug'.

My 'guests' were already on the porch… And among them, he who'd arrived… Not too tall in height… A somewhat strange type… Dressed like a shop assistant but someone who worked in an expensive shop – neat, clean, and the clothes he wore looked expensive… His suit – nothing much to look at, but I'd say it was from Brioni… Then again, his tie, too, was most likely from Valentino or Moschino… Hard to work out exactly… For he was constantly wrapping himself in some variegated cloth… What was he trying to hide? A weird one, this… Then, something was wrong with his hands. One looked normal but the other one was lifeless… Clearly, another chimera… But who was it?

Meanwhile the entire hangout was jumping up and down with joy of their meeting… Even started dancing a bit… Holy cow – the things happening at this farmstead… And in the world as a whole?

By now the whole caboodle was dancing like mad. The girls couldn't see what was what, but from my vantage point I suddenly got a clear view. As he was stretching his leg in a dance move, it got exposed, and looked – my word! – like a leg of a goat… On a very high heel! I felt my entire body started quacking… Could it be someone… wearing a disguise? Had my grannies never told me what to look for, I wouldn't have been able to spot it… But as it was, I could clearly see the one who shouldn't be remembered before going to bed…

Suddenly the first girl found her voice and hollered:

'Volodia, look here! Can you walk up and down solo? Solo or by solo – what's the correct was to say it?'

They all stopped, mouths gaping. Waiting for something.

'*Why not?*' smiled the newly-arrived visitor. And covered the mouth with his hand, as if slightly embarrassed.

'Great stuff, Volodia my darling! On you go, my sweet thing!' joined the other.

So Volodia unhurriedly peeled off his kaftan, dropped it on the ground… Underneath was the shirt – in white, navy, and red colours!

'See? How he loves his country?' shrieked the third girl. 'Whatever he wears shows only national colours!'

'Wow! If only every one of us loved our country as much…'

'We-e-ell…' there was clearly some friction among them…

'Nothing to it! Things do happen in life! The respected sir wants us to be as one with them. Not to wander Devil knows where…'

'Can't it be decided? I'm sure it'll get sorted out… So that we could have it good, them, too…'

Meanwhile dearest Volodia was already whirling around in that devil-may-care dance, solo. His shirt was swelling like a sail, bigger, and bigger still… By then the Russian flag was much clearer, visible from every side…

It was pure phantasmagoria. As if it wasn't taking place here and now, but in some distant lands…

Finally, his devilish solo was over. He picked up his kaftan from the ground, put it back on.

They all flocked together, stood around whispering…

He put fingers in his mouth and gave such a piercing whistle! Must've been heard even in Myrhorod… Then yelled:

'*That's it, my lovelies! Enough! Stop knocking about, off we go!*'

'Where to?' the girls were all agog with excitement.

'*Who cares? Away and forward!*'

'Hoy! Hi! Hey!' was coming to me.

The guy with the accordion momentarily produced some devilish screech. And the other one – gave such a *whack*! to his tambourine…

They all squeezed themselves tight into that chariot that looked as if it was swelling. Then the 'weird' one whipped the horses with all he had! They charged forward and, in an instant, everything vanished.

Thus, they left. But as for me – what was I supposed to do?

I just couldn't wrap my mind around any of it. OK, the outlander – everything was more or less clear on that front… They guys were probably his henchmen… But the girls? Looked sort of normal, if only a touch on the brazen side. But how was it possible that they also came under his spell?

I could be absolutely sure of only one thing: as soon as I got back home to Kyiv, I would take myself straight to a church. Maybe even go round all of them… light a candle to every saint imaginable… I'd pray fervently, drop to my knees in ardour. It wasn't a joking matter anymore… But that would have to wait… The main thing now was to somehow plot my escape…

This important decision made, I realised that the next most pressing task was to go to sleep… Somehow… How would I be able, otherwise, to survive all this stress? I simply had to recover before the following day…

I grabbed hold of my pills – three at once. Got myself a glass of water, my teeth chattering against its rim… Somehow managed to swallow some…

Now, three pills – wasn't it over the odds? On the other hand, if I were to collapse the following day, at least it would be brought on by the sleeping pills, not those mad happenings, the guys in fancy dress, the frantic girls… Perhaps, those were not even the girls but female hobgoblins, who could tell?

The morning after my head was full of lead. Still, I managed to get some sleep, even it had been troubled…

I tried to pull my thoughts together. Who was that person that had arrived in the farmyard and pranced around with the girls? Besides, someone fresh from Russia? God Almighty! All of it happened exactly on the day of Candlemas! The day of fortune-telling! Perhaps it was a special emissary sent by our neighbour in the north? Or could it have been *Himself*? Posing as a regular reconnaissance guy?

Horror of horrors! The thoughts in my head…

How could I have possibly forgotten? Today was the sixteenth! Perhaps we'd been already under attack but I still wasn't aware of the news?

I hastily picked up my phone, opened a random news site. Nothing… And another one, and yet one more… Nothing there, either… They all insisted that something was about to happen but nothing had, yet.

'Narrow escape? God be praised… Looks like the forecasts don't always play out. Even if issued by the Americans…'

My thoughts turned again to the adventures of the night before… Could it be that I'd gone nuts? For at a time like this nothing could be ruled out, nothing at all. On the other hand, could it have just been a bad dream? A hallucination of some kind? Enough to send me round the bend?

I promptly approached my grannies.

'Did you hear anything? Last night? There were some things going on here… weird things…'

'Where? In our place? What on earth could it have been?'

'Bah! Nothing untoward has ever happens here… Seeing as we're away from all and sundry, what could it possibly have been?'

That was the sum total of our exchange. Well, what was new? Long story short, I had to go and find Pyvynsky. Spill the beans…

* * *

'I've got a question for you, Anatoliy Semenovych… Much as my principal mission is in relation to the original sources for *The Dead Souls*, there's something else emerging now…'

I stopped, short for words.

For some reason he grew solemn. Even gloomy…

'OK, go on…'

'In some circles of the capital city…' I started from afar, 'it's accepted that, allegedly, there exist some serious reasons… Well, generally speaking, looks like our neighbours…'

I grew silent and gave him a questioning look. But he wasn't hurrying me up!

'…long story short… there are reasons to suspect that over there, in the across-the-border country there is… how shall I put it? '

I was faltering again.

But Pyvynsky – he kept mum! Most likely he felt that what was about to come would've made the whole conversation very undesirable.

Ah well, what the hell! I'd get it all off my chest and then – come what may.

'Well, you must be aware that the president of theirs… is hatching some devilish plans about us… Most cunning and dangerous ones… And he…'

And yet Pyvynsky wasn't saying a word!

'… and seeing that ever since the times of Gogol it's been believed that the craftiest and most scheming evil forces are all coming from the area of Myrhorod… so… OK, there's this thought that's making the rounds now… Allegedly, the Devil – irrespective of where in the world he's residing now – could've become so street-wise and unpredictable that he's simply got no other way forward but to turn to Gogol's *oeuvre* – in order to get well-versed in black arts… That's exactly what Gogol warned us against…'

Phew, finally got it all out and now was expecting a response. Even closed my eyes.

Suddenly I was struck by a thought. What if all my blabbering was pure insanity? And I would be kicked out of Shyshaky as a result of all this nonsense? Stood to reason… What if he responded to all of this in some unexpected fashion? That would really be a catastrophe!

For a while, Pyvynsky remained motionless. Gradually his complexion started picking up colour, turning red and then burgundy. His breath got ragged – he was gasping convulsively.

'What? You… you're trying to say… that the president of a country… a huge country – one-sixth of the entire earth surface! That he's the spawn of the Devil?'

Bloody hell! What had I done putting forward those insane allegations of mine? I felt little chills running up and down my spine. My heart was pounding. What if Pyvynsky would grab me in his clasp and press me to the wall? To shake the innards out of me? To commit me to the forces of law and order? The Big Brother of some kind?

But Pyvynsky had already pulled himself together. He clasped my hand.

'Sh-h-h… Let's say, the timing is wrong now for such contemplations. Look here… Don't peep a word to anyone! Of course, we live in a democracy and one can speak one's mind… But nowadays, when our side is jumping out of their way so as not to provoke this very neighbour in any way!!! Meanwhile you, a dewy-eyed ignoramus, come up with such statements! You can easily get arrested! As an agent provocateur! In a word – you've opened your gob to me, but that's it! Not to a soul!! Don't you dare!'

However, it suddenly looked as if something occurred to him.

'But to tell you the truth... This deduction of yours... I'll be frank, I'm impressed with the scope of your analysis. Do tell... This, too, is the rector's influence?'

Something inside me started snapping and lapsing – by then I was properly scared. Who could tell what sort of a person that Pyvynsky really was? Could it be that in confiding to him I'd overstepped the mark? After all, he was on first-name terms with everybody here, and even in Poltava. What if he reported me under the heading of 'danger to state security?' In which case it wouldn't be just me, the rector would come under the same cloud as well...

My God, what a fool – to put him in the harm's way like this!

I started mumbling:

'Regrettably, that is... luckily... no! The rector's got nothing to do with it. It isn't even my own assumption...' trying to wriggle out of a potential danger of being responsible. 'It's just that I... overheard some rumours circulating in Kyiv... Can't even remember where... Might've been at some market... I was getting some batteries and hears some lasses nattering...'

Spun the whole yarn, in short...

He puckered his brow:

'A market, some batteries, some lasses... My advice is this: stay well clear of those shady areas. Completely! It's a slippery slope. And you and I – d'ya hear me? – never had this conversation!'

He remained silent for a bit... Then gave me a curt smile, slapped me lightly on the shoulder and briefly put his arms round me – as if trying to ward the evil forces off...

So how could I possibly tell him, after all of this, about things that had happened to me at the farmstead the previous night? It made no sense... None at all...

* * *

The day before I was due to leave – it was February the eighteenth, the three of us got together: Pyvynsky, Yanovsky and me, in the boss's office. The only topic of conversation was the possibility of invasion.

'They said – the sixteenth... Americans were adamant about that date... But nothing ever happened! There was no attack!' cried out Yanovsky and even slapped himself on the knee. 'So much for their celebrated intelligence service!'

'And Zelensky said: "Our intelligence service is every bit as good! And we've got no evidence to support their conclusion"!' Pyvynsky agreed. 'And then went on with his pet refrain – stop scaring us! Stop inciting panic!'

'Ha! They were threatening us with the sixteenth. Like hell!' Yanovsky was clearly in a cheerful mood. It wasn't clear, though, whether he believed what he was saying or was just taking the mickey. 'Even the Day of Unity passed without a hitch! The train choo-chugged across the entire country – from Rakhiv and all the way to Mariupol! Didn't we punch them where it hurts with this train of ours! Stick it where the sun don't shine, grandpa Putin and all your Ru-u-u-u-s-s-ia!'

'Well, don't get carried away!' Pyvynsky reigned him in a bit. 'Such a shame, our Yanovsky here is disillusioned with the American intelligence services. The only thing is…'

'The only thing is that still, the American services are probably better…' I joined the fray. 'They've got more resources… A different scope… And the rest of it…'

'Still…' Pyvynsky's face puckered and he became sombre. 'The Americans are now insisting on a different date – allegedly, it's the nineteenth… The recent developments give little reason to be happy – the situation in Donbas is escalating all the time. Meanwhile the Department of State is warning us that this escalation will be used by Russia as a pretext for launching an operation against Ukraine…'

'Could it be that our side is aware of this?' I was either asking a question or contemplating out loud. 'There's another breaking news: starting from the nineteenth, that is from tomorrow, the Chornobyl zone will be closed indefinitely for tourists. Officially, for "engineering works". But in all likelihood, it's related to the possibility of invasion and the proximity of the Belarusian border.'

'You know what?' Yanovsky added in a whisper. 'I'm about to say something seditious…'

'Well?!' Pyvynsky clasped his hands. 'Shoot!'

'The tension is extreme… Everybody everywhere is so strained… Me, too… And there are times when I have this criminal thought… By Jove, may at least something finally happen! I'm trying to drive it away but it returns… It's simply unbearable! Un-bea-rable! Such is my criminal mindset… Will you shame me now?'

'Indeed, it's criminal to think like that…' Pyvynsky rose abruptly from his armchair. 'But I do understand you perfectly… For I, myself… I have similar urges at times… Roll on the day when it goes either this way, or that! True, it's impossible to live in this state of continuous stress!'

'There's this thing, too, that I find suspicious,' Yanovsky again. 'The oligarchs and members of the pro-Russian party are promptly doing a bunk…'

'Yeah… It is definitely a telling sign,' conceded Pyvynsky. 'Perhaps someone gave them a warning? Oksana Marchenko, Medvedchuk's wife, was reported yesterday as crossing the border with Belarus. Had to be for a reason…'

'Oh, but that's truly grim! Maybe their chum Putin gave them a signal? Warned it was time to leg it?'

'So, she, what? Scarpered without her husband? What about Medvedchuk himself?'

'Who the heck knows?... He is, after all, "under arrest and tagged"...'

'She's sure as hell aiming for Russia, this Oksanochka of his. What's there to keep her in Belarus?'

We sat in silence for a while.

'What do you reckon – from where will Putin attack?' I dared to ask.

'He's sure to barge in from all directions,' answered Pyvynsky not missing a beat. 'Kyiv's a must. He needs it as a symbol. He's got a bee in his bonnet about it – "the bloody mother… of all Russian cities"…'

'Bloody indeed!' chuckled Yanovsky.

And the president added convincingly:

'Our example of democratic development is a showcase. Especially for those post-Soviet countries that are currently under authoritarian regimes. For we're something like a "stepping stone" into Europe – the free and civilised world. I don't even know how much time they'll need to at least catch up with us… Within the last 30 years – Jeez, we've made such a break-through… Worlds apart from where we were!'

'Yes, we'd like now to become a fully-fledged member of Europe… Doesn't quite work like that, though… For all that, there's progress – this association agreement. Visa-free travel, too. But as for moving forward, that's to accede to the EU – it's a different story. That's a proper bottleneck.'

'And what would you expect? The EU is grappling with a host of their owns problems. Why would they want to shoulder ours as well? Besides, we are situated in such a dangerous place – the fault line of civilisation runs through our country! And no one really wants to mess around with Russia…'

'Still, NATO is making some funny announcements. They keep saying, over and over again, that they won't give up an inch of their members' territory. Which means a carte-blanche to Putin in respect of the countries that are not in the alliance. Apart from Ukraine, it's also Finland, Sweden, and Moldova[69]… But Russia has aggressive plans not only about Ukraine. In the end, they are against the entire civilised world. The way I see it… He is as if invited to go forward? What an irresponsible thing to say! As for him? He's quite capable of attacking them too… Say, swallow the Baltic countries in a week. Poland would probably take a month. By the time NATO came to their senses… By that point

---

[69]   True at the time when the action takes place. Finland and Sweden have subsequently joined the bloc.

in time, Berlin – if you please – will be only some hundred kilometres away!
For an armada of tanks – no distance at all. For all one knows they may even
capitulate without engaging…'

'It's a shame that Europe is so spineless, thinking only about themselves…
We don't really have any true allies there except our immediate neighbours.
But they, like us, are facing a direct threat of military intervention. And may
find themselves as helpless against this heavily armed monster…'

'And the leader of this neighbour of ours? Their tsar, the one who's in power
for over twenty years, what does he say about our sovereign country with its
multi-million population?' Yanovsky raised his figure. "'Is this truly a country?
A mistake of history! Cobbled together from scraps of other powers"…'

'That's it! Allegedly, it's imperative to put the historical record straight! And
what's the best way to achieve this? Simple: they get what used to belong to the
Russian Empire. And what once belonged to Austro-Hungary – let it be shared
among the surrounding nations. We'll get what's ours, and you get what's yours.
Restore, so to say, the original fairness.'

'He is inciting such proprietary interests in those states, preparing a tasty
present for them!' agreed I whole-heartedly with their analysis. 'Sort of, take
it – period. Such a prominent "historian", such a specialist on geopolitics!'

'He's throwing transparent hints: who cares where those Ukrainians are
going to end up? Some will live here – they'll assimilate painlessly for we are
"one people", even if they are reluctant to admit it. And some of them – let
them find themselves in your countries. If they adapt – great, if not – let them
live in isolation…'

'What's Putin train of thought? "You say – the Final Act signed in Helsinki in
1975? The Budapest Memorandum on Security Guarantees of 1994? Our joint
Russian-Ukrainian Friendship Treaty of 1997? Forget it all. It never happened.
Full stop. I'm telling you – put it out of your mind"…'

'Just listen to what they're hollering!' Yanovsky was getting ever more excited.
"'Your history is all wrong! And those pathetic ringleaders of yours that, for some
reason, you venerate as heroes! Every single one of them was doing something
wrong, and in general – they all are criminals…" But if you ask me – each nation
has its own history and its heroes… Stay away from ours!'

'The Russians have an acute psychological disorder…' Pyvynsky summed it
all up. 'They believe themselves to be a "great people"– whilst simultaneously
being devoured by complexes because the rest of the world doesn't agree. They
are perceived like any other nation. And that riles them beyond any measure.
And they conclude: "How is it possible? The whole world is against us? But
that's collusion! They all wish to see Russia weakened, and humiliated. Even
destroyed"…'

Dear God, the things we discussed then… Deep inside, all three of us were aware of the fact that a catastrophe was imminent. Still, we all harboured a spark of hope: what if a miracle happened and it all became dispelled like smoke?

My soul in turmoil, all I wanted was to get home as soon as I could…

On Saturday the nineteenth of February, came the day to see me off at the local bus station, with all due pomp. In the foreground stood the members of the presidium, behind them – the Society's activists. President Pyvynsky made a short but emotional speech. There was the general applause, I was presented with a luxurious copy of *A Guide to Gogol's Country*… The buxom secretary leaned over to a friend of hers, and I pricked up my ears.

'To start with, we were scared stiff, took him for an auditor or something,' whispered she. 'That's how they look nowadays when on a mission – mediocre as you please, so that no one would suspect a thing. Yet this one, turns out, is kinda academic… By the look of things, not too bad at it, either… Anatoliy Semenovych, they said…'

A giggle in response.

The president took me by the elbow and gently steered towards the bus:

'Do come back to us, Kiril!'

'By all means – with a ready script and a film crew in tow!' His deputy, Yanovsky, was ensuring my progress, supporting me on the other flank.

Pyvynsky shook my hand.

'And… sincere greeting to the dear rector!'

He leaned over to speak straight into my ear:

'Perhaps it's not playing out all that bad, at least for now… I mean that intervention…' he explained. 'Look for yourself – the sixteenth been and gone, and nothing bad has happened. All's peace and quiet. Relatively speaking, of course… There is a report, however, that big landing craft carriers entered the Black Sea. And huge portions of it have been cordoned off by the Russians – allegedly, for the drill. Today, as you know, is the nineteenth, and still – everything is OK. No one has attacked us. So, looks like the level of alarm is going down. Then again, who can bloody tell? Perhaps it's just a reprieve… The Americans, though, just won't shut up – constantly riffling out some new dates…'

We made eye contact. Our shared anxiety was palpable. How could it have been otherwise?

I was leaving with a genuine sense of relief. Had I had to stay in Shyshaky another several days – I'd have probably started wailing at the moon. It wasn't even that I was all that superstitious but at times it was really too much… It felt like all those demons, vampires, house spirits and witches were about to drag me into their macabre whirlwind from which I would never emerge alive…

Still, now I was on my way back home, and even feeling quite proud of myself. You bet! I had accomplished my mission. Hundred percent! All rector's instructions had been carried through to a successful resolution. I had even achieved something over and beyond! He'd be satisfied, no doubt about it.…

After all, I had done absolutely everything he asked. I visited every locality and interviewed everybody I could. Did some good digging around in the local archive. Conducted quite a few interchanges with the elderly, asked them lots of questions, recorded everything diligently. Immersed myself into those heathen rites to nearly a breaking point. Visited Pyvynsky's farmstead. But the most important of all – I simply rambled around all over those famous places associated with the name of Gogol, saturated myself with their healing vibes…

When presenting my material to the rector, I wouldn't have to blush. I'll pass over to him whatever I'd got. Without exception. Whether or not I was going to use it for my own purposes – that was something I wasn't yet sure about. As for him, to make his way into the Corresponding Members, all that was unquestionably useful.

What else? Aha, I'd put on about two kilos, Mum would be happy. Just one thing… Was there something I could've done and didn't? Say, develop an idea for my script? As inspired by the mysterious localities enfolded in two hundred years of arcane history? To outdo Gogol, or what? Ridiculous thoughts…

I turned to my research into the origin of the idea for *The Dead Souls* with renewed ardour. I even started forming some ideas in my head. But was it really my cup of tea? I did have to think it over… What I badly wanted was modernity! So how was it feasible to bring together that notorious 'ethno-component' with the worries of our times?

Gogol, after all, was describing his demons, house spirits and mermaids two hundred years previously. It was all exciting then, the readers had been reading themselves stupid. But now?

Again, and again! What I was painfully eager to do – was to write about our times! Nothing to stop me, though, from putting in, here and there, a sprinkling of things bygone… Yet, I still wasn't totally sure of what my story was going to be…

February 2021 – February 2022.
The Panther About to Pounce

On the morning of February 20th, I finally made it home. I'd spent a sleepless night on the train and felt dog-tired.

Once there, I collapsed onto my bed and into sleep but when I finally came to, I felt zoned out right up to the evening, so didn't even call anyone.

What was there to tell? Two weeks in Poltava Oblast had flashed by in a blink of an eye. In the evening, I read everything that I'd entered into my files, then reread the whole lot again. How could I sum it all up? I'd never managed to identify even some initial pointers for my script. The conclusion was suggesting itself: alas, in all the time spent nearby Myrhorod I'd failed to work out how to fuse the Gogolian themes with modernity. Although, it didn't mean that a project like this would be impossible. The problem was me. Someone else would've definitely come up trumps.

So, for the time being, no ray of light was going to break the clouds for me. I'd pulled a blank with those foreign – read, Asian – contemporary motifs. And as for the past – in this case our own history – it also proved to be a dead end.

And all the while, needless to say, I kept following the news… Alarming news at that… As recently as the nineteenth, the Americans alerted us to the fact that between 40 and 50 percent of the RF ground troops deployed near to the Ukrainian border had taken up positions enabling them to launch an attack. The very next day, Russia's First Deputy Permanent Representative to the United Nations, D. Polyansky responded that Russia doesn't trust declarations coming from the intelligence services of Great Britain and the United States… He stated as well that they talked about 100 thousand and now it's already 130 thousand. So, which is correct? Instead, Ukraine keeps 120-thousand-strong military presence along the demarcation line in Donbas… Whatever the case, Russia is on its own territory and anyone should tell it when to conduct or not to conduct a training exercise. Russia carries out drills on its territory and this shouldn't be a source of worry to anyone…

Later on, I joined an online chat and learnt that our group was getting together on Tuesday, February 22nd. And thus, on the morning of that Tuesday – still no attack! – I schlepped to the institute…

First of all, I popped over into the rector's reception.

'He's at a meeting… But he's constantly asking about you. I'll let him know you're here…'

Within a minute the door flew open and the rector came out of his office.

My notepad was already in my hands. Or, to be more precise, his notepad, the one he'd given me back then…

'Well? Has it worked? Yes, or no?' His words were gushing out as if from a submachine gun. 'Just be brief, I've got visitors…'

'Your theory is confirmed… It all comes together – to a tee. It's incredible! I've got it all recorded here…'

I extended my hand, holding the notepad, towards him.

'Atta boy! Well-done!' his face broke into a broad smile.

He accepted this notepad, and examined it with a kind of awe.

I offered him the memory stick.

'What's that?'

'Some explosive stuff. Enough to blow your head away, at least twice… I don't want to talk about it now. Let it be a surprise for you…'

'Oh ya, Zhalovaha!'

He grabbed my hand and pressed it gratefully.

'Let's do it this way: first, I'll go through it. And in a couple of days, you'll come by…'

His gaze directed at me was full of respect, or at least it seemed that way.

I wished he didn't, for I felt tacitly consumed with this contemplation: *So, after all, who? Gogol or Dostoyevsky? And what you gonna say once you've been through my notes?*

But his eyes conveyed some fiery mischief too. Something bordering on impish. I could even read an evanescent message there: 'You've brought along all this Gogol stuff – that's brilliant. But nowadays Dostoyevsky, too, is extremely topical… You know yourself what's going on around us now… So, for the moment, I'm not sure who's gonna come on top: Gogol or Dostoyevsky. Nothing's clear for now, Kiril… Not at all…'

With this, he disappeared through the door.

Letter Z in the Offing

Shortly after I ran into Taras. We stopped in the corridor, and I complained about my lack of success. Funny but my misfortunes didn't seem to bother him at all. Just like before, he was confident that everything was transitory and would work out in the end…

Meanwhile, on our horizon appeared Spyridon, Bolik, and Alla with Liubchik. Taras immediately shot them a question:

'Well, has anyone heard anything about this intrusion? What gives?'

'Sure thing, Paliy, there's news, what's more – some strong stuff!' Spyridon clasped his hands in excitement. 'Russian social media are brimming with pictures and videos: they now draw a Latin letter "Z" on the flanks of their military equipment… In bold brushstrokes, in white paint, within or without a square. Scrolling it, the bastards, on anything that moves: tanks, military trucks, howitzer weapons…'

'Shit!' Taras couldn't contain himself. 'I saw it too. Looks like a swastika cut in two… What could it possibly mean?'

'Must be some markings, what else?' suggested Bolik. 'Sort of: this equipment belongs to us. So's there's no confusion. That's what I think…'

'Stands to reason,' I wedged in, too. 'One can assume that this is exactly what one does before intruding somewhere…'

'Come on, wait a minute…' Taras sounded amazed. 'Who's intruding where? Just because someone is drawing some weird letters?'

'But our side is adamant: it's all pure bluff!' Spyridon was getting worked up and eager to put forward his version of events. 'They say it's not worth taking any of this on trust…'

'Precisely!' Alla waived her hand. 'They were expected to attack on the twenty-second. So it's the date today! And where's this "attack"? Looks like our guys were right when they kept banging on about scammers from the Kremlin?'

'Um-hm… Top leaders often misread the signs,' Bolik scrunched his face. 'Remember Stalin? They kept telling him that Germans were actively preparing for an immediate attack! But his only retort was to tell the well-wishes go and screw themselves. I hope what's happening now isn't something similar…'

'Whether or not the top leaders get it wrong – that's one thing,' Liubchik's face was now profoundly sad. 'But normal people are watching it all from their separate belfry and arrive at their own conclusions… Don't you know that there's already a stampede out of the city? OK, perhaps not a stampede yet, but it's gaining momentum…'

The bell rang.

We all shuffled off towards the auditorium. What was there to say? Anyone could sense it by now – something really bad was definitely about to happen…

As for the letter 'Z' adorning their weaponry – there might've been a simple explanation. Perhaps, the soldiers simply had nothing better to do with their spare time?

Something's Brewing... Dismantling of Ukraine?

Well... The puzzle of those developments was coming together.

As is well-known, no intelligence services ever share their findings. But Russia's preparations for an intervention into Ukraine ushered in a stage that was an exception to the rules. As a result, something unprecedented happened: the British and the American secret services, acting as a kind of united front, decided to inform the world! They started small, by offering information in measured doses, but gradually leaking everything they had into the public domain...

Initially, the alarming signals started showing in February of 2021. The situation in Donbas was exacerbating, and suddenly, both in Russia and Ukraine, appeared predictions of a major war. In spring of 2021, Russia relocated to the Ukrainian borders about 100 thousand troops – thus achieving the highest concentration of her military presence around Ukraine since the year 2014. The justification given was a military drill.

On March 31st, on the initiative from the American side, Mark Milley, the Chairman of the Joint Chiefs of Staff of the US Army, and Valery Gerasimov, the Chief of the Staff of the Russian Armed Forces, conducted a conversation. Shortly afterwards, Milley telephoned his Ukrainian opposite number.

On April 1st, D. Peskov, press secretary to the Russian president, declared that Russia was moving its armed forces around its territory at its own discretion, and this 'shouldn't be a cause of worry because it poses no threat to anyone... As for the involvement of the Russian forces in the conflict on the Ukrainian territory, the Russian army have never had any role in it and will not have any such role in future. All of it is exclusively an inter-Ukrainian conflict.'

On April 22nd, the Russian Defence Minister Shoigu made a public announcement about a successful completion of the training exercise and return of the armed forces to places of their permanent dislocation.[70] Yet, the military experts pointed out that despite the official assurances, Russia had left *in situ* a certain proportion of their military potential, most of all – the heavy-duty weaponry. Meanwhile the social media brimmed with posts on new Russian contingents being brought closer to the Russian-Ukrainian border and also into Crimea.

The picture started taking shape by the summer. The American intelligence services had reached a conclusion that 'the plans for a full-scale invasion into another country were being actively hatched within the higher echelons of

....

[70] **Sergei Shoigu:** Minister of Defence of Russia from 2012 to 2024.

power in Russia. Thus, it was understood that in order to bring Ukraine back into her sphere of influence, Russia was preparing for decisive actions, including the use of force. Clearly, Putin was aware that the window of opportunity was getting progressively narrower…'

On 12 July 2021, the official site of the Kremlin carried Putin's article 'On the Historical Unity of Russians and Ukrainians'. In his article, the president of Russia presented his vision of the history of the two countries – starting from the days of Ancient Rus and right until our times. He stated there that Russians and Ukrainians were one people. Ukraine's attempts to free itself from the clutches of Moscow, according to Putin, were exclusively a result of pressure from the West that 'had always dreamt to undermine our unity'. He insisted that Ukraine today was 'being managed from outside', as a result of which it was being transformed into the 'poorest state in Europe', where the Russian-speaking population were undergoing an 'enforced identity change' and 'coercive assimilation'. In the final passages of his article Putin made eight references to the anti-Russian project that, according to him, the Western powers were eager to implement within the territory of Ukraine. 'Step by step, Ukraine has been drawn into a dangerous geopolitical game aimed at converting it into a barrier between Europe and Russia, a launching pad against Russia. Inescapably, the time has come when a concept of "Ukraine is not Russia" is not acceptable anymore;[71] we will never agree to it…' Putin referred to contemporary Ukraine as a 'an offspring of the Soviet times – root and branch'. 'The Bolsheviks had arbitrarily re-drawn the frontiers, distributing generous territorial "gifts". And that's how Russia was robbed,' was his conclusion.[72]

Already the following day, the prominent historians – Ukrainian and Russian alike – responded in unison: the article had been a mixture of pseudo-historical, paranoidal and conspiracy-theories-inspired imaginings that had no relation whatsoever to the facts of history. 'Over a lengthy period of time the German nationalists have been outspoken about their belief that there never existed such a country as Holland, that the Dutch language is nothing more than Low German. Well – and? Linguistic contiguity and shared historical realia could be identified in practically all border-sharing countries'…; 'Putin's views are a hotch-potch of ignorance and aggression. What is evident is underhand manipulation and a banal absence of any ethical considerations. All of this is designed for the internal consumption'…; 'Undisguised lamentation one could hear increasingly often on social media, stating that Ukrainians are true Slavs whereas "Muscovites" – they

---

[71]   A reference to *Ukraine is not Russia* (2003), a book by Leonid Kuchma, the second president of Ukraine.

[72]   See the website of the president of the Russian Federation, 12 July 2021: http://kremlin.ru/events/president/news/66181

are, so to say, diluted by the Asian influx,'; 'A morbid phobia caused by the fact that Ukraine has, yet again, chosen the Western way – the same as several centuries ago. Had Russia followed the same route – something that Putin reiterated himself during his first presidential term – Ukraine and Russia would have been walking now hand-in-hand, like Czechia and Slovakia, Croatia, and Slovenia. But Russia has pitted itself as a Western opponent while Ukraine, defending itself against the Russian aggression, is gravitating towards the European Union and NATO,'; 'What is lurking behind this article? Is it pseudo-historical research or an overt threat, by now stripped of all camouflage?'

There were numerous references to a famous quote from Zbignev Brzezinski's article of 1994 – 'The Premature Partnership': 'Russia may only be an empire or a democracy, but never both at the same time… Without Ukraine, Russia stops being an empire. However, with Ukraine – first, corrupted, then subordinate, Russia automatically transforms itself into an empire.'

Within two weeks President Zelensky also responded to Putin's treatise: 'We are definitely not one people… Both of us have our own way to follow…'

The prevailing thought seemed to be that Putin's article was a manifesto of sorts, proclaiming the need to eliminate Ukraine. Such attitude should have alerted the higher echelons of the Ukrainian power. Did they arrive at the adequate conclusions?

June 16th. Biden and Putin met in Geneva. Information on Ukraine is scanty, practically non-existent.

Soon after, the American and British services learnt that Russia had formed a task force comprising of a variety of specialists in various fields for the purpose of developing plans for such an intervention.

The same summer, all of a sudden, appeared an article by Vladislav Surkov,[73] one of the Kremlin ideologists, alleging that such was Russia's historical mission – creating and enhancing chaos, which, according to him, spelled out her historical mission. Russia would use whatever possible to spread this chaos to her neighbouring nations and beyond, so that it would then be possible to bring them under her control.

At the same time, the American analysts came to a consensus about Putin's obsession with Ukraine, and his view of Ukraine as a break-away part of Russia that should be brought back into Russia's embrace. Presently he is apparently guided by the following considerations: should Ukraine get cosy with the West,

....

[73] **Vladislav Surkov**: first deputy head of the Russian Presidential Administration from 1999 to 2011, during which time he was often viewed as the main ideologist of the Kremlin. He proposed and implemented the concept of "sovereign democracy" in Russia.

the options for bringing it back into his fold would be shrinking; the West was dissociated and weak; the time for taking a calculated risk was ripe...

Some factual materials started appearing too. The data were uncorroborated but Russia allegedly planned to usurp the bigger part of Ukraine. The armed forces moving from the territory of Belarus and adjacent Russian territories were expected to take Kyiv in three or four days. Special operational units were to remove President Zelensky from power and reinstate a puppet government friendly to Moscow. Other forces, progressing from the north, east and Crimea, having completed a series of military operations, were to line up along the thrust line running from Belorussia in the north to Moldova in the south. The timeline for this was several weeks. The western part of Ukraine was to remain free – seeing that it was populated by 'incorrigible neo-Nazis and Russophobes'.

August 30th. Zelensky arrived in Washington D.C. by plane. Initially, his conversation with President Biden was supposed to take 40 minutes but instead they had a two-hour-long conversation, its results shrouded in mystery. What the American President said and what the Ukrainian President replied, remained unknown. It was only reported that the conversation had been very difficult... The briefing, as was to be expected, offered nothing of substance.

In the first part of September, Andriy Yermak[74] and Dmytro Kuleba[75] rushed off to Washington too. It was assumed they flew there for the sake of more specific information. While at the US Department of State, they were welcomed by 'some individual' who then took a seat, getting rid of his cup of coffee. That was the first time they heard the phrase that later on became legendary: 'Well now, guys! Go and dig your trenches!'

The Ukrainian party were somewhat sceptical... Registering their stunned gazes, the individual added: 'Yes, and get down to it straight away! You will find yourselves under attack!'

The guests asked; 'What gives you grounds for such conclusions?' Allegedly, they got no supporting intel.

Later, Kuleba would comment: 'But where is the problem? You are told: " We see it's all moving towards war!" After which there is a full stop and no additional information is ever offered. Meanwhile, the situation is clearly dire: the Russians, no doubt about it, are getting themselves ready for a war... But

---

[74] **Andriy Yermak** – appointed by President Zelensky to serve as the Head of the Office of the President of Ukraine from February 2020. He has been described as Zelensky's right-hand man.

[75] **Dmytro Kuleba** – Foreign Affairs Minister of Ukraine (March 2020 – September 2024)

the Normandy process is still alive.[76] In other words, what's going on is a big diplomatic game involving political super-stakes – like "who blinks first". In other words, Russia would like us to provoke her in some way… Suddenly it's clear that they are playing out a scenario whereby we're going to be responsible for provoking them in some way… The same partners then drop a hint: "God forbid you give them any reason…' And on the other hand, they say: "Go and dig your trenches"…'[77]

The Secretary of the National Security and Defence Council of Ukraine (NSDC) Olexiy Danilov: 'On 6 September 2021 came out a remarkable article by Shoigu – "On New Cities in Siberia". Having scrutinised it we realised – the article expressed a desire to enhance Siberia at the expense of our citizens…'[78]

On September 22nd M. Milley and V. Gerasimov held a meeting in Finland. Their conversation lasted over six hours and became 'an extension of negotiations about reducing the risks and resolution of conflicts'. The parties undertook not to divulge the details of these negotiations.

By October the Americans had accumulated new information. The Biden Administration had held several sessions on the subject of Ukraine. Some of those in attendance had trouble appreciating the scope of Russian President's ambitions. They found it hard to believe that 'a reasonable country would behave in this way…'

On the basis of conclusions drawn at those sessions, President Biden decided to follow two courses of action simultaneously: inform the NATO allies about the preparations for an invasion and convince them of the need for concerted efforts to oppose Russia and help Ukraine. Also, to warn Rusia about the inevitable consequences. This communiqué was passed on to Kyiv where it met with a certain degree of scepticism…

At the same time, municipal authorities in Lviv were not as optimistically minded as their colleagues in the centre. They set about putting together an alternative system of energy supply for their water board. No electricity – no water, no water – no life…

....

[76]   The **Normandy Format**, also known as the **Normandy contact group**: representatives of Germany, Russia, Ukraine, and France which met from 2014 forwards in an effort to resolve the war in Donbas and wider Russo-Ukrainian issues.

[77]   Gordon, 15 August 2022, https://gordonua.com/publications/kuleba-v-sent-jabre-2021-ho-v-hosdepe-nam-s-ermakom-skazali-nu-chto-rebjata-kopajte-tran-shei-1621358.html (accessed 30.06.2025).

[78]   LB, 22 April 2022 https://lb.ua/society/2022/04/22/514319_kreml_planuvav_st-voriti_kontstabori.html (accessed 30.06.2025).

October 15th. Optimistically minded or not, but there was a leak that some of the Ukrainian top brass were taking the threat seriously. And that day the NSDC approved Ukraine's defence plan in the event of a Russian attack.

October 31st. *The Washington Post,* quoting their sources within the American and European military, and certain civil servants, wrote about Russia moving its armed forces to the vicinity of the Ukrainian borders. Meanwhile videos and photos placed on social media started showing Russian military echelons transporting equipment to the south and west of the country. The situation reminded of the spring of the same year – 2021 – when Russia had engaged in similar activities.

A short time later, M. Zakharova, an official representative of the RF Ministry of Foreign Affairs, announced that at least three American publications were pushing forward these accusations and denied them.

For all that, the military experts disagreed: 'It looks nothing like a military training exercise. Something else is going on…'

On 1-2 November 2021, CIA Director William Burns paid an unexpected visit to Moscow. No official notice had been issued. The whole world was watching with bated breath – why on earth did the chief American security official find it necessary to embark on this mysterious mission? What could it all mean?

Mr Burns, however, made the purpose of his visit clear to the Russians. He brought a message of warning: the USA were confident that Putin was getting ready to invade Ukraine. Should he decide to go ahead with these plans, he was to face comprehensive sanctions from the united West. That was when some of the top Russian officials first realised that their country was about to attack Ukraine – they learn it from Mr Burns.

Putin at the time was at his Black Sea residence in Sochi. Mr Burns was put through to him on a secure line. Putin made no effort at all to counter Burns' accusations. Instead, he quietly listed Russia's grievances regarding the fact that the USA had allegedly been ignoring the Russian interests in the security sphere. As for Ukraine, he added, that was not a real country anyway. A 'contrived country, spun out of thin air…'

The visit proved momentous. To start with, many NATO member countries paid no heed to any of those warnings. No one could believe that a war like that was possible in Europe in the 21st century. Their intelligence agencies kept banging on about Russia being fully integrated into the commodity-driven business with Europe, and therefore couldn't possibly be interested in unfolding a full-scale military campaign in Ukraine. Some even assumed that Russia was misleading the West deliberately. For example, the 'old Europe', led by France and Germany, believed that Putin was bluffing and expressed their strong mistrust of the American data. The countries in Central and Eastern Europe that had only recently joined the bloc were convinced that should Russian aggression really take place it would be on a limited scale. And only Great Britain, Poland and the Baltic countries accepted fully the possibility of a full-blown invasion.

2 November 2021. At the International Climate Change summit in Glasgow, US Secretary of State Blinken shared his intelligence information with President Zelensky and described the storm moving towards Ukraine. It was a difficult conversation since in the past Ukraine had been a target of 'numerous tricks' pulled by Russia. Zelensky was understandably wary of an economic collapse brought about by a state of panic. Besides, he considered the information somewhat speculative. And another factor: although the Americans issued warnings, they made no offers of help with weapons for self-defence. You can repeat your warnings of an invasion a million times, said Zelensky, mocking the West, but if you don't provide the weapons we need, it's all empty words.

November 18th. For over a month the Russian foreign policy had concentrated on an active strategic campaign aimed at putting an irreversible halt to NATO's expansion to the east. At the extended session of the RF Ministry of Foreign Affairs Putin's instruction was 'to raise, without fail, a question of providing Russia with reliable long-term guarantees to ensure our security' and 'to keep the West on tenterhooks.' The narrative was being pushed that in the late 80s or early '90s an agreement had supposedly been reached whereby NATO undertook – in exchange for the reunification of Germany – not to extend eastward. But it had extended in that direction, nevertheless.

At the same time Moscow knew perfectly well that no such guarantees had ever been issued in writing to either the Soviet Union or the post-Soviet Russian Federation. The most that occurred were some informal oral discussions, nothing else…

November 21st. In an interview with an American publication *Military Times* Kirilo Budanov, the head of the Main Directorate of Intelligence in the Ukrainian Ministry of Defence, pointed out a high concentration of the Russian forces along the Ukrainian border. He produced a map and expressed his conviction that the attack would take place in the January to early February. 'The attack from the Russian Federation will probably consist of air strikes, offensives by the artillery and the armoured vehicles, followed by airborne infantry attacks in our east, amphibious assaults in Odesa and Mariupol and a smaller-scale intrusion from the direction of neighbouring Belarus… '[79] Peskov responded to information from Ukrainian and Western intelligence services about preparations for an invasion of Ukraine by calling it hysteria.

At the same time some other top security officers of Ukraine remained confident that the build-up of the Russian military presence was an act of psychological pressure. 'We do not envisage a classic intervention in the style of the Second World War – with tanks, artillery, infantry and support from the air.'

November 26th. The internet was overflowing with more and more new photos and video clips showing the westward progress of Russian military equipment. NATO Secretary General J. Stoltenberg announced that in case of her attack on Ukraine, Russia would have to face grave consequences. He stressed this was the second time this year that Russia had achieved an unusually high concentration of forces in this area: a considerable amalgamation of tanks, artillery, armoured vehicles, army units … The West, he said, could no longer be sure about Russia's intentions.

December 1st. Mr Stoltenberg declared that despite the fact that Ukraine was a valuable partner of NATO's it could only count on the Alliance's support measures. It could have no access to security guarantees and collective defence available to the member countries. In the course of several days, he kept reiterating that should Russia attack Ukraine, the Alliance would take no part in active fighting.

December 1st. A. Yermak in an interview to *RBC-Ukraine* on the probability of a full-scale intervention: 'Let me put it like this: the risk is high but I hope it won't happen…'[80]

December 2nd. RF President Putin proposed to enter into negotiations to eliminate NATO's advancement to the east and to obtain written legal guarantees since the oral ones could be ignored. Once more was sounded the narrative that Ukraine's accession to NATO was tantamount to crossing 'the red lines'.

NATO responded that this issue belonged exclusively to the Alliance's jurisdiction and that Russia had no vote and no veto.

December 4th. President Biden on Putin's statement about the 'red lines': 'I do not recognise anyone's "red lines"…'[81] Still, a lot of hope was placed on the telephone negotiations between Biden and Putin.

[79] Ukrainska pravda (UP), 23.02.2024, https://www.pravda.com.ua/podcasts/63f90 cc807994/2024/02/23/7390928/ (accessed 30.06.2025).

[80] Babel, 1 December 2021, https://babel.ua/texts/73572-golova-op-andriy-yermak-dav-velike-interv-yu-rbk-ukrajina-vono-pro-krashchogo-prezidenta-zelensko-go-viynu-ta-shtati-yaki-silno-vklyuchilisya-perekaz (accessed 30.06.2025).

[81] Golos Ameriki, 4 December 2022, https://www.holosameryky.com/a/baid-en-chervoni-linii-putina/6339340.html (accessed 30.06.2025).

The United States and Great Britain unexpectedly approved the decision on a large-scale information leak. This step – to place the intelligence data in public domain – was completely unprecedented. Yet it reflected their attempt to force Putin to renounce war or at least limit his capability for spreading disinformation. It was also decided to reveal details about a puppet government that Russia meant to bring into power in Ukraine. All these actions produced a powerful impact: the attention of the whole world was now focused on the possible intervention.

Thus, on December 4th, *The Washington Post* published the documents provided by the American secret services and bearing witness to the fact that the Russian troops were concentrating in four locations: nearby Yelnya in Smolensk Oblast and in the oblasts of Voronezh, Rostov, and in Crimea. The intelligence service concluded that Russia was intending to attack Ukraine simultaneously from several angles. It was planned to engage 175 thousand personnel.

On the same day, *Bild* – the biggest German daily with a circulation of over 1.5 million – carried a material on the same subject. They published a map different to the one provided by *Military Times*, but with a similar image showing multiple directions. The intervention would be carried out in three stages. The best-case scenario – annexation of two thirds of Ukraine. The material quoted some big-shot commentator: 'The Ukrainians will fight but they won't be able to withstand a massive attack launched by the Russians.'

Certain news items were leaked through the British media too.

Putin's press secretary Peskov retaliated by calling those publications hysterical.

But then, none of it caused any undue concern in Ukraine either. At the time there was quite a lot of ridicule aimed at the map – since *Bild* wasn't a serious source but a regular tabloid. On that map Lviv was shown as Lemberg – a name that had been obsolete for a long time. The military experts offered their own interpretation: plans of this nature were too complicated, and on close inspection resembled operational plans from the times of the Second World War. Even if Russia had enough capability, it wouldn't reach beyond Donbas.

Yet from that moment on, the Americans and the Brits started issuing regular warnings regarding this specific threat. Kyiv, as before, was taking the risk of Russian invasion with a pinch of salt. Eventually the Ukrainian position was formulated: 'If you are hundred percent sure that an assault is going to happen, why don't you launch your preventive sanctions? Why waiting till after the event? Introduce them as a matter of urgency! Make their life difficult straight away!'

December 7th. A two-hour-long negotiation between Biden and Putin took place in the format of a secure video link. Prior to that, the American President had discussed the situation along the Ukrainian borders with the leaders of Italy, France, Germany, and Great Britain. The Kremlin announced that the conversation would be routine and no breakthroughs were to be expected at that time.

The White House Press Office made the president's position public: the USA and its allies were concerned about the build-up of the Russian military presence along the Ukrainian borders; decisive economic steps, along with other measures, would be taken in case of a military escalation; Ukrainian sovereignty and its territorial integrity were confirmed.

Some days later S. Lavrov, Russia's foreign minister, announced to A. Blinken that Moscow needed long-term guarantees of security on its western borders.

December 12th. A summit of G-7 Foreign Ministers took place in Liverpool. Its agenda was concentrating on the situation along the Ukrainian borders. The countries that had been doubtful before, by then were gradually abandoning their sceptical stance. At least in their final communiqué the summit participants issued a warning to Russia that 'she would have to pay a dear price for the gravity of the consequences'.

Throughout December the Americans and the Brits were constantly warning about the existence of a threat.

December 12th. In response to an article published by Bloomberg on a possible Russian operation against Ukraine, Peskov referred to it as an unsubstantiated attempt to whip up tensions and emphasised that Russia posed a threat to no one. However, he simultaneously drew attention to an increased number of 'incendiary incidents' initiated by the West. At the same time, Russian Deputy Foreign Minister Ryabkov declared that in case of NATO's spreading towards the east, the Alliance would have to meet with 'grievous consequences'.

December 14th. In an interview given to the Italian *La Repubblica*, President Zelensky shared his view that Russia was accumulating its forces along the borders for the purposes of blackmail. 'However, if the number of Russian troops continues growing, this would mean an even crueller blackmail and could be interpreted as preparation for enhanced aggression against our country and, possibly, the entire region… Russia started this war in 2014, and ever since we've been ready for any scenario. Regrettably, the same does not apply to all European countries. Our country gave up its portion of the Soviet nuclear arsenal – the third most powerful in the world – in exchange for guarantees – among others, from Russia – that our security and borders would be respected. All this has now been thrown into the dustbin of history… It's surprising to hear Russia demanding any guarantees when the RF itself has broken so many promises.'[82]

....

[82]   Army inform, 14 December 2021, https://armyinform.com.ua/2021/12/14/volo-

As for Ukrainian society, it was split along the lines of people's expectations. Only a little more than one third of the population perceived the agglomeration of the Russian troops as a realistic threat.

Russia stated that it was concerned not so much with Ukraine's formal membership in NATO as a noticeable presence of the United States and NATO on the Ukrainian soil, given that Ukraine was not a member. That was precisely what Russia saw as a threat to her national security. Moscow put forward a demand that NATO should retreat to its positions in 1997 (that is, without the Baltic countries, Poland, Czechia, Slovakia, Hungary, Romania and Bulgaria as member states) and guarantee that Ukraine would not join the bloc. Which meant that Russia was unequivocally proclaiming the entire Eastern Europe the sphere of her influence.

That was an unrealistic demand because meeting it, NATO would have had to renounce its fundamental principles. Much as everyone understood that, realistically speaking, membership in NATO of either Ukraine or Georgia wasn't on the agenda any time soon, the West couldn't and wouldn't make promises that these countries would never join the Alliance. Also, NATO absolutely couldn't renounce its proclaimed 'open door policy'. As for the demand to withdraw its troops from eastern Europe, from the countries who were already members, it was simply impossible. J. Stoltenberg has said that each nation must choose its destiny independently and that this is the cornerstone principle behind security in all of Europe...

December 16th. O. Danilov still maintained that there was no immediate risk of a full-scale intervention by Russia. 'There are some calculations, a period of preparation, a certain amount of time... that they must allocate... At the moment, 92 thousand Russian troops are positioned nearby the Ukrainian border, but should President Putin decide to invade he would need many more – at least 500-600 thousand soldiers manning the border in order to maintain control in case of an invasion...'

Moscow kept banging on about some pre-planned military drill.

December 17th – totally unexpected news. The Russian Foreign Ministry published a draft agreement about 'reciprocal guarantees of security'. Russia proposed that the NATO members should commit to the non-proliferation of NATO, which would include non-accession to the Alliance of Ukraine and other countries. Moreover, Moscow underscored that those published drafts were not a menu from which one could pick and choose. The Russian proposals

....
dymyr-zelenskyj-v-intervyu-la-repubblica-rosiya-pogrozhuye-ukrayini-shhob-shan-tazhuvaty-zahid/ (accessed 30.06.2025).

could only be accepted by the West in their entirety! Moscow went on to issue a direct threat: should the West not treat those proposals seriously, they were ready to resort to a 'military-technical alternative'.

In essence, it was an ultimatum. There had never been a precedent to any of this. So, a question logically arose: what were the negotiations all about then? When negotiating, both sides should be prepared to make concessions. Whereas here was one side – Russia – put forward such demands that the whole process could be summed up thus: 'either this way, or not at all'! Unheard-of!

For NATO this stance was unacceptable. The organisation's General Secretary had already rejected several Russian demands of similar nature. Meanwhile Germany and France kept dropping hints that the situation should be resolved peacefully, through negotiations.

The White House was not opposed to negotiations but was of the opinion that Russia had no real need for any of that. Simultaneously, the United States started openly increasing their military presence in Europe. Joe Biden let it be known that in case of Russia's invasion of Ukraine, Washington was ready to undertake steps that had not been taken back in 2014.

December 22nd. Peskov explained that the 'military-technical response' mentioned by Putin did not mean a new arms race, but a 'complex of measures to ensure Russia's security.'

December 23rd. Putin made a statement asserting that aggravation of the relations between Moscow and the West had started in 2014 – the year of a 'coup d'état' in Ukraine. Prior to that, he said, Russia had been cooperating with all governments in Kyiv and that the situation had changed radically with the 'bloody upheaval' in Maidan. He also claimed that Ukraine had made two attempts to resolve the situation in Donbas through the use of force during the presidency of Petro Poroshenko.[83] And that Russia was under the impression that Ukraine was preparing a third military operation…

December 25th. The Russian Defence Ministry issued a news bulletin announcing that the military training exercise that had been planned and conducted was now completed.

Lviv. Municipal authorities began preparing for the arrival of displaced persons from other areas. Mayor Andriy Sadovyi[84] started regular Zoom sessions with the mayors of towns and cities in Western Ukraine, suggesting that a quota should be put in place to identify the local capacity for receiving the new arrivals. All of this was his personal initiative, there had never been any

....

[83] **Petro Poroshenko:** the fifth president of Ukraine (2014 – 2019).

[84] **Andriy Sadovyi:** mayor of Lviv, Western Ukraine.

instruction from above. Yet there was a clear understanding that people from the affected areas should have somewhere to move to.

December 28th. After Vitaliy Klitchko, mayor of Kyiv, declared that a special command unit was to be set up in the capital city and tasked with developing a system of territorial defence (in preparation for the Russian invasion), the Ministry of Defence insisted this was beyond its sphere of competence: 'matters pertaining to the defence of our nation are not a suitable subject for political PR.'[85]

Meanwhile the prevailing sentiments among the general population were rather those of scepticism… Some even joked: 'Listen, you, Russians – invade after January 1st if you must but let's have a normal festive season over the New Year!'

At the same time K. Budanov and his deputies were racking their collective brains trying to work out the most efficient way of presenting the info on the invasion to the higher echelons of power. They decided to move cautiously, in a measured fashion – but to get the point across – yes, the invasion was now a certainty.

At all events, the New Year celebrations were held in relative peace.

However, already on 10 January 2022 the world's attention was concentrated on events in Geneva, where the USA and Russia entered into negotiations about security guarantees. After a seven-hour-long discussion no diplomatic break-through was reported.

January 11th. The Russian army started another drill involving the use of small arms. The drill was conducted on training grounds intended for combined arms and situated in the vicinity of the Ukrainian borders – in the oblasts of Voronezh, Belgorod, Bryansk, and Smolensk.

On January 12th the negotiations picked up in Brussels, by now in the format Russia – NATO. Representatives of the Russian Federation and 30 Alliance members talked over the threat of an armed invasion by Moscow and the demands put forward by Russia to NATO. The Alliance made it clear that they would never agree to a compromise over the Russian demands – NATO would never denounce their policy of 'open doors'. In his comment the head of the Russian delegation had this to say: 'If it proves impossible to parry threats to her security by political means, Russia will employ an armed response.'[86]

....

[85]   BBC news Ukraine, 28 December 2021, https://www.bbc.com/ukrainian/news-59807802 (accessed 30.06.2025).

[86]   New voice, 12 January 2022, https://nv.ua/world/geopolitics/peregovory-rossi-ya-nato-12-yanvarya-2022-vse-podrobnosti-sammita-onlayn-poslednie-nov-osti-50207827.html (accessed 30.06.2025).

January 12th. W. Burns visited Kyiv in secret. The Americans had accumulated much more new evidence about the Russian invasion, and Mr Burns presented President Zelensky with their specific findings. Envisaged was a blitzkrieg attack against Kyiv, mostly stemming from Belarus with a purpose of beheading Ukraine's central power.

He exposed the key element of the Russian plan: the assault would start with landing an advance group of troops at the Antonov Airport in Hostomel, nearby Kyiv, for that airport was capable of receiving large transport aircraft carrying air cavalry. The President and his family were in personal danger. It couldn't be ruled out that those charged with the task of eliminating him were already *in situ* in Kyiv. The city was supposed to be taken within two or three days. Mr Burns warned: in case of an attack, you won't survive for more than 72 hours! And offered Zelensky an escape route. Zelensky answered that he would stay put.

Mr Burns left. The majority of the top officials in Ukraine remained convinced that Russia would never be able to amass sufficient human resources and requisite hardware for realising such grandiose plans and occupy a sizeable part of Ukraine. The same clichés kept being reiterated: Russia would never attack, what with a high probability of internal destabilisation and large-scale sanctions introduced against her.

January 13th. The third round of negotiations, this time in Vienna under the auspices of the OSCE.

All rounds of negotiations had been completed. The parties failed to come to an agreement – both sides held their ground. Russia, as before, was demanding guarantees that neither Ukraine nor Georgia would ever be accepted into NATO but was given a reply that no one was allowed to interfere in those spheres. The Western countries refused to accept Russia's key proposals on drawing up legally-binding commitments preventing NATO's expansion and deployment of offensive weapons near the Russian borders. From the Western perspective, the whole exercise was rather a dialogue aimed at reducing tensions along the Ukrainian national borders. Meanwhile Russia thought it was not a dialogue but negotiations, and that the agenda was all about guaranteeing the security of Russia. As a result, there was no further clarity about whether Russia was going to withdraw her troops away from Ukraine.

Upon completion of all those meetings, Russia's Foreign Ministry announced that the West had to 'make up its mind': either comply with the Kremlin's demands of 'guarantees for security' or face 'manifest risks for all

OSCE member states, risks fraught with irreversible consequences.'[87] After that Mr Stoltenberg feared that there was a real risk of a new armed conflict in Europe.

January 14th. Following the three rounds of negotiations with Russia, Europe was in a state of discomfiture and incomprehension. The main question went thus – what on earth had just happened? Referring to its sources within NATO, a German magazine *Der Spiegel* explained that there was no joint understanding within the Alliance either, yet work had started on a scenario of dealing with Russia on several fronts. This lack of unity within NATO proved to be yet another complicating factor – there was no consensus there on what to do even in a case of Russia possibly attacking the Baltic countries. To say nothing about Ukraine…

For all that, the world leaders were getting increasingly convinced that in the course of negotiations Russia had made it abundantly clear that she was not interested in any compromise suggested by the West; that she was ready to go to war should her ultimatum not be accepted in its entirety. The editor of an influential Western publication wrote: 'This week has revealed that Putin is ready to inflame the military situation to the point of conflagration. The only remaining question is whether or not Russia is ready to cross the line.'

Within the Alliance itself it was accepted as possible that Russia could use her enhanced military presence in the Mediterranean, North Atlantic and Arctica so as to thrust forward on a wide front, including an assault against the countries that belonged to NATO. Although NATO had no specific evidence to this effect, the probability of such a development was considered quite realistic. Should this prove to be the case, the Alliance would not be able to fight back sufficiently promptly – neither on the battlefield nor in the cyberspace. NATO was investing week after week in trying to divine what Putin was after when drawing his troops into vicinity of the Ukrainian borders. Essentially, his principal demand had already been met: a membership in NATO, promised to Ukraine and Georgia back in 2008, was no more discussed in any practical sense – allegedly because of internal territorial conflicts unfolding in both countries.

The Kremlin leader had achieved yet another of his goals: President Biden was now negotiating with the Kremlin directly. Russia had re-entered the global arena as a superpower. The Europeans had been recast as extras. Putin's provocations proved efficient in mercilessly exposing the weaknesses of the West. So, a question was waiting to be asked: how far were the USA and Europe really prepared to go in case of a need to defend the Baltic countries? Forget

---

[87]   TASS, 13 January 2022, https://tass.ru/politika/13422215 (accessed 30.06.2025).

Ukraine in all of this… The United States couldn't even be certain if Europe could be persuaded to introduce harsh economic sanctions against Russia if she decided to attack Ukraine. Such a step would clearly result in sharp hikes in fuel prices in Europe. Then appeared yet another item of news: the NATO member states had held a discussion on the subject of Ukraine's chances, should the war turn out to be not a local conflict but a full-scale invasion. The consensus was that 72 hours – and then nothing would be left of Ukraine…

January 16th. After the negotiation's fiasco Russia issued a warning: she was prepared to resort to stern measures. True enough, two days later a large-scale cyber-attack against the sites of multiple Ukrainian state institutions took place. It had been assumed by some that it was directly related to the failure of the negotiations.

In the meantime, Moscow and Minsk[88], simultaneously, announced that a joint military exercise was to take place in Belarus in February; the Russian officials continued denying any plans of launching an offensive against Ukraine.

Against this background, the USA State Department announced that Blinken would visit Kyiv.

January 16th. Two transport aircraft of the British Royal Air Force landed at the Boryspil International Airport carrying a cargo of anti-tank defence systems. The aircraft had to fly along a circuitous route, bypassing the German air space. UK Secretary of State for Defence Ben Wallace explained that the equipment was sent to Ukraine with a view of increasing its defence capability within a context of a dangerous concentration of the Russian armed forces.

CNN reported that in the course of their telephone conversation, President Biden and President Zelensky disagreed on the subject of possible gravity of the Russian invasion. Joe Biden was certain that the attack was imminent while Zelensky insisted that the threat emanating from Russia was 'serious but ambiguous.' At the same time the Ukrainian authorities turned to their partners: sanctions against Russia should be introduced as a preliminary measure – they would be of no importance in case of an active invasion. The US State Department rejected this idea – 'the deterrent effect will be thus lost.'

There's a leak that during a telephone conversation with V. Zaluzhny, M. Milley, chairman of the US Joint Chiefs of Staff, expressed a wish to be acquainted with Ukraine's defence plan in the event of a Russian attack (as approved by NSDC on October 15th). However, Zaluzhny did not share this with him.

....

[88] Minsk: the capital of Belarus.

On January 19th Blinken arrived in Kyiv and told Zelensky that he was acting on behalf of President Biden because the agglomeration of the Russian troops near the Ukrainian borders presented a direct threat. 'Russia's goal is to sow discord among our nations. We cannot allow them to succeed… You and us, we must act in concert with each other, promote our unity and enhance it. This is the most important message for today, especially in view of a possible aggression from the side of Russia,' formulated Blinken.

It was suggested to V. Zelensky that it was imperative to ensure the un-interrupted operation of the structures of power. He received a promise of support whatever his decision. The possible options included him staying in Kyiv, moving to the west of the country, or Poland. He announced that he would stay in Kyiv.

The responsible sources confirmed that Ukrainian president treated this information with all due attention. However, to the State Secretary's conster-nation he continued insisting that any appeal to mobilisation would result in general panic and a drain of capital – that would be a serious blow to the Ukrainian economy, not overly stable at the best of times. Answering questions from the journalists about Russia's plans to attack Ukraine, he tried to quell the wide-spread worry. 'If we sow chaos on the eve of an invasion, the Russians will simply eat us whole. The thing is – when chaos reigns, people flee from the country.'

On the same day – for the first time in those two weeks of disquiet – the president finally addressed the nation. The video was entitled 'No to Panic. With Faith in Ukraine and Peace' and must have been designed to calm the agitation. After the initial general contemplations about tensions in society, in the sixth minute he voiced this question: 'What should you do?' And answered it himself: '… Calm down and do not rush to supermarkets to stock up on buck-wheat grain and matches.' He reiterated his appeal to refrain from panic since everything was under control and developing according to plan. 'Soon we shall celebrate the Day of Unity, after which we shall inaugurate the long-awaited bridge over the Dnipro River in Zaporizhzhia. Shortly after, it'll be Easter and we'll enjoy our shashliks… And then – collectively dig up our orchard plots and, sure thing, make merry at weddings…'[89]

But not a word about the real state of events, and what preventive meas-ures were planned by the authorities… Immediately, everyone was doubtful. The president was amazed as the sentiments of panic started spreading in the society? Blaming the Ukrainian mass media for whipping up hysteria? While

....

[89]   Official website of the President of Ukraine, 19 January 2022, https://www.pres-ident.gov.ua/videos/bez-paniki-z-viroyu-v-ukrayinu-ta-mir-prezident-volodimir-ze-1981 (accessed 30.06.2025).

simultaneously avoiding any reference to a possible full-scale invasion planned by Russia and dominating international news for several weeks running? Omitting the American statements assessing the risk of invasion as the highest since 2014?

January 20th. The eighth aircraft arrived from Great Britain as part of the aid programme.

January 21st. For the first time a high-altitude, remotely-piloted surveillance aircraft RQ-4 Global Hawk was used by the US Air Force to monitor, for the benefit of Ukraine, the borders with Belarus and Russia. It took off from the airbase within the UAE and entered the Ukrainian air space from the south. To start with, it made several circles in the north – between Zhytomyr and Konotop, after which it headed towards the city of Izium in Kharkiv Oblast. Ukraine granted access to its air space to foreign aircraft and remotely piloted aerial vehicles with a view of monitoring the situation within the occupied Donbas and Crimea. The reconnaissance data, thus obtained, was passed on to our military command.

Commander-in Chief Zaluzhni gathered his inner circle and said: 'Not all our people believe it, but I think the Russians will come at us. It is impossible to negotiate with evil, so get ready to fight.'[90]

January 22nd. Despite Kyiv's attempts to apply 'calming measures', informational leaks were already occurring on a mass scale. The UK Foreign Office claimed, based on their intelligence data, that Russia was planning to bring a pro-Russian politician to power in Ukraine. The front-running contender for the post was named as Yevhen Murayev, a former deputy of the Verkhovna Rada of Ukraine[91]. Also named were another four Ukrainian ex-politicians 'maintaining connections' with the Russian special services. They were Mykola Azarov, prime minister in Victor Yanukovych's presidency; Serhiy Arbuzov, first vice premier during the same period; Andriy Kliuyev, who had served both as vice premier and head of Yanukovych's administration; and Volodymyr Sivkovych, the former deputy secretary of the National Security and Defence

....

[90]   Reporters, 21 February 2023, https://reporters.media/gotujtesya-bytysya/ (accessed 30.06.2025).

[91]   The Verkhovna Rada (Supreme Council) of Ukraine – is a one chamber parliament consisting of 450 people's deputies. For various reasons currently it numbers a bit less than 400. De jure the pro-presidential 'Servant of the People' party has the majority. De facto they often resort to agreements with other factions. Both the President and the VR were last elected in 2019 for the term of five years. The Constitution forbids holding elections at wartime. That makes that both the President's and the VR functions have been automatically extended.

Council of Ukraine. It was emphasised that several of those listed above were directly involved in the 'planning of an attack against Ukraine'.

Y. Murayev, who was to be placed at the head of the puppet government, achieved notoriety through his pro-Russian pronouncements: called the Maidan Uprising a 'coup d'état' and the war in Donbas – a 'civil conflict'. Quite naturally, Murayev said he knew nothing of this and basically he was a good guy. Some sources also mentioned the former president V. Yanukovych ('an extremely legitimate contender') and Oleg Tsaryov – formerly, a deputy of the Verkhovna Rada.

At the same time the Ukrainian Ambassador in London stated that the main question was not whether or not Russia was going to attack Ukraine but the actual scope of such an invasion.

January 22nd. Military assistance started arriving during that night from the USA: 90 tonnes of airborne weapons to be used at the front line. Secretary of State Blinken declared that should Russia bring her troops into Ukraine, the retaliation would be swift and deadly. The Ministry of Defence informed that Russia was bringing tanks, artillery, and ammunition into Donbas.

January 24th. The Ukrainian authorities gave a reserved response to their Western partners regarding the threat from Russia. President Zelensky's advice was to remain calm, while Foreign Minister Kuleba urged Ukrainians 'not to fall for those bogeyman stories'. It felt odd – given that a blitzkrieg in Ukraine continued making frontpage news in the West.

O. Danilov expressed his thoughts on this subject too: 'We are aware of Russia's plans and intentions… What we need now is self-control and thoughtfulness, everybody should go about their business as usual… It is of paramount importance for the Russian Federation to see the internal situation destabilised, whereas our task is to carry on as normal, remaining level-headed and in control… Are we ready for their active interference? Yes, we are. Will they put their plans to the test? We cannot know for sure, but we are making ourselves ready. We understand it all and give account of the *status quo*. We've been acting in this vein since the first intervention in 2014, which resulted in the annexation of our territories but provoked no reaction from the USA or the UK in their capacity as guarantors of the Budapest Memorandum…'[92]

January 24th. The US Department of State announced the start of evacuation of the families of diplomats and some supporting staff, whereas US citizens were insistently advised to refrain from any trips into Ukraine. The Kyivan

[92]   Radio Svoboda, 24 January 2022, https://www.radiosvoboda.org/a/news-rn-bo-danilov-panika/31669157.html (accessed 30.06.2025).

embassy would operate as usual and the USA remained unswerving in their support of the Ukraine's sovereignty and territorial integrity – a pledge envisaging supplies of weapons.

January 25th. The third aircraft arrived from the USA carrying 80 tonnes of Javelin weapon systems. Estonia, Latvia, and Lithuania got a permission to supply American-manufactured armaments. It applied to the same anti-tank missile complexes Javelin, portable air-defence systems Stinger, and anti-tank light weapons NLAW. The weapons of this type were expected to be just right for preventing Russia from quickly taking Ukraine by storm.

January 25th. Western secret services expressed their certainty that some Russian troops would cross the border from the side of Belarus. The US Department of State warned Belarus about a 'quick and decisive reaction' from the USA and their allies in case they would make their territory available as a launch pad for an aggression against Ukraine.

January 26th. Germany undertook to supply 5,000 helmets to Ukraine. The German defence minister stated: 'This is an absolutely clear signal that we are on your side.' Andriy Melnyk, Ukraine's ambassador to Germany: '… A purely symbolic gesture… a drop in the ocean… Ukraine expects the federal government to make an about-face, to genuinely alter the paradigm…'[93]

January 28th. President of the German Federal Intelligence Service Bruno Kahl: 'Russia is ready to attack Ukraine and can use a thousand ways to do so. Yet the final decision is still to be taken.'[94]

January 28th. 'We are witnessing the reformatting of the world's politics, economics, and culture…', said Alexander Lukashenko, president of Belarus, in his annual message to the Belarusian people and parliament: 'But no compromise has yet been found. In effect, what's in stake is the destiny of humankind – either new agreements or new rounds of escalation and a new world war… Thus, Question Number One for our society is: will there be or won't there be a war? Yes, there will be war but only in one of two situations: in the case of direct aggression against Belarus which would lead to a hot war. And another scenario: there will be war and Belarus will take part in the event that our ally, the Russian Federation, is exposed to a direct attack and the same aggression takes place within the Russian Federation. I would like to offer my response to the collective West. They are asking a very important question: will there be troops deployed within Belarus? If our country falls victim to aggression, there will be hundreds of thousand Russian troops here who will, alongside hundreds of thousands of

[93]   DW, 26 January 2022, https://www.dw.com/ru/germanija-postavit-ukraine-pjat-tysjach-voennyh-kasok/a-60563387 (accessed 30.06.2025).

[94]   European Pravda, 28 January 2022, https://www.eurointegration.com.ua/news/2022/01/28/7133248/ (accessed 30.06.2025).

Belarusians, defend this sacred land… In this war there will be no victors. We all stand to lose. So, we don't want another war, we've had our share of fighting. Our nation lost millions of lives in the wars of the past. We want to live and work in peace. We've never caused our neighbours problems, never been a problem for other nations. And never intend to do so in the future. Not only because we are peaceful people but also because we have no need to do so…'[95]

February 1st. Boris Johnson in Kyiv.

February 2nd. Upon his return to London, he spoke with Putin over the telephone and tried to deter him by offering assurances that Ukraine was definitely not going to accede to NATO any time soon. Allegedly at some point Putin said to Johnson that he would hate to hurt him but 'in case of a missile strike, it'll only take a minute…' Was this a joke or a genuine threat?

February 2nd. Russia continued building up her military presence near the Ukrainian borders, especially in Belarus, Crimea and its western territories. Within the framework of Union Resolve – 2022 joint military exercise, Russia transferred several thousand of her army personnel into Belarus. The exercise was to take place between February 10th and 20th on training grounds in the immediate vicinity of the Ukrainian borders. The West was concerned that this was just a cover for starting an invasion. Moscow and Minsk resolutely rejected those suppositions.

Satellite surveillance picked up the exact locations of troop concentration. Compared to the images dating back to January 19th, the numbers had grown substantially. There was clear evidence that military tents were set up in the places of deployment – an unequivocal sign that not only military hardware, but manpower, too, was relocated into the field camps. In came Iskander missile complexes with target range of up to 500 kilometres.

No official numbers were yet quoted for the Russian military personnel arriving in Belarus. Yet the observers recorded the highest concentration of the Russian military capability in Belarus in the entire post-Soviet period. S. Shoigu, Russia's defence minister, stated that the numbers did not exceed the parameters established in the Vienna document of 2011 (i.e. 9,000 persons), and therefore placed no obligations on Russia to explain the goings-on. Yet the Western intelligence counted at least 30 thousand military personnel. The new development – by that point, Russia was not only brining in the armed forces but also the Russian National Guard.

....

[95] Official website of the president of Belarus, 28 January 2022, https://president.gov.by/ru/media/details/aleksandr-lukashenko-28-yanvarya-obratitsya-s-ezhegodnym-poslaniem-k-belorusskomu-narodu-i-nacionalnomu-sobraniyu (accessed 30.06.2025).

According to the official announcements, the training exercise was to use Tochka missile complexes, Triumph C-400 missile systems, Pantsir anti-aircraft gun-and-missile complexes, Iskander operational-tactical systems, and Su-35 fighters.

The first posts about the Russian soldiers in Belarus appeared in Belarusian social media on January 18th. The locals complained about the railways being used for accommodating heavy equipment, thus damaging the facilities. Small loading stations proved unfit to handle such heavy weaponry that was destroying loading ramps and causeways. There were frequent cases of heavy technology collapsing off the platforms. Once the loading was complete, behind were left the armour vests, helmets, personal safety apparels. During an unloading, the soldiers would throng the tracks, taking off only when an incoming train was some 200 metres away. Engine drivers were forced to use emergency braking. It was reported that the army drank a lot, selling off diesel oil and leaving behind piles of refuse. 'There are bags bursting with rubbish at about 20 metres interval… All over the place – empty vodka bottles, used plastic containers, empty boxes formerly containing biscuits…'

Early February saw a new leak of confidential documents – the USA and NATO responded to Russia's demands concerning guarantees for national security. The USA declared their readiness to consider such agreements but warned that if Russia continued increasing her armed forces or launched a war of aggression against Ukraine, it would trigger a response from Washington and its allies. NATO then stated that they were not seeking a confrontation with Russia but would not consent to a compromise undermining the very principles on which the Alliance was founded.

On 4 February 2022, both *Bild* and *The Washington Post* wrote, yet again, about the plans of invasion of Ukraine. Once more, they reminded their readers of three stages in such an invasion. There was something new, though. *Bild* made it known that the RF was finalising plans to create 'camps for detaining pro-Ukrainian activists' and drawing up lists of those to be sent to these camps. The newspaper concluded that Russia's main objective was to form a new 'union state' consisting of Russia, Ukraine, and Belarus.[96]

Practically straight away, Lavrov, the Russian foreign minister, in an attempt to countermand this statement, confirmed that Russia had no plans involving invasion of Ukraine.

....

[96]   Priamyi, 5 February 2022, https://prm.ua/bild-opublikuvalo-plany-rf-pislia-vtorh-nennia-v-ukrainu-kontstabory-referendum-ta-soiuzna-derzhava-z-rf/   (accessed 30.06.2025).

The Ukrainian top officials still remained convinced that Russia wasn't about to launch a full-scale war but if anything did come to pass it would only concern the eastern territories.

Top military brass also continued to prepare for a conflict in Donbas, most likely a head-on collision. But a 'great war'? Unrealistic! Hardly anyone believed in an attempt to approach the city of Dnipro from the direction of Crimea, and simultaneously from the north, via Kharkiv; also, an encirclement of the largest and most battle-ready military force in the east seemed improbable… A full-scale attack against Kyiv? That idea was perceived as even less credible – everyone was too scared to give it serious consideration.

Just then appeared some extraordinary news: field agents of the FSB established regular communication with the Russian airborne assault troops.[97] In view of this unconventional development, certain quarters were shifting towards a conclusion that it meant joint operational planning.

By that point the politicians in Europe had obtained their own, more detailed, intelligence. They assessed the Russian invasion of Ukraine as unlikely but the situation caused alarm. Whatever their beliefs, the Europeans made some convulsive attempts to appease Putin.

On February 7th Emmanuel Macron took a flight to Moscow, hoping to persuade Putin to deflate the tension. Prior to his meeting with Putin, he was supposedly offered an injection of the Russian anti-COVID vaccine. Macron turned the offer down. He was, therefore, given a place at the opposite end of a seven-metre-long white table. The conversation lasted six hours. Putin delivered a lengthy lecture on the 'historical unity between Russia and Ukraine'. He referred to the hypocrisy demonstrated by the West. The French President kept trying to steer the exchange back towards a discussion of the situation and ways to avoid a military conflagration. Putin responded with another chapter of his lecture.

At their joint press conference Macron, talking about a hypothetical plan of peaceful resolution, decided to butter up the Russian President: 'It must be done in a way respectful to Russia that would take account of the contemporary traumas faced by this great nation and great country.'[98] Macron's agenda was to highlight the 'exceptional role played by France' in the security of Europe and his personal contribution as a successful peace-keeper. It was all the more topical in view of the fact that in several months' time France was to hold its

....

[97]   **The Federal Security Service** (FSB) of the Russian Federation: Russia's principal security agency and the main successor agency to the Soviet Union's KGB.

[98]   BBC news Russian service, 7 February 2022, https://www.bbc.com/russian/news-60288898 (accessed 30.06.2025).

presidential elections and the contest promised to be tough. Putin was also flattered by all this renewed international attention and recognition of his power.

At the same press conference Putin mentioned that the Ukrainian leadership found the Minsk agreements underwhelming and allowed himself a crude joke: 'Whether you like it or not at all // Suck it up, my pretty girl... It's the only way...'[99] Such an insulting statement didn't go unnoticed.

On the same day President Zelensky parried: 'Ukraine is unquestionably pretty but as to being "his" – that's laying it on a bit thick... As for the ability to show patience, I personally believe that Ukraine is very patient for this is a sign of wisdom.' In other words, he was displaying wisdom for the sake of preventing further escalation of the conflict.[100]

The phrase itself created a buzz and sparked animated discussion. Social media even suggested that it had been a reference to a track by the notorious punk band Red Mildew where a similar line was used to describe a scene of rape. Press secretary Peskov was forced to comment: the Russian president, he said, had simply been quoting a folk source, nothing more. Pernickety commentators, however, did some digging around and discovered that if indeed this was a folk source, it alluded to the racy folk rhyme 'That my love has kicked the bucket// Doesn't mean I cannot f*** her// Whether you like it, or not at all//Suck it up, my pretty girl.' The rhyme had been popular in the '70s – the decade of Putin's youth which saw him make a start in his career in the security services. The conclusion was thus clear: most likely, the president of Russia had been referring to Ukraine as already dead, placed in the coffin of the Minsk agreements. Putin would have liked to see Ukraine submissive and to subjugate the Ukrainian nation completely. Implementation of the Minsk agreements in the sequence that was desirable for the Kremlin – 'first the elections in Donbas, then reinstatement of Kyiv's control over the borders' – would serve just that purpose.

The administration of the president of the United States published the following response: 'Any joke about rape is an outrage.'[101]

Whatever the inns and outs, everybody agreed that with this phrase Putin had achieved a new personal low.

....

[99]   **The Minsk agreements** (signed on 5 September, 2014): a series of international agreements which sought to end the Donbas war fought between armed Russian separatist groups and Armed Forces of Ukraine, with Russian regular forces involved and playing a central part.

[100]   UP, 10 February 2022, https://www.pravda.com.ua/rus/news/2022/02/10/7323-531/ (accessed 30.06.2025).

[101]   Meduza, 9 February 2022, https://meduza.io/shapito/2022/02/09/terpi-moya-krasavitsa (accessed 30.06.2025).

February 8th. Macron arrived in Kyiv. He told Zelensky that Putin had personally assured him there would be no new escalation.

February 8th. The Armed Forces of Ukraine began the Blizzard 22 command and staff defence drills in various regions of the country to perfect procedures of managing troops in active combat.

February 10th. A new meeting between political advisers to the Normandy Format heads of state (Normandy Four) started in Berlin. The first one had taken place on January 26th in Paris, following a period of lengthy inactivity. At the end of nine-hour-long deliberations, the parties failed to agree even on the formal joint document. A. Yermak announced that 'the next meeting will take place in the nearest future.'[102]

February 10th. The White House appealed to their citizens to leave Ukraine as soon as possible. 'Russia may start an important military operation against Ukraine any minute, and should it prove to be the case, it will unquestionably start with air strikes and missile attacks which will have an impact on departure logistics and threaten civilian lives.' This message from the USA government prompted other countries to call upon their nationals to leave Ukraine ASAP. Such countries as Great Britain, Australia, Canada, and the Netherlands followed suit.

In their turn, the Russian Foreign Ministry announced the existence of a' collusion' between Western powers and the mass media whose aim was 'to whip up artificial tensions around Ukraine by means of coordinated placing of comprehensive fake information that serves their geo-political interests, and is designed to divert attention from their own aggressive intensions.'

In the Verkhovna Rada D. Arakhamia suggested holding a sort of 'rehearsal'[103] – for how to run 'a vote in an extreme situation. In order to know who is in charge of what. I was collectively gagged: "Whatever on earth for? It would be a clear signal that there would definitely be war…" '[104]

S. Deyneko, head of the State Border Service: 'Yes, western intelligence has kept on warning us. We have listened carefully to this information. On the other hand, we have our own border intelligence, which works quite effectively in related countries, especially Russia and Belarus. I made a report to the president that the war will take place. Russia will attack us in the Chernobyl zone from the territory of Belarus'[105]

....

102   DW, 11 February 2022, https://www.dw.com/ru/peregovory-normandskoj-chet-verki-ne-prinesli-proryva/a-60738374 (accessed 30.06.2025).

103   **David Arakhamia**: head of the (propresidential) Servant of the People political party in the Verkhovna Rada.

104   UP, 23 February 2024, //www.pravda.com.ua/cdn/cd1/reconstruction/a6.html (accessed 30.06.2025).

105   UP, 23 February 2024, UP, https://www.pravda.com.ua/podcasts/63f90cc807994/

February 11th. The USA authorities continued with their deliberate policy of publicising intelligence on the situation regarding Ukraine – in an effort to discourage Russia from an armed invasion. The USA also warned the leaders of all NATO members that Russia had identified the date for the campaign – February 16th. An abundance of details was aired at secret briefings: comprehensive description of the routes to be taken for the attack, and even tasks to be performed by various military units. The discussions also covered possible missile and air strikes at the facilities of military infrastructure. The partners were adamant: if it was to be war, it would include 'all relevant nuances' – the elimination of country's leaders, and also creation of filtration and concentration camps. It was emphasised that Chairman of the Joint Chiefs of Staff M. Milley was not only actively engaged in a dialogue with his NATO colleagues but had made two telephone calls to the commander-in-chief of the armed forces of Ukraine, V. Zaluzhny, and even to the chief of the general staff of the armed forces of Belarus, V. Gulevich.

Yet again, the analysts were unanimous in their conclusion that the USA kept placing secret intelligence data into the public domain deliberately – in an attempt to thwart Russia's interventionists plans.

According to some sources, the supreme military command of Ukraine took the warnings of their American colleagues very seriously, while at Bankova Street the threat was taken on board, but the prevailing opinion was that there would be no full-scale intervention.[106] Yet another source announced that the Ukrainian secret services had already moved the better part of documents and equipment to the country's west. The embassies of several countries, including the United States, had reserved premises in Lviv for the eventuality of having to move from Kyiv.

February 11th. R. Wallace, the UK defence secretary, arrived in Moscow. S. Shoigu, his Russian counterpart, offered him personal assurances that Russia would not move into Ukraine. 'I know Ukrainians. I've been there five times, and they will fight,' stated Mr Wallace. Shoigu replied: 'My mother is Ukrainian [incorrect: she was simply born in Ukraine]. It all is part of our country.' Wallace reminded him of the possibility of sanctions. Shoigu: 'We can suffer like no one else. We will never reconcile ourselves to Ukraine choosing a pro-Western course.' The British delegation was already on their way out when Shoigu stopped Wallace and locked eyes with him: 'We have no plans to invade Ukraine…'[107]

....

2024/02/23/7390928/ (accessed 30.06.2025).

[106] **Bankova Street**: a street in central Kyiv. Most of the street is pedestrianised and closed off since it houses the Presidential Office of Ukraine.-

[107] Suspilne noviny, 16 August 2022, https://suspilne.media/271901-zavilis-podrobi-ci-ranise-ne-opublikovanoi-rozmovi-uollesa-ta-sojgu-the-washington-post/ (accessed 30.06.2025).

February 11th. Western security services registered an increased number of Russian saboteur groups within Ukraine. Mercenaries from a variety of private military companies arrived in secret, most probably tasked with causing a tumult in the society by way of assassinating specific targets and the use of special devices. It could not be ruled out that Russia planned various provocations that could be used as a pretext for intervention.

On the same day the National Security and Defence Council of Ukraine (NSDC) held an offsite session in Kharkiv. NSDC chairman Danilov said that Ukraine was 'perfectly aware of the intentions of the RF to provoke us. Yet we do not know where and when such provocation may take place. We've heard about the Crimean Bridge, about the Chornobyl power station, about the occupied territories of Donbas and Luhansk, and other facilities too... This is done with the purpose of shifting blame onto our country and our armed forces... The task we are facing is this: our territorial defence system must expand to two million citizens ready to defend our country in case of need. Additional battalions and brigades are being actively put together in all regions. Commanding officers have been appointed to practically all these units, and they are currently busy recruiting personnel.[108]

The first half of February saw a considerable increase in the rate of arrival of the aircraft bringing in military assistance: two or even three a day. So, on February 9th the ninths such aircraft landed from the USA. By February 11th, Ukraine had received, in total, 25 aircraft delivering help from the Western partners.

February 12th. Experts from the Ukrainian Centre for Defences Strategies concluded that there was a clear insufficiency of the accumulated strength and capabilities needed for a wide-scale campaign aimed at seizing the entire territory of Ukraine or any significant part thereof. Therefore, forecasts for the probability of such scenarios could not be confirmed for the immediate future. They considered such scenarios unrealistic for the foreseeable future.

For all that, a new poll of the population revealed that 39% of Ukrainians considered this invasion probable or imminent.

February 12th. President Zelensky visited the site of a special tactical drill conducted by the Ukrainian Internal Affairs Ministry in Kherson Oblast. From February 9th to 12th law enforcement agencies practised methods for dealing with public disturbances, disarming armed criminals, and liberating captured facilities belonging to critical infrastructure. 'This drill is happening for a purpose, it's taking place in all cross-border oblasts and is a result of concerted

....

[108]   Army inform, 11 February 2022, https://armyinform.com.ua/2022/02/11/u-harkovi-vidbuvsya-bryfing-za-rezultatamy-vyyiznogo-zasidannya-rnbo/ (accessed 30.06.2025).

efforts of the national police, the State Emergency Service, and the National Guard. This is exactly how our state should have been operating back in 2014. We and you, we understand that an assault or occupation always starts with destabilising the situation within, with operations carried out by saboteurs and reconnaissance groups. As we can see today, everything is perfectly under control, and the drill will continue for several days. The military training exercise will run in parallel,' announced the president after inspecting the training exercises in the village of Kalanchak. He also commented on the risk of a Russian invasion of Ukraine. He assured society that the situation was under control, yet added this: 'There is more than sufficient information to suggest a full-scale war.' He went on to say that we should count on our own resources, that Ukraine was grateful to the USA for the intelligence they gave us, but our secret services were active, too. The American data were taken into account but nevertheless still needed analysing. 'We are aware that we can expect "surprises" at any time... The most important thing is to be ready for anything... We are ready for any steps taken by anybody from the direction of any border. I am convinced that our specialists, our teams, the army, the ministries – all are operating at a very serious level... The NSDC convened for a session yesterday; we are acting according to plan. We are not afraid of anyone, there is no panic, everything is under control.'[109]

TV coverage from Kherson Oblast: 'Everybody feels the growing tension. But to say that Russia will start a war? Practically no one believes it... All routes leading out of Crimea, the adjacent fields, too, have been rigged with mines; anti-tank trenches are in place, as are barbed-wire fences. The organisation of the Territorial Defence has been practically completed. Security has been stepped up at key facilities of the infrastructure...'

February 12th. The border guard services intercepted telephone calls placed by Russian army personnel deployed at the military training exercise in Belarus. They were calling their families and, just in case, saying their goodbyes. The nature of those conversations made it clear that invasion was only days away. Head of the State Border Guard Service reported these findings to the president, underscoring their conclusion that Russia would definitely attack from Belarus and move in along the Chornobyl zone. The border guards evacuated all secret materials on personnel from Mariupol, Berdiansk, Kramatorsk, Lysychansk, Kharkov, Sumy, Chernihiv, Zhytomyr, Lutsk, Odesa, Kherson and Boryspil.

....

[109]   Official website of the President of Ukraine, 12 February 2022, https://www.president.gov.ua/news/na-hersonshini-volodimir-zelenskij-pereglyanuv-navchann-ya-si-72853 (accessed 30.06.2025).

February 12th. On Biden's initiative, another telephone conversation took place between him and Putin – that was their last direct contact. They spoke for several hours. The conversation was 'professional and amicable'. They agreed that their teams would continue cooperating over the crisis resolution. An American insider warned that Moscow 'would venture to go forward with her military operation whatever', and should this prove to be the case, 'the damage for Ukraine, the security in Europe and Russia herself would be huge.'

February 12th-13th. The USA started evacuating their personnel from the embassy in Kyiv. It was envisaged that the entire staff should be transferred to Lviv within the ensuing 24-48 hours. The move continued even on a Sunday – February 13th. According to the journalists, it was in support of disseminating the classified intelligence with a view of thwarting the Russian plans and deterring the Kremlin leader from any acts of aggression. By the same fell swoop, the Ukrainian powers were given yet another cue.

February 13th. Within just one day 20 chartered flights and private jets left Ukraine with some prominent businessmen on board. Allegedly, it was the final day to extend the aircraft insurance policies with the Western insurance providers. All this – shortly before February 16th – the date named by the Americans as a starting point of invasion and the reason for a temporary suspension of the respective policies. Everybody talked about little else.

February 13th. Prior to planned visits by the German chancellor, Olaf Scholz, to Kyiv and Moscow, the Ukrainian Ambassador in Berlin emphasised that it was the last chance to resolve the conflict around Ukraine through diplomatic means. That there was a sense now that war was becoming increasingly inevitable… And that the Ukrainian government was ready for a worsecase scenario under which Kyiv might be bombed within a matter of days…

February 13th. Out of all her fleets, Russia pulled together practically everything potentially usable for an invasion by sea. By that moment, 46 warships were deployed in the Black Sea and the Sea of Azov. Under the guise of a massive military drill, during the interval between February 13th and 19th, the Kremlin *de facto* effected a naval blockade of the Ukrainian Black Sea shoreline. An unprecedented concentration of the Russian combat vessels was registered in the Mediterranean Sea – 17 in toto, transferred over from all Russian fleets. Nothing like this had happened since the days of the Soviet Union's breakup. It was envisaged that even a possible entry of the US multi-purpose aircraft carriers into the eastern segment of the sea should be blocked.

J. Biden had a telephone conversation with V. Zelensky. As usual, in the end the parties exchanged generalities… Although our leader did insist that it was imperative 'to prevent the spread of panic…'

February 14th. Chancellor Scholz paid a visit to Kyiv under the umbrella of 'the diplomacy in crisis'…

Meanwhile, the satellite images registered an extremely high concentration of Russian military equipment and manpower in Crimea. A proper strike force, ready for an offensive, was thus ready. At the same time the Russian TV channels showed Defence Minister Shoigu informing President Putin in a routine meeting that agglomeration of force was nothing more than a massive army drill that was coming to an end.

It was announced that from February 14th to 19th the police in Kyiv were to be placed on a regime of maximum security. The streets were suddenly full of enhanced patrols, the critical infrastructure was brought under tighter security, there was a round-the-clock monitoring of the situation in the city.

Airlines started mass-scale cancellations of flights into Ukraine. A *de facto* blockade of the Ukrainian air space could no longer be ruled out.

The evening of February 14th. After an in-camera meeting with the Rada deputies, Danilov, the NSDC secretary, issued the following statement: 'As of now, we see no risk of a full-scale invasion. Could there be problems instigated by the Russian Federation? Yes, there could. We are ready for this eventuality. But we do not understand how in the 22nd year of the 21st century a country can say that they will be killing us. Tell me, please, how is this possible? What is the proper name for this: genocide? Terrorism?'[110]

An opinion started making rounds in the corridors of power that Ukraine's Western partners were using Ukraine as a bargaining chip, that the West and Russia were jointly 'scamming' the president to make him agree to concessions over the Minsk agreements. At the same time Moscow kept reiterating that 'Kyiv was getting ready for an offensive in Donbas.'

Suddenly, it became known that Zaluzhnyi, the Commander-in-Chief of the Ukrainian Armed Forces, was insistently trying to persuade president Zelensky to mobilise the reservists and start building fortifications along the borders. The president refused, reluctant to sow panic among the population…

Certain generals were reported as flaring up in private conversations: 'Christ Almighty, what are they waiting for, the guys up there? Still full of doubts? Relying on private channels of communication with the Kremlin, that some staff members have access to? Still hopeful that all of it will sort itself out somehow?'

February 14th-15th. New information came from Belarus concerning the joint training exercise. The military vehicles and manpower were spotted not

---

[110]   LB.ua. , 14 February 2022, https://lb.ua/society/2022/02/14/505566_danilov_mi_bachimo_ymovirnosti.html (accessed 30.06.2025).

only in the areas earmarked for the drill, but all over the place. For example, on February 14th-15th, Russian military equipment was being unloaded at the railway station in the town of Khoinyky in Homel Oblast. Tracked vehicles rolled down the town streets. The soldiers were put up in tents, erected in the surrounding forests. Khoinyky was only 50 kilometres away from the Ukrainian border.

The morning of February 15th. The Russian Defence Ministry announced that upon the completion of the training exercise, it started a stage-by-stage withdrawal of its troops from Belarus. The statement had come a day earlier than February 16th, the day identified by the western intelligence services as a possible date for the Russian invasion into Ukraine. Press secretary Peskov supplied an ironic aside – he suggested that the Ukrainians should set their alarm clocks for the hour identified by the West to be ready: 'They (the Ukrainians) should better set their alarm clocks for this precise time to be personally convinced...'

Yet the Western intelligence community dismissed this 'quip'. Besides, researches from the Conflict Intelligence Team, supported by the surveillance data, issued this statement: the preparatory work for the Russian intrusion into Ukraine had been practically completed or would be completed within a matter of days.

February 15th. From Kyiv Chancellor Scholz flew to Moscow. Supposedly, he was also offered an injection of the Russian vaccine. Scholz was trying to convince Putin that NATO were not an enemy of Russia, and if Ukraine were to join the bloc it wouldn't happen within the next 30 years. And if he did harbour plans of attacking Ukraine, the reason was 'totally absurd', whereas the real intention would be seen as 'conquering a neighbouring country'. Putin delivered a similar lecture to Scholz – on the subject of 'the Russians, Ukrainian and Belarusians being one people with similar languages and identity. They only became separated as a result of manipulations by various politicians. Belarus and Ukraine should not be separate countries.' Councillor Scholz was horrified: 'He was really ready to run his felt pen across the European landscape. And then to say: "This belongs to me, and that – to you".'

The German Chancellor replied that the international order was based on recognition of the existing borders – irrespective of when and how they had been drawn. He also warned Putin that the West would never condone the re-tailoring of the borders established in Europe. The sanctions would be rapid and harsh. And the close cooperation between Germany and Russia would come to a stop.

Answering Scholz's question about the intervention, Putin said: 'Our plans are in accordance with the situation...'

In line with their attempts to pacify Russia, Western politicians continued to 'lull Kyiv'. These were the incoming messages: 'Don't press Putin… Don't irritate him or make him nervous… Don't provoke him…' In other words, the same old refrains from the years before, the same advice that had failed completely. The only negative consequence of these 'lullabies' for Putin was annoyance.

One could understand the position of the German and the French: they were prepared to maintain peace in Europe at any cost. Even if it meant giving up the interests of Ukraine…

February 15th. A massive cyber-attack had hit the Ukrainian banks and state establishments, and first of all, the headquarters of the Armed Forces and the Defence Ministry. The attack proved to be multi-dimensional – coming from various countries and costing millions of Dollars. The officials voiced their disbelief that hackers could afford budgets of this magnitude. Assaults on this scale could only be sanctioned at a country's national level, to be carried out by either special services or criminal gangs under the country's control. 'The only country interested in such reputational attacks against us is, alas, Russia. The key objective is destabilising Ukraine and driving our population into frenzy.'

February 15th. In Belarus a pontoon bridge was erected across the Pripyat River, only six-and-a-half kilometres away from the Ukrainian border. The route to Kyiv from there was a little more than a short-cut.

The morning of February 16th. The anticipated intrusion from the Russian side, something vociferously predicted by the Western secret services, had not taken place. By then, a new prediction was announced – most likely, February 19th.

February 16th. The command-and-staff drill of the Armed Forced of Ukraine and other security and defence services took place at the Rivne combined-use training ground within the framework of Blizzard 22. Training involved the use of combat aviation, home-made and imported remotely-controlled aerial complexes, cannon artillery, multiple-launch rocket systems, Air Defence Systems, and modern weaponry supplied by our foreign partners: Javelin, NLAW, Stinger, and the others. The drill was planned to last throughout February in all regions of the country.

February 17th. News started arriving from Dzhankoi and other Crimean railway hubs about accumulation of the Russian convoys carrying cargoes of military equipment… On the whole, there was an impression of a 'powerful thrust'. Despite all this, the official Kyiv line was still to accuse the West of groundless panic-mongering. The circles closest to the president blamed the alarmist sentiments for a slump in the country's economics and the loss of the country's attractiveness to investors. All of this, they asserted, may lead to a hike in prices…

Much as it used to be the Conflict Intelligence Team that followed the progress by the Russian crawler machinery across the railway platforms and tank transporters, it was now obvious to everyone that the equipment was on its way towards the borders with Ukraine. 'The machinery is evidently moved to a launch site for a possible assault.'

As for the Ukrainians, by that point they were tired of living in fear of a new intrusion and believed it to be less and less likely. The result of yet another poll showed that a bare 19% of those polled estimated its likelihood as high (only several days prior to that, the figure had been 28%).

February 17th. A restricted-access chatroom revealed the following: allegedly, our military command had realised that the resources and manpower employed by the RF in the training exercise in Belarus were sufficient for forming a number of robust battle groups. Clearly, Kyiv would be attacked from several directions, so the time had come to start preparing. The General Staff issued respective instructions. It was decided that the defence headquarters would be set up in Kyiv. Colonel General Oleksandr Syrsky was appointed leader. 'We've started preparing ourselves, but there isn't much time. Today, no one wants to believe it. Or they believe that after all there won't be an invasion. Yet the mechanism has been set in motion, and we have started making adequate arrangements...'

It was decided that the 72nd brigade would be the basis for the defence group. This was not nearly enough: it covered only a quarter of minimal needs. Syrsky made the decision to form shooting battalions at higher education institutions and to create consolidated artillery units at training centers.[111]

February 17th. President Zelensky left for the front line to inspect the Ukrainian defence positions in Donetsk Oblast. While there, he gave an interview to *RBC-Ukraine* – a Ukrainian news agency. The was to be the last interview he gave before the war. The main points for discussion were membership of NATO, the Minsk agreements and security guarantees for Ukraine.

'We confirm that we have embarked on the road towards our membership of the alliance. NATO today is effectively the only existing security alliance which Ukraine could join. They have an 'open-door' policy towards us. But the road is long – years and months, especially if there is an escalation. Yet we expect to be given a package of guarantees. If only theoretically, this should be in line with what's accessible to NATO member countries...

[111]   UP, 24 February 2024, https://www.pravda.com.ua/cdn/cd1/reconstruction/a7.html (accessed 30.06.2025).

'Today, no one can be 100% sure that something untoward won't happen to them tomorrow. Even if they belong to this or that union… Therefore, if you, our partners, say that these are our shared values, let us invest in them together. And no, not from altruism, but because you will be attacked tomorrow. And the attack will go on and on, and this means a refugee crisis. Among other things… Allocation of financial resources to the army: that's question number one. So that there will be a powerful independent army in Eastern Europe, in Ukraine, one that could defend Ukraine, and not only Ukraine, by virtue of being able to keep in check any subsequent encroachments…

'We do realise that no one is prepared to die for us. We say: thank you. Moreover, we wouldn't like to end up as a country that deludes itself and believes that others would die for the sake of our wellbeing – but when a war of aggression starts, we must be ready…

'Why do we talk about the risks existing at the border? Because, more often than not, what the Russian authorities say and what they do are two different things. The risks are a result of the high concentration of their military presence. Had the numbers been considerably lower, no one would have even mentioned the fact…

'A meeting with Putin will definitely unblock relations between Ukraine and Russia because at such a meeting the presidents would have to find a solution. The mere fact of such a meeting would signal the intentions of the parties. We would meet, express what we consider important, hear each other's arguments, and understand whether it makes sense to meet again in half a year's time to continue our discussion… A president may come out of the meeting and say, "Nothing's going to work in the next five or ten years, that's how it is… It won't happen in our time; it will be down to subsequent generations. But for now, we would like to bury the hatchet and let our countries develop on different planets, though we live on the same Earth." This, too, would be a good result for Ukraine because nothing's worse than living in uncertainty…'[112]

The follow-up comments branded the interview 'extremely important as it has shed at least some light on what's going on… It is a pity, though, that the president, speaking from the bottom of his heart, sincerely hopes that "this, too, would be a good result for Ukraine" – is something that may suit Putin… Putin will only pursue an option that would be bad for Ukraine. None other…'

'It's clear that given the complexity of the situation Zelensky is clutching at straws. But still – all those hopes – God forbid they may become our undoing…'

<hr>

[112]   RBC Ukraine, 17 February 2022, https://www.rbc.ua/ukr/news/vladimir-zelens-kiy-prohodya-put-nato-ukraina-1645105487.html (accessed 30.06.2025).

Right… I detached myself from the news for a minute… It was quite hard to navigate this abundance of information, especially since some items were contradictory. Luckily, Taras had somehow managed to gain access to a restricted chatroom that posted quite a few additional leaks. He never explained how he did it, but what the hell. The important thing was access to yet another reliable informational channel.

I immersed myself in the news again…

18-23 February 2022. Six Insane Days

On February 18th President Biden informed several allies that Putin had finally approved the decision to invade Ukraine. The invasion would start within days and target Kyiv. 'We have substantial intelligence capacity and have reason to believe these conclusions.'[113]

Instead of an abstract threat, the situation was becoming real. The word got out that the Russian side had drawn up a list of Ukrainian politicians and public figures that would have to be 'sorted out'. Russia remained steadfast in denying these accusations and insisted that she had no plans to attack her neighbour.

February 18th. The heads of the self-declared Donetsk and Luhansk Peoples' Republics (DPR and LPR) made public plans to evacuate their population to Russia 'due to an increased threat of an attack from Ukraine'. People were sent to the cross-border Russian oblast of Rostov. The offer to evacuate was first extended to women, children, and people of advanced age, however, the men aged between 18 and 55 were not granted leave to evacuate.

The news caused serious concern to the supreme military command of Ukraine. The certainty grew that a 'full-blown war' was going to happen after all… As a result, having taken additional security measures, the army started transferring all their command offices to the in-field locations. The General Staff ordered withdrawal of the troops away from the borders so that the Russian army could move in, hoping for the best, but would stretch itself out to a maximum.

February 18th. The American reconnaissance continued its 24/7 monitoring of the Ukrainian borders. An RQ-4 Global Hawk remotely-controlled aircraft started operating in the Ukrainian air space, keeping tabs on the borders with Russia and Belarus in the north, and the frontline in Donbas. Its trajectory was followed by eight thousand people all over the world, thus proving the developments to be of prime interest.

A well-known American military expert indicated that: 'The major problem of the Ukrainian armed forces is the relative weakness of their aviation, the

---

[113]   Radio Svoboda, 19 February 2022, https://www.radiosvoboda.org/a/news-biden-putin-uzhe-uhvalyv-rishennya-pro-napad/31710709.html (accessed 30.06.2025).

systems of air defence and the navy. Over several recent years, the Ukrainian troops on the ground have considerably improved their operational capability but Russia will dominate the sky and the sea. Thus, Ukraine is practically defenceless against any air and missile strikes delivered by Russia.'

Yet scepticism still reigned in the higher political echelons of Ukraine. As before, Kyiv was confident that the attack would only include Donbas, while a thrust towards the capital city – something permanently reminded of by the Western countries – was nothing more than a decoy plot designed to distract attention. In an attempt to deflate tensions, Danilov announced that Kyiv saw no signs that an integrated operation was mounted by Russia. The intent of this provocation was to 'force Ukraine into a powerful military retaliation' and then shift the blame for such a provocation onto the Ukrainian side.

Kyiv appealed to allies to disbelieve the propaganda fakes and insisted that the only way forward to liberate Ukrainian territories was through finding political and diplomatic solutions. Meanwhile practically all embassies had completed their transfer to Lviv and nearly all air carriers had suspended their services into Ukraine.

February 18th. The presidents of Russia and Belarus met in Moscow to discuss the Ukrainian crisis and possible sanctions against their countries. Answering questions from the press, Putin suggested that Kyiv should urgently open negotiations with representatives of the two Donbas People's Republics. Lukashenko pointed out that people were already fleeing Donbas. He accused Western politicians of 'feebleness' and a 'morbid desire to skirt round the issue'. Putin added that he paid no heed to Western declarations concerning an invasion of Ukraine. 'To keep responding to this is more trouble than it's worth. We do what we think is necessary and will continue doing so.'[114]

February 19th. Lukashenko's visit to Russia was extended. Together with Putin, they attended a military drill.

On February 18th-20th, the Security Conference was scheduled to open in Munich. Americans tried to dissuade President Zelensky from attending – the invasion could start any minute. They reminded him of their forecast regarding February 19th, and that his absence would give Russia an ideal time-point for a first strike.

Yet how could Zelensky not attend a conference on security when his own country was in such a situation?

....

[114]   Slovo i dilo, 18 February 2022, https://www.slovoidilo.ua/2022/02/18/novyna/
polityka/putin-lukashenko-vyslovylysya-shhodo-zahostrennya-donbasi (accessed 30.06.
2025).

On the morning of February 19th, there was no intervention and Zelensky took the flight. Prior to his speech, he had a meeting with Kamala Harris, the American vice president, who emphasised that the invasion was inevitable. He requested that sanctions be introduced against Russia, and that Ukraine should start receiving military aid. The Americans were not convinced it was acceptable.

And then he made a speech. He practically 'squashed' the political weaklings of the West.

'What is the result of appeasement? The question of 'Why die for Danzig?" led to the need to die for Dunkerque and lots of other places in Europe and the world and cost millions of lives.

'The main question is this: how is it possible that a war is being waged, yet again, in Europe in the 21st century? It started in 2014 in the Donbas. Why are people dying? Why has this war now outlasted the Second World War? How have we allowed the biggest security crisis since the days of the cold war? To me as president of the country that has lost a part of its territory and thousands of people, the country whose borders are threatened by 150 thousand Russian military personnel, equipment, and heavy-duty weaponry, to me – the answer is self-evident.

'The global security architecture is brittle and requires an overhaul. The rules agreed upon by the world, the rules that have been in place for several decades, do not work anymore. They are not up to the new challenges. They are just cough syrup when what we actually need is more like vaccination against COVID. It was here that 15 years ago Russia announced her intent to challenge global security. What was the world's response? Appeasement. What followed was the annexation of Crimea and aggression against my country. In the 21st century there is no longer such a thing as somebody else's war. The annexation of Crimea and the war in Donbas: that's a blow to the whole world. And this is not a war in Ukraine, it's a war in Europe. I talked about it at summits and forums, in 2019, 2020 and 2021. Will the world finally hear me in 2022? What's needed is action. It's the world that needs practical deeds, not just us…

'We will defend our land with or without the help of partners, whether we are given hundreds of units of modern weaponry or 5000 helmets. We appreciate any type of help, but everyone should understand – this is not charity that Ukraine's asking for or has to keep reminding others about.

'These are not noble gestures for which Ukraine should bow profoundly. It is your contribution towards security of Europe and the world, where Ukraine has been a reliable shield for over eight years, where for eight years it has been deterring one of the world's biggest armies. This army is now at our borders, not the frontiers of the EU.

'Come hell or high water, we shall defend our beautiful country, whether our borders are threatened by 50 thousand, 150 thousand or a million soldiers of whatever army. To really help Ukraine, you shouldn't tell us how much manpower or equipment is out there, but how many we all are.

'To help Ukraine, it isn't necessary to keep naming the dates for a possible intervention. We shall defend our country, whether it be on February 16th, March 1st, or December 31st. We have a much greater need of other dates, and everybody knows perfectly well what I am talking about.

'This applies to NATO too. We are told: the door is open. But for now, it's admittance to authorised personnel only. If not all alliance members would like to see us in or all members of the alliance don't want to see us in – be frank about it. The open door is well and good, but we need open responses, not questions left hanging for years.

'In exchange for renouncing its nuclear potential – the third largest in the world – Ukraine was given guarantees of security. We don't have those weapons anymore. Neither do we have security. Nor a portion of our country whose area exceeds Switzerland, the Netherlands or Belgium. Most importantly, we don't have millions of our Ukrainian citizens. We do not have any of this anymore.

'Starting in 2014, Ukraine has tried three times to convene a consultation of those countries that act as guarantors of the Budapest Memorandum, and all three of these attempts have failed. Today Ukraine will do this for the fourth time, although for me personally it's the first time in my capacity as president. But neither Ukraine nor I will do this again. I announce our initiative to conduct consultations under the auspices of the Budapest Memorandum. Our foreign minister has been instructed to convene this meeting. If, yet again, the meeting does not take place or fails to provide guarantees for our security, Ukraine shall have every right to believe that the Budapest Memorandum does not work and to call into question all comprehensive decisions taken in 1994.

All these questions need answers.

'For now, all we get is silence. For as long as this silence lasts, there will be no silence in our country's east. That is to say, in Europe. That is to say, in the whole world. We hope it is finally clear to the whole world, to Europe...'[115]

Everyone was profoundly impressed by his speech – powerful, urgent, and non-compromising, a harbinger of the new Ukrainian politics. Ukraine didn't ask, it demanded. All aspects of the speech were of a fundamental importance for the whole world, effectively a road map for future actions!

....

[115] Official website of the president of Ukraine, 19 February 2022, https://www.president.gov.ua/news/vistup-prezidenta-ukrayini-na-58-j-myunhenskij-konferenci-yi-72997 (accessed 30.06.2025).

The partners listened attentively but did not believe in Ukraine's ability to hold out in a full-scale conflict with Russia. In backstage conversations, various interlocutors suggested to Zelensky to stay behind, to create a 'government in exile'. Some were sincerely curious if he would use his visit to Munich as a pretext for not going back, before the bombs started falling. Zelensky's answer to all those suggestions went like this: 'I had breakfast in Kyiv (before taking a flight to Munich) and I shall have my dinner there too!' (In other words, he returned the same day.)

It became known that Chancellor Scholz had made a last attempt to settle the relations between Moscow and Kyiv. He suggested that Zelensky should renounce their aspirations to join NATO and declare neutrality under the umbrella of a broader security agreement between the West and Russia. Such pact would be signed by Presidents Putin and Biden who would jointly guarantee Ukraine's security. In response, Zelensky reminded him that Putin could not be trusted to adhere to provisions of such an agreement, and that the majority of Ukrainians wanted a membership in NATO. His reaction troubled Europeans who could see that chances for peace were evaporating. Zelensky, on the other hand, got an impression that even his closest allies had written him off...

Meanwhile, rumours started circulated around the couloirs. Allegedly, those leaders he'd had meetings with during that trip, were not sure if they would ever see him again.

The same evening president returned to Kyiv.

Thus, there had been no intrusion on February 19th, which only served to further convince the authorities that Russia did not have sufficient resources, or budget, to go through with the plans to occupy a sizeable portion of the country. Like before, the majority of the population played down the chances of a fully-fledged war with Russia: 'If it were to pass, it would be complete madness!'; 'This can never happen! And that means – never!'; 'This is just new Russian tricks...'

The majority believed that if anything did happen it would be an intervention on a much smaller scale, an attempt to win back the areas in Donbas, those still under Ukrainian control.

But the Americans came up with a new date – the intervention would start on February 22nd...

Like this... It was extremely difficult to get one's bearings among all those conflicting forecasts. The foreign leaders were saying one thing while our own insisted on the opposite...

February 19th. Putin addressed the Federation Council to seek permission for using the army abroad, allegedly, to defend the DPR and the LPR.[116]

February 20th. Defence minister Reznikov in a live broadcast: "As of this hour, the strike group of the Russian Federation has not yet been formed in any place where they have surrounded Ukraine. Therefore, to say that there will be an attack tomorrow or the day after tomorrow, in my opinion, is inappropriate. But this does not mean that the risks are low. This does not mean that there is no threat."[117]

February 20th, Sunday. President Macron still clung to the hope of a peaceful resolution. Yet again, he telephoned Putin.

Putin accused Macron of supposedly trying to 'overhaul the Minsk Agreements' and advised him to take on board the 'peaceful proposals' put forward by the self-proclaimed DPR and LPR. A tense exchange alluding to Moscow and Paris diverging in their interpretation of the Minsk Agreements made Macron lose his temper: 'I don't know where your lawyer got his degree. All I am doing is looking at the texts and trying to put them into practice. Which lawyer would insist that in a sovereign state draft laws are tabled by separatist groupings and not by a democratically elected power?' Putin: 'There is no democratically elected government over there. They came to power as a result of a bloody coup d'état, with murders and arson, with people being burnt alive. This Zelensky of yours is part of the same gang!' Marcon: 'It's all the same to us what the separatists have to offer. We demand that the Ukrainian laws be observed!'

By the end of their conversation Macron suggested that he should organise a meeting between Putin and President Biden in Geneva and 'take into account your enquiries about NATO and Ukraine'. Putin replied that he had nothing against this and suggested they should leave details to their assistants. Macron: 'I'm glad you agree. I propose that our teams put together a joint statement based on the results of this telephone conversation.' Putin: 'First, I'll play some hockey, then I'll talk to my advisers. Frankly speaking, I was looking forward to this hockey session. I'm talking to you from my gym…' The conversation lasted nine minutes.[118]

....

[116] **Federation Council**: the upper house of the Russian parliament.

[117] TSN, 10 September 2022, https://tsn.ua/ato/naperedodni-velikoyi-viyni-yak-ukrayinska-vlada-zustrichala-24-lyutogo-hronika-podiy-2153590.html (accessed 30.06.2025).

[118] Mind, 28 June 2022, https://mind.ua/news/20243731-v-nih-nemae-niyakoyi-demokratichnoyi-vladi-pro-shcho-govorili-makron-i-putin-za-4-dni-do-pochatku-vijni (accessed 30.06.2025).

February 21ˢᵗ, Monday. Neither Chancellor Scholz nor President Macron nor even Prime Minister Boris Johnson, who had unlimited access to intelligence data, believed that 'this' was about to start…

Meanwhile a good many deputies of the OPZZh had fled Ukraine,[119] as if having received a private warning. Stars of show business also rushed towards the 'exit door', taking with them their parents and children from previous marriages.

S. Naev[120]: 'The armed forces are not a separate actor. They are a tool for the authorities. The law on defence clearly states what is done in peacetime and what happens in wartime. In the event of armed aggression against Ukraine or the threat of an attack, the president makes three decisions: on the use of the armed forces, on the introduction of martial law, and on the announcement of mobilization. After that the chain of making the armed forces of Ukraine and other military formations ready to repel aggression is set in motion. [This did not happen…] On February 21 I was at my command point. Of course, I read news and I followed what was going on. There was a feeling that trouble was approaching. There were seven commanders online with me, and I told them: "All the forces that we have should be forwarded to the task areas!" I went beyond my authority. I did so at my own initiative, on my own… General Zaluzhny also – orally, without giving a written order – allowed us to go forward, to start deploying… But my generals know the law. Some of them said: "Give us written confirmation." And on February 23ʳᵈ for those who asked, well… for all of them… I signed a written order. I did not have that authority as well; it was my own initiative….'[121]

February 21ˢᵗ. At the traditional morning briefing Peskov suddenly announced that an enlarged session of the RF Security Council was planned for that day.

At 4 p.m. Kyiv time (9 a.m. in Washington, D.C.) – some breaking news! The White House confirmed President Biden's preparedness to attend a summit with Putin. This had become possible after a series of telephone conversations between Macron, Biden, Putin, Zelensky and B. Johnson. The summit agenda was to be worked out by the US secretary of State Blinken and Russia's Foreign Minister Lavrov at their meeting on February 24ᵗʰ in Geneva.

....

[119] **OPZZh** (the **Opposition Platform For Life):** a pro-Russian and Eurosceptic political party in Ukraine.

[120] **Serhii Naiev** (b. 1970): lieutenant general who served as commander of the Joint Forces of the Armed Forces of Ukraine from 2016 until 2024.

[121] UP, 10 February 2025, https://www.pravda.com.ua/rus/articles/2025/02/10/7497449/ (accessed 30.06.2025).

Macron declared that possibly a way had been found out of one of the most dangerous European crises in decades. Yet the White House specified that President Biden agreed to this meeting 'in principle' and only on condition that there would be no Russian intrusion into Ukraine. 'We are always open to diplomacy. We are equally ready to provide a fast and astringent response if Russia were to choose war instead.'[122]

Just at this time (5 p.m. in Moscow and 4 p.m. in Kyiv), the Russian federal TV channels had interrupted their regular broadcasts in favour of the session of the Security Council. The journalists noticed that Defence Minister Shoigu's watch showed 12:47. The same time could be read on the watch worn by the director of the Foreign Intelligence Service Naryshkin. Thus, admittedly, the broadcast was not live but taking place five hours after the event. In other words, the recording could thus have been edited and all undesirable details redacted.

The session had opened with Putin's address. He explained that 'they have convened today to discuss the situation around Donbas and adopt relevant decisions.' Putin sat alone at his table. The Council's members were seated about 10 meters away, on chairs. After his address, they started approaching the microphone, one by one, to make their speeches. Some sounded excited and confident. Zolotov, head of Russia's National Guard, said: 'We are not neighbours with Ukraine, we have no joint borders with Ukraine. These are the American borders because they are masters in that country, and everyone else are their vassals. And the fact that they are propping them up with weapons in an endeavour to create a nuclear arsenal – it will come back to haunt us in the future. It goes without saying that it is necessary to recognise the republics. We should move forward in order to defend our own country.'[123]

Some were losing the thread, searching for words, their hands visibly trembling. Putin was particularly displeased with temporising demeanour of the Foreign Intelligence head Naryshkin – and so he subjected him to a public dressing-down.

To start with, Naryshkin suggested 'giving Kyiv one last chance' to try and settle the situation in Donbas. When Putin asked him to 'avoid ambiguity', he came back with 'I support this decision.' When Putin asked him which decision he had in mind, Naryshkin answered, irresolutely and unexpectedly: 'I support

[122] Detector media, 21 February 2022, https://detector.media/infospace/article/196691/2022-02-21-bayden-pogodyvsya-provesty-bezpekovyy-samit-z-putinym/ (accessed 30.06.2025).

[123] Gordon, 21 February 2022, https://gordonua.com/ukr/news/war/glava-rosgvardiji-mi-ne-majemo-kordonu-z-ukrajinoju-tse-mezha-amerikantsiv-1596426.html (accessed 30.06.2025).

the decision to include the Luhansk and Donetsk people's democratic republics in the Russian Federation.' 'We are not discussing that today,' replied Putin. 'I support the decision to recognize their independence,' Naryshkin corrected himself. He looked like a schoolboy before a ruthless class mistress, eager to justify himself after having dodged his homework…[124]

The only member of the Russian leadership who made a lengthy statement justifying the fallacy of the decision to begin hostilities in Ukraine was Dmitry Kozak.[125] Kozak's performance was removed from the minutes of the meeting and from the television report.

It was a sinister assembly! In essence, Putin was leaning on everyone to approve an attack on Ukraine. It was *de facto* a declaration of war. Judging by all indications, most Security Council members, unaware of things to come, felt shocked and unprepared. However, *de jure*, Putin was trying, albeit rather naively, to cover his tracks – for example, his demonstrative intention to implicate the entire supreme leadership of the country: everyone attending was on film, and thus, everyone sullied their reputation. It was clear that Putin, should something go wrong, was reluctant to be the only one responsible. The Security Council members looked dumbfounded; it was probably dawning on them that one day they may have to answer for the decisions they had publicly approved. By way of conclusion, Putin said that he had heard the opinions of his colleagues: 'The decision shall be approved. Today.'[126]

On the same day, late in the evening, TASS, the Russian News Agency, communicated that in his telephone conversation with the leaders of France and Germany Putin had warned them of his plans to recognise independence of DPR and LPR. Afterwards he reiterated this decision in his TV address to the nation. Russia had acknowledged the DPR and LPR as independent states, and moreover had acknowledged them as states within the administrative borders of Donetsk and Luhansk oblasts, and thus within territories controlled by Ukraine!

Putin called the Ukrainian state 'an artificial concoction of the Communist era that became possible at the expense of historical Russian territories.' In the same breath, he denounced Lenin's approach to setting up the USSR because

<hr>

[124]   Radio Svoboda, 21 February 2022, https://www.radiosvoboda.org/a/radbez-rosiyi-putin-vyznannya-lndr/31714861.html (accessed 30.06.2025).

[125]   **Dmitry Kozak**: deputy head of Putin's administration, was 'in charge of Ukrainian affairs' as the Kremlin's principal negotiator.

[126]   UNIAN, 21 February 2022, https://www.unian.ua/politics/rishennya-pro-viznannya-ldnr-bude-priynyato-sogodni-putin-novini-ukrajina-11712025.html   (accessed 30.06.2025).

it had envisaged the right of the republics to secede from the union: 'That was worse than a mistake. That is how Ukraine came to be – thanks to the efforts of the Bolsheviks. That should be an apt name for it – "Lenin's Ukraine" since it was he who also forced Donbas into this entity. And nowadays, over there, they are pulling down his monuments and running a campaign of de-communisation. You want de-communisation? It suits us to a "tee". We are ready to show you what genuine decommunization is all about,' said Putin,[127] his hands twitching, his face a distinctive contorted mien – just like Hitler in one of his speeches.

Later, there followed a broadcast showing the Russian President and the DPR and LPR bosses signing the requisite paperwork – in the same assembly hall as the Security Council.

All of it inspired depression, even if the plans to recognise the DPR and LPR had been bandied around for some time. But the thuggish speech made by Putin, his words about our country – that was beyond anything imaginable... It felt like an advance warning of an impending war...

Kyiv's reaction. Security Secretary Danilov: 'Russia is deliberately creating a *casus belli* – a pretext for declaring war on Ukraine... We shall not yield to provocations. We shall not open hostilities against our population. President Zelensky's plan provides for de-occupation of the territories through political and diplomatic means. The RF has launched a powerful information campaign against Ukraine... We must maintain self-control and refrain from panic... The defence and security sector is operating 24/7.'

For his part, President Zelensky discussed the developments with Macron, Scholz, Biden, B. Johnson, and President of the European Council Ch. Michel, and, in view of a new spike in the tension, he initiated a new round of meetings under the umbrella of the Budapest Memorandum; an emergency session of the UN Security Council; an extra-ordinary session of the OSCE; and an emergency summit of the Normandy Format. 'We are committed to resolving conflicts through political and diplomatic means; we reject provocations. Our borders are reliably secured; we have created a system for territorial defence. Our partners support us.' The president went on to say that it was imperative to separate provocations and military aggression and added that 'at the moment there aren't any reasons to start acting chaotically. We are on our own land. We are afraid of nothing and of no one. We do not owe anything to anyone. And we shall yield nothing to nobody. We are certain of all of this. It is now February 2022, not February

....

[127] BBC news Ukraine, 22 February 2022, https://www.bbc.com/ukrainian/features-60480944 (accessed 30.06.2025).

2014. We are a different country now, with a different army. Our goal is peace. Peace in Ukraine.'[128]

February 21st. An official representative of the USA circulated this important news among their NATO partners: President Biden's previous assertions on Putin's decision to bring his troops into Ukraine received corroboration from intelligence data: the Russian command had received an order to get ready for an attack. Targets for future strikes included not only Kyiv but other cities, too.

February 22nd, early morning. All was quiet. Once again, the American date for the invasion had been proved wrong. However, in the morning the USA brought this most recent intel to Ukraine's attention – Russia was definitely going to mount a full-scale military campaign, most probably within the following 48 hours. Its thrust would be towards Kyiv, proceeding from the direction of Belarus. 'Of special concern' was security of Kharkiv.

In response, a source close to the President's Office stated that the information had been duly received but it was the third such warning issued by the USA in February alone that had proved inaccurate.

At the same time, NATO announced: the intelligence of its allies also pointed towards a 'threat of invasion that would take place in the nearest future.'

February 22nd, morning. Ukraine's Defence Minister Reznikov telephoned Khrenin, Defence Minister of Belarus. They talked about the concentration of the Russian army on the Ukrainian borders. Answering the question about them crossing the border from the side of Belarus, Khrenin categorically dismissed this option and gave 'his word of an officer'.

February 22nd. Following Russia's recognition of the DPR and LPR, Biden and Blinken announced that Putin's speech bore testimony to Russia's insincerity when alleging her commitment to methods of diplomacy. Biden: 'His speech showed the world his distorted vision of history. He directly refused Ukraine a right to exist. He indirectly expressed a claim to territories that belonged to imperial Russia, including territories that nowadays belong to democratic states and members of NATO. He was clearly issuing a threat of war – in the event that his radical demands would not be met. There is therefore no doubt that Russia is an aggressor. We are making you aware of the challenges that you are now facing.'

Blinken: 'A seriously worrying speech made yesterday evening by President Putin demonstrated to the whole world his views of Ukraine. According to him, it is not a sovereign state that enjoys a right to territorial integrity and

<hr>

[128]   TSN, 10 September 2022, https://tsn.ua/ato/naperedodni-velikoyi-viyni-yak-ukray-inska-vlada-zustrichala-24-lyutogo-hronika-podiy-2153590.html (accessed 30.06.2025).

independence but a "creation" of Russia and thus should be subjugated by Russia. This is the greatest challenge to security in Europe since World War Two. Washington will not allow Russia to maintain a façade of democracy. Now, when we observe the beginning of an invasion, and when Russia has clearly indicated that she renounces diplomacy, we see no reason for a meeting with Lavrov, the head of the Russian Foreign Ministry, planned to take place on February 24th in Geneva. I have sought the advice of our allies and partners – the decision is unanimous…'[129]

In an intercepted telephone conversation, a Russian army man complained to his wife that for several days he had been very short of money. Yet on February 22nd he told her that she shouldn't transfer him any money now, for in several days' time they would be in Kyiv and he'd procure for himself over there…

It felt like the authorities did all they possibly could to preserve an illusion of normalcy. Zelensky held conferences, prepared for meetings with deputies and businessmen, received foreign visitors.

2 p.m. Reznikov had spent a whole hour convincing journalists at the Kyiv Officers' Club that there wouldn't be a major war and that the Kremlin's decision about Donbas may yet prove beneficial. The defence minister insisted that 'Putin would not dare bomb "the second Jerusalem – Kyiv". '

At the same time British intelligence intercepted several conversations between the Russian military command and heads of the battalion tactical groups: 'Move over to your positions.'

At the owners' demands, numerous aircraft were removed out of Ukraine. And – more! The deputies with a requisite clearance level received envelopes labelled – 'In case of war'. They complained that there was nothing useful inside, just some generalities…

* * *

On the same day, February 22nd, at lunch time we flocked together by the classroom, all glued to our smartphones, avidly following news updates. Putin's speech the previous day was hotly discussed on social media. We all had bad presentiments, yet the majority still hoped that the worst would simply dispel.

'They write here that the remaining oligarchs, those who hasn't done it yet, now scarper in their private jets,' Alla turned her phone's screen over, for all to see. 'Must be for a reason. Something's really brewing…'

....

[129] European Pravda, 23 February 2022, https://www.eurointegration.com.ua/news/ 2022/02/23/7134467/ (accessed 30.06.2025).

'Look like they have their own intelligence,' mused Spyridon. 'Perhaps even more efficient than the state one…'

'Must be true,' Bolik agreed. 'Any oligarch has access to immense resources. Of course, the state facilities are lagging behind…'

'Oh my… To start with, I didn't even want to tell you…' Liubchik's face was all worry.

'You probably don't have a clue… I was the first to learn…'

'What?'

'You learnt what?'

'Well, our Arkady did a vanishing act, too… Or, to be precise, his family did. So, he went along, goes without. Even if they're nowhere near real oligarchs, looks like they picked up something on the wind. And we, we are left behind…'

'It couldn't have been any other way!' Spyridon's raised finger was supposed to convince us all. 'To swan off to the West like that, requires decent dinero. You can't cook it up in a week. Even if you've stashed something for a rainy day, you won't survive for too long staying in hotels. It takes a nice private nest somewhere. And a healthy bank account…'

'True!' Alla summed it up. 'That's just it – the rich dudes have spent years weaving nice private nests over there…'

'My God, what does this evil one want with Ukraine?'

'Ideally, that Ukraine should cease to exist as a state. He started its dismantling back in 2014 when he'd annexed Crimea. He then went on, moved on to Donbas…'

'What's so hard to understand?' Liubchik sounded aggrieved, even annoyed. 'Yesterday he surreptitiously declared war on Ukraine. So, the question really is: when? And in what way?'

'Blast it! The shortest distance to Kyiv is from Belarus…' Alla buried her face in hands. 'And now… Lukashenko… Tell me, for God's sake – will he really have the nerve to let the Russian troops through Belarus?'

'Enough talking shit! All we do is worry ourselves to death…' concluded Spyridon. 'Let's break up. By the way, we do all remember that we work independently tomorrow?'

'Sure thing…'

'So, we'll meet the day after tomorrow, on the 24th. It will be Thursday…'

On my way home I passed by the Radisson Blue Hotel, the one in Bratskaya Street in Podil.[130] Just then a black van pulled up, carrying the Qatar Airways

....

130 **Podil**: a historical district of Kyiv (Lower City) on the Right bank of the Dnipro where traders, craftsmen, and fishermen used to live. Today considered one of Kyiv's fashionable districts.

crew: pilots, crew hosts and hostesses, all sporting their signature burgundy uniforms.

It was a wonderful sight, since practically no one was flying into Kyiv anymore. But the Qatar folk were clearly staying overnight! Most likely they would be the only guests there, as the hotel showed no signs of life…

For some reason it occurred to me that it might be the last ever passenger flight. The street was empty too – no cars, no pedestrians. The crew paused briefly, carry-on bags and all – and gave me a once-over, as if thinking – *Tomorrow we, inshallah, will make it out of here on the last flight. And this one – what nerve! – he'll stay behind…*

I returned their collective gaze and thought that they, too, had balls – to have flown in in such a situation…

I veered off Bratskaya Street towards Contract Square – the fairy wheel operated as normal, what else could be expected? But few customers, if any, were prepared to ride it. It felt like the city lay in wait, biding its time. I picked out my usual trajectory: on the right – the Kyiv-Mohyla Academy;[131] on the left – the monument to Skovoroda.[132]

By then my step grew rhythmical, my head pulsating with just one word: Putin, Putin, Putin…

My God, what sort of a demon was he? What sort of a person was this Volodymyr Volodymyrovych Putin? A smooth operator chasing his fortune? A deranged person who'd left the vestiges of sanity behind? Or just a common bluffer?

Surely, I wasn't the only one to ask these questions… In the USA alone, experts specialising on the Kremlin and its politics counted many thousands. But it wasn't just them, the entire planet buzzed with the same question. After all, if something did happen, the consequences would spread out and reach everyone…

On the other hand, perhaps he was overly demonised? The Russian leader did spout bluff in spades. More than once, his resonating statements about Ukraine had been proved to distort history. No wonder that for Putin Ukraine's love of freedom was a pain in the neck. And so, he was adamant that Ukraine should be taught a lesson…

At the same time, clearly, he and his Kremlin advisers knew very little about the dynamics of developments in Ukraine. Say, this assertion that lots

....

[131] **Kyiv-Mohyla Academy:** a higher educational institution established in 1615 (now: the National University). It is located in the buildings of the historical Kyiv-Mohyla Academy and positions itself as the latter's successor.

[132] **Hryhorii Skovoroda** (1722-1794): a philosopher, poet, teacher, and composer of liturgical music.

of Ukrainians had a burning desire to join the 'Russian world'! Allegedly, the spanner in the works were the malevolent West Ukrainian 'fascists'. Allegedly, the same crowd who'd usurped the power in Kyiv at the time of Euromaidan. Which meant that Western Ukrainians now controlled the entire country, while they, themselves, were nothing more than puppets of the omni-present USA.

The Kremlin never took seriously any polls of public opinion in Ukraine – a most important indicator! Overall, their perception of the sentiments as expressed by the majority of Ukrainians was off-kilter. The Kremlin believed wholeheartedly that their troops, when they barged into Ukraine, would be greeted with flowers, given a welcome suitable for real liberators. Such an act would signify triumph of justice! Whereas, in reality, all it would achieve would be installation of the pro-Russian puppet regimes.

Putin's believed that such a scenario would mark a 'historic' unification of the Russian and Ukrainian peoples. On the other hand, did he even know what the Ukrainians themselves really thought?

There was yet another factor, a very important one: a new young generation had already grown up in Ukraine and didn't accept any other identity. The Russian leader clearly discounted this fact. Then again, perhaps he was aware of it but feared that the gap between the two countries and their peoples was getting wider with every passing year? That might have been yet another reason to act swiftly and decisively… So, what did it all mean?

Their most probable course of action would be a battle march towards Kyiv (as opposed to any other routes) – a sort of a new blitzkrieg. Putin, most likely, was confident that the population of Russia would greet the 'liberation of Kyiv from fascists' with particular joy and incredible enthusiasm.

Another plus – according to his way of thinking. If he managed to grab the power in Kyiv, the Ukrainian regions would be left in a vacuum. In the absence of a leader and the authorities, it would be much easier to thwart them individually.

There was, however, a more stretched-out option. News started seeping through about possible elimination of the Ukrainian army in field conditions, laying siege to major cities while infiltrating them with rings of agitators. Those would be tasked with creating pro-Russian local bodies of government that would 'come to an understanding' over surrendering their cities. Once the bigger cities were all under complete control, a semblance of a 'Veche' would be put in place,[133] delegates to which would be properly vetted by security ser-

---

[133] **Veche**: a popular assembly in ancient Slavic countries. In Novgorod and in Pskov, where the *veche* acquired great prominence, it was broadly similar to the Norse *thing* or the Swiss *Landsgemeinde*.

vices. This 'pre-parliament' would form a basis for an ersatz-government and facilitate introduction of a puppet regime. A classic multi-move game... The scheme had been used by Moscow many times, often successfully.

Ri-i-ight... I turned it all around in my head and reached a conclusion: Putin's plans could be edited by events. Just as before, no concrete assumptions were feasible.

On my way home my smartphone told me that Valentina Matvienko, the speaker of the RF Federation Council, had announced: 'President Putin's official request regarding the use of the Russian army abroad has been received. I am adding this item to the agenda for today. The request has already been considered by the FC committees.'

There was also a report that the staff of the US embassy, currently stationed in Lviv, were now removed to Poland.

Meanwhile Zelensky continued receiving foreign guests. Bankova Street kept hoping that Putin wouldn't dare attack Ukraine if it was playing host to a foreign leader. Thus, the entire diplomatic corps of Ukraine was working to ensure a visit of some kind for every day. That day the visitor was President of Estonia Alar Karis. At their joint briefing, the journalists asked Zelensky about probability that, given Moscow's blatant preparation for a war, Ukraine should introduce martial law. 'We believe there won't be a war,' answered the president without a moment's hesitation.

Once home, I put on the TV. They were showing a patriotic rally attended by over a thousand residents of Mariupol – raising their voices against the Russian invasion, carrying slogans 'Mariupol is Ukraine!'. The participants in the rally were chanting: 'We are here to prevent the repetition of 2014! We don't want to live like they do in DPR! We don't need to be liberated!'

I moved over to my computer.

There was confirmation of the news that the American diplomats were moved to Poland – in view of fears of a Russian intrusion. I didn't get it, though, if they were moved for only one night...

There was a post about pontoon bridges being shifted from Crimea to Sivash.[134] Was it just a broadly advertised drill? Nothing like this had happened in all eight years...

In the evening, I got a call from Taras. He offered some new info from his restricted chatroom. Supposedly, Zelensky had invited over heads of all factions of the Supreme Rada. The aim was to bring together powers that be

....

[134]   The **Syvash or Sivash**, also known as 'the Putrid Sea' or 'Rotten Sea', is a large area of shallow lagoons on the west coast of the Sea of Azov dividing Crimea from mainland Ukraine.

and the opposition, thereby creating a 'defence coalition' to ensure speedy decision-making for the sake of enhanced defence capability.

Faction leaders expressed their solidarity with the president. The only one who abstained was the OPZZh leader Boyko. After the politicians, the security men spoke too, one by one. Given their high security clearance, faction leaders could be involved in a frank discussion.

Zaluzhnyi stressed that the army was getting ready for various possible scenarios.

Bakanov and Reznikov expressed their doubts as to the probability of a full-scale war.[135] 'What is possible is Russia engaging in psychological manipulation and, worst-case scenario – escalation in Donbas.'

Budanov was the last to take the floor. His was the weightiest, and possibly, the most accurate report. He talked about horrendous things: Russians can start war outside the Donbas! They could threaten Kherson and Kharkiv, there is a threat to Kyiv, Russians can try to come from Belarus via Chernobyl zone.. He produced a map and showed the main directions of assault. Kharkiv and Kherson were under threat. Kyiv was also in danger – the Russians would try to use a shortcut through Chornobyl.

The top leaders responded to his presentation with a degree of annoyance. He was clearly perceived as a sort of younger brother – not really worth listening to closely. That was why the others didn't give his speech full attention. It was generally believed that recognition of the pseudo-republics of DPR and LPR may yet come to nothing – a figure of speech in Putin's pronouncement. It was later presented as a joint opinion of the entire president's team.

There was a publication about the response of business: money had been leaving the economy during the entire period between December and February. The authorities, fearful of a domino effect, had placed no restrictions. Taras's comment was this: 'as they say, business knows what's what…'

February 22nd, afternoon. From a speech made by Lukashenko: 'You remember where I stand: we have always advocated peace. From this important podium I would now like to address, yet again, the Ukrainian people and their leadership before they have crossed the red line – let us, the Slavs, always live in peace and accord. All passes, all gets forgotten. The whole problem is what type of scars will be left on our Slavic hearts after the conflict. Therefore, I suggest, once more: halt, wave your masters from over the ocean away. They won't give you

....

[135] **Ivan Bakanov**: a Ukrainian politician who from 2019 to July 2022 served as Head of Ukraine's security service.

any joy. As soon as you cease to suit their purposes, they will throw you into the dustbin of history. This is our way – a way of peace and goodwill…'[136]

At 10 p.m. Zelensky turned to the Ukrainians with an urgent address: 'Accepting independence of the occupied areas of Donetsk and Luhansk oblasts may signal Russia's unilateral withdrawal from the Minsk Agreements and her disdain for the decision made within "Normandy". Russia legalises her troops that had, factually, been stationed in Donbas since 2014. We draw a clear line between provocation and an assault by an aggressor. Truth is on our side. And we shall never hide this truth from you. At this stage there is no need for a general mobilisation. What we need is urgently to bring the Ukrainian army, along with its units, up to its full strength. In my capacity as supreme commander of the Ukrainian Armed Forces, I have issued a decree that authorises calling up reservists for the duration of this special period. Let me emphasise: we are talking about citizens included in the operative resource. If we see the situation change, if the risks start to augment – we will inform you accordingly…'[137]

Concurrently Reznikov changed his rhetoric… This was him addressing the Ukrainian army: '… the Kremlin, through its actions, has taken a new step toward resurrection of the Soviet Union. The only stumbling block in its path is Ukraine and the Ukrainian army. Our choice is simple: to defend our country, our homes, our families. Nothing has changed for us. Ahead of us is hardship. Losses. We will have to go through pain, conquer fear and lack of faith. But we shall inevitably win for we are on our own land, and truth is on our side. The Ukrainian army has the support of our people. This popular faith is a sign that we are doing everything correctly.'[138]

Just then we learnt from the evening news that Putin had been granted permission to use the troops abroad, ostensibly, to defend the DPR and LPR. As if playing to the Ukrainian authorities, that it's only in the Donbas that something is planned, and nowhere else… Anyway, there was this general feeling of unease, or even worse – it felt like descending into darkness…

Presently came a warning that in the nearest future a formidable cyber-attack may be launched against the sites of the Ukrainian government and banks.

<hr>

[136] LB.ua, 22 February 2022, https://lb.ua/world/2022/02/22/506386_lukashenko_zvernuvsya_ukraintsiv.html (accessed 01. 07. 2025).

[137] UNIAN, 22 February 2022, https://www.unian.ua/politics/zelenskiy-zvernuvsya-do-ukrajinciv-onlayn-translyaciya-novini-ukrajina-11713288.html (accessed 01. 07. 2025).

[138] Lb.ua, 22 February 2022, https://lb.ua/news/2022/02/22/506335_reznikov-zsu_poperedu_vazhki.html (accessed 01. 07. 2025).

It was hard to put it all in words… Those February days flashed by like some images in an insane kaleidoscope. Someone wrote a post: 'Everyone understands everything… Yet no one wants to believe the worst… Thing is, it isn't just madness but madness of a particularly twisted kind. Therefore, it just cannot be. And thus, no one wants to believe it. Apart from those who've left Ukraine in good time…'

Hmm… Whichever news one read, there was only worry. But what could I, personally, along with millions of my compatriots do in such a situation? Absolutely nothing…

The only thing to do was wait for developments…

So, it was imperative to take my mind off things, if only briefly…

If only I could quickly fall asleep. Even if the following day I was supposed to study independently, there were lots of other things to do…

February 23rd, Wednesday. I woke up very early, hardly slept at all… The anxiety kept me awake… I rushed to my computer for the news updates. The previous night a flight had arrived from Canada carrying aircraft armament equipment. Meanwhile, in the last 24 hours Donbas was shelled nearly a hundred times, which included, starting from the early morning, its territories under Ukrainian control.

I had a quick wash and popped into the kitchen for my breakfast and a brief exchange with mum, then back to the computer – to follow the avalanche of news.

In his morning message of greeting to Russian citizens on the occasion of Defender of the Motherland Day, Putin underscored that 'the international situation was far from straightforward', that Russia was facing the threat of 'her system of arms control being eroded, and of ambitions displayed by NATO', while her demands 'were left unanswered'. He threw in some frighteners: 'We've put on red alert the weapons that are second to none in the whole world'. He also added that 'the most advanced weapons are controlled by people, therefore it is important for them to be not only knowledgeable and well trained, but to be patriots.'[139]

07:12 a.m. D. Kuleba, at the time on a visit to the USA, emphasised that Ukraine had two options: diplomacy or war. 'Option A involves the use of all instruments of diplomacy for deterring Russia and avoiding any further escalation. If it fails, Option B means fighting for every inch of our territory, every town and village. To fight till a complete victory, of course.'[140]

<hr>

[139]   Lb.ua, 23 February 2022, https://lb.ua/world/2022/02/23/506449_putin_pohvalivsya_zbroieyu_yakiy_nemaie.html (accessed 01. 07. 2025).

[140]   Slovo i dilo, 23 February 2022, https://www.slovoidilo.ua/2022/02/23/novyna/bezpeka/vijna-rosiyeyu-kuleba-ozvuchyv-dva-osnovni-plany-ukrayiny-protystoyan-

09:12 a.m. Another carrier from Canada brought the second aid cargo of aircraft weaponry. The specific nature of that weaponry was not disclosed. However, behind the scenes the partners' aid was branded 'rather decorative'. It looked like out there few believed in Ukraine's ability to hold out.

Taras called. Incredible! In all evidence, that chatroom of theirs had learnt specifics of the NSDC morning session! Its agenda had included a complicated dilemma of whether or not to introduce martial law ahead of the attack. Small wonder – preparations carried out by Russia and her satellites in Donbas gave cause for serious concerns.

Commander-in-Chief Zaluzhny and Defence Minister Reznikov had insisted that a state of emergency may not be sufficient and suggested introducing martial law, although only in two or three oblasts in the east. However, the majority of those present had been reluctant to provoke Russia, especially taking into account these past several weeks, when their TV channels had been shouting from rooftops about Ukraine getting ready for a massive offensive in Donbas. A state of martial law might let Russia off the leash and provide a formal pretext for an intervention. It might seem that Ukraine was about to initiate hostilities and had, therefore, put the country on a military footing. The session had decided that they should refrain from provoking Moscow, and introduce a state of emergency instead. The president signed the appropriate decree and the NSDC Secretary Danilov took it over to the parliament for approval that required at least 226 deputies voting in its favour within the following 48 hours.

It was reported that the head of the Ukrainian Border Guard Service had telephoned his opposite number in Minsk once more. He asked a direct question:

'Is it true that the Russian troops on your territory are about to invade Ukraine?'

'Out of the question!' came the response. 'Nothing could be further from our mind!'

10:15 a.m. Reservists drafted into active service for the term of just over a year.

Colonel general Syrskyi convened a session of military commanders in charge of the defence of Kyiv. Also present were the municipal bosses. He used the occasion to outline his defence strategy. The session approved a chain of command and interaction, presented leaders of various defence sectors. And then it turned out that the state of affairs was disastrous – absolutely insufficient military capability meant that the city wasn't ready to defend itself. Thus, a desperate measure was called for – setting up rifle battalions of cadets and students.

ni-ahresiyi-rf (accessed 01. 07. 2025).

10:43 a.m. The Foreign Ministry of Ukraine issued a 'recommendation to refrain from any trips to Russia whereas those already in this country should urgently leave its territory.'

10:50 a.m. A plume of smoke rising over the building of the RF Consulate in Lviv triggered an emergency response from the municipal services. It later transpired that there had been no fire – in all probability, it was the staff of the diplomatic mission burning documents.

11:30 a.m. News from Kharkiv: 'The Russian Federation is building up its military presence on the border with Kharkiv oblast. Manoeuvring and repositioning of troops can be observed along the entire border. They have acquired 45,000 body bags for corpses...'[141]

11:24 a.m. In the south of Belarus – in the vicinity of the Ukrainian border – images from Maxar satellites picked up the arrival of a hundred units of military equipment. Scores of tents had been put up for the men. A field hospital was being erected. Also spotted were the motor carriers suitable for transporting tanks, artillery, and other heavy-duty equipment.

Noon. In his speech at the Rada, NSDC Secretary Danilov elucidated the reasons for introducing a state of emergency. He mentioned the current risks but assured the deputies that the situation was under control. 'This includes measures to ensure civil order, also enhanced security for the facilities providing vital services for the residents and the state. It may include restricted operation of certain types of transport, additional spot-checks of the same transport, random inspection of personal IDs and other documents. In other words, these are preventive measures designed to maintain peace and enable the economy to function. Should it prove necessary, a state of martial law will be introduced without delay. For the time being, it is not considered necessary, but we are ready for any eventuality. We can call up 36,000 reservists. Most of these have experience of active combat, they know what's what. Should Kyiv or any other city find itself under attack, the response will come like a flash. Our army is ready...'[142]

In other words, the country would be put on a military footing in case of a full-scale war. At the same time the Mayor of Kyiv Klitchko announced that once the decree had been approved by the Rada, the city would tighten controls over arrivals and departures, introduce a ban on mass rallies and, possibly, curtail operation of certain types of transport.

....

[141]   UP, 23 February 2022, https://www.pravda.com.ua/news/2022/02/23/7325092/ (accessed 01. 07. 2025).

[142]   Suspilne noviny, 23 February 2022, https://suspilne.media/210057-rada-rozgla-dae-zaprovadzenna-nadzvicajnogo-stanu-v-ukraini-nazivo/ (accessed 01. 07. 2025).

01:00 p.m. Traders all over the world expecting the threat of intervention to force the buyers of wheat, maize and oil to go elsewhere in search of supplies – a problem in its own right. Ukraine and Russia supplied 29% of the world's wheat, 19% of maize and 80% of the sunflower oil. A hike in prices was clearly on the cards. Wary of the military risks, the ships avoided entering the Black Sea. Supplies had been already interrupted.

A video started making rounds in the afternoon: a many-kilometre-long column of the Russian weaponry moving towards Kalanchak[143]. Another video showed the Russian army near Chongar.

03:00 p.m. Beginning of the evacuation of every Russian diplomatic mission outside of Ukraine. The Russian Embassy in Kyiv brought down the Russian flag. Odesa residents saw the staff of the RF Consulate leaving the premises. The last one to leave hoisted down the Russian flag and took it with him. The flag was removed from the Russian General Consulate in Lviv.

03:00 p.m. Finances were taking a hit, too – the value of hryvnia (UAH) had dropped.

03:15 p.m. Presidents of Poland and Lithuania (Andrzej Duda and Gitanas Nausėda) were in Kyiv on a visit of solidarity. The presidents of Ukraine, Poland and Lithuania signed, in the Mariyinskyi Palace,[144] a joint application in support of granting Ukraine the status of an EU candidate state.

At their joint briefing President Duda said: 'The situation created by Russia's acts of aggression is a serious test of unity within NATO and the EU. With its behaviour, the RF is threatening not only Ukraine but the entire eastern flank of NATO and the European Union. We hope the war won't flare up. We call upon President Putin, those who make decisions, to refrain from condoning armed aggression against Ukraine. We are all walking a tight line between war and peace, and it is yet to be seen where this will take Russia and the whole world. The West is watching every step taken by RF President Putin closely. It isn't just a question of Ukraine's' sovereignty but of our global security architecture…'

Asked by journalists if he believed that Putin would attack, Zelensky gave an ironic reply that Putin's plans, unlike weather forecasts, were unpredictable. 'However, I know perfectly well, without any forecasts, how our army will respond. I beg your pardon, but it's between me and our army which specific actions shall be taken regarding our defence capability and the security of our state. But believe me – we are ready for anything.'[145]

………………………………………………………………

[143]   **Kalanchak and Chongar**: settlements in Kherson oblast, southern Ukraine, that have border-control facilities on the border with occupied Crimea.

[144]   **Mariyinskyi Palace:** the ceremonial residence of the President of Ukraine.

[145]   Official website of the President of Ukraine, 23 February 2022, https://www. president.gov.ua/news/ukrayina-polsha-j-litva-yedini-v-tomu-sho-majbutnye-yev-

04:00 p.m. A new mass cyber-attack launched at the government sites. Down went the sites of the Cabinet of Ministers, the parliament, the Security Council, and the Defence Ministry.

04:32 p.m. A bomb scare announced in the building of the Supreme Rada. No one was allowed onto the premises. The extraordinary session to approve the President's Decree on a state of emergency was planned for 05:00 p.m. Did someone want to derail approval of this decree?

05:40 p.m. In view of the Russian threat, Kyiv started setting up blood banks – for the needs of the army.

All the time, three reconnaissance aircraft – from the USA and the UK – continued their simultaneous operation over Ukraine. The American drone entered our airspace above Chernivtsi oblast and started monitoring southern and eastern areas. It then moved on to continue operating along the border with Belarus. Another aircraft was an American Boeing RC-135W Rivet Joint. This one crossed the Ukrainian border from the side of Poland and started monitoring the southern boundaries. Another one, a British Boeing RC-135W flew in from Poland where it had been monitoring the southern border of Belarus. At six in the evening these aircraft were still carrying on.

06:30 p.m. While still in the States, Foreign Minister Kuleba addressed the UN General Assembly: 'Russia's pronouncements and actions inspire dismay but are targeted not only at Ukraine. No one will be able to wait this crisis out. If the RF President Putin so desires, he can export his aggression to Europe. Your countries and nations will then have to face those morbid challenges – along with our country and its people. This is why we must grab this last chance to act and stop Russia in her current tracks. It goes without saying that Putin will not stop of his own accord. Launching a full-scale war against Ukraine will spell an end to the world order, and Russia's impunity may encourage other countries. It is imperative to stop the Russian war machine for otherwise it will initiate a bloodbath where thousands will die, suffer, and be wounded... Several years ago, we offered to host a UN peace-making mission. Till now, the Security Council has not approved of the requisite decisions... We hope that the global community will do whatever it takes to douse the fire in the heart of Europe, the fire that is about to break out.'[146]

07:00 p.m. The head of local administration announced that in case of need, the Trans-Carpathian Oblast could accept up to 50 thousand relocated persons.

....

ropej-73085 (accessed 01. 07. 2025).

[146] Novynarnia, 23 February 2022, https://novynarnia.com/2022/02/23/pro-movu-kuleby/ (accessed 01. 07. 2025).

07:10 p.m. The Rada had been debating the president's decree on the introduction of a state of emergency since lunch – they definitely took their time. The 'Defence Coalition' created in the president's office the previous evening had crumbled within less than a day. Most opposition factions that had promised support only the day before, entered into a tug-of-war with the authorities, keen to eliminate from draft the points concerning political parties and curtailment of the mass media. They kept re-writing various sentences and re-shaping definitions. As a result, no result. Danilov lost his temper: 'We can sit here looking for problems with every comma. But do you realise that tomorrow, perhaps, we'll have to vote on a state of martial law?' Yet the factions carried on regardless.

07:20 p.m. I hurriedly switched over to CNN – just in time for their material on a most recent poll among the Russians. According to the Americans, about half of the Russian population approved of using military force to prevent Ukraine from joining NATO. But the Russian sociological services quoted an even higher percentage. Herein lay the answer: it wasn't down to Putin alone, even if liked wielding his machete– the majority of Russians were like that!

07:45 p.m. Quoting Ukrainian, American, and European sources, the mass media cited Macron. Back from his trip to Moscow he told the journalists that the Kremlin leader had become much more abrasive: 'He is not the same person I last saw back in December 2019… This new person is a much more withheld, profoundly affected by ideology and security concerns.'

I tore myself away from the computer.

The only thing reconfirmed by this abundance of news – throughout the whole day the situation continued escalating. Generally speaking, it was obvious that a major war was to break out any minute. But to understand didn't mean to accept. As before, people's sentiments remained mixed. The minority were sure Russia would attack. Others – the overwhelming majority – believed that such madness was simply inconceivable. Even if something did come to pass, it would be like a second Donbas. There were those, too, who either headed westwards or started packing quietly. Some simply waited. To tell the truth, many felt confused by so many invasion dates wrongly forecast by the Americans.

However, after the Federation Council approved the use of the Russian army abroad, the most far-sighted citizens raced to their banks – to draw their money out in cash and to tear up contracts on deposit accounts.

The situation was so inflammable that it was felt even by the young school children. The price of real estate in Lviv sky-rocketed. People started considering other areas in Western Ukraine. The drain of people from Kyiv continued, drip by drip, because – oh the wonder of wonders! – it was still possible to buy train tickets.

Deep down, we probably envied Arkady – he was sure to find himself a bolthole from which no mobilisation would ever pick him out. And if a huge conflagration boomed upwards here, he would watch all this horror from a very safe distance. As for us? If we were called up, we'd go…

Still, the Russian sites kept churning out their usual tales about Ukraine. There was a lot of stuff like this: 'This is a contrived state, in effect, it's our state. Fascists and Nazis have pulled off a coup d'état. The Kyiv regime came to power and is creating an "anti-Russia".'

There were numerous quotes from Donald Trump responding to the recognition of the DPR and LPR: 'This is genius… Putin declares a big part of Ukraine independent. Oh, that's wonderful… very savvy…'[147]

More and more photos and videos in social media showed the letter 'Z' endlessly slapped onto their equipment. Then two other letters appeared: a 'V' and an 'O'. And finally, a lower-case 'z' placed inside a square. Needless to say, gave rise to very ominous sentiments.

I switched the TV off. Zelensky was reported to have invited owners and managers of 50 biggest Ukrainian companies for a meeting at 5 p.m. Some oligarchs had even arrived in their private jets from abroad – all within a space of one day. They sat there, on edge. There were serious reasons to believe that Ukraine would shortly close its airspace and they wouldn't be able to return to where they had arrived from.

The president entered the assembly chamber 'worried but keeping himself together'. His complexion was of an unhealthy sallow colour.' He asked those attending to show an example – make investments and stay in the country.

'Let me say it right away – I have gathered you here not to ask for money. It's very important now that you should help the country. I'm asking you to support the economy and your employees. On our part, we will do our best to resolve the conflict by diplomacy. We are exploring all possible channels…' After his opening speech Zelensky gave the floor to the law enforcers.

Reznikov's address failed to impress the businessmen.

Zaluzhnyi emphasised that the army was ready for any possible developments.

Budanov held back certain intelligence about Putin's plans – unlike the parliamentarians, these businessmen lacked the requisite clearance. Yet his meaning was perfectly transparent, and thus the level of danger was obvious.

---

[147] Politico, 23 February 2022, https://www.politico.com/news/2022/02/23/trump-putin-ukraine-invasion-00010923 (accessed 01. 07. 2025).

Then it was the businessmen's turn to speak. Overall, the speeches were commonplace…

It was getting progressively less interesting. The audience started whispering among themselves: some were saying that everything would start at four in the morning. However, when it was their turn to speak into the microphone, they said nothing of this.

08:00 p.m. The TV reported the meeting as closed. There was a barrage of questions from journalists. This was what they heard:

'Our side does not believe that there will be a full-scale invasion. We've had an exchange of views and opinions on who's going to play which role. The meeting was substantive: we heard one other and expressed our mutual support.'

'Zelensky told us he's not in contact with Putin anymore. He's looking for intermediaries, international partners to facilitate negotiations with the Russians, but so far without success. Nevertheless, he comes across as a person who, for some reason, believes that he'll manage to settle it all peacefully. He told us: don't panic, make investments, don't flee…'

'After him came the security men: the defence minister, the commander-in-chief of the Armed Forces, the bosses of the Security Service and Intelligence. They explained various scenarios and what the government's response would be in every case.'

'The principal message is: the Russians are trying to wear us down and, as usual, they are bluffing…'

'Aha! There's one more thing… Yermak was seated next to Zelensky and they kept whispering to one another…'[148]

* * *

Mum had descaled some fish and, despite the late hour, I had to go outside to throw the package with the innards into the bins. In the courtyard I spotted our neighbour – a tough businessman, who was busy stuffing the bags and cases into the boot of his car. This guy had bought two adjacent flats in our high-rise, built himself a cosy nest. I once lent him a spanner, so after that we'd been on speaking terms.

I threw my rubbish and headed back home but he beckoned me with his finger. His face anxious and eyes bloodshot, he gave me a wink and leaned closer.

....

[148] UP, 5 September 2022, https://www.pravda.com.ua/news/2022/09/5/7366190/ (accessed 01. 07. 2025).

'I've got these mates, so they furnished me with some info, for friendship's sake...'

'Which means?'

'Up there, some astonishing things are whispered about... It's said that when parting with the Polish Duda Zelensky told him: "I'm sure Ukraine will be attacked within the next several hours"...'

I felt as if someone had hit me in the solar plexus.

'And then he said this: "The Russians think we won't fight back but they got it wrong. We've got experienced guys who'd fought in the east for eight years now, got plenty of combat skills. It's a different Ukraine and a different army now, not like it was in 2014... Dear Andrzej, maybe we won't see each other again... Anything's possible...'

I gasped spasmodically, trying to breathe at least some air.

For a while we just stood there, transfixed, looking at one another with crazy eyes.

'And...' the words were failing me. 'Now? What now?'

'I, for one, am getting ready to hit the road tomorrow.'

'Going far?'

'I've got this cosy summer house in Ternopil Oblast. It'll all be clear to-morrow morning. If mother Russia does barge in, I'll already be far away...'

'Right,' I was still fighting for breath. 'Damn it! So, it means... But just now, when meeting with the business, Zelensky insisted...'

'Hmm. Zelensky... He comes before an audience and says: "What attack? Nothing of the kind! Sleep peacefully! We'll have a barbeque in May!" He does his best not to egg on this Puttie-guy, not to arm the wanker with a pretext... But in reality...'

He momentarily grew silent, then gave me push on the shoulder:

'Well, see ya. I'm off to get my other bags. I've told you everything. Think it all over, together with your mum.'

On my way back up to our floor, I was thinking – *Wait a minute! Hold your horses. It's necessary to digest it rationally. Where has he found the mates with access to such info? They would've had to stand next to the president! And when saying goodbye to Duda, Zelensky would've had to yell – to be overheard. But such conver-sations only ever take place tête-a-tête! And sotto voce! So, it all looks doubtful. Must be complete rubbish! Cock-and-bull! Mates in high places? Not likely!*

Back in the flat I hurriedly went to my computer.

The evening of February 23rd. A. Sadovyi: 'Numerous press bureaus from many countries have now moved to Lviv, along with about a hundred em-bassies. Yesterday I arranged a reception for the ambassadors; quite a few of them came along. From about nine o'clock onwards, the ambassadors started leaving, saying they had urgent business to attend to. On the morning of the 24th I must fly to Kyiv to attend an agreed meeting with Minister Chernyshov and discuss alternative facilities for heat generation.'[149,150]

08:00 p.m. American intelligence communicated to the Ukrainian authorities that a large-scale offensive was to be promptly mounted by Russia any time soon. The Russians planned to start with Kharkiv. In addition, several Russian military units had already been seen crossing the Russian-Ukrainian border in Donbas, at a spot not controlled by the Ukrainian border guards. The intervention would start at night and involve a march towards Kyiv from the direction of Belarus. The mood in Washington was 'extremely pessimistic'.

08:30 p.m. Because of a new round of escalation, airports in Kharkiv, Dnipro and Zaporizhzhia discontinued all incoming and outgoing flights. Runways were blocked with mobile units to eliminate any possibility of the hostile aircraft being able to land with assault troops on board. The airport in Kherson was being prepared for closure, too.

That was that, the airports were being closed. A senseless thought kept churning round my mind: *Looks like all the oligarchs that'd wanted to leave had managed to do just that. At least this looks positive. At least someone gets his portion of luck in life...*

08:47 p.m. The president's decree on the introduction of a state of emergency kept being footballed around the Rada. Finally, the contestable provisions had been eliminated from the decree. Zelensky 'had taken onboard everything suggested by the Rada' – they should finally move in and vote in favour! Every hour was worth its weight in gold... The vote was expected to take place shortly...

Bah, February 23rd turned out to be an extremely eventful, nerve-racking day...

08:53 p.m. CNN announced that certain Russian units were now stationed only five kilometres away from the border. Eighty percent of the Russian troops had taken advance positions and were ready for action. Some other sources confirmed that 'they can move forward straight away, given the right order.'

09:00 p.m. Another curious piece of news arriving from Crimea: Russia had blocked two checkpoints: Kalanchak and Chongar.

....

[149] **Oleksiy Chernyshov:** minister for communities and territorial development, 2020 – November 2022)

[150] UP, 24 February 2024, https://www.pravda.com.ua/cdn/cd1/reconstruction/a5.html (accessed 01. 07. 2025).

But what about our border guards? Nothing to write home about. Doing their duty. Just like before...

Taras had dropped some excerpts from his chatroom into my email. Allegedly, the security services had received some super-secret information, about Putin's approval of the date and time of intrusion. The information was presented to the top leader of the state. He made adequate instructions. Yet what information and which instructions was never explained. Something else became clear, though: if there really was to be an intervention, we hardly had any time to prepare properly. There was more there, but my computer started misbehaving, so I never got to the end of Taras's news. Damn it, at the most interesting bit!

Suddenly, my computer was back on and I caught the final phrase: 'Will they move in openly or under somebody else's flag – like during the past eight years? Who can answer? And what are those at the top doing? Dragging their feet, and dragging their feet... On the other hand, perhaps their tactic is correct. Training the army on the sly, while keeping the population at ease...'

Then Taras called me himself, his voice breaking with nerves.

'That's the trick, man. There won't be any limited-scale assault, like Donbas. What's gonna happen will be a real attack from all sides. Including the capture of the country's capital in the shortest time possible. That's what it's gonna look like!'

Then he was yelling:

'Once this information's been received, the sentiments up there went through a complete about-face. All in all, everything's abuzz now. Russia isn't even hiding her intentions anymore. Imagine: Zelensky's spent the whole day convincing the country that the situation was under control but now he's assembled his advisers and started reading out notes for his TV appearance! His face looks proper grim, concentrated to the full...'

He rang off.

09:49 p.m. The Rada finally approved Zelensky's decree on introducing a state of emergency in some regions of Ukraine. The decision had been voted for by 355 deputies, four of them abstained, and no one voted against. This regime was to be put in place as of midnight of February 24th – that is, as of tomorrow – for the period of 30 days. This parliamentary fuss looked quite ludicrous, especially if contrasted with the newest data emanating from the USA. The Rada was putting forward a counterargument – their conduct was a direct consequence of the president's attitude towards the danger of intervention.

10:10 p.m. A flight arrived carrying military aid from Latvia. Most importantly, it had brought Stinger surface-to-air missiles. I'd lost count of the number of aid aircraft sent by our partners over the several previous days.

10:50 p.m. A state of emergency announced in Kyiv. No curfew yet but one had to carry one's passport at all times.

The day was drawing to a close. I'd spent all of it – weird! – at home, overcome with some inexplicable inertia. I kept kicking around the flat: from the computer to the kitchen, from the kitchen to the sofa. I couldn't be bothered to do anything: limp, all over, but tense, too – what was about to come?

10:55 p.m. at that moment was, perhaps, the ace news: the gang leaders of the pseudo-republics of DPR and LPR simultaneously appealed to the Russian president with an official request to help with rebuffing attacks from the Armed Forces of Ukraine. They reiterated their assertions of Kyiv attacking near-the-border areas in Donetsk and Luhansk Oblasts and thus, 'forcing the peaceful residents of Donbas to flee to Russia.' For some reason, that appeal was dated February 22nd. Even this was doctored... Try as they might, nothing came out 'pure and pretty'...

However, formally it all was above reproach. Volodymyr Putin had a bee in his bonnet about things being 'legally watertight'. Funny these appeals had appeared so late, practically at night. Hardly anyone was going to read any of this since most people had been cosily tucked in in their beds...

Well, one couldn't rule out that Putin, as per usual, was raising the stakes. Tomorrow would show if it was really true.

11:47 p.m. That must've been the last update: Zelensky had conducted the negotiations with Macron. Phew! This unusually hard day of the twenty-third of February was finally about to end. Only a few minutes before it was over. I switched the TV on – no, it hadn't been the last update. They had just started broadcasting Zelensky's address to the peoples of Ukraine and Russia...

First, the president appealed to Ukrainians, then to Russians:

'I am addressing Russian citizens as a citizen of Ukraine. Today I requested a phone conversation with the president of the Russian Federation. The response was silence. Although it is in Donbas that silence should reign. We are separated by over 2000 kilometres of state border. Along this border your army now stands – nearly 200,000 soldiers, thousands of military vehicles. Your leadership has approved their next step: to move into the territory of a different country. This step may ignite a major war on the European continent...'

Referring to the claims of 'Nazism' spread by Russian propaganda against Ukraine, the president reminded everyone of the fact that over eight million Ukrainians had given their lives in the fight against fascism during the Second World War. He emphasised that Ukraine wanted peace but also adherence to principles, including the right to self-determination. 'We know for certain that we don't need war, either cold or hot or of any hybrid type. However, if troops start advancing against us, if attempts are made to take away our country, our freedom, our lives, the lives of our children – we shall defend ourselves. We won't attack anyone but defend ourselves. When on the offensive, you will see our faces.'

The president denied that Ukraine could pose any threat to Russia and pointed out that at this moment Kyiv did not belong to any defensive alliance.

'Ukraine's security is linked to the security of our neighbours; therefore, it makes sense to talk today about the security of Europe as a whole. Yet our primary concern is peace in Ukraine and the security of our citizens. To achieve this goal, we are ready to discuss it with anyone, including you, in whatever format, in whatever venue…

'I know that my appeal to you will not be broadcast on Russian TV, but Russian citizens must see it, must learn the truth. And if the Russian leadership rejects the ideas of peace and does not come to the table of negotiations with us, perhaps they will enter into negotiations with you. Will Russians want war? I'd love to be able to answer this question, but the response depends only on you…'[151]

That was it. He completed his speech. It lasted 11 minutes – I'd timed it.

Suddenly I stopped in my tracks. In fact, in his appeal the president said… He announced, in plain language, that the intrusion was likely! Even imminent! In other words, it wasn't a supposition, it was complete certainty!

I felt as if a jolt went through my body – no, something was terribly wrong. It was not possible that the president should talk about an intervention in such terms! Did anyone else understand it the way I did? Perhaps I was the only one? It felt weird, though – no one was bright enough to cotton on, just me. What if something was wrong with me, and not somebody else?

It had to be all this pent-up tiredness, and stress… All those horrors made my head pound, they set my mind on fire. What I needed was a good night's sleep, and the next day, with a clear head, I should be able to make sense of it all…

My smartphone buzzed – Taras again.

'Have you watched Zelensky? Me too… Awesome. Christ knows what's going on. He addresses the Russians in Russian, and pleads with them to prevent a war in Ukraine. It's quite obvious, though – he talks about this intervention as a done deal. Could it be true?'

He made a pause and added:

....

[151] 23 February 2022, https://www.youtube.com/watch?v=QsPP-q-ZhnQ (accessed 01. 07. 2025).

'On the whole, I'm not just sitting in this restricted chatroom, I'm reading social media too. Lots of up-to-date stuff there. There are videos of the Russian tanks, howitzers, armoured vehicles and MRLs concentrating near Chongar on the territory of Crimea.[152] They're writing about pontoons near Syvash. A many-kilometre-long column of the Russian battle vehicles is deployed near the check-up point in Kalanchak. What do'ya make of it?'

And he answered his own question:

'Come to think of it, nothing funny is likely to happen today. Although, it's not today anymore, the twenty-third… It's the twenty-fourth already, the clock says 00:10… Night-time… Time to hit the hay, so's to get up early to follow it all, not to miss anything…' he gave a stretched-out yawn.

My God, what an unbearably long day had the twenty-third of February proved to be…

Just then Alla called.

'Look, I've just read that the LPR turned to Russia with a request for military support. Ukraine is calling an emergency meeting of the Security Council…'

She talked about something else, and finally:

'I don't know anymore who to believe. Will they attack? Won't they? I don't even believe myself anymore…'

She yawned.

'That's it, Stinger, I'm off to bed. You and Taras should go, too… Don't call me tonight.'

Mum came up to me, exhausted:

'Really, get off the phone. I'll tell you from my personal experience: life is full of idiotic stuff but this whole story with a full-scale intervention is beyond the pale. Do go to bed. The day tomorrow will be just like the other ones before.'

'Ahh-haaaa…' I, too, yawned audibly.

Already in bed, I still had one eye on the notebook screen. Much as it was already night-time, the comments in social media kept running. So, out there were people who, like me, couldn't sleep. Despite the insane developments of February 23rd, the majority still did not believe in a possibility of a full-scale attack: 'They'll target Donbas. The kerfuffle will blow up over there!'; 'Maybe not only Donbas, they'll head towards Berdiansk too… Towards Melitopol and Henichesk – to cut through an overland corridor towards Crimea!'

But the others were already posting about a great invasion.

OK. What was that about the check points? No change, they never got opened. Although why opening them for the night?

....

[152] **MRLs**: multiple rocket launchers.

As for those check points – it's really funny. Have they shut them down for long? I wonder if there's some sort of 'manager on night duty for the country' who monitors such things? who keeps tabs on all of this? Someone who could make decisions if things go wrong? There must be. After all, we are a state, we have all the relevant institutions. A state... Such a powerful, proud word... concept... definition...

'Ahh-haaaa...' Overcome by fatigue, I just couldn't control my yawning anymore. Sleep had avoided me for a couple of days, and I felt out of focus, barely able to process the incoming information. Tomorrow everything would be clearer...

I finally got into bed, arranged my pillows. As for my notebook, I switched it off – what else?

Since the Russians have shut the check points for the night they won't reopen them till the morning. As for our state, it rests on numerous institutions: those dealing with law enforcement, with gathering of intelligence, security, and guarding the borders... Then there's the army too. All of them are strong dignified institutions... They are in control of everything that's going on... Besides, there's got to be somebody 'managing the country' even if it's night already... As soon as something goes wrong, they'll make the right decisions...

'Ahh-haaaa...' I should be careful not to damage my jaws – the sleep was finally enveloping me... The day had been exhausting, overcharged with tension. I hadn't slept for nearly 48 hours, so felt far from sharp...

Still, I must mull over the state institutions some more. No doubt, we've got those institutions... Those who are responsible for everything. And high-ranking state officials, charged with responsibility for the entire country, gather there. And they are protecting my sleep... Although, why only mine? The sleep of all our citizens... All... all... I can't take anything in... Can't anymore... I'm collapsing into sleep... I'm already asleep... And all, all-all... in our country... are asleep... While they protect us... Think of us... take care of us...

My head twitched...

Tomorrow it will all become clear... Now it will have to be tomorrow...

My head jerked again, and again.

That was it. I was asleep.

24 February 2022. Blitzkrieg –
Drama of the First Day

At four-thirty in the morning of the twenty-fourth of February – even before the daybreak – all hell broke loose. Suddenly, everything around was trembling and vibrating – the air and the earth, the buildings, and the trees. It was coming not just from below but from above, too – bombs and missiles. It was all exactly like in 1941 – at night, and without any formal declaration of war.

Fu-u-u-u-u-ck!

Now, why do all dictators believed that the best way forward was an attack on your peaceful neighbours, conducted at daybreak? For some reason, they all preferred four o'clock in the morning. It must have felt like a most suitable hour. Convenient, too – the adversary's soldiers being peacefully asleep in their barracks… Bring in the bombs – kaboom! Also, the complete airport infrastructure would thus go to rack and ruin, aircraft included. So clever!

It must've 'tasted' divine – to attack at four-thirty. And dictators of all times loved the 'taste'.

At 05:30 in the morning (Moscow time, 04:30 in Kyiv) the Russian TV channels broadcast Putin's address:

'Dear citizens of Russia! Dear friends… I have approved the decision to launch a special military operation. Its aim is to protect the people who for eight years have been abused and subjected to genocide by the regime in Kyiv. That is why we shall demand demilitarisation and denazification of Ukraine. We shall also demand that those who have instigated numerous acts of bloody carnage against peaceful communities, including citizens of the Russian Federation, be put on trial.'[153]

It was all topsy-turvy! Their signature style…

And the bombs, shells and missiles came flying in our directions. They had started 'protecting people'…

....

[153] Official website of the president of Russia, 24 February 2022, http://kremlin.ru/events/president/news/67843/videos (accessed 01. 07. 2025).

Fu-u-u-u-u-ck!

* * *

To tell the truth, on that morning of February 24th, exhausted by my night computer vigil, I was asleep and heard nothing.

Mum came into my room, patted me on the shoulder, then gave a gentle push.

'Get up, son! And you… Just don't get too upset… But you know, it's started. It's war!'

She perched on the side of my bed.

'I only woke up some ten minutes ago myself… Car alarms suddenly all went off… The missile and bombing raids are going on not only here, in Kyiv, but all over the country…'

No, I didn't spring from the bed and didn't rush to the window… For a while I just lay there, stupefied. It had just gone five.

'It's in the north, and the east, too… Coming from the south, as well. From all sides…' clarified mum. 'The invasion on a massive scale. Involving all branches of the armed forces and from all directions!'

To start with, things around me started swirling round as if in a fog.

Then followed a kind of a stupor that quickly spread all over my body.

It must've been shock.

Shock, shock, shock!

This state of shock washed over me before I started, little by little, to come to. So, there it was – a full-scale invasion…

I finally tumbled out of bed and sprinted towards TV. All channels were transmitting Putin's morning speech in which he announced the start of a 'special military operation'. However, if one discarded this newspeak, this was a declaration of war on Ukraine.

'… We cannot accept any further enlargement of NATO and their initiative to colonise Ukraine militarily. The point, of course, isn't NATO as such – it is nothing more than an instrument of the foreign policy of the United States. The point is that on adjacent territories, our very own historical territories, they are creating a hostile "anti-Russia" that is under total control from outside, enhanced by the armed forces of the NATO members and pumped to busrting with contemporary weapons… The pace of developments as a whole and our analysis of incoming information show that Russia's collision with these forces is unavoidable. It's only a question of time. They are getting ready and are only waiting for a suitable point in time. Now they're also laying claims to nuclear weapons. We shall never allow this to happen! Russia cannot feel secure, develop, and exist if there is a continuous threat emanating from contemporary Ukraine… The circumstances call for decisive and urgent action on our part. The peoples' republics in Donbas have appealed to us for help…

'In this connection I am addressing the citizens of Ukraine.

'Much as it may be hard, please understand this. I am appealing for your cooperation, so that we can turn this tragic page as soon as possible and move forward together.

'I must address the personnel of the Armed Forces of Ukraine (AFU). I urge you to lay down your arms immediately and go home…'[154]

I hurriedly opened some sites, started surfing through them.

The initial updates flashed across my screen in capitals: WAR came at 04:55.

They reported that, before it had even gone five in the morning, missile strikes had started hitting military facilities all over Ukraine – from the borders in the east and all the way to the west. Explosions rang out in many cities. Massive fires enveloped Mykolaiv. Kharkiv experienced numerous attacks aimed at the military infrastructure. Powerful air strikes in various districts of Kyiv…

Final Preparations

Ri-i-i-ight… Clearly the day ahead meant sheer insanity… Full of mind-boggling events…

First of all, I had to take myself in hand and concentrate. Also, work out the main points. If only because that day – the way I saw it – was going to be the longest day in the life of my country. On the other hand, it hadn't just started, it had started back in… Ye-e-es, piles of news snippets, diverse updates, the materials from Taras's restricted chatroom started falling into place within the initial puzzle. And it looked like the accursed twenty-fourth of February had started much earlier.

I frantically leafed through my notes.

'The Ukrainian and Russian villages of Milove and Chortkove are separated by Friendship of Peoples Street. It feels like some poisonous sneer – the "friendship" petered out back in spring of 2014…'

In February of 2022, the local residents started regularly informing the Ukrainian border guards about activities of the Russians. But it was obvious anyway: for no apparent reason, the Russians had suddenly increased their numbers of border guards in Chortkove. Previously, everyone had known

---

[154]   Official website of the president of Russia, 24 February 2022, http://kremlin.ru/events/president/news/67843/videos (accessed 01. 07. 2025).

them by sight, but by that time no one could recognise anyone anymore. They were all wearing body armour and sported more personal weapons than usual.

February 22nd. Police, the Prosecutor's Office and other Russian authorities had all left Chortkove. From that moment on, the Ukrainians border guards started wearing body armour at all times.

Danilov: 'Already on the 22nd, at approximately 19:20, I received information on the invasion being planned for the nearest future. Following protocol, I informed the president, prime minister, their security services, the minister of the interior, other appropriate authorities…'[155]

'Ok,' they wrote later in Taras's chatroom, 'the statesmen and responsible services have all been warned. But what about the population? People now say: "We could've prepared ourselves somehow… At least taken our children some place… Stocked up on some foodstuffs… In any case, there would've been fewer casualties…'

However, the authorities have some powerful arguments in their favour. First of all, they were trying, at any cost, to avoid provoking Russia. Secondly, it was absolutely necessary to avoid showing that the Ukrainian General Staff knew about the attack and was taking appropriate measures.

Thus, the outcome was harsh: those who'd kept their wits about them and made correct guesses – and besides, disposed of the appropriate means – ensured their own safety and the safety of their families. Those who didn't cotton on, or had no means – didn't.

Had we believed that an invasion would take place? There were numerous obvious signs that the majority of Ukrainians preferred to ignore. Or rather they saw the signs but rejected the inevitability of war. It was clear as bell that Russia's incursion into Ukraine would mean huge casualties and losses. And people were simply tried to protect themselves psychologically – by refusing to accept the possibility of such a horrible prospect…

Kuleba: 'By the end of February 22nd (approximately, 23:00 by Kyiv), while in Washington D.C, our ambassador, Oksana Markarova, and I were going from one meeting to another. Oksana received a telephone call from the White House: "Come along, we'll arrange a meeting between the minister and National Security Adviser Sullivan." The car took us to the wing that houses his office, that's next to Biden's. We were asked to wait… As a rule, Biden doesn't receive foreign ministers of other countries. Unless you're a president or a prime minister, such a meeting can never be guaranteed.

---

[155]   UP, 22 April 2022, https://www.pravda.com.ua/news/2022/04/22/7341301/ (accessed 01. 07. 2025).

'The door opened, and out came everybody referred to as "Biden's inner circle." Some were wearing military uniforms; the others were in civilian suits. Blinken came out first and said: "We've just had a briefing on Ukraine…" In his wake came a real crowd. They all shook my hand, sighing in sympathy and looking at me as if trying to bid farewell. It felt as if they'd just stepped out of a medical concilium where it was confirmed that I had the final stage of cancer. So now everyone was coming out to look at the patient and sigh heavily – "Ouch!"

'Following this, Blinken showed us into the Oval Office.

'Biden confirmed that according to their most recent intelligence it was all about to take off: "There will be war. We will stand with you through thick and thin, till the bitter end…" But by then we had received many pieces of information suggesting otherwise. We knew that NATO members had discussed Ukrainian prospects in the event of a full-scale war, not a local one. And their conclusion was unanimous: after 72 hours there would be no longer be any Ukraine…

'Then Biden said: "Discuss specifics with Tony…" It goes without saying, I left that meeting in a mood that was far from serene since I realised we were unavoidably devolving into war. Whether it was going to take another day, or two, or three – that was less important… I headed to the State Department… A guy there showed me a map, and on it something that looked like tiny specks: "These are the airfields… On those airfields are stationed the air freighters, ready to take off…' I felt as if struck by lightning. As soon as I was out, I reported to the president. He'd been receiving all kinds of information: from the military, the security, the diplomats. By that time the president hardly slept or ate, he was completely consumed with developments. He said: "Ok, we'll take it into account when putting together the bigger picture"…'[156]

The evening of February 23rd. The security services had obtained specific intel on the invasion. Budanov: 'Putin made his final decision on D-Day at about 15:00 on February 23rd. Before lunch he'd still had some doubts… (Previously) he could have implemented any scenario. The decision was his own – no one had any significant influence. He personally got in contact with the commanders of all groupings, listened to their official reports confirming they were on standby and gave his official command to open aggression. (Since it became known) that the intervention would start tomorrow – on February 24th at four in the morning – my wife and I quickly packed some bags and drove to where I work. We moved into my office. Went to a food shop and laid in some pro-

[156] Gordon, 15 August 2022, https://gordonua.com/ukr/publications/kuleba-u-veresni-2021-ho-u-derzhdepi-nam-iz-jermakom-skazali-nu-shcho-khloptsi-kopajte-transheji-1621358.html (accessed 01. 07. 2025).

visions… Next, we had to urgently prepare a special task force because, whatever the cost, we had to prevent the enemy troops from landing at Hostomel Airfield…'[157]

Sometime around 9 p.m., right after the reassuring meeting with business representatives where optimism had still reigned supreme, the grim news finally reached Bankova Street. It was corroborated with interceptions on the Russian troops receiving orders to take their battle positions.

[One of the reasons for Zelensky's scepticism regarding the Kremlin plans was precisely the fact that up till that point the Ukrainian interceptions had not picked up any info on the Russian advancement to operational sites, whereas the technical equipment available to the Americans and the Brits was of higher quality. Most importantly, in Moscow the information had been classified at the highest level, with only few individuals having access, while the army and the security services were kept practically in the dark. And the ploy had worked…]

Thus, at this point our top leaders' reading of the status quo went through a radical change. Suddenly, everything was frenzied activity. At last, the long-awaited instructions were finally issued. The AFU commanders, too, finally took it onboard that the Russian army would direct their main thrust towards Kyiv and Chernihiv. Thus, it became imperative to urgently figure out a new lay of the land and put in place at least some arrangements. Seven hours before the attack, the troops had received a command to move towards Kyiv. Such a transfer, though, could never be completed quickly, therefore, at the time of invasion many Ukrainian units were still on defence duties in the east of the country, with those who had already set off still in transit.

S. Naiev: 'On February 23rd I received intelligence confirming the time of attack as 04:00 on February 24th. I personally called all the generals under my command and ordered that all units be put on red-hot alert. At the same time the commander of the navy received an order to start planting mines in the Black Sea harbour.[158]

February 23rd, evening. Several AFU units stationed near the Belarusian border received a warning of Russian activities on the night of February 24th. By that point it had been expected from the daily emergency drills and the fact that some detachments had been placed on standby.

[157]   Espreso, 24 May 2022, https://espreso.tv/u-rozvidtsi-rozpovili-koli-putin-ukhvaliv-ostatochne-rishennya-pro-napad-na-ukrainu (accessed 01. 07. 2025).

[158]   UP, 10 February 2025, https://www.pravda.com.ua/rus/articles/2025/02/10/7497449/ (accessed 01. 07. 2025).

Ukrainian checkpoint at Milove village, Luhansk oblast. The Russian checkpoint on the other side of the border slowed down the passage of Ukrainians crossing the border to Russia. At 10 p.m. crossing was cancelled altogether.

At midnight the Ukrainian customs personnel started packing their belongings and property.

'What's up? What's going on?' asked their own border guards.

'Everything's fine…' was the answer while continuing to pack the files and computers.

Budanov's wife: 'On the evening of February 23rd I was watching the first Special Task units undergo training. They were to leave for Hostomel shortly. The soldiers were issued with weapons and ammunitions. They were waiting for the word. At midnight they were still at the base, eating hamburgers from McDonald's…'[159]

As for the president's office, there had been practically no interval between the days of the February 23rd and 24th. They all left for their respective homes at about one o'clock in the morning. The borderline between the events of those two days had been eroded not only in Zelensky's office. It was erased everywhere – in Kyiv and all over Ukraine, in Europe and all over the world.

Arakhamia: 'On February 23rd we were in the President's office, waiting for yet another forecast of "intervention" to play out but in was nearly one in the morning and nothing had happened. I was the first one to lose patience, and said I was going home, to bed…'[160]

It felt funny – to wait for an attack at night because world history confirmed that hostilities would normally start in the early morning. Be that as it may, they just sat and waited. They already had reliable information about the attack but still did not believe it. Because it was simply impossible to believe in this… The situation was truly difficult. If you were to take decisive action of any kind, this could be regarded as provocation and then you yourself would be blamed. Incidentally, it was not just Russians who would be likely to blame, but even some partners. So this too had to be taken into account…

Zelensky: 'I remember I got home quite late. Thing is, all day (that is, until February 24th), we'd had conferences, and I think an NSDC session too. We discussed those issues too, all of us. We prepared documents and mapped out

....

[159]   Gordon, 1 October 2022, https://gordonua.com/ukr/news/war/druzhina-budanova-uvecheri-23-ljutogo-cholovik-skazav-meni-shcho-o-p-jatij-ranku-rozpochnetsja-povnomasshtabne-vtorgnennja-1628992.html (accessed 01. 07. 2025).

[160]   UP, 23 February 2023, https://www.pravda.com.ua/cdn/cd1/reconstruction/a6.html (accessed 01. 07. 2025).

what we were going to do… We knew that if things started, the state should carry on as a single entity. [There was] an understanding) that there should be someone ensuring operation of financial bodies; we and the National Bank made certain arrangements in advance – to secure the state reserves, too. Safety was ensured, let's put it this way…'[161]

Yermak: 'I left the president's office at half past one in the morning (01:30 a.m., February 24th). The president left at about one o'clock too. We'd been in session all the previous day… I got home by about two…'[162]

February 24th.

01:30 a.m. Those residing in Milove could hear the rumble of the Russian military columns approaching.

01:30 a.m. One of the nine Russian battalion tactical groups (BTG) left the Palmira training ground in Belarus (near to the town of Khoiniki in Gomel Oblast). Its personnel mostly consisted of Pskov Airborne Cavalry. The order of the day included these time pointers: 03:15 (head of the column) – 04:50 (tail of the column) – pontoon crossing over the Prypiat River (six kilometres from the Ukrainian border); 04:00-05:30 – Belarusian village of Belaya Soroka on the border with Ukraine (the village was unpopulated: its residents had been evacuated following the Chornobyl disaster); 06:30-08:00 – the village of Cherevach (Ivankiv District, Kyiv Oblast; residents of the village had likewise been evacuated; 09:00-10:30 – the town of Ivankiv, Vyshhorod District on the Teteriv River); 13:00-14:30 – the village of Babyntsi (Bucha District by the Zdvyzh River, 20 kilometres west of Hostomel and 54 kilometres from the centre of Kyiv); 14:15-15:50 – the village of Stoyanka on the Kyiv-Chop motorway (by the Irpin River, several kilometres from the administrative border of Kyiv along the Zhytomyr motorway, and 23 kilometres to the centre of Kyiv); after which 'to concentrate forces on the city's administrative border in order to block Kyiv from the west.' This route of over 200 kilometres had to be covered in about 12-13 hours.

Another 10 BTGs remained in reserve in Homel Oblast near the Ukrainian border.

[So, this elite grouping of the Russian army carrying the 'V' insignia of the East (Vostok) Military District on its equipment's flanks was assigned the decisive role in the capture of Kyiv. Its subdivisions were to advance along the Dnipro's Right Bank, take possession of the deactivated Chornobyl nuclear

[161] UP, 23 February 2023, https://www.pravda.com.ua/podcasts/63f90cc807994/2024/02/ 23/7390928/ (accessed 01. 07. 2025) (accessed 01. 07. 2025).

[162] UP, 24 February 2024, https://www.pravda.com.ua/podcasts/63f90cc807994/2023/02/ 24/7390928/ (accessed 01. 07. 2025).

power station, enter the pivotal thoroughfare connecting Kyiv and Chop (via Zhytomyr), and block it. This achieved, they were to proceed southwards toward the railway hub of Fastiv, while the vanguard units were to gain control over Hostomel Airfield. The aim was to facilitate transportation of airborne assault units tasked with capturing the governmental quarters in Kyiv. Simultaneously, another grouping was to thrust towards Kyiv from the Russian oblast of Bryansk and, passing through Chernihiv, the oblast centre, block the capital from the direction of Brovary on the Left bank.]

Naiev: 'At about two in the morning the general in charge of the Air Force reported that a command aircraft fitted with airborne radio relay had taken off from Belarus. This is an aircraft used for aerial targeting. I asked him: "Has it ever happened before?" He replied: "It's a first." So I said: "Well, in that case we definitely have to expect invasion.'[163]

A Ukrainian journalist: 'I got home at about two in the morning and set my alarm for four o'clock. The alarm went off – nothing... I thought then: "Yet another spook story has just been deflated." I listened to the news – nothing there either... I did have reasons to be concerned, but nothing was going on...'

About 02:00 a.m. Urgent! The White House was in receipt of urgent intelligence. There was a 'high probability' that intervention was already underway. The Russian troops were on the move. The war was about to start...

02:45 a.m. The European Union Aviation Safety Agency (EASA) reported that the Defence Ministry of Russia had urgently warned Ukraine of the high risk to flight security due to the use of weaponry and military equipment, starting from 02:45 on February 24th, and requested that the Ukrainian air controllers suspended all flights. As of 02:45 on February 24th the air space of Ukraine was closed for civilian users. Just then a Sky Up plane had taken off at Boryspil Airport but was ordered to immediately return to base. Flights were banned over the Russian and Belarusian territories adjacent to Ukraine. FlightRadar24 monitoring service showed planes reversing their course before entering the Ukrainian air space and heading back.

Yermak: 'At about two or three in the morning, Reznikov was on the line. He said that he'd just received a call from the defence minister of Belarus, who said: "...I think you should urgently get in touch with your Russian colleague." Reznikov answered that he "had no channels for communicating with him. Then again, why call him, what's up?" It was clear by then that things were coming to a head. We'd accumulated a lot of info by then...'[164]

....

[163]   TSN, 7 October 2022, https://tsn.ua/ato/yih-treba-biti-general-nayev-rozpoviv-pro-pochatok-viyni-ta-nakaz-zaluzhnogo-2175244.html (accessed 01. 07. 2025).

[164]   UP, 23 February 2024, https://www.pravda.com.ua/podcasts/63f90cc807994/2024/02/23/7390928/ (accessed 01. 07. 2025).

03:00 a.m. Chongar, the administrative border with Crimea. Military personnel were raised in the dead of the night, and by that point everyone was awake.

Budanov: 'At about 3:30, Yermak gave me a call: "Well, it's half three by now, all's quiet. Perhaps, it'll blow over?" We chatted till about four, me completely psyched up. For me it was such a challenge! If I, as a security boss, had spread the wrong information, it would've been total dishonor for me...'[165]

(Yermak: 'For all that, practically within an hour, or an hour and a half, both the security guys and the military had informed me of the start of hostilities... So, I quickly got myself together and sometime around 5 o'clock in the morning was already in the president's office.')[166]

03:30 a.m. A fully-equipped Russian sabotage party of eight infiltrated the village of Zorynivka in the vicinity of Milove. On duty that night were six Ukrainian border guards. Denis Tkach, in charge of the detail, ordered a withdrawal. The Russians opened fire and Tkach was killed. First blood and the first casualty. The war came from the side of Milove...

04:00 a.m. Major General Sokolov, commander of the AFU southern group, was at his operations office in front of a computer display, on which Virazh-Planchet, an air control app that was monitoring movements of vehicles, picked up a massive take-off from Crimea. 'To start with, we tried to work out the total number of aircraft but lost count at about the thirtieth. They first circled over Crimea, thus giving hope that they would fly around for a bit and then land at their own airfield. That had happened before...'[167]

04:00 a.m. The border control office and police headquarters in Milove were shelled by Grad, a multiple rocket launcher. The border guards had an emergency plan in place, developed for the eventuality of an attack. In order to hold the line, they were urgently relocated to Bilovodsk, which was further back in Luhansk Oblast. Within an hour, a Russian military column had entered Milove.

04:00 a.m. Two Ukrainian army men came outside for a smoke – their unit was patrolling the forest within the Chornobyl Exclusion Zone. All of a sudden, the sky above lit with a barrage of bright lights. One of them: "I saw flashes all over the forest. I first thought it was the car lights. Then it dawned on me

[165]   UP, 16 October 2023, https://www.pravda.com.ua/news/2023/10/16/7424364/ (accessed 01. 07. 2025).

[166]   UP, 10 March 2022, https://www.pravda.com.ua/articles/2022/03/10/7329989/ (accessed 01. 07. 2025).

[167]   UP, 18 September 2023, https://www.pravda.com.ua/articles/2023/09/18/7420200/ (accessed 01. 07. 2025).

that it was the Grads. They were shooting at us. By the time I'd finished my cigarette, the war broke out"…'

The first Russian vehicles started crossing the Ukrainian border…

04.00 a.m. Commander of Kyiv defence Syrsky receives a call from the commander -in -chief Zaluzhny; 'It all started. Everything is action. They started…'

04:00 a.m. The Russian columns started moving through the Crimean checkpoints.

The mayor of Kyiv, Vitaliy Klitchko, had also received reliable warnings from security services of the intrusion that would start at four in the morning on February 24th. He set the alarm for three, woke up and didn't go back to sleep. At four he received a telephone call confirming that it had really started…

04:15 a.m. Debris from a kamikaze drone strike ripped apart the tent in which the off-duty Ukrainian border guards slept. They had been in charge of the Ukraine-Belarus crossing point. Several minutes later the launchers opened fire. They left 20 metre-crates – no one had ever seen anything like it before…

04:15 a.m. Missiles started landing throughout Ukrainian territory… Budanov: 'The strikes started in earnest at about 04:20, since it had taken some time for the rockets to reach their targets. Our priority was to derail the landing of assault troops in Hostomel…"

04:15 a.m. Minister of the Interior Monastyrskyi received a call on his mobile. The head of the National Border Guards informed him that his units were engaged in active combat with the Russians coming from three directions, and that the Russians were advancing in columns. It thus became clear that what was underway was not just a limited attack in the east, as had been believed by the majority of the Ukrainian top brass.

Well… And who was the first to inform Zelensky about the start of war, by phone or message? According to Monastyrskyi, he was the one to dial Zelensky's number:

'It's started…'

'What do you mean precisely?'

'Judging by shellfire coming from different sources, it looks like a full-scale intervention…'[168]

Those were the first minutes when the initial horrendous strikes were delivered by the Russians: the missiles were destroying the Ukrainian Air Defence units, radio location stations, the ammunitions depots, airfields, and delivery bases…

....

[168] TSN, 27 August 2022, https://tsn.ua/ato/pochalosya-golova-mvs-prigadav-yak-skazav-zelenskomu-pro-pochatok-viyni-ta-pershi-godini-vtorgnennya-2143942.html (accessed 01. 07. 2025).

Closer to five in the morning the entire Kyiv was woken up by missile strikes.

Zelensky: 'I heard the explosions. I was already on my way; I was almost going out. I received some calls before the explosions started. We were on alert for this, so everything was followed by intelligence and the military, we understood where the offensive was likely to come from. So as soon as they started, I received a call.'[169]

Olena Zelenska sprang up in alarm,[170] saw that her husband wasn't by her side. He was in the room nextdoor, already fully dressed – a dark grey suit, no tie.

'What's going on?'

'It's started,' Volodymyr Zelensky was brief.

'What shall we do about the children?'

Now it was imperative to wake the children up and get them ready to evacuate. Behind the windows, explosions continued to boom…[171]

Then he left. The motorcade had set off directly, heading from the presidential residence at Koncha-Zaspa towards Kyiv.

Ever since then, Zelensky hadn't been to either his Kyiv flat or the out-of-town residence. Ever since then, he and his closest colleagues didn't just work on the premises of the President's Office, they lived there.

Later, O. Zelenska reminisced that on 'the first day of war I felt as if I'd ended up in a parallel reality, as if all of this was just a bad dream. It was a surreal feeling, similar to a computer game, where you have to go through several levels to end up at home.'

Without doubt, the news of the Russian aggression staggered President Zelensky. He was, most likely, really hopeful that the situation would somehow be discharged. Yet this new real threat inspired him with a sense of huge responsibility. It was imperative now to rouse the country, previously lulled through his own efforts. It was necessary to pull together all available resources and rebuff the blow. Zelensky was facing many challenges, the paramount among them being to prevent the country from falling…

'I was thinking only about us, our country. I immediately set off to the office, was ready and collected. I wasted no time on contemplation – straightaway we all got together, and the military committee assembled too. We were ready to

[169]   UP, 23 February 2024, https://www.pravda.com.ua/podcasts/63f90cc807994/2024/02/23/7390928/ (accessed 01. 07. 2025).

[170]   **Olena Zelenska**: the president's wife.

[171]   TSN, 9 April 2022. https://tsn.ua/ukrayina/todi-vin-vostannye-odyagnuv-bilu-sorochku-zelenska-rozpovila-pro-pershiy-den-viyni-i-koli-vostannye-bachilas-ya-z-cholovikom-2032867.html (accessed 01. 07. 2025).

strike back. The most important thing at a moment like this is to make decisions, not muse over things that might happen tomorrow or the day after. It's important to think of now…'[172]

And thus, much as intelligence leaks organised by the partner countries had been unprecedented in terms of the sheer scale, and much as they had been aimed at ensuring Ukraine's safety, they failed to stop Russian aggression…

* * *

February 24th. 04:00 a.m. in Kyiv, 09:00 p.m. of February 23rd in New York. Ukraine convoked an emergency meeting of the UN Security Council. The meeting was chaired by the Russian Ambassador Nebenzia.

Reznikov: 'Valeriy Zaluzhnyi called me just after four in the morning. I had set an alarm on my phone for six – the thing was, the day before, the foreign ministers of the friendly powers of Latvia, Lithuania and Estonia had flown in, and Dima Kuleba had asked me to take them on a trip to Donbas. I had booked a plane and left it on standby at Zhuliany Airport. We had planned to leave at eight in the morning, get to Kramatorsk and then arrange a visit for them to see the army. And then that call… I saw it was Zaluzhnyi: "Oleksii Yuriiovych, they've launched an attack…" I said: "Got you, I'll be over there in 20 minutes." Before, if you had made your way into the Defence Ministry, you had to pass through several control points, and the guys manning those wore uniforms. But now they all had body armour on, helmets, assault rifles and their mags. In other words, they were on high alert. It was visually striking. Immediately, there were piles of sandbags everywhere, used as fortifications, as combat lines…'[173]

04:30 a.m. Chornobyl. Introduction of a state of heightened alarm was closely followed by an announcement that this wasn't a training exercise and that evacuation was about to start.

04:30 a.m. Kyiv time (09:30 p.m. in New York). Everyone attending the Security Council meeting heard their mobiles buzzing! So, everyone snatching them as one, they all read the same message: the intervention had started. A phone was carried over to Chairman Nebenzia. He read it and carried on…

....

[172] UP, 8 March 2024, https://www.pravda.com.ua/podcasts/63f90cc807994/2024/03/8/7397132/ (accessed 01. 07. 2025).

[173] UP, 8 March 2024, https://www.pravda.com.ua/podcasts/63f90cc807994/2024/03/8/7397132/ (accessed 01. 07. 2025).

Sergiy Kyslytsya, Ukrainian ambassador to the UN, addressing Nebenzia: 'The Russian Federation should resign as acting head of the Security Council! Would you like me to play you a video showing your president [Putin's speech announcing the start of the 'special military operation']? Mr Ambassador, would you like me to do this? So you can confirm it?'

Nebenzia: 'I'd like not to be interrupted…'

Kyslytsia: 'Call it what you like, but you have declared war. The responsibility of this organisation is to stop wars. Therefore, I am appealing to all of you: do what you can to stop war!' [Addressing Nebenzia]: 'Shall I, after all, play the video where your president declares war?'

Nebenzia: 'Don't put any question addressed to me while I'm making my speech!'

Kyslytsia: 'Call Putin, call Lavrov. Stop the aggression. I welcome the decision by some members of this council to call an emergency meeting as soon as possible in order to approve the requisite resolutions and condemn your aggression against my people. There is no purgatory for war criminals. They go straight to hell, Ambassador!'

Nebenzia: 'I must reiterate that I am grateful to the Ukrainian Ambassador for his presentation and for the questions, which I do not plan to answer. Whatever I know today I have already explained. I have no intention of waking up minister Lavrov at this hour. We said we'll provide you with information on developments. Do not call it "war" – it's a special military operation in the Donbas.'

Representatives of the USA, the UK and France admitted that 'while we were trying to stop war, the Russian president declared a special military operation in Donbas. Thus Russia chose war…' [Hm… Can it be that in the first minutes western diplomats too, following Nebenzia's example, preferred to speak only of a 'special military operation in the Donbas'?]

Nebenzia: 'I must emphasise that our intrusion is aimed not at the people of Ukraine but at the junta that has usurped power in Kyiv. There are no more points left on the agenda, and the session is thus closed.'[174]

After 04:30 a.m. The aircraft that had circled over Crimea spread out over the Sea of Azov and the Black Sea and started massive air strikes aimed at the continental Ukraine, targeting our army dispositions, managerial offices, air defence start-up points, airfields.

....

[174]   Partially: European Pravda, 24 February 2022, https://www.eurointegration.com.ua/news/2022/02/24/7134559/ (accessed 01. 07. 2025).

The Chornobaivka airfield nearby Kherson was under fire. In Mykolaiv – Kulbakino airfield and Ochakiv naval base – under multiple rocket attacks. Concurrently, there started bombing of the airbase near Vasylkiv, Kyiv oblast. The missiles hit the runway and the facilities housing air defence equipment. The airport in Myrhorod, Poltava oblast, was also shelled, although the planes, allegedly, got away unscathed as they had taken them off the ground and were in the air.

Shortly before five in the morning, Naiev: 'About five in the morning was the start of the full-scale intervention. I urgently presented my report to the commander-in-chief. General Zaluzhnyi's first reaction was: "Fight them back!! Got it?" I answered: "Aye, I got it." We estimated that they had 90 battalion tactical groups and 140,000 men. '[175]

Reznikov: 'In Zaluzhnyi's office [most likely, he'd never left it that night] commanders from various areas were putting in their reports: what was happening, where, and what was moving in which direction. Those in receipt provided adequate responses. It went like this: "This and this is happening, we're doing that and that." OK. If, for example, Zaluzhnyi saw that what was required was artillery support – an [enemy] column was moving in – he would dial the number of the person responsible for artillery: "Can you defeat them? OK, give them comms!" It was commanding the troops in real time, through all channels, using all types of telephones that existed. We have our special communications (military), also protected phones, and in addition there were the ordinary messengers that everyone can use – we used them all.'[176]

It sure sounded beautiful and well-organised. In reality, there was confusion and chaos, with officers tearing up and down the corridors, the numerous doors banging. It was as it should've been, of course, for even if the preparations had been made, with something like *this* going on, no one could amble round between offices leisurely. It would have been the same in any country, in any General Headquarters.

Also, they must have used a more colourful language there, in that office, something along the lines of 'fuck them all sideways till the feathers go flying from their asses!' Small wonder, those were the army men in extremis, clearly, they were not the ones to mince words. Say, a command worded thus – 'Be so kind as to deliver a powerful blow from you cannons!' – would've been a sure sign of idiocy.

....

[175]   TSN, 7 October 2022, https://tsn.ua/ato/yih-treba-biti-general-nayev-rozpoviv-pro-pochatok-viyni-ta-nakaz-zaluzhnogo-2175244.html (accessed 01. 07. 2025).

[176]   UP, without date, https://www.pravda.com.ua/cdn/cd1/reconstruction/a3.html (accessed 01. 07. 2025).

Zaluzhnyi: 'From the very early morning I was on the phone calling the commanders, but some of them contacted me directly. Conversations were brief... People would sign off with "Stand firm!" or "Hold fast!" There was something else that struck me. The same early morning a certain person got through to me on the phone... From abroad, of a very high rank... And that person asked for my forgiveness...'[177] (Jeez, could it have been someone from Russia? The most supreme commander?)

Arakhamia: '... [I was got out of bed by an insistent call from] Yermak. It was something like four in the morning. He said: "It's started, get over here"...'[178]

Yermak: 'Close to five in the morning, I was already at the president's office. They put me in the picture – the fighting along the border, the bombings... When I arrived at Bankova Street, the president was already there.'[179]

Minister of Infrastructure Kubrakov received the news of war in his office. During the night he'd been in communication with airport managers who continued blocking their runways, and with leaders of Ukraerorukh, Ukraine's State Air Traffic operator, who had closed the airspace above Ukraine at half two in the morning.

R. Stefanchuk, the head of the Supreme Rada was also woken up by the sound of explosions. Interior Minister Monastyrskyi called – he told me it had started, that the Russians were moving in, making their way from the border. Then Yermak called and asked me to come to the president's office as soon as possible and to organize a meeting of the Verkhovna Rada promptly: "We need to administer martial law, no time to waste!" So I quickly went over to the president's office from my Left Bank – that was before six o'clock. The president came out in his white shirt (later he adopted a military outfit) and said: "Well, it's started..."' He then added: "We've been chosen by fate..." No one was panicking, but everyone realised we had to make decisions and work out a way for Ukraine to avoid ceasing to exist during those crucial days...'[180]

From the off, the Kremlin propaganda announced that the Ukrainian air defence was no more. Following the bombardment, the invasion was developing along the two thousand kilometres of the joint border, the one that in a blink

[177] Ukrainsky noviny, 13 May 2023, https://ukranews.com/news/932538-zaluzhnomu-utrom-24-fevralya-pozvonil-chelovek-iz-za-granitsy-chtoby-poprosit-prosheniya (accessed 01. 07. 2025).

[178] UP, 11 July 2023, https://www.pravda.com.ua/articles/2023/07/11/7410729/ (accessed 01. 07. 2025).

[179] UP, 10 March 2022, https://www.pravda.com.ua/articles/2022/03/10/7329989/ (accessed 01. 07. 2025).

[180] UP, 8 March 2024, https://www.pravda.com.ua/podcasts/63f90cc807994/2024/03/8/7397132/ (accessed 01. 07. 2025).

of an eye transformed into the front line. The longest front since the times of the Second World War.

Approximately at 05:00 a.m. Putin and Lukashenko spoke over the phone. 'Volodymyr Putin informed his Belarusian colleague about the developments on the borders with Ukraine, and in Donbas.'

Approximately at 05:00 a.m. Prime Minster D. Shmyhal notified Minister for Communities and Territories' Development Chernyshov of the start of the war and the need to urgently arrive at work. He had an important mission to perform…

05:00 a.m. The Border Guard Service of Ukraine announced that the Russian troops had crossed the Ukrainian border in the north. This act of aggression was committed 'with the support of Belarus.'

05:00 a.m. An on-duty traffic controller at Boryspil Airport finally managed to get in touch with Hostomel airfield: 'Boryspil is under attack. A similar one may be aimed at Hostomel. I suggest you leave the air control tower…' A rapid-reaction force unit of the National Guards was urgently drafted into the operation – to defend the airfield.

And again, at 05:00 a.m., Russia closed the Sea of Azov and the Black Sea. Their intention, apparently, was to start operations in the Sea of Azov and near Odesa, which would involve landing the troops of the Black Sea naval fleet.

Zelensky was the first to reach the premises of the President's Office, it was a bit more then five in the morning. He had only one thought: 'The Russian missiles – right now! – are flying above my children, above all our children… And before long, a devastating number of people will die…'

Yet he was confident that all Ukrainians shared his sentiments and would mount a fierce resistance to the occupiers. On the third floor he got out of the lift and proceeded to his office. He didn't remain alone for long. The first one to arrive was Monastryrskyi.

Several minutes later along came Danilov: 'Right away I went to the president's office. The interior minister was already there. Zelensky had a white shirt on, and I… you know… somehow remembered it…'[181]

Arakhamia: 'To the right of Vita-Poshtova a structure of some kind went up in roaring flames, a base of some sort… [182] I had no idea what it was but pressed

---

[181]   Korotko pro, 22 April 2022, https://kp.ua/ua/politics/a648332-oleksij-danilov-vtorhnennja-rosiji-pochalosja-o-340-u-luhanskij-oblasti-o-5-j-nastup-pochalosja-skriz (accessed 01. 07. 2025).

182   **Vita-Poshtova**: a residential village to the south of Kyiv.

down on the accelerator, rushing through red on traffic lights. It normally takes me about 40 minutes to get there, but this time I reached the president's office in 15. Everyone in Zelensky's office looked somewhat phased out. When we first got together there was no real info about what was going on. What if Kyiv was to fall within an hour? And everyone was calling everyone else; telephones got overheated: "This damaged, that destroyed, this destroyed, that damaged." That is to say, the picture as a whole was being put together from those morsels. And then everyone cottoned on to the fact that there was fighting over here, and fighting over there… It took some time to pull ourselves together and get down to normal planning…'[183]

Arakhamia: 'At the very beginning we didn't know anything at all, we didn't know what would happen. But we gradually started realizing: ours were fighting here, ours were fighting there. And there is time to get mobilized and get down to normal planning.[184]

Presently, the other NSDC members started arriving at Bankova Street and stared, in shock, as the monitors displaying tracking images of hundreds after hundreds of Russian tanks and other armoured vehicles crossing the border. They moved in columns, reviving memories of the fascist onslaught at the start of the Second World War. They came and came, and there was no end to their progress… It was excruciating to watch, even harder – to accept, for even the top military command couldn't imagine anything like it. Accept that in the 21st century there would be a war on this scale, involving the use of aviation, strike tank groupings, and missile attacks! The principal question, though, was this: how far would the enemy manage to get with their enormous concentration of offensive troops?

05.30. Start of a session of the NSDC.

The topmost priority was to approve the introduction of martial law in Ukraine. Danilov: 'Everything happened instantly. Everything had been prepared and printed out… [We had] different packages for different scenarios. All that was needed was the president's signature under Presidential Decree No 64/2022, Point 1 – "To introduce in Ukraine martial law from 05:30 a.m., February 24th, for the duration of 30 days". The document then had to be registered… And that was that, the document was ready to be taken over to the Rada for approval. The day before, on February 23rd, the NSDC had discussed intro-

[183]   UP, 11 July 2023, https://www.pravda.com.ua/articles/2023/07/11/7410729/ (accessed 01. 07. 2025).

[184]   UP, 23 February 2024, https://www.pravda.com.ua/cdn/cd1/reconstruction/a6.html (accessed 01. 07. 2025).

ducing the state of emergency, and there had already been proposals to take the martial law route, but they had decided it was best not to provoke Russia...'[185]

Reznikov: 'Everything happened instantly. Everyone arrived, a brief report was given, and the document was immediately taken to parliament for the president's signature'.

Danilov: 'We had everything prepared, everything printed out - different packages of documents for different scenarios. We just received the president's signature and are registering it. We were preparing for everything, but we couldn't tell anyone about it, not even our relatives'.[186]

Last days of peace. First minutes and hours of war

In those last days, everything connected with the war was officially denied by both the Russian and Ukrainian sides. However, an observant citizen could still notice something here and there. They eagerly shared their observations on social networks...

Sudzha, Russia: 'On the evening of the twenty-third of February I was at one party. Most of the conversation was about whether or not there'd be war. Thing is, one could feel it in here. Not so long before, I'd been driving along a forest strip and saw lots of tanks and soldiers, sitting around campfires, their military trucks nearby. It was a bit strange but I didn't pay much attention. Anyway, was it a big surprise for out militarized country? At the party me and some other friends kept trying to convince everyone that war was out of the question: 'Are you off your rocker? What are you talking about? What war? Why would Putin need it?' We were absolutely sure that Putin was out simply to scare everyone...

Belgorod oblast, Russia, near the Ukrainian border: 'On February 15th we'd been told there'd be no war, it was just a case of flexing our muscles. Before that we'd been dragged from one exercise to another. Even if I suspected something, I thought as well that it was pushing our chest out in front of Zelensky. And no one around me thought it would be a fully-fledged invasion. A demonstration of power as I said...'

[185]   UP, 5 September 2022, https://www.pravda.com.ua/articles/2022/09/5/7366059/ (accessed 01. 07. 2025).

[186]   UP, 5 September 2022, https://www.pravda.com.ua/articles/2022/09/5/7366059/ (accessed 01. 07. 2025).

Sumy oblast, Ukraine: 'On February 23rd, me and my girlfriend we had been to the countryside and stopped to have a snack. We could easily see the planes flying over. There were several of them, one after the other. They flew fast and low. I realised that something was wrong. The rumours about war had been going round in our quarters for several months now, some people had been leaving...'

Kharkiv, Ukraine: 'We first felt something significant was afoot on the evening of February 23rd. I was driving towards a petrol station, and the number of cars queueing there amazed me. The people looked tense and kept filling their tanks to the full. So, I did the same. At night I listened to Zelensky's desperate appeal to the Russian people, still I failed to take onboard the scale of what was going on.'

The Russian-Ukrainian border: 'In the morning of February 23rd our unit commander had us lined up and said: "In five days' time you'll be home. The Ukrainians won't fight to defend their oligarchs." Prior to that, we'd lived for a month in tents. Now our trucks joined a column of equipment on the road, and that was how we spent the ensuing 24 hours. It was freezing, getting really cold and we were so sleepy... We didn't want anything and we didn't think of anything...'

'A single official order was ever pinned to the notice board. They instructed us orally – we were on a march now, and we to go forward. Where to, for what? But our army doesn't function the way: 'Soldiers, you're off to move forward and capture this and that!" No way. You're sitting around like a blockhead, till the officer sends you an order: "Ahead! Follow this vehicle!" Tens of thousands received an order just like that. It's the army. You can't reply: "Oh no, I won't." You mind isn't engaged at such a moment. The more you think, the madder you get. Army is madness.'

'Till the last we believed there'd be no war. But then you're stuck in a column deployed in a forest somewhere near Kursk – and what's there to do? Say – no, I'm not going anywhere? I was what, going to go home?'

Village of Khoyniky, Belarus. 'In the morning, we set off from our tents... We had no emotions. The only thing we wanted at that point was to get home as soon as possible... After when we'd entered Ukraine, I realised that our army wasn't battle-worthy. We just moved on, bombed all the time. Then we approached Kyiv, and got to a standstill there, yet again. Bombed, of course. That was the entire beginning of war for me, nice and all.'

Belgorod, Russia. 'At 04:50 my mom woke me up, hysterical. "It's war!" We lived in a southern outskirt, on a high-up floor, and our windows were facing the border. I got up and looked through the window. Indeed, it was 04:50 on the clock, and it was February, so it had to be dark but the entire horizon was aflame. I had a clear view of other buildings and of everything on the horizon. As if the sun had risen ahead of time. That was Ukraine burning, Kharkiv burning…'

And here is Ukraine.

Chernihiv: 'We were raised by the sound of explosions nearby, and immediately realised it was war. We started packing hurriedly. But the bombardment was so heavy that we decided to stay indoors. Our friends called and said that the best would be to get to the corridor, or to the bathroom. Other people called and said that we better criss-cross the windows with scotch so's not to be wounded by shards of glass. Then, we pulled the wardrobes towards the windows, and everything else that we could drag…'

Kharkiv: 'We were shaking all over… that was so… unusual… Throughout the day the shelling intensified, we could hear the fighter aircraft flying around. It all was so scary. We ran towards the Metro to hide ourselves. On our way we saw long queues in front of the cash points and food stores where people were buying everything in sight. No one had the slightest idea of what was to follow. The planes kept dropping bombs and it felt like they could drop one on you at any minute. When we'd let ourselves inside the Metro station, there were already lots of people inside, all completely panicked…'

'I rushed to pack some things… All I took with me was a backpack with personal documents. a change of clothes, food, notebook, medicines. With this in hand, I hurried out of the apartment… in the street there were crowds all over – in front of shops, at bus stops. Everyone was agitated. I also panicked and realised that I had not just walk but run away towards Metro… In the course of a day I didn't eat anything. And I didn't want to…'

Chuhuiv, Kharkiv oblast: 'I looked at the horizon and saw something I'd never seen before: the horizon was smouldering – explosions everywhere and plumes of rising smoke, the entire skyline was on fire. It filled me with terror and a sense of all-enveloping war. 'My life as if has started anew today. I have nothing else to add…'

Sumy: 'On the evening of the 23rd, I was privately warned by the servicemen that war would start in the morning of the 24th but I took it with a pinch of salt.

Nevertheless, a sense of danger was in the air, a feeling that something terrible was round the corner – after all, Sumy Oblast is on the border. And so, I spent a sleepless night, constantly checking up on the news on my mobile. My TV was tuned to the Russian channel. Thus, I learnt about the beginning of the war directly from Putin…

Nizhin, Sumy oblast: 'It was so strange when I went out: some people rushing towards the supermarkets, the cars speeding up and down, here and there. Amazingly the public transport operated, so without any trouble I got to my place of work – side-by-side with a military base. Over there, all was in an even greater state of commotion: trucks shuttling back and forth, armoured vehicles everywhere, also, crowds of soldiers, and officers, clad in helmets and body armour… In the office we received an instruction to pack up the most valuables documents and transfer them to the basement. We did it all very quickly because we realised that the neighbouring base was very likely to become a target for an air strike. That was how I'd spent the first day of invasion. It was the longest day for me…'

Kyiv:
   'I was hiding all day long in the corridor inside the flat. By the evening there appeared information that the Russian army was approaching Kyiv. I lived in the left bank so in order to leave Kyiv for anywhere in the west of the country, one had to cross one of the bridges towards the right bank. From day one, there were roadblocks and huge jams there. I knew that if their army did come close, I would never be able to leave Kyiv. So, I called my parents to say a final goodbye – I thought I would never see them again.'

'I spent the first week in Kyiv. All this got merged in my mind into one hazy day. We never slept properly then. During the night, we took turns to be awake for three hours – to stay on top of the news and wake everybody up in case of an emergency. Yet one couldn't sleep anyway, for the house kept trembling. it's only now that I realise that it was air defence working. On the first night their powerful thuds had been virtually five minutes apart. I still cannot believe that I've lived through it all. I think the people who stayed in Kyiv have really showed their mettle. If I stayed there for more than a week, I'd go mad. But my parents didn't want to leave, simply didn't want to abandon their flat. They said: "If it's meant to be, we'll die. You can't escape your destiny".'

'Originally, I'm from Donbas. I was lucky to have escaped the war in 2014. We'd managed to get out just a couple of days before Russians started bombing everything. So I didn't know some things. But my relatives who stayed there learnt quite well to tell the difference between the sounds of planes arriving or leaving, types of shooting going on, and from which range. I remember while telephoning there they patiently explained to me all those things. And I thought: would I have to learn it all too? And now the people in Kyiv can decipher the lot, no problem.'

Now back to Russia. There was one inquisitive Muscovite: 'I was shocked by everything that was happening... Closer to lunch I decided: I need to go to downtown and see – what are people doing, how are they reacting? I walked along the central streets – I didn't see anything "like that". Everything was as usual. Then I went out onto the main thoroughfare – Gorky Street. Nothing! Someone was walking with a briefcase on business. Someone stopped near the shop windows – looking at some shoes. A pensioner was walking his dog... On Pushkin Square, near the monument to the poet, only pigeons were playing around... And some women were sitting in the windows of the cafe, sipping something from their glasses, calmly talking... This can't be! I need to go further – to the Red Square. It is the most important one in Russia: the Kremlin is there, all life is there! Something must definitely be happening in it! In five minutes I got there. No one! The huge Red Square was empty! The great country of Russia did not care at all what it was doing to its neighbour...

* * *

There appeared first official notices.

05:45 a.m. 'The territory of Ukraine is under massive missile strikes. Russia has targeted centres of military management, airfields, armaments depots in Kyiv, Kharkiv, Dnipro-city. The explosion could be heard in the eastern boroughs of the Ukrainian capital and the outskirts: Vasylkiv, Brovary and Boryspil.'

Social media confirmed that resounding explosions could be heard near Boryspil Airport.

I started receiving first calls, for some reason from those living on the Left Bank. It turned out that starting from six in the morning the streets over there had been chock-a-bloc with cars. The bridges over the Dnipro and the areas on their approaches tuned into one huge traffic jam. Everyone rushed out toward the Right Bank. The fear was that the Russkies would destroy the bridges, thus closing a way out.

Just then Liubchik called, her voice trembling with fear:

'It's complete horror here, on the Left Bank. Some dreadful detonation could be heard from the side of Boryspil. They 're already saying it's all ablaze over there!'

'Wait a minute...' I tried to put in a word in the edgeways but she'd have none of it.

'That's it! We are packing. Dad is yelling that if they hit the bridges we'll be cut off.'

True enough, after the initial scare of windowpanes rattling and the car alarms wailing in the streets and courtyards, some Kyiv residents hurriedly started packing the essentials into their cars, eager to take their families out. Straight away, queues appeared by the petrol stations and the cash points.

The Right-Bank-streets started being clogged with cars, too, jams everywhere.

05:50 a.m. The TV showed prospekt Peremoha in the direction of the exit from the city to the west.[187] All one could make out was a long line of red rear lights. Four lines of traffic were crawling forward. In some places, they even clogged the pavements. People were not simply leaving; it was a mass exodus. Good grist to the Russian propaganda mill. Goodness gracious, people were about to be 'liberated' but, instead, they skedaddled out. On the other hand, those propaganda hacks would be able to explain even this fact away...

Enormous queues not only on the westward motorway (towards Zhytomyr) but heading south too (towards Odesa). The atmosphere thickened as tempers started flaring. Police were urging the drivers of damaged cars to have them quickly pulled to the side of the road to free the evacuation route.

What amazed me was the speed with which some people got ready to leave. Less than an hour– and that was it, already on the way. How did it come about? Perhaps someone wasn't asleep and saw the president's address, and right away got wise to the situation? Or did they get it on the 'grapevine' straight from the intelligence's mouth? Or possibly, the shock from the missile strikes was so overwhelming that they got ready to leave ASAP, leaving with only min-imal baggage? Some must have managed to do it in a space of mere minutes – grabbed the essentials, the kids and raced towards their cars... They were leaving behind their flats and houses, only to go away, away. Away...

The incredible had happened. Kyiv got off as one and headed west and south. No one issued any instructions, any advice... It must have been taken onboard intuitively: a dangerous treacherous enemy was at the gate, there

....

[187]   Proskept Peremoha (Victory Avenue): the main thoroughfare connecting with the Kyiv-Zhytomir-Lviv motorway, which with its extension to Chop runs to the country's western border.

would be no way to live normally under occupation, so there was only one
way to follow…

In a word, everyone was either on the way already, or busy packing hastily…

To leave or not to leave wasn't something that we had ever discussed with
mum. Supposing, we'd decide to leave – to where? Besides, it would mean access
to some hefty money. Also this: to leave – how? We should've left the day before
by train. One could only imagine what was going on at train stations. To leave
as a 'ticketless' passenger, at that point, required real courage.

Mum let herself into my room:

'What horror! What would your late dad have to say about it all?'

I didn't answer. At times I thought – he'd been lucky to have been spared this
nightmare. He'd been mowed down by the ghastly disease two years previously.
But if he'd survived, this war would've done for him.

Alas, but he'd been an idealist. He was convinced that we could and should
co-exist peacefully with Russia, seeing as she was powerful. Even after 2014,
he kept hoping that democratic changes would take place over there, and…

'And then – what?' mum would ask him. 'They'll give back all they've appropriated, innit?'

Dad remained silent. Perhaps he was coming to realise that his idealistic
hopes were unfeasible? Who could tell…

Finally, mum said:

'Perhaps, you and Alla should also leave, eh?'

'And you?'

'Not me. This is my place. Granny's here, too. But you – you're young. What
if you screw up your life this way?'

'No. I'm staying.'

I said nothing else. I thought: *I want this experience in my life.* I didn't know
why, but it felt important for me. That was the word – important.

I cast my gaze towards mum. I had a sense that she, by some innermost
instinct, was also aware that I *needed* this…

∗ ∗ ∗

Taras called with his news.

His Olga was packing, about to leave, urging him to go along. She didn't just
ask, she was adamant. Taras, meanwhile, refused point blank.

'I want to see it all with my own eyes. The defence of the city. But even
if they do get in, I want to see and live through it, too. This is a unique life
experience!'

'Get lost, you and your life experience,' Olga wailed in the telephone. 'Can't you see what's going on? They are serious, they're bombing us, as if it were the Second World War! Even those who believed in invasion thought it would be just tanks and armoured vehicles, no missiles, no rocket horror! Can't you get it? Idiot! Incorrigible… You'll be caught, and then… Not enough for you to learn what they're doing in Donbas with those who are pro-Ukraine?'

My God, she was sobbing by then.

'If it gets extreme,' Taras cut her short, 'I would always be capable of breaking loose. Through vegetable patches, wastelands, and village tracts… It's not possible there won't be some loophole somewhere.'

Long story short, it all ended up a proper row. At the end, Olga told Taras that she never wanted to see him again. Well, must've been in the heat of the argument…

Then Alla called:

'You leaving?'

'No.'

'So, I won't either.'

Mum increased the volume of the sound on TV. The news was gushing forward non-stop…

05:55 a.m. Following air strikes and the use of artillery to soften up our positions, the RF troops crossed the border near Kharkiv. Enormously long columns of war vehicles started rolling forward.

06:00 a.m. Those Russians that passed the Crimean checkpoints proceeded in two directions: towards Kherson and Melitopol. They bypassed the Ukrainian positions and, where possible, moved in on our army. Our guys, when they could break out, retreated in the same two directions: via Antonivka Road Bridge towards Kherson, and to Melitopol.

06:28 a.m. The tanks continued pouring out of Crimea. Many-kilometre-long columns of Russian troops went through the checkpoint on the Ukrainian border with Belarus.

On TV screen, the Mayor of Kharkiv Terekhov was choosing his words with care: 'Dear residents of Kharkiv! Today I ask you to stay indoors. Due to the new distressing circumstances, schools, kindergartens, and other facilities will stay closed today, until further notice. However, public transport operates as normal.'

But the Mayor of Kyiv Klitchko was decisive: 'Dear Kyivites! Here, in Kyiv, we can also hear the bombs roar. Our worst enemy now is panic. Let's remain in control of ourselves! If you're not an employee of critical infrastructure or services, stay in. The city government is in place. We are busy ensuring

continuity of the city's functioning. We hold the fort! We must hold on!'[188] He
advised the city residents to put together their IDs and other documents, also
bare essentials, and keep them handy.

After six o'clock Zelensky was back in his office after the National Security and
Defence Council meeting to join his closest colleagues. The president pulled out
his iPhone, scrolled down to the number he needed and activated the speaker
mode. At the other end answered the voice of Great Britain's Prime Minister
Boris Johnson. Even if London was two hours behind, he was already on the
job.

'Boris, we shall fight! Boris, we shall never surrender!' cried out Zelensky.

The British prime minister vigorously assured him of unconditional support
for the Ukrainian people – they had been on good terms ever since Johnson's
first visit to Kyiv; they even took the liberty of contacting one other by mobile,
bypassing secure channels.

Afterwards, the president did switch over to the secure connection: he called
US President Biden. Zelensky was distressed. He was asking Biden to urgently
get in touch with other world leaders and jointly convince Putin 'to switch it
all off'! He also asked for intelligence to be made available in its entirety. 'We
shall fight! We shall defend ourselves! We will be able to hold the line! But we
do need your support...'[189]

The very next thing he did was get behind his desk and write the text of his
video address to Ukrainians.

At 06:42 a.m. this emergency appeal went live. Zelensky was in a civilian
suit and white shirt, with no tie, his eyes bloodshot – perhaps, he hadn't even
slept that night.

'Today, in the morning, President Putin announced a "special military operation" in Donbas. Russia has landed strikes on our military infrastructure,
border guards and border troops. Explosions could be heard in many Ukrainian
cities. We are introducing a state of martial law across the entire territory of
our state. A minute ago, I spoke with President Biden. The United States have
already started bringing together international support. What's required from
you today, from everyone, is calm. If possible, stay at home. We are working.
The army is working, as is Ukraine's entire security sector. Ongoing communication with you will be taken care of by me, the NSDC and the cabinet of
ministers. I will get in touch again shortly. No panicking. We are strong. We

[188]   Liga.net, 24 February 2023, https://news.liga.net/ua/politics/news/kak-nachinal-
as-bolshaya-voyna-hronika-liganet-ot-24-fevralya-2022-goda (accessed 01. 07. 2025).

[189]   UP, 5 September 2022, https://www.pravda.com.ua/articles/2022/09/5/7366059/
(accessed 01. 07. 2025).

are ready for anything. We shall win over everyone, for we are Ukraine. Glory to Ukraine!'[190]

The address was concise, only one minute and seven seconds long…

Then followed a string of telephone conversations with other world leaders. First of all, Zelensky dialled Macron; at the time, France was presiding over the EU.

'They are on the approaches to Kyiv. We, in Kyiv, we are fighting, Emmanuel! They are spreading all over: towards Kyiv and Odesa, they've sprung from Belarus! And Ukraine is fighting them off its territory! We could never imagine it! It isn't like it was in 2014. It's much bigger…'

'So, total war…' was all Macron could add.

Zelensky urged him to talk to Putin and forcibly emphasised the need for an anti-war coalition.[191]

To be put in action, the president's decree on martial law had to be approved by the Rada. Things simply couldn't progress in an orderly fashion, given the state of overall confusion that reigned on the morning of February 24th. Fearing that the governmental quarters may be bombed, the deputies turned to their party chatrooms trying to arrange that the session would be shifted from the regular assembly hall to a chamber under the monument to Mother Ukraine. They started pitching up there, in tracksuits and carrying holdalls – 'we are to be evacuated'.

Arakhamia: 'First we planned to assemble on alternative premises and vote by show of hands. We practically needed to run just one vote – on a state of martial law. Then we decided to pop into the regular session hall, quickly vote and disperse. I wrote to everyone: "The task is for everyone to survive. Await further instructions through the chatroom." And that was that. No one knew what would come next, and how. We realised that the parliament had to stay functioning, which meant 226 votes across the entire body. That is, if someone got killed or captured, we still could ensure a quorum elsewhere. Yet we didn't know where that "elsewhere" would be tomorrow – perhaps in Uzhhorod, or Lviv, or Odesa, no one could tell. We didn't know if the communication systems would still be there. That is to say, if TV and radio had been cut off, disinformation would start spreading like fire over Telegram channels. Tymoshenko wisely suggested that we signal to all regions that the central power

---

[190]   24 February 2022 https://www.youtube.com/watch?v=Peq96VbpvqI (accessed 01. 07. 2025).

[191]   Liga.net, 8 September 2022, https://news.liga.net/ua/politics/news/my-srajaem-sya-v-kieve-emmanyuel-voyna-totalnaya-zvonok-zelenskogo-makronu-24-fevralya (accessed 01. 07. 2025).

is functioning and in control of the situation.[192] "The country has to see that the authorities are in place and everything is functioning!" Yet everyone was jittery, the situation was very bad...'[193]

Stefanchuk[194]: 'We decided that after all we should assemble in the building of the Verkhovna Rada at 5 Hrushevsky Street.'[195] This was the correct decision for had the session been broadcast from an alternative auditorium, Russian propaganda would have made use of this fact to allege that the Ukrainian authorities had already fled the capital.

People's deputies headed towards Hrushevsky Street, increasingly crowded. Many were frightened – not only the deputies but the administration personnel, too – after all, no one knew what was about to happen. There were spontaneous debates on whether to evacuate the parliament and thus ensure the country's vital functions. The opponents of this move insisted that it would be a clear signal for everyone to take flight from Kyiv: 'We must stay here to show our determination, that we have no intention to surrender Kyiv!'

* * *

I called my granny, and on hearing my voice she burst out singing:

The date was June, twenty second,
In the morning, precisely at four –
We were told that Kyiv'd been bombed
That was the start of the war.[196]
'Granny, how are you?'
But she just carried on:

....

[192]   **Yulia Tymoshenko**: leader of the Batkivshchyna (Motherland) political party and faction in the VR (pro-European); 'the lady with a plait': an iconic figure in the Orange Revolution of 2004-2005; the first woman to be twice appointed prime minister; ran three times for president.

[193]   UP, 23 February 2024, https://www.pravda.com.ua/cdn/cd1/reconstruction/a6.html (accessed 01. 07. 2025).

[194]   Ruslan Stefanchuk – speaker of the Verkhovna Rada (since October 2021)

[195]   UP, 8 March 2024, https://www.pravda.com.ua/podcasts/63f90cc807994/2024/03/8/7397132/ (accessed 01. 07. 2025).

[196]   Highly popular song composed in the first week of the war between Nazi Germany and the Soviet Union. It spread throughout the country in no time. The main theme is that Kyiv was bombed at four o'clock in the morning. The plot of the song was repeated in full during Putin's own attack on Ukraine.

The war – it was dawn, when it started,
So as to kill one and all.
The parents were sleeping, their children were sleeping
That's when the bombs started to fall.

'Gran, still, how are you?' I wasn't going to give up.

'Kyiv was last bombed 81 years ago. And now this… The Moscow leader acts totally in accordance with this song. And again, in early morning. When everyone was asleep… Innit symbolic? Who's that who likes mischief in the morning?'

'Gran, shall I take you some place? Taras has someone in the countryside… Us too, we've got some family there, a distant one but still…'

'Over my dead body…'

I hurriedly got back to my computer where some military expert was already busy explaining reasons for the morning bombing. It turned out, the first reason was unexpectedness. Moreover, the first day always required a most elaborate planning. This day was decisive. The other reason was the number of casualties. Everyone was asleep, so it was imperative to kill as many as possible. Besides, the most battle-worthy air defence personnel on duty would have been exhausted from the day before, so relaxing. The third reason was psychology: it was time to break the spirit, to thwart the will to resist. And a very specific reason was symbolic: that 'precisely at four' bit, give or take half an hour. Putin had already been already sussed as having a penchant for symbolism – or even numerology, when it concerned military operations. Say, in Georgia it had all happened on 08.08.2008 – symbolic or what?

07:00 a.m. Sirens piped up; one couldn't hear them before. Why there was a lag – I wasn't sure. Perhaps, it was just our district.

07:01 a.m. Hostomel. The enemy delivered a strike at the National Guards unit with a winged missile, which, to tell the truth, flopped near a residential block.

07:02 a.m. The situation in Western Ukraine described on social media. Hostile attacks registered there as well: a TV tower blown up in Lutsk, air raid alerts in Kolomyia, airstrikes at the airfield in Ivano-Frankivsk and a helicopter detachment in Lviv Oblast.

07:03 a.m. Appeal by Defence Minister Reznikov: 'Dear Ukrainians! The enemy is now intensively bombing our forces in the east, along with military centres and airfields in other regions. Our army is doing their utmost to defend you and to deprive the aggressor of a chance to break through. The best way you can help now is to remain calm and keep believing in the AFU.'[197]

....

[197] Radio Svoboda, 24 February 2022, https://www.radiosvoboda.org/a/news-reznikov-

07:04 a.m. Yermak telephoned Arestovych,[198] with whom the President's office had parted a month previously, and suggested that he should return. Arestovych was a far-from- straightforward person but the Office decided that his return at that point was advisable.

07:25 a.m. Kharkiv deafened by the non-stopping boom of explosions.

07:30 a.m. Information streaked in from Donetsk Oblast under Ukrainian control: people were loading up their cars and leaving, queues at petrol stations. Explosions could be heard in Mariupol, lots of locals had left the city, yet there was no chaos in the streets. The internet and mobile networks operated as normal.

The picture in Kyiv was a mixed one: some people had just woken up, traffic jams were sporadic – some routes were navigable, yet endless queues had formed at petrol stations. Explosions could be heard only irregularly, and many people were clearly not yet aware of what was happening. The metro and taxis were operating as normal. Banks and shops were open, and one could pay with plastic.

07:30 a.m. Security services confirmed that Antonov airfield (Hostomel, 10 kilometres from the capital city), just as the Americans had warned, was selected as a springboard for capturing Kyiv. It had a unique landing strip suitable for receiving most heavy-duty aircraft, that is why the Russians had planned to capture it, within several hours, with the help of helicopter-delivered strike force. After that, they would be able to land freight air carries bringing in thousands of troops. In this way, it would become a toehold for springing assault troops against the government quarters. Similar plans for overpowering foreign capitals had been tested in Prague in 1968, and Kabul in 1979 – both times, successfully.

The military command was aware that the Russian operation was aimed at Hostomel. This would enable their lightening-speed capture of Kyiv and the Russian flag over the President's Office within the third day of attack at the latest. However, if landing were to be delayed, the plan was going haywire from the off. At the moment, our guys had blocked the runway with special vehicles. They were taking their positions, getting ready to shoot down freight aircraft, using air defence systems and portable complexes.

What our top brass had been so reluctant to see – intervention was in full swing via the Chornobyl Exclusion Zone. It really was a short-cut towards Kyiv!

....

zvernennia-napad/31719795.html (accessed 03.07.2025)

[198]   **Oleksii Arestovych:** assisted the office of the President of Ukraine as communications adviser from February 2022 to January 2023.

The same in Chernihiv Oblast: about 30 battle units, 30 thousand altogether, crossed the border from three directions to press forward towards the capital of the oblast. This contingent's operational task was the same: first capture the oblast centre, then blast towards Kyiv. Combined with the manpower landing at Hostomel air base, they expected to pincer Kyiv…

It was impossible to even watch the news anymore: massive destruction, blood, people moaning… Everyone cursing that deranged leader and that crazy people…

* * *

Spyridon and Bolik called – together with their Teutonic lasses, they were fighting their way towards Dachna Bus Station on Peremoha prospekt, and then off to Berdychiv (Zhytomir oblast) where Spyridon had some relatives. He already had been in touch with them by phone – they were ready to receive their complete hangout as they lived in a voluminous private house. He asked if Taras and I would like to leave with them? If the answer was yes, we had maximum half an hour to pack.

Meanwhile Liubchik left with her parents towards some distant summer house.

Me and mum, we had neither a summer house, nor close relatives in the country, so we decided to stay put.

Taras, on the other hand, had relations all over, but he had announced his decision to me before. He wanted to stay. Alla was staying too. Whatever the reason, I felt warmer at heart – come what may, it would be easier to navigate this chaos if there were three of us.

Alla called again:

'You shouldn't condemn anyone, Stinger. Those who've left towards their safe destinations… Everyone has their reasons: family, children, parents… Plans, come to think of it…'

'Far be it from me to condemn…'

About eight in the morning, people's deputies started filing into the session hall of the Verkhovna Rada: some in tracksuits, women with no makeup, all carrying 'emergency suitcases' to accommodate emergency circumstances. Danilov arrived from the President's Office carrying with him the NSDC's decision on introducing martial law. 'The audience was tense, atmosphere electrified since a lot of decisions had to be made at the very beginning of the war. Someone wanted to leg it, others were eager to take out the savings they had…'

08:00 a.m. Russian Special Task Force base near Mozyr, Belarus, was getting ready to depart. One of the commanders goes around the place with a camera taking a video, which he titles: 'Souvenir for descendants.' Moscow time was 09:00 a.m. Special Task hadn't been raised at three in the morning like the other troops – they had to be properly rested and ready to perform an extremely important mission. They climbed into covered trucks and headed to the military airfield in Mozyr.

08:01 a.m. The assembly hall at the Rada. Speaker Stefanchuk appeared in the presidium area and announced that the only item on the agenda was introduction of martial law.

This decree (No 65/2022), like the Decree on the State of Emergency discussed a day earlier, was presented by Danilov: 'Today, at 05:30 in the morning the president convened a session of the National Security and Defence Council of Ukraine which approved the emergency measure to introduce a state of martial law in our country. I urge you to support this decision, this presidential decree; we desperately need it. Our army is fighting, resisting the onslaught; everyone is in their place, we won't yield our country to anyone. It is our country, and we shall defend it!'[199]

There was applause from the deputies. Three hundred deputies voted in favour, yet only 10 hours previously, when voting on a state of emergency, the votes 'pro' had counted 335. Most likely, the drain to the west had already started. Among the deputies supporting the decision were also those representing the pro-Russian Opposition Platform – for Life. They looked visibly shocked by the turn of events and acted reserved and inconspicuous. Stefanchuk: 'It's hard for me to assess their state of mind, but they showed up, voted in favour, and looked flabbergasted by the developments. I wouldn't want to be in their place on that day.'

Great, 300 deputies, but what about the rest? After all, they were 420… Little by little all became clear. The total number of those absent was as many as 113. Some had left abroad in advance. Some were in transit – either to some foreign destinations, or to the western regions of the country: to sit out this stage and get their bearings… Some may well have been somewhere nearby, at their dachas near Kyiv.

There was this important question, too: how to ensure the parliament's continued operation under any circumstances, for example, if Kyiv was besieged. There was an explicit need for some alternative venues where they could bypass the Rada system when voting.

....

[199]   UP, 8 March 2024, https://www.pravda.com.ua/podcasts/63f90cc807994/2024/03/8/7397132/ (accessed 03.07.2025)

On the whole, the session was completed in good time. Unlike the experience with voting on a state of emergency that had taken the whole day, the decision on martial law was approved in 10 minutes. Stefanchuk summarised it all thus: 'Dear colleagues, all people's deputies shall stay in Kyiv. I appeal to you to make sure that in case of need we shall be able to convene straight away in a specified place at the appointed time and continue working for the benefit of the Ukrainian state. Those who leave are traitors. Dear colleagues! Glory to Ukraine!'[200]

Stefanchuk: 'After that I and my colleagues, the vice speakers, agreed to disperse: I was to stay in Kyiv, and they all went to different places. This was necessary to ensure the Supreme Rada's ability to operate.'[201] The vice speakers were issued special folders specifying a sequence of their actions in case of Stefanchuk's death.

08:00 a.m. Social media were describing the response of the population: 'The situation in Kherson thickens. Since the early morning, the thunder of explosions, the wailing of sirens. The city's in a state of mild panic. Queues have formed by the ATMs, and the petrol stations too. Exit roads from the city are choc-a-bloc. The airport's on fire.'

Long queues at ATMs across the country...

08:40 a.m. President Zelensky on social media: 'I spoke with the USA president and also Olaf Scholz of Germany, Ursula von der Leyen, president of the EC, and Andrzej Duda as well as Boris Johnson. I am appealing to everyone to stop Putin immediately, to stop the war.'[202]

08:40 a.m. The mayor of Kharkiv: 'Shortly, within more or less half an hour, we shall open all sanctuaries and bomb shelters – in residential blocks, at infrastructure facilities. If the situation worsens, you are free to use them. I am appealing to the residents of Kharkiv yet again: please stay indoors and, if possible, stay calm.'[203]

08:45 a.m. The first briefing at the President's Office. Zelensky himself attended at the beginning, only for several minutes: 'I am constantly in com-

[200]　UP, 8 March 2024, https://www.pravda.com.ua/podcasts/63f90cc807994/2024/03/8/7397132/ (accessed 03.07.2025).

[201]　UP, 8 March 2024, https://www.pravda.com.ua/podcasts/63f90cc807994/2024/03/8/7397132/ (accessed 03.07.2025).

[202]　Liga.net, 24 February 2023, https://news.liga.net/ua/politics/news/kak-nachinal-as-bolshaya-voyna-hronika-liganet-ot-24-fevralya-2022-goda (accessed 03.07.2025).

[203]　Liga.net, 24 February 2023. https://news.liga.net/ua/politics/news/kak-nachinal-as-bolshaya-voyna-hronika-liganet-ot-24-fevralya-2022-goda (accessed 03.07.2025).

munication with you…' After that the briefing was chaired by Podolyak and Arestovych [204]

09:00 a.m. AFU Commander-in-Chief Zaluzhnyi: 'Exercising their right to self-defence under Article 51 of the Charter of the United Nations, the defence forces of our country are giving a fitting rebuff to the enemy's attempts to break through the borders. The situation is under control. The Russian troops are sustaining losses. We are on our own land, which we shall never surrender. Together for victory!' [205]

After the Rada voted on the state pf martial law, it was agreed that the president would meet the leaders of factions. Shortly before nine, they headed for the president's office.…

By that time, the building at Bankova Street was probably the busiest in the entire governmental quarter. No one – be it the ministers, deputies, or journalists – had yet realised the danger of being in the vicinity of Object No 1. Reznikov: 'At that time, in the first hours, there still wasn't a proper understanding of the need for security… That we shouldn't all gather in the same building at once. Or we should get together on some protected premises. However, that was something that dawned on us all during the course of the day.' [206] Anyway, the military were already busy carrying bags with sand; they used the bags to line windows and built fire points.

09:00 a.m. From the president's office at Bankova Danilov ran the first teleconference with all heads of oblast administrations who, from that moment on, became heads of military administrations.

10:00 a.m. In an assembly chamber within the President's Office, Arakhamia updated the faction heads on the army reports of new missile attacks and the situation at the fronts. He tried to spice it up with obscene words and even tried to wisecrack…

Those present acted tense but collected. The president entered the session, along with the Prime Minister Shmyhal and the Head of Office Yermak. The president told the parliamentarians that the main challenge of the moment was to maintain legitimacy of power and asked them to proceed from scratch: 'We don't have opponents at this point. We have one enemy – Putin. We should

....

[204] **Mykhailo Podolyak**: chief communications adviser to the presidential office Head (Yermak).

[205] Horyn info, 24 February 2022, https://horyn.info/news/prezydent-ukrayiny-vid-dav-nakaz-nanosyty-maksymalnyh-vtrat-zagarbnykam/ (accessed 03.07.2025)

[206] UP, 8 March 2024, https://www.pravda.com.ua/podcasts/63f90cc807994/2024/03/8/7397132/ (accessed 03.07.2025)

forget our past disputes and act as a team, in a concerted way...'[207] He received unequivocal support. Then he said that he knew where the strikes had landed. The next thing to do was to mobilise all army men and all paramilitary forces – in fact, the entire defence sector, in order to form some acceptable front lines. He asked the premier to oversee logistics while he was dealing with international affairs: it was imperative to call everyone, put everyone in the picture, ask for help, etcetera.

His proposal was unilaterally approved: 'We'll help with whatever we can. Count us in!' After which they all went to be issued with private weapons. They had no doubts that the weapons would come in handy when defending Kyiv.[208]

Another point of critical importance. The head of the Supreme Rada was, *de jure,* to become an acting president, should something happen to the president himself. Therefore, the Rada passed a decision that Stefanchuk and the president shouldn't be present in the same place at once. Zelensky approved of the decision for Stefanchuk to leave for Khmelnitsky, an oblast capital in Western Ukraine.

Stefanchuk: 'As we were about to depart, I was instructed yet again to leave Kyiv. When alone with the president, I told him: "During martial law I am ready to carry out any decision of yours apart from this one. I will move out of the governmental quarter but will stay within 10 minutes' drive of the centre".'[209] From that moment on, he was on a merry-go-round – moving around, constantly changing his lodgings, but remaining in the city, so as to be there if needed.

Suddenly, at about thirtieth minute of the meeting, the head of presidential security burst into the room. Security services had just learnt that the Russian hit squad were already active in Pechersk,[210] only a few blocks away from the President's Office. Moreover, there was a real danger that a missile strike would target the office itself. In an instant heavily armed officers from the State Security Department steered the president, practically manhandling him, out of the room and into a 'safe location' (it later transpired, a secure bunker). The people's deputies and the journalists, urgently summoned to the Office, were asked to leave the premises, and to make haste leaving the President's Office.

[207]   UP, 5 September 2022, https://www.pravda.com.ua/articles/2022/09/5/7366059/ (accessed 03.07.2025)

[208]   UP, 8 March 2024, https://www.pravda.com.ua/podcasts/63f90cc807994/2024/03/8/7397132/ (accessed 03.07.2025)

[209]   UP, 8 March 2024, https://www.pravda.com.ua/podcasts/63f90cc807994/2024/03/8/7397132/ (accessed 03.07.2025).

[210]   **Pechersk**: a district of Kyiv that contains governmental quarter

Soon after, the deputies received a message from their faction leaders: "At the Main Directorate of Police on Vladimirskaya Street you may obtain weapons." The deputies rushed there: police officers were indeed distributing machine guns and pistols after only a cursory check of passport and deputy's certificate. Very soon the pistols began to run out; it was decided that they would now be given only to women deputies.

There started appearing first recorded witness accounts of the Russian intervention. The video dated February 24th, 04:00 a.m., showed the Ukrainian checkpoint in Kalanchak. Even though the previous day Russia had closed it down, it showed the administrative border being crossed from the Crimean side by some civilians with cases. At the same time the Ukrainian border guards were looking elsewhere, clearly distracted by something. Perhaps, by the sight of a large formation of the Russian tanks approaching their checkpoint?

Another video, 04:02 a.m., entitled 'Crimea! Kalanchak outpost under fire. The Ukrainian military and peaceful residents in flight.' Concurrently came the news that all three checkpoints on the Crimean isthmus – Chongar, Kalanchak and Chaplinka – were crossed simultaneously.

I tore myself away from the news, overcome with a new sensation. A kind of morbid amazement persisted: had it really happened? Was this madness conceivable in our day and time? It had been expected... disbelieved... and yet it had happened...

At the same time, a kind of calm had descended, all anxiety of the previous months had finally evaporated. It wasn't 'if it did happen' anymore, but 'it had happened.' It was 'here and now'. Everything had come to a head...

After a while, anxiety returned. The sense of reality was swamping me. Ah well, it had to be accepted: it was war, and it was incontrovertible...

Would our guys withstand the blast? Or, as the Americans had insisted – 72 hours, and there wouldn't be any Kyiv anymore? And after some 10-14 days, and nothing would be left of our city, our country and any of us?

Somewhere in the future we would be asking each other this fundamental question: had we prepared properly? Had we done all we should have? But those were the questions for the future...

But at this point in time... Perhaps the army, unlike the civilians, did read the situation accurately and had done something in advance?

We didn't have all that many close relatives but they all called. And everyone invited us over: 'Give it a day or two, the Russian will be in Kyiv. Don't you see what it means? Constant shelling ... Life in a basement... Death...'

* * *

'Since we're staying put, let's not waste time,' mum sounded determined. 'Let's pack "emergency necessities" – documents, medical supplies. What else is essential? What if we have to flee from the flat at once, at least we won't do it empty-handed...'

I started feverishly packing my backpack, stuffing in some stupid things. I kept pulling them out and packing them all over again. It all felt wrong... Ah well, the most important were the papers and the pills... What else, though? I'd read it on some site what one should pack ahead of everything else but for the life of me, couldn't remember any of it...

Then there was this nagging feeling that so much had to be done in those first days, that I shouldn't forget anything. Yet I couldn't shake off the feeling that I was watching myself as if from outside.

My God, how funny and incomprehensible it felt... People all over the country must've been asking the same questions: 'Where are you?'; 'How are you?'; 'Been bombed?'; 'Hit or miss?'; 'You alive?'; 'Are you leaving?'; 'Why not?'

The Russian aggression did bring back the memories of a blitzkrieg. TV informed that following the massive missile strikes all over the country, the Russian troops had started moving in from four sides: Belarus, Russia, Crimea, and Donbas. Their progress was fast. In order to capture Kyiv, they would also proceed from several directions: aiming at Brovary from Chernihiv; from Sumy; and advancing from the Belarusian border – via the Chornobyl Zone and the Zhytomyr Highway – they'd move towards the Odesa route. Thus, Kyiv would be encircled. It couldn't be ruled out that the landing troops from Belarus would be used for taking control over the nuclear power plants in Rivne and Khmelnitskyi.

The non-stop shelling went on. The blasts of explosions came from various regions of the city.

The shock washed over me yet again. The shock from the fact that it wasn't just the ground weapons used, this could've been somehow accepted, albeit with difficulty. The worst was this *bombing*, delivered by aircraft and missiles. Majority of those who believed the invasion probable had imagined tanks. But bombs? At half four in the morning, from the air, just like the fascist Germany? No one could even conceive of anything like it. That would've been pure insanity...

Whoever you asked, everyone was stunned – not by the fact of invasion *per se*, but the way it was going forward. Some even couldn't decide who was worse – bloody Russians or the fascists. There were even those who admitted that the fascists hadn't been so unhinged.

My, oh my. The comparisons like that – pure lunacy.

Perhaps it was the shock talking… For example, 'the Germans had never had missiles like that …'; 'They never were so ferocious, at least to start with… They did wage their war, true… But…'; 'But this… This inexplicable brutality, this overwhelming hatred towards us, from the very first hours…'

I popped out of our flat, rushed downstairs, to the street. I wanted to get at least some idea of what was going on around us.

Putin's ardent dream was taking shape – the city was gripped by panic. The drain from the city before February 24th had been 'child's play'. By that point, the cars were fighting for every patch of the passable road, ruthlessly shoving each another aside, to gain exit. Yet no driver ever popped out to scream about scratches on his fender. By then, other things were dominating everyone's attention.

So, by now it was all proper 'adult stuff'. I read later that that a queue of such length, crawling forward at such snails' pace – from the city centre to the country's western fringes – had never happened before. The cars were idling in the streets and highways for hours, edging forwards by centimetres.

Fu-u-u-u-u-ck!

It was coming from everywhere:
'This is fuck knows what!'
'Bastards!'
'A horde of barbarians!'
'Right you are – it's above anyone's head!'
'They're common scum, that's all!' – these were the most common exchanges.

War – now? Between Russia and Ukraine? Such as Hitler's Germany had unleashed in 1941?

That was the stuff of nightmares.

Insanity…

The Dark Ages…

Bedevilment…

Fascism!

I rushed back home. Ok, fine. Since we weren't leaving, we were to stay here. But the Russkies were moving forward at a breakneck speed! What if our side hadn't prepared properly? What then? Could it mean a siege? And then – God forbid – occupation? What would that be like? In a word – what was to come? And how?

For a hundredth time I was trying to concentrate on what had to be done first, seeing as we'd decided to stay. What if water and electricity supplies became damaged by bombs?

I filled every single vessel we had with water, then had a shower, washed my hair, for really – what if there would be no water?

Mum got round to doing the laundry, for again, what if our water got disconnected?

And if there were no electricity, all we would have left would a battery-operated radio. No internet, no TV. Although, if we had radio, it would be something.

And what about the smartphone? Somehow, I hadn't even got myself a power bank.

I called Taras:

'Most likely, it's too late,' commented Taras but then had an idea: 'Even so, get your ass over to Pochaina,[211] lots of shops over there sell electronic goods. If you do find it anywhere, it's got to be there.'

'No, sweetheart, we first must stock up on foodstuffs,' mum chipped in. 'Besides, your electronic shops are still closed, it's too early. In case of a siege, we must horde some food. Let's run for the supermarket.'

We popped out. Lots of cars on Mezhyhirska Street, this transport artery, zooming forward at an insane speed, but by the time we'd reached the supermarket, the street was already congested. One could only imagine the goings-on in the streets leading to the Zhytomyr and Odesa motorways. The entire city scampered in the directions of Lviv and Odesa.

The sirens continued blaring non-stop. But what else could we do? We carried on to get our food supplies, that was all there was to it.

The queues by the two nearest supermarkets – Silpo and ATB – were not too bad. It took us a mere half an hour to make our way inside. Basically, everything we needed was still available, so we stocked up. The only wrinkle was buying bread – little choice and all stale, baked days before. One couldn't tell whether there would be a new supply.

'Why are we buying so much, mum?'

'We'll make croutons…'

On our way back we could overhear snippets of conversations:

'Did you hear? They say Zelensky did a bunk…'

'Well, I never! To where?'

....

[211]   **Pochaina:** a station on the Kyiv metro. Contains a large number of supermarkets.

'Like everyone else, to Lviv… Russkies announced. I've got the satellite, so am watching ours and the Russkies too…'

'Wait a minute. How do you mean, a bunk? Let's look at it all from the state's point of view. If those bastards – God forbid – get into the city, tomorrow or the day after, what can he to do from here? He's got a country to run. So, he'll do it from somewhere else…'

'They also say that Putin appealed to our army generals: sort of, take the power in your own hands, do away with those druggies and Nazis…'

'He's a complete wanker to blabber like this. As if our generals gonna listen to him… Fat chance!'

On the whole, the situation in the city was complicated and odd in equal measures: some residents were in a hurry to leave, the others roamed the streets, or even shuffled on to a place of work. Some were completely immersed in their own affairs. Visually, anxiety manifested itself only as long queues snaking in front of the ATMs, pharmacies, and food stores. However, those queueing acted calm, behaved amicably, even if many faces looked grim, the eyes alarmed, attentive…

One more thing: everyone around was glued to their phones, eager to learn what and where was going on. How quick were the fuckers moving forward? Where had they got to? What next?

We'd brought purchases to our house.

Our neighbour – that cool businessman – turned out to be truly sagacious. He wasn't just leaving by car; he 'd procured a trailer, too, and was busy loading it up.

'People are funny, if you ask me,' he even clicked his fingers. 'All they can think about is Lviv. As if there aren't any other cities in Ukraine… Take this Ternopil, for instance – a little gem of a city.'

'Perhaps if you live in a capital city…' I did my best to offer something sensible without betraying my amazement over his trailer. 'To find your feet in a city of a hundred thousand… Or even if it's half a million…'

'True enough. But to sweat over something like this now? Lviv will be overwhelmed, overcrowded to a bursting point… Yet Ternopil is beautiful! You did see the reprint of that map in *Bild*? Russia moves in and forms a line – from Belarus in the north to Moldova in the south. And the entire Western Ukraine remains ours. There's no way they'll make it as far as Ternopil. And we'll build a nice bolthole out there…'

He was loading in earnest, probably taking with him all valuables from his flat. We saw the porters carefully carrying across even his home plants, pots, and all…

Back at home I got back to the news...

The biggest fear was this – what if mobile service went down? What, then? Be cut-off completely? Now, that would be real horror.

09:29 a.m. Kharkiv's outskirts had been bombed by *Smerch* self-propelled missiles. A 20-thousand-strong grouping was moving from Russia towards Kharkiv, expecting to take the city within a space of two days.

10:00 a.m. The world leaders announced that a package of harsh sanctions against Russia was about to be implemented.

10:00 a.m. The Russian troops in the south made lightning-quick progress. Apparently, they had already appeared near Nova Kakhovka (on the Dnipro River), having effortlessly covered the distance of 150 kilometres. Other sources alleged it had been taken by the landing troops. A Russian flag was flying over the hydro-electric plant...

Me, I still couldn't get my head round the fact that some people had managed to organise their exit from Kyiv within a couple of hours. Photos and video clips continued showing enormous auto queues on all roads, endless line-ups at petrol stations. Those incredible agglomerations kept growing. As for traffic regulators – they did try to introduce some law and order, true. For all that, it was chaos everywhere.

Yet there were other queues, too, forming by the doors of the call-up points. One could see all kinds of people there: young ones and those advanced in years, boys and girls, moneyed folk, and those of humble means. Many looked stunned by this message from the commissariat's personnel: 'No vacancies left, leave your number, we'll call you.' Army service had momentarily been transformed from a duty to a privilege. In a 'corrupt country', as some western politicians sometimes call Ukraine, people were practically ready to offer bribes to join the AFU.

Reznikov: 'I remember it all in detail: I was told that huge queues had formed at military commissariats and weapon-dispensing centres. That people had started enlisting in the Homeland Defence, that we were running out of sub-machine guns. So I gave an order: bring in more automatics!'[212]

At the same time, they started putting up roadblocks on all roads.

10:40 a.m. News started arriving from Serpent Island.[213] The island had been approached by two vessels of the Russian Black Sea Navy, including its flagship – the cruiser *Moskva*. The aggressor had used an international channel so as to reach our border guards in safety and demand that they surrender: 'I am a Russian

....

[212] UP, 8 March 2024, https://www.pravda.com.ua/podcasts/63f90cc807994/2024/03/8/7397132/ (accessed 03.07.2025).

[213] **Serpent Island**: situated in the Black Sea, 120 km from Odesa.

warship. You are in complete isolation now, and within our shooting range. In case of resistance, you will be destroyed. Your chances of survival are zero. Think about your children, your loved ones who need you, who are waiting for you at home, alive and in full health!'

The reply rang out: 'Russian warship, go fuck yourself!' This phrase would shortly become famous all over the world.[214]

11:00 a.m. A call from a student in a parallel class: '11:00 a.m. Khreshchatyk is practically empty… Rare cars at speed… Shops and cafes are closed…'

11:00 a.m. Belarus, Mozyr airfield. Special Task Russian troops completed loading up into helicopters. The video carried this caption: 'Departure of the main force.' Thirty-four Mi-8 and Ka-52 helicopters took off towards the Belarusian-Ukrainian border, with 200-300 elite landing troops on board. Combat helicopters were paving the way…

And what was happening in the south?

These bitter updates were posted on social media: 'The situation in Kherson is depressing. On the night between February 23rd and 24th, police, security units, National Guards and border guards kept leaving in columns, heading to Mykolaiv and Voznesensk. The exodus goes on. Police precincts are closed. The military commissariat personnel who are still here, go around in civvies. It feels like no one is in charge of defending the city. There are no channels of communication between the local authorities and the local population…'

11:05 a.m. News from Kharkiv: four Russian tanks had been hit and burnt on the perimeter road. Yet, the Russian vanguard first appeared in the city's outskirts by 11:00 a.m. There they were met with fire from the man-portable air defence systems.

Meanwhile a pensioner was spotted on the bridge in Kyiv – fishing, as if nothing had happened. 'Where should I flee to? I'm at home here. How could the world condone it – that a peaceful country, in the heart of Europe, is being torn to shreds?'

Another story: the Mayor of Kyiv Klitchko arrived at a building in Obolon that had been hit by a Russian missile.[215] A very agitated elderly person came running towards him:

....

[214] Graty, 24 September 2022, https://graty.me/chomu-rosiya-ne-hoche-viddati-ta-ta-istoriya-zahisnikiv-ostrova (accessed 03.07.2025).

[215] **Obolon:** a residential district on the Right Bank of the Dnipro river.

'Mister Mayor! Do you see this hole in our building? That's where my flat was. God led me outside, into the courtyard, a couple of minutes prior to the strike. I am homeless now, but elated. I'm alive!'

Klitchko offered him to be evacuated to the west of the country or abroad.

'I'll stay in Kyiv. Only give me weapons…'

* * *

Meanwhile, Taras, in his chatroom, had come across something else. Apparently, Zelensky had been agitated but at the same time trying to stay calm. Later, he described his state of mind at the time: 'Everybody – civil servants, the army – they all look up to you. You are a symbol. You must behave as befits a head of state.'

The information arriving at the President's Office was updated at five-minute intervals – it was getting increasingly threatening and scary. Too much was happening at the same time, what's more – all over. And one had to respond quickly and make prompt decisions. Zelensky was told of a risk of Russian strike groups landing in Kyiv whose sole task would be to capture and assassinate the president and his family. Barricades started appearing around his Office at Bankova, built of any kind of materials. By then, Zelensky's comrades-in-arms were arriving, many with their families. Like the president, they were all issued with body armour and sub-machine guns. Windows were protected with sandbags, personnel were forbidden to use their mobiles, and an electricity-saving regime was introduced. The nearby streets had all been converted into a warren of barricades and roadblocks. Those with urgent business in the 'governmental triangle' were asked a secret password by security.[216]

Security and advisers kept insisting that Zelensky should move to a safe location outside the capital, and eventually, possibly, to the west of the country: 'Volodymyr Oleksandrovych, this isn't just a question of your personal honour. It's a question of the defence of our country. You are a symbol; you are the commander-in-chief. Imagine if something were to happen to you? The morale will collapse straight away. The roads are to be cut off, and getting out of Kyiv will be extremely difficult. The enemy is advancing on several fronts; they have an advantage in manpower. Your office is already a target. It will be hit by air strikes, as well as aimed at by saboteurs. Even your bunker isn't safe enough. They could block it off and use gas. You should be able to stay in command at all times. As for us, the best we'll manage here will be several hours.

------

[216] **Governmental triangle**: colloquial for the governmental quarter containing the Office of the President, the Verkhovna Rada, and the Cabinet of Ministers.

We are finished! There's an option of breaking out but it's risky. All in all, it's not escape we're talking about, but a transfer to a different place where it's safe and you should be able to supervise our defence.' Zelensky answered: 'Would you like to fall out with me? Whatever happens, we stay here.' The defence guys shrugged and left.

The partners also believed paying proper attention to his own security, the president would avoid the risk of creating a vacuum of power. However, Zelensky believed in the exact opposite: if he fled, he would surrender the heart of Ukrainian power to the enemy without fight. And this would bring the entire system into an unavoidable crisis. Also, what would the army at the front feel like if the president of the country just disappeared? He decisively rejected this option. And thus, he never left. Instead, he just stayed in the same bunker into which he'd been taken by security, the same one that'd been built back in the Soviet days.

The chatroom asserted that high-placed Kremlin functionaries, members of the Cabinet of Ministers, the elite of business in Moscow couldn't believe their own eyes. They turned to Lavrov for elucidation – who could've ever advised Putin to act like this? The Foreign Minister, painfully aware that he, himself, had only been informed of the invasion several hours prior to its commencement, and Putin's fixation on the sacredness of certain historic personalities, snapped back in irritation: 'He's got three advisers: Ivan the Terrible, Peter the First and Catherine the Great!'

11:00 a.m. Prime Minister Shmyhal assembled the secure videoconference with members of his government. He announced the already approved decisions: to ensure the manageability of the country, the Cabinet of Ministers was to be divided in two.

The first one was to stay in Kyiv. The second – in case of unexpected developments – while keeping a quorum of 13 ministers, would be empowered to approve the necessary decisions while physically residing elsewhere. The latter group was to depart on the same day, by a special train, to one of the relatively safe western areas. The ministers involved in defence were to stay in Kyiv and join governmental sessions from their various locations: a bunker, or an unknown office, or the friends' place. The other group would be signing in from the west of Ukraine. These measures would ensure stability of the governmental system. Chernyshov was appointed acting chair of the latter group.

11:00 a.m. At a briefing with military personnel, Lukashenko emphasised that Belarusian troops were playing no part in the Russian special operation in Donbas. 'We have no troops there! However, if it becomes necessary for

Belarus and Russia, they will be there.'[217] Yet the news – for the time being, conflicting – started seeping in from other sources, asserting their involvement in the areas adjacent to Ukraine.

11:30 a.m. The head of the Office Yermak received a telephone call from Moscow. When he identified the caller, he was initially beside himself, but after the phone continued to ring insistently, he regained self-control, picked it up, and heard the voice of Kozak, deputy head of the Kremlin administration – who said that the Ukrainians should abide by the ultimatum put forward by the Russian Federation. Yermak deployed a string of fierce expletives and rang off. [This is the Ukrainian patriotic version. Sources report differently: Yermak called Kozak at the RF presidential administration: "What can we do to stop this madness?" "I'm in touch with Arahamia. Talks must begin immediately as a matter of urgency," – replied Kozak. So, apparently there was no theatricality, no one sent anyone to anywhere, and no one slammed down the phone].

11:30 a.m. About 20-25 helicopters landed on the Antonivka Bridge near Kherson. Russian landing troops took up position on this strategic site, an evacuation route not only for the army but civilians as well. Probably, that was why it hadn't been blown up, just as other bridges across the Dnipro River had not been. Had that been done, evacuation would have been impossible. Lots of peaceful residents were trying to break out of the southern areas of Kherson Oblast. The Russian commandos wouldn't let anyone through and execute people by shooting through the forehead.

11:30 a.m. At a briefing President Zelensky called on the population to rise to the defence of Ukraine. 'Everyone who has combat experience and could join the Ukrainian defence forces, should immediately report at a relevant recruitment centre. The Interior Ministry is engaging the veterans, too. We shall issue weapons to anyone who is prepared to defend the country. Get ready to support Ukraine in your cities. We have cut off diplomatic relations with the Russian Federation. From now on, we and Russia are on opposite sides. Citizens of Russia will have to make their personal choice as to where each one of them stands.'

Thus, the principal message was not to think about tomorrow but try and somehow make it through the current day.

It became known that the president had sent to the Supreme Rada the 'Decree on General Mobilisation'. 'This Decree shall come into force after it has

[217] Slovo i dilo, 23 February 2023, https://www.slovoidilo.ua/2023/02/23/info-grafika/polityka/lukashenko-sluzhbi-putina-yak-zminyuvalasya-pozycziya-bilorusko-ho-dyktatora-shhodo-vijny (accessed 03.07.2025).

been approved by the Supreme Rada of Ukraine.' However, were there any deputies at the Rada? After all, the plenary session had been reported as closed...

11:38 a.m. The helicopters carrying the Russian Special Task Force from Belarus entered the Ukrainian air space. For a while, they hovered over the Russian columns of military equipment on the ground, then flew, at low altitudes – to avoid being noticed by our air defences – over the water along the western shore of the Kyiv Sea towards Vyshhorod.[218] Ukrainian Air Defence spotted them too late — literally on their approach to Hostomel, opened fire but their supplies proved insufficient. Some of those had been destroyed by the Russians – their whereabouts having been disclosed by an airport employee's son recruited by Russia.

11:40 a.m. At the same time, the city followed its own course. By that point, here had been big queues in front of all supermarkets. Same at the bus stations, people eager to board the services leaving Kyiv.

The western areas developed their own problems. For example, scores of cars tried to cross the Transcarpathian border and enter Slovakia; checkpoint Uzhhorod reported overwhelmed with queues and crowds.

* * *

Mum said:

'Do you think they'll get into the city?'

'Perhaps, some outskirts. But then what? From wherever you get in, it's about 50-100 streets and crossroads before you make it to the centre. And at every one of those, unpleasant surprises would be lurking. After all, we're not completely helpless and good for nothing. Edging forward in a city where a blast can come from any window, any attic – it's far from straightforward. However, we can't rule out that the city will eventually be encircled...'

'OK, let's make one more trip, if that's how it is. God forbid, the city does fall under siege, what shall we eat then? How will we survive?'

We ran back to Silpo and ATB. By then, the pharmacies and the bank machines had been thronged. Like before, the sirens kept howling but people wouldn't disperse. The bombs overhead spelled danger, yet no one had yet been taught how to survive with no medication or cash...

---

[218] **Kyiv Sea:** an artificial lake to the north of Kyiv formed by Kyiv Hydro-electric Plant in Vyshhorod.

Although the queues were now much longer, they were still moving forward, if slowly. As to the range of products available, within three or four hours, there'd been drastic changes. By then, there was no bread left at all...

While in the queue, I kept reading news on my phone.

11:58 a.m. The Russian helicopter-borne landing troops approached Hostomel. The airport was under fire, the aim being to capture the air control tower and the landing strip. The helicopters kept arriving in waves, intent on destroying the Ukrainian forces that defended the strip and managed to down several helicopters. Fierce fighting was going on.

Around 12:00 p.m. The units of the Russian 1st Guards Tank Army had reached the outskirts of Kharkiv but failed to gain access into the city.

12:02 p.m. The tension in Kyiv intensified. Monastyrskyi urgently appealed to city residents: 'The citizens shall be issued with weapons thorough the system for territorial defence. All you need is to produce your passport.'

12:20 p.m. Russian Special Task Force troops started unloading from helicopters at Hostomel. The battle ensued on the ground. The Russians tried to unblock the runway. Allegedly, heavy-duty personnel carriers were getting ready to take off from Russia, or maybe they'd already left.

By then we, too, could hear the sounds of explosions travelling from the western outskirts of the capital, that is to say, from Hostomel! The bursts weren't coming from the air, that was fighting on the ground! Social media started posting videos of Hostomel enveloped in smoke.

Out of the supermarket, mum joined the queue leading into a pharmacy. Sure thing, in case of a force major, top priority would be food and medications. Christ almighty! When had it ever happened before – such lines in front of pharmacies? I relieved mum of our food bags and rushed back.

Back home, I started cutting bread to make croutons. The air inside the flat was hot and scratchy, the pieces would dry up in a day or two.

Taras's chatroom reported that Zelensky was under a continuous pressure to leave: 'All our partners say we'll have it hard, with little chance to succeed. We won't have any huge support throughout the initial days, for they would want to see if we were capable of defending ourselves. May well be that they would be loath to see the Russians ending up with sizeable amounts of their weapons. To top it all, the Russians have perfected their plans to assassinate or kidnap the president. The stakes are way too high...'

True, the Kremlin had all reasons to expect that Zelensky would flee. Eight years previously, President Yanukovych had fled from Ukraine to Russia. There were other precedents too: in 2021, when the Taliban had taken Kabul in a pincer, President of Afghanistan Ashraf Ghani had also taken flight...

Oh, but this electronic conundrum had gone straight out of my mind. I made a dash to Pochaina – popped into the Metro station rootling thorough my pocket for the multi-trip ticket.

'State of martial law, access is free,' said the lady on duty. 'Get through.'

Very few people around, clearly, everyone was elsewhere. Those leaving – in cars, sitting out the congestion. Those staying – in queues for food, cash, and medications. The most daring ones – in queues by the military commissariats.

I got off at Pochaina. Well, I never! All electronic shops were closed. Even if there were scores of them here, and not a single one was open. The only store operating was Fozzy supermarket, where one could still buy batteries and even power banks!

People shuttled between the isles loading their trolleys; there still was stuff to choose from. The sections with sugar, grains, and flour were continually replenished by staff, who kept pulling new packages from their carts. It looked like the supermarket was trying to clear its stocks, sell as much and as quickly as they could, and then close down and pull the plug.

I got us another load of grains, sugar, and tins from here too. At the tills, people paid for the contents of their groaning trolleys with thousand-hryvna notes. I noted that many had enormous packs of toilet paper. It felt weird...

All the time, I kept one eye on my phone.

In the governmental quarter, the army and volunteers kept erecting the barricades.

01:00 p.m. At a briefing at the Presidential Office Podolyak announced that enterprises, the Nuclear Power Plants (NPPs) and Hydro-Electric Power Plants (HEPPs), as well as transport thoroughfares were operating as normal, except those under attack from the RF. The banks were also operating as they should, although a limit of 100 thousand hryvnas had been introduced for withdrawals. There had been some interruption to processing of payments for good and services with cards, but that had proved to be just local consequences of cyberattacks. The NPPs and HEPPs worked; security had been already tightened there several weeks back, but it had now been further improved. The major motorways were operating as normal, even though there was an increase in traffic heading westwards. Petrol stations had encountered a speculative hike in demand, which had triggered shortages of fuel supplies. Trains were circulating in the direction of the west and towards the centre; evacuation trains were available from Luhansk and Donetsk oblasts. On the whole, the railway service was operating under extraordinary conditions. Certain east-bound train routes had been cancelled. As for food supplies, the major supermarket chains still had stock sufficient for 15 days in their warehouses. The situation might be exacerbated by speculative demand, but measures would be taken in the nearest future. [Later he admitted: 'By about lunchtime it had become clear that the system of management was coping. There was a steady stream of information, continual analysis, understanding of everyone's role. It was also becoming clear that the situation was coming under control...')[219]

01:00 p.m. The state border transgressed, from the side of Belarus, at yet another checkpoint – Vilcha in Kyiv Oblast, this one being closer to the oblast of Zhytomyr. The enemy's military equipment started pouring in, there, too.

01:30 p.m. Defence Minister Reznikov emphasised that Ukraine had moved to a regime of total defence: 'Anyone who is ready and knows how to handle weapons may now join the ranks of the AFU Territorial Defence directly. Weapons shall be issued upon a direct request to the brigades and battalions of your local Territorial Defence branch. We shall supply with weapons all patriots who have no reservations in using them against the enemy. All you have to do is show your passport. Everyone – to the defence of Ukraine!'[220]

01:30 p.m. Well, at last. Peskov – Putin's press secretary and his 'talking head' – showed up in the Kremlin to face the journalists. The first chance to learn at least something 'from the horse's mouth'. After all, the situation was ambiguous: on the one hand, it was all about defending DPR and LPR, but on the other – invasion was afoot along the entire perimeter of the borders.

'Bloomberg: What is the Kremlin's definition of denazification? Does it involve a change of government in Kyiv?

Peskov: Well, ideally, it's necessary to rescue Ukraine, cleanse it from Nazis. From pro-Nazi people and ideologies...

Bloomberg: Are the president and the leadership of Ukraine pro-Nazi?

Peskov: I shall refrain from any other explanations...

Bloomberg: Is Russia prepared to stop its military operation on the territory of Ukraine and under what conditions?

Peskov: The operation has its goals. They must be attained. The president has said that all decisions have been approved and the goal shall be achieved.

CNN: What does the clean-up of Nazis involve? Does this mean organisations or Nazis in the government? Who is it?

Peskov: I cannot be more precise.

CNN: Is the operation going to be carried out only in the territories of the DPR and LPR or any other oblasts of Ukraine?

Peskov: That's a question for army officials.

....

[219] 24 February 2022 https://www.youtube.com/watch?v=zQ-NpZYSihs&list=PLctE-8jw7TIKjc3pQinTD5i3pKYW3ynJAV&index=4 (accessed 03.07.2025).

[220] Suspilne media, 24 February 2022, https://suspilne.media/210205-ukraina-pere-hodit-u-rezim-totalnoi-oboroni-reznikov/ (accessed 03.07.2025).

Reuters: To somewhat paraphrase the question: does "cleansing from Nazis" involve the Russian army going through the entire territory of Ukraine?

Peskov: Next question, please. I've already answered that question.

Ekho Moskvy: Has the Russian president set the task of capturing the Ukrainian cities of Kyiv, Kharkiv and Odesa?

Peskov: Let's move on. Guys, I've given my answers. If you keep asking the same question, it doesn't mean I'm going to answer it.'

There it was: a measured avoidance of responding. On the other hand, what was there to elucidate? The main thesis had been voiced: 'Ideally, Ukraine should be rescued, cleansed of Nazis. Cleansed of pro-Nazi people and ideologies...' Somewhat later, Peskov admitted the possibility of negotiations between Zelensky and Putin: 'Why not? If Ukraine is prepared to discuss Moscow's concerns in the sphere of security...'[221]

* * *

Meanwhile, by then the war was absolutely real and nothing could stop it.

01:40 p.m. The army urgently needed help: 120 trucks that could bring in the partners' help across the border into Lviv. The AFU would provide the fuel.

01:55 p.m. Roskomnadzor decreed that mass media,[222] when covering the 'special operation in Ukraine', should only publish information from the official Russian sources. Non-compliance entailed 5-million Ruble fines and a risk of being blocked.

01:55 p.m. Video 'Attention – 18+. Destroyed Russian vehicles and bodies of enemy's soldiery near Kharkiv.' Horror of horrors! The body parts scattered around the entire perimeter...

01:58 p.m. Podolyak's briefing. 'Protracted combat at Hostomel near Kyiv. One of the goals pursued by the occupants is to remove the country's leadership and gain access to the governmental quarter. This may involve the use of Russian landed troops.'

It was pure hell. Our troops in Hostomel were running out of ammunition. Our army was retreating...

By then it felt like a catastrophe. Arestovich's wife: 'Shortly after lunch, Oleksii called and said that the Russians were landing near Hostomel. "No doubt,

....

[221] Meduza, 24 February 2022, https://meduza.io/feature/2022/02/24/v-ideale-nu-zhno-neytralizovat-voennyy-potentsial-i-zachistit-ukrainu-ot-natsistov (accessed 03. 07.2025).

[222] **Roskomnadzor:** the Federal Service for Supervision of Communications, Information Technology and Mass Media, this is the Russian federal executive agency responsible for monitoring, controlling, and censoring Russian mass media.

they know our address and will use it for their purposes!" We didn't know then that their attempt had been unsuccessful. Oleksii cried in agitation: "You've got ten minutes to leave the building! Go west!" I got dressed very quickly, packed some bags, grabbed Sasha, our son, and we left… By the time we'd reached our destination, our plans had changed several times…'[223]

Spyridon, Bolik and their Teutonic girls had managed to fight their way into the Dachna Bus Station.

'You can't imagine the goings-on here!' Spyridon was yelling into the phone. 'A sea of people… An ocean… I don't even know if we manage to squeeze ourselves into a shuttle van of some sort…'

Alla called:

'I fear for the windows… I've criss-crossed them all with sticky ribbons, just one's left, but is it really gonna help? You know, if there are no windows left, in the winter it's little joy. How're you? Putting ribbons up? Take care! I still have to do the last one…'

02:00 p.m. The NATO secretary general avoided an answer regarding provision of aid to Ukraine while at the same time making it clear that NATO troops would definitely not be in Ukraine.

Thank God, Taras stayed in touch and kept me in the loop with the info from his chatroom.

Kubrakov: '… (From early in the morning) we were looking for a train to evacuate ministers, their families, and classified documents. All around us: war and chaos. I called nearly all managers of the Ukrainian Railways before we were able to put together two trains from what was available. The trains pulled in, but then they could not depart. They were scheduled to leave at noon. They didn't. Then at 1 p.m. – still no joy. The first of them left at about 2 p.m.'

About 02.:00 p.m. Chernyshov: 'At approximately 2 p.m. two special trains left in a westward direction. The decision about their destination – and there were several options under consideration – was taken already en route.'

While half the government travelled west, life in ministries that had stayed in Kyiv entered a stage of frenetic activity – for reasons of security, some ministries were dispersed around the city.

....

[223]   RBC Ukraine, 3 September 2022, htt ps://www.rbc.ua/ukr/styler/zhena-arestovi-cha-vyskazalas-voyne-semeynoy-1662176140.html (accessed 03.07.2025).

Kubrakov: 'We were in a state of complete disarray: people were dashing about, transferring something from one place to another, disposing of stuff. Out in the courtyard, secret documents were being burned – in accordance with protocol. In a word, it was pandemonium, but of a managed variety...'[224]

By the way, certain foresighted institutions had started evacuating in advance: had their archives boxed in good time, and urgently sent to somewhere.

Hmm, then there was this: they had started putting up roadblocks in the streets.

Some stuff was funny, though. To frustrate any plans to land the troops near the monument to Mother Ukraine, some people from 'European Solidarity'[225] came up with an idea to place two heavy machineguns atop the Kyiv-Pechersk Lavra's belfry – after all, it was 96 metres tall! And so, they tried to locate some monks and make arrangements, but found no one: the sacred premises had been totally deserted...

02:40 p.m. On my way home from Pochaina I watched the city change before my very eyes. When heading there, some little shops were still open, even small cafeterias, too. But as I stepped out of the Kontraktova Ploscha (square) metro station, everything was in the process of shutting down: little shops, pharmacies, banks. People were preparing for the worst...

Yet the supermarkets still worked, even though casting a quick gaze through the windows I saw practically empty shelves, cleaned off of any goods. I bumped into some casual friends on their way back from a shopping trip. According to them, the water, most cereals, groceries, and other stuff had already run out.

I finally made it home, unloaded my purchases. There was a slew of calls from those on the highways, nervously enquiring about the state of affairs in Kyiv, describing their own adventures: jams everywhere, cars spilling over and across all lanes and hard shoulders. Apparently, those who'd left by major routes got hopelessly stuck while the smarter ones made a much better headway choosing to drive on the B-roads. At the same time those travelling to Kyiv had to fight their way forward against the flow of the oncoming traffic, by side strips.

'Are there any check-up posts?' I asked. 'Any controls in place? Say, checking the IDs?'

'Nothing so far. No one controls anything.'

---

[224]   UP, 8 March 2024, https://www.pravda.com.ua/podcasts/63f90cc807994/2024/03/8/7397132/ (accessed 03.07.2025).

[225]   European Solidarity: a faction in the Verkhovna Rada led by Petro Poroshenko (the fifth president of Ukraine).

It later transpired that the jams towards all city exits, and further along, on the Zhytomyr and Odesa Highways, had been paralysing traffic until noon, and then the tension started easing off a bit...

Back to my computer.

Taras sent me a message, an update of his chatroom's reaction to the dramatic events of that morning. The first chat member went thus: 'Only now Putin's tactics have become clear. Using a false bait – he was escalating the situation around Donbas. Made us to believe that their troops concentration on our borders was for intimidation. He was distracting attention from the real goal. And he succeeded in this. Our people bought it. In short, he deceived...'

Another: 'The army hasn't been deployed; practically, the entire northern flank was exposed. The alarm had been raised at night, and the soldiers leapt out of their bunks. What a catastrophe! During those initial hours, but for the people who'd rushed out into roads and streets, armed with whatever came handy, keen to defend themselves through their own efforts, it's impossible to predict what would've happened!'

The other one: 'The morning of the 24th was very stressful. Organizational chaos... Complete confusion. What's there to say? Everything was in a muddle: the President's Office, the General Staff, and the entire country. The people were panic-stricken... Hundreds of thousand, if not millions, had left in haste, heading westward...'

The forth: 'Basically, it was a perfectly normal situation for the initial several hours of war... Tell me, where has it ever been otherwise? For all that, by about lunchtime, the General Staff started piecing together a picture of directions and the scale of invasion... They came to and got completely on top of the situation.'

The chatroom confirmed that nine battalion tactical groups were advancing towards Kyiv through the Chornobyl Zone, while 10 BTGs stayed in reserve in Homel Oblast, near the Belarusian-Ukrainian border.

At the same time, the Russian troops were moving forward from another angle, from Sumy Oblast, via Chernihiv area, towards Brovary (20 kilometres from Kyiv) on the Left Bank.

Fierce fighting at Hostomel had raged until 02:00 p.m. That was where Kyiv's fate was decided. Following this, the National Guards retreated to a safe distance, waiting for the arrival of our air force. True enough, at about 02:50 p.m., heavy artillery started shelling the runway, following which, the strip was further destroyed by our two bombers. Even if the air carriers had taken off from Russia, they would've had to turn around and fly back.

More news on Hostomel. It turned out that the insurance policy on the world's largest aircraft – *Mriya (Dream)* – had been suspended on February 22nd on an initiative of the Western insurance providers. In view of this, *Mriya* had to be evacuated to Leipzig-Halle Airport in Germany but the relevant order had never arrived. It was mind-boggling! So, it meant that *Mriya* was now at the heart of a hellish storm. Right?

And there was this, too: Reznikov received a telephone call from Khrenin who said: 'I'm acting as in intermediary between you and Minister Shoigu. You should sign the Act of Capitulation and then it would be possible to put a stop to all of it.' Reznikov replied: 'Thank you for trying to act as a kind of a transmitter. Feel free to pass it on that I would sign the Act of Russia's capitulation, and then we would be able to put a stop to all of it.'

03:00 p.m. The enemy reached the outskirts of Melitopol in the south.

03:05 p.m. Ukraine requested that the EU should urgently provide medical help.

03:10 p.m. Hostomel. After our army had retreated and the artillery and the aviation had destroyed the landing strip, the Russians entered the airfield. However, by then it was good for nothing. In other words, the blitzkrieg had gone tits up! Immediately, there followed a much livelier exchange about negotiations. Peskov: 'Putin is ready to negotiate with the President of Ukraine but on one condition: Ukraine must be prepared to discuss "neutrality of status" and "refusal to deploy weapons".' The term "occupation" does not apply to the actions of Russia. The Russian special operation pursues two goals: demilitarisation and denazification. Ideally, it is necessary to free Ukraine, rid it of Nazis, pro-Nazi people and ideologies. Russia's aims include neutralisation of Ukrainian military potential, which has recently been considerably enhanced through the active efforts, among others, of foreign countries.'[226]

Hmmm… Sure thing, the blitzkrieg went haywire, so it became possible to 'negotiate'. Clearly, much as they were advancing, the plans became frustrated. Besides, the losses were rather too high. So, things weren't as great as they'd been planned in those high-placed Kremlin offices. For all that, those negotiations were exclusively designed to agree everything on Russia's terms…

As if on a prompt, the Belarusian President's site showed excerpts of Lukashenko's verbal exercises at a briefing with the army people. He outdid himself there. As for us, one thing was clear: since the attack against Kyiv and Chernihiv Oblast had been launched from Belarus, *de facto*, their country was also an aggressor.

[226] BBC news Ukraine, 25 February 2022, https://www.bbc.com/ukrainian/news-60495999 (accessed 03.07.2025).

Lukashenko: 'I've just read: "At approximately five in the morning, the state border of Ukraine that is in the vicinity of Russia and Belarus sustained an attack by Russian troops with support from Belarus." Bastards! Our troops took no part in the operation! But, if need be, if Belarus and Russia need it, they will!

'Last night, before the start of the operation, he (a representative of the Ukrainian military command) asked for a conversation (with our military leadership). He was advised to urgently get in touch with the RF Defence Minister, with the Russian General Staff – in order to prevent a bloodbath. Did he place this call? He didn't! Aware of a possible conflict, he didn't even call Moscow! Look, there were precedents in history, when Khrushchev had called Kennedy at night, and thus they prevented a thermonuclear war. But here you are, if you please, it's below him to pick up a receiver and make a call. What a scoundrel!

'They (the Ukrainian powers) did nothing to prevent it (invasion). Stop!!! Who is going to resist – the most powerful nuclear state! What's in it for you? But no, they won't listen. Do you think they are unaware of the fact they're not ready to fight against Russia? Of course they are aware. Another question: why, then, do they worsen the relations? Because they are shoving those warriors into a fight by sticking bayonets in their behind! And thus, they join the fray. And they received a good answer... Well, they'd been warned, point by point, what had to be done. They didn't do it. So, they wanted this war. Let them now sort it out by themselves – see who's incited them...

'Putin announced – what a great guy: "We're not occupiers, we have no plans to occupy Ukraine!" What else do you need? This is a basis for negotiations. And it's true, he's not going to occupy. Whatever for? Who needs this headache? No one is going to bring in troops and a new government. It's a starting point for negotiations. Let us proceed from this and develop an agenda and adopt decisions...'

And these were his pearls at a meeting with the press.

'That is why the best course for Ukraine now is to come to their senses and approve of this decision [on opening "constructive" negotiations]. Naturally, it will be in line with Russian demands about security...'

'Look, we've spent the entire night sending them (the Ukrainian side) the signal... Why don't they get in touch with the President of Russia and say: "Yes, we are ready to demilitarise (at least this). We are ready to some other steps." And there would've been no conflict! But no – "I called Putin but there was no answer!" So go ahead and call him 10 times! What's there to discuss? He (Putin) always says: Ok, let's meet and talk, but what about? "I won't abide by the Minsk Agreements; I won't do this or that..." What's there to talk about, then? That's why I say this: the list of questions and draft decisions is to be elaborated by specialists, as always. [After this] the presidents meet, 'waive their incense burners, deliver their benediction, sign and leave. That's how things should be done…

'Imagine that tomorrow there will be no Russia – it got beaten, destroyed and so on. Who will be dragged into this funnel? We will disappear in a split second. No "balcony" (top leadership), nothing. Tomorrow we shall be under attack from all sides. That is why all has to be pieced together, and you should understand what politics I'm pursuing here, and what knife-edge I have to balance today…

'(I remember how in the days of Yeltsin), at an early meeting between presidents of Belarus, Russia and Ukraine I suggested that Kuchma should incorporate amendments [to the Ukrainian Constitution]. [227] Yeltsin told me: "Listen, go to them and help him write [the draft]." I said OK. And help I did. It was a stringent constitution, similar to ours, the one in Kazakhstan and Russia, but we did alright. But he (Kuchma) never submitted it to the Rada for ratification. And that was that. It all was thus ruined…'

Oleksandr Hryhorovych,[228] just as always, applying his inimitable "rustic common sense", explained it all and enlightened us, the ignoramuses, making everything as clear as a bell. He loves giving it large when dwelling on 'lofty' subjects. Which never got in the way of him allowing something like a thousand political prisoners to rot in his torture chambers. What a man, a famous adviser on the affairs of Ukraine…

Whatever the background story, a concurrent signal arrived in Kyiv from Moscow via Minsk: 'Well, now we could come to an understanding…'

Taras called again:

'What gives? Managed to lay in at least some supplies?'

'Sort of…' I answered.

He was silent after that, me too.

To tell the truth, before the invasion, it would've been hard to call us some super-patriots. But when it all came to be – something in the brain had shifted. No one had the time to blab about patriotism – the situation was too tense, bordering on dramatic.

So, what was there to do – to sit around at home, staring at the computer screen with its flowing avalanche of news?

Suddenly, Taras suggested:

....

227 **Leonid Kuchma**: the second president of Ukraine and the only president of Ukraine who has served two terms (July 1994 to January 2005).

228 **Oleksandr Hryhorovych**: Alexander Lukashenko.

'Look, perhaps we'd pop over to the military commissariat? At least we'll see what's going on…'

'Makes sense.'

We raced towards the commissariat. And what did we find there but a gigantic queue!

'Come on, dudes!' we clearly amazed a guy who was standing there, already dressed in fatigues.

We were amazed ourselves: he was unhurriedly pouring himself some coffee from a thermos, pulling some crackers from his backpack. Clearly, a smart guy, who'd come prepared.

He turned to us, sounding somewhat caustic:

'Have you been asleep until now, or what? It takes good five to seven hours only to get inside. Also, you've got to have some provisions, to stay the course…'

Then he softened up and even offered an advice:

'You students or what? They aren't likely to take you on. There's more experienced folk here than is needed. Try to work your way into the Territorial Defence (TD), you might get lucky…'

So there. How would we get there? It became clear that acting officially we would achieve bloody nothing.

Taras started calling some people he knew. He got in touch with somebody who was already in the TD and promised help.

'Lots of things are still not clear,' he explained. 'Everything is being put together on the hoof. TD has some practically fully-fledged army units, they're already receiving uniforms, sub-machine guns, modern devices that are really gonna be helpful when fighting back. But there are some volunteers, too – those that go on sentry duty and organise roadblocks. You could get in this way. In a word, wait, I'll find out.'

Some ten minutes later he got back to us, told us where to go. But it would have to be tomorrow, for at the moment it was completely overcrowded.

We headed home, registering with our naked eyes that within some 10-12 hours the city had become deserted.

Taras switched on his smartphone radio. Good timing – four in the afternoon was the time for a news update. Reports emphasised that from the direction of Sumy 'the situation is difficult. Fighting continues in Okhtyrka, Konotop, and near Sumy. The Russians rolled through the town of Hlukhiv, while in transit.'

Another item was about Kyiv. The National Guards were blocking bridges over the Dnipro, allegedly to plant mines. Should the enemy break through Brovary, coming from Chernihiv or Sumy, the bridges would be immediately blown up, thus impeding their progress across the river. Therefore, if someone hadn't been able to flee by car – tough luck. The only way from the Left Bank to the Right was by Metro. But even this, in the absence of air raids.

'Clearly, if they are mining the bridges after all, it means that the Russkies are barging forward non-stop,' wistfully, Taras summed it all up.

As soon as I let myself into the flat, Spyridon called, yelling in the receiver:

'By some miracle, we've squeezed into a transit van. It's a total horror! It's packed to its gills; people are travelling astride boxes in the isle...'

Bolik snatched the phone from him:

'To cut it short, we've got out.'

'How fast are you moving?'

'We aren't. We're stationary. A jam. A hopeless one...'

'How are Greta and Brunhild? Hanging on?'

'Brunhild is OK... Greta, though, went to pieces, cries all the time...'

'Doesn't sound too Teutonic to me,' I tried to inject some levity. 'Teutons they are... how to put it? Strong as iron...'

'Sure. Still, she cries...'

I hastily returned to my computer to get some fresh news. The Russkies were reported as suffering huge losses... That was American help put to good use. In the area near Hlukhiv (Sumy oblast) the army used some Javelins, destroyed a column of 15 T-72 tanks. It cheered me up. For all that, they kept advancing...

03:45 p.m. A column of Russian armoured vehicles entered the Chornobyl NPS, defended by 169 of our National Guards. After an enforced negotiation, they had to surrender. One of the sources revealed that starting from November 2021, Russia had been infiltrating Ukraine with her agents. Their task was to establish human contacts with those in charge of defending the Chornobyl NPS and ensure its surrender without a fight. Another advantage was its proximity to a shortcut towards Kyiv.

04:07 p.m. Two warships of the Black Sea Fleet – *Moskva* and *Vasiliy Bykov*, remained near the Serpent Island and started shelling it with their naval artillery. Our border guards rejected the Russian ultimatum of surrender and held the fort.

04:35 p.m. At a briefing, Podolyak underscored that Russia was trying to destabilise situation in big cities, especially Kharkiv and Kyiv. 'Severe fighting continues in the south where the Russians target Henichesk, Skadovsk and Nova Kakhovka. Nevertheless, the Russian shock attack against Ukraine has failed, as have their overall plans.' He also reminded of a threat that there would be an attack against the governmental quarter.

Like other embassies, the EU representation in Ukraine was preparing for the worst, including seizure of this institution by the Russians. The representation's staff copied the contents of their servers to Brussels; many documents were sent there with diplomatic mail; many were destroyed. They also destroyed all information system encryption technologies. (On February 24th seven EU diplomats still remained in Kyiv. On the 25th they all left).[229]

05:00 p.m. Mayor Klitchko: 'Starting from today, a curfew shall be effective in Kyiv between 10:00 p.m. and 07:00 a.m. the following day. During this time there will be no public transport. The metro, as a bomb shelter, shall be accessible around the clock.'[230] The curfew in Kharkiv started at 10 p.m., too. The Metro trains in both cities stopped running, the Metro itself being only accessible in its capacity as a bomb shelter. It was possible to stay there overnight, the authorities had put in the toilets and organised a supply of water.

Another update: for reasons of security, access to the governmental quarter was henceforth granted only to the people's deputies, government officials, certain executives, and accredited mass media employees. By then, the quarter had been encircled on all sides with fortified blockades.

Displaced residents started arriving in Lviv. Sadovyi: 'As of today, Lviv has become the world's largest humanitarian hub. The Western press simply cannot understand how it all works. They expected disarray, spectacular mishaps. Yet everything works as if in an ant colony. Everyone knows their role and carries out their duties. Our train station has become one of the symbols of war. We finished refurbishing the square in front of the station before the start of the war. Otherwise, it would have been Armageddon. But now here it is, this spacious square. Public transport is allocated its own area, private vehicles are parked in the other. There is a lot of room for setting up kiosks where people can get information. We expediently took all the flexible decisions that enable people to wait out their time while the trains are getting ready to leave for Poland. We have also put in place new bus routes heading in the same direction. For all that, quite a few people prefer to stay in Lviv.'[231]

[229]   European Pravda, 6 December 2024, https://www.eurointegration.com.ua/rus/articles/2024/12/6/7199623/ (accessed 03.07.2025).

[230]   Radio Svoboda, 24 February 2022, https://www.radiosvoboda.org/a/news-kyiv-komendantska-hodyna/31721204.html (accessed 03.07.2025).

[231]   UP, 24 February 2024, https://www.pravda.com.ua/cdn/cd1/reconstruction/a5.html (accessed 03.07.2025).

The Russians rolled through Sumy Oblast, and fast – driving their tank columns towards Kyiv. The Ukrainian Army retreated its main forces but left ambushes in their wake.

Then there appeared images of the Kharkiv perimeter road – it had stayed ours!

05:00 p.m. With enormous effort, the Russian landing troops had seized practically the entire perimeter or Hostomel airfield. However, the AFU had kept control over both the landing strip and the Russian units that had landed under fire from our artillery.

Meanwhile the daylight was receding in Kyiv, and street traffic had come to a complete stop. No people around, either. As the twilight got denser, only few residential windows lit up. Some buildings remained completely dark.

Finally, some inspiring news from the motorways. The chaos of the early part of the day and the afternoon had gradually subsided. There had even appeared traces of primitive organisation. After strenuous hours spent waiting in queues, the cars started slowly edging forward. Yet many damaged vehicles had been abandoned in the curbs.

Those already in Lviv wrote about endless queues on the Ukrainian-Polish border. Hundreds of cars, idling. The waiting time at every checkpoint was getting longer with each passing hour. Despite operating in fast-track mode, the border guards couldn't process more than fifty cars in one hour. It was real pandemonium, much as the previous day there'd been hardly any cars. The license plates originated from all over: Kyiv, Dnipro-city, Chernihiv, Sumy, Odesa. The pedestrian crossings were as bad: horrible queues. Lots of people travelled with children, they all were waived through, men included. The border guards said: 'No restrictions for now. Should a car carry children under three years of age, we can let those though ahead of all others.'

Where were they all going? Some must have been planning to stay with their relatives. Yet the majority had no idea of their destination: where they headed, and what to expect in the unknown 'somewhere'. First, they had to get over the border, and only then look for some asylum.

05:58 p.m. Troubling news! Allegedly, 18 Il-76 freight aircraft had left Pskov for Kyiv, with landing troops on board. If those aircraft managed to land, the Special Task Force would be immediately relocated towards Kyiv. An incursion could start at any point!!!

That was when Taras sent me some new stuff from his restricted chatroom. Allegedly, it was an intercepted post from a Moscow 'source' detailing their plans of invasion into Ukraine.

'Under the operational plan of the RF, the Special Task Force was instructed to capture either Hostomel airfield, or the air base in Vasylkiv. The first contingent of the landing troops is to arrive from Belarus, either by helicopters or light aircraft. [Hmm... We saw that that is exactly what had happened.] That group is to facilitate the arrival of the main force, transported by the Il-76 aircraft – from four to ten thousand men and light-weight armoured vehicles. The landing operation is to be overseen from the Belarusian and Russian air space by A-50s [early warning and surveillance aircraft]. At the same time, the troops already *in situ* in Ukraine are to sabotage the electric grid and sub-stations aiming to cut off significant portions of the city from electricity and communications, thus creating panic among the population. Certain groups are to instructed to burn and loot so that the panic would intensify, and the law enforcement agencies, instead of hunting down the sabotage parties, will concentrate on stabilising the situation. All this will take place concurrently with a massive cyber-attack targeting the organs of power and other sites of vital importance. Prior to that, there would be intensification of activities at the frontline, possibly, provocations along the entire length of the border which will force their military and political leadership to reassign the bulk of their battle-worthy forces to the task of defence, and thus only few troops will stay behind in Kyiv. The landing troops shall block Kyiv, its communication lines, troop management channels; capture/blow up armaments' depots, exacerbate chaos to the maximum, create conditions for an "uncontrolled exodus from Kyiv of the columns of refugees" who will thus block the roads/highways, and impede manoeuvres of the army and the law enforcement agencies along the said routes. The next stage will be to capture and keep under control the government agencies: the President's Office, the General Staff, the Cabinet of Ministers, the Supreme Rada; and proceed in this vein, until the arrival of the main troops. The landing operation must be completed within 24 hours; it shall start as soon as everything is ready – late in the evening or at night. The date of the operation is yet unknown but expected to start within the next few days, depending on the weather, the evolution of the global political situation and the processes of negotiations. The desired result will be to capture the country's political leadership and force them to sign a peaceful treaty on Russian terms, blackmailing them with a possibility of killing massive numbers of civilians. Even if some leaders have been evacuated, someone from among the pro-Russian politicians shall accept the responsibility and sign the requisite documents, motivation being the flight of political leaders from Kyiv. As a result, Ukraine may be split into two parts, similar to West and East Germany (or North and South Korea). At the same time, the Russian Federation shall recognise legitimacy of the part that has signed the agreements and stays loyal to the RF. The overall principle shall be: "He who controls the capital city, controls the entire country".'

R-i-i-ight… Thank God, that information was already available to our security services.

And so, landing troops were about to enter the fray. It was also clear that there was a number of saboteurs already operating in the city.

Taras continued sharing his insider's information: 'The President's Office functions under siege conditions. Zelensky's closest circle are now convinced that it's impossible to defend the capital, and therefore evacuation is the only answer. "We shall never survive"!' That was when Zelensky exploded: 'I don't want to listen to this! Listen, I'm a live person. I don't want to die, just like anyone else. But I know it for sure – if I allow myself to think like that, I'm dead already!'

06:00 p.m. Zelensky arrived for a briefing in his Office wearing a standard issue T-shirt of bottle green. It looked that from that point onwards it was going to become his usual get-up. Perhaps, even an inalienable detail of his new image. Someone on his team had advised him to start dressing 'military'. He followed the advice and must have found it more convenient, realising, too, that it would send a message to the people. 'This is war, after all, and it would be weird to show up in a suit.'

Then he addressed the Western countries: 'Dear European leaders and leaders of the world, if you don't provide us with some significant help, tomorrow you'll find war knocking on your own door.'

In his turn, Danilov ran his last teleconference for the day that involved all leaders of the regional military administrations. It had been reported that by 06:00 p.m. so many saboteurs that had been exposed in Kyiv and taken down. Meanwhile, at last the Ukrainian army started brining up their troops into Kyiv's vicinity.

06:37 p.m. The Ukrainian Railway had started evacuating people from the east of the country where active combat was in progress.

07:20 p.m. Hostomel. The airport had finally been seized by the Russian army. Yet the aggressors realised that it wasn't fit anymore to receive freight aircraft. They had been reported as having to turn round in the Belarusian air space and head back to their base in Pskov.

The north was producing its own news. The speedy advance of the Russian army had brought it to Chernihiv – that was one direction. Allegedly, in Sumy, another corridor towards Kyiv, they had burst into the city centre. They had reached Konotop, and there the progress of this 300-item-strong column was interrupted. That provided the AFU with a respite and a chance to prepare their defence.

07:40 p.m. Commander-in-Chief Zaluzhnyi appealed to the world in English: 'Thanks to all our foreign partners. But now it is time to act, not to discuss.'

And then he continued in Ukrainian: 'Russia hasn't managed to pull off a blitzkrieg, they will drown in their own blood.'[232]

By then, contradictory rumours had already been in circulation, insisting that during the night the city would be taken by storm, and not by landing troops but by those units that had approached Kyiv directly during the day. Therefore, ammunitions and weapons were to be issued to any volunteer who declared their readiness to defend the city from aggressors. Within an hour, over 10 thousand items of armaments had been distributed. Just like the authorities had promised – everything was done in a simplified fashion. All one had to do was to produce a passport, which was then entered into the database, enabling its carrier to receive a submachine gun registered to their name.

08:00 p.m. Deputy Defence Minister Malyar: 'If you throw a flask with combustible mixture off your balcony or open fire with your side arms against enemy vehicles carrying hostile manpower – all that will mean irreplaceable losses for our adversary!'[233]

08:40 p.m. Several other cities had also decided to introduce a curfew. During those hours, the citizens were banned from staying outside. Roadblocks were erected at all points of entry and exit. The police checked personal documents, stopping vehicles, inspecting cars and their cargos. The cities with curfew in place allowed exit but not entry.

It wasn't clear about the others, but before the curfew kicked in, our city had become totally deserted.

In the evening, Brussels convened an extraordinary summit of the European leaders. Later on, a 'pale and exhausted Zelensky joined in and announced straight away that perhaps it was the last time that the partners would see him alive. For all that, he kept asking them insistently whether Ukraine would ever be allowed to join the European Union? His five-minute-long speech produced a bigger impact than the months spent talking about a Russian threat. That was the president of a European democracy who, by then, had taken residence in a bunker, ready to die and see his country occupied.'

[232]   TSN, 6 August 2023, https://tsn.ua/exclusive/general-21-stolittya-batko-zsu-ta-ukrayinska-legenda-valeriy-zaluzhniy-2385259.html (accessed 03.07.2025).

[233]   RBC Ukraine, 25 February 2022, https://www.rbc.ua/ukr/news/odna-butyl-ka-zazhigatelnoy-smesi-balkona-1645740324.html (accessed 03.07.2025).

* * *

By the end of the day, it became clear that most friends and the people we knew had managed to leave the city and make progress along the roads. I felt happy for them…

On the other hand, this mass exodus was depressing. Even despite the fact that the three of us had stayed. I felt like I was face-to-face with something inexplicable… Unexpected… Even eerie…

To make things worse, the TV kept urging everyone to descend to their bomb shelters. They showed some footage from the Metro – people had secured places in good time and were getting ready for the night.

Mum tried to calm me:

'It's panic. They flee, try to hide… I've spent the whole day mulling it over. One shouldn't feel ashamed, shouldn't beat one's chest. It's human nature – to be afraid and seek survival. Fear is normal. Besides, some are so overcome with panic that they cannot see anything clearly and descend into despair. Still, others can pull themselves together and regroup, which later transcends into determination, anger, and a desire to act…'

More news.

09:00 p.m. The USA and over 30 partner countries approved hellish sanctions that would hit Russia where it hurt. Bullet points from the President Biden's statement on Russia's intervention in Ukraine:

The USA will put in place harsh sanctions against the leaders of Russia and their families;

The sanctions will apply to a number of Russian banks whose assets amount to a trillion dollars;

The leaders of G-7 will curtail Russia's ability to conduct business in dollars, euros, yen, and other international currencies;

The USA will send additional military equipment and manpower to NATO countries in Europe, but the American contingent won't take part in the conflict on Ukrainian territory;

In his conversation with Zelensky Biden gave assurances that the USA would provide comprehensive assistance to Kyiv. 'Putin has attacked the very principles of international peace and security. Putin and his supporters have never cared about security; all they want is to restore the empire. Putin is an aggressor. Putin has chosen this war and now he and his country will have to face the consequences.'[234]

....

[234] New view business, 24 February 2022, https://biz.nv.ua/ukr/economics/bayden-

A message from Scholz: 'We shall act decisively. Putin will not win this war. Peace, supremacy of law and democracy – these are the aims for Europe and Ukraine.'

09:00 p.m. The General Staff reported that fighting was going on on the outskirts of Chernihiv. Also, they announced that in the south the Russians would try to go round Kherson in order to attack Mykolaiv. According to their plans, Mykolaiv should be encircled in two days' time, and Odesa – in three.

09:00 p.m. A landing operation started near Hostomel airfield – this time, conducted by the Ukrainian troops. Ferocious fighting ensued, all around. Eventually they did manage to kick the Russians out of their positions and bring the airfield back under control of the Ukrainian army. The Russian Special Task Forces fled into the neighbouring woods and were mopped up.

The news somewhat lifted my spirits.

After the airfield had been reseized and the Russian freight aircraft had flown back, assurances were issued that the capital was now secure and no offensive would be launched at night. At the same time, we were encouraged to work out the whereabouts of a closest bomb shelter, within easy reach, in case of an air raid.

It was mentioned, though, that one couldn't rule out a possibility that the enemy would try to land their troops near the Museum of the History of Ukraine during the Second World War, and the Mother Ukraine Monument, since the site in front was convenient for helicopter landing. If this happened, the governmental quarter would be a bare couple of kilometres away. My unease returned.

On the evening of February 24th Stefanchuk got to the Supreme Rada. He was consumed with fear that if Kyiv were captured, sacrosanct objects would fall into the enemy's hands. The Flag of Independence was immediately removed– the same flag that had been brought into the Rada's session chamber on August 24th, 1991. 'We believed that those bastards have no right to touch it. Neither the flag, nor the master copy of the Constitution, nor the Act of State Independence should ever go over to those orks! We have taken these things with us… [At a later date he said: "this flag spent the following two months in my bodyguards' backpack, travelling with me around the outskirts of Kyiv.")'235

....

anonsuvav-nishchivni-sankciji-proti-rosiji-ostanni-novini-50219772.html   (accessed 03.07.2025).

235   UP, undated, https://www.pravda.com.ua/cdn/cd1/reconstruction/a4.html

09:35 p.m. S. Tykhanovska:[236] 'Belarus has become a stepping-stone for Russia's invasion of Ukraine. Lukashenko agreed to this as a pay-back to Putin for the latter's support during the presidential election of 2020.'

10:00 p.m. After bombing it from air and the sea, having destroyed the entire infrastructure, the Russians had gained control of Serpent Island.

Still, there were some positive developments too – it became clear the enemy had been definitely stopped near Kharkiv.

Zelensky responded immediately: 'The country has managed to withstand the first wave of the Russian invasion. The Ukrainian army, border guards, police and Special Task Force put the brakes on enemy's attacks. Using the terminology of a conflict, this could be called an operational pause.'

Subsequently, he appealed to the EU leaders for help during Ukraine's standoff with Russia. He asked for guarantees of security from the European perspective: 'The fate of Europe is decided in Ukraine. If Putin doesn't receive a proper rebuff, he will go further… Our people are dying while defending the freedom of Ukraine and Europe! We have been waiting beside an open door for quite some time now. We have asked about membership of NATO but received no reply…' [237]

11:00 p.m. The press service of the AFU Army command: 'As of 21:00, over 60 Battalion Tactical Groups, out of the total of 90 BTG, have been moved into Ukraine. Thus, the perfidious plans of the Russian aggressors have been exposed for all to see. The principal aim of the operation is to block Kyiv, create an overland corridor to the Crimean Peninsula and the self-proclaimed Trans-Dniester Moldovan Republic.'

11:00 p.m. President Zelensky signed a new decree – on general mobilisation (No 69/2022). This was identical to the morning's Decree No 65/2022,[238] with the only exception being removal of Point 10, that is 'This Decree shall come into force after approval of the Supreme Rada of Ukraine'.

Conscription of those liable and reservists, as well as re-assignment of the means of transportation for the needs of the armed forces, were to take place in accordance with targets established by mobilisation plans.

....

[236] **Svitlana Tsikhanouska:** a Belarusian political activist. After standing as a candidate in the 2020 presidential election against Alexander Lukashenko, the current president, she has led the political opposition to his authoritarian rule through an oppositional government operating from Lithuania and Poland.

[237] Suspilne noviny, 24 February 2022, https://suspilne.media/210628-v-ukraini-virisuetsa-dola-evropi-zelenskij-zvernuvsa-do-lideriv-es/ (accessed 03.07.2025).

[238] Official website of the president of Ukraine, 24 February 2022, https://www.president.gov.ua/documents/692022-41413 (accessed 03.07.2025).

And then came this update, as if a follow-up to the above: 'The National Border Guard Service notifies that as a result of a state of martial law in Ukraine (which, in essence, is a law on mobilisation) a temporary ban shall be put in place preventing departure of a specific category of citizens, which includes every male between the ages of 18 and 60.'[239]

Whoops, only those who'd used the 'window for departure' during the day of February 24th managed to get away…

* * *

On the very first night of the war the Russians hadn't abandoned their attempts to penetrate the 'governmental triangle' – with their infantry, saboteurs, or some other landing troops. The Zelensky family at that point remained within this very triangle. The USA and UK kept trying to persuade him and his team to leave for Poland and create a government in exile. In response, the president used a phrase that made headlines all over the world: 'The fighting is here! I need ammunition, not a trip!' His security personnel suggested moving him to a secure bunker outside Kyiv, the one that would be capable of ensuring a lengthy survival in case of a siege. He rejected this offer too.

Deep down, the president suspected that some of his foreign interlocutors would have welcomed a speedy resolution of the conflict where Ukraine would surrender to Russia. He stressed that he wasn't clinging to his post: 'I came into politics not for this (to have power), and I will leave if you tell me that this will put a stop to the war.'

11:43 p.m. In his late-evening appeal Zelensky said: 'We have information confirming that the enemy's subversive groups have made their way into Kyiv. I stay in the governmental quarter, together with everyone who is needed to ensure the functioning of central authority. My family is staying in Ukraine. We are not a family of traitors but of citizens of Ukraine. However, I have no right to divulge their exact whereabouts. I have been confirmed as Target Number One for the enemy. My family is Target Number Two. They would like to eliminate Ukraine politically, to destroy its head of state.'[240]

In a word, the night assault wasn't ruled out, after all.

The president went on: 'Today I asked 27 leaders of Europe: will Ukraine be accepted into NATO? It was a direct question. Everyone is afraid, they do

[239] Suspilne noviny, 24 February 2022, https://suspilne.media/210619-v-ukraini-zaprovadzuetsa-obmezenna-na-viizd-colovikiv-za-kordon/ (accessed 03.07.2025).

[240] UP, 24 February 2022, https://www.pravda.com.ua/news/2022/02/24/7325590/ (accessed 03.07.2025).

not reply. And us – we are afraid of nothing. We are not afraid to defend our state. We are not afraid of Russia. We are not afraid to talk to Russia. We are not afraid of any subjects, of discussing guarantees for our security. We are not afraid to discuss neutral status. After all, at this point, we are not a member of NATO. So which guarantees are thus possible? And most importantly: which countries will provide them?'[241]

Taras's secure chatroom asserted that the fate of Kyiv was hanging by a thread, apparently the enemy's advantage over the AFU was 12-fold. And if the defence line collapsed against the attack of the Russian army, the fighting would move to the streets of Kyiv. And again, they talked about a complete impossibility of containing the enemy on the border when the invasion had started.

Most Ukrainian units had been redeployed to the eastern flank, thus depleting the defence capability of Kyiv. In terms of tanks, the only unit available was 72nd mechanised brigade, clearly insufficient for defending such a big conurbation. That was why they used the only possible tactic – 'territories in exchange for time'.

Colonel General Syrsky was confirmed as the appointed head of the Kyiv defence. His initial command had been to create two circles: one in the outskirts, the other one – in Kyiv itself. The city was divided in ten sectors. Their bosses were authorised to make tactical decisions without seeking the headquarters' approval. In order to dilute the enemy's 12-fold advantage, the Special Task Forces had been urgently moved from their various duties to the capital. Another measure was to use the forces in reserve, for example the cadets and instructors from military academies and the territorial defence.

Meanwhile, there was news from the American side. Addressing the Congress, Secretary of Defence Lloyd Austin asserted that several Russian armoured infantry units had moved rather close to Kyiv and stopped at only 20 miles away. OK, I converted it into kilometres, and got the figure of 32. My God, so close… State Secretary Blinken added that they disposed of some preliminary information on Russian plans to lay siege to the capital.

There was a lot about the affairs in the south, too.

'The goings-on in Kherson area are hard to work out. The situation is disastrous. Perhaps, it's already a catastrophe. For some, Russia's invasion from Crimea was predictable. For the others, alas, not so. The Russians passed all three checkpoints on the Crimean isthmus – Chongar, Kolonchak and Chaplinka – in one swift move. But the Chongar Strait, as well as the narrow isth-

....

[241]   24 February 2022 https://www.youtube.com/watch?v=F7J77qu5Sbw (accessed 03.07.2025).

mus between the Crimean Peninsula and the continent (from the direction of Kalanchak and Chaplinka), given properly organised defence, were considered insurmountable. Another natural obstacle for military vehicles was supposed to be a network of irrigation canals criss-crossing the entire Kherson Oblast. Therefore, the Ukrainian General Staff believed that the enemy would be bogged down in the minefields. Great stuff! But the bridges had never been blown up, and even if there had been reports of damage to some bridges and canals, none of those reached critical proportions. At the same time, mine fields stayed intact. How come that none if it has worked? It's a miracle.'

'The situation is horrible. After all, Kherson Oblast was referred to as "potentially vulnerable to a possibility of the Russian invasion from Crimea." Observers have been constantly drawing attention to a speedy buildup of the Russian armaments over there. During the years of occupation, the peninsular has been turned into a powerful military base. They have built numerous camps, depots of weaponry, relocated aircraft and helicopters. And here we go: 35 thousand Russian troops moved in from Crimea, to be faced with a much smaller Ukrainian contingent. That's why Ukraine cannot yet fight back properly. That's why, even after engaging in combat, we have to withdraw. That's why in the morning the Russian troops could easily cross the Crimean administrative border, not meeting with any significant resistance, and start their lightening-like advance into the depth of Ukraine, moving along the motorways.'

'They captured control over sizeable territories… Anybody trying to flee from Henichesk District, have to be vetted by the Russians over their connection to AFU. In the town of Tavriysk, they have captured the main facility of the North Crimean Canal. And after they've seized Kakhovka HPP, a huge armoured column moved across its dam and then started descending from north-east, by this point moving along the right bank of the Dnipro, practically threatening the Ukrainian defence from its own rear.'

'The Antonivka Bridge – that's nothing short of tragedy. During daytime they managed to kick out the Russian landing troops, and for some two hours, our army and vehicles had been fighting their way, under fire, out of encirclement. Big trucks, other vehicles and equipment kept rolling and rolling. People sat on top and were clutching to the sides. Lots of civilians… Alas, not everybody has managed to break through…'

'The Russians show rather good dynamics, so it remains unclear whether we'll manage to stop this onslaught or will they reach Kyiv? On this first day, no one could understand anything anyway. A total discoordination of the army. A commander's field of vision is severely constricted: his position, his company, battalion. And he has no idea of what's going on some 10 kilometres away.

All is chaos, no point denying it. Just like any major war at its start. Besides, territorial defence had only been conceived about a month before all of this…'

Apparently, Reznikov said this: 'In our warehouses we have no body armour, no helmets. We have some summer uniforms but nothing for the winter, not at all. As for the ammunition in the depots… So, the prospects for our warfare are like this. Zaluzhnyi was quite outspoken: we've got what it takes, theoretically speaking, to keep us going for two months, maybe more, after which – "goodbye, my friend, goodbye".'[242]

'The main thing is that air defence has survived, that the aviation hasn't been destroyed. We have practically withstood the first blast, the front line In fact, we withstood the first massive blow, the front line crumbled almost nowhere… Kherson Oblast? Yes, that crumbled, true, there wasn't enough of our presence there. They were physically short of the people needed to hold such a long stretch on the Ukrainian-Russian border. Whereas to increase the army by 300-350 thousand would've meant a significant increase in budget allocations. The president was against it, that's why what happened happened.'

'It's all true. But still, by hook or by crook, we've survived this first day. Our priority now is Chernihiv and Kyiv. For as long as Chernihiv stands, Kyiv holds on. And as long as Kyiv holds on, Ukraine will fight.'

I broke myself away from this exchange. It was physically painful to read it…

By Jove, I had so many questions as to what was happening. But criticising the country's leadership that day would mean supporting the enemy. That was not the time for discussions of any type. This time would come later, after our victory…

So there. One way or another, that horrendous day was ending. *In toto*, 160 missiles had been fired at the Ukrainian territory. The Russian troops had managed to make considerable headway inside the country. The most dramatic developments – excepting Kyiv, Kharkiv, and the directions leading to Sumy and Chernihiv, had clearly taken place in the south. The invader had reached Melitopol, abutted on Kherson, from where the direct routes opened up to gain access to adjacent oblasts: those of Mykolaiv and Odesa.

Ok, those were the hair-raising developments here. But what had happened that day in Moscow? People must have been discombobulated, not to say stupefied. Even the high-placed officials had been unaware of an imminent full-scale invasion into Ukraine…

....

[242]   UP, without date, https://www.pravda.com.ua/cdn/cd1/reconstruction/a3.html (accessed 03.07.2025).

And what about the army? They were so confident of an easy and speedy victory, that the Russian fighting cocks had been sent to the frontline without any proper training or supplies. Some of them had even thought they were going on a drill…

That came from a Russian soldier: 'We never got warned about no "special operation". We went to take part in a training exercise. They moved us from one location to another. On February 23rd, we arrived at this place and just sat around, waiting for something. Then we were told to put on our body armour and keep it on, they issued us with sub-machine guns. Shortly before, they'd brought into our unit a lot of ammunition, much more than is used in a regular drill. No one explained anything at all, just told us to load the ammunition into trucks, and that was that. They said the place of deployment would change. No one knew what was going on. We still thought it was a drill. I guess the commanders did know in advance, and were getting ready for a "special operation" but they kept it from us, the soldiers. All they said was that there would be a route march to over there (towards Ukraine). On the twenty-fourth, our brigade opened fire from our artillery units: "aim to where we tell you." We didn't know what we were firing at. But when the fire was first returned, we twigged that something was wrong. It looked like Ukraine started firing back and defending itself… I had my mobile on me and read in the news that Russia had started… an invasion. We realised that our armed forces had attacked Ukraine. It dawned on us that it was really war. It was a proper shock, all round. We hadn't been ready for such a turn of events…'

Several hours after the start of invasion it became clear: allies of Ukraine assessed our chances for success as zero. Based on Zelensky's initial telephone conversations, one got the impression that some of his opposite numbers would like to see this 'conflict' resolved ASAP, even if it meant surrender of Ukraine. 'No one of those who called me believed that we were holding on. The reason was this demonization of the Russian leader, his power, his philosophy, the massive promotion for the might of the Russian army… They thought we'd be dealt with in two or three days, five at the most, and then everything would be over…'

The principal conclusions of the first – insane! – day of the war:

Under the fierce attack by this heavily armed monster, Ukraine hadn't collapsed. It held the line and gave it as good as it could be. The vital military decisions had been approved and a viable power structure had been put in place. Even in a worst-case scenario, the legitimacy of power was thus secured.

But how would it all develop after that?

What would then happen in the days to come?

That was a question no one could answer.

The most immediate task was to hold the line…

25 – 28 February 2022.
If Only We Could Hold the Line…

'Dismantling of Ukraine'

On February 25th, the second day of the invasion, one could physically sense the tension in the air. War was everywhere, underway full blast – on land, in the air, on the sea. Not a local conflict this time, but an actual war…

It was hard to know whether we'd slept at all that night, because the sirens wailed and the rockets pounded non-stop, so both mum and me kept waking up. How could it be otherwise? What it felt like was a drowsy semi-consciousness.

In the morning, I leapt out of bed, peeped out of our enclosed balcony. In the distance, the entire horizon was on fire, plumes of black smoke rising upwards. One simply couldn't tell where our army was and where the 'liberators' were.

I went into the room with the TV.

Mum was already watching it, sound reduced, so's not to wake me up.

'And? What's going on?'

'There are places where ours are fighting back… But here and there, they're withdrawing. And those – some of ours are fighting back… Some are retreating… And those bastards barge right on in…'

It was mindboggling. Outside – it was war, and what a war! Yet the TV operated as per usual. Presenters in their studio narrated something… Showed footage… Something about Mars… Meanwhile, breaking news kept arriving from all over. One update after another…

At a session on the night of February 25th, the European Union agreed on a package of sanctions against Russia. Charles Michel, President of the European Council, said: 'In this dark hour our thoughts are with Ukraine and the innocent casualties – women, men and children – facing this totally unprovoked aggression, fearing for their lives. We shall call the Kremlin to account!'[243]

....

[243]   X. com, 25 February 2022, https://x.com/eucopresident/status/14967106363567 47266?lang=bn&mx=2 (accessed 03.07.2025).

The TV reported that thousands of Kyiv residents had spent the night in bomb shelters, and inside the Metro. Not everyone, though – there was footage recorded at three in the morning at a weapons distribution station. The queue in front of it was a kilometre long. The night was cold and gusty, but they just stood there, waiting in the snow: men and women. We were about to be 'liberated from Nazis', so the people decided to defend themselves.

They kept showing Blinken's statement practically on the loop: 'All available data prove that the Russians intend to surround Kyiv.'

True enough – a huge number of tanks and various other vehicles were moving from Sumy Oblast towards Kyiv. Meanwhile, enormous mechanised convoys bypassed Chornobyl and had reached Dymer and Ivankiv, the latter being half-way between the state border and the capital. In an attempt to impede progress of the tank convoy towards Kyiv, the bridge had been blown up over the Teteriv River. And once they'd reached Dymer, the way would open both to Vyshhorod and Hostomel, where just then the battle was raging on.

Ever since early morning, in Vyshhorod, the sound of roaring guns kept growing in volume. This intensifying audibility meant that the enemy was really close. On TV we saw people racing around, with bags, children in tow. Those who could were leaving by cars. The AFU land forces warned of a possible Russian incursion into Vorzel and nearby settlements: 'Meet the invader with fire! All to arms!'

Yet it was possible to reach Kyiv from the side of Chernihiv, too. At that point Chernihiv was shelled heavily, fires burning everywhere. Yet the Russian troops failed to seize the city in one easy move. They partially blocked it and moved on, for the main target, after all, was Kyiv. Chernihiv would get its comeuppance later.

There was this interesting piece, too. It was reported that on its way forward, this armada had run against a single tank brigade, two thousand-strong, under the command of Leonid Khoda, who had forced the enemy's convoys disperse over the side roads, difficult to negotiate, where the enemy kept getting stuck in the fields and marshes – already thawing out after the winter, where it was ambushed by the regular forces and the territorial defence. At the same time the vehicles moving along the highways either tripped the mines or become an easy target for our mobile weapons. A military expert posted: 'Their problem is conceit. They believe that in comparison to them Ukraine is small. That's to say, they expected to simply crush it underfoot, roll their tanks across it, and call it a day.'

OK, I more or less got on top of the situation in Kyiv.

But what about the south? Over there, things were grim.

On the Kherson direction of approach, the AFU were most likely retreating from the Antonivka Bridge over the Dnipro towards Chornobaivka on the Left Bank. If they failed to keep their position there, they'd have to start regrouping towards Mykolaiv.

Another southern route of retreat led to Melitopol. It had proved impossible to keep the city, the AFU troops had withdrawn northwards and entrenched some 44 kilometres short of Zaporizhzhia, and the reinforcement joined them there.

07:00 a.m. The Polish radio stated that nine centres had been set up on the border to welcome Ukrainian refugees.

08:50 a.m. Odesa – there, thank God, the air defence systems had operated quite successfully.

09:00 a.m. Kharkiv: the Russian troops had tried to break into the outskirts, approaching simultaneously from several directions.

I tore myself away from the news for a minute. If only I could concentrate… But truth be told, I didn't even feel like contemplating… Imagine if 'something' hits your building, then what? There'd be no other thoughts then, all you'd do would be imagining your own death. For no one could guarantee that you would survive the day. And even if you did, would you be able to make it through the day after? Survival was a problem, even if you hid in a basement. God Almighty, did it really mean that my life would come to an end – and at my age? Could it be possible?

There-there. I had to calm down. Keep myself in check. Somehow gain control over my own mind, work out a way to fit in. To try and live on, under those new and horrendous realia.

But no! Why just 'try and live on?'

I had to do something! By all means, I had to act.

In the morning, Taras and I ran to that address, God alone knows what it had been before, perhaps a warehouse. And again, the first thing we found was a crowd! We reckoned it had to be some sort of headquarters – what with men of all ages everywhere, inside and outside, yet no jostling, arguing or swearing. Some were seated, some lay on the floor. It turned out to be a queue for firearms. Were they issued to everyone or what?

Somebody shared:

'The queue in Troieshchyna is a kilometre long![244] The folk wait for hours before they get their side arms! Also, they are only issued to those who stay. Who are ready to take part in defence!'

....

[244] **Troieshchyna:** a large dormitory district in Kyiv, located on the city's north-ern-left bank.

'But in other places,' somebody piped in, 'like hell will you get anything even if it's your turn in the queue. They say not just anyone can get arms. Also, you've got to have the proper documents on you, and proof that you've done your service, have the skills. Only then they'll sign your contract and issue the weapons. What's gonna happen here, dunno. But look, someone's coming out, armed, praise be to God.'

'Oh man, what a pity one couldn't make a documentary in a place like this,' Taras whispered into my ear. 'You see, who'd need a script? Nothing to write, and no one to chase for an endorsement. No need for a director, either, who'd be delaying things. You see, man, no need for any of this at all!'

It was truly inspiring – so many people, motivated to come to the rescue of their own city!

This spectacle just couldn't leave you indifferent. This had to be the future of Ukraine, heatedly debated throughout the last 30 years…

Long story short, Taras and I had been sent to another headquarters, the one in charge of the defence posts. I wasn't even sure if they registered us, in accordance with all the rules or just waved us through. It wasn't all that important…

We galloped to this other place – and saw yet another sea of people, all waiting and scanning news. And so, we, too, immersed ourselves into our phones.

The air was almost cracking with electricity: the invader was speedily making headway towards the capital city, approaching from three directions. They moved especially fast from the direction of Belarus. They had come within a stone's throw of the Kyiv's outskirts in the north and north-west. Apparently, their leading armoured groups were already on the Zhytomyr's Motorway, as well as heading towards the district of Obolon in Kyiv.

09:15 a.m. A massive cannonade could be heard in Obolon. The Minsk district was under fire. The Defence Ministry announced: 'A group of enemy saboteurs had positioned itself in Obolon. We request all citizens to keep us informed about the enemy's vehicles movements. Make Molotov cocktails, destroy the invaders! Residents – please stay vigilant.' Arrival of the enemy's landed troops was announced as a possibility.

It later was reported that a Russian hit squad, having seized two AFU's cars, changed into Ukrainian military uniforms and sped towards the city centre. In their wake drove several trucks. Their aim was to get inside the governmental quarter by passing themselves off as reinforcements. Once close to the President's Office, they were to engage in a fight with the security. After an intense shoot-out, the group had been taken down.

10:00 a.m. News came from the city of Dnipro. Properly reinforced roadblocks had been erected around its perimeter. There were no updates about the shelling attacks – allegedly, there had been so many, that it made no sense to keep writing about them.

Yet there was practically no Russian advancement in Donbas. Well, this was to be expected: it would've been really hard to break the Ukrainian defence lines over there. Besides, that was exactly where our main forces had been concentrated.

11:00 a.m. Russian helicopters headed, yet again, towards Hostomel airfield. They were expected to be joined by the units moving from the side of Belarus – the Russians had managed to seize the airfield for the second time.

Boyko, the leader of the pro-Russian OPZZh faction in parliament, contacted his "colleague" and close ally of Putin and asked only one question: does Putin know that Russian troops are bombing Russian-speaking Kharkiv, Sumy, and Odessa? The answer was: "Yes, he knows."[245]

11:00 a.m. Italian Prime Minister Mario Draghi sounded agitated when announcing that President Zelensky had not been in touch with him, despite their earlier arrangement.

Eventually, Zelensky did show up and took part in the Extraordinary Summit of the European Union. Prime Minister of Sweden Magdalena Andersson noted: 'He spoke from somewhere that looked like a cellar or a bunker. Told us about the situation in Ukraine. When signing off, we were all aware that we may never see each other again. It all depends on the developments over the next several days.'

11:20 a.m. An avalanche of testimonials about Russian military vehicles making speedy progress through Belarus: convoys rattling on, military aircraft flying by, among them – some freighters.

10:00-12:00 a.m. The two trains carrying the second party from the Ukrainian government arrived [one of them somewhat earlier; the other, shortly afterwards] in Ivano-Frankivsk. Chernyshov: 'I haven't divulged their time of arrival. The passengers hadn't been informed, either, for reasons of security. And then there was this moment when we arrived, when some of them, including the ministers, were amazed to find out where we all had ended up.'[246]

'Ha!' sneered Taras. 'They must have hoped to end up in Lviv, a city with a million inhabitants. Where all the embassies are by now. Where everything is bright and shimmering. Also, the border's just round the corner... OK, I'm kidding.'

<hr>

[245]   European Pravda, 6 December 2024, https://www.eurointegration.com.ua/rus/articles/2024/12/6/7199623/ (accessed 03.07.2025).

[246]   UP, 8 March 2024, https://www.pravda.com.ua/podcasts/63f90cc807994/2024/03/8/7397132/ (accessed 03.07.2025).

Whatever the reasoning, the managerial decision about Ivano-Frankivsk was the correct one – by that point, Lviv was already bursting at the seams.

The telephone rang, sounding unusually cheerful:

'Hooray! We've made it!' Spyridon and Bolik both yelled excitedly into the receiver. 'We sat in this jam all the way to Zhytomyr! Might still be there if we continued travelling west. But we veered off left, towards Berdychiv. You know, this whole trip used to take two and a half hours but it's taken us 14! How did the driver survive it at all! Everyone was so grateful...'

Hmmm... They did manage to break out. Several days later we learnt that on that very motorway – Kyiv-Lviv – our 'brothers' had gunned down several vehicles with refugees. Eventually, the motorway came to be known as the 'Road of Death'.

We were approached by a man. Middle-aged, corpulent, strong – nature had been generous to him.

'We are about to start erecting a roadblock near Zhovten cinema. I've been told you are filmmakers. Makes sense to send you there. Follow me.'

He walked around, selecting several more guys, and we all set off after him.

He was an imposing guy – had fought in the ATO,[247] and the wound he'd received in that previous war in the East had left with a limp. With this new turn of events, he tried to rejoin the army but was told: 'Hold on. Can't' you see what's going on around you? Defence posts are mushrooming all over the place, some of them official, some unofficial. Lots of people got their hands on the arms, got cocky. Some even started bragging. Your work here is cut out for you – someone's got to take charge. Weapons should be used against the enemy whereas this crowd is ready to treat nearly every passer-by as a saboteur. You are assigned two sites: this roadblock, and later you'll arrange a firing ground on the Rybalsky Peninsular.[248] Some of these guys haven't handled arms for a hundred years, and some – never at all.'

For some reason, we all started treating him as our 'battalion commander' and calling him 'Commander' for brevity. He might even have been one in the days of the ATO, who could tell. Although, none of it was all that important. And thus, he became Commander.

....

[247] **Anti-Terrorist Operation Zone**, or **ATO zone:** a term used by the media, publicity, the Ukrainian government, the OSCE, and other foreign institutions for Ukrainian territory in the Donetsk and Luhansk oblasts that was under the control of Russian military forces and pro-Russian separatists.

[248] **Rybalsky Peninsula:** on the Dnipro River, located in the Right-bank Podil neighbourhood of Kyiv in the vicinity of Kyiv Harbour.

Back at the headquarters, a bespectacled guy also attached himself to our party. He looked about 40. 'I'm Gennady,' he said. 'We're Kiril and Taras,' we answered in unison. In short, we were thus introduced.

Before we even left, the Commander had put in an application for some concrete slabs, sand, and the Czech hedgehogs, following which, he engaged in a heated argument with somebody. In the end, he dangled before us a bunch of massive keys: 'What did they expect? That we should end up without any refuge?'

It turned out he had managed to wrangle some kind of a cellar for our use. That was where we'd headed and started to settle in. The people must have spotted our crew from their windows and started bringing in whatever they could: some sleeping bags, Coremats, all types of food. And the restaurant round the corner – I did wonder what it was they were doing with themselves in times like that? – they even sent over some hot meals.

We were all waiting for a moment when, either that very evening or the day after, the Russians would try to fight their way into the city centre. No big words were used but we all knew that we were there to defend our country, our city, and in that case – the entire borough. There was this feeling of a shared goal. And everyone realised that the first thing to do was to fortify the crossroads. Still, no materials had been made available as yet.

A bit later a dump truck did arrive and unloaded a pile of sand.

'Well, now, boys. Our dear Western "allies" haven't supplied anything apart from the "guerrilla" weapons, but even those are thin on the ground. They only started sending something on the eve of the actual invasion. So that's my question to you – will those Russkies kick our asses or are we worth something after all?'

'"Cause we are...' Taras stuttered awkwardly.

'I've just got a call from yet another jerk who's bringing us our sacks,' the Commander interrupted. 'The bastard even tried to lecture me on how a hundred should be enough to start with. A fuckwit!'

The Commander spat on the ground, clearly in anger.

'OK. Talking of barricades – let's see what you, lot, gonna come up with for me.'

Well, sacks with sand it was going to be.

'Chins up, the young 'uns,' he softened somewhat. 'We'll work, all of us, not just you. Me included, whatever I'll be good for...'

The sacks arrived and we started loading them with sand. Someone found a barrow from somewhere, so we set about erecting something like a defensive dike. After several hours I was as tired as never before in my life.

We did need the Czech hedgehogs, though, the Commander was close to yelling. Still, no hedgehogs...

'Most likely, none are left,' the Commander was explaining things to our crew. 'They've first got to be cut out of some metal, then welded together. Now, if we're talking about the governmental quarter – I've just been called – they delivered them there yesterday.'

No 'hedgehogs', but they did supply us with concrete slabs, even if nowhere near enough – only enough to hide behind if the Russkies did push through.

During the breaks we continued monitoring the news. Like before, the developments were alarming. I wasn't sure about the state of our preparedness for this war but the Russian army had gained control over Kherson Oblast easily and quickly. As early as the day before they had made a substantial inland advance and approached Kherson from the left bank. Today, they will try to cross the Dnipro over Antoniv Bridge.

And here parts of the Russian column advancing from Belarus got even closer to the capital – from the direction of Obolon and Sviatoshyn. It felt like a genuine apocalypse.

It was impossible to see what was coming next. Should they gain access, it would mean that our defence post, and the other posts like ours, would have to come face to face with them. The road from Obolon ran directly towards us. We were stationed on Mezhyhirska Street, a transport thoroughfare. They would have to veer off a bit first, but after that the access would be unimpeded. And so, we kept glancing in that direction. Neither Taras nor I could even start imagining what this possible clash with the bloody Russkies would be like. And so, we kept our counsel and refrained from asking questions. Then again, no one talked much. The Commander was the only one with some vision of the situation. At least, that was what he kept repeating: 'As for me, I get it all.'

12:00 p.m. Reznikov: 'We have decided that the Territorial Defence should include patriots over 60 years of age, morally and physically capable of resisting and overpowering the enemy. In Kyiv alone they have distributed 18,000 submachine guns, complete with ammunition, and the process is continuing. Thousands of people are joining the Territorial Defence, ready to take on the enemy. I am proud of every one of you!'[249]

Scores of experienced military pilots, from captains to generals, had returned to the Air Force. But the young ones proved themselves too: one of them received a nickname – the Ghost of Kyiv, and had already downed several aircraft!

....

[249]   LB.ua, 25 February 2022, https://lb.ua/society/2022/02/25/506800_reznikov_sil_teroboroni.html (accessed 03.07.2025).

By the way, at that point we'd become friends with this bespectacled Gennady, and a kind of a social circle had emerged. He shared with us a news item he'd found on his iPhone.

12:55 p.m. Russian Foreign Minister Lavrov: 'Russia is ready to negotiate on the subject of Ukraine – as soon as the Ukrainian army lay down their arms.'

'True to form,' was Gennady's comment.

At which point came a hope-inspiring update: our army had blown up the dam, along with its bridge, in Kazarovychi – the place where the Irpin River flows into the Kyiv Reservoir. The aim was to prevent the Russian tank convoys from crossing the river and continuing their advance towards Kyiv. The water flooded, thus creating a natural obstacle for their onslaught. All our guys had to do was to observe the Russian armoured vehicles making desolate circles over the other bank, stripped of a chance to move on. Not bad! Not bad at all! The manoeuvre was sure to gain some time, and so better prepare for the defence of Kyiv!

But in other places, too, our army did not hesitate to bomb the highways and rail tracks – anything that could hinder the bloody Russian invaders. It was asserted that this 'scorched-earth policy' would play a significant role in deterring the aggressors and preventing the seizure of Kyiv. Apparently, our troops needed another two to three days to complete equipping themselves and move forward towards the defence positions. And if it proved possible to hold the line, the Russians should ready themselves for an increased number of unpleasant surprises.

All things considered, the Irpin-Bucha-Hostomel line near Kyiv remained a challenge. That was where the Russians were attempting to break through. We watched, in dismay, the developments taking place slightly to the north, in the village of Moshchun. That was the final obstacle on the road to Kyiv.

Up till noon, fierce fighting had continued in other regions of Ukraine. The Russians had fought their way into a city populated by a million and a half of residents – Kharkiv, only 40 kilometres away from the border. They were thrown back, but continued their attempts to encircle the city.

What else? Obviously, the south. It was painful even to think about it.

The Crimean isthmus had been surrendered for incomprehensible reasons; the impression was that the southern cities had been hardly defended, if at all. The Russian speedy advancement on Kherson and Mariupol did look suspicious. One thing was clear, though: while the war was raging on, certain questions should better not be raised. For the time being, it was best to forget about political strife and expression of opposing views.

Still, this thought kept pounding in my head: why? Why? There were so many different questions… The main one among them: why did the enemy have to be stopped not on the border but in the urban boroughs, where each shell meant indiscriminate death to so many people?

Closer to one in the afternoon Zelensky put forward, yet again, a proposal to come to the negotiating table – 'to stop people dying.' In the same breath, he called the Russian aggression not just an 'invasion' but 'opening a war on Europe. On European unity. On elementary rights of individuals in Europe. On all rules of coexistence on this continent. On European powers refusing to reallocate borders through use of force.'

Zelensky appealed to Europe itself, urging it to become more active in helping Ukraine: 'How are you going to defend yourselves if your help to us is so sluggish?'[250] He addressed citizens of European countries, inviting them to come to Ukraine and join us in our efforts to defend Europe.

The afternoon outside was cold and miserable. We'd shortly dropped back into the cellar – to get warm. We'd heard that some forward-deployed parties – either Russian regular troops, or saboteurs – had made their way into certain quarters within the city.

02:00 p.m. Klitchko: 'Kyiv has entered the stage of defence. Shots and explosions are ringing out in some areas of the city. The army is neutralising Russian agents of sedition. Everybody capable of joining the defence must do so and help our fighters!'[251] He also advised the city residents to create their personal water reserves, lay in supplies of food and items of first necessity.

Certain announcements were bordering on hysteria: 'Kyiv may fall!'; 'Zelensky may be kidnapped or even killed!'

Zelensky himself was appealing to the people, advising them to fight back with Molotov cocktails. The Kyiv residents, eager to join the defence efforts, continued to receive arms. Over a hundred of the people's deputies, the first to be armed, were ready to come to the rescue of the capital. It was asserted on the grapevine that the allies kept up their pressure on Zelensky to leave Kyiv temporarily, so that both him and the first party of the government followed the example of various diplomatic missions and moved to Lviv. It was possible to govern the country on Zoom. Another option was to carry on into Poland, where he could create a government in exile. And from there, continue to fight. Biden and Johnson both expressed their willingness to grant Zelensky and his family asylum – either in the USA or the UK.

[250] LB.ua, 25 February 2022, https://lb.ua/news/2022/02/25/506819_zelenskiy_ievropi_yak_zbiraietesya.html (accessed 03.07.2025).

[251] Kyiv official website, 25 February 2022, https://kyivcity.gov.ua/news/vitaliy_klichko_stolitsya_vstupila_v_fazu_oboroni/ (accessed 03.07.2025).

Everybody froze in suspense: would Zelensky stay in the city?

But he uttered that phrase of his: 'Fighting is going on here. I need ammunition, not a pleasure trip.'[252] He enunciated it with precision. Then, he categorically refused to leave the beleaguered capital city. People's faith in the president instantly soared.

Somewhat later the bespectacled Gennady shoved his mobile towards us once more:

'Everyone's discussing Peskov's statement about the negotiations and agreements on Ukraine's neutral status!'

'Ha! The bastards now feel their nether regions itch!' Taras spat in disgust. 'I don't get it, though… They started such a war, and now they are ready to negotiate? Weird…'

'Sure thing!' came back Gennady. 'This "liberation" is nothing short of bestial. The world community is also quite agitated. Their losses are quite high, too. Most likely, they never counted on this degree of resistance.'

'So, they really want negotiations?' I wanted to be sure.

'They sure do. Us too. Our authorities will clutch at any straw. But that's hardly the point – the Russians want it all on their terms. That is, we surrender, end of story. Look here…' Gennady pointed to another bit of news on his mobile. 'They've just reposted Putin's reply from Moscow. He's ready to send a delegation of those representing the Defence Ministry, Foreign Ministry, and the Presidential Administration to Minsk, to open negotiations with the Russian Federation.'

And that was what we'd learnt about the enemy's losses.

02:30 p.m. The command of the AFU ground forces: '… The Russian army has lost over one thousand men. In the entire period of its existence, Russia has never experienced such a level of losses during a similar length of combat in any armed conflict she has initiated.'[253] Shortly followed a statement from Konashenkov, a spokesman for Russia's Ministry of Defence: 'Russia has sustained no losses during its conflict with Ukraine.'[254] Hmmm… In other words, furious fighting was going on, but they somehow managed to avoid any losses. Uncanny…

....

[252]   X. com, 26 February 2022, https://x.com/UkrEmbLondon/status/149750613469 2970499

[253]   Novynarnia, 25 February 2022, https://novynarnia.com/2022/02/25/hronika-ob-orony-ukrayiny-den-2/ (accessed 03.07.2025).

[254]   Novynarnia, 25 February 2022, https://novynarnia.com/2022/02/25/hronika-ob-orony-ukrayiny-den-2/ (accessed 03.07.2025).

And then, most likely the best news of all. The landing strips at the two airports – Zhuliany and Boryspil – had been drowned in oil, blocked with vehicles, and then, mined. The enemy's aircraft could not land there anymore.

'That's the end of the game for them, with their blasted blitzkrieg!' The Commander clapped his palms in excitement. 'Hostomel, Zhuliany, and Boryspil are now inaccessible! What's left is only Vasylkiv. You mark my words – they'll thrust through there. No other way.'

Another piece of news: several days before the invasion, President of the German Federal Intelligence Service Bruno Kahl had flown into Kyiv to take part in the consultations on the current situation. On the first day of war, he hadn't been able to make it to the evacuation station assigned to German citizens, so the Special Task Force had urgently evacuated him to the Polish border.

The general turmoil continued, in everything and everywhere. You could cut the air with a knife – it was so tense. Isolated Russian reconnaissance groups kept pitching here and there, all over the city. The situation was extremely volatile, changing by the hour.

Then came a frightening update: Russians were at the Kyiv HPP! From the hydroelectric station's dam, right-bank Kyiv is like the palm of your hand! It was only six and a half kilometres to the city's boundary, 15 – if you continued straight on – to the city centre. Ho-o-o-o-o-rror!

By then, those who stayed in the city restarted their frenetic shopping, buying up whatever was still available. The shelves became practically empty.

'Wha' you talking about? We are not getting any supplies anymore. We've run out of any new stuff. And very near to running out of what's left…' warned the shop assistants.

The goods being scooped up was to be expected. But if the fighting was to start inside the city, how long would it take? What if it were a drawn-out affair? And one wouldn't be able to step out of one's flat?

Mum gave me a call, sounding alarmed:

'Sure thing, defend the city, like everyone else. But think about yourself too. A security expert has just spoken on TV: "The citizens should make sure that they stay as far as they can from the epicentre of fighting. You shouldn't indulge your curiosity about what's going on around you. Hide, hide, and hide again, so's not to catch it in the neck." That was his advice. Be careful, sweetheart.'

Christ Almighty, what was going to happen? Would the city really be encircled? Or worse, would the enemy get inside?

And then, at last!!: About an hour earlier, the AFU had started bringing in their equipment into Kyiv, getting ready to defend the city. The residents were asked to refrain from filming it.

04:00 p.m. Current Time TV was showing footage from the Ukrainian-Polish border:[255] 'Due to high concentration of people and cars, the situation is far from simple. We've spent last evening, the night and a better part of today sitting in a jam that started some 12 kilometres ahead of the border. The traffic has been progressing extremely slowly, with no wardens to regulate it; spontaneous quarrels flared up here and there – everyone was nervous. Besides, there are no toilets or services. Approximately by midnight, our queue started creeping forward. Closer to the border security area, the wardens appeared and explained that under a new decree, males aged between 18 and 60 could no longer leave Ukraine. Somebody tried to argue, but the majority simply turned round and left, perhaps in search of a different control point. Police on the Polish side of the border exercises total control. Straight away, you are approached by volunteers who, without even asking about your nationality, offer help, especially medical assistance. Many cars are waiting nearby, people are ready to give you a lift to your destination. When crossing the border, citizens of Ukraine have it easier because of their visa-free status. On seeing our Belarusian passports, the Ukrainian border guards asked – not quite disdainfully but with a clear sense of hurt: "Why have you treated us like this, you, our Belarusian kinsfolk?" For a split second we lost the power of speech, then tried to explain that it wasn't the entire nation acting in this way towards Ukraine, that the Belarusians respected the Ukrainians, that all the goings-on in Belarus are masterminded exclusively by Alexandre Lukashenko...'

04:20 p.m. With enormous effort and significant losses, the Russian army broke through Kherson defence line, thus gaining control over a route into the city, i.e., the Antonivka Bridge.

All throughout the day, the news was pouring in from Mykolaiv. Seizing this city was one of the invaders' main objectives, a key to the Russian strategy of cutting off the southern coast of Ukraine. Control over this city would open up the route towards Odesa, which, in its turn, would enable creation of an overground corridor towards the Trans-Dniester Republic.

Major General Marchenko arrived in the city, having been put in charge of its defence. 'By four in the morning, there was not a single roadblock there, not a single patrol, nor any army man or policeman. The city was completely deserted... Still, Mykolaiv has something that Kherson didn't have – time. We're gradually putting together a system of defence. The city has been divided into four parts; each has its own officer assigned to it. Signal posts are being

----

[255] **Current Time TV:** a Russian-language television channel with an editorial office in Prague, created by the US organisations Radio Free Europe/Radio Liberty and Voice of America.

installed at each point of entry into the city, complete with piles of tyres and incendiary mixtures. Should the tanks get near, the tyres are to be set on fire to give a signal and a reference point to anti-tank groups. Unlike Kherson Oblast, we shall blow up the bridges.'[256]

06:15 p.m. Municipal authorities of Kyiv appealed to the residents of high-rises with access to the roof space, to run urgent checks up there, in order to identify the presence of potential markers for missile strikes. 'Should you discover anything of the kind, please cover it with soil or place something on top.'

Whoopsie! The first 'swallows' foretelling the future logistical cock-ups. Because of problems with supplies of fuel and provisions, the Russkies had to come to a halt near Konotop. The tank drivers roamed around with their empty jerry cans, trying to find a way to fill them. The soldiers extorted food from the local population. First reports arrived of the local retail establishments being looted.

Our outfit grew – the Commander brought in a new guy in the evening.

He explained in whisper: 'I wasn't all that keen on him. He's odd somehow. But I was given a direct order…'

And then in a loud voice: 'We've got reinforcements from Uzhhorod. He's sprinted right to where we are, to join us. Other folk do a bunk to over there, and he's done the opposite. He's, well… In a word… A true patriot. Practically, a hero!'

And the guy goes: 'Why such big words? We need to defend ourselves, and that's all there is to it.'

We all stopped in our tracks. The dude was kitted out in a super-cool uniform. I wondered if something like it was even available within NATO. It boggled imagination – from where, I wondered, could he have sourced all that beautiful stuff? His personal kit was even more impressive – all those gadgets, hanging off his wide belt! Little canisters, whose purpose was yet to be identified, a pair of gloves with spikes, various chains, huge protective dark glasses that could cover half his face. Also, a knife in its sheath, a gas mask, a helmet and even a pair of handcuffs – all that dangled from his back. How did he manage to even walk around, carrying all this stuff along? Must have been made of some super-strong but super-light alloys.

'Wow, this guy does have some gear!' Taras communicated his message with his eyes. 'Fit for any scenario in combat! The dude comes prepared…'

<hr>

[256]   Inshe.tv, 31 January 2024, https://inshe.tv/important/2024-01-31/825409/ (accessed 04.07.2025).

'Unlike you and me,' I answered with my eyes, too. 'We're like some kinder-garten kids. Still, what on earth does he need those handcuffs for?'

'But of course! You take a Russian prisoner, then what? How to keep him in check till someone comes along to take him away? But here, he puts the handcuffs on, chains him to a lamppost, and is free to mind his own business.'

'He's got a satchel, too! I wonder what else could be inside?'

'Perhaps, an inflatable mini-raft? To cross the Dnipro without sweat? Let them shut down all bridges, he won't mind!'

Still, the main point was none of this. He also had a kind of a snub-nosed gun, too!

We all stood around, of course, admiring his gear, and only our Commander frowned and looked at the guy with suspicion.

The dude's name turned out to be Denis. He was older than the rest of us, perhaps 25. As a matter of fact, he'd hoped to get on active service, so dashed, like us, into a recruitment office. They had him registered: 'And now wait for word. At this point, we've got enough people.' In other words, same as us. If they did need somebody at that point, it would be someone with experience.

In a word, Taras and I, compared to this Denis here, were complete spring chickens.

On the other hand, was it all that important? The main thing was that he was here, and would also do his bit, putting his gear to good use.

'This is what interests me,' the Commander cut into our silent exchange. 'How has it happened that several precious days before the outbreak of war have been wasted? Say what you want, but it was clear they'd go ahead!'

'Someone in power did explain it yesterday,' I felt a need to but in. 'He said, it was impossible to accept. After all, one of the tactics used by the Kremlin is to instigate chaos.'

'Sure thing. An exhaustive explanation.' The Commander didn't try to hide his irony. 'It's always easier to explain things away. Especially after the fact...'

He pushed his hat to one side, wiped his forehead with a kerchief, smiled mischievously:

'This "political leader" over there... He's committed an irreversible mistake. They placed their stakes on people rushing out to welcome them with flowers! Fuck knows who they employ as "analysts" in that Kremlin of theirs!'

'They never had any clear understanding of the situation,' piped in the be-spectacled Gennady. He was the wisest of us, although we still had no idea what he'd been before the war. Even the Commander listened to what he had to say. 'The crux of the matter is that our peoples have a vastly different attitude to-wards power. In Russia, they almost worship it. Always ready to drop to their knees. Whereas here, we've never really trusted it. Whoever the president, we never were in a rush to genuflect. Nothing could be worse for a Ukrainian than to express faith in some disingenuous politician. Zelensky, too, was first elected on a wave of long-cherished hopes. Yet, some time had passed, and they got less exulted. Nowadays is a different story. It's war! Force major – and he's proved to be a genuine leader. That was when people's faith in him bounced back up. Meanwhile what we see in Russia is a supine, slavish subjugation to power, bordering on adoration. Yuk!'

Phew! We were finished for that day which, again, we'd spent loading up sacks with sand –brought in by another truck – and building the rampart. My whole body was aching from this unprecedented excursion. Some of the sand, though, was still left for the following day. Good. It would help to relax the groaning muscles. Hmmm… Hopefully, we would avoid being seized by storm.

In the evening, Taras and I, being the green ones, were kicked out from the defence post for the night – to have fewer people milling around the post and the cellar.

'I just got a call,' the commander clicked his fingers in our direction. 'Some of our territorial defence battalions have received short-range NLAW anti-tank guided missiles. Excellent news!.. But you… You – go. Don't hang around,' 'Stay ready, though. Would be a good idea, too, to have a couple of hours' kip. Get back for the night. And don't be late!'

Back home I sat staring at the darkness. After all, the Dnipro was just round the corner, so cold air was wafting in from that direction. The night had long since enveloped the city. The lights were coming up in sequence – that was the streets. Well may be, they would switch it all off in the near future, to deprive the Russkies of landmarks. The windows were triple glazed, and it did shut out the sounds but not entirely. In the distance, or perhaps, not that far away, something kept crashing – bang-bang-kaboom!

I got myself into mum's room and hit upon a TV footage from the scene of main action.

It was drizzling and muddy. The road was clogged with refugees. There were endless lines of people who didn't run but trudge, must have been on the road for some time. They looked dead beat.

A carriage of some sort was carrying little children. In their arms, they held even younger ones, toddlers.

A little boy was dragging a dog by the lead, but it looked like he had hardly any strength left to go forward himself.

The most exhausted would take a break, slumping onto a kerb, straight into mud, some already lying down.

Two older women shuffled along, with their old man…

In their wake – a woman, a baby in her arms. The other one, an older child who could barely put one foot in front of the other, she was pulling forward by hand.

A body in the road-side ditch, someone who died, having given up.

In the distance one could make out flashes of light – the Russians moving on, bombing, destroying everything on their way and yet, advancing.

The rain grew heavier. The exodus of people continued. The 'Nazis' were retreating, yielding a portion of their territory to the Russians…

I returned to my room and immediately plunged into the news.

Propaganda on Russian websites – I entered them out of curiosity – was reporting joyfully: the Ukrainian capital had been blocked from several directions. Kadyrov, the Chechen leader, announced he would send to Ukraine something like 10,000 of his troops, to be used in the hottest spots: 'If you'd really like to meet us, we'd be happy to meet you over there!' he announced pompously and suggested Zelensky should apologise to Putin before it was too late.[257]

And then that, really worrying: the Maxar satellite images picked up significant build-ups of the Russian ground forces, especially several hundred units of military equipment, in the south of Belarus and also, about 150 military helicopters, some 30 kilometres off the Ukrainian border. That was to say, all of this was ready to start moving forth in our direction, coming from the 'fraternal Belarus', and in the nearest future.

Taras didn't forget to forward me the new stuff from his chatroom.

They confirmed something we'd been aware of, anyway: in the beginning, the ratio between the Russian and the Ukrainian forces near Kyiv amounted to 12:1 in favour of Russia. The best prepared and equipped AFU troops had been concentrated in the east of the country, at the demarcation line. They'd been placed there because everyone believed that was going to be the place for a future hullabaloo. Some individuals who had 'access to information' asserted that the AFU's leadership were seriously concerned about whether or not they would be able to stop an advance towards Kyiv. There was a clear shortage of military presence here. Apparently, the command is in despair, waiting for things to happen and become apparent…

As for the President's Office – they were already under siege. The rumours confirmed that the living conditions at Bankova Street were dire. They hardly

....

[257] *Kommersant*, 25 February 2022, https://www.kommersant.ru/doc/5236561 (accessed 04.07.2025).

ever ventured out, no catering arrangements to speak of, some slapdash meals at best. Apparently, they'd been supplied with instant Mivina that they diluted not with boiling but lukewarm water.[258] It didn't even get properly soaked. The shower had been put in, right in the corridor. And the top management were in the subterranean bunker.

And everywhere – in corridors, on stairs – stood, sat, and lay the armed soldiers. They even slept in turns, because of the lack of room. The weapons and ammunitions piled up in every corner, every Office employee was armed, too. Everyone was psyched up to return fire if ever an attack were launched at the Office. The president was armed too, he had a pistol on him. And supposedly was saying: 'How can you even think about it – the president of Ukraine, taken prisoner?' he might have been wisecracking, but perhaps not. 'But what if,' someone was horrified, 'if something were to pass… You?! Like this?' – 'Never you worry. Suicide isn't even an option. I'll be fighting back!'

And then he told his team: 'Ah well, they keep banging on, claiming that we've left for somewhere. We must put our faces out, if only so that people can see us. To say: we're here! We all are here!'

OK – there was some quite interesting stuff going on in Taras's chatroom. And now: why not switch the TV on to see what was going on in the informational sphere?

07:45 p.m. Just think of that! A video recording had been broadcast: practically all the country's leadership lined up in front of the President's Office. And that with the shots ringing out in the centre of Kyiv, and rumours circulating about Zelensky being the newest target for the Chehcen hitmen! But here he was: out with his entire team, making a video recording for the whole country to view – he was going nowhere! He was in office!

Zelensky said:

'Good evening to you all! The faction leader [D. Arakhamia, leader of the Servant of the People Party] is here; the head of the President's Office [A. Yermak] is here; Prime Minister Shmyhal is here; Podolyak [adviser to the head of the President's Office] is here; the president is here. We all are here, our army is here, our community [literally: "citizens of society"] is here. We all are present. We will defend our independence, our country. And that's how it's going to go on in future. Glory to our defenders, men and women. Glory to Ukraine!'

Those present at this improvised rally responded in force:

'Glory to heroes!'

----

[258] **Mivina:** a popular Ukrainian brand of instant noodles.

The prime minister raised his mobile to demonstrate the hour and the date.[259]

It was an important moment. Even if only short, this video allowed the entire country to see that no one had fled, that everyone was in their place.

Straight afterwards, came an update: a Russian landing force had tried to attack Thermal Power Plant (TPP) 6, in Troieshchyna. The enemy was very keen to seize it – the biggest power plant in the city, partially supplying our borough, too.

Nice stuff – had they been successful, we'd probably already be without electricity. How prudent had been that jaunt of mine to Pochaina, to get the batteries! Still, our guys had done a good job and taken out 60 saboteurs!

I went into the kitchen and found a video on my iPhone.

A Russian POW: 'Mum, I'm in Ukraine, taken prisoner!' 'Why did you even go there?' 'We all did…'

Another clip: 'We'd been told we would be taking over Ukraine… Our task was to seize Kyiv. We got in from Belarus. We were side by side with the Belarusians. In the outskirts of Kyiv, we came under fire. We ran out of ammunition; I was taken prisoner. I am sorry, I deeply regret my actions. One should not assault people who are one's brothers…'

All of them, once captured, either 'didn't know anything at all', or – in a rare case when they admitted anything! – were 'filled with remorse and repentance'. It became quite a template…

We returned to the defence post, and at ten in the evening, the air defence sirens howled: the first rockets were being fired on the city. After only five or ten minutes, we had already heard of severe damage to buildings and of fires everywhere. But by that point our army was taking position, especially in the city centre.

Some alarming news came from Vasylkiv – 33 kilometres south of Kyiv. Starting from the evening, the enemy had been bombing our troops and the airfield.

Another worrying development – an increase in the concentration of the Russian troops in Belarus. In addition to their existing presence, some 90 helicopters had been placed in the vicinity of the Belarusian town Khoiniki.

11:00 p.m. Mayor of Kyiv Klitchko: 'As morning approaches, this night promises to be very difficult. Kyiv is now defending itself. The bridges in the

259   25 February 2022, https://www.youtube.com/watch?v=RSQTnJh9dso (accessed 04.07.2025).

capital have been placed under enhanced protection and control, military equipment has been deployed there, and the AFU is keeping watch.'[260]

11:00 p.m. Zelensky's press secretary confirmed the president's readiness to negotiate with Moscow: 'We've given our consent; the parties are making arrangements regarding the place and time for such negotiations.'[261] Well, that was that, then. Clearly, at a time like this one had to clutch at any straw.

11:20 p.m. And then Zelensky himself announced that the Russians would try to take Kyiv by storm: 'This night will be harder than the day. Chernihiv, Sumy, Kharkiv are under attack… Kyiv is our priority, we cannot afford to lose it. This night the enemy will engage all their resources, eager to thwart our resistance. They are acting villainously, cruelly, and inhumanely. This night they will step up their assault. This night we must stand our ground!'[262] Meanwhile, the air raids in Kyiv continued.

11:30 p.m. Finally, some news from New York. As predicted earlier, Russia had vetoed the UN resolution to denounce her actions in Ukraine. Eleven out of 15 Security Council members had voted in favour, including permanent members – the USA, the UK, and France. Three countries abstained – China, India, and the UAE. The US Ambassador to the UN expressed her regret that the resolution had not been approved and emphasised that the UN had been created in the wake of the Second World War specifically with a view of preventing wars like the one unfolding in Ukraine. And the UK Permanent Representative to the UN called the situation absurd.

But for the Russians, all of this was like water off the duck's back. Russia's Permanent Representative to the UN Nebenzia arrogantly exclaimed that the purpose of the 'special military operation' would soon be achieved, that there had been no confirmed civilian casualties and that Kyiv was using peaceful residents as a 'live shield': 'Russia isn't waging a war against Ukraine and the Ukrainian people but is fighting "nationalists" and defending residents of Donbas.'

It did sound weird: they kept banging on about defending Donbas while attacking everyone and everywhere and bombing the entire territory of Ukraine. This obsession had really sent them off their rocker…

And another thing: Nebenzia declared that responsibility for the war stayed with Ukraine and the USA.

....

[260]   NTA, 25 February 2022, https://www.nta.ua/sytuacziya-dlya-kyyeva-zagrozlyva-nastupna-nich-bude-duzhe-skladnoyu-klychko (accessed 04.07.2025).

[261]   Radio Svoboda, 25 February 2022, https://www.radiosvoboda.org/a/31723818.html (accessed 04.07.2025).

[262]   Radio Svoboda, 26 February 2022, https://www.radiosvoboda.org/a/news-zelensky-nich-bude-vazhkoju/31723878.html (accessed 04.07.2025).

The second day of war was drawing to a close. The Russian plans for a blitz-krieg had gone pear-shaped. Yet they hadn't abandoned their intentions on that score. Everything would be decided in the following days. Or perhaps, even that night...

Kharkiv and the East held on.

The Left Bank had collapsed in the south. The situation in the south of the Right Bank was unpredictable. No one could be sure whether events out there had been a result of treason or criminal ineptitude. Most likely, both. And quite likely, something else – it was nothing short of tragedy.

Evidently, the next step would be an attack against Mykolaiv and Odesa, aimed at gaining access to Trans-Dniester area. And eventually the country may be cut off from the Black Sea...

As for Kyiv... The fighting in the routes of approach had been going on all through the day. The Russian armada was moving in from two sides. The city was in mortal danger. And no one could predict what was to follow...

Ah well. It was the twenty-sixth already. The clock said it was five to one in the morning.

The Commander came up to us and said, addressing Taras, the bespectacled Gennady and me:

'OK, for now, have some rest, the other shift will keep watch. But stay alert. I do have a first-hand knowledge of how those bastard saboteurs go about things. At seven in the evening, the pills are distributed among them to knock them off straight away. Then, at two or three in the morning, they are raised and sent off on their missions. The time when all the normal people are asleep is when they engage in their underhand activities.'

We schlepped to our cellar where, by then, we'd had beds, and bed-side tables, and even a wardrobe. The Commander turned out to be quite an operator – ca-joled all this stuff out of some house-management office. He explained to them that no war ever lasted for a week or two, and we were to remain in that cellar for quite some time...

At two-thirty the Commander showed up, the other shift in tow.

'These guys should take a break now, and you – time to go on duty. No assault as yet. But I'm familiar with this tactic: for sure, they are now busy infiltrating the entire city with their hit squads... And if they sniff out a weak spot somewhere, that's where they'll strike. Our task is to keep our eyes peeled.'

On our way back to the defence post he gave us an update: on the previous day, which meant the twenty-fifth, late at night, several vehicles with flashing beacons had pulled up by the gatehouse of the Vasylkiv airfield. People wearing the National Police uniforms killed the security, after which the helicopters started disembarking the Russian landing troops. Severe fighting ensued and was still raging on. After the airfield in Hostomel had been put out of commission, and the facilities in Boryspil and Zhuliany had been proved not fit for purpose, that was their last option. Which meant they still clung to their brazen idea of engaging their transport aircraft. Immediately after the helicopters, an Il-76 airlifter followed. However, approximately at one in the morning our guys shot it down. Hopefully, that plan of theirs would also be frustrated…

Here we were again, on duty, keeping a close watch over the things around. Our brief had been somewhat extended: in addition to holding the fort – in case of the enemy making headway in our direction, we also had to monitor the surroundings and spot suspicious behaviour. If anybody was ambling around at night, especially, if it was more than one person, it had to be saboteurs, for it was them who would snoop around the borough in small groups.

'Bigger hit groups,' mused the bespectacled Gennady, 'are unlikely to reach us. More and more roadblocks are being put in. Police and security people are doing a great job spotting them and taking them down, but still, they keep popping up from somewhere…'

'At least it's quiet here, but the stuff going on elsewhere!' the Commander finished talking to someone over the phone and turned round to face us. 'Fighting in Peremoha Prospect and Dehtiarivska Street. A military base has been attacked. Shortly before three o'clock, there had been shots and machine-gun fire in the vicinity of the zoo. Fighting and explosions in other areas of the city, too. No other word for it – what's going on is active combat! So, don't drop your guard.'

Reports started pouring in from everywhere – those accursed saboteurs were being apprehended and disarmed. Finally, at four in the morning, the Kyiv Mayor's Office posted this announcement: 'Urban warfare has broken out in our streets. We appeal to you to stay calm and exercise maximum caution. Do not leave your shelters. If you are at home, do not approach windows and do not go out on balconies. Hide in an enclosed room, for example a bathroom. Cover yourselves with something that will protect you from being wounded by debris.'[263]

Then, at a quarter past five, this: 'Shots ring out even in Bohdan Khmelnitsky Street, in the city centre!'

---

[263] 26 February 2022, https://t.me/KyivCityOfficial/2122 (accessed 04.07.2025).

'You see,' the Commander addressed the bespectacled Gennady gently but reproachfully. 'You've said we are practically in the centre, and they won't reach us. They are crawling out of every crevice…'

By hook or by crook, by the time the morning came all the hit squads had been taken out, and their equipment destroyed. Long story short, at least by that point their attempts had been rebuffed.

At six in the morning the Commander let me and Taras return home for several hours. His message was clear: the students had worked through some very turbulent hours and earned some indulgence. He looked questioningly at Gennady and Denis, too.

'No, I'll hang around for a bit. I'll go to the cellar to get warm,' the bespectacled Gennady clapped his palms together, even if he had his gloves on.

'I'll go to the cellar, too,' called back Denis. He wasn't clapping his hands, though, perhaps his unusual-looking gloves were self-heating.

As for Taras and me, we quickly dispersed.

I raced back home, and mum looked at me closely:

'Well? What gives?'

And I went:

'I need tea! Hot tea!'

I urgently switched on both the TV and the computer. There was a real avalanche of news.

At night, there had been an attempt to seize Mykolaiv. Our army had kept the city.

Again, at night, after some protracted fighting, the AFU had regained the Kyiv hydro-electric station! Hooray! The personnel had returned to work out of the bomb shelter and re-assumed their duties.

06:10 a.m. According to the Ministry of Defence, the Russians had sustained considerable losses: up to three thousand men. Large numbers of armoured vehicles had been put out of commission, along with 14 aircraft and eight helicopters, cannons, etc.

07:57 a.m. Zelensky appeared on TV – in front of his office at Bankova: 'Good morning, Ukrainians! A lot of fake information has popped up on the net – supposedly, I am calling on our army to lay down arms, and evacuation is underway. Not a bit of it: I'm here. We won't lay down any arms. We will defend our country, and our arms are a tool of the truth. And our truth is the fact that this is our land, our country, our children. And all of this we shall defend. And that's that. That was all I wanted to say. Glory to Ukraine!'[264]

....

[264]   26 February 2022, https://www.youtube.com/watch?v=quy6_RS7euc (accessed 04.07.2025).

08:00 a.m. The fighting in Vasylkiv was petering out. It had lasted throughout the night. The city's mayor: 'Russian landing troops have been parachuted into our fields, forests, and villages. Decembrists' Street got it the hardest – it was completely ablaze. They wanted to gain control over our airfield, but our 40th Brigade repelled the attack and is busy mopping up.'[265]

Ho-o-o-o-ray! Thus, yet another potential springboard for attacking Kyiv had been eliminated. Also, it turned out, the helicopters spotted in Belarus had stayed idle.

However, Lviv reported an alleged landing of Russian troops near Brody. What followed was a frenetic influx of volunteers wishing to form their own units. Bandera smoothies were now being produced on a mass scale,[266] crates with bottles stacked up nearly in every house. Everyone was ready to shoot out of windows, taking aim at the encroaching tanks with shot-guns and rifles, and throwing Bandera smoothies, too.

08:42 a.m. At the Polytechnic Institute Metro station, the tannoy made this announcement: 'Because of the fighting in Peremoha Prospect, the red Metro line will stay closed today. All stations of the line have been sealed.'

09:04 a.m. Mayor Klitchko: 'The night was hard. There are no enemy troops in the city, but raiding squads are still operating.'[267]

Right. And what about the approach routes to the city?

A convoy of about 100 Russian armoured vehicles was moving towards us via Vyshhorod District. The suburb of Irpin was being shelled nonstop. Our army guys carried civilians across the damaged bridge in their arms.

10:10 a.m. The National Guards issued a warning: Russian commando groups had made repeated attempts to land on Kyiv's left bank. 'The Ukrainian army and law enforcers are keeping the bridges under control and are prepared to shoot to kill at targets attempting to cross the river in the direction of the right bank. Kyiv residents are requested not to use the bridges leading in that direction. If need be, the Ukrainian army will blow them up.'[268]

Just then we were warned that saboteurs operated in civilian clothes. Residents were urged to stay vigilant and report anybody suspicious to the police.

....

[265] Glavcom, 26 February 2022, https://glavcom.ua/news/u-vasilkovi-vzhe-ti-ho-armiya-zachistila-rosiyskih-desatnikiv-mer-825133.html (accessed 04.07.2025).

[266] **Bandera smoothies**: a variation on the name for a Molotov cocktail.

[267] Novynarnia, 26 February 2022, https://novynarnia.com/2022/02/26/hronika-oborony-ukrayiny-den-3/ (accessed 04.07.2025).

[268] Novynarnia, 26 February 2022, https://novynarnia.com/2022/02/26/hronika-oborony-ukrayiny-den-3/ (accessed 04.07.2025).

And again, saboteurs. Shortly before eleven in the morning, a Russian column was destroyed in Peremoha Prospect.

11:40 a.m. In came updates from the Zhytomyr Motorway – the 'road of life', leading to the western area of the country. The AFU had blown up the bridge near the village of Stoyanka, sitting practically on the borderline between the city and Kyiv Oblast. The road was closed. Did it mean that it wasn't possible anymore to leave Kyiv, heading towards Zhytomyr and on to Lviv?

Those who hadn't left Kyiv straight away found it hard to work out what to do. People kept calling each other endlessly, exchanging news. Yet the situation was going from bad to worse. So, when a red glow flared up over the Zhytomyr Motorway, those who still hesitated made up their minds: it was time to leave, driving along the Odesa route. Until it got cut off, too. So, there would be even fewer people left in the city…

And finally: the Metro had been totally converted into a shelter. From that point on, there would be no transportation of people.

This abundance of news kept me awake after my shift. In addition, Taras was continually forwarding me posts from his chatroom – lots of new stuff.

It became known that during those first days our president had been trying to reach Putin on the secure telephone line but with no success. He commented: 'When a war starts, you try to rationalise it. If a great power is onto you, it's vitally important to learn: is it really an act of aggression, or have they simply… "got confused" over borderlines during their exercises. But Russia is not responding.'[269]

It was also stated that Russia's failure to seize strategic airfields as footholds for future advancements had dealt her a crushing blow –since there was no Plan B. The Russian leadership were totally convinced that the way to success was straightforward, and the unforeseen landing of thousands of men, artillery and light armoured vehicles would meet only a token resistance from the Ukrainian side.

The site also insisted that a Wagner Group unit,[270] 400 men-strong, had entrenched itself in Kyiv. The subdivision belonged to a private military army commanded by Yevhen Pryhozhin, one of Putin's close allies. Five weeks previously, those mercenaries had been pulled out of Africa and redirected, via Belarus, into Ukraine. The Kremlin had set them a task – in return for a sizeable fee, to kill Zelensky and his closest associates. Their 'execution list' included

....

[269] TSN, 11 September 2022, https://tsn.ua/ato/na-pochatku-vtorgnennya-zelens-kiy-namagavsya-zatelefonuvati-do-putina-podolyak-2154949.html (accessed 04.07.2025).

[270] **Wagner Group:** a Russian state-funded private military company.

the prime minister, the entire Cabinet of Ministers, and the Mayor of Kyiv Vitaliy Klitchko. Thus, it would enable them to seize power and then transfer it to a puppet regime. That plan had been revealed to Kyiv that morning. In an attempt to cleanse the city from those saboteurs, it was decided to introduce an unprecedentedly severe curfew.

It was even asserted that between 2,400 and 4,000 mercenaries had been smuggled into Ukraine as early as January. The group based in Kyiv allegedly had shadowed Zelensky, tapping his mobile and those of his colleagues, aware of their whereabouts at any point in time. For the time being, on the eve of the 'peaceful' talks between Russia and Ukraine, the group supposedly was instructed to hit the brakes.

At last, some comforting news: for reasons unknown, the Russian troop advances had started to stall. By the third day of war, they reportedly were exhausted, as a result of the AFU's vehement resistance. Numerous enemy's convoys had been apprehended and destroyed near Kyiv, Chernihiv, and Sumy. This success had been brought about by modern high-precision light anti-tank and air-defence equipment and drones. Of huge importance, also, had been a continuous intelligence support whereby our Western partners kept us abreast of the enemy's movements. It was becoming increasingly obvious that Putin's plans to overtake the capital in one fell swoop, to overthrow the Ukrainian power, or force the leadership to flee, were far from realised.

American and British intelligence also confirmed the loss of momentum in the Russian advancement and were saying that Russia has met much stronger resistance than expected. Counting on speedy progress, with no response from the AFU, the Russian troops had started out in convoys, foregoing the combat deployment. Once opposed, they had been forced to regroup into battle order and, from that point, fight their way forward. High intensity of combat activity brought about, for the Russians, a deficit of ammunition, fuels and lubricants, provisions, and other resources. All this impedes their progress and necessitates the use of reserves stashed in Belarus… .'

Enough! I switched off the computer and collapsed, exhausted, into bed. We still had a shift to do that evening…

Something like Somalia…

By the time I made it, running, back to the defence post – hooray! – another truck with sand had arrived. We got back to putting it into sacks and building up the rampart.

One way or another, we were getting ready – an attempt to take us by storm was still more than possible.

Well, by then it was official: the curfew in Kyiv was to last from 05:00 p.m. on Saturday, February 26th (that same day) to 08:00 a.m. on Monday, February 28th. Which meant 39 hours in toto. Klitchko: 'It is strictly forbidden to leave your homes. During these hours, any civilian spotted outside shall automatically be considered a saboteur.'[271]

And shortly afterwards, Monastyrsky: 'The residents of Kyiv have received over 25,000 sub-machine guns and about 10 million rounds of ammunition. There's no question: Kyiv will defend itself! Defend and fight till the very end. I must emphasise the high level of our people's self-organisation. I am proud of how they have defended their cities, villages, streets, and houses!'[272]

Hmmm… Weapons distributed, the situation in the city had become odd: commandos were spotted all over. People would fire away at anything that seemed suspicious. For some it felt advisable to shoot first and ask questions afterwards. There was even this joke – a saboteur was somebody who got himself killed. What to say? It became easy to whack one of our own…

'Look here, the city is in the grips of a real commando-phobia!' exclaimed Gennady. 'I've asked around – the city's a real Somalia now! Everyone's armed, no one knows anyone, and everyone suspects everybody else…'

Taras and I traded glances – of course it was scary.

'That's completely true. Everyone's on a lookout for things looking "strange" – markers on the land, suspicious individuals, unrecognised cars, weird pink lights in the windows – it all is now seen as a hit squad's' activity,' the Commander offered his explanation. 'On the whole, it's only natural at the start of any war. The demarcation lines are being identified – us versus them. It's the initial stage of getting used to war and what it means, of adapting to new circumstances. Besides, there are crowds of armed people in uniform everywhere – the Territorial defence is formed as we speak. It's truly frightening. People who never did their army service, and have no proper training, now come to the fore. And hence this phobia.'

'I've got a friend,' continued Gennady, 'who told me this. It takes two days to bring in supplies from the western oblasts into Kyiv: you've got to go through innumerable roadblocks, and at some of those you get shot at, thrown face-down to the ground and frisked. That's the best-case scenario. He said sometimes people didn't recognise their own, and friendly fire had caused fatalities…'

'Sure, it's harsh,' agreed Denis. 'The only excuse is that we get lots of challenges now…'

....

[271]   Novynarnia, 26 February 2022, https://novynarnia.com/2022/02/26/hronika-ob-orony-ukrayiny-den-3/ (accessed 04.07.2025).

[272]   UNN, 26 February 2022, https://unn.ua/news/v-kiyevi-uchasniki-teroboro-ni-otrimali-ponad-25-tisyach-avtomativ (accessed 04.07.2025).

The Commander calmed all of us down: 'Hysteria won't last. I'm sure it'll be contained soon enough. It could happen even in the most advanced armed forces. They're already introducing armbands you could affix with Scotch, the passwords, and the roadblocks are put into a system of sorts...'

No arguing there – by then, quite a few roadblocks had been erected all over the city. Also, there were lots of people in uniform around, carrying arms. Once in a while, a car would barrel past, fast as an arrow, presumably travelling on some super-pass. After all, the roads were empty of people, cars, and traffic lights, so one could drive at any speed one wanted.

Still, much as the threat of a hostile invasion hadn't disappeared, the city started showing first signs of organisation.

Taras read the news on his mobile – turned out, those bastards had penetrated into the city as far as the St Michael's Golden-Domed Monastery![273] But they got neutralised...

He shared this piece with the Commander and then asked, curious: 'They also say that those hit squads vary in size, could count from three to something like 50 militants. Some wear the AFU uniform but on top is Russian body armour!'

'May well be, but they still are dangerous!' the Commander even wagged his figure at him. 'By now it's possible to admit that a kind of "Brownian motion" had dominated the city over the first two days. Including – what a tender term! – this "friendly fire"! It's taken some time to line up all the law-enforcing agencies, and coordinate all efforts against the saboteurs. Back when the city was divided into 10 defence sectors, an operative investigating group had been assigned to each one of them, consisting of security guys, police, and special services. So that they could respond immediately to any emergency. As far as our roadblocks go, the system has only started emerging. We've got the reps from the National Guard and police put in charge. You can see for yourselves, lots of things have been put in order, under control...'

'Sure, we can,' Taras gave me a wink. 'We also know there are roadblocks where folk don't get along with one another ... The situation there is like this: he who shouts louder gets to be a commander.'

'But at our roadblock,' I am answering him with my eyes, too, 'thank God, it's nothing like that. Perhaps because our Commander is an experienced guy and has a good grip on it all...'

....

[273] **St Michael's Golden-Domed Monastery:** a 12th-century monastery on the edge of the right bank of the Dnipro River.

That must have been it. Also, the Commander appointed the bespectacled Gennady head of our shift. He was given some special telephone number – in case something suspicious did take place, he would be able to inform police under his own steam. There were vehicles on standby there, they'd send somebody over straight away.

The main news after that was that we all received our own arms! Our institute had included military training as part of our curriculum, so we did have the idea of how to handle them. Even so, the Commander gave us a brief ABC course too. Also, we received our proper pass papers from the headquarters that would enable us to move around after the curfew. The Commander was quite adamant, though, that it meant only within our borough. It all was because of the extreme circumstances. After all, an enormous convoy of Russian soldiers was heading towards us from Belarus, reinforced with inexhaustible equipment supplies. Most likely, that was their reserve, made up of those ten battalion tactical groups…

Oh my. It did look like, after all, we would have to come face to face with it in the nearest future… Us – against the tanks and the armoured carriers? What fun…

The Commander must have been reading our thoughts:

'The main thing is not to be afraid. Much as it's harsh and nothing can be ruled out, for the time being it's all under control. They've failed to capture airfields, which equals disaster to their original strategic planning. Let me assure you, something went horribly wrong for those Russian fascists…'

Taras and I exchanged quick glances: it was a charged message. Inspiring some hope… On the other hand, that was him all over – not only there to command but, also, fill his subordinates with hope.

'Our main task is not to let the commando groups through. Remember, it's not a given that they would seep forward from the outskirts. So many of those special task force had arrived well before the invasion, took lodgings with the "willing home-owners", sat around, waiting. And now they've started creeping out. Some single individuals are hanging around too. Although unclear how they'd move around during this curfew marathon. We'll see…'

Ah well, yet again, Taras and I were treated like children. Late in the evening we'd been sent home again. Just when the most important thing was about to start.

The Commander kept insisting:

'That's my order. We've decided, once and for all – you spend your nights at home. Unless something out of the ordinary happens. As if they could show up in front of you within the next five minutes! First, they have to fight their way through. As soon as they make an incursion, I'll be warned. That's for starters. Besides, we are not alone on this route, quite a few other roadblocks have been set up too. I'm telling you: as soon as it gets hot, I'll call you immediately. Just remember this: my cellar is not a spa. How many beds are there? People have to relax from time to time: it's winter, it's cold. But you – you live nearby, so why should you waste two beds? So, God speed.'

We turned round and left.

He yelled after us:

'Here! I've got a new message – another truck arrives tomorrow. So here by nine, on the dot. We'll get on with filling the sacks!'

As per usual, once at home I went straight back to the news.

Fierce fighting was underway in Kherson and Mykolaiv Oblasts, that direction also being a priority by Russia. The Ukrainian troops retreating, the Russians are already heading to Kherson over the Antonivka Bridge; their destination is Odesa.

Furious battle broke out to gain control over Mariupol. Kharkov and Chernihiv were also under heavy artillery fire. The Mayor of Chernihiv called on the residents to be ready for street fighting.

Taras sent me a message – *U asleep?*

I dialled his number.

'Listen, once you're still awake let me read you something. Commander-in-Chief Zaluzhnyi writes: "Dear reservists of the AFU Territorial Defence! I salute you! There are already 37,000 in your ranks! I thank you for putting your dependable shoulder to the wheel. Together we'll win."[274]

'Ha!' I cried. 'It includes us, too!'

'There's more. The chatroom discusses the eventuality of Russkies popping up in our neck of the woods! Apparently, they've moved in as far as the tram terminus at Pushcha-Vodytsia.[275] "The enemy may break into the city. As for the governmental quarter – in theory, it's possible too. However, thousands of arms have been distributed already. Same with anti-tank weapons. Besides, it's possible to open fire out of every gateway, off every roof. If already now – when there is no enemy in the city –"friendly fire" is ringing out here and there, one can only imagine what's going to happen when they do show up. Another

....

[274] Army inform, 26 February 2022, https://armyinform.com.ua/2022/02/26/rezerv-istiv-syl-teroborony-zs-ukrayiny-vzhe-37-tysyach/ (accessed 04.07.2025).

[275] **Pushcha-Vodytsia**: a neighbourhood in the north-west outskirts of Kyiv.

10,000 small arms supposedly have been issued today. Say what you may, but when the troops on offensive find themselves under fire from an ambush, it really strikes horror.'

Taras carried on:

'Quite a positive post, this. But it concerns the right bank. Now listen to what they're writing about the left bank: "On the left bank the Russian have approached Brovary, so, effectively, Kyiv. Yet the authorities publicly advise the people "not to succumb to panic", and, in the same breath, earnestly discuss how to blow up the bridges – so that the Russian army would abut on the Dnipro but won't be able to proceed to Pechersk and take the governmental quarter." How do you like it? It goes on: "Kyiv will defend itself, that much is true. But to listen to you, the bloody Russkies will cancel their attack out of fear. It looks so beautiful on paper. But those barging on are not kids, they're professional soldiers. And heavily armed with armoured vehicles..." Got it? The things people write. Don't bother to comment. Let's hit the hay, we're on in the morning tomorrow.'

Before going to bed, I tried to sum up the day.

By the end of the third day, it became clear that even if the Kremlin's plan to take Kyiv in a matter of days had gone down the drain, the Russians were on the cusp of entering the capital. True, they'd failed to bring in their landing troops, either through Hostomel or Vasylkiv but the situation was far from rescued. Next would be an offensive on land and a 'classic' attempt to take Kyiv by storm – if not through sabotage, then by using regular troops. The threat of Kyiv falling remained completely real.

Clearly, the situation called for maximum prudence. Therefore, Zelensky stayed in a bunker. His 'heir' Stefanchuk – in case something, God forbid, happened to the president – hadn't left for Western Ukraine and stayed in Kyiv but lives in hiding and intends changing his overnight locations.

OK, the Russians had come a-cropper with their original plans. Still, it wasn't over. Blitzkrieg hadn't been called off. It had only become a stretched-out affair.

'Putin Cannot Kill!'

In the morning, I was jolted out of bed – it was the twenty-seventh already! The fourth day of war!

I left the computer and TV in peace but raced to the window – what if the enemy's convoy was already rattling down our street?

A complete lull. God be praised! And not a person, not a car around, as if we were on Mars...

Yes, that morning marked the 72 hours since the start of hostilities. The forecast from all our 'well-wishers', predicting Kyiv falling within this space of time, hadn't come true. But still, no clarity about the things ahead. The Americans, for example, had become more specific: Kyiv possibly won't fall as quickly as Russia had planned and we had anticipated, but it would fall all the same. Russia had more tanks, artillery, fighters, missiles. The odds were against Ukraine.

Anyway, we hadn't fallen yet. Moreover, the advancement of Russian fascists had been contained. And in some places, their ass had been properly kicked.

'See? The night is over, but no offensive!' Mum came into my room, her face swollen, her eyes red. 'Looks like the AFU are holding their ground?'

I squinted at the clock – it had gone six.

'Are you afraid, son?'

I had managed to catch some sleep but mum, apparently, had just tossed around in her bed, awake.

'Well, ahem…' I tried to clear my throat.

'I know, you are. Me too.'

Mum clasped her palms together.

'How shall we live? In a siege? Or even under occupation?'

I said nothing. It was scary even to imagine it.

Horror! Real horror!

I had to pull myself together. Drive those thoughts away, as far as possible!

I switched on my computer. The news flowed in.

Miraculously, the night in Kyiv had been relatively quiet, nothing more than several skirmishes with saboteurs. Yet, enough weaponry and ammunition had been issued to the civilians and thus, the city had transformed itself into a huge military base. It wasn't going to take anything lying down!

But around the capital… At about one in the morning, an oil depot in Vasylkiv had been hit by a missile and went up in flames. Flashes could be seen even in Kyiv.

In the western outskirts, the enemy attempted incursion – scores of hostile vehicles kept proceeding from Bucha to Irpin. In an attempt to deter them, the local bridge had been blown up. The Russian tanks, also heading towards the capital, rolled through Makariv. Against them stood the regular army and volunteers. The main AFU forces had been pulled out of Hostomel, but our artillery continued pummelling its outskirts.

And what about social media? Well, more of the same. Some panicked, some criticised. Everyone was stunned at how quickly the Russians had come close to Kyiv's perimeter. In essence, the authorities had been caught unawares. Not only in Kyiv but everywhere... In the beginning chaos reigned everywhere – there were no precise instructions on what to do and how to do it. The mayors of captured cities and towns in the east and south found themselves in a particularly tight spot: stay on in your occupied city – and you would be called a traitor. Leave – you'd be branded a coward. About ten mayors, presumably the ones who had refused to cooperate, had been simply kidnapped by the Russians. Some posts called for a measured approach. In other words, the authorities' cockups could be forgiven since the country was holding on. It wasn't the time to apportion the blame. It all would have to be analysed only after we'd won.

Some alarming stuff: the satellite images picked up the Russian convoy advancing from Belarus. The convoy was 4.8 kilometres long and headed towards Ivankiv.

In the morning, Zelensky made a TV appeal, addressing the citizens of Belarus: 'Regrettably, in the war that has now been unlashed we and you are on opposite sides. The forces of the Russian Federation are using your territory to launch their rockets at Ukraine. They set off from there to kill our children, destroy our houses, and try to eliminate everything that has been built up over decades. Be Belarus, not Russia!'[276]

Somehow, I'd been pottering around for too long, so popped out of the flat at the last minute. God forbid I'd be late! I'd promised to arrive on time! I rushed out of the house towards Shchekavytska Street, no time to glance, as per usual, at Naberezhno-Khreschatytska Street and see the Dnipro. I raced further, on to Pochainynska, a famous street, one of the oldest in Kyiv. In the beginning it had followed the local terrain, and so was narrow, and winding. But after the Great Fire of Podil in 1811 it had been restructured.[277] The name came from the Pochaina River – a right tributary of the Dnipro. Its mouth used to house a port (*Prytyka*), a stopover on the route from the Varangians to the Greeks.[278] The word *Prytyka*, on its own, was quite fun – there'd been no words for *ports* at the time. So, there it was, a *prytyka*, a place to which ships had been carried by the river – *prytykaly*. Closer to the Dnipro stood the Church of St Ilya, a

....

[276] Interfax Ukraine, 27 February 2022, https://interfax.com.ua/news/general/8030 78.html (accessed 04.07.2025).

[277] The **Great Fire of Podil** occurred in this historical and commercial part of Kyiv on 9 July 1811. The fire lasted for three days and almost destroyed the entire neighbourhood.

[278] The trade route 'from the Varangians to the Greeks' is the conventional name of the waterway that ran along rivers and led from the Baltic Sea to the Black Sea, to the shores of Byzantium. This was one of the key routes of Ancient Rus, important for its trade and cultural ties.-

successor to the first Christian temple in Rus. And on our side – the Church of St Nicolas on the Water, with its monument to the victims of the Holodomor.[279] It was in front of this monument that they buried the martyred body of Georgiy Gongadze.[280]

But I had no time to stop and muse, so I hurriedly passed the 'count's mansion' and momentarily reached Voloska Street, another street that survived from the times of Kievan Rus, its name coming from the name of pagan god Volos.[281] What a thought! It had existed even before Christianity had been accepted in these parts, in 988 A.D.!

I crossed it and trotted towards the Gordon building,[282] then over to the other side of the street, towards the Podil synagogue and on to Shchekavytska Hill, where, according to legend, Shchek, one of Kyiv's founders, once resided. Sometimes people called it Oleh's Hill. Supposedly, one day Oleh, a Kyivan prince, came to this hill to pay homage to the remains of his horse that had died in battle. He picked up some skull and started scrutinising it. But out of the skull sprang a snake and bit him! And so, he was buried there, too. His grave is believed to lie underneath what in later days was the old observatory.

Well, researchers still argue about the grave's exact location. What is indisputable, though, is the location of the radio mast, 136 metres tall, lording it over the hill and all of Podil. The mast was built in 1951 on the former site of All Saints Cathedral, the oldest part of its graveyard. The mast's height should also include another 180 metre above the sea level. That mast, among many others, was used for jamming the western broadcasters, thus blocking the Soviet citizens any access. The amount of electricity it had used was enormous, but the

....

[279]   The **Holodomor** of 1932-1933 – an act of genocide in which the Ukrainian people were subjected to artificial mass famine. Organized through deliberate measures taken by the top leadership of the Soviet Union under Stalin and the Ukrainian SSR, it was intended to suppress the Ukrainian national liberation movement and to physically destroy the larger part of the Ukrainian peasantry. The Holodomor occurred as a result of large-scale collectivization: hundreds of thousands died in 1932, millions in 1933. Unlike in other regions of the USSR, where many people also died from starvation, the famine in Ukraine was an act of genocide because it was deliberately directed against the Ukrainian nation. It is recognized as such by many countries.

[280]   **Georgiy Gongadze:** a Ukrainian journalist of Georgian origin who promoted freedom of speech and civic liberties in Ukraine. He was kidnapped and murdered in 2000.

[281]   **Volos:** a deity in the ancient Russian pagan pantheon, the "cattle god". According to the theory of the main myth, one of the central deities in Slavic mythology; living on earth, he is an antagonist of the thunderer Perun, who lives in heaven.

[282]   **Dmytro Gordon:** a Ukrainian journalist and interviewer. In the RF he is on the list of extremists and on the federal list of wanted persons.

Soviet power did not mind. The most important thing was to protect the 'holy cow' of ideology. The mast continued to function until 1988, after which the hill was finally opened to the general public, even if, only shortly before, a little stroll in that vicinity could have easily resulted in an undesirable rendezvous with the security offices.

I ran further along Shchekavytska, my beloved street, in existence since God knows when. Shchek must have used it as a shortcut towards the Dnipro – to wash himself. What other options for maintaining personal hygiene would have been available at the time?

Huh! Finally, got to Mezhyhirska – our site! I'd managed it in the nick of time, down to the last second. The Commander checked his watch, put on an amazed face, yet said nothing, for it all had worked out. I kept my word!

I was fighting for breath and looking around. After all, our post was situated on a transport artery. I glanced to the right – nothing. No people, no cars. No Russians either, at least by then. I looked left – about a kilometre away, the street abutted the semi-circular main building of the Kyiv-Mohyla Academy. Nothing was really far. If their tanks did break through, would their armoured vehicles go forward down Mezhyhirska? To poison us with their stinking exhaust gases? And get themselves over to the Academy? And once they reached Kontraktova Square on the right, they'd arrange themselves in columns… The soldiers would get a breather, and then, refreshed, follow down Sahaidachny Street, climb the Volodymyr Hill and proceed onto Hrushevsky Street, and straight into the governmental quarter, a mere two kilometres away. No distance at all for a tank. Some ten minutes, perhaps, and this only because the road went uphill.

Enough. I should put all this nonsense right out of my mind! To get the full measure of the situation I raced along Shchekavytsky Gardens in the direction of Kostantynovska Street. All looked quiet, everything was in its place: Zhovten cinema on the left, the fountain on the right, and straight ahead – this odd building with a spire on the roof and the enormous windows. I trained my eyes upwards – as before, the radio mast stood atop Shchekavytska Hill. Oleh's grave was somewhere there too, underneath either the observatory or the graveyard. In other words, also where it belonged.

And thus we continued stomping the sand in sacks, and the buildings around us stared in amazement – what on earth were we after, hustling like that around this plot which had been lived upon for centuries? Astonished they were, no less…

Phew, a short break after lugging our sacks back and forth. Also, a chance to look around, taking in the surroundings and the buildings, each with its own history, as if ready to tell its own tale. For example, Zhovten cinema could explain that it was the oldest in Kyiv. And although the authorities have long since taken a course on decommunization, they are not touching it. Its name was left be for it had become a brand. So now the cinema was the first to be amazed but stayed silent.

That building with a spire on its roof that sat at the confluence between Shchekavytska and Kostiantynovska, kept staring at us through its enormous windows – who had decided on their size? It silently observed the commotion as well, probably contemplating like this: 'What's with the sacks? What's the point? Why haven't I been consulted?'

And the mast – it, too, exuded criticism: 'Anyone thought of asking my opinion?'

And a voice, perhaps belonging to Oleh, boomed up from the underground in wonder:

'Well, what do you say? Shall we surrender to our "brothers"? Or shall we fight back?'

'What sort of a question is that? Of course, we'll fight!', I answer him.

'Well... then look, don't let me down...'

Yet again, I sank into my reflections. Russia aside, clearly there were huge problems with Belarus, too. Based on various sources, Lukashenko could decide, any day, to send their armed forces into Ukraine to fight alongside Russia. Belarusians might not even be told where he was sending them. Besides, their TV space was overflowing with statements about 'Nazis' in Ukraine. Also, they might be unaware that Russia had sustained huge losses. That was why Zelensky's appeal to them was rebroadcast repeatedly – the one where he was urging them to be 'Belarusians and not Russians.'

* * *

Shortly before lunch the Commander had brought along another three guys:

'Here, new recruits,' he introduced them. 'They sing in the famous Capella choir.'

He clicked his fingers:

'It'll be more fun now. Singing always lifts one's spirits.'

We started introducing ourselves. Two of them – Platonovych and Mykolaiovych – were professional singers. The third one – Andriyovych[283] – joined them as an amateur performer, being a journalist by trade. We bandied news and quickly realised that he had access to some quality information. Well, we'd be even better informed.

....

[283] **Platonovych, Mykolaiovych, Andriyovych**: a respectfully familiar Slavic way of addressing a person is to use their patronymic. In this case the fathers were called Platon, Mykola, and Andriy.

We chatted some more and quickly realised that Mykolaiovych loved irony, Platonovych was a swashbuckler, while Andriyovych was rational. A journalist after all, it went with the territory.

A truck had delivered the hedgehogs – they proved heavy, the bastards. But together we somehow managed to drag them down off the truck and along the site. After this we arranged them in a zigzag on the tarmac, thus blocking passage. This way no armoured vehicle could get straight across. Spirits lifted somewhat.

Our breath back, we returned to the monitoring of the things around. Everything looked peaceful and we all plunged into news on our smartphones.

The bespectacled Gennady was the first to cry out – he'd spotted something on his iPad.

It turned out Reznikov had shared his views on 'street defence': 'Within the first two d ays roadblocks have popped up on every street: some on the left, some on the right, some beyond a parade of houses – all sorts. A lot of arms are in use, too. That's why people are tense, people are frightened. Anything's possible, including "friendly fire". We are gradually taking it all in hand.'[284] Well… we are perfectly away of the situation with these roadblocks and a "Somalia", too. It's not news to us…'

One of the choir singers, Andriyovych, the rational one, added:

"Tis true, all sorts of things happen. Because of this chaos someone even threw a government's minister face down on the asphalt. He shrieks: "I'm a minister!" And they don't give a damn. He calls the Minister of the Interior, who says: "I can't give you a trouble-free passage! Most roadblocks are out of control.'[285]

The news cheered us a bit, everybody started laughing and wisecracking. It was as if we were either in our Huliaipole,[286] or in African Somalia that materialised on the Ukrainian land in the 21st century…

....

[284]   UP, undated, https://www.pravda.com.ua/cdn/cd1/reconstruction/a3.html (accessed 04.07.2025).

[285]   UP, undated, https://www.pravda.com.ua/cdn/cd1/reconstruction/a3.html (accessed 04.07.2025).

[286]   **Hulyaipole:** a city in Zaporizhzhia Oblast. After the 1917 revolution Huliaipole was variously held by Austro-Hungarian forces, the Red Army, the Ukrainian People's Republic, the Hetmanate, Anton Denikin's White Army and Nestor Makhno's Insurgent Army, among others. The city became widely known as the headquarters of the Revolutionary Insurgent Army of Ukraine and the capital of the 'Makhnovshchina' movement.

There was this, too. Everybody knew of a huge number of calls placed from Ukraine to Russia, people reaching out to their family, friends, and colleagues.

'What are you doing? You are killing us!'

'But that's your imagination! Putin cannot kill!'

'How d'ya mean – imagination? You are dropping bombs and firing missiles!'

'It's not us bombing you. You're doing it yourselves!'

I was completely sure that there wasn't, anywhere in the world, a pharmaceutical company, no matter how famous, that could medically bring around residents of that fucking country.

Everybody returned to their smartphones.

Zelensky announced that he'd had a telephone conversation with Lukashenko. 'We agreed that the Ukrainian delegation would meet the Russian one without any prior conditions on the border between Ukraine and Belarus, near the Pripyat River. Oleksandr Lukashenko took it upon himself to guarantee that during the time that the Ukrainian delegation was in transit by air – there and back – and during the negotiations proper, the helicopters and missiles deployed on the Belarusian territory would remain on the ground. The conversation was very substantive. I don't want the missiles, planes, and helicopters to fly from Belarus into Ukraine. I don't want the troops moving from Belarus into Ukraine. And he gave me his assurances.'[287]

Meanwhile Denis came across something horrible. Only at that point – several days later! – they announced that in the battle of Hostomel serious damage had been caused to *Mriya*, a unique cargo aircraft, the biggest in the world. To repair it would cost billions. And take years of painstaking work. And therefore, I wondered – why hadn't they removed it from there beforehand? Was it an act of sabotage? They had, after all, evacuated five An-124-100 *Ruslan* air freighters to somewhere outside of Ukraine. Why hadn't they done it with *Mriya*? No one could answer.

The Commander was sighing heavily, his jaw muscles playing. And us – we only silently clenched our fists in anger.

Taras and I descended into the cellar to make some coffee and suddenly my Viber pinged.

I checked the Caller ID – Pyvynsky! We used to have the same mobile operator, but now he was calling me on Viber.

[287] UNIAN, 27 February 2022, https://www.unian.ua/politics/zelenskiy-pro-rozmovu-z-lukashenkom-domovilisya-pro-zustrich-z-rosiyskoyu-storonoyu-u-rayoni-richki-prip-yat-novini-ukrajina-11720788.html (accessed 04.07.2025).

'Yes, I'm calling on Viber,' he could still read my thoughts even from a distance. 'What if you'd left – and not simply for Western Ukraine but have outsmarted everyone and done a bunk to somewhere nice in Germany? Eh? Do come clean…'

'Not at all. I'm here. My friend and I, we've joined the Territorial Defence.'

'Uh-huh! Well-done, then. So, how're doing then, seeing that you're over there?'

'It's alright. We are on duty right now, at the block house. Some ten kilometres away, though, it's real hell.'

'But you're holding your own?' this time it was Yanovsky. It was only natural for them to be side by side.

'With us, it's not too bad. There are several similar roadblocks ahead. Even if a hit squad does show up, it's as likely to be neutralised before they even reach us. So, with us, things are rather neat. One could say we're waiting. Identifying suspicious individuals, upkeeping order. In a word, nothing special so far. The main events are over there… where the army is.'

'Come on – nothing special. Everything is special now.' Pyvynsky took the phone back. 'And what's your take on Zelensky staying on?'

'What's to say? Praise to him. He hasn't run away, not to the West, not into exile.'

'He's a hero, that much is true,' Pyvynsky even clicked his tongue. 'Still… There's this. Let's put it this way – to leave after he's said all those words about forthcoming barbeques would've been unthinkable. People would've called him a traitor. I don't know if everything would've crumbled or not, but it definitely would've been a severe blow to the entire country.'

'I'll add a couple of words, too.' Yanovsky was on the line again. 'His departure would have been political suicide. He would've been signing his own death sentence. And power would've fallen into the hands of whomsoever would've stayed. He who stayed and headed resistance would've come on top.'

'Hmmm… wise words,' I agreed. 'And how are things with you?'

'Yesterday evening they bombed the military aerodrome near Myrhorod. Looks like we've got away with it, though. But good stuff in Kharkiv, apparently the invaders been kicked out.'

'Still, not everything is great,' Yanovsky lowered his voice. 'They say the Russians are close to Enerhodar. And that means the Zaporizhzhia Nuclear Power Station, the biggest in Europe!'

'Blast it all,' Pyvynsky winded up the conversation. 'We'll be in touch.'

After the shift Taras and I went our separate ways but instead of going home, I turned towards Naberezhno-Khreschatytska, to cast my eye over the Dnipro. What a big and wide river it is!

At that time of year, the river looked grim and mysterious but still beautiful with a kind of wintry beauty. That was not the point, though, the point was the problem facing those residing on its left bank. It just so happened that the left bank, with over a million residents, had become the largest dormitory district in Kyiv, with practically nothing there apart from residential blocks. Back in the Soviet days it had been a site for several industrial complexes but eventually enterprises had been permanently closed, and they erected numerous apartment blocks instead. And thus, at a time like this, crossing the river into the right bank became a huge problem. At the first sound of an air raid, they shut the bridges but could do it any minute they saw fit – after all, the enemy was near Brovary. Also, all bridges had been mined and if they decided to detonate them – this would be a true catastrophe. How would people that had decided to stay ever get out of the left bank?

Back home I read this. Our pilot nicknamed the 'Ghost of Kyiv' had already shot down 10 Russian aircraft.

Right on the heels of this news came a statement from the General Staff: 'As of 18:00, the enemy had lost 4,500 men. Twenty-seven aircraft (to be confirmed) have been brought down, along with 26 helicopters, about 250 tanks, over 700 armoured vehicles, approximately 150 cannons. It is difficult to keep track due to the intensity of the fighting.'[288]

Wow, the Russkies had lost a lot of their equipment, the count was already in hundreds. The manpower losses were even more striking – on average, over a thousand a day. That was why they became ferociously violent in the occupied territories. You bet! They had expected to be welcomed with flowers, but instead hundreds of their bodies remained scattered along the roads and in the fields.

For understandable reasons, they didn't quote the losses of our side. We knew they were lower but still, losses they were. And those were our guys… Our defenders… Alas…

Zaluzhnyi, the AFU's Commander-in-Chief, made a statement: 'We are fighting against one of the biggest armies in the world. But we are stronger! And day in, day out, our ranks are gaining new strength! In just two days 100,000 people have been mobilised in Ukraine!'[289]

....

[288]   Army inform, 27 February 2022, https://armyinform.com.ua/2022/02/27/moralno-psyhologichnyj-stan-okupaczijnyh-vijsk-nyzkyj-strokovyky-zs-rf-gotovi-sklasty-zbroyu-i-zdatysya-v-polon-genshtab-zsu/ (accessed 04.07.2025).

[289]   LB.ua, 27 February 2022, https://lb.ua/news/2022/02/27/507226_mayzhe_100_tisyach_ukraintsiv.html (accessed 04.07.2025).

In general, news was getting ever more worrying. Late at night the Russians had taken Berdiansk in the south.

I continued reading exchanges in Taras's chatroom:

'When the war started, Putin was far away from Moscow, apparently in a bunker. He spoke on TV to announce his "special military operation" in order to "demilitarise and denazify Ukraine." He was still on air when Ukraine came under missile fire. Following several months of hypocritical diplomacy, posing as a "victim" and lying through his teeth on the international arena, the Kremlin made its choice.

'The whole concept of invasion was to move extremely quickly, so that the international community would have no time to respond. The troops were to bypass the spots of resistance and continue their progress towards their destination. According to the plan, 10 days after invasion, that is to say, on March 6th, the AFU would stop their organised efforts to rebuff the aggression, the power representatives would flee, be killed or taken prisoner, after which it would be possible to start stabilisation efforts, supported by the Russian Guards and the RF security services. Those measures included putting together administrative facilities on the occupied territories. The Russian Guards would be in charge of clamping down on possible hotspots of unrest. Their convoys, destroyed during the first days of the invasion near Kyiv and Kharkiv, had been carrying shields and gum clubs. To render impotent any further attempts at resistance among the Ukrainians, effective filtration was to be carried out in a network of camps. The population in overtaken territories was to be divided into four categories: those subject to annihilation; those to be terrorised and forced to remain inactive; those who could be convinced to cooperate, and those ready to cooperate voluntarily.

'The Russian General Staff kept their intent to attack Kyiv secret even from their own troops. Most units had received the order to join less than 24 hours before the actual invasion. Although keeping this information top secret had allowed the Russian forces an advantage of surprise, eventually this very secrecy came back to bite: the troops ended up short of ammunition, fuel, provisions, and most importantly, understanding of their further actions.'

The insiders also wrote: 'Supposedly, the AFU command learnt that the main thrust of the Russian invasion would be aimed at Kyiv and Chernihiv literally several hours before the invasion. There was therefore hardly any time to issue the relevant instructions. Another vital component of the Russian plans to destabilise the Ukrainian military system was to neutralise the AFU top brass. After the start of hostilities, many generals received personal messages from their Russian colleagues urging them to surrender, and assurances that Russia's actions would not be detrimental to Ukraine. Thirdly, the Russian "plan-makers" have failed to consider that the Ukrainian authorities would not be afraid to distribute arms among the civil population – something that took place during the first couple of days after the invasion.'

Another chatroom member added: 'Obviously, the Russians started preparing for an invasion of Ukraine some time ago. It would be sufficient to remember a series of explosions – here, and there. Then, the biggest armament depots caught fire. It was a targeted attempt to wipe us out'.

'Many individuals among the Ukrainian top officials, especially the top brass, did not believe that Russia would start a fully-fledged war. Even several days prior to the actual intrusion, and despite numerous warnings from the international partners insisting that Kyiv would be a primary target, the military command still believed that an intense assault against Donbas would be a safest course of actions for the enemy. Allegedly, encircling and destroying the Ukrainian forces in that area would have undermined political equilibrium in the country. At the same time an offensive launched from Homel, Belarus, was viewed as a distraction, needed in order to draw the Ukrainian forces further away from Donbas. And now we have to admit the bitter truth: by endlessly ginning up the subject of Donbas, the Russian trick has worked! To withstand a possible attack on Donbas our military command has kept 10 war-ready brigades out there – half the AFU's mobile forces. Now they use excuses: "We thought it was just a muscle-flexing game. In January of 2022, Germany allowed the completion of Nord Stream-2 gas pipeline, thus putting a tin on this thorny issue. Putin achieved what he'd been insistently angling for. True, we didn't believe it, since from the military point of view the invasion was simply absurd. They had insufficient concentration of forces in every direction. Something like 120 thousand men against the entire Ukraine? Nothing behind them, either. Logistics non-existent. They had combat capability for carrying out a thrust up to a certain point, after which what was needed was extra fuel, reinforcements, warehouse facilities. So, all of it lacked logic. They had insufficient manpower, dispersed, with no support. All had pointed towards hostilities breaking out, if at all, in the east, within boundaries of the oblasts of Donetsk and Luhansk.'

There was another line of reasoning, too: certain high-placed influential individuals suspected that the West and Russia were jointly trying to 'dupe' Ukraine so that it would be compelled to agree to some concessions regarding the implementation of the Minsk Agreements.

Yet another one wrote this: 'Nevertheless, approximately a week before the invasion, personnel and equipment had been gradually pulled out of certain bases. Also, they had relocated all operations control posts "into the fields", bringing them closer to the direction of a possible offensive. Aviation was ordered to leave their permanent bases and move to remote sites, away from the obvious targets for bombing. The rest of the aviation, in case the attack did take place, was supposed to urgently take off and stay airborne. As a result, when the Russians air strikes did start, they often hit vacant grounds.'

Some person provided a truly marvellous insight: 'As for Russia herself, before the start of the war, an FSB outfit responsible for Ukraine had been substantially beefed up: it had grown from employing 30 officers to 160. The stake was to nurture a broad network of paid "sleeping agents" planted at various levels of authority in Ukraine. Several days before the invasion, some of them had received coded messages instructing them to pack up and leave for somewhere safe but leave the keys to their flats behind. In other words, those flats were then to be occupied by Russian pros whose brief had been put together in advance – to eliminate the top leadership and establish a pro-Kremlin regime. "Have a good trip!" – that was an FSB officer parting with his collage, leaving for Kyiv on this mission. They expected to take Kyiv quickly. That would've created a "domino effect" – the central power out of the way, the provinces would disintegrate in panic and chaos, and everything would've crumbled by itself.

'The Russian leaders viewed Ukraine as a state where the God-damned nationalists had treacherously usurped power and put the entire population in bondage – the people essentially Russian but calling themselves Ukrainian on a whim. Therefore, what was needed was to overthrow that government, carry out 'denazification' and liberate the miserable people, horribly oppressed.

'However, there had been this unexpected cause for alarm. The secret polls commissioned by FSB revealed that Putin was extremely unpopular in Ukraine and no one was going to welcome Russians with flowers: 84% of those polled said they would assess any "enforced approach" as "occupation', with only 2% terming it "liberation". Yet the most unexpected turned out to be this. When asked: "Are you ready, if need be, to defend Ukraine?", 48% answered in the affirmative. And now – having these data available, how was it possible to end up construing the situation in such an idiotic way?

'There is this opinion that the situation had been read correctly and unequivocally. But no one dared present those killer-facts to Putin. Instead, they told him about flag-waiving liberators and nice bouquets of flowers. Of some importance was the overall contemptuous viewing of Ukraine as a weakling.

'For all that, the operation had been planned with a lot of pathos: Kyiv taken over in several days, the Ukrainian president defecting or eliminated, the ensuing political vacuum expediently filled in with a pro-Kremlin regime...

'Of special note was the fact that Western analysts also proved to be myopic. Boris Johnson talked about the Western attitude – prior to February 24th – towards a possible Russian invasion into Ukraine. Different countries had different views; the opinions diverged profoundly. Germany believed that in case of war, Ukraine should better surrender. Yes, it meant a catastrophe but it would be in everyone's interests to have it done and over with ASAP. They even offered some rational justification – the gigantic economic losses it would ensue. France, until the last minute, hadn't really believed that invasion would really start. Italy had confessed that it couldn't afford to side with the countries raising the alarm – they were too dependent on Russian fuel.'

This one was also interesting: 'Zelensky in the bunker, Western leaders can hardly connect with him. The NATO secretary general was unable to organize a call in the two days after the war started. At that time there was a strong fear that Zelensky might soon be killed. But when the call happened, as Stoltenberg himself says: "The conversation was quite difficult. Most of the time was dedicated to the no-fly zone. Zelensky demanded it. And I could not give it to him…".'[290]

There also was this important message: 'Kyiv remains in serious danger since Russian fascists can still launch an attack. However, it looks like their troops have lost the advantage of surprise, having failed to achieve their aims in one fell swoop. In addition, it has become clear that the Ukrainian army has impressive combat skills. By now it's proved – it is perfectly capable of fighting against the Russian army.'

And the last post from that chatroom: 'There appear signs of the city being eventually encircled. Zelensky received a report stating that the Odesa Motorway may be taken over, and thus Kyiv would be surrounded. The president issued instructions to procure and bring into the city whatever possible, whatever was still available to buy – flour, pasta, etc. He asked his staff to call round all supermarkets and retail networks, urging the latter to lay in supplies. If the city ended up besieged, at least for a month or two people should have some comestibles and water.'

(Arakhamia subsequently recalled: 'Once, there was this little incident. Our bodyguards rushed in, acting all pushy, and told us to start evacuating straight away. We had an hour in which to decide. Then the president got all of us together and said: "Guys, I understand everything, but I'm staying. For even if Kyiv ends up encircled but the people know the president is here, it will be such a symbol of resistance! And then, sometime later, we will be liberated. At least it gives us a chance for this to happen. But if we leave, everyone will leave too, and Kyiv will fall. Still, you have families, children. I won't judge you. Everyone should decide for themselves. And then, possibly, it's time for you to evacuate."

[290]   RBC Ukraine, 4 October 2024, https://www.rbc.ua/rus/news/rozmova-bu-la-vazhkoyu-stoltenberg-rozpoviv-1728069632.html (accessed 04.07.2025).

'So, we discussed it with our families – over some five minutes – and everyone decided to stay. No one left. That was the first time, probably, when I realised that 90% of us would be taken prisoner. That was security's interpretation, too. I went in search of the building's custodian, found him, and tried to establish who might have known about the whereabouts of the bunker, who had access to technical drawings, knew about the air ventilation system, etc. After all, the building had been built back in the Soviet days and the FSB might well have had access to these data, enabling them to pump some gas in, or whatever. That was how psyched up we all were. Later we got used to it somehow, because we knew that at the same time guys were actually at the front line. To evacuate or not to evacuate – to even face such a dilemma was luxury. But those guys had no such choice. It helped me understand that we were really privileged in comparison. Irpin residents couldn't even leave their homes. After that, I firmly kept these points of reasoning in mind…')[291]

OK, it was time to sum up the fourth day of war. The situation in Kharkiv and the Kyiv's outskirts was grim. Everyone was aware of the fact that even if his blitzkrieg had failed, Putin would change his tactic but still try to encircle, enfeeble, and eventually capture the capital of Ukraine. The situation was so unpredictable that apparently somebody at the top was already advocating surrender of the left bank because the Russians were within a hair's breadth from Brovary. All the better to keep the right bank and entrench ourselves there.

Then this, too – everybody's attention was fixed on the forthcoming negotiations in Belarus. For some reason, many believed that there would be some 'solution', forgetting the fact that as far as Russia was concerned, yet again, it was pure deceit. In all things, at all times. Those of more realistic views harboured no special hopes.

* * *

February 28th, the fifth day of war. The aggressor was fiercely rebuffed everywhere, yet we'd failed to deter them. Ever since midnight, the attempts to break Kyiv's defence had continued, and the Russian convoys had repeatedly stormed the outskirts. If such a convoy moved along an autoroute, the soldiers would be firing at the buildings along the road – afraid of being met with the 'Molotov cocktails'. Despite serious losses to the west of Kyiv – near the settle-

---

[291] UP, 23 February 2024, https://www.pravda.com.ua/cdn/cd1/reconstruction/a6.html (accessed 04.07.2025).

ment of Makariv, in the east Russian vehicles had made headway and reached the outskirts of Brovary. Clearly, the intent was to encircle Kyiv, to pincer it.

A curious fact. According to the satellite images, the Russian convoy moving from Belarus continued growing even further. By that point it was 15.5 kilometres long. In effect, Belarus had been drawn into the conflict – it was from its territory that the rockets were fired, aircraft took off, the troops advanced. Their entire infrastructure – aerodromes, warehouses, rail network – was actively used against Ukraine.

Meanwhile here, in Kyiv, things were changing fast, like in a kaleidoscope. House numbers and street names had all been removed – to baffle the Russkies if they did get in. It was important to remember that they were only ten kilometres away. Anything could happen…

Finally, after the enhanced curfew of 36 hours had expired, those who stayed in Kyiv could venture outside. Some said it felt like being born again.

The shops, pharmacies and some public transport started operating again. But the Metro trains were much less frequent than in the time of peace. Some stations remained closed. An average interval between trains was extended to 40 minutes!

Some other stuff. The Russians had finally cut off the main thoroughfare leading out of Kyiv to the west – to Kyiv-Zhytomyr-Lviv motorway, and so it was out of bounds. And that was why those who still tried to leave could only count on the Odesa route, whereas those who had left earlier and even got as far as Lviv discovered that numerous roadblocks had been erected at all entry points, and the need to check all in-coming cars resulted in huge queues. The authorities had brought in over three thousand men to operate as patrols. Lviv had really become a transit hub for hundreds of thousands of refugees. The country's western border – the one with Poland – was daily crossed by about 120 thousand people.

Mum and I watched some footage showing the border crossing. A little boy, about six years of age, alone, was paddling along. At a distance – two files of people. In his hand, the little guy had a package, empty, buffeted around by the wind. The little boy walked and walked, crying, perhaps unable even to see the road behind his tears. On and on he trudged, out of his country, to God knew where. They all went along, and he did too…

And then the two Polish helicopters brought our delegation into Belarus from Poland, in order to take part in the negotiations with Russia – in other words, the location had been shifted from the Ukrainian-Belarusian border to the Polish-Belarusian one. The public attention was enormous. Some even hoped for a 'breakthrough'. The others said – 'What are you talking about? Come to your senses! They are sure to put forward unacceptable terms. This is an attempt to humiliate us by an ultimatum, and declare: we've brought them to their knees! A classic Russian set-up!'

Somewhere closer to the afternoon they'd already televised the meeting between the two delegations. The whole country gasped. The participants were clasping their hands in a handshake so firmly, as if attempting to tear each other's arms off. Our guys were beaming forth, broad friendly smiles across their faces...

Mum turned the TV off. I returned to my room, looked at the house plants, spotted some leaves covered in dust. I should wipe it clean with a wet cloth. Perhaps it was the plants' last chance to breathe normally? For plants were like people...

By two in the afternoon, I'd set off back to the block house – it was our shift. On my way I looked around, taking things in. True, there were by far fewer people in the city. Still, one couldn't say that there was no one around. Rumours had it that out 3.8 million residents some three million had left in the course of the several previous days. Yet the municipal authorities insisted that about one million people were still there, simply not all of them visible. May well have been true. Those still here stayed almost permanently in, including those advanced in years – at this point in life, they had nowhere to go, and at this age change was difficult. So, the 'stayers' had hoarded provisions and kept indoors. Easy to understand – the possibility of the Russians breaking through was still high, what with the vehement street fighting that was sure to follow... If this proved to be the case, they would have to peek out from behind their window curtains, in stealth. For what else was a peaceful civilian supposed to do?

As in previous days, there were practically no cars around: the owners must have moved them to safe places, if only to adjacent courtyards. If tanks appeared in the city, would their drivers pay attention? They'd barge on, wiping everything off the face of the earth on their way. Still, our courtyard was enclosed, and a coded lock had been installed on the iron gate. And so several cars were left parked inside, at least somehow protected by their owners.

I walked towards the roadblock along Voloska Street, bypassing the hostel, none of its earthlier inmates were still there, everyone gone. The faces inside were new – the hostel was filled to capacity with people from Sumy Oblast. For the umpteenth time I was accosted by a hulk of a man who must have been hanging around at the time.

'You can't imagine things that're going on out there! It's complete horror! Nightmare!'

And he kept telling, narrating… He even grabbed my sleeve, to make sure I'd listen. But I made no attempts to leave – I knew, he had to get it off his chest.

Went without saying, our defence post was abuzz with our thoughts about the negotiations. Everyone was stunned by those firm handshakes and amicable smiles.

'Handshakes and smiles – that's protocol,' the Commander tried to reassure us, although he, himself, was somewhat taken aback.

'But they shook those hands so vigorously! I feared they would pull each other's arms off!' Mykolaiovych was not the one to waste a chance for a dig.

'I won't be surprised if ours are entertaining them now, telling jokes!' Platonovych added fuel to the fire. 'Over here, they are bombing the entire country, raising everything to the ground while the ones out there…'

'Look, it's called opening up channels of communication,' the rational Andriovych tried to calm them down. 'Who can tell what's best? Our situation now is so sticky that, perhaps, it makes sense to butter them up a bit…'

'Sticky…' Mykolaiovych's voice was like an echo. 'It's turned out the south was completely exposed…'

'Why south?' exploded Platonovych. 'The north too, and Kharkiv has been retained by miracle. It's no time to think of the south or the north. All attention now is on Kyiv.'

After that no one returned to the negotiations.

And thus, the slippery subject of the handshakes was glided over. It felt like a much a better plan to immerse ourselves in news.

The hottest spots at that point were Mariupol and Volnovaha in Donbas. Still, there were others: Sumy, approached from all sides by the enemy vehicles, was facing a threat of street fighting.

Other news… By now, according to international organisations, seven million Ukrainians had already been forced to flee their homes.

Elon Musk granted Ukraine access to Starlink, his new satellite communications service.

The stars of Hollywood, at the Guild of Actors' awards ceremony, had expressed their solidarity with Ukraine. The world-famous directors and actors wore pins with the colours of Ukraine's flag on the red carpet: Michael Douglas, Jeff Kravitz, Lady Gaga and many others: 'We are proud of this country's people!'

Well, that was Hollywood, far away and across the ocean. But this one came from a neighbouring country, an EU member into the bargain: 'Hungary will not allow transit of the EU's lethal weapons across its territory into Ukraine. Such supplies may be targeted by hostile forces. We must ensure Hungary's security… to prevent it being dragged into this war…' [292] Statements of this kind coming from European leaders became increasingly perplexing.

'It's not perplexing. It's scary,' Taras somehow guessed my thoughts.

'To start with, zero empathy,' echoed him Platonovych. 'And secondly, a true European leader shouldn't say things like that.'

And thus, the negotiations between Ukraine and Russia had closed by the time evening fell, having lasted five hours. The parties returned to their countries for further consultations. Straight afterwards, in a telephone conversation with Macron, Putin recalculated the terms for a peaceful settlement with Ukraine. It wasn't hard to work out which ones he had in mind. In other words, they put forward an ultimatum.

Well, it was common knowledge that they were cynical louts. However, despite the fact that their advance was somewhat slowing down, and our resistance kept growing up in intensity, one couldn't ignore their achievements. In the south, the enemy had reached Berdiansk. Kherson was under siege. Whichever way one looked at it, within several days they had invaded the territory bigger than Switzerland. They'd also tried to take Mykolaiv, thus far unsuccessfully, but their troops had come near and the front line was some 20-30 kilometres away. The city and its oblast were shelled practically daily.

Social media, as usual, went through the roof – and no one could gag them when discussing the recent developments: 'What's so hard to understand when the adversary keeps building up its military potential along the national border? When the world's best security services keep banging on, for an entire half a year, about this threat? And when the president of the world's most powerful country constantly and unequivocally talks about it? How hard is it to understand that he's not wasting his words? Why is it so complicated to read the situation adequately when residents of Crimea and Belarus continuously report new facts of this build-up? By that point there wasn't even a need for any security intel!'

Danilov commented: 'The country's leaders had advance knowledge of these plans. It was very important, at that point, to keep the informational space closed. Had we revealed our knowledge of the attack against Hostomel, of future developments, they would have activated Plan B. And that was something we had no knowledge of. The task we faced was by whatever means possible to

....

[292]   European Pravda, 28 February 2022, https://www.eurointegration.com.ua/news/ 2022/02/28/7134926/

prevent panic in the country! Just imagine if the president had come out and announced that in two weeks' time there would be war. The chaos that would have ensued would have been ungovernable. And that was what the Russian Federation was counting on.'[293]

Social media countered: 'But if at the top level they knew about the Kremlin's plans, why hadn't they brought in, in advance, some proper troops capable of defending Hostomel? Why hadn't they blown up the Chongar Bridge? And other bridges? Why had they mined the fields but not the roads? Certain things could still have been achieved even at the eleventh hour. Especially when it was reported that the ratio between us and the enemy was 15:1 to their advantage? Therefore, why keep the bridges intact?

'Talking privately, the military say: "We didn't have sufficient manpower or resources. The enemy concentrated their troops along a huge territory – from Belarus to Crimea. We started war as if operating under conditions of peace: no new military groupings had been created, no martial law, no mobilisation. In all those years we'd never created a fully-equipped defence line. In the south, a 35-thousand-strong enemy force met with about a thousand and a half of ours.'

'Come on now! We've channelled everything we had towards the defence of Kyiv that was hanging in the balance. We came within a whisker of losing the entire country, at that point no one even thought about the south.'

'And that's how we stumbled into war. The reservists had not been called up, a state of martial law had not been introduced, army regiments had not been deployed. Oblasts leaders, local authorities did nothing to prepare their defence, since they did not believe in the Russian invasion. They weren't brought up to speed, even after the centre had got the picture! But if mobilisation had been carried out not by the end of the first day, but in advance, there would've been no need to send untrained people to the frontline. They could've had the time to acquire at least some skills!'

'You see – they didn't believe it. Still, one doesn't have to believe in order to prepare. That's what a smart person would've done!'

'How do you mean – they didn't believe? In 2003 the Russians had been building the dam near Tuzla.[294] In 2014 they annexed Crimea, then a portion of Donbas. They promised the troops a safe passage out of the encirclement around Ilovaisk, and then gunned them down at a close range. Throughout the

....

[293] New voice, 23 February 2023, https://nv.ua/ukr/ukraine/events/yak-armi-ya-rf-pereyshla-chongar-u-2022-i-chomu-zsu-ne-zupinili-okupantiv-novini-ukra-jini-50306207.html (accessed 04.07.2025).

[294] A crisis in Russia-Ukraine relations broke out at the end of 2003 caused by Russia's claims to ownership of Tuzla Island (2 km from Crimea) and its construction of a dam in the Kerch Strait leading to this island. The dispute raised fears of an armed confrontation.

entire 2021 they kept increasing their battle numbers along the entire perimeter of the Ukrainian borders. For half a year, the two best intelligence services in the world kept warning us of invasion, sending maps of the directions of attack, other data. The top leadership had no right "not to believe". They duty was to assess the risks independently of their "beliefs".'

However, the more moderately-minded appealed: 'It is incorrect to insists that the Ukrainian army surrendered Kherson lying down. They were desperately trying to withstand the attack for as long as possible. Still, on February 26th they had to retreat to Chornobaivka, and then towards Mykolaiv...'

'True enough, the country wasn't ready to operate under extreme conditions. But that was when the inherent Ukrainian ability to self-organise, self-control and self-govern kicked in. Principles of self-help, in a word. It's also known as the "bee code". The Russians didn't understand that the Ukrainian army wasn't 200 or 400 thousand, the Ukrainian war force was 40 million, it was all of us...'

'It's not the time to sort it all out now. The most important thing now is to fight the bastards off. Everything else can wait.'

Goodness gracious, the time was flying. Shortly before midnight I went home.

No one in the streets. Little wonder – the time was after the curfew.

By now, it had become customary that Taras would send me whatever he'd accumulated in his chatroom.

This military expert talked, yet again, about us going into war in a state suitable for peaceful times: 'No single unit of ours had been brought up to a full strength in terms of war-times manpower. And then – those unbelievable developments. Tens of thousands of people had joined the Territorial Defence in the very first days of invasion. This strategy had met with difficulties. Eventually, a correct route had been chosen, foreseeing the enemy being confronted not only by a professional army but a trained and armed community that needed no additional motivation, because the main thing for them was to defend their homes and families. When on February 24th the Russian troops had invaded Ukraine, they had to have to deal not only with a regular army but local volunteers too, who had immediately started forming resistance hotspots, billeting, and feeding the soldiers, climbing the trees in search of a mobile signal, thus enabling them to transmit the updates of the hostile advancement to our intelligence.

'The first columns of the Russian equipment that had entered the territory of Ukraine expected no resistance. Accordingly, they met practically none when crossing the border. They were spontaneously crying out, encouraging one another: "On to Kyiv!"; "Hooray to blitzkrieg!" Yet the invaders did not expect that they would find a road ahead blocked with a bulldozer and a cement mixer, and a slogan attached on top: "Welcome – to hell!" And those hadn't been regular Ukrainian units but a handful of volunteers from Irpin and Bucha. Among those were people who had never handled arms in their lives: a psychoanalyst, a bus driver, other representatives of peaceful professions. Yet they made the Russian occupiers turn and flee!'

Another chat member: That's what Danilov was saying privately: 'The worst days in Kyiv were February 26-27. The streets emptied. The top team is in the bunker. And those of the tops that remain outside it gather in the GUR, Budanov's office. That's because he was the best source for information about coordination of special units of all levels in Kyiv. Everyone was subordinated to that center'.[295]

Another one: Me too, I can add something that has been said privately! By Zelensky himself! This is what he said: 'In the first days of the war, when Lukashenko called, he apologized. He said: "That was not me... Yes, missiles were launched from my territory, but they were launched by Putin." Those were his words, I have witnesses. He also said: "I apologize. Believe me, Volodya, that was not me. I don't control this, they were just missiles, and that was Putin..." I told him: "You are the same killer, and I say it to you in simple words." And he told me: "Understand, you can't fight the Russians." I said: "We didn't start this. The missiles flew from your land, from Belarus. How could you allow it!?" He said: "Well, come up with a response!" I still remember this perfectly well, him saying that to me: "Hit the oil refinery. You know how much it means to me. Mozyr Refinery."[296] I told him: "What are you talking about? What sort of response?".'[297]

Chatter: And what about the Russian Army invading from Belarus? Why didn't Zelensky mention that?

Yet another chatter: 'Whatever you say, but we've managed to contain the enemy within those first couple of days, thus enabling our forces to be at least partially replenished and start forming a line of defence. This stage is now over. By now, the top brass have identified what constitutes a subsequent pressing task – that of severing the Russian logistic lines…'

---

[295] TSN, 31 August 2022, https://tsn.ua/exclusive/kozhnogo-dnya-zbiralis-u-budano-va-danilov-rozpoviv-pro-naystrashnishi-dni-viyni-u-kiyevi-2147590.html (accessed 04.07.2025).

[296] **Mozyr:** a city in Belarus, 50 km from the Ukrainian border. It is the site of a very large refinery.

[297] UP, 6 January 2025, https://www.pravda.com.ua/rus/news/2025/01/6/7492145/ (accessed 04.07.2025).

'During the initial three of four days, our Western partners didn't believe that we would act effectively. That was why they were reluctant to send us any heavy-duty equipment. They remembered how the Talibs had re-emerged in Afghanistan, and had been wary of their weapons ending up in the Russian hands. Instead, they suggested a guerrilla war. Therefore, at the very start, we had to rely only on our own resources. But now, having seen how we've fought back, they start gradually coming round…'

'Pooh-pooh! Don't talk to me about them. Those Westerners haven't shown themselves in the best of colours. Don't you have the whole picture? Our Ambassador to Germany was ready to hand over a list to one of their ministers, pleading for urgent help. In response, they made a compassionate gesture with their hands: "My dear chap! Let's be frank. Why should we help you, if in 48 hours it will all be over and a new reality will have arrived"?'

'By the way, Yermak is regularly sending pictures of the killed Ukrainian children and damaged buildings to the mobile numbers of the civil servants all over the world. Those horrible images must be keeping them awake at night. He is harassing them with those circulars. True enough, many do wake up after that.'

Another correspondent shared this information. Allegedly, three days before the invasion Putin had summoned the Chechen leader Kadyrov into Kremlin. That was when they developed a special strategy of sabotage. Kadyrov had been charged with two missions: to take out the Ukrainian president and take over the governmental quarter in Kyiv. While Kadyrov's squads were in training in Belarus, he wrote to Zelensky through his Telegram-channel: 'The time for clowning has come to an end!'[298] For Kadyrov, it would've been desirable to kill Zelensky – a kind of the Kremlin's bonus to the Chechen leader.

A telephone interception revealed that Kadyrov had been informed of an incursion into Ukraine on February 25th. He knew of 1,500 men – select units, best fighters, that were to move forward in three convoys of armoured vehicles.

Yet – despite best plans of mice and men… The attack had proved unsuccessful. The first group, practically in its entirety, was eliminated on approaches to Kyiv, while the other two had to regroup and stall, without completing their mission. Later on, Kadyrov's troops came to be used as retreat-blocking forces, preventing the Russian soldiers from escaping the battleground. Those who did try to retreat found themselves under submachine fire. Kadyrov's units were also dispatched to already captured towns and villages, where they interrogated and tortured residents, organised shakedowns in order to flush out partisans.'

....

[298]   WSJ ,16 December 2022, https://www.wsj.com/articles/chechen-warlord-kady-rov-putin-dirty-work-ukraine-11671204557(accessed 04.07.2025).

That was all I'd learnt from the restricted chatroom. I tried to put the day's events in a sort of an order.

First of all, that Russian convoy looked increasingly intriguing. By the end of February 28th, having incorporated reinforcements, it had grown to 24 kilometres and showed a tendency to grow even further. Most likely, it was those 10 reserve BTGs, intended to join their vanguard units and, thus, thrown into battle for Kyiv. The convoy moved forward through the same Belarusian village of Belaya Soroka, and along this route: Chornobyl – Dytiatky – Ivankiv – Nove Zalissia – Zdvyzhivka – Hostomel aerodrome. On the whole, including the first nine BTGs, the grouping moving out of Belarus looked formidable. I felt it in my bones – the heat was turning up.

OK, what else was there? In the course of the day, heavy fighting had taken place all over the country. The General Staff reported that the enemy had sustained grievous losses in manpower and equipment: about 5,000 men killed, nearly 200 tanks and 30 aircraft wiped out. Although the occupiers had slowed down, they tried to make up for this elsewhere.

For all that, the eyes of anyone who cared – both here and all over the world – were on Kyiv. The situation had turned critical. The city was being gradually wrapped up. The space around was shrinking at a catastrophic rate. Would Kyiv survive? And if the answer was yes, it would mean a huge boost to the whole country's morale, justification of its dreams and expectations.

It looked like I'd rationalised all the main points. The clock said several minutes to midnight.

In a very short while the month of February would be over. It was hard to believe. Those last five days in February had been horrible but it felt as if February had dragged on for a whole year…

* * *

Just like the life of anyone in Ukraine, on February 24th my life had changed irrevocably. Some heard the bombs exploding, some hadn't – it made no difference. Everybody's reality had been merged. What baffled belief had become actuality.

The sirens blared, something boomed and exploded in the distance. I asked myself if a new life was about to begin. What sort of life would it be? God alone could answer this question.

During the first several days there had been throngs of people by every shop, pharmacy, ATM. Everybody stood there, deep in concentration, stern. What was the point of recollecting any of it?

Those who were not here, ended up hemmed in elsewhere – sitting in their cars, in endless jams.

The sirens continued to wail and we were urged to descend into air-raid shelters. Still, many people did run out of their homes and, yet again, raced towards the shops – what if something had appeared there? Everybody knew that if the city got encircled, hunting for food would be pointless. We'd just have to tighten our belts to the last notch. Perhaps, not at once, but then again, who could tell how long it would last?

Some people, for all sorts of reasons, had children staying here, so obviously, they were the ones who descended into shelters every time. Some even moved into there. Someone, by the way, came up with an idea of how to explain it to the children: the war, the shelling, the air-raid shelters. It felt advisable to turn it into a game. Say, mum and them were tiny innocent mice, and had to escape from a wicked cat. Ahoy, who'd reach the shelter first, running? That one would get a sweet – there still were some available. Come on, quick, hurry up, run!

Hey-ho, games or no games, the children felt baffled. Or perhaps they could sense that something scary was going on: they cried and refused to be placated by any sweets...

In the dark, only few windows lit up in the house across the road. But even those were curtained and illuminated by one weak bulb. Those were the instructions. In some blocs there was no light whatsoever. Could all of them have left? No, some did stay. Most likely, they put up some very heavy fabric and it was blocking out any light – as was the authorities' advice.

Suddenly, for some reason I remembered our rector and his plans for a monograph. So ridiculous... The Russian fascists were within a stone's throw from Kyiv, or maybe in places already inside it. That wasn't the time for Gogol, not at all. The theories about original sources for *Dead Souls* had receded into the background too. As for Dostoyevsky – even more so. What was the point of the rector's monograph anymore? Under the conditions of martial law, everything closed down, our institute, too. Everything had gone to the dogs...

* * *

Those who hadn't left in the first days along the Zhytomyr Motorway were trying to break away on the Odesa route. Those who had stayed, seldom ventured outside – no point, unsafe, with practically nothing left in the shops. The city felt almost dead. By the way, living in a city like this was also a unique experience.

Psychologically, getting used to all of this was hard. Only shortly before, I'd lived in a metropolis that was abuzz with energy. In a stream of people and cars, I remember swearing at nearly every turn, cursing those who'd parked on the pavements. Then what? Almost no one in the streets. And hardly any cars at all. Everything looked extinct and felt surreal. Life on a remote farmstead could've been livelier.

There were so few people in the city that the authorities virtually begged those who stayed: to prevent the supplies of energy cut down, please use electricity! Do your laundry, cook, don't save – use it any way you can! Who would've thought that the war had this among its consequences...

Therefore, those still around sat at home in front of their computers, and kept both their TV and radio on. There was a lot of news, all coming in around the clock. Something had exploded, something was on fire. Some of our guys advanced, the others retreated. And all over the place, the people were dying.

We were constantly warned about the sabotage squads: 'Numerous subversive groups are active in the city. Their main objective is to kidnap the country's political leadership.' Allegedly, their top priority was to assassinate the president.

In other words, to murder? A person elected by the people? Discharge his official duties? But that was pure villainy! Although... Villainy was all around, unmitigated, and unremitting.

God in Heavens, why was this to become our fate? Had there been a spell cast over our land, a place of our birth, and then everyone tried to have a go at us? All kinds of tsars and tsarinas, and those Soviets? Everyone – from the Soviets to Hitler? And from Hitler to the Soviets? And now – Putin? A vicious circle, no less. Why wouldn't all of them just let us be and live normally?

One theory stated that it was all about fertile black soil. Not many countries in the world could equal our land's fecundity. Allegedly, during the WWII, the Germans had been transporting our soils back home by trainloads – whether or not it was true. Our chernozems were, unquestionably, an irresistible lure; so productive, you could almost eat it on a piece of bread. The topsoil that was feeding, apart from its own country, 400 million people all over the world.

Sweet Lord Jesus! How could we continue to stand firm? To hold out against that onslaught?

Truth be told, I didn't want to ruminate anymore. What if something came flying and hit our house? What then? The only thing to ruminate about was the probability of one's death. On any given day, who could guarantee that you would survive it? And if you did, would you survive the day after? For even a shelter wasn't a complete panacea. To say nothing about being exposed at the roadblock. Danger lurked everywhere, what with the hit squads and all?

On the other hand, when on the roadblock duty, at least one had a sense of making a difference. Perhaps it was ludicrous but one felt inspired.

Also, the roadblock proved to offer very handy protection from the winds of March for those could be really violent. Apropos the roadblocks – their number kept growing. That did give substance to the hopes that we would hold our ground – however briefly.

Yes, for several days running, the city had been getting ready to meet the enemy. We kept trying to work out the rate of their daily advance toward us in kilometres. Obviously, from our Mezhyhirska Street we had no clear view of their progress but the booming explosions made it possible to calculate the distance, since the sounds travelled well down the gradient of the thoroughfare. By hook or by crook, the Russkies were getting closer.

'Looks like this is where Taras and I will die – like heroes, or without any pomp, if after all, say, we do have to engage…' piped in a small voice inside my head.

But I immediately shushed it: 'Don't be an idiot! What's that – "if after all"?'

'Come on,' came back my *alter ego*. 'You get it all yourself, just keep showing off, refusing to accept reality…'

And I, so as not to be overheard, snapped at myself in whisper: 'Away with those bastardly thoughts! What a wanker you are, dear Kiril, if you allow yourself to think like that! Shame on either you, or this other creature inside your head, for you are one and the same. Here, on the home front, and such an attitude! While the real warriors, perhaps your age-mates, are in much greater danger!'

In short, my two inner 'me's had had a fight. Let them. I didn't even feel like apologising for that dialogue, for the tension was mounting. Even if you are 'backstage', coping with all of this wasn't easy.

But the little voice came again:

'Dear me, could it be that my life will end, and at my age? How can it be?' my inner adversary just wouldn't be silenced.

That's it, I had to pull myself together. Somehow bring my brain into gear, fit into the context. Somehow to try and live, whatever the circumstances.

But no, what was all that – 'to try and live'?

I had to do something. By all means, do something.

'But what?' exclaimed the small voice.

'What I'm doing here! Being on duty! And this, however insignificant, is action!' retorted my first 'me', not without pride.

* * *

During those crazed days, the headiest period between February 25th and 28th, when the Russian burst-through into the city was quite real, all that was left was to carry on somehow.

We were at the defence post practically all the time, except the hours when the Commander let us go home.

So then, five days after the outbreak of war, the top news for us was realisation that the Russian blitzkrieg had definitely gone tits up. And that gave ground to hopes that they would eventually get bogged down in all else.

Within those five days Zelensky had become something akin to a national hero. His daily televised appeals were a proper boost to everyone's morale. Nothing but determination! Not even a shade of doubt that we would be victorious! His ratings soared. No one even wanted to remember that not so long before he'd been sceptical about a possibility of invasion. Alas, but that was the real reason why we'd late preparing.

Only five days, and yet so much had happened. It had become clear that the Ruscists were opening the bloodbath. They'd twigged that things were going haywire and saw red. By then it wasn't an operation to 'liberate' but a bloody mayhem.

One of our guys narrated this. His friends were on their way out of Kharkiv Oblast, by three cars – families, small children, some even babies. The Russians flagged them down, telling to stop, checked and saw that it was only civilians inside – 'Drive on!' They did, unhurriedly, so as not to irk the occupiers. Which was when they opened machine-gun fire. Only one car got away, the first one, the other two had been gunned down, from a close range.

The specialists commented on this horrific phenomenon thus: in each war, there would be a point when the second war was unleashed. When an aggressor felt they were failing, it rankled, and so they would become indifferent to the fact whether it was civilians or the regular army. Nothing would deter them, and no rules would apply. They would shoot at women, old people, children. By that point, it was all the same to them. They would blast at the windows, cars, the civil population – so that no one would be left.

That would probably explain why, by then, there appeared a new word for them – swine of dogs. Who had invented the word, which linguist – that much was unknown. Although, clearly, it was folk getting creative.

Just like Granny Horpyna – before the invasion – had been calling the invaders the 'accursed demons'. Bull's eye it had turned out to be, for they were monsters.

People kept coming up with the inventive names. For example, the pro-Russian party – the Opposition Platform for Life (OPfL) came to be known as 'Oops-Asses'. Which contained a multitude of meanings. Those very parliamentarians had been among the first to do a bunk out of Kyiv. Out of forty-odd their deputies, few were left in the Rada. The rest had moved on, in search of a foreign billet and ration. In other words, this hated Europe.

Yet Mother Russian remained true to herself. Anything outside of the beaten track – 'No can do!' Under this instruction from Roskomnadzor (the state censor), it was forbidden to: 'refer to the special military operation as an attack, invasion, or war.'

Did everyone get it or not? A ban was introduced on using those words, otherwise arrest, a sentence, and the time inside. Just to be sure: it was not war! For those who were slow – it was a 'special military operation'.

(Later, Syrsky would describe the beginning of the war thus: 'The first day was really hard. Several days later the situation became more or less clear: we got a hang of the methods that the enemy was putting in place, realised where they were headed, assessed their potential and resources, the routes they were going to use. A particular characteristic was that most of the fighting had erupted in densely populated districts. That meant, directly in the streets, children's playgrounds, near supermarkets – where the enemy's armoured assault vehicles were parked alongside regular cars. Vehicles had caught fire; all around were the bodies of enemy soldiers and our guys who'd died defending our land. Of course, it was out of the ordinary for us, but for civilians it was pure shock. No one had been prepared for anything like this. Besides, there were countless other problems: a huge number of unprepared people had been drafted in; lots of arms had been issued. The enemy had tried, repeatedly, to land their troops, including by river. Landing troops disembarking from river boats had tried to take a site near Lyutizh and Petrivtsi, next to the Kyiv Reservoir and the dam. It was then that I realised that a new period had started in my life, although not only mine, but the life of the Armed Forces and the entire country, something unforeseen and unpredictable. And that was that – we had to go on, whatever the conditions.'[299])

March 2022. The Capital City Semi-Besieged

All the people I knew who'd stayed in the city talked about little else but this column. The March 1st images showed that it had already grown to 56 kilometres! To tell the truth, the whole business was quite confusing. Clearly it was aiming at the capital but why was its progress so slow? According to some updates it wasn't moving at all. Why it was like that – no one said anything coherent, horror being the dominating emotion. Perhaps the intent was to amass an even bigger striking force?

....

[299]   UP, 24 February 2024, https://www.pravda.com.ua/cdn/cd1/reconstruction/a7. html (accessed 04.07.2025).

All in all, the initial days were hardly bearable. The Russians were getting ever closer to Kyiv. We heard that the ring around the city was about to close, the only remaining escape route being the Kyiv-Odesa Motorway. One could go to bed, and just then they would capture the city. Seemingly, if nothing depended on you, a good idea would be to have to at least a several hours' kip. Yet sleep was evasive, driven off by all this horror.

Aha! There was this clarification: that endless column consisted of hundreds of tanks, trucks, and other vehicles, and stretched out from Ivankiv to Hostomel – by that point, being already 64 kilometres long… Apart from the military machinery, it also included pontoon equipment, tankers filled with fuel, and lorries with ammunitions and provisions. Roughly speaking, also about 15 thousand personnel…

The Commander presented me with a barrow and a 10-litre plastic container.

'Go get some water – we need to drink, also, make some tea or coffee…'

So, I set off along Voloska Street towards the standpipe. People popped up from time to time. We would exchange tense glances – sort of, here we were, those who'd stayed and got cut off from any other form of life. Living in a big city, would anybody normally clock the strangers? If only for a split second, to avoid collision. Yet by now it was like living in a village – anyone, even walking along the other side of the street, was an object of close attention. To meet anyone in the street now felt eventful.

Three men walked towards me. I could spot their odd clothes from a distance – not just tattered, but genuinely odd. Yet the worst was their eyes – completely wild. Homeless? But the eyes of a homeless person looked different. These guys weren't local, that much was clear. Homeless people from Kyiv were somehow – how to put it? – genteel. Then again, not many of them were around anymore, perhaps sitting it all out in some boltholes. Whereas these guys were disconsolate, as if shuffling under an eerie cloud. If not homeless, what then? Buglers or something? They looked capable of anything. And not a living soul around, just them and me. Our eyes met. I tried to curb my fear, putting on my best imitation of someone whose insides didn't tremble and boil…

And suddenly it dawned on me: they must be from Chernihiv or Sumy! Or some smaller town, but from out there, from the north… From where the real horror was unfolding. So, they must have simply fled away, leaving everything behind, chattels and baggage. Poor bastards… Trudging towards who knew where…

We came level, sneaked a peek at one another, and went our separate ways, as if nothing had happened.

When already at a distance I looked back. Another guy was walking to-wards them. I could sense his wretchedness but they silently bypassed him, too. I thought – OK, today those three miserable souls were here. But what about the day after? One could easily imagine that a number of ghosts like that would only grow...

I wondered if our city had been spell-bound. This territory that had once belonged to the glorious and powerful Kyivan Rus. Over the centuries there had always been somebody eager to butt in and inflict distress and misery. Such a beautiful wonderful city with such a dire fate...

And to think about what could arrive in the nearest future! Something similar had happened once already, a hundred years ago. Kyiv had been pro-foundly shaken by the events of 1918-1919. Various regimes had been flick-ing past non-stop, but it had been the return of the Moscow Bolsheviks that marked a real start of severe bombardment and bloodshed. The occupiers had taken to killing the locals for speaking Ukrainian, or wearing the tradi-tional embroidered shirts, or keeping a Taras Shevchenko portrait on a wall at home...

But they had only become entrenched the second time round, and after that lasted long seventy years. Then followed the 30 years of independence, breezing out in relief had become possible. But no. A hundred years later, a new adversity loomed large again, but stemmed from the same direction. To top it all, if by that point they'd made up the lists of the undesirables, then next thing would certainly be filtration.

Christ in Heaven! Dear Mary! Did you see all this? Did you cry? Or didn't you? Hard to tell...

I lugged the canister back into the cellar and plopped down onto a bed, to rest up. I decided to have a quick whirl around social media. Just as I thought: while in the thick of it, more and more people accused the authorities of al-legedly underestimating the danger. The posts were combustible:

'It's imperative to work out what's just happened, and not only here, in Kherson Oblast. When the Russians came over the Belarusian border, were our guys fully prepared? What about in the oblasts of Chernihiv and Kharkiv? The Russians easily reached Trostyanets in Sumy Oblast by eight in the morn-ing on the twenty-fourth! A column of a hundred vehicles! And after that, their combat equipment kept passing through on a daily basis! As for our ill-fated Kherson Oblast – there's nothing to add! Everything was exposed. TV channels were competing with each other as to who would broadcast the meeting with oligarchs on February 23rd. So much so, that Bankova had become one big scrum of elite motors. They should've been not arranging a meeting like this but regularising – even at the eleventh hour – their defence lines! Digging trenches near the border, planting mines, and setting up ambushes!'

'My mum called me from Kharkiv early in February. She said there would be war, and a proper one at that. She is a normal pensioner, not somebody with a security background. She said that everybody in their milieu knew they should be ready for invasion. I didn't believe her then…'

Volodymyr Zelensky explained: he had bypassed the subject of that danger in order to prevent panic, and to keep the economy operating. What would it have looked like if he'd come out on TV with a statement along these lines: 'Look, here, get ready. Stash your money, hoard provisions', and so on. Had we said something like this – and certain individuals whose names I wouldn't name had insisted we should – I'd be losing seven billion dollars a month. And the Russians, when they did come, eventually, would have overpowered us in three days. Had we created chaos before the invasion, the Russians would've swallowed us whole.'

He also referred to the warning signals from our Western partners: 'When somebody insists they were sending us signals, I kept telling all of them: "Send us armaments!" I was talking sense then, and am convinced of it even now.'[300]

It was leaked that even before the war Deputy Kremlin Chief of Staff Dmitry Kozak had been negotiating with Ukraine. Allegedly, he had been granted relevant authority by Putin. As a result, Kozak brought him a draft agreement totally consistent with the Russian demands. Ukraine had yielded on some points: for example, it had agreed to forego its membership in NATO and a lot of other things. In other words, this agreement would have rescinded the need to attack Ukraine.

If that was true, Zelensky's train of thought became somewhat more understandable. He was facing a powerful adversary. The West had no confidence in his ability to withstand any of it, and therefore, they kept dragging their feet over the military support. Eventually, they had started sending us some stuff suitable for defence, but offensive weapons weren't' even on the agenda – such was their lack of faith in the Ukrainian abilities. So, what was one supposed to do under those circumstances? Engage in negotiations, agree to some forms of compromise, and avoid anything that could have provoked this enemy! The other way round, it had been imperative to keep sending out peaceful messages while assuring the Ukrainian society that no danger of invasion was imminent. That would have been the logic.

....

[300] Suspilne noviny, 16 August 2022, https://suspilne.media/271842-zelenskij-rozpoviv-comu-vlada-ne-poperedila-ukrainciv-pro-vtorgnenna-rf/ (accessed 04.07.2025).

Yet Putin had rejected that plan masterminded by Kozak, intimating that those concessions were now insufficient. He gave a temperate response: the invasion had acquired new objectives, much broader ones…

I took a plunge into comments on the news sites – my, the passions were really boing over there!

'As for Kherson Oblast, the whole thing was truly weird. Little reason to feel joyful over the summarised conclusions. Within a matter of days the Russians have taken over a huge territory, including key ports, and blocked the Dnipro – the main aquatic artery. They've assumed control over supplies of drinking water from the river into Crimea, the junction between all three bridges over the Dnipro in the area: the Antonivka Bride near Kherson, suitable for use by vehicles; the adjacent railway bridge, and the other one, of dual purpose, running along the HEPP dike in Nova Kakhovka. Their final purpose is to cut through the "overground corridor" towards the occupied peninsular…'

'How is it possible? Two weeks prior to invasion we'd heard about being "ready for any incursion coming from any angle", and in the end, not ready at all? To have practically the entire Kherson Oblast occupied within a week? No one expected such quick progress. What we've got is occupation, chaos, and disarray. We are reaping it all now…'

'How has it happened that've surrendered the south? Why hadn't the combat units been deployed in relevant positions? After all, wouldn't it have been possible to advance all troops forward, under the cover of the night? To spread them around and sit waiting. Seeing as everyone knew perfectly well that they would advance from Crimea, plus they knew about those multi-kilometre columns. So, it would've been possible to simply bring down heavy fire, employing whatever means available…'

'The Russians started preparing on the evening of the twenty-third. It's impossible that our counter-intelligence knew nothing about it. As for the Americans… They had simply overwhelmed us with intelligence of theirs…'

'The border guards told me themselves that hundreds of combat vehicles had been brought in from the other side. It was half two in the morning. And they did send their reports upwards!'

'The control points in Kherson were all stormed simultaneously. It wasn't even a storm – the Russians simply drove through. I'm a live witness of how the war started. The Russians were having it easy: moving forward, shooting in the air, having fun, getting a high…'

'Why hadn't the defence redoubts worked? Say what you want, but we had it all available: the mines, the artillery… Targeted explosions of the passage routes wouldn't have stopped the Russians but definitely would have impeded them…'

'Yet again, let me explain – our army didn't want to provoke them. In the evening of the twenty-third, they knew the invasion was about to start, but right up to the last minute they still had hope and didn't want to give the Russians any pretext for what they were about to do. Got it?'

'What's to say? In the first several days, things really were hanging in the balance. We've held our ground thanks to the independence and initiative shown by the lower-level commanders as well as the local residents…'

'Lots of people in the south have been bought. It was they who undermined the defence there.'

And those thoughts applied to a wider range of issues, not just Kherson Oblast:

'They say they knew about the inevitability of war but tried to keep people calm so as not to incite panic? And at the same time the army had not been brought up to the full strength? They knew about the war but did nothing to prepare the army?'

'Even a lay person could see it all: if an armada like that has been dragged towards the border, there's no way it'll remain idle…'

'One could hear no sirens in Mykolaiv, none at all: first, only the rumble, and then the planes. I don't know what they meant when talking about preparations in the south, for in our oblast lots of occupiers had been shot by regular people, capturing the tanks from the Orks.'

'Anywhere you look, they've missed their chance. They'd only managed to give the enemy a proper welcome in the ATO area.'

And so on, and so forth.

Still, several sympathetic posts.

'The start of a war always means panic, bunches of traitors and saboteurs. What's going on? Where to? Why? One doesn't know what to cling to. In the end everything falls into place, settles down, more or less, and that's when a new round of fighting begins…'

'Everyone got simply scared and took off – it's the human factor. It's one thing to exercise to look like Rambo, but when explosions go off!!! The bodies get blasted to bits… A normal reaction – let's get out of here. And the commanding officers failed to control this panic. That's all there is to it.'

Well, those were comments on the sites, mostly anonymous, so no one could contain their agitation, and they were free to say whatever came into their heads. Officially, though, at this time of war, there was a political lull. Everyone realised now was time to stick together. Yet one day you would have to take responsibility for your actions…

How had *that* happened?

It was already possible to list at least a dozen of those 'thats'…

Yet the main thing was clear. What happened had been a regrettable miscalculation, no point denying it.

Yes, it was the wrong time for burning and painful questions, stubbornly refusing to go away and impossible to brush aside. Looked like the leaders knew 'what' but not 'when'. Even if they had understood it all, they still believed that anything newsworthy would only flare up in Donetsk and Luhansk Oblasts where the Russians would be fighting for Donbas within its administrative borders.

Was it, after all, possible that by endlessly insisting on 'recognition of the DPR and LPR', and constantly emphasising the subject of the East Ukraine Putin had managed to dupe the Ukrainian top leadership?

So – had the authorities been preparing? And if yes, had the measures been adequate?

What was true and what was fiction? Enough material waited for competent analysts in the future.

But what about Moscow? They had their own bickering to deal with. According to one opinion, the Ukrainian fiasco revealed systemic faults within Russian intelligence services: the use of unreliable sources – clearly, someone had willingly accepted payments in exchange for cock and bull stories. Also, lack of professionalism in data processing; a weak analysis...

Their analysts had insisted that in view of the fact that petty Nazis had usurped power in Ukraine and mercilessly repressed the local population, the reasonable solution was a blitzkrieg: 'We count on things over there going into a downward spiral: the leaders will flee; some residents may succumb to panic, whereas the majority will welcome us with open arms. Our forces accumulated along the border can easily cope with a task of this order.'

Opinions were voiced that Russia had planned on capturing at least two-thirds of the Ukrainian territory. Putin's personal view had been that 'there'll be no resistance, everything will be like it was in Crimea, and things will fall into place automatically.' In any case, the active phase of the military operation should have been completed within a maximum of ten days. At the same time, it had been planned that the Russian Guards would be transferred to the occupied cities, along with the Chechen Special Forces and police, thus enforcing 'order'.

According to prominent analysists, military strategists in Putin's entourage believed that Russia, assisted by special agents, would only need a limited military capacity, and no more than several days, to make Zelensky resign, flee, or capitulate. The same strategists had even suggested that it would be possible to capture Kyiv by only using the ring of agents, even before the

Russian troops came anywhere near the capital. And thus the rationale provided by the FSB and GRU led to the Kremlin approving such an ill-judged plan of attack.[301]

Such a comprehensive failure of the FSB caused amazement. After all, this organisation had been spying on Ukraine for decades, planting its moles into state institutions, bribing officials – doing whatever it could to stop Ukraine drifting towards the West. They'd spent astronomical amounts of money on these activities...

But in the end, they failed to paralyse the government machinery or instigate anything resembling a pro-Russian movement. Let alone a plan to overthrow our leaders. To add insult to injury, after the invasion Moscow discovered that while some agents continued obeying orders to sabotage the Ukrainian defence, there were those who had received the money but following the start of hostilities ignored any instructions.

And thus, it became clear that nothing went according to plan. The Ukrainians kept resisting which meant that practically all of them were Nazis. From which followed that the FSB either hadn't read the situation correctly or had been too afraid to communicate it all to Putin. Therefore, Moscow was compelled to start changing the 'special operation's' strategy on the hoof. The official propaganda, as well, had to introduce corrections: now a Russian soldier on a seized territory had to run his independent 'filtration', aiming at purification of the population. They were to inspect the bodies of the suspects, trying to establish whether or not they carried any 'Nazi' symbols – for example, the insignia of the Ukrainian state. And if the answer was yes, those unquestionably were Nazis.

But what was going on among the Russian population *per se*? Nothing special. Those few capable of thinking for themselves were mercilessly clamped down upon by the authorities. Some remained indifferent, yet the overwhelming majority continued with their unconditional support. The question was – what a person was supposed to do in the name of all of this? Most likely, everyone would try to protect their vulnerable existence, keep themselves to themselves so's not to get involved. That suited the powers that be just fine – stay inside, don't put your heads above the parapet, and you could get a mortgage and credits, perhaps even advance your career...

And the military personnel? Some of them really had no idea where they'd been sent, some – did know. They were hardly overjoyed, and most likely just followed the orders, automatically, went where their commanders told them they should. But with all said and done, they all did take part in a war. In the

....

[301]   GRU: RF military intelligence.

beginning, it could have been automatic, but getting more engaged with each passing day. And finally, they developed this bestial hatred...

* * *

So, these five insane days had come to an end. February became March – Taras's chatroom continued exchanging thoughts. They quoted AFU Commander-in-Chief Zaluzhnyi's words explaining the initial days of the war. Zaluzhnyi insisted that Ukraine's military command had an integrated plan: 'To start with, we had many options as to how to act. I analysed them all in my head. At times I felt terrible, but what urged us on – me and the military command – was the need to understand what to do when the adversary had all the advantages, could attack from practically everywhere, and could act with power and speed; when Russia's strategic aim was to eliminate Ukrainian statehood. [And we found the only correct solution]: to inflict on the adversary the maximum losses in the shortest time possible. To bleed them to a point where they would have to give up any plans of moving deeper into Ukraine. And that was what we did...'

From about early March Zaluzhnyi realised that his plan had proved effective. OK, we were retreating, but we'd shrunk the frontline and saved the army. We'd identified the best lines of defence. We'd lured the enemy deep into Ukrainian territory and started 'mauling' him from all angles. The Russians were systematically decimated by our defence, yet our real agenda was to go on the offensive. The Ukrainians decided to reject the paradigm enforced on them by the Russians, one that Russia had used many times in the previous 100 years of her military history. The AFU started attacking the Russians on weakened sections of the front, approaching from behind, severing supply channels, and thus undermining the morale of the Russian army. The Russian armed forces had clearly been psyched up for a short-term 'special military operation' and a triumphant march towards Kyiv, not a dragged-out war. That was why they had engaged in hostilities with their support services unprepared, their artillery not quite up to snuff, and with scrambled radio electronic methods of war. Another thing was extremely important. Ukraine had managed to withstand the onslaught by using its own resources – initially there had been practically no outside help. Our Western partners had been convinced we would never hold our ground against the 'second army in the world.' Presented with the facts, they acted somewhat annoyed with our being 'not totally au fait with the entire range of problems.'[302]

....

[302]   Chas, 13 May 2023, https://chas.news/current/voni-diyut-yak-orda-golovni-te-zi-z-velikogo-intervyu-valeriya-zaluzhnogo (accessed 04.07.2025).

Another user wrote this: 'Some comforting news is now arriving from even the ill-fated south. At long last, one can be sure that the AFU have completely recovered and are capable of more than just defence. On March 1st, having botched their attempt to take Mykolaiv (our reinforcement had arrived promptly), the Russians tried to bypass the city and move forward, in a gigantic convoy, towards the town of Bashtanka. From there they could've built their attack onto Kropyvnytsky and Kryvyi Rih. On March 2nd, they weren't just marching into Bashtanka, they opened fire on the way. Yet, they've finally overreached themselves. It was hard to believe but the local residents organised themselves and brought the huge enemy's convoy to a halt! They then called in for help from the Ukrainian troops, and the latter duly completed the smash up. The Russians were forced to abandon their equipment. The enemy suffered significant losses, hundreds of their vehicles were destroyed and captured. And the soldiers simply dispersed – the Territorial Defence are still busy catching them from all over...'

'Guys, that's not all! On March 2nd, another Russian column moved onto Voznesensk. To capture the town would've opened a route towards Odesa, and what's more, from an unexpected angle in the north. So here, too, residents created numerous roadblocks and blew up the bridge, and this attack also stalled. So, in March the Russians started rolling back, abandoning their equipment. The enemy ran into a frenzied local resistance: rank-and-file locals were digging trenches, helping the soldiers. Hunters, their rifles at the ready, were keeping watch at the roadblocks; enemy vehicles were set on fire. That was a turning point for the AFU – realising that there was grass-root resistance, they acquired a new faith in their own efforts. Thanks to successful defence of Mykolaiv Oblast, the onslaught against Odesa had floundered. In other words, this example alone proves that it was possible to avoid a catastrophic fiasco in Kherson. Destruction of the bridges, early mobilisation, timely deployment of troops along the border, adequately arranged systems of communication and city defence – all of this could've produced a totally different result of the Russian incursion into the south of Ukraine.'

'Sure, Bashtanka and Voznesenk were two sizeable operations, they became a turning point in the battle for the south. But there were quite a few others, even if not so full-scale. So, it became clear from early March: Russian invasion didn't just lose its momentum, it has been deterred...'

'On the other hand, precisely on March 1st Russia launched missile strikes targeting Freedom Square in the centre of Kharkiv. One of the missiles hit the HQ of the oblast administration, the devastation was horrific. That was when most Kharkiv residents decided to get out of the city. Just then, on March 1st, because of the lack of communication between the municipal authorities and the city residents, unsure of what to do next, some people started to organise themselves in Kherson. They assumed responsibility for creating the units of Territorial Defence. They came out in the morning, armed with Molotov cocktails and submachine guns. When they all assembled in the Lilac Park, the enemy's armoured vehicles moved in against them. Nearly all of them died there. Afterwards, the Russians just entered the city, and that was that.'

'Bloody hell,' that was the last comment in the chatroom exchange. 'In a war it's always the same: obvious achievements but also, errors of judgement...'

* * *

There was no access to the government quarter. Every street leading up to the President's Office, the Cabinet of Ministers or the Supreme Rada had been barricaded and blocked with all sorts of equipment.

Verification was required at every step – you could only pass through on producing your passport with your place of residence stamped into it. The questions were asked in Ukrainian and your answers were attentively listened to. A Russian saboteur, even if with some knowledge of Ukrainian, wasn't that hard to spot – they couldn't help making stupid mistakes, there were things they just couldn't pronounce properly...

Yet at our roadblock things were much more straightforward.

Alla dropped in, wrapped in some funny furs, perhaps something inherited from her granny.

'How are things? Everything tip top?'

I sent her a sidelong glance. She dipped her eyes, for both of us knew – things were seriously far from 'tip top'.

'It's miserably cold. How do you bear it, when you're on a shift?'

Turned out that in the meantime she had joined the volunteer movement. Anyway, right now she brought us two thermoses with tea and coffee.

'Look, you know things. What's going on in the institute?' I asked.

'Calm sea.'

'And where're the bosses – the rector, head of department, Dmytro Petro-vych?'

'It all closed down. Like everything else. And who's where – I've no idea.'

Why did I ask her that? As if I didn't know the answer myself. Sure thing, it was all closed. Which meant that the rector had a lot of time now to work on his treatise. I was more than sure it would be on Gogol. For Dostoyevsky – as a subject, at that point? The grim view of the world, all that mental imbalance, conservative views, a supporter of the Russian empire – what would the rector do with any of this at such a time?

Alla cut into my thoughts:

'Give me your cups. Do you ever wash them?'

"You bet!' Taras gave me a wink. 'As for rinsing them – we sure do, as sure as the next thing.'

I winked back at him, sort of, yeah, we were all sticklers for cleanliness here, at the roadblock. Just give us a cup, we'd make it shining clean.

'Can you imagine? There was this popular writer,' Alla flung her arms up, 'a real "master of human souls"… Some years ago, the whole world couldn't get enough of his books… So now he's blurted something out of his far-away Latin American bolthole…'

'Which is what?' the bespectacled Gennady bristled up.

'Either something about the "mysterious Russian soul", or the "great Russian culture"…'

'Ha! Can't' you understand the subtext?' Denis moved in to join us. 'Will you give me a splash?'

'That tired myth about the "mysterious Russian soul" can go fuck itself!' Gennady wasn't the one for mincing his words. 'And I feel like saying the same thing to all those defenders of the "great Russian culture" – fuck off! Your "great Russian culture" at the moment is bullshit. Who has it nurtured, this "great" culture?'

'There you are… I feel like many assumptions will have to be reconsidered today,' Alla summed it all up. 'As for this maestro, I was rather indifferent before any of this. Trash, but OK. But now, for me, he's a nonentity. I will not open a single book by him. Let the rest of the planet go gaga and starry-eyed!'

The Russian fascists were making many new assertions, mostly stupid and absurd. For example, that Ukraine… allegedly… had threatened Russia! Just think of it! Russia being a powerful country, armed to the eyeballs… Along with the USA, the owner of the biggest nuclear potential – to say nothing about her bottomless natural resources. And then, suddenly, it spotted a danger to her security from the side of Ukraine! A much weaker country. How on earth was it possible? Although, true, we presented a danger by being a democratic country – a clear threat to an autocracy…

Then there was this statement of theirs: the future of Ukraine was much more important for Russia than to Ukraine itself. Lu-u-u-u-nacy!

So, there we were, trying to extricate ourselves from the bondage imposed on us by our neighbouring country. By now, we had climbed a very high summit and our task was to enter the community of European countries as an equal, full-bodied partner. All we had left was that leap. We were standing on a mountain top, buffeted around by winds, waiting for a European ascent…

Meanwhile the Europeans were still overly cautious, waiting out for something. Even if nearly all of us had been killed here, they would still avoid a decisive cause of action.

'They fear Russia,' explained the bespectacled Gennady. 'Putin has masterly assumed the role of a mad leader. And this sends them into a trance. Don't they get it – and it can't be ruled out! – that after us they may be the next ones torn from limb to limb?'

It was going to be my shift now. My surroundings were visible to me from two angles: either if I tried and made something out in the distance, in between those tiny isolated lights, or if I cast my eyes upwards, at the sky. What was that above the city? Nothing but the dark frosty sky, and the stars timidly poking out. Strategically – nothing special. Nothing to look for.

The main task was to look ahead, although you wouldn't see anything, however hard you tried. Still in the global scheme of things that wasn't all that important. If the Russkies did start advancing we would get an instant message over the two-way radio. Therefore, how important was it, us standing guard? On the other hand, of course it was important. It was our duty – to keep sentry and cover all the risks. Besides, saboteurs were everywhere, their prime time being at night and at dawn.

Still, from time to time I was raising my eyes to the sky, looking at how the stars were growing bigger and bigger. Meanwhile, the same thought was going round and round in my head: 'OK, for now it's all working out, the Russians haven't popped up. But what about tomorrow?'

The day was dawning. The stars paled and disappeared. I didn't shiver with cold anymore, the body must've got used to it. All was quiet around me; a suspicious silence had descended. No explosions, no sirens. 'What do you want?' asked the same small voice inside my head. 'After all, the soldiers get tired, too – ours and theirs alike, so their commanders allow them some sleep before morning…'

* * *

I woke up with a start, and for a while couldn't clear my head. Then as if a jolt went through my body – it was the third of March! Well, the war had already lasted a week.

Kyiv was enveloped in this deceptive lull. The sirens still howled, but not as frequently. By then, we'd had quite a few new people at our roadblock, thus making it possible to sort out the shifts.

And then came a call from Spyridon.

'How are you?' I asked. 'All settled?'

'How we are here is beside the point. It's much more important how *you* are. The danger is monumental.'

'We are hoping for the best. Positive thinking… you know it yourself… is quite useful.'

'Look here, man. I've got a favour to ask. Maybe it's something that's within your power.'

'What's up?'

'Before the war I ordered some super vitamins and bio supplements for our whole group. We'd trained together. Well, you know, we were building our muscles with Bolik. As we were leaving, that was the last thing on my mind. I know, there's no transport now, no wheels, and to get from your place to ours is quite a schlep. But I'm having a greed attack. I did live in the strategic district, Darwin Street, smack in the centre. Those bastards are sure to be billeted in our vacant flats, for our landlady's left too. And if they come across such stash – they'll heartily gorge the lot. Fresh from the USA, my Lord… And then push on against our guys with redoubled muscle force? A finger to them! You could get the keys from the neighbours, I'd call them.'

'Why don't the neighbours move into that flat themselves? Simple as that?'

'No go. They want to leave too, tomorrow. And they're unlikely to take those vitamins with them, for the car isn't elastic. The Zhytomyr direction is cordoned off but it's still possible to try one's luck towards Odesa.'

'Got you. I'll try.'

'Bring a biggish backpack, also a holdall or something. Take all the stuff to your roadblock, distribute among the guys. Those nice vitamins would really come in handy, 'tis winter and all. It ain't much, but still, my tiny bit for the victory. By the way, scoop all the grub out of the fridge. Some grains in the cupboards – empty the lot out.'

Well, vitamins and bio supplements, it wasn't bad. I reasoned the Commander would give me leave to repossess the goodies.

OK, Shchekavytska Street to Darwin had to be on foot. Before leaving, I picked up a city map to try and work out a shortcut. Although I could see it even with my eyes shut.

I set off at about eleven in the morning, so's to be heading back while it was still light.

I reached the corner at Voloska Street, and all my local acquaintances brightened up. Oleh's Hill was the first to call out to me: 'You say Zelensky hasn't done a bunk? I am here, too. Although I probably couldn't do it anyway…' Then came the voice of Oleh himself, ringing out from his grave: 'If you see a bloody

Russky – say, you do! – tell him from me that they've hatched up such a crummy plan. I really don't like it one bit!' The mast couldn't stay silent either: 'Where are you trudging off too, you poor thing? Are you out of your mind? Everyone's sitting at home, silent as lambs, not even daring to peep out of their windows, you're the only one who's putting his head over the parapet...'

I used this opportunity of a direct dialogue and posed a question to the mast:

'Perhaps at least up there, at this height of yours, it's clearer as to what's to come?'

'Oh my, a very good question. You see, there's no direct answer even at Bankova. Perhaps the Hill has a better idea, after all, it's older...'

'Something's gonna happen, that much is clear,' the Hill piped in. 'No doubt about it. Let Oleh say something.'

And the Hill started rocking his grave with one of its buttresses. So Oleh joined in:

'From my cramped quarters I can see nothing and understand even less...'

Goodness gracious, were they really talking to me or was it all in my imagination?

I trudged on. I passed Yaroslavska Street and both Vals – Nyzhniy and Verkhniy[303] – funny distinction, for if was one street but with different names for each side.

From there, I entered Kontraktova Square and passed by that famous building, a rare example of classic architecture – a place where the contracts had once been agreed at those celebrated fairs. I paused briefly in front of the monument to Hryhorii Skovoroda. I looked the philosopher in the eye – what if he had a view on our situation? But I registered no response. I glanced to the left – in the direction of the Kyiv-Mohyla Academy Perhaps the Academy would suggest something? It stayed silent too, apparently the time being too complex for any forecasts. I veered off a bit – towards Ilyinska Street, to have a look at one inscription. Quite some time ago, the students had scribbled this on a stone fence: 'On Vitaliy Klitchko's initiative, developers are demolishing the genuine Kyiv!' This slogan used to be endorsed by painting new crosses, constantly added underneath. But by now – not a single new one. There was no one left to add the crosses. Then again, the demolition had come to a standstill; allegedly, all the developers had successfully vanished, to re-emerge somewhere in the south of France. Walking along Ilyinska one could reach the Dnipro and see the oldest church in Kyiv, the one dating back to Kyivan Rus. The river was straight across the road, as was the place where Kyivites had been baptised in

....

[303] **Val** (Bulwark), **Nyzhniy** (Lower) and **Verkhniy** (Upper): streets in Podil.

the distant year of 988 AD. A nice opportunity to have a contemporary look. But that was not the route suitable for now.

Straight in front of me was the Ferris wheel and the Greek monastery. The monastery remained proudly silent, all right and proper, while the wheel looked gloomy. People taking a ride and paying their coins to have a good look around – that had been to its liking. But to try and wriggle an answer out of it, and pay no coins… Still the Wheel snarled at me: 'See? The way it goes? You think the Russian soldiers will take a ride on me? To have a better look at Podil and the Dnipro? Paying me in Roubles? Oh, woe to me…'

There was nobody around. Everything was still, everyone was keeping to themselves, everyone was hiding. Perhaps I really was the only one like this, off my trolley. What if the Russian fascists would break through at that very moment, bringing in their convoys of tanks and armoured vehicles? While I, like a complete half-wit, was crossing the entire city in order to rescue some American bio supplements? Total lunacy! Ah well, nothing doing. Once started, the road had to be covered. Besides, my aim was noble – so that not a single precious vitamin fell into the enemy's hands. I was a bloody 'hero', that was who.

I reached the Fountaine of Samson. The popular myth insisted that if one drank some of its water, one would stay in Kyiv forever. I came closer, but there was no water. It must have fled the Russian fascists too. Now my route lay along the rear façade of Hostynnyi Dvir towards St. Andrew's Descent.[304,305] Bright people always insisted that was the place to be visited by illuminating thoughts. The place itself was conducive to this: from time immemorial it had marked a borderline between the two parts of the city. Upper Kyiv – rich, administrative, aristocratic; and the Lower Town – a place of commerce place for craftsmen, traders, common folk. And also – God have mercy on me for those thoughts in such times – a venue for various carnal pleasures. In a word, that descent was keeping a close watch over the things going on up there, but in the down quarters too. No other way to sum it up – it was keeping its ear to the ground. And thus, I started climbing uphill, moving carefully – it was slippery, easy to fall. That would've been a bummer. God forbid I would twist my arm or my leg – what was the situation with the ambulances?

I continued my climb upwards. Across the road was the black box of the Theatre on Podil, the one that had been so controversial. Yet none of it felt important now. At the turn of the descent, I glanced downwards – Podil spread

....

[304] **Hostynnyi Dvir:** a trading complex (bazaar) built in Kyiv in 1813 to a design by Luigi Rusca.

[305] **Andriivskyi Descent** or **Andrew's Descent:** a descending street connecting Kyiv's Upper Town with the historically commercial Podil (Lower Town) neighbourhood. It is often advertised by tour guides and operators as the 'Montmartre of Kyiv'.

underneath. What a powerful view, filling you with excitement, even in those horrible times.

Ahead loomed the huge bulk of St Andrew's Church, the Italian Rastrelli's masterpiece. It stared down at me from its height – attentively, even reproachfully. As if saying – *where are you off to in times like this? Everyone's inside, things happen. And you should be home, too. Aha, it's the vitamins... So that the enemy wouldn't get them? Alright then, off you go. Just keep your eyes peeled!*

I promptly reached the upper platform, the beginning of Volodymyrska Street. Oh, what a magnificent place! It was right here, in this neighbourhood, that the great princes of Kyiv had built their palaces – in the days long bygone...

On the right stood the Church of the Tithes, the oldest in Kyiv, with only parts of its foundation surviving. I followed down Volodymyrska Street, crossed over Great Zhytmomyrska, and there it was, another towering presence. Magnificent edifice! Under Imperial Russia it had been the place for governmental agencies, but in our days it housed the municipal police. But what a surprise! That was where life was in full swing: cars emerging out of the forecourt and zooming right back in. Armed personnel going in and out. Every passer-by scrutinised me attentively: was I a saboteur by chance? Generally speaking, normal people had no business hanging around the city... It all was somewhat disturbing. For all that, my mug must have fitted. No one stopped me.

I got myself into Sophia Square, with its monument to Bohdan Khmelnytsky right ahead of me. That would've been the place to stop and have a proper chat. Alas, it was unsafe – if I stopped, the policemen would have surely run up to me. So, all I managed to snarl in passing was this: 'Why did you, esteemed Bohdan, ever put so much faith in them, those Muscovites? After all, the very next day after the Pereyaslav Agreement had been signed, [306] the boyars deceived you

....

[306]   The need to break free from the Polish-Lithuanian Commonwealth and the inability of the Zaporozhian Sich to independently achieve unification of all Ukrainian ethnic lands into a single state prompted Bohdan Khmelnytskyi to appeal to the tsar of Muscovy for a union between the hetmanate Ukraine) and Muscovy. In January 1654 Khmelnytskyi convened a military council in Pereyaslav, attended by representatives of the Cossacks of only three regiments and residents of Pereyaslav. Numerous representatives of the Cossack elders, the Zaporizhzhya Sich, and the Ukrainian Orthodox Church refused to support this agreement and swear an oath to the tsar of Muscovy (later, with the help of *streltsi* [soldiers] who came to Kyiv, Moscow forced the metropolitan to take this oath). As a result of the Pereyaslav Agreement (PA) and subsequent negotiations between the hetman and tsarist governments, a military-political alliance of the two states was concluded. The Cossacks were given a tsarist guarantee of the hetmanate's rights as a state. Subsequently, with every passing year, the government of Muscovy departed further from the terms of the PA. In 1667 a separate treaty (the Andrusivsk Treaty) was concluded between Muscovy and the Polish-Lithuanian Commonwealth. This

all – you, and your elders.' I reminded him how Ivan Sirko,[307] before signing a document on friendship with Muscovy, had warned: 'I's easier not to let them in now than it will be to drive them away afterwards.'

My Lord! A sort of miracle happened! As if some divine energy hovered over me... It felt like all the bells on St Sofia's Cathedral's belfry were about to start tolling. More! The clouds parted and instead – the fiery ball of the Sun appeared in the sky! What a moment for Bohdan to answer! Yet somehow he had no wish to respond, and the belfry had a change of heart too. The clouds rejoined and the ball of the Sun momentarily disappeared...

From that huge cathedral – yet another one dating back to Kyivan Rus – I took a left and followed Sofiiska Street down to Maidan of Independence. Over there, the roadblocks and entrapments on the opposite side had been reliable and solid, after all, the governmental quarter was right behind.

Bypassing the building of the Main Post Office, I walked along the odd-numbered side of Khreschatyk. I paused in front of the metro station of the same name (side by side with the city's central McDonalds, which was closed at this moment, like everything else in the city). This was the best place to cross over towards the odd-numbered side of the street. Not a single car in Khreschatyk, only recently so alive. Four lanes one way, four – in the opposite direction, but I crossed this broad thoroughfare without having to descend into an underpass. I wasn't even rushing, there was no sense. The little forecourt in front of the metro and that same McDonalds used to be the main meeting point in the city. Life used to be in full swing here. But now: not a soul around.

So, I set off along the odd side of the street towards Bessarabska Square, the venue of a world-famous market. In Soviet times they used to bring foreign tourists here to take excited photos of colourfully attired peasant women displaying agricultural goods. Across the street there had stood a monument to Lenin, the Bolshevik leader who, according to Putin, had created our state, much to Putin's irritation. Lenin on his pediment had had his arm stretched upwards, his fingers splayed. People used to joke he'd been telling off the market traders, sort of, *Ok, by all means sell your bloody petit-bourgeois goods, but keep your prices reasonable for working class people! Otherwise, we'll set our workers-and-peas-*

violated the terms of the PA and agreements with Khmelnytskyi and other hetmans and thus established the forcible division of the Ukrainian ethnic territory between these two states along the Dnipro River into two parts – Right-Bank Ukraine and Left-Bank Ukraine. In August 1775 Catherine II signed the Manifesto On the Liquidation of the Zaporizhzhya Sich and its Affiliation to the Province of Novorossiysk.

[307] **Ivan Sirko** (c. 1610–1680): a Ukrainian Cossack military leader.

ants inspectorate on you and you'll regret the day you were born! Yeah, that had been the golden age, the heyday of the glorious Soviet past… Alas, the sellers from the countryside had long since disappeared, the roost was now ruled by ordinary and uninteresting dealers. Equally, the great leader had also bit the dust, the 'ungrateful' Ukrainians had overthrown his monument, the very same ones for whom he'd created their state. Paradoxes abounded…

The road from the market went uphill, along Krutyi Descent. I reached halfway, stopped to rest. A mighty roadblock was looming ahead. But strange thing: not a single person nearby! I can imagine our Commander having a look at this disorder! He would have raised hell… Calming down, I closed my eyes and saw the city of Moscow with its population of many millions. The capital of the country that had attacked us – its streets clogged with traffic jams, crowds everywhere. Was anyone there giving a passing thought to what was happening here? Supposedly, the majority of them supported this nightmare. The initial days, when things were new and full of triumph, had passed. So, by now they felt simply satisfied. Or perhaps they gave no thought to any of this at all. The 'Special Operation' – harped on about constantly for their benefit, but in truth horror with an admixture of death, blood and screaming – was far away, threatening nobody and nothing. Most likely, they didn't even think about it all that much. Like in any big city, some people there had carefree faces and broad grins, the others looked downtrodden, immersed in their thoughts and affairs. A city whirlpool would always consist of a stream of cars, snatches of conversation, the sound of feet shuffling on the asphalt. Although, perhaps I was mistaken and some of them thought: 'The battle for Kyiv is raging on. OK, we've failed to take it in three days. But that's fine, we'll manage within two weeks, those petty peasants aren't going anywhere. As per usual, our country will get additional territories, especially this much-coveted Ukraine. Complete with the fabulous city of Kyiv, which will finally return to where it belongs after the lengthy period of "oppression and humiliation" imposed by the Polonised folks of Galicia…'

Sure, they craved a conquest as significant as possible: the entire southern area on both sides of the Dnipro. They dreamt of Odesa: a city with a million residents, a 'pearl by the sea'! Although, a Russian-speaking place, it was mostly populated by ethnic Ukrainians! Plus, a complete southern mosaic of ethnicities had struck root there: Russians, Greeks, Jews, and lots of others, peacefully living side by side and flourishing for several centuries! Once the Ruscists got Odesa, naturally, they would reach out for smaller 'sea pearls' – Mykolaiv and Kherson: 'It will all belong to us! For that's what we want. For where a Russian soldier has planted his foot – is Russia. Haven't you heard of a slogan like this? So there. Our stertorious 'ho-o-o-oray' will resound shortly all over your country, through the glory of our weapons!'

And that was that. At the very end the Krutyi Descent curved off to the right, and I was already in Darwin Street. A little further – and there it was, the entrance to the house where Spyridon and Bolik had been renting a room. Now to get the keys from the neighbours and on to their room, where vitamins and supplements waited for me, along with grains in the cupboards. So that not a gramme of those goodies would fall into the enemy's bloody hands.

I managed rather quickly, stuffed everything into my backpack and the holdall, and was off. Even with the weighty bags, now it was easier since the road went downhill. I deliberately walked from Khreschatyk to Podil by St Volodymyr Descent, so that at no stretch I would have to climb the road.

Back home I realised that the round trip had been something like 10 kilometres, and took about four hours. It was winter after all, and the pavements slippery in places, one had to walk with care. It would've been much quicker in the summer.

OK, so what was the current situation in the city? Public transport – zero, oncoming cars (if one disregarded former imperial governmental agencies) – also zero. In all four hours, I had met as many as eight frightened passers-by, which was nice – there still were people in my home city!

Mum was out. One hour passed, another one.

Suddenly I heard the key turn in the lock and mum let herself in, carrying a huge package.

'Here. I've bought some medications!' she plonked it on the kitchen table.

'So many? Whatever for?'

'Let it be. Things could go wrong. What if those bastards get in? Then we won't be able to buy anything at all!'

'Mum! How can you have doubts like that?'

'I don't. But the meds – it won't hurt to keep them. I'm not twenty-two anymore, not like you.'

She continued:

'From the pharmacy I went to the supermarket and was returning home with my empty bag, and then those people stopped me: "Lady, go to the children's outpatient clinic, the one round the corner, they give out some dairy there!" And indeed, I received a bottle of milk, several tubs with yoghurt, a selection of cottage cheeses. All they asked was how many people were in my household. The quantity issued depended on that. For free! Amazing!'

* * *

On the whole, compared to the very first days the panic had considerably subsided. There were even some feeble signs of optimism. The overwhelming majority felt certain that the state would be able to withstand the Russian invasion. The performance demonstrated by the authorities – at both the national or local levels – met with an unprecedented degree of approval in the society. Which was amazing since nothing like that had ever happened before.

By the way, I wanted to know how many people had been using the Metro as shelter. The number was announced as 15,000. In other words, most residents still stayed home. At several central stations where the trains did not stop, people settled in carriages – those taken out of circulation and left stationary along the platforms on a closed-down sideline. Only one train continued operating on the Blue Line, running along only one track. The train shuttled between the two terminuses, and arrived at any given station at about 40-minute intervals, sometimes even longer...

At the railway station, now, that was where panic flared up from time to time! The first several days felt like excerpts from the films about the Second World War: thousands of people desperately trying to leave westward, among them many refugees from the eastern and southern provinces, sites of heavy fighting. The clockwork operation of the train schedules had become a thing of the past, one couldn't buy a ticket. All was chaos. The crowds stormed the ticket offices, spent hours in queues in search of information and couldn't get any. Finally, it was announced that now there was no need for tickets, the travel was free! Additional trains were brought in, but no advance announcements were made – to avoid a stampede. As soon a train would approach a platform, everybody rushed forward, eager to gain seats by storm. Ten or twelve people would squeeze into compartment designed to carry four. Many of those travelling were women with small children...

And again, my thoughts returned to the new lull that had settled on Kyiv. Superficially, all felt calm. But this impression was deceptive. One minute all was silence, and the next – gunshots again. Same with the weather: March was a fickle month – the sunshine replaced a blizzard, or rain, or snow. It had always been this way. Yet at this point in our lives the weather was only one of many worries. Everything was worrying now, and everything had become important, but no one could predict anything – neither a common person nor an official at the highest level. How would it all develop and where it would all lead to – no one could say...

And again, no one could work out the situation with that enormous column. Since its length had reached that awful 64 kilometres – no joking matter. What was it expected to achieve? It was standing still, moving neither forwards nor backwards. What was its infernal intention towards Kyiv? Clearly, the order was to capture. But why had it been at a standstill for several days running? The panic was reinforced by rumours about the creation of a filtration camp near Gomel, Belarus. Supposedly, our prisoners of war are being held and tortured there...

If you cast your gaze westwards from Zhovten cinema – either down Mezhyhirska Street, or Kostiantynivska, some breathtaking vistas opened. The entire skyline was visible. Amazing arterial roads. Even if Mezhyhirska eventually veered off and high-rises in the distance somewhat blocked the view, nevertheless the eye could see all the way towards the city's outskirts. That was where the main events took place: we heard a constant thunder of explosions and volleys of gunfire, coming from about 10 kilometres off our roadblock. And it was all that separated us from the real hotspot. Still, events in the outskirts weren't exactly clear, we only knew that everything was up in flames, that it was a life-or-death struggle, all for the sake of preventing them from breaking through, along Mezhyhirska and Kostiantynivska, towards our cinema house...

In the beginning of March there was a stream of unnerving news. Russians had entered Kherson and even started settling in. However, there was a real backlash from the local population, numerous protest rallies. To start with, the occupiers paid no heed. But eventually they started taking active counter-measures – using flash-crash grenades, shooting in the air, apprehending active participants.

Mykolaiv. Every day that had passed made it clearer that the enemy was running out of resources needed for an ambitious push on the southern frontline – in some places the Ukrainian army started overtaking the initiative. Russian supply deliveries had failed, and their troops were forced into a partial retreat.

March 2nd. Mariupol encircled.

On March 3rd, the Russians got onto the Kyiv-Zhytomyr-Chop Motorway, although previously all they had managed was to sweep it with fire. The motorway was closed – not even a Road of Death anymore, for who was still using it?

All this was really close to Kyiv, some 30 kilometres towards the city centre. As for the city boundaries, those were a stone's throw away.

The Russians were ecstatic because that was where the parade columns were to be formed so as to proceed onwards to Khreschatyk – the intended place for the parade itself.

What they hadn't expected was that the Ukrainian long-range artillery would join the fray and blow nearly the lot of them away. Those who survived were afraid to stay overnight in private houses. They were sleeping in the dugouts in the forest instead.

A Russian POW soldier:

'We had problems with sustenance. First, one ration was to be shared by two. Then we ate what we could procure ourselves. Of course we had to hunt around, looting people's homes...'

Finally, some comforting news! In the first days of March, due to logistical complications, the Russian attack on Kyiv had become mired down – the column travelling from Belarus was still stationary. Simultaneously, followed violent clashes in various localities: Bucha, Hostomel, Vorzel. Irpin, too – about 7-10 kilometres from Kyiv's sleeping boroughs. On the opposite side of the city the Russian had reached Brovary. Therefore, the General Staff had to announce that the Russian main objective was to encircle Kyiv.

Since the Russian progress along the Vyshhorod Highway (from the side of Chornobyl NPP) had ceased, and resistance to them in Irpin and other towns close to the capitals' west was vehement, on March 6th Russians started looking for alternative ways to get into Kyiv. They believed their best bet to be a breakthrough across the forest near Moshhchun, a settlement abutting on Kyiv's outskirts in the north-west. This little village was like a gateway into the capital, only three kilometres from Pushcha-Vodytsia, administratively, already within Kyiv. Thus, the battle of Moshchun became one of the key episodes of the defence of Kyiv. To make things worse, the following day Russians seized a better part of Hostomel and started using it as a hub.

In nearby Hostomel itself some residents took cover in the bunker attached to the glass factory. On March 6th, the Ukrainian units retreated and the occupiers entered the town. One woman recollected: 'I asked them what we should do. If we kept the doors locked from inside, they could think that we were hiding some of our military personnel that who hadn't managed to escape and either break in or drown us, who knew? If the doors stayed open, they could simply gun the lot of us down. That was the choice. We decided to keep the doors unlocked.'

The three of them approached. She remembered that the first was a fair-haired guy, with dark eyes, their pupils huge. *'Why are you looking at me as if I were a fascist? We are not fascists. It's your Ukrainian war dogs... they are fascists.'*

Another catastrophe. On the night between March 6th and 7th, Kharkiv was subjected to an intense shelling, heavier than in any previous days. The city was significantly damaged, lots of residential houses had been razed to the ground.

The anxiety among Kyiv residents also intensified. The people were shocked by the news of attacks against civilians, large-scale missile strikes and bombings. Everyone kept their ear to the ground, expecting an escalation of fighting around the capital. The municipal powers yet again warned of the enemy's intentions to encircle Kyiv. More and more primitive barricades appeared in the city streets, mostly sacks filled with sand. Through-highways and numerous streets were obstructed with anti-tank 'hedgehogs' and piles of sand dumped straight off lorries onto the asphalt, without even erecting any roadblocks anymore. It was just that – an additional obstruction.

Aha, something curious! According to some sources, after February 24th Putin had practically lost interest in the 'affairs of peace', and his inner circle contracted even more. He concentrated exclusively on the idea of an imminent victory and the creation of a puppet regime.

Announcement started pouring in, explaining the options for such a puppet government. Allegedly, the Kremlin had no final plan for appointments, so it was unknown who was going to be what. Several nominations were tipped for accession to the throne in Ukraine. As the expression went, you couldn't have too many spares. An attractive option was to restore Yanukovych in his erstwhile position and then announce the reinstatement of the 'legitimate president'.

Yet this would have been just a formality. His real role would've been to announce an early 'presidential election'. During this time, the government would've been headed by Medvedchuk. It was him that the Russians viewed as president at the end of the 'transition period'. Medvedchuk himself, too, only saw himself in a leading position. As for Yanukovych – ah, well, just a stop-gap marionette.

Yanukovych was ordered to get ready. Indeed, on March 2nd, his plane had landed in Minsk – closer to the 'scene of action', especially in view of the fact that Medvedchuk had gone AWOL. Allegedly, Yanukovych himself, aware of the Ukrainians' attitude to him, wasn't all that happy. Yet an order was an order: he had to board that flight and head the group already assembled in Belarus: the 'government in waiting'. The other group, comprising ex-members of the Party of Regions,[308] was getting together in the temporarily occupied southern territories of Ukraine.

For all that, the events had taken an unexpected course. The political network masterminded by Medvedchuk had started falling apart even before inva-

....

[308] **Party of Regions:** a banned pro-Russian political party in Ukraine. Formed in late 1997, it became the largest party in Ukraine between 2006 and 2014.

sion: about ten of his closest associates had taken to their legs and did a bunk in very good time. Some others – right after the start of hostilities. The plan with the capture of Kyiv also went haywire. Yanukovych saw no point in sticking around in Minsk any further. Before taking a return flight to Moscow, he addressed Zelensky in writing. This 'appeal' of his was tirelessly broadcast by the Russian channels. Yanukovych issued this statement:

'As one president to another, or even somewhat avuncularly, I would like to appeal to Volodymyr Zelensky. I realise perfectly well that you have numerous "advisers", but it is your personal responsibility to stop the bloodbath at whatever cost and achieve a peaceful settlement. That is what is expected from you in Ukraine, Donbas, and Russia. The Ukrainian people as well as your Western partners will be grateful to you.'[309]

He scribbled this 'appeal' and on March 7th flew out of Minsk...

Taras grabbed me by my jacket, took me away and whispered, 'They're writing in the chat that "on top" every day is unlike the previous one since it's so difficult to plan anything in detail. But the vertical of power works... Also, they sleep for 3-4 hours at different times of the day... Zaluzhnyi didn't sleep the first three days at all and still has this sleeping problem because of the continuing stress... The president has 10 phone calls every day, with some leaders he talks several times a day. There's Yermak's interesting admission as well. "We didn't believe until the last minute that this would happen... Yes, there was a lot of information from our partners.... But, still, we did not believe... We were preparing, of course... And that is why we are now seeing results – for the second week we are fighting quite successfully... And... [before the invasion] it was very important that until the last minute our entire society, our country, lived a normal life... The military were preparing, we were preparing... but we did not believe until the last...

* * *

That day, for the first time I brought along my script pad.

The Commander was busy sorting things out with the bosses and Taras had popped out to somewhere, so I pulled it out and made a couple of entries.

'I can't stand it when they say that all of this has been started by just one person.

It's lies.

---

[309] UP, 8 March 2022, https://www.pravda.com.ua/news/2022/03/8/7329341/ (accessed 04.07.2025).

The truth is this. One person put them up to this, but he was supported by this entire vicious country.

Those few who are against are only several percent, and they make no difference.

I can't stand it when they say that they didn't or don't know.

They "didn't know" it but enthusiastically welcomed it anyway. By now – they all know. Yet quite a few continue insisting that they know nothing. It's more comfortable this way.

In our technological age, it's only possible to stay ignorant if you live in some God-forsaken village.

It's just that people's minds are attuned to this setting: to be anti-human, barbarian, fascist… They like the way they behave. They are… getting a high! Each newly acquired foothold brings a massive release of adrenalin. A flash of bestial "patriotism"…

"Denazification"? That's not about us. That's what should happen over there, in their own country.

Yet in Russia it will take much longer, for they also have to go through "de-imperialization"… Which is a much longer procedure…'

Finished, I looked around me. I wasn't keen for anyone to see that I was writing.

A minute later, I pulled my pad out again.

'Fascism was born in Italy. Germany picked it up. The two great nations had erroneously allowed themselves to be dragged into this ideology. They had been fated to go through all of this.

Seemingly, the Second World War finished – the regimes overthrown; fascism annihilated. What was ahead was an era of peace and prosperity. Yet the "rational" West – the leaders, politicians, analysts – for some reason failed to notice, or understand, that right under their noses, for quite some time, fascism had been brought back into existence, that it had become the national ideology.

The Russian people (if they exist) have to go through this. Just like the Germans and Italians did it, in their time.

That will be a long road, running through blood of their neighbour states…'

Now was the time to close the pad and hide it away securely. I wanted to make several entries, so that no one would see, and I managed to do it. Hooray! Could it be that I would start working little by little? Starting from that day?

As for 'no one would see'… I wasn't sure. Perhaps, it was my rabbit's foot…

Denis showed me his iPad. An expert was sharing his views about the encirclement of Kyiv: 'The Russian grouping approaching Kyiv via Chernihiv and

Sumy has run into logistical problems. To ensure a speedy advance, they were bypassing our troops. In the end they stretched themselves out across approximately 200 kilometres – from the border to the outskirts of Kyiv. Moving through this area, mostly consisting of woodland, they've found themselves constantly under fire from our manoeuvring units, who attack them from various ambushes and cause significant losses. The AFU's effective and spirited countermeasures on the approaches to Kyiv have made the Russian general staff review their original plan for the campaign since the troops proved to be unprepared at the tactical level. Ten days after the start of the military campaign, the Russians were still incapable of breaking through the line of the Kyiv defence on either bank of the Dnipro… Another point of interest: they have been using old maps from Soviet times. And miscoordination among subdivisions led to a situation where various units were using the same route, getting mixed up and clogging junctions, thus impeding their rate of advance. All this has been deduced from interceptions at brigade level, most of which focused on the whereabouts of regiments and individual units and only 10-20% dealt directly with tactical control.'[310]

Meanwhile Taras returned to the roadblock from the cellar and showed me his mobile.

'Their conversations are intercepted. They are euphoric – *We are successfully liberating Ukraine from the Nazis!*

Hmmm… Those must have been interceptions from different sources…

* * *

Anatoliy Semenovych Pyvynsky gave me another call from Shyshaky.

'You see, Kiril, the type of "movie" we have to work on.' He sighed heavily. 'Can't be any worse…'

We stayed silent for a while – what was there to say?

'Yet there are some good signs!' he perked up. 'After all, Putin's underestimated the reaction of Ukraine. And the response in the West. They have responded, and mightily. Thank God, unlike 2014 when the Russkies had annexed Crimea. Do you remember how Obama behaved then? With extreme caution. That's why it's all coming to a head now.'

'You bet!' I agreed.

'And what d'ya think about the second round of negotiations that took place on the third of March? That term – "denazification"– wasn't even bandied around

[310]   New voice, 6 March 2023, https://nv.ua/ukr/ukraine/events/bitva-shcho-vryatu-vala-ukrajinu-rik-tomu-rosiyan-vitisnili-z-pid-kiyeva-yak-vidstoyali-stolicyu-rekon-stru-50314634.html (accessed 04.07.2025).

much anymore. By now it's just a vacuous slogan with no substance. Are there narrow-minded interests within the Ukrainian power structures? Something of nationalist orientation? Nope. There aren't any "representatives" like that, either in the government or the Rada. So, what's with this "denazification" then?'

'Sure thing.'

'Or this, for example – the war is in full swing but the leadership look ahead. Now they're trying to resolve the issue of security guarantees. Since NATO is dragging their feet and act skittishly, our leaders put out their feelers to identify potential guarantors. Some of them are quite odd – Turkey, Israel… Whatever happens next, the issue of NATO membership will be raised again. That's the only realistic guarantee…'

He sighed again, then fell silent.

'Our country is truly special,' was Pyvynsky's conclusion. 'There are lots of zones of conflict in the world but our country is somehow unique. Isn't it?'

'I agree.'

The following day Yanovsky called me too. His main interest was the position of China.

'Americans showed this video on China. They think it's lying in wait, holding its horses, observing. China's interest is understandable, they want to see if the USA manage to show that they're up to snuff. Then they'll draw their conclusions. There's also this talk: the fact that we've survived for longer than three days has profoundly shocked many Europeans – the military and the diplomats. Remember when Putin snatched Crimea and a portion of Donbas – everybody pretended that it wasn't a war, not really – just some local conflict. The West failed to realise then that Putin's most ambitious project is restauration of the USSR.'

'Um-hum,' I agreed with this too.

'It's a pity that new protests in Russia are insufficiently powerful and small-scale. Besides, it'll all peter out soon anyway. Russia will only be impacted by her defeat in this war.'

'Looks like it.'

A silence fell. He promptly said goodbye and rang off.

And I felt awkward. Both he and Pyvynsky called to discuss the painful subjects, wanting to share, and I'd been 'sure thing', or 'um-hum'. It really wasn't nice of me…

By the way, when a missile was in flight, the sound was…peculiar. I wouldn't have ever imagined it to be like that. The missile was fast but the sound was sort of sluggish, droning…

Missiles were flying above us every day. They were shot down, crashing down on top of buildings. It wasn't too bad when missile fragments tumbled onto a roof, causing a fire that was put out. It was worse if a missile hit a flat. Try and escape in that case!

One such missile fell nearby but people had already learnt to calculate the distance based on the sound:

'This one is some five kilometres away!'

'This one – some seven or eight.'

'If they reverberate, it's already in the outskirts.'

The people's eyes – that was something to remember! 'So what's the story with this super-long column? When will it set off? Will our guys be able to fight back? Will they be able to defend us? What if… they fail… Then what? How shall we live then? 64 kilometers, my God…'

In an attempt to conquer stress people turned to sedative, tranquilisers, some herbal infusions…

Ah-ha, more people started appearing in the street. At times, even a private car would whisk by. The food stores, though, were open only for few hours a day. No queues anymore, the panic of the initial days had subsided. Besides, there was hardly anything worth buying anyway: no dairy, no fruit or vegetables, flour, or grain. All that was available was super-expensive imported stuff: a pack of some French kefir cost nearly a hundred Hryvna. You had to be lucky to happen on bread – it hadn't been even baked in the first several days, they'd stopped all the industrial bakeries. At the time, other things required attention.

Like before, no lights went on in the evening, or perhaps people had switched to using extra-dense curtains. It all was to prevent houses being tar-geted with shelling. Responding to an appeal from the humanitarian centre, private pharmacies had reopened – and the queues in front of them were even not too bad. And – miracle! – some medications were still available.

I cycled over to my granny's – to bring her some food, sedatives too. An en-terprise like that had to be undertaken very carefully, for those drivers who'd stayed and been issued with passes, were clearly throwing their weight around, zooming past at breakneck speed. That was why most people were scared to walk across the street – they dashed ahead, besides no traffic lights were now in operation. Also, they introduced a ban on alcoholic drinks, but the foresightful had laid in a stash beforehand.

I found my granny in tears – she'd run out of heart drops. She was 87 years old, and her childhood had started and was spent under the fascist occupation. Then followed many peaceful years, full of hope – seventy-seven of those, to be precise. And now, already so advanced in age, she had to live through it all over again. Just like in her childhood?

'Yes, my darling, on its circuits the wind returns. That's what the Bible says. See, dear Kiril, how it's all come to be. And you didn't want to read the New Testament, just kept saying: "Let me, let me"…'

I returned home and mum said:

'I also want to be useful. I asked Alla to put my name down too, for volunteering. Why should I stick around inside? Meanwhile they need people. People bring in lots of clothes – for adults, for children. It all has to be sorted out, prepared for dispatch.

'Even if we live with the sirens howling, and the missiles are flying – of course, it's scary, but can you even compare it to what's going on in the outskirts? Or in Chernihiv, Kharkiv or Mariupol? And how many other places…'

On the whole, one could get used to anything. When sirens started going off ten times a day, you got used to this too. By now, if it happened in our central boroughs, hardly anybody bothered to rush to a bomb shelter. It didn't seem all that reasonable. The outskirts and suburbs – that was a different story, since over there the bombardments were intense, incessant, and accurate. Out there, people spent most their days in shelters and basements.

* * *

We were already twenty at our roadblock. There weren't enough beds in the cellar, some of us had to put their sleeping bags right on the floor. Thank God, we had new recruits – it had become bestially cold, no way to survive without rotation.

But the Commander was dissatisfied:

'What sort of personnel numbers are these? Not enough even for a section! Just a couple of platoons!'

The Commander developed special respect for bespectacled Gennady, always attentive to what he had to say. The day before he had even appointed him second in command, since he, himself, was like a hamster in a wheel: this minute he had to deal with the district HQ, the next – with a municipal one, then the shooting range that he'd been instructed to organise. And should an emergency happen at some roadblock, he was asked to go over and sort things out. A man in great demand!

I spotted Denis stealthily putting his hand into the flask with vitamins – grab! – he scooped up as many as ten capsules, unaware that the Commander lurked nearby, all eyes, and then, all of a sudden, pounced on him, seized hold of his palm.

'Where you off to? Take only one! As per the mode of usage! What are ya doing, building a stash?'

'Aye-aye, sir!' Denis dropped his head, embarrassed.

He popped one capsule into his mouth, emptying the rest back into the flask. Talk about hygiene…

And then they said that the Territorial Defence was, of course, all well and good but still not quite the army. I wouldn't know – had not served in the army, but at times what we had here felt just like active service…

Our choir guys once started contemplating about 'good Russians'.

'Let's not indulge in wishful thinking,' Andriovych gave a wave of his hand. 'About a hundred people in Russia signed the petitions, and several tens of thousands came out in protest demonstrations. They had to pay the price, of course. Hundreds of thousands legged it, pronto, to various other countries. But who can say whether they are against the war or for it? It's incontrovertible that the majority are pro-war, wholeheartedly. They hate us with bestial hatred. They are ready – not just the army but tens of millions of bloody Russians – to tie our hands, torture us, carve their red stars on our backs!'

'That's just the way it is,' Platonovych voiced his agreement. 'They would happily kill every one of us, by any methods available. Say what you want, we are enemy. So they are, accordingly, too. That's the reality. And it matters not an iota, what bright picture they are painting on the subject of "fraternal peoples" – be it President of France Macron or Pope Francis, or any other world leader. '

'All of this is classic European politics. Banging on about "ideals of humanism" till everybody's eyes gloss over, whereas the harsh and bloody reality is here,' summarised Mykolayiovych. 'And there's nothing else left for us but to fight. Till the last drop of blood – so that we could survive, we as individuals, and as a nation. As for those grandiloquent European assertions, they are irrelevant now. We need other things. Everyone should come together and join our defence, not hide behind their wonderful humanity. But none of this is straightforward…'

Spyridon and Bolik took to calling me practically every day.

Bolik once sighed grievously:

'Ah… What's to say? Take us, for instance. We just got cold feet, that's what happened. To call a spade a spade…'

And Spyridon added:

'It just somehow happened like this. Everyone was leaving, so we did, too. Or to be totally honest, we were numb with fear. Elementary, we got a proper fright! But you, guys… you are heroes…'

'Cut it, you two, what're you talking about? We're scared, too, at times, and how. This talk of heroes… Stop it this minute. OK, we are hanging around the roadblock, waiting, lest something should happen. But to tell the truth, we've seen no war. And generally speaking, everyone was really afraid. Same now, too. And… long story short, it's normal, bros. It's human nature. Even the soldiers are afraid. The difference is – they know how to master their fear. Real heroes is them!'

'Still, it's hard,' Bolk sighed again. 'In a word, it sucks.'

* * *

That evening a piercing wind was blowing through our roadblock. No clouds in the sky, and the bright stars started peeping out. The night ahead promised to be frosty.

The bespectacled Gennady and Denis dragged in a bunch of firewood from somewhere, built a fire. Our entire hangout moved in around it. By that time, we were quite a motley crew. Still, everyone gravitated towards the choir guys.

For a while they sat around silent, like everyone else, immersed in thought. The sign of times. Suddenly Andriyovych said:

'That's what I'm thinking about. Evil exists, OK, that's clear. Yet there is also *absolute*, global evil. The one that's happening here, on our earth…'

The Commander gave him a close look, probably wanted to add something but thought better of it.

'I've got this neighbour, Irina, she's Russian,' Andriyovych carried on. 'What's more, not one of those who, thank God, are in majority, the ones who wholeheartedly support Ukraine. No, this one is a died-in-the-wool Russian, an admirer of Putin. And this Irina once said: "*What happens is a rift among the Ukrainians. So, sort it all out among yourselves*".'

'Funny how she's not afraid to blurt out things like that!' Platonovych sounded really hurt. 'If I found myself in Russia in a context like this, I would've kept my counsel. Or they'd nick me at once!'

'This little lady must be one of those who are "waiting for their guys".' Mykolaiyovych didn't waste a chance to put in a barb. 'She's clearly certain they'll arrive. And a lady like this will report on you, Andriyovych, straight away, if it did happen. Look for yourself: you are singing in a Ukrainian choir, joined the territorial defence. You speak the language of those Ukes. Thus, if they do make it to here, you're finished.'

After that we all grew silent. What could one say? We all have heard it a hundred times that 'sleeping agents' (assisted by volunteers like Irina) had long since put together 'blacklists' of candidates for immediate elimination! Or else, processing in a filtration camp, with all due diligence.

Ethnic Replacement: 'Ukrainians, Fuck off!
Now This Is a Place for Russians!'

During the first ten days of March, the enemy had received new reserves and relaunched their offensive. Russian groupings renewed their attempts to encircle Kyiv from the west and to sever its communication lines. Makariv stayed under Ukrainian control, but fighting continued. The situation in Irpin, Bucha, Hostomel, Vorzel and other suburbs was similar. The Russians were trying to solidify their position on the Zhytomyr-Chop motorway and threatening to break through southwards towards Fastiv. The enemy was clearly trying to expand their launching ground so as to cut off the Odesa motorway. Simultaneously, they were making attempts to fight their way into the city from the east – having stopped in the vicinity of Brovary, a suburb of Kyiv. The situation remained tense, heavy fighting raged on. So it was logical to assume that in a matter of days there would be yet another attempt on Kyiv. The Russian military presence around the city was getting ever more concentrated.

And yet, most importantly, there was this new understanding that Kyiv, while remaining in great danger, was now unlikely to be taken by storm. The number of Kyiv defendants was already reported to exceed the Russian manpower. The AFU were as yet unable crush such a sizeable enemy force but were actively wearing them down.

That came from a military expert: 'The Russian units are battle-bled and demoralised after their 300-kilometre-long march, carried out under AFU fire. Will the enemy's capacity be sufficient to overpower Kyiv? To overpower it – no. Goes without saying that the enemy may try and risk storming it. But Kyiv is huge. And close engagement within its boundaries would be horrible. The Russians are tactically unprepared for street fighting; our defendants continue fitting Kyiv out with engineering structures, preparing toeholds. If the enemy decided to take the plunge and attack directly, it would mean a sure defeat. To reach the city centre through streets leading from the outskirts is unrealistic. Any incoming vehicles would find themselves hemmed in and targeted from well-established positions. Even if they decided to use their landing troops, we can exsanguinate them with our Stringers, the man-portable air defence systems installed at some vantage points. Each hour of such "advancement" will be working against the invaders...'

Inspiring expert forecasts... Notwithstanding, the Kyivites continued their preparations for defending the city. At their disposal were small arms and portable anti-tank equipment manufactured in the USA, UK, and Germany. Mayor Klitchko: 'Fighting goes on in Bucha, Irpin and Hostomel. All I can say is that we remain in Kyiv. If need be, every house, street and roadblock will fight till the end. No one wants to die, but if that's what's required, we shall defend our children and families…'[311]

Taras's chatroom announced that on March 4th, the ninth day of the war, Chancellor Scholtz spoke to Putin over the phone.[312] On the same day he discussed it with Macron and supposedly said that the situation had not got any better. Putin continued expanding on his views of Ukraine, talked about demilitarisation and denazification. Then he asked for recognition of Crimea as part of Russia and of the independence of the so-called DPR and LPR. When Scholz asked him if a meeting would ever be possible between Macron, Scholz, Zelensky and him, Putin, he didn't brush it aside out of hand. But he did name two conditions. Firstly, it shouldn't be used as a pretext for suspending hostilities. And then he only mentioned the three leaders without Zelensky. Macron, who had spoken to the Russian leader earlier, replied to Scholz that Putin had told him exactly the same.

Meanwhile the Kyiv suburbs were a proper inferno. During the first days of the occupation the locals had been in shock. The Russian invaders had allowed no 'green exit corridors.' Anybody intent on breaking away on their own initiative risked ending up under the Russian bullets. The occupiers had set about fiercely destroying the infrastructure: gas and electricity grids, retranslation. They shot cars at close range.

In villages, they had been breaking into homes, plundering whatever came to hand: first of all, matrasses, rugs, clothes, and blankets – after all, they did have to sleep on something. Also, food – the same story, they had to eat. If a daily ration originally had to be shared by two people, and later there were no rations at all, beggars couldn't afford to be choosers. But in general, they looted whatever they could, even ripping the lace curtains off the windows. If anybody tried to reason with them, those words either fell on deaf ears or even led to threats to use their weapons. Whatever they couldn't carry away, they damaged and destroyed. They were simply subhuman… Barbarians…

By the way, the Orks (our name for the invaders is a borrowing from both Roman and Greek mythology, where Ork was the god of the underworld – an

---

[311]   Priamyi, 2 March 2022, https://prm.ua/voroh-proryvaietsia-do-stolytsi-u-buchi-irpeni-ta-kyievi-tryvaiut-boi-klychko/ (accessed 04.07.2025).

[312]   Radio Svoboda, 4 March 2022, https://www.radiosvoboda.org/a/news-scholz-putin-perehovory/31736779.html (accessed 04.07.2025).

idea which was later used picked up by Tolkien) had been promised that in return for their participation in this 'liberating mission' they would be allocated apartments. And they took to fighting like mad, seeing that an apartment in Ukraine was worth it. It was definitely better than a dog-like kennel somewhere on permafrost. To lay one's hands on such a valuable accommodation was worth fighting for.

That was what they were saying:

'Those Ukes are degenerates. We need to drop more missiles and bombs on them, cause total devastation. So that all of them, the bastards, legged it. And we'll live in their flats and houses…'

'Oh, what a luxurious land! The soil is so fertile! And when you hear stories about summers here, your mouth waters… Fruit trees that grow right in the city streets! Have you seen anything like it? Apples, pears, plums – everything juicy and ripe, simply falls down on your head! One should take care not to get hit on the head. We'll wait it out till the summer and then it'll be dropping down on our own heads!'

'I heard that their apricots are like honey. They fall on the ground and no one even bothers to collect them…'

'They've had it too nice for too long, the scum!'

'I'll tell you what – this Ukraine here is surely a nice place to live! Not too cold in the winter, and the summers are free from this exhausting heat…'

'Wow, we'll make life here buzz! Under the Kremlin strategic plans, the Nazi Ukes will be decimated, left to rot, and buried. And Russian humanity will live in their houses. Historical justice – according to Putin – will be restored!'

Those were the plans for the future as described by the occupiers.

But once taken prisoner, every single one of them insisted that they had known nothing and been drafted by deceit. So, what about the dress uniforms found in their damaged tanks and vehicles after battle? Complete with medals and other bling – carefully stored to be worn on a parade along Khreschatyk! They even brought a military orchestra along, to turn the parade into a properly ceremonial occasion. And right after that – they would be off to their newly-seized homes.

They were getting ready to call their wives and relatives: *'Get packed, come over! There'll be enough room for all of us!'*

They had thought out the reverse plans – how to deport the Ukrainian population. Hundreds of thousands were already taken to Russia, children included, and sent through filtration camps. Those more or less sympathetic to all this, and with no 'Nazi' background, were treated according to one scenario: mostly sent to northern areas, for someone had to reclaim those territories. The Russians themselves were fleeing those parts, so let the Ukes take up the torch.

Well, but if a person turned out to be a 'die-hard Nazi' – their destination would have no exit route.

* * *

The segment of the Kyiv-Lviv train route that ran through suburbs and previously had required 15 minutes, now took at least three hours.

The carriage attendant would pop out into the aisle and yell:

'Blinds on all windows – down! Now! Everyone on the floor! Stay put till I say otherwise.'

The train would pull out and immediately come to a halt. Then barely clink off, and stop. And again, and again...

Finally, once out of the danger zone, the train would gather momentum.

'You can all get up now!' the attendant would command.

And then the train would continue non-stop.

The suburbs – Irpin, Bucha, Hostomel – bore the brunt of the battle for Kyiv. Those daring to step out of their communal entrance could momentarily get a bullet through their back. Or their head – anything was possible. The logic followed by the invaders in an occupied outskirts went thus: 'But h*ow do we know who's who? They all are Nazio-nalists.*'

Lord Almighty, where else to be "Ukrainian nationalists" if not in Ukraine itself?

A dog heard the explosion – perhaps a missile or a bomb, gave a start of surprise, and toward the undercarriage of a car. That must have been its 'bomb shelter'.

And people... they were becoming accustomed to everything, even inhuman suffering. The process had long since been described by psychologists. In order to survive, people would adjust to anything.

But what about pregnant women? They were giving birth in basements, bomb shelters, on the Metro, at train stations. Wherever they happened to be when the time came...

Apropos the metro. More and more people became homeless as every day passed. They sat and lay on the steps of escalators, some even erected plastic sheets to cordon off little corners of the vestibules between the entrance foyer and platforms, thus creating a tiny personal space. Inside, they lay on matrasses, some even managed to produce something like bedside tables.

University metro station became one of the most overcrowded bomb shelters in Kyiv. Curfew would kick in at eight in the evening, and the escalators stopped. That was a signal for switching on the airlock – special doors that sealed the tunnel, capable of withstanding a missile strike, or even a nuclear attack. Several minutes later, the station would be hermetically sealed. And that was that – the people inside would be cut off from the outside world till morning.

The TV in the vestibule showed news, then – a speech by Zelensky.

Most people here came for the night but about thirty of them stayed permanently, practically not even venturing upstairs at all.

The best living place was inside carriages, where towels and underwear would be drying on handrails, mattresses be rolled out on seats and the floor, and the ledges underneath the windows be cheek by jowl with arrays of water bottles, food, paper cups and napkins.

In the first days, people tried to pick up every sound: what if those blasted Russians were already barrelling down the tunnels, ready to execute everybody?

Lights-off came at ten, signalling the time to rest.

And in the morning, the service toilets were unlocked, everyone filed over – to answer a call of nature or simply wash themselves, however inadequately.

There were those who intended to stay here for some time… The others planned to somehow make it to the station and leave for Lviv…

Each was attending to their business: watching the news on iPhones, reading, darning something, applying iodine to a lacerated wound on the leg…

One could discern a sharp smell of alcohol: that was a female nurse disinfecting her hands in order to give some person a drip.

Each told his own story here. That was one of them:

'We were speeding out of Borodyanka and came under fire. Also, a bastard Russian threw a grenade at us. We were showered by shards from the window. I never heard the explosion, only the sound of glass shattering. All I could see was the bits of my skin and flesh flying in all directions. I didn't even twig it at once – that my wife was grievously wounded. I only started coming round when I heard my son shriek: "Mummy, don't die! Please don't die, I beg of you"!'

'We ourselves are from Irpin. They shot at us non-stop. The bridge leading into Kyiv was blown up in the first couple of days. Our military were carrying us, exhausted, in their arms across the bridge. I hate the lot of them, those bastard Russian, with all my heart!'

* * *

March 10th. By now Ukraine had been at war for 15 days. The General Staff announced that the rate of the Russian troops' advance had slowed down.

As for that Russian column, 64 kilometres long, the one that continued to threaten the city and fill everyone with horrible fear… Suddenly guesses started filtering through: what if it was stuck in a dreadful jam, created by themselves? After all, their vehicles remained stationary for days. And day in, day out, the column was targeted from all sides: by both the Ukrainian troops and the local residents. And thus, the column was gradually getting weaker. What would be the reason, then, for keeping it there? It was truly bizarre…

And so, we, here, felt somewhat relieved, even if things weren't all that easily comprehensible. Yet the missiles and bombs, like before, continued hitting Sumy, Kharkiv, Mariupol and other cities. We heard an ever-increasing number of accounts of them falling on residential buildings or maternity hospitals.

And here no visible change, though, could be observed at the line of defence – compared to the initial days of war. After lunch the Commander told Taras and me:

'Off with you, go home, rest up, catch up on sleep. For all that, I can't rule out that I'll summon you for the night shift.'

I barely had the time to cross the doorstep, a call had already come from Taras, his voice breaking, almost vibrating:

'Listen, they are showing such things on TV, put it on at once! Lukashenko is now in Moscow – he and Putin lounging in their armchairs, giving it large for the benefit of the cameras. Luka's dishing it out, making no fucking sense at all. A real stream of consciousness, James Joyce aint' even in the same league!'

'What, total gibberish?'

'Well, main points do come across. He assures everyone that they did it all correctly. That otherwise Ukraine would've been the first to attack! Master class!'

I put it on, and several clicks later, here it was.

…To start with, Lukashenko informed Putin that Ukraine had nurtured plans to carry out an attack against the joint Russian-Belarusian training exercise. Then he said that when they had met in Moscow on February 18th, Ukraine had opened pre-emptive fire, targeting the Belarusian border. Later (!) he would produce maps reflecting Ukraine's preparations for an attack against Belarus, he had them ready. 'It wasn't us who opened hostilities; the AFU executed pre-emptive strikes when you and I were at your place, two days earlier. We were on board a helicopter and they kept reporting [to us] non-stop. It was they who started it all! Let me show you from where they'd intended to commit an assault against Belarus. And if six hours prior to their operation there hadn't have been a pre-emptive strike against their positions – there were four of them, let me show you, I've brought the map with me… They would have attacked our troops, the Russian and Belarusian troops that were training. So it wasn't us who unleashed the war; our conscience is clear. We've done well to get involved: biological weapons, the largest nuclear stations – [they] were prepared to blow up the lot.'[313]

Lukashenko was banging on while Putin was looking at him in amazement – could it be that he also felt stunned by that drivel, that mind-blowing gibberish?

I went online to check the response on social media, which proved to be tumultuous:

'Shame on the Belarusian nation – a laughing stock all over the world!'

'Batska,[314] have you had one spliff too many?'

'Both of them dissembling gossips, puppet masters. Candidates for a loony bin.'

'My God, what a complete…'

The Commander had some Belarusian roots, and often spoke of him harshly:

'Just listen what he's on about! "Belarus isn't an aggressor! But we shall support Russia!" Vintage Lukashenko: hot behind his collar and slippery like an eel! But that's what he thinks, that his country is not an aggressor. We, here, view it differently. He's converted his country into a springboard for the Russian army! That's from where that armada started out towards Kyiv! And army aircraft took off from their aerodromes! And the missiles pelt from their launches! And this country isn't an aggressor?'

The Commander whacked his fist against a sack.

'And those Belarusian brigades that allegedly had been spotted on the march towards Kyiv? He must have sent them forward deliberately! If the blitzkrieg had worked, he would've been yelling from all rooftops: "What d'ya think? We've contributed with all our might!" And would've laid his claims to a slice of the trophied pie. But as soon as the blitzkrieg started stalling, Lukashenko momentarily twigged where the wind was blowing from and pulled his troops out…'

* * *

February in Kyiv was a winter month, and early March was no better. Even if the temperature did crawl above zero it would be only a few degrees. To find oneself without a roof over your head? Ouch, that would be grim…

And the bombs continued falling. Pounding everything. The 'brothers', purportedly, aimed only at the military facilities. What a lie! They laid waste to residential blocks too…

....

[313] 11 March 2022, UP. https://www.pravda.com.ua/news/2022/03/11/7330394/ (accessed 04.07.2025).

[314] **Batska**: father in Belarusian, a nickname for Lukashenko.

The neighbour from across the landing told mum:

'Take my advice, it won't cost you anything,' people tried to make it light even now. 'You must keep your windows ajar…'

'Why? Whatever for?'

'If a bomb goes off nearby, you'll save your glass panes. Your flat is generally well-appointed, it faces in two directions. The stream of air will gush in through the semi-opened window, and on the other side it will escape securely through a similar opening. And your glass will stay intact!'

'But it's cold!'

'What's better – being cold or keeping your panes in one piece? And if those are smashed into smithereens, then what? Cold and no panes?'

Actually, the neighbour's made it all easy to understand. He must have been right. But it was frigging cold outside! In the event, we decided that when at home we should be paying special heed: as soon as a siren started wailing, we'd promptly open the windows. But if setting off to somewhere, we should leave them slightly open…

On that day's shift we were bursting our sides. TV brought us a story about this daughter in Ukraine whose mother was in Russia. On February 24th, the day of invasion, the daughter called her mum and started yelling into the receiver: *'You've attacked us!'* And the mother, without batting an eyelid, came back: *'No, it's yours who attacked ours!"*

No, really, we laughed till our bellies ached. But it was laughter through tears.

And another story. Those two had been friends since the kindergarten days. By now he was in Moscow and she – in Kharkiv. He called her: *'How are things with you?' 'I'm inside the Metro, there's an air raid, we are being bombed.' 'It's impossible. Everything's fine. Go home.'*

That one was beyond laughter.

Lavrov made a fool of himself too. A journalist asked him: 'Who are you going to attack after Ukraine?' Lavrov answered solemnly: *'No one. We didn't attack Ukraine either.'*

The entire audience burst out laughing. It was surreal. One could never discuss anything with those people. Nothing at all.

If our shift was in the evening, we tried to get leave to catch the evening news digest at eight. One had at least to catch a glimpse of the tele-marathon: whom our valorous army had smashed, how many aircraft had been downed, how many tanks bit the dust on unsurfaced roads by the hand of our partisans. And of course, what damage had the orks inflicted on us…

As for the Territorial Defence, the word was that the Russians hadn't expected any of it. People picked up their hunting rifles and little by little started encircling those warriors in their own villages, forests, and fields. After all, the locals knew every tree and bush by sight. After a couple of shots and a command 'Give up!', sometimes the Russians did.

March 9th. The war had been going on for two weeks already. Out of all big cities the only one under Russian control was Kherson. Regarding the massive onslaught, the enemy had decided to take time out. However, the air strikes continued at full bast. Having realised her failure with a blitzkrieg, Russia decided to alter her tactics. Anything and everything continued to be shelled, especially the residential quarters, kindergartens, clinics, and maternity hospitals. What did they have in mind? A scorched-land approach? A desire to intimidate? Most likely the latter. With all said and done, it was now an all-out warfare aimed at annihilation of the Ukrainian nation. Kharkiv had it very hard – the enemy was practically raising it to the ground and had it already semi-encircled. Kyiv, too, was semi-besieged...

So, how was it possible that all those people, who once upon a time had been born by their mothers, and taken, by hand, to playgroups and the first day in school, those same people decided to commit to such atrocious slaughter? Which theories and 'learned' treatises on history could have possibly motivated this course of actions? No, those weren't people. They were monsters in human form.

A good question: why would anyone want to bomb civilian facilities? Would the objective be to undermine morale and monger panic? Easy to see that panic would undermine the effectiveness of the military force. Also, the Russians might have believed that this or that structure was an obstacle on their route forward. Or a place from which the locals could open fire. So it's better for them to first bomb it themselves...

Did the Kremlin nest, whose children and grandchildren resided in London and Paris, really believe that any of this was normal? That millions of people, up till now living in peace and safety, were now seeking refuge 'between the two walls', in blacked-out rooms, to the accompaniment of endlessly howling sirens and unremitting bombing? While keeping an 'emergency bag' handy at all times? And constantly guessing whether their house would take a hit or perhaps it would pass over this time?

Those days, human scum had ended up in power and in command of our lives...

Once again, my exhausted mind started churning over the thoughts about this 'great Russian culture'.

Oh, the mysterious Russian soul and culture, something that Western intellectuals loved waxing lyrical about! It had been a 'schtick' with them – to worship all things Russian… So where was this 'great culture' now? A Russian poet once said – whether because he was feeling lyrical or filling his lines with philosophical subtext:

Russia is not to be grasped rationally,
Common yardsticks do not apply.
The essence of Russia is a thing apart –
All you can do is believe in her.

Only four lines… Whether fully understandable or not, they gave off a whiff of recondite hauteur. The message they carried was clear enough: just look at us, so exceptional! The only ones in the whole world! All loud and clear…

OK, let it be. What if we phrased the question differently – why would one want to understand such wisdom? Hmm… Go and work it out.

So, where was this great Russian culture? Really, where?

Yet it had existed, no doubt.

But now the Russian culture had become undesirable not because it lacked talent, was derivative or boring. It was no longer implicitly wanted because if one looked closer at its users and proponents – from the raping guards to writers, actors and musicians who had daubed the letter Z on their breasts…

It all was logical. That wasn't a case of some targeted Russo-phobia. It was exclusively considerations of social hygiene: to protect oneself against something venomous and dangerous. The fairytale about the 'mysterious Russian soul', armed with a hatchet wrapped up in a piece of cloth (Dostoyevsky), and simultaneously suffering 'over a child's tear' stopped being a fairytale. In reality it all turned out to be simpler, scarier, and more treacherous.

Indeed, this culture was no more at this moment! It had sunk without trace. All that showed on radar screens was the letter Z.

Bitter Flavour of Mundanity

The times were such that no task could be performed without involving good housekeeping skills. Nothing at all could be thrown away spontaneously. For example, there would be no kefir left in a pack. But if you snipped the tip off, you'd find that several grammes of the valuable product would still be left inside. Something always stayed deep in the corners and wouldn't be poured out with the rest of the contents. I'd never paid attention to it before but my attitudes changed. And another piece of advice: the best bit was smeared around the internal sides of the pack – thick and nourishing. For some reason, the best was always to be found up there.

By now I'd understood what bread was all about. I fully realised its value. Or the value of the dairy products. Or vegetables…

We had a good supply of various grains. Yet those lack-lustre daily porridge recipes did call for at least something more exciting.

If you'd brewed tea, you could use the leaves once more, having added some boiling water. If the tea was of really good quality, the second brew came out amazing. Well, the third go, though, was clearly trash. So what? They had used tea dregs before the revolution?[315] The masters had enjoyed the fresh brew while the servants used the dregs and had been quite happy with the second-hand result. In a word, there was always something useful one could discover in the sphere of the culinary.

Truth be told, it was still possible to happen on some lower-grade tea. Yet one had to be careful about the money too. Money didn't grow on trees, and no one could know how long all of this was going to last.

If you put a slice of the last remaining lemon (out of the pre-war stash) into coffee (we still had some), one should never throw it afterwards. The same slice could last for some time, till it disintegrated completely. And let me tell you, the aftertaste from this lemon was miraculous. True, it wasn't the lemon's flesh anymore, it was its rind. Still, it was tasty. I would never have imagined any of this earlier!

If someone complained that we, here, were in a real squeeze, you shouldn't believe it, it would be a case of somebody losing heart. For all that, things were really sinister in the outskirts where the Russian fascists were setting fire to whatever they could. Whereas in Kyiv itself, just not in the suburbs, it was still somehow possible to live a life. Although there still was no clarity – that very 64-kilometre-long column with Russian men and equipment was still only some 25 kilometres off Kyiv. It was clearly waiting for something, and looming large over our heads…

Mum was unwell – could have been a head cold, or perhaps stress caused by all recent developments.

'Shall we make some borsch, sonny?' she offered. 'It's not costly and we'll have food for several days in just one go. The longer it sits the tastier it becomes, because it infuses. And I'll teach you how to go about it.'

We found several potatoes, a beetroot too. All that was left from a cabbage, though, was a depleted core. Not a single carrot. I scooped out the last spoon-

....

315   Revolution: the October Revolution of 1917.

ful of tomato paste left in a jar. Then I rinsed the jar with boiling water and emptied it into the pan. Not a gramme should go to waste! Force major meant force major. When cooked, borsch had to sit for at least half an hour. We sat to our meal – what could I say? The taste was funny, unusually sharp. An acquired taste, in a word. But for all that, edible.

What had Putin said about Ukraine? 'Whether you like it or not, take it on your chin, my beauty!' Blurted out something so vulgar. The world's community had been shocked – to allow oneself such language talking about your sovereign neighbours? For all that, we'd heard him say worse...

However, hand on heart, what was so surprising? A very specific nation. How many of them, out in the sticks, still wore homespun worsted coats? And in place of a toilet, had used a battered wooden cabin in the backyard? Their villages – dusty, foul, sitting on pockmarked roads. And worse – not all roads even had asphalt.

Yet the arrogance – off the radar screen. A superpower, no less!

* * *

The supermarket that had operated around the clock now worked from 11 to 5 p.m. The Metro was shut, trolleybuses didn't run, lots of bus routes had been cancelled. The workforce did have to get to their place of employment somehow, that was why they still kept some transport running but cut back on the hours. Some shops were opening at the actual time when the employees had made it. And then at 5 p.m. they were already closing – people had to make it home before curfew.

Out of the eight flats in our shared entrance, only three were still occupied. Mayor Klitchko announced again that half the city had left. In reality, it was probably more, must've been two thirds.

The first ones to leave our house were some foreigners who'd been renting – they must have had a sixth sense, warning them of imminent danger. Then the family who had fled Donetsk. By the way, they were Russians, so had a better understanding of what the 'Russian world' was all about. After that it was a proper exodus. Not everyone who left had children, but one could understand them anyway.

Previously, the rubbish bins had been emptied daily: a juggernaut of a lorry would pull up and tip their contents over, filling its huge belly. By now it happened once a week. But this was rather an attempt to maintain public health – evacuating whatever was there. Practically, it now took a week for at least some rubbish to end up in the bins. Previously, the residents would have used large plastic sacks for this purpose – so much had been consumed. Now everyone took out some pithy packages – there was practically nothing to throw out.

For all that, yet again, the life here, in the centre and adjacent boroughs, was tolerable. We had water, heating, and electricity. Even if on a limited scale, they reopened deliveries of foodstuffs. The municipal authorities did try their best. Utility companies operated. In a word, even if we all lived in permanent anxiety over our own fate, the fate of our families, and dear and near ones, life still went on. It was intimately better if compared to goings-on in Kyiv's out-skirts, or Kharkiv, Mariupol and other places. So, one had no right to whinge.

Mum and I enjoyed our borsch once more. After a period of rest, it had tasted different, so yummy. And great even without carrots. As for that cabbage core – that had been pure inspiration.

Somehow, I'd managed to cook that borsch with some requisite ingredients lacking. And all that was happening in Ukraine – the world's largest agricultural producer! In the past, no one would've paid any attention to those beetroots, or tomato paste, or. Who would have predicted the times like ours?

Difficult ones, horrible, with everything hanging by a thread…

Suddenly mum started singing, in a small and faltering voice:

Oh, but in a meadow a red viburnum is bending low
Why is our glorious Ukraine now saddened so? [316]

She brushed away a tear but suddenly gave me a wink, sort of, cheer up, my son! I clapped my hands and happily joined in:

But we'll go and raise this viburnum,
And we'll go and cheer up our Ukraine!
Hey-hey!

Christ Almighty, who would have thought that the 'Anthem of the Ukrainian Sich Riflemen (dating to the remote year of 1914) would be resurrected imme-diately right after the start of war in 2022 by Andriy Khlyvniuk, the lead singer of the band BoomBox![317] (On the 27th of February, standing with his rifle at

....

[316] **Viburnum:** a symbol of Ukraine. Ruby viburnum berries, according to popular beliefs, symbolize the courage of people who shed their blood for the motherland in the fight against enemies. Viburnum is also a symbol of the native land, the fatherland, the father's house.

[317] **The Sich Riflemen:** one of the first regular military units of the Ukrainian Peo-ple's Army. Operating from 1914 to 1918, the unit was formed from Ukrainian soldiers

the ready, in a completely deserted Sophia Square – the Russian fascists were on the brink of breaking into Kyiv – Khlyvniuk made a video, burst into song, belting out at the top of his voice, *a cappella*:

> *But we'll go and raise this viburnum,*
> *And we'll go and cheer up our Ukraine!*
> *Hey-hey!*

Some time later, on the same Sofia Square, the chapel thundered these words in chorus! The very same where our roadblock singers sang. One could feel the little chills running up and down your spine. And straight away the song had become a symbol of the Ukrainian resistance.

And then the song started conquering the world. Thanks to Khlyvniuk's performance, the British singers David Gilmour and Nick Mason brought together their legendary rock band Pink Floyd and released their first track in 30 years – 'Hey, Hey, Rise Up!' This was performed on the night between the seventh and eighth of April 2022.

Within two days the song came top of the charts in over 20 countries. All proceeds went to the humanitarian aid to Ukraine.

Listening to this song, the people all over the world had tears streaming down their faces.

As for us, the song made us proud, for that was us – holding on regardless, and even with a Russ-scist muzzle against our temples, repeating tirelessly: victory would be ours!

* * *

The first reports that vanguard Russian troops were running out of fuel and had started clogging up the motorways were intercepted several days after the invasion. As a result of technical cockups and the activity of the AFU, they ended up cut off from their supply lines. As for that extra-long column moving from Belarus in order to render support to the vanguard troops, it was now clear that it had come to a final halt 25 kilometres away from Kyiv. Most ve-hicles remained stationary, thus disrupting supplies of water and provisions, ammunitions and fuel, medications and spare parts allocated to the spearhead troops. Obviously, it reduced their fighting effectiveness even further. The

....

of the Austro-Hungarian army, the local population, and former commanders of the Ukrainian Sich Riflemen in Austria-Hungary. The word *Sich* roughly means a **camp** and dates to the days of the Cossacks.

huge logistical problem that now arose could not be resolved in several days, or even weeks.

Behind this logistical collapse had lain various blunders and miscalculations in the original concept for the entire operation. After all, the Russian leaders had countered on speedy progress and paid little attention to logistics. As a result, vanguard elements of the Russian Armed Forces had been carrying only enough fuel, ammunition, and provisions to last them three to five days.

And thus, that column had become a problem not only for itself but for the vanguard divisions that had ended up without the requisite resources. Meanwhile, after getting stuck on the motorway, the column continued using the resources for its own needs: the food for rations and the fuel for heating.

Eventually even those supplies had run out. According to social media, as a result of this logistical mess and because of the inability to provide rations for their own personnel, both the column and the vanguard elements received an order from their superiors – to switch over to 'self-sufficiency'! And that was how looting became legalised. Thousands of civilians living nearby found themselves in really dire straits. Looting became ubiquitous, laying waste to people's homes and shops.

As for us, we had our own portion of hardship. On March 11th the Russians carried out an all-round attack on the nearby village of Moshchun. The ensuing fighting was extremely intense. After several days the Ukrainian units were forced towards the outer boundary of the village. It was feared that on March 14th they would have to retreat completely. But everyone understood that for the Russians Moshchun was a gateway into Kyiv. That was a really critical juncture…

They also stepped up their activity in the north-east – Chernihiv was almost under a complete siege. The situation in Brovary (near Kyiv) was also exceedingly dangerous. Authorities were even forced to start evacuation of the local residents. To top it all, the Russian air strikes had set fire to a food supply depot in the same area, one of the largest in Europe. Some 50 thousand tonnes of food had been destroyed. This must have been an attempt to have Kyiv starve, the same way they had done it in Mariupol.

Mykolaiv was a hotspot too – the invaders had encircled the city. Approximately 250 thousand out of the total population of 480 had left the city in the first several days of fighting, heading towards Odesa. Despite heavy losses in manpower and equipment, the Russian troops continued with the siege and bombing of the city, obviously still adhering to their plans to take it over. Like before, they controlled the villages 20 kilometres away, with only the Pivdennyi Buh River impeding their advancement. Mykolaiv residents – adults and their children alike – were assisting the military in building barricade of car tyres and mixing Molotov cocktails.

At one of the intersections, a little boy was standing at a crossroads, shivering with cold and fear. The adults, engrossed in other extremely important business, entrusted him with keeping guard over the road juncture. He was nervous – would he be able to ignite the cocktail and lobe it at the tank?

Then Danilov, too, made this interesting statement at the tele-marathon. The presenter asked: 'When did you realise, personally, that a full-scale war, predicted by Western partners and the media, was inevitable?' 'When I started wearing the black uniform. You might have noticed that before I had only ever been seen in civvies. But in November I took to wearing my black uniform. And that was a sign that we were getting ready. But we couldn't announce it to general public. It was unacceptable since it would've been to our enemy's advantage, it would have played havoc with our economy. We had a clear vision of what it would've meant.'

That was our life now – full of questions, with no straightforward answers, at least for now. While the danger persisted.

The Whole World is Looking at Ukraine

It was nearly three weeks since the invasion. Those had been truly the hardest days and until mid-March, the state of affairs had been catastrophic.

We later learnt that the twenty-seventh of February (the fourth day of war) had been earmarked as the date for Putin's speech. He was supposed to declare a 'complete and irreversible victory over the Nazis'.

Instead, the whole world ended up glued to their TV screens watching Ukraine. And worrying on our behalf.

But there was some regrettable news too. The mayor of Lviv Sadovyi: 'Since February and March all international organisations have fled Ukraine. Especially organisations that were supposed to aid us in these troubled times, including those supposed to aid refugees. We have been holding regular briefings in the City Hall forecourt, and at one such meeting I spoke exclusively about the international community. I said: "Hello, where are you? After all, you're getting your budgets from the UN and various international bodies. Come over here, we're waiting for you, we need you!" After that they gradually started showing up. The international community wasn't ready. They all thought it would quickly be over and they wouldn't have to put up any HQs. Meanwhile, during this time we've handled over five million people. And on some days we had two million people present in the city. In other words, practically every family here was putting up displaced people. We have also accommodated many state institutions that are critical for the functioning of our state. All of this required that adequate measures be taken to enable these institutions to function: from supplies to passes and clearance options, we arranged the whole lot.'[318]

* * *

A pregnant woman was carried out by rescuers on a stretcher, evacuating her from the maternity hospital. The picture was somewhat fuzzy but there was clearly a lot of blood. Aha, the image got sharper: looked like she had a shattered pelvis and, also, one of her legs had been blown off. But she was carried out. And now she prayed that her baby would be born, even if it meant losing her own life.

An ordinary guy, salt of the earth, broad-faced, with a moustache. His duffel coat unbuttoned and untidy, his hair standing on end, he was shown in front of a pile of broken bricks – must have been his house – screaming: 'Putin, may you drop dead!'

Lord, did you hear this?

And the principal culprit, as if nothing was amiss, was sitting somewhere in his bunker…

A seventy-year-old woman, in a village of Vinnitsa Oblast: 'This Putin… I would've smothered him with my own hands! Do you hear? With these very hands of mine…'

A young woman, fashionably dressed. 'I'm from Kharkiv. The city is being reduced to rubble. We don't know where we're headed. Where we'll stay. We don't know if we find a refuge of any sort. At least, some roof over our heads. And also… We really hope that we'll be able to return to our home…'

Bloody hell, she said all this with a smile. Like nearly anyone from Kharkiv, and like many people all over the country, she spoke Russian. But she wanted to live in her native Ukraine. The country that would be independent and free…

In Ukraine, many people who regard Russian as their native tongue, considered themselves Ukrainians. There it was, the *real* truth…

The woman saved by rescuers out of the maternity hospital died and never gave birth to her child. The child died in her womb. The mother who never

---

[318]   UP 24 February 2024, https://www.pravda.com.ua/cdn/cd1/reconstruction/a5.html (accessed 04.07.2025).

became one, died together with her unborn child. The god-awful vampire, in his bunker, never even realised any of this…

TV showed the same guy again, down to earth, and, obviously, sincere. He kept screaming: 'Putin, may you burn in hell!' He was also yelling things that they'd omitted from the footage the first-time round: 'May you perish, you Kremlin scum!'

Dear God, why didn't you respond to any of this?

Must've been reluctant to get involved in this earthly filth. Or, perhaps he was simply too high in heaven from where he saw and heard nothing…

They continuously showed railway stations, trains, and roads chock-a-block with cars. A huge exodus of refugees, comparable in its scale with what had been going on during the Second World War. The human river was flowing towards Europe…

Zelensky had become a national hero – in his military get-up, visibly unshaven. By now no one would even recollect the times when he had stubbornly rejected the possibility of war. He wasn't your typical politician. And didn't speak like one. A stereotypical politician would have long since collapsed.

Brain-damaged Russians were posting this on social media: '*We are so strong that they tremble with fear! Folk in Odessa and Lvov hide from us in the metro!*' (This was precious, in view of the fact that neither Odesa or Lviv had their Metro.)

'*Putin's right! Do the lot of 'em in!*' the Russians continued their verbal contest on socials. Were any of them bots? Unquestionably. But Russia wasn't populated only with bots…

All we heard in the centre of Kyiv was the echo of distant explosions and the wailing of sirens. Yet all this time from the outskirts, and especially the suburbs, which were under horrific fire.

* * *

It felt like Putin, at times, was losing interest in the contemporary events and lived in the past. He had become obsessed with his dreamt-up idea and lost all ties with reality. Thing was, he'd been nurturing plans of 'restoring Russia's greatness' for quite some time. He believed that the West had profited from Russia's enfeebled state in the '90s, thus moving the NATO's borders to her proximity.

Yet by now Putin had decided that the West was rather weak too, and the time had come to revenge the erstwhile humiliation and translate the dream of his entire life into reality. He had turned 70 and was aware that if wanted to leave a trace in history, the time to act was now. Now or never! In his view, the Russian people needed a ruler whom everyone would obey unquestioningly. He insisted that the Ukrainians were not a centuries-old nation but 'Russians by origin'. He was convinced that the Russian army was so powerful that it would enforce a coup d'état in a neighbouring country within a space of several days.

And that was where he met with his great disappointment. Whatever happened to those Russian-speaking Ukrainians who were supposed to welcome his soldiers with open arms?

In real life, those Russian-speaking locals turned out to be no different to their Ukrainian-speaking compatriots! And united, they proved themselves capable of organising fierce resistance to such a strong adversary.

Generation Z

Coming back to the letter Z... The photographs showing Russian military equipment with this incomprehensible marking on its flanks had first appeared on social media several weeks prior to invasion. This white letter had been daubed with broad brush strokes, sometimes within a square, on the sides of tanks, military lorries, howitzers, delivery trucks. Eventually, some other letters started showing too: V, O, and a low-case z inside a square. It later transpired that the letters simply meant that this or that vehicle belonged to this or that military district. In the beginning, the Russian Defence Ministry had even argued that the letters had no symbolic importance and carried no additional message.

Yet the propaganda specialists had had other ideas, or perhaps the initiative had been put forward by the Kremlin itself. Whatever the real story, it was suggested that the letters should take on specific meanings. And so Z started being read as 'Za (*For*, in Russian) peace'; 'Za our guys'; 'Za stand-up guys'. This transformed the letter Z had from a sign for a military district into a propaganda tool. Several days later, this Latin letter had undoubtedly become the emblem of the 'special military operation', a military symbol of Russia's war in Ukraine. An official and eerie attribute of invasion. In the end, there had appeared the main slogan – 'Za victory!' And thus, step by step, the letter Z had turned into a principal marker of contemporary Russian life.

Then – lo and behold – a Russian gymnast, full of triumphant fervour, appeared at the awards ceremony dressed in a sporting uniform adorned with the letter Z.

In the University of Kazan, the management organised an event at which the young people, letter Z prominent on their clothes, were encouraged to thrust their arms forwards and upwards. It looked painfully familiar. Later, the students insisted they had been forced.

Flashmobs using this symbol took place in many Russian cities, often attended by civil servants, students, or children driven there by threat or coercion.

In Khabarovsk, teachers and students organised a lineup in a square, and shaped it like a huge Z.

Here and there, young school pupils were shown forming a Z-shaped line – the children hardly aware of what it all meant. They must have been told it was good, it was how it should be. And then there was a group in a kindergarten – the children holding up signs with the same letter. For some reason, the kids were on the knees.

Similar examples numbered in hundreds.

Out there, in Russia, they didn't even see how illogical all this was, for the Z wasn't a Cyrillic letter, much the invasion was dressed up as an attempt to 'rescue of the Russian world'.

It would be interesting to know who had suggested that the Z and other Latin letters (instead of Cyrillic ones, which would've been more consistent) should be used as insignia? That was unknown. Most likely, some general from the Russian General Staff. He'd just liked it, ok? Although it wasn't all that important.

What was important, though, was the fact that it became the world view of tens of millions of people. An alien letter (the letter Z that did not exist in the Russian alphabet) had morphed, according to Russians themselves, into a most significant symbol of the 'Russian grandeur'. And simultaneously, according to the rest of the world – a symbol of the bloody massacre instigated by the Russians.

And another thing. The polygonal zigzag of this letter became a good reflection of Russian mentality – broken and twisted.

Watching, yet again, some footage from contemporary Moscow, showing young people walking down the streets, smiling, waving arms, laughing, even guffawing, I felt that I was in a very bad place. It was as if nothing was happening, next door, as if life went on as normal…

How could it be?

* * *

'Listen, here's a perfect paradox,' Platonovych was extremely agitated. 'By the eighteenth of March the main Russian convoy moving towards Mykolaiv has been wiped out, the remaining troops have retreated towards the administrative border with Kherson Oblast. Seemingly, there's nothing for them to be happy about. And then right on the eighteenth, yesterday, they showed the Luzhniki Stadium in Moscow. Did you watch the news?'

'Sure, we did,' Taras bobbed up and down in agitation. 'Folk gathered around the stadium too, perhaps a couple of hundred thousand. Just to think of it – an event attended by Putin himself! The eighth anniversary of the annexation of Crimea! They bellowed so loudly that one could possibly hear them beyond the confines of Moscow: "Russsssshia! Ru-ssssh-ia! Vic-to-ry"!'

'Those attending behaved like people possessed,' confirmed bespectacled Gennady. 'A case of mass psychosis… Must have been worse than in the days of Stalin.'

'Demons…' I gasped involuntarily.

'What's that?' Gennady didn't hear me properly. 'You said something?'

'Before the war I'd spent two weeks in Myrhorod region, dossed down in the house belonging to two old ladies. Collected ethnographic materials. And they told me lots about all sorts of evil creatures. Especially demons. At the time, it was only rumoured that Russians might invade us, no one knew anything for certain. And my grannies told me that demons weren't extinct. That if we were to be attacked, it would be by genuine devils. It's clearly an allegory but…'

'Your grannies were right, that's what they are – demons and devils!' Denis was angry.

'That zombified populace don't even suspect that their Fuhrer has long since prepared a peaceful nest for himself and his family, in case of a force major…'

'How do you know? And where, in which country?'

'This political expert has posted some info on YouTube, but didn't name the country. He said: guess for yourselves, it's not rocket science…'

'Well, this is a conspiracy theory,' grimaced Andriyovych. 'All the rage now. So, which country, what d'ya reckon?'

'Deuce knows. Somewhere in Latin America, or Africa. Either would do, really. Then again, lots of good pals around. Warm, too. Besides, the radioactive dust – if it gets to this – is unlikely to blow that far…'

There was a moment's silence. Everyone was trying to imagine life in that warm nameless country…

Denis spoke again:

'There's this talk of his ill health. Allegedly, he's got a bouquet of complaints. That he's got not that much left. When travelling, he's accompanied by at least ten physicians. And all this war-related hullabaloo probably means he's in a hurry…'

'May well be,' summed up Mykolayovych. 'He's twigged that his physical life will soon be over. Yet he's so eager to go down in history. Physically you'd be here no more, and yet still here for centuries to come. Lording over everyone like a monument. Sort of a new-fanged Peter the Great. Must've been one the reasons for the operation he's started.'

'The German chancellor, too, has excelled himself.' Platonovych raised his hand to attract our attention. 'His fellow countrymen supposedly hurt his feelings with their attitude towards visiting Russians. So he's hit back: "The Russian people are not to blame. This is exclusively Putin's war".'[319]

'Amazing to hear that a high-ranking European politician would talk like this,' that from Andriyovych.

'Isn't it clear that he isn't waging this war by himself, seeing as he's sitting around in his bunker? And who elected him president several times? The very same Russian people, 80% of whom support him. They are prepared to follow his lead "till the triumphant end"! It's Putin's war and his people's war. Dear me… Nothing's gonna fall into place until the European leaders get the message. And their support will be lukewarm. Neither do they realise that all we want is to live like them – in peace and harmony. Yet those "neighbours" strive to wipe us all out without a trace. In other words, to kill us all.'

Since no one was looking at me, I pulled out a pen and pad, turned away for a minute and started making rapid notes:

'What is really curious is this. There are Russians in Ukraine, too, and quite a few. Mostly they are normal people, free of this slavish dependency. The people who've shed this burden of "imperial sublimity". Also, there are ethnic Ukrainians who prefer to speak Russian but are pro-Ukraine, pro-democracy, pro-Europe which, in this case, means anti-Russian. Not everyone but the overwhelming majority. Whether or not Russia likes the fact…

'What I'm trying to say is this. A person is predominantly shaped by their environment, things they see and hear. Including the stuff shown on TV. The Russians in Russia are imbued with this imperial self-perception, a sense of their obscure but inflated "grandiosity". But lots of those Russians who live in Ukraine are free from all of this. Within thirty years of living in a free country, they've been cured of this complex…'

Afterwards everyone was buried in their mobiles: socials were bursting with posts on intercepted conversations between the Russian soldiers and their families, and videos of the blasted Russkies plundering all and sundry.

....

[319]   UP, 17 March 2022. https://www.pravda.com.ua/rus/news/2022/03/17/7332281/ (accessed 04.07.2025).

They'd got into somebody's home and opened various jars with home preserves: 'Wow, those Ukes do roll in clover... Nice jam, nice marmalade...' They'd started spreading it on bread, stuffing their faces.

Intercepted phone calls were equally eloquent.

'Tis OK... We're fighting... I happened to shoot this little kidda ... It just happened...' a Russian soldier had told his wife.

'*Well, I never,*' that was her, in response. And that was that. Just a normal everyday conversation.

'*You know I'm looting things a bit...*'

'*Seen anything interesting?*'

'*Not really, just got this blender...*'

'*Wow! Very useful. Great stuff.*'

A POW called his mother in Russia, she spoke back in semi-whisper:

'*Sonnie, don't tell me anything about yourself, I beg of you. They will come here and put me in prison...*'

A Russian slacker soldier called home:

'*Mum! I'm scared... The things that happen here...*'

'*Have you been paid yet?*'

The generation 'Z' had grown up in Russia before our very eyes.

So, as they were having those telephone conversations, we were burying our fallen citizens ... in parks and enclosed tree-lined squares. Sometimes directly in urban streets – if it proved possible to find a piece of ground not covered with asphalt. Who would bury anyone in a cemetery now? You'd have to get there first... And riding on what?

* * *

These bastards more or less calmed down only at night, their long-distance explosions only hammering the city from time to time, infrequently. But closer to the daybreak, at about four, they probably were getting a wake-up signal, prompting them to resume their bestial duties.

Finding themselves in limbo, after several weeks of war they changed tack. Their emphasis shifted to cruise missiles, also ballistic ones. Those missiles were of a different class, launched either from Belarus, some Russian territories, or the sea, targeting the most important facilities: Antonov aircraft manufacturer, Promin R&D institute (guided missiles and rocket complexes) – which meant destroying decades' worth of research data, and the years spent building airports. Even runways and landing strips would not be rebuilt all that promptly.

And then there was this question: could it be that the West would leave us to our fate – a 'cruise-ballistic' annihilation?

The missile strikes, coupled with the use of long-distance artillery meant that every building in Kyiv was now in danger… And every person, too.

A psychologist spoke on TV. That we were all patriots, he said, was incontrovertible. However, as for danger assessment and attitudes towards a threat, there was a certain hierarchy of priorities. It wasn't some abstract academic analysis but scientifically proven data. So, the top priority was those closest to us: children, spouses, parents. After that – close relatives, friends, and good acquaintances. Motherland, of course. He didn't specify its place in the hierarchy but everyone realised it was among the topmost ones.

Another interesting thing: they said on TV that Russia reciprocated the sanctions introduced against her by introducing her own. From that point on, Joe Biden and Justin Trudeau were banned from entering the territory of the Russian Federation. Who could tell if they would be able to cope with this tragedy…

* * *

The Commander had left for his shooting range and we all relaxed somewhat, just sat there, chattering.

Denis spat derisively and clenched his fists:

'A commander, my ass! I don't give a fuck about commanders like this!'

'Come on, there-there,' the bespectacled Gennady gave his sleeve a tug.

'Why, then, he's always breathing down my bloody neck?'

'Don't you know, Denis?' Taras tried to calm him down too, waved his hand in front of Denis's face. 'It's all because of this NATO uniform of yours, or wherever else it's coming from. Time to come clean – where did you nick it from?'

'Too flashy,' Andriyovych moved closer, also eager to offer some words of wisdom. 'The Commander fought in ATO but wears a regular uniform. And you, who's hardly been anywhere, are good to go on a fashion show. Pockets alone – must be at least 40 of those, one wouldn't know what to put them. It vexes him.'

'Well, what's to be done?' Mykolayovych joined in too, offered Denis a placating sweet. 'Have a sweetie, go for it. It's not like it was in the days of peace when you could just drop into a shop and buy it.'

'Fuck it all!' Still, Denis seemed somewhat recovered. 'Would be great if they accepted us into NATO asap. It's unbearable. He's already taken all of you to the shooting range, and you did some shooting, received some training. And I'm like a shabby relative...'

'Just a minute! You've dropped NATO into the mix...' Platonovych gave him a sly squint. 'What d'ya reckon, Denis, they must accept us?'

'You say "would be great" and "be accepted",' Mykolayovych was clearly ready with a gibe of his own. ''Tis easier said than done...'

'How much longer will we have to wait?' That was from a sad Gennady.

'What d'ya mean?' Denis leapt up at that. 'You have doubts?'

'And you don't?' summarised Andriyovych. 'I have this feeling... Why would they want all that extra trouble? And on such a scale?'

* * *

More often than not, when a political debate flared up at our roadblock, Taras and I kept ourselves to ourselves. There were much wiser people around.

'It looks increasingly likely,' Gennady offered us some new arguments, 'that what's going on is Realpolitik at its clearest. Sort of, let them continue slaughtering Ukraine but as for us – we'll see Russia weakened and send a clear message to China regarding their hypothetical actions in Taiwan.'

'The Kremin accuses the West of their alleged desire to spark a revolution in Russia.' Andriyovych disengaged himself from his mobile and joined in. 'But that's not how it is, at all. It's much easier for the North Atlantic bloc to isolate Russia through a cold-war-style military standoff than to seek a change of regime in such an unpredictable nuclear power. To top it all, ethnically, Russia is far from homogeneous. That's yet another source of danger. What if it ends up torn asunder into numerous national entities and its nuclear potential falls into God knows whose hands?'

'Yeah... I'm sure the Westerners have reached a consensus and believe that trying to change the Russian regime spontaneously from within may create even greater problems,' pointed out Platonovych. 'And if Russia does disintegrate into a multitude of separate territories, tens of millions of refugees will be headed for Europe. And what about religious radicalisation in some of the Russian regions? And the possibility of a dangerous energy crisis... Not to mention a string of revolutions in other post-Soviet republics.'

'Sure thing,' Gennady nodded his agreement. 'That's why they would like to create something like a "manageable neighbourship" with Putin's regime. In their opinion he should be deterred by a new iron curtain – much more preferable to any confrontation that could inflict a deadly damage on Russia.'

'What we need is security guarantees for the future,' Platonovych chopped the air with his hand. 'Most urgently – a bloc with nuclear powers, perhaps even without NATO. Otherwise, it's impossible to imagine how we're gonna live side by side with such a neighbour. But instead, they offer us funny "guarantors" – Turkey, Izrael. Some guarantors they are! But even Germany and France cannot clearly identify their stance. For now, it's nothing but talk. The only real guarantor is the United States of America. And Great Britain– they too have clear principles.'

'A bloc that could be efficient!' I couldn't contain myself. 'NATO today includes too many tiny member-countries who cannot do much themselves but when it comes to throwing a spanner in the works – that's where they're at the forefront. I'd like to see those "independent" states defending themselves under attack. So, this other bloc should bring together countries with more guts when defending democracy. Less bureaucracy and more determination!'

'An alliance like this couldn't do without Ukraine. Its army is among the most powerful in Europe, if not the most powerful,' added Gennady. 'It's been through baptism by fire, and its commanders have skills acquired not only in a classroom but on a battlefield.'

'You heard the news?' Mycholayovych's eyes twinkled.

Ri-i-ght, he was about to drop a bomb of some kind.

'I don't know if it's true or not but allegedly, on the twenty-third of March, Roman Abramovich, the Russian oligarch and, as they say, one of Putin's "wallets" who is currently acting as an intermediary between Moscow and Kyiv, delivered to the Russian president a note personally written by Zelensky. In it, there were possible options for a compromise acceptable to Ukraine. Putin, extremely irate over multiple failures in the Kyiv offensive, snapped at the envoy: "Tell them I'll destroy them". That's how it goes…'

* * *

Finally, it became possible to reverse the situation in Moshchun, and the Russian troops were forced back. The word got through that the AFU might shortly liberate Irpin and Bucha.

Failed Russian attempts to attack Kyiv had lasted till March 19th – our guys continued methodically annihilating their manpower and equipment. The Russians had been forced to abandon their damaged vehicles, switch over to a defence mode and start entrenching. And on March 21st, the AFU kicked them out of Makariv and completely liberated Moshchun. The fighting had left the village practically raised to the ground – approximately 2 out of 2.8 thousand houses had been destroyed…

While the Ukrainian TV audiences mulled over the 'fur coat storage room',[320] in Kharkiv there died a 96-year-old called Borys Romanchenko – his home was shelled by the Russians. Romanchenko had survived four Nazi concentration camps, returned home, and reached a respectable old age. But he hadn't survived the death campaign orchestrated by Putin – his plans for 'denazification' as applied to real life.

Another horrible example. There was this lady who for a whole month had been hiding inside a Metro station in Kharkiv. She'd stayed there permanently. Then one day somebody told her that the day outside was sunny and beautiful. She'd decided to venture upstairs, to see the sun. And got killed by shrapnel.

That was happening in Kharkiv, a city with one-and-a-half million residents, an intellectual and academic hub, home to over 40 higher educational establishments. Now it was a place where hundreds of houses and structures had been destroyed, and this number was only growing. The city where practically everyone considered Russian to be their mother tongue. Were they also the 'Ukrainian Nazis'?

The other cities steamrolled by the Russian war machine were Chernihiv, Sumy, Mykolaiv. All those oblast capitals continued to hold up heroically.

As for Odesa. Compared to other cities, it had been lucky. Odesa residents had access to catacombs – two thousand kilometres of those, no joking matter. During the Second World War the population had been hiding there from the fascists. Now it was a hiding place from the Ruscists – the only difference being a slight difference in spelling.

And there were us, here in Kyiv. During the first several days of war, many people had left for suburbs and villages within the oblast. And ended up in a trap, where the worst was happening – a real inferno. As for the city centre and the adjacent quarters, for the time being the destruction there was not so vast, even if life was extremely stressful too: something was flying over us all the time. It felt like a roulette – may pass you by, may not.

By the way, today in Kyiv was a relatively quiet day. Perhaps those basted Russians started gradually fizzling out? All we had to cope with were occasional missiles.

Goodness gracious. Today was exactly one month since the war had started but it felt like hostilities had been going on forever. The enemy was sustaining grievous losses but showed no inclination to stop.

....

[320] **Fur coat storage room:** one of many de lux facilities discovered in the palace belonging to Viktor Medvedchuk after his arrest on charges of corruption and treason. His wife was known for her weakness for fancy dress.

At our roadblock things were pretty much the same. Just like before, we went on shifts, checked the passing vehicles, kept tabs on the situation around us.

However, that was not entirely true, there was one point of difference. I took to bringing along my notepad and making occasional notes on my observations. At times, new impressions simply gushed in. Taras was very happy to see me do it:

'That's wonderful, man! I can see you coming back to life. I mean, in the creative sense. That's the spirit. Record our life here, describe the roadblock, and you'll produce a classy script.'

Even the Commander offered his opinion (already aware of my dallying with the script):

'It's this… Do write, you know? But only what's allowable. No divulging bloody secrets…'

And then he failed to specify which secrets he had in mind.

On the other hand, there was no need. We got each other's meaning perfectly well.

The Russians meanwhile had worked out a new dress code: if your dress included anything blue and yellow,[321] you could be stopped: 'Hey you, take care! It's an extremely disgusting combination!' Also, the doors of anti-war activists' homes now could show a message: 'A traitor lives here!'

The Russian propaganda machine ran into its own problem – it had become very hard to source coverage. They'd anticipated that they would come across just a few 'Nazis' in Ukraine – only to discover that all Ukrainians were 'Nazis'.

Mum kept the TV on practically non-stop – the informational avalanche continued. Now they were asserting that Russia needed 'de-Putinisation'. Quite possible. But if over there up to 80% supported him, it meant that up to 80% of Russians were die-hard 'putinists'. Could one de-Putinise them all, then?

There were some 'forward-thinking' citizens in Russia too. Those contemplated thus: 'Oh, the whole thing has been kick-started by politicians. They had an axe to grind with each other but it's the regular people who have to suffer.'

A very smart way of reasoning. If you referred to 'politicians', was it the Russian ones you referred to, or the Ukrainians too? So, what exactly had the Ukrainian politicians done – to your leader and you personally – to justify a war that you'd started against us?

....

[321] **Blue and yellow**: the national colours of Ukraine.

Then there was this opinion, too, much more explicit. One after another, top Russian officials declared: 'Yes, we have attacked them. But only because they *had been preparing to attack us themselves!*'

Christ in Heaven, how could a normal person bear it all?

Life in the Bunker

The time did fly. It was nearly midnight; I was on my way home after my shift. Not a soul in the street... Sure thing, it was already past the curfew hour...

As was by now customary, Taras would send me whatever had accumulated in his chatroom during the day.

The first thing discussed was that period at Bankova Street – several days and nights – when time had simply condensed. Days and nights had merged, and no one could tell them apart. 'In the first days no one could make any sense. We were all deep underground, in a bunker, practically in the same room. It was an insane marathon.'

I carried on reading.

'Top officials – not only the president but the speaker of parliament, prime minister, defence minister, commander-in-chief of the AFU – had to stay in secure locations. Those who for whatever reason were outside the bunker had to constantly change their locations, moving from one place to another, every night.

'As is already known, on the morning of February 24th (at approximately 10:30 a.m.) heads of parliamentary factions were invited to the President's Office, and suddenly the president's security detail burst in, yelling loudly: "There's movement in the direction of Bankova. Everyone must urgently go down into the shelter!" They took Zelensky to the bunker. He was followed by Yermak and several of his deputies, Prime Minister Shmyhal with his team, Arakhamia, and Podolyak. In the general commotion the Speaker, who had a separate block down there never made it to the bunker, but some who were admitted should not have been there under the protocol.

And thus, practically from the first hours of war on February 24th, commenced the life and performance of duties of the president and his team at Facility No 1, in a shelter/bunker, deep underground. Once upon a time, it had been built to protect the top Ukrainian Communist Party leadership against a nuclear attack. In terms of amenities, however, it turned out to be humble.

It was very deep underground. To go there one had to make a long descent in a lift, then some stairs followed, finally – a heavy door. Afterwards – long corridors... Not having fresh air, it was quite hard psychologically. Later an idea came to pop out from time to time in order to catch have some fresh air. Also, the problem with light. Since it was electric it was impossible to say it's day or night outside.

The rooms were tiny: some intended for work, some for sleeping in.

From the very start Zelensky found himself in a really tight spot. Besides there were nearly always some four-five people in his small office. New visitors came down to talk to him every day and his protection service was not happy about it. More to that – he induced them to stay and work from there.

Naturally, there was a lot of chaos in the beginning. People were coming in and out reporting their cases, no one observed any rules and it was with time that some order was put to that.

The only advantage of the president's 'room' was an ensuite shower but even this perk didn't last for too long.

But then, what sort of life was possible in a bunker? Those who were there nowadays recollect that, initially, everyone was surviving on adrenalin. The food was samey and scarce: Mivina instant noodles, canned meat, stale bread, and chocolate.

The first several nights people that were in the bunker slept for just several hours. Zaluzhnyi regularly popped over with the news via video conference, reporting what was happening and where. The news was always bad. Here something had been taken, there – someone killed, elsewhere – places got bombed to bits. There was also a string of negotiations, consultations, conference calls and communication by phone. It was all one turbulent never-stopping flow. The telephone rang incessantly? at night as well. And at about five in the morning, Zelensky was already receiving the first precis of updates. The first days stayed in memory as one block. What and when happened there – impossible to single out today.'

Eventually, some time later, daily life in the bunker had been straightened up: hot meals had been organised, primitive fitness equipment brought in, and the morning reporting been shifted back to seven a.m.

Zelensky stayed in constant communication with another bunker from where Commander-in-Chief Zaluzhnyi – together with other generals, managed the defence of the country, operating on air and in manual mode. The Chief Commander's secure dwelling was in a bunker near the General Staff. Zaluzhnyi, reportedly, hadn't even slept throughout the first three days and nights, being at all times in touch with the commanding officers from various regions. The conversations had been brief but to the point. His 17-story bunker capable to take inside up to five hundred people was a real underground city fitted out to withstand a nuclear war. The officers sat in large, well-appointed rooms – like they showed in films, surrounded by monitors, huge maps, and such like. It was easy to see that the area under consideration was not just a separate segment of the frontline. It was a hub in charge of the whole war effort, where decisions had been taken on actions in the north, on defending Kyiv, Kharkiv, Mykolaiv… Lots of maps, lots of people, lots of everything.

There are many such protected command posts in the Ukrainian military. They also exist in all ministries. However, after the war, the entire network will have to be overhauled because most of these facilities are situated in Kharkiv, Chernihiv, and Sumy oblasts – in view of the fact that in Soviet times the danger always supposedly stemmed from the West. As for the Russian 'fraternal and friendly' neighbour – it hadn't been a source of danger at all. And that was why nearly all secondary command stations ended up located smack on the vector of the contemporary source of danger.

The key contributing factor to the efficiency of our defence was probably the fact that all top political and military officials had been isolated and concentrated in those two places. A message to the army, or an instruction from the military – all was processed very quickly, inside the same office room. the same for the government – its sessions were held twice a day: in the morning and in the evening. And all consents, decisions, everything – no bureaucracy – was issued very promptly. In the first days or weeks, the decisions were taken momentarily, no one thought about anything else but – let's go! Everyone understood the risks, especially for Kyiv. The capital was half-encircled, all that was left was the motorway between Kyiv and Odesa. The same applied to foreign partners – they also were very quick. A minister could call his counterpart: "We need fuel!" "OK, we're looking for what we can do." And so on.

OK, that was the bunker. But what about developments upstairs, inside the President's Office? Sacks with sand everywhere… national guards lay on the floor along the corridors. The visitors who came to see the president would step on somebody, apologise. Thing was – it was dark, no overhead lights, and everyone had to pick out their way by the flashlights on their mobile phones…

The House of Death. The Street of Death. The City of Death

The name Mariupol sounded so nice. 'Pol' came from the Greek – 'polis', a town or a city. But most locals referred to it tenderly as 'Marik', or 'our Marik'.

And then Mariupol-Marik, a port city, a centre of metallurgy, had been struck by disaster. There was no Marik anymore. It practically stopped to be, having been levelled to the ground. Its population – half-a-million people, mostly Russian-speaking, was being annihilated by the Ruscists. Our 'Russian brothers' according to some Europeans. And as a result of continuous bombing, this city would stay in history alongside Coventry and Dresden.

Mariupol was defending itself heroically – its extremely important role being to distract considerable chunks of the enemy force.

The TV coverage of its bombed-out ruins was unwatchable. The houses reduced to rubble, tens of thousands of people living in basements and cellars, for days. And still, every new day hundreds of air bombs were dropped onto the city…

About a thousand adults and children had found shelter on the premises of the Mariupol Drama Theatre. They wrote on the asphalt by the entrance, in ginormous letters – 'Children'. The hope had proved futile. A Ruscist pilot eagerly dropped on them a 500-kg bomb. Another one hit a swimming pool – a refuge for pregnant women.

Beasts. Scum. Barbarians!

Testimonials:

The father of a family stated: 'Not so long ago, life was great – everything was on the up: houses were built, schools and kindergartens, the roads were laid… New public transport appeared, too, the city was developing actively, becoming prettier by the year. We lived a full, happy life. But now for several weeks we've been sitting in the basement of our house. Just recently everything around started trembling, and people wondered: how was it possible? Could the shells and bombs be targeting just our house? But once outside, we saw – they'd hit everything. The city now, end-to-end, is just one big ruin. A pile of rubble…'

His wife added: 'They don't just bomb our city, they roast it. I hate this Putin! And the Russian people? It isn't just one person who's doing this. They do keep re-electing him, keep idolising him, and chanting "Well-done"!'

'The hardest thing about living in Mariupol is lack of water. It used to be delivered by trucks. The queues with containers reached stood? around the clock. The last ones in the queue could have to go without. It could be just three or four sips a day – and that was that. Food was a problem too, but we had a sack of potatoes. We used to boil two potatoes per day. Sometimes we made carrot soup on the bonfire in the courtyard. Once we went out to get some water and ended up in an air raid. My son's leg was hit with something. Turned out, it was a piece of asphalt ripped out by a mine. If it'd been a fragment, he'd been left with no leg.'

'It's scary not only when they make you lie face down on the ground. It's really scary when you get up and start walking, for behind you is a soldier with a submachine gun. The only question then is – will he shoot, or won't he? You can never know what's on their minds…'

Just imagine – what once had been 'Marik', now was a martyr-city. According to the most recent news, on March 24th, the Russians had advanced towards the city centre.

And everywhere – not only in Mariupol – they burnt with this desire to eradicate the local population. People were sitting in basements and shelters all over the occupied territories: no electricity, no heating, no food, no water. If it snowed, they would melt the snow and use it for drinking. That was the plan of 'denazification' of Ukraine as devised by the intruders.

A sharp increase was registered in the numbers of premature births, brought on by stress, poor diet, and horrible living conditions.

And the refugees… They were everywhere: in cars, on trains, on foot… The war had created a migration catastrophe unheard-of in Europe since the '40s. Millions had gone abroad; millions were in transit within our country.

'My God, our only fervent wish is that you, beastly Russia, would crawl back to where you belong! You've got no business here! Also, you shouldn't just bugger off but pay huge reparations. That's the only term available because it's impossible to work out the real figures. The visible losses entail other, invisible costs. One type of grief is closely associated with another. One case of unfairness – and then an outpouring of other evils, each one more horrible than the other…

'And how to evaluate the moral damage? Do such yardsticks even exist? And the health problems? The impact on people's mental health? And how does one measure those tears – in litres?'

'Effing Russia should pay for everyone killed. How much is due to a family of someone who's died in an air crash – according to international standards? Something like a hundred thousand Dollars? So, she owes us a hundred thousand Dollars for everyone who's been killed. Even this wouldn't be enough…'

'To decimate, like this, such a country, in full bloom? It's impossible to let them off scot-free. Enough to say that the world, for a long time, has allowed a lot of things – as regards Ukraine – go unpunished…'

I could imagine how Lavrov's creatures – in all venues, diplomatic and judicial – would strike up their disgraceful song: 'But we've never attacked Ukraine! Nothing was further from our minds…'

And if the world this time, too, freed them from responsibility, it would be impossible even to imagine what would happen next…

As for Putin, one could understand just one thing: his total panic caused by our democracy. He was horrified to think that a day would come and a 'colourful revolution' would erupt in Moscow, too!

The previous year Navalny had shown a film about Putin's luxuriant palace situated on a seaside.[322] It had cost billions to build! Two million views! One would think, it was time to draw conclusions… And what? And nothing. They had watched it, said their 'ah-s' and 'oh-s', and persisted being fascinated by him.

And one more prominent thing. While Moscow oligarchs' children and grandchildren hopped around European capitals and enjoyed exclusive resorts, those who fought with us, the 'Nazis', were the endless Ivans and Pyotrs from the sticks. Some of them had even come to the end of their earthly road here. Some notorious celebrity – I'd read somewhere – was insisting that all people had herd mentality. I wouldn't be so sure. However, if it was true, the herd that had formed itself in Russia was exceptionally large…

Break Away from Hell and Keep Running…

February 24th irrevocably split the lives of most Ukrainians, initiating a tectonic shift in their existence. The 'brotherly' nation nextdoor had come to save them from Nazism. For some reason this involved rockets, bombs, and shells. And then, in a bid to save themselves from this 'liberation', millions of people fled their homes and ran away, under fire – just like in films about the World War Two…

You might have thought yourself the luckiest person in the world – successful in business, married to your sweetheart, you'd just bought a a new apartment, but in no time all this went to hell…

Your windowpanes began wobbling, explosions made your walls reverberate. Car alarms suddenly started screaming everywhere. People heard these sounds and rushed to their windows to see that a nearby petrol station had burst into flames. Within minutes everything around was ablaze. It wasn't safe to stay in your flat – people were popping out into the frosty morning, darting back and forth in panic… Someone switched on the radio in his smartphone: Russian tanks, it was reported, were attacking the city and Ukrainian troops were fighting back…

In the morning huge queues formed in front of shops and pharmacies. People were buying up whatever they could. But when you'd bought something, there was another problem: it was now dangerous to remain in a residential area. People raced towards basements for shelter. Those with relatives or friends living in the 'private sector' hurried off in that direction – because

....

[322] **Alexei Navalny** (1976-2024): a Russian opposition leader, lawyer, anti-corruption activist, and political prisoner.

those houses had cellars![323] You could sit it all out, waiting for things to subside. Many of those who left didn't know at the time that they would never see their homes again.

Nights were the worst. Someone in each family had to stay awake and on guard for air raid alarms. But those who were supposed to sleep could not – the drones were overhead at low altitudes and made a lot of noise. Sometimes thing exploded – and it felt like your building's roof was about to collapse. People lay paralysed with fear, rolling down onto the floor, covering their heads with their hands, although they knew that this was of no use.

The days dragged on…. Stunned, people spent their days mostly inside, without speaking. When an air raid siren started yelling – you would rush to the basement. People took tranquilisers. Yet every morning the same thought as you rolled over: I must live with this horror for a while more, then hopefully everything will somehow be sorted out and it will be possible to go back home. But every night the bombings continued. And on TV the same awful scenes: bombs falling, screams, death…

You waited until the news came that a Russian bomb had practically destroyed either your own or an adjacent building. Then, days later, a shell would hit your friend's private house. And the Russian troops were getting closer and closer. Everything got complicated. People around about would succumb to hysteria, lash out, become aggressive and spiteful. The time had come to take a serious decision: leave. Head westwards…

But yours was not the only family to take such a decision. Lots of people were already on the move. To leave the city was already problematic – the jams were insane. And a terrible fear: what lay ahead? It was one big unknown…

Even if it was early spring, the weather was more like winter. The roadsides were covered in snow. Horrendous traffic jams bloomed in the mass exodus. The city left behind was blitzed. There was no petrol at petrol stations. Spot a station with petrol and it was a stroke of luck. They would only let you have a few litres, but, still, it was something.

The first part of the route was one huge traffic jam. Left and right, all was boundless fields and darkness. You just sat in your car and waited.

Explosions boomed all the time. The road was slippery – cars skidded on the black ice, crashing one into another. At times somebody would slide out of the queue and try to overtake the other traffic by driving on the oncoming side of the road or the hard shoulder. In response the other drivers would jump out

---

[323] **Private sector**: in Soviet (post-Soviet) urban planning 'private sector' is the name for an urban district where families can build privately owned single-family homes.

of their cars, bats in hand: keep calm and obey the rules, everyone here is in the same boat! Then an order spread from car to car: switch off headlights. An attack was expected, but there was no place to hide – both ahead and behind were only cars…

Happily, for those with babies finding a place for the night was not a problem: just post on social media – people were quick to offer accommodation.

A hundred kilometres could take you half a day… But finally, you arrived somewhere, and it was a different planet. At least, this was the first time you could wash yourself and change into clean clothes.

Relieved? No way. You start thinking: everything has been ruined, there is no home to return to. And the future: a total blank. And then: the shock. What to do? Where to run next? Total horror! Your previous life has been wonderful, but now you are homeless, you have neither money nor abode. Now life is just passing by… And another thought: there's no going back, you have to keep moving. To Western Ukraine or further – to the border…

Those without a car departed on an evacuation train. As soon as a train arrived, people started storming it. Men who were seeing off their families forced their way inside to help their wives, children, and mothers board. None of the rules of peacetime applied anymore. Little kids lay on the floor, tucking their legs under themselves. Old people were pressed against walls. Adults stood…

Outside, it was quickly getting dark, so it was impossible to see where the train was going: all signs showing names of train stations had been either masked with fabric or boarded up. And there was a ban on loading maps onto phones; people were told to switch their phones off – an evacuation train had to be invisible.

It took one and a half days – at snake's pace – to reach one of the cities in Western Ukraine. Children were taken by volunteers to a hostel, where they were given mattresses, hot meals and a chance to use a shower. The adults stayed at the station prior to taking a decision: what next? Others – women and children – switched to trains going abroad… The men had to go back and join the army…

Many of those who stayed in besieged cities in the east believed it would be like in 2014: after some shooting the people at the top would come to an agreement. And everything would return to normal. So what was the point in going away? And when they realised this was a totally different war, it was too late. The enemy was closing the circle…

So they had to live a terrible existence. Day after day of shelling and bombing.

Electricity became irregular and then was simply cut off. There was no heating, no water. All communication with the outside world ceased.

Ukraine was making attempts to agree "green corridors" so that locals could evacuate, but nothing came of it. Shells started falling on residential buildings. With each passing day fewer and fewer windows in houses remained intact. Those with windows were lucky – it was a trifle warmer inside. Those who were not so lucky had to move onto landings with a lift shaft at one side. They lined the floor with sleeping mats and rugs.

But hard times came to the luckier ones as well – as the shelling intensified, fragments started flying into their flats. Sooner or later the day came when there was a hole in your wall, or there was no wall at all.

Later, Russians began targeting houses specifically. Parts of buildings were in flames – both communal entrances and flats. Residents came running out. Some were in luck: it wasn't the whole building that had taken a direct hit and was on fire but just a number of flats. Then the neighbours would try to smother the flames to prevent it spreading to other flats. Sometimes, to stop the fire, they had to force out the doors in several flats whose owners had left. Usually, men were on standby all through the night.

With the wind changing direction, buildings were often on fire for several days – the wind kept the sluggish fire going. Because of the lack of intact flats people bedded down in whatever had survived. They ventured outside only briefly to local semi-destroyed shops or to get water. Or to boil that water on an improvised stove several metres from the house entrance. By the time they carried the kettles back upstairs the water would be cold again. The temperature inside was usually around zero but at night would drop lower.

Older people would reject food even if it was available, preferring to die. Their neighbours would be too scared to take out their bodies: gunshots and the whining of shells came from everywhere. Once they did manage to carry a body outside – just in front of the communal entrance – they would hastily dig a shallow trench, place the body inside, lightly cover it with soil, and rush back inside. But there were more and more dead bodies lying around. So you had to carry the immolated corpses further away and leave them by the roadside.

Particularly heavy bombardments caused houses that had already been partially destroyed by fire to tremble. It was like being in a storm at sea. The rain was also difficult to cope with: residents of houses with damaged or destroyed roofs had to take everything that fell from the skies.

In cities that came under Russian control life was no easier. Security checks at every step in the city itself, filtration camps erected at exit points from the city, but at least you could go outside your building and walk many kilometres to get water.

The camps varied: in some people had to undress, were humiliated and put through every trick in the book, ostensibly in the name of a thorough identity check. The guards demanded that phones be unlocked and then closely examined them. Everyone was afraid of this step in the proceedings. You could never tell if you'd be considered suspicious, especially if you had contacts that were outspoken supporters of Ukraine.

Oh, my… People have always lived for the sake of aims and dreams. But now they were forced to live minute by minute and hour by hour. They felt exhausted. They had little energy – either moral or physical. They'd like to see it all end soon. And then to start their lives again… from scratch… But was that possible?

* * *

The story of Mariupol was repeating itself throughout Ukraine. The local residents had no opportunity to leave towards the Ukrainian side. In between air strikes, they had been shifted in only one direction – towards Russia. In the absence of choice, it meant coercion. After that, everyone had to go through filtration. Further on – a railway station in Rostov where they had been issued with a one-way ticket to an assigned region. People had been trying to flee from that station, go to a different one, for example, to be able to go to Taganrog, or buy tickets to Minsk and continue onwards. But they had been told: "What are you talking about? Tickets to Taganrog? Your destination is Siberia or the Far East, all according to quotas. That's the only option that's open to you…'

Mykolaiv… At night the Ruscists had aimed six missiles at the barracks of our marines. Many were killed. A young guy was shown lying in a hospital bed – both legs shattered. He was crying. Not because he was in pain – he was on pain-killing injections, but because of what had happened to his legs. He sobbed. It was impossible to watch…

The smell of war. The weather was completely still today, and so, Kyiv was enveloped in a dense smog and nauseating stench of burning. Reportedly, we now had the highest level of smog in the world. Residents were advised to keep the windows shut and, if at all possible, stay inside. The authorities explained that a rubbish dump had caught fire. Perhaps. Only one could smell fuels and lubricants. But there was burning human flesh, too. After all, there were lots of dead bodies everywhere…

M. Zakharova, Russian Foreign Affairs Ministry spokesperson: 'Our armed forces do not target civilian facilities, no matter how many photos and video clips you post.'

And again, Mykolaiv, the same hospital. The young lad with damaged legs asked a Western correspondent: 'How many more casualties and deaths would it take for you finally to *see*?'

* * *

For the life of me I couldn't follow their logic. Since you'd come here to bring us 'liberation and happiness' in the image of the 'Russian world', you should have acted in a way that would ensure respect of those you'd set out to 'liberate'. So that they would see all advantages of a life under your leadership. In other words, under no circumstances you should behave like animals!

Theoretically, during the first couple of weeks, when chaos had reigned and people couldn't work out how to survive, you should have behaved 'humanely'... Besides, at that point you had no reason to be embittered yourself.... So, even if the AFU had been pummelling you at the time, what did it have to do with the civilians?

Yet everything that had happened and continued to happen was the exact opposite. You had been bursting into people's homes, kicking the owners out, locking them up in sheds and root cellars, to keep them out of the way. And then, having 'processed' it all, and ransacked the cupboards and pots, you had to urinate in every corner, and also, leave a turd!

Although, to defecate in a corner was no great fun – good for weaklings, not ambitious enough for the 'great Russian people'. But to climb into a bed, with its snow-white sheets, in your muddy boots, and leave those blasted Ukes your excrement – that was the ticket. Good enough for the 'Russian world'!

And just before leaving, after another go around the rooms, to do something really cheeky: say, gun down a TV. Or TVs, if there was more than one.

And by way of saying goodbye, to call out to the terrified owners in their cellar:

'Hey you, down there! Hear me, bastards? Be grateful that all we did was take a shit and bang up your TVs. And didn't bump you bastards off, while at it!

Well, our heartfelt 'thank you' for leaving us alive.

Cordial thanks for the fact that practically all houses where you'd hung around were left drowning in faeces. Nearly everyone returning home testified to this with one voice. The sheets had been fouled and folded. Then fouled and folded again – a kind of a 'rolled cake' of their shit. Let those blooming Ukes sort it out for themselves!

It had been exactly the same during their notorious Chechen campaigns: afraid of stepping outside in the dark, they'd been emptying their bowels in the same 'caking' way.

And one more thing to add. Not a single Russian oligarch should receive a cent out their foreign stashes! Which applied, too, to the Russian national assets. Losses should be reimbursed! And grief and suffering should be paid for, many times over!

* * *

Wiretapping the conversations of the Russian military at various sections of the Kyiv defence bore witness to a gradual change in their morale. Erstwhile enthusiasm was giving way to disappointment and panic. Kyiv was holing up and the problems multiplied. Russia was whitewashing her losses and the offensive started crumbling.

In the course of March, the AFU launched several crushing attacks against the enemy groupings, and in some sectors had even managed to mount a counter-of-fensive. The first month of war had demonstrated how flexible the Ukrainian army was in their approach to fighting: they delivered pinpoint strikes at the principal targets, not just places of maximum agglomeration of troops. This had become possible due to modern technology and intelligence – supplied by our Western partners, advising us of the enemy's whereabouts and change of position.

Dispersal over a significant territory, separation from the logistical units and establishments, shortages of fuel, communication and ammunitions turned most of the enemy's battalion-tactical groups into convenient targets for our artillery and aviation, especially the self-piloting Bayraktars. Taking advantage of diversity in terrain and supported by intelligence, the AFU dealt crushing blows to the enemy, practically in real time, while sustaining only minimal losses. Thus, the Russians were now facing a choice: either to continue building up their presence around Kyiv – against the background of an increasing fuel and ammunition deficit, the AFU exerting pressure on the flanks while there was a lack of options for bringing in the artillery – or to withdraw.

And so, the last week of March saw a kaleidoscope of events.

March 24th. Our military rebuffed a new attack on Brovary and went on a counter-offensive. They started gradually regaining control over some localities within the district.

March 25th. The Ruscists destroyed an automobile bridge over the Desna River, thus cutting Chernihiv off from the outside world. The mayor said that in the end the city hadn't been fully encircled. By that point, half of pre-war population had left.

March 29th. Putin had unleashed the war proceeding from a catastrophic underestimation of the AFU resistance and overestimation of his own army's potential. He had quickly realised that his plans went belly up, and tried to bring the war to an end. On the other hand – and that was an open secret – from the off, some in the West had been putting pressure on Ukraine to enter into a negotiation and accept the Russian terms. The delegations of both countries had been in online communication throughout March, and on March 29th, met in Istanbul in person and held a three-hour-long round of talks. It was noteworthy that the venue for this event was now Turkey, and not Belarus.

Since the Kremlin's 'plan-maximum' – Ukraine's unconditional surrender – had become unrealistic in the first few days of war, after the attempts to capture Kyiv by storm had been frustrated. Also, it appeared that the absurd demand to 'denazify' had also been dropped.

Therefore, the Ukrainian delegation put forward this key proposal: legally viable security guarantees provided by several countries, among them the nuclear-empowered ones: the USA, China, Great Britain, Turkey, Germany, France, Canada, Italy, Poland, and Israel. However, which ones of them would agree to put their signature under the final document remained an open question. It was further suggested that the negotiations on the issue of Crimea should be held within the next 15 years and preclude the use of weapons. The issue of the occupied Donbas territories was to be singled out as an agenda for direct negotiations between Zelensky and Putin. In whatever case, Ukraine recognised its borders as those in 1991. In response, Ukraine was prepared to consider a neutral nuclear-free status, refusal to place foreign military bases on its territory, execution of training exercises without consent of guarantor states, and renunciation of its plans to accede to military-political alliances. At the same time, Ukraine was to receive guarantees of an EU membership and financial support. To be implemented, this decision would have to undergo a certain procedure: a referendum and then ratification by the guarantor states.

In her turn, Russia announced a step towards de-escalation – a radical curtailment of hostilities around Kyiv and Chernihiv. Head of the Russian delegation Medinsky: 'This is not a cease-fire but it is our desire to gradually achieve de-escalation at least in those directions.' [At the same time, there was a shared understanding that the Russians were stuck around Kyiv, their situation there evaluated as catastrophic.] Whatever the case, the Russian delegation called the negotiations 'constructive'; there was something to take back to the Kremlin.

Although for the time being it was just proposals and a stage for swapping ideas, many in Ukraine had voiced their sharp criticism. There was an immediately feedback from Blinken: 'There are things Russia says and things that Russia does. We focus on the latter.' According to him, there were no signs that Russia meant to conduct peace negotiations in earnest, and not to use the occasion to mislead everyone.

March 30th. The RF Defence Ministry announced that they 'had fulfilled all their tasks on the routes leading to Kyiv and Chernihiv and were now engaging in a planned regrouping.' The Ukrainian leadership, along with the partner countries, accepted the report sceptically. Moreover, the very same day the Russians promised to stop shelling Chernihiv but resumed bombing within several hours.

March 31st. The Ukrainian army regained the Chernihiv-Kyiv Motorway, thus putting an end to the siege of the city. The Mayor of Chernihiv declared that it was the first quiet night since the start of hostilities. On the same day the AFU took Irpin. Yet the neighbouring towns of Vorzel, Bucha and Hostomel remained under the enemy control and constant air strikes.

And still, news came from everywhere – the Russian troops had really started to pull back quoting a 'planned relocation towards the route to Donetsk'. All those goings-on were craftily termed by the Russians as a 'good-will gesture'!

And so, as if by magic, the Kremlin lot changed their tune: only a few days previously, Peskov – Putin's 'talking head' – had been complaining that not all aims had been 'achieved', that it was necessary to 'continue working'…

Yet now – lo and behold: they sent an urgent message: 'We've reached our main goals! From now on we concentrate our efforts on the liberation of Donbas!' Translated into a plain language: 'We've had enough, fighting near Kyiv. We are withdrawing back. But our colours fly high and nothing is over yet!'

My, oh my! It was already clear that things in Donbas would blow up to a new high. Most likely, the whole thing would burst up in a matter of days…

For Kyiv, those thirty-six days – from February 24th to March 31st of the year 2022, had been the days of borderline uncertainty. And every one of them had been scary, from the first to the last…

Yet for Putin, this withdrawal from our city had become his most shameful mistake in 22 years of his rule, the one resonating on the international arena. Generally speaking, this invasion of his had really gone belly up. To top it all, a new situation had emerged, the one altering the entire security architecture in Europe and setting it against Moscow, isolated Russia to a level unheard-off since the days of the Cold War. To the amazement of the whole world, an attempt on the Ukrainian capital culminated in a humiliating retreat. To add insult to injury, it had exposed inherent systematic problems within the Russian army – after all, billions had been spent on its 'modernisation'!

Obviously, God had sided with Kyiv. Lots of things had happened, many of them quite miraculous: the airports had never been converted into landing bases; the blitzkrieg had been thwarted. The multi-kilometre-long column got stuck on the approaches to Kyiv. Just one Ukrainian tank brigade had proved able to block a 30-thousand-strong Russian grouping advancing on Kyiv from the direction of Chernihiv. On top of it all, in the course of the battle for Kyiv our military had captured 1,300 tanks, armoured vehicles and lorries. All of it would now benefit the AFU.

Thus, in March of 2022, the Russian plans of rapidly conquering Ukraine bit the dust. However, the danger had been real. Later, the president would say: 'We were in an extremely difficult situation, we were practically occupied – at least in the central areas our country's logistics, roads, railways, food deliveries – we were totally blockaded…'

April 2022 – Irpin, Bucha, Borodyanka, Hostomel… A Massacre…

'Carve Our Red Stars on the Backs of those Uke Brats!'

On March 31st, Kyiv's suburb Bucha was liberated – its streets lined with scores of dead bodies; hundreds of mutilated cars riddled with bullets; tens of wrecked tanks and APCs. Our innocent people, murdered – piles of weapons scattered everywhere: along the roads, on pavements, and near building sites. Everything scorched, shattered, blown into smithereens…

No people anywhere, just corpses, corpses, corpses… The bodies of those who had died.

Survivors started crawling out of their basements, confused – who had entered the town? Could it be ours? They just couldn't comprehend any of it. Why was it so quiet, why no gunshots? Why was it so different compared to the previous four weeks? God Almighty, what was all of this?

Meanwhile our military moved on, bypassing the burnt and demolished houses. Or rather, their foundations. Although, as it turned out, people had lived there too. Then a courtyard – and in it, a row of graves. Further on – more dead bodies, thrown all over. The lucky ones had been buried in shallow graves, hastily dug up, and covered with loose soil. At least, they would have had a Christian send-off. The unfortunate ones simply lay around.

Bucha was essentially no more – high-rises in ruins, private houses burnt to the ground. Horror! And again, and again – remains of those who had never been buried.

This sickening footage was transmitted for the whole world to see.

Only now, when the occupiers had left Kyiv Oblast, the full horrible picture emerged. Kyiv's suburbs – Irpin, Bucha, Vorzel, Borodyanka, Hostomel – had borne the brunt of the capital's defence. It would not be an exaggeration to admit that Kyiv had been saved at the expense of its perished outskirts and suburbs.

But now, those who'd survived could narrate their experiences.

They had spent an entire month in basements and cellars with no food, light, or heating. A sortie into one's courtyard meant a bullet in the back of one's head.

Women had been raped in front of their children's eyes, young girls – with the family made to watch. A well-tested practice, this, a weapon against civilians, a deliberate act of subjugation.

The residents of liberated towns and settlements told that the first Russians to have appeared were the air assault forces: 'They were extremely cruel, drove everyone outside into the street and ordered to hand over their keys – keys to people's homes and cars, as well as mobiles and money. The occupiers pocketed the lot. Anybody trying to resist got shot. The remaining residents were forced into basements while the Russians moved into their houses and flats. Then this lot was transferred somewhere, to be replaced by some normal guys. All they did was drive around in tanks and shoot. They were young, with only fluff on the upper lips. Lots of them had Asiatic eyes...'

Christ in heaven! What an evolution of the word 'normal'! 'Normal' now meant tearing about in a tank and shooting...

As for those ones, the ones with the 'Asiatic eyes', that had been the bunker strategist's cunning plan: to conquer Ukraine by using small ethnic groups – Buryats, Daghestanis, Tuvans, whatever... True, in the early days of the invasion there had been lots of them around. So that the vicious old man had surmised: if there had to be losses, let it be those, the ones with Asiatic eyes! Seeing as they were expendable. And only later, when the blitzkrieg had gone pear-shaped and they had to call a mobilisation, they'd started sending more of the 'great Russian people' to slaughter. For all that, the 'preference' was still given to those coming from distant and depressed regions. On the other hand, all things considered – that had been their lucky chance to make some money, and with the proceeds, buy a wife or a girlfriend a fur coat. And if, God forbid, that Ukraine would cost them their lives, their families would still benefit by being able to afford an inexpensive car from China. So, say what you like but this very 'special operation' did have its advantages. It wasn't all that bad, after all.

A man had been executed here. And the spot nearby had been selected as a place for the Russian soldiery to hang out – so handy, seeing as there were some benches, too. Better than having to trudge elsewhere. Faceted glasses at the ready, one only had to remove the cap off a bottle with booze, open the tins, carve the sausage. All of it looted from a shop nearby. The place to celebrate, here and now. Also, a place to brag before each other about who had done in more Ukes ...

They had shot down a dog. Not in one go, but eventually they'd managed. Somehow, it hadn't felt enough: they had doused it in petrol and set on fire.

With blunt indifference, they'd been shooting at targets and elsewhere, just for the fun of it as they'd finally managed to get their hands on some weapons. The bliss of a total anarchy! Back home in Russia no one could squeak without leave, each cog being firmly tightened into its place. Whereas here they'd had a field day. Make merry, bros, with this fucking 'free Ukraine of theirs!' Our feral amusements had been pardoned in advance! Who would miss a chance like that? Only a total idiot…

A dead woman near her reversed bicycle. Iryna Fylkyna was an employee of Epicenter company. She was identified after a photo of her hand with bright red nail polish was published by the Reuters agency. At least 15 bullets were fired into it. This photo made rounds in the world press. She was 52 years old. Her stylist recognised her by this manicure – Irina had been taking lessons in the art of make-up, planned to attend the concert of a Ukrainian singer. The last class had taken place on February 23rd. She had said then: 'I've realised the main thing – you've got to love yourself and live for yourself. Finally, I will live as I want!'

Irina had never managed to start this new life of hers…

For a month, twenty-five young women and girls had been kept in the same cellar, routinely gang-raped – the whole thing being put on an industrial footing. Nine of the victims ended up pregnant.

The Kremlin's response to goings-on in Bucha was crafty – what else could it be? *'It's all stage-managed by the English! If anyone knows how to do this, they do. And those ones… the Ukrainians… have joined in, too. It's all lies! Disinformation! They have launched against us this attack of fake info! Russia's got nothing to do with any of this…'; 'Bucha is a mass-scale production in the best traditions of Hollywood!'; 'Dead bodies in the streets? What dead bodies? Those are not dead bodies but Ukrainian actors, dressed accordingly and wearing stage make-up!'*

'We've never even been there!' – for some reason, they'd omitted this signature phrase.[324]

....

[324] **"We were not there"** or "they're not there": a Russian-language Internet meme reflecting Russia's constant denial of its military presence in hybrid wars in one country or another – above all, on the territory of Ukraine, starting in 2014 (the year in which Crimea was annexed and military action was taken in Donbass as part of the undeclared Russian-Ukrainian war). The term has gained great popularity and is now a common name for Russian military personnel without insignia who take part in military actions abroad.

They lied cynically and glibly. So, did it follow that Ukraine had executed its own citizens? Tied up their hands and shot them in the back of their heads?

All that had happened in Bucha could only be summed up thus: 'a complete massacre'.

The situation in the countryside hadn't been any better. They had stationed their cannons in people's courtyards to take aim at Kyiv, having locked up the owners in their own cellars.

A woman had been forced out of the cellar:

'*On your knees, bitch!*'

A second-long discomfiture.

'*On your knees, or we'll throw a grenade into your cellar!*'

But down there had been the children. She dropped down, genuflecting.

'*Ask Russia for forgiveness, you fucking whore! Plead the great Russian people for forgiveness, you piece of shit!*'

Children in the cellar, a Russian soldier in front of her – a grenade in his hand, she, standing on her knees, realised that it hadn't been such a big deal – to "apologise".

'*Forgive me... Forgive me, Russia!*'

'*And the people... Ask the great people too!*'

'*Forgive me, the great Russian people!*'

She had knelt, entreating that she should be forgiven by Russia, and the 'great Russian people'...

The soldiering scum had kept their word – had never thrown that grenade. And then left. And the children in the cellar had stayed alive...

Talking about children – those were excerpts from wiretapped mobile conversations. An occupier's wife had told him that she had a burning desire to 'carve our glorious red stars on the backs of those Nazi sons of Uke whores!' In other words, the children. She was 30, working in a Russian children's hospital.

In another conversation she'd professed her hatred of the Ukrainian children. 'They all are tiny Nazis! I'm ready to machine-gun the lot. Why on earth Putin keeps inviting them all over: "Do come to Russia, do!" Those half-wits. It would be good to go and kill them all, while you're in that Ukraine of theirs. I'd be happy to inject them with drugs, the sleazebags, looking into their eyes and repeating: "Perish, you fuckers!" I'd even cut off their tiny todgers! And each day – an ear or a finger – to make them suffer, the fuckers...'

This guy, visibly scared, had accidentally bumped into a Ruscist patrol.

They yelled:

'*Wha'? Wonna live? Fuck out of here, you scumbag! In double-bloody-time!*'

He'd started running, and sounds of gunshots rang out in his wake: bullets sent through his head, his back…

They hadn't allowed the dead to be buried. The fallen had become prey for stray dogs …

And thus they'd lived till March 31st when the invaders started withdrawing from the Kyiv area. Those located in the north headed for Belarus. Those in the east set off to Sumy Oblast via Chernihiv, then onwards. After all, a new priority had been announced – a 'complete liberation of Donbas'!

The Ruscists had pulled back from other suburbs too. Same as in Bucha – tens of corpses in the streets, some of them – with tied-up hands. Some of them teenagers…

There were people with their limbs chopped off; some had been shot in the back of their heads. All over the place – maimed and brutalised cars. Next to a sign saying 'Children' – lots of bullet holes.

So, that was what a mass-scale genocide looked like. Each day, more and more bodies of tortured and killed civilians were uncovered on the liberated territories: strangled, raped, and immolated… And lots of them had their hands tied…

Mass graves were a separate story. Lots of bodies had been simply hurriedly shoved inside, for lack of body bags… Hundreds of people had been buried this way.

* * *

Mum switched off the TV and buried her face in her hands, shoulders shaking, her body racked by sobs.

'Bucha… Mariupol… Borodyanka… Kharkiv… Children… Killed, raped, wounded… A slaughter… A bloody pulp… But they did live before! In their houses and flats! Had plans for the future… Their eyes sparkled with joy! And now none of this will ever come true. I'm looking into myself, deep into my soul, and all I can see is an abyss, a black hole. But this isn't the end, I'm sure… There will be scores of other towns and villages. I don't know how to live with this…'

'Mum, stop watching! You're killing yourself…'

'How can I not watch? *Those are our people*! They're ours!'

'Still, don't.'

'But I will! I want to remember it all!'

We switched the TV on, regardless. On the screen, there was a boy, at a railway station, crying. He couldn't work out what had happened to his mum

and dad. Some guy was trying to placate him: they would turn up, don't worry!
A woman came closer and whispered into his ear: 'The little one doesn't know
yet, but his parents are no more.'

The boy continued crying, as yet unaware that he was now an orphan…

At that point debates flared up on whether or not it was genocide. And here
Macron, who from the early days of tensions and the outbreak of war had
been trying to play a role of a peacemaker, excelled himself, yet again. Sure
thing, he pointed out that 'the situation was unacceptable and what was going
on amounted to war crimes on a scale unprecedented in our European home',
yet he kept pushing forth a message about 'fraternal peoples'. But if one 'fraternal nation' committed such atrocities against the other one, at the very least
it would seem indecent if one continued harping on like this. A definition
of 'fraternity' simply did not fit the *status quo*. As for Ukrainians, such pronouncements caused not only bewilderment but a very understandable sense
of outrage.

My Lord, where were they now, all those European intellectuals who had
been always giving it large on the subject of the 'great Russian culture'? In which
dens were they hiding, waiting till the whole thing had blown over?

One could use any term one liked – genocide, ethnocide, something else.
Whatever the name, it was a 'new Srebrenica'. In the year two thousand and
twenty-two. In Ukraine. Instigated by the Russian Federation and its 'great
people'.

How sickening it was to hear the tired old arguments: 'The Russian people
are not to blame! It's all Putin! This is only his war!' 'And you and Russia – don't
you know? – are fraternal peoples!'

Fuckwits, the lot of them! Of the worst kind!

Poor ducklings, those European politicians! 'Unable' to comprehend that
it wasn't just Putin at the core of it all. Things were much deeper and more
hideous. What had emerged in Russia was genuine fascism. Of a Russian variety. And anybody more or less capable of thinking for themselves would name
Russia a rogue country. The worst criminal in the world.

Would the massacre in Bucha force the West to reconsider their worldview?
What had been viewed, from the times immemorial, as dreadful, and horrible
in all wars, had now emerged as hundred times more dreadful and horrible.

A Surviving Empire

My writing pad was filling up, bulking out with notes and various inserts.
Also, the abundance of thoughts, some contradictory or even counterintuitive.

Sooner or later, I would have to sort it all out, analyse in detail. Clearly, no time for that now, only for jotting down things that came to mind and were useful or interesting. Like this, for example:

'Back in the 19ᵗʰ century emerged this idea of a "Russia's special path". After all, this is a country that combines the traits of East and West, and is "absolutely unique" in culture and spirituality. This idea of "specialness" allegedly entitles it to a special place in the world as well as special rights. Therefore, those who live in Russia are above everyone else because of their "special mission". And it's only natural that they feel a need to interfere here and there, just not in their own country.

'The Russian Empire wasn't a standard case – externally, many of its characteristics seemed European, yet it largely possessed an Asian mentality while propped up by the Orthodox faith. Russia spreads over two continents and, unlike most erstwhile moderately-sized European empires with colonies overseas, concentrates a huge contiguous territory. In other words, it's landlocked, and the borderline between the centre and the peripheries has been stretched out and indistinct – that's one of its peculiarities. This is, by the way, the reason it has survived while all the others have fallen apart. It may go on for some time yet – who can tell?

'Their imperial mission statement boils down to this – "Russia should have no boundaries". Basically, it's nothing new. In essence, it's a textbook definition of an empire, for they don't recognise borders. "Where we've managed to get to, is ours. Where we haven't got to yet, is yours. When we get there, you will have to leave. It will be ours. But if you stay, you will be under us."

Nowadays this formula has been practically legalised. Today, Russia's overall strategy goes thus: we bite off a mouthful and then recognise its legitimacy and independent status. Based on this recognition of this new territory's legitimacy and independence, we can move on and usurp something else and incorporate that new territory too.

'For Russians, Ukraine has always been a pleasing and coveted country. For them it was south – a different type of climate, warm conditions, fertile soils… And lots of other advantages into the bargain.

'It has so happened that several million ethnic Russians now live in Ukraine. They are all different. Among them are those whose houses and flats have been destroyed by the Ruscists yet they whole-heartedly support Russia. They are brimming with this imperial grandeur and hauteur, for they are – in their own estimation – the best. So much they have conquered! And this virus is devouring them. Those are the people who for decades have been brainwashed by various "Russian ideas". Allegedly, they are representatives of a 'Chosen people who will bring the Light of Truth into the whole world.'

'All this hallucinating nonsense first spouted by philosophers and writers in the 19th century should long since have been deposited in a dustbin of history. It's so clearly blown out of any proportion… Russia should've clung to a really genuine idea – to provide a long-awaited prosperity to the nation residing in the world's richest country in terms of its natural resources. So that it became a huge new Norway, nothing less. That would be a worthy purpose! Not this hazardous rubbish.

'It will take decades, if not centuries, for all of this to evaporate. Thank God, Russians like this in Ukraine were in the minority, and now there are even fewer of them left. Thing is, as the Russian troops were pulling out from the occupied territories, some of those die-hard Russians left in their wake. Reportedly, when the Russian units retreated from the right-bank Kherson Oblast, they had been followed by over a hundred thousand people. Hard to say whether this figure is correct. It will be corroborated later.

For all of that, most Russians consider themselves citizens of Ukraine and support its sovereignty.

Then this, too. I've come across it by chance.

A blogger writes: "There's more than a million Russians in Germany. Which percentage among them share the Kremlin principle: where there're Russians, it's Russland!"

And another blogger: 'Lyonia Brezhnev had been building this (relations with Germany and Europe on the whole) for twenty years, while Vova Putin has ruined it all in six months"!'

We spent a long time today debating the subject of the Russian culture with the choir guys. From time to time, I kept popping out – round the corner, or to our staff quarters. I used all sorts of pretexts but what I really did was enter their contemplations into my pad. As usual, I wasn't all that keen for anyone to spot me doing it. So, I wrote:

'I believe that this war is a crushing blow to their worldview and the Russian language. A catastrophic one – like an atom bomb dropped onto the Russian culture as a whole, because the most important is this: their "lofty and advanced" culture has failed to raise people of integrity. And we've seen other Russians: aggressive, wicked, despicable. Execution basements in Bucha – that definitely hadn't been the people of a great culture.

'Nowadays one can frequently hear the Russian culture being called impe-rial – through and through… It has injected its population with slavish men-tality, which it then continued to nurture.

'It's true, the Russian culture has a significant imperial component, and now it's time to see through it. The history teaches that the best time to analyse reasons for an empire's collapse is the actual time of such a collapse. But does the "imperial element" apply to the Russian culture in its entirety? After all, the body of work produced by this or that author may not give us a whole story. May we look for imperial ideas in the work of this or that author? We may and we should. But at the same time is it a good idea to necessarily accept or reject this author's entire output?

'A culture is never a sum of its imperial ideas. Say, the German imperialism wasn't the sum total of the entire German culture. Or, the British imperialism wasn't equal to the British culture. It's there, you can trace its influence but it does not disqualify the British culture as such, neither does it negate this culture's important contribution towards global achievements.

'Most likely, this is what is going to happen to the Russian culture. The most shameful features will drop off. The most important ones will remain: Tolstoy, Chekhov, Tchaikovsky – they are here to stay. But it's not for here and now. The time is wrong. The degree of rancour against "them and theirs" is too high. It's off the radar screen.'

I had to make a note about this one as well:

'It's being said they've stolen a lot from us and go on stealing. Say, they are trying to appropriate the Kyivan Rus. In principle, small wonder. What sort of an empire wouldn't try to appropriate the best?'

Also, this.

'The contemporary Russian authorities have managed to desecrate all important values: "president", "parliament", "freedom", "democracy"… Also – "Motherland". To say nothing about "patriot" or "fascist". Their dirty hands have touched everything, they've befouled it all…'

And this, about various spurious theories. Although, I think I had already written about it…

'Philosophers and writers have invented all types of drivel, like – "the Russians are the Chosen people". All this is tightly wedged into their heads. You bet – they are special! And the rest of the world treats them as common sort. For them, it's a source of profound annoyance. Even enragement…'

It was worth mentioning too that the world was clearly splitting. I found this on socials: 'The whole, as they say, "civilised" world supports Ukraine. But what about India with its population of a billion and a half? Similar numbers in China. There soon will be half a billion Arabs? OK, the Chinese and the Arabs have their own specific agenda. But India, who proudly calls itself "the largest democracy in the world"? So now, when the Russians commit atrocities, the Indians find it hard to "disengage" themselves from Russia…'

* * *

The suburbs had been liberated but remained dangerous to return to – the land-clearing and demining were still underway. Before pulling back, the Ruscists had mined even the dead bodies.

The liberated outskirts started receiving aid from all over. Yet the mayors there pleaded: 'Don't send us any children's food. All children have been killed.'

April 1st. President of the European Parliament Roberta Metsola arrived in Kyiv. She later called Stefanchuk and said: 'As I was leaving Ukraine, I felt ten years older...'

So, what it was all about – this Russia? Could it really be a country so savage, blinkered, and browbeaten? Was her entire population really completely zombified? Ready to be rejected by the global trend for years, decades and centuries to come?

While Moscow propaganda gurus kept foaming at the mouth about the Hollywood fakes – allegedly staged by the Brits and using Ukrainian actors – Bucha stayed on everyone's lips, not just here but all over the world. But Bucha wasn't the only place. The same had happened in Vorzel, Borodyanka, Hostomel... There were lots of such 'buchas'...

Significantly – not only around Kyiv but in other areas, the situation was similar. One of local dignitaries wrote: 'This was where the people fell sick and died. The live ones had to stay cheek-by-jowl with the dead. Hunger. Thirst. Fear. Pain. Despair. Toilet – over a bucket. Stuffy heat. Women and children. Whatever happens after that, the enemy must be called to account.'

Even by this point, thousands of residential and public houses had been damaged or destroyed. How many more would there be in a week? In a month? In a year or more?

It had been impossible to take the dead ones over to the cemetery, so they had been buried in courtyards. Emerging out of their house entrances, the people would see the graves of their dear ones. Or their neighbours...

Even if those houses were rebuilt and made suitable for living, would the residents still have to look at the graves, for the time to come?

* * *

Taras and me were getting ready to leave our defence post when we overheard the Commander tell Gennady:

'What a dangerous "neighbour" we've got there! Our children and grandchildren must learn this home truth from the off. But listen to what I've got to say about Lukashenko! Putin is talking him into launching a strike in the Lutsk-Lviv direction. It would cut off deliveries of weaponry from the West.

But Belarusian military aren't burning with a desire to get involved in a war like this. And the population is mostly unsupportive of this hypothetical incursion. So, yesterday this crafty Luka came in with another portion of his "musings": "Anything that Belarus could and has to offer to Russia had already been done. Thus, we have no need whatsoever to take part in this special operation." When he said "anything", he meant the territory and the infrastructure already made available to Putin. To paraphrase: you've made your bed, now lie in it...'

Back home mum was watching TV where an analyst was explaining what Europe and the USA had done and what they hadn't.

'Europe... USA...' Mum flung her hands up in desperation. 'My word, I'd show 'em...'

'Mum...'

'Don't defend them!' Mum yelled. 'They do nothing!'

'How d'ya mean – nothing? But for their aid...'

'Too little too late! Don't you dare argue with me! If they did the right thing, none of this would've happened.'

'But...'

'But what? No tanks, no aircraft... No long-range artillery either, to say nothing of multiple rocket launchers. It's a crying need, it is, but they give us nothing! And in general, the USA have chosen a good strategy – a strategy whereby they exhaust Russia. And since it's a long shot, what if the war were to drag on forever? And while it's all going on, Russia is annihilating everything here – the cities, the infrastructure! Can't you see it for yourself?'

'That's true. Still, they're helping us...'

'Just look at those sly foxes! We know what they're after! We should become this sanitary cordon between the snow-white Europe and a crazily unpredictable Russia! The only one responding adequately is Great Britain and its Boris Johnson!' Mum was flying off the handle again. 'And stop arguing! You hear me?!'

Ah well, being ordered around like this in my own home...

* * *

The following day I returned to our roadblock and retold the Commander my mum's lamentations about the insufficient aid from our partners.

'I know,' he nodded. 'Our position is crystal clear: "Give us what we need, we'll do the rest ourselves..." But for now, they won't. Or we receive something with a great lag. Putin's regime has been nurtured by Western politicians who, for years, have been consistently ignoring Ukraine's cries for help. What is there to say on this subject? They are so smart and pragmatic... perhaps too much so. This pragmatism is now coming back to bite us. Them too, by the way...'

I kept reasoning with myself. According to our Western partners, in the aftermath of 2014, the main thing was not to provoke the Russians even more. So that the Russians wouldn't 'take umbrage and see red.' They've grabbed something in the South? Infrastructure is going to the dogs? People are dying? Well, a war is a war – casualties happen. Most important is that they shouldn't go too far...

But 'go too far' was exactly what they'd done, and the whole world witnessed thousands of victims – raped, tied-up, killed and dumped into mass graves. Killed with inhuman bestiality.

There were those 'analysts' who kept insisting: 'It's an inherent feature in all democracies. The task is to avoid escalation. But if something does happen, don't rush into anything. Especially if a war is already raging on – in the times of war, politicians act extremely slowly and are late to wake up.'

Sure thing. Putin had attacked Ukraine not because of the 'imagined Nazis'. The real danger had been that Ukraine's successful ability to resist dictatorship. To him, Ukraine had become a most threatening precedent. That was why it all required a 'radical' resolution. Also, an apt opportunity to maul off a piece of territory and thus enlarge the empire even more! His programme maximum would have been to completely pull out this vexing thorn from his flesh and annex the lot. OK, perhaps offer some leftovers to the neighbouring countries – at least trying to give it a lick of respectability. Oh, and also, smear some dirt on them too, if they ever agreed to this underhand proposal.

* * *

I suddenly became aware that increasingly often, deep inside me, rang out the Ukraine's national anthem. I wanted to mull it over properly and perhaps make a note but there was a call from Pyvynsky. He went like a machine-gun:

'How's it going? Mum? Your gang? Quite a hotspot, this city of yours was! They are getting closer to here, too, this halcyon Myrhorod land of ours. Took to bombing us... But our guys are fighting them right back! Serves them right, the bastards! And this negotiation – any thoughts?'

But not waiting for an answer, he offered his own analysis straight away:

'As for me, I never believed it, not for a second, that it'd do any good. They never abide by any agreements. Never! If it's in their interests, they'll scratch your eyes out and insist on strictest adherence, to the last comma. But if not, they simply won't do it. Woodenly ignore the whole thing, not to be barged with a tank. Such a unilateral "commitment".'

'How true. It's enough to remember…'

'… that "famed" Budapest memorandum where we'd been promised all sorts of guarantees. They've scrapped it without batting an eyelid.'

'And the so-called "Magnum Treaty"?'

"'On Friendships, Cooperation and Partnership between the RF and Ukraine"? The one of 1997? Didn't miss a beat either. I said it already – they never deliver on promises. And that's all there is to it. I've got to go, here's Vasyli Mykolayovych.'

'Hi there, hi!' Yanovsky talked nineteen to the dozen. 'I've only got one question. Tell me this – after all you, over there, live in a metropolis, the newest ideas and the like. So, tell me – what's gonna happen to Ukraine?'

The suddenness of the question left me nonplussed. True, I did live in the capital city, but I hadn't held a candle to Pechersk Hills (meaning: I had no access to top-secret information).[325]

And suddenly it all started pouring forth.

'It is right here that history is being made! And if that's so, we shall have a bright future!'

'Bah… Don't you feed me all this "propaganda". We here aren't against enthusiasm but pray, stick to specifics. Are there plans now to make us sort of neutral? Outside of NATO?'

'A good question. I don't know exactly what the thoughts are at the very top, but whomever I talk to, all believe that eventually Ukraine will be a fully-fledged part of the Western world. It must join the EU. NATO, too… They say that neutrality won't save us, it'll only enrage the "bear" even more…'

'There you go! Say to those wise people that I'd be happy to shake their hands. And generally speaking, pass on a heartfelt hello from our Myrhorod country!'

* * *

Life in Kyiv was gradually picking up. Groceries started appearing in shops: I dropped into Silpo – lots of dairy products, I counted nearly 20 lines! I continued to the butchery – meat was now available! Not a huge choice, but still, available, for the first time in many weeks!..

Even if the counters started filling up, still, the sirens kept wailing, perhaps not so frequently. As if the enemy was sending a message across: 'I'm here! Close

---

[325]   Pechersk: the district where all Ukraine's governing structures are concentrated; situated on the Right bank of the Dnipro.–

by! In the Belarusian forests… I'm lying in wait, rocket complexes and all, and am watching. Tee-hee, you, Ukes, it's too early to relax!'

Something else occurred to me… Of course, those spared the atrocities had been in luck – despite all tribulations and suffering, constant anxiety, and stress – physical, psychological, moral. Yet compared to the experience of those who had come face-to-face with those indescribable horrors, all of it was a mere trifle.

* * *

The city's main method of transportation, the metro, mercifully continued operating, although still on a reduced schedule. I didn't know about other directions, but, as earlier, one and only train was running on the only track on the Blue Line at 40-minute intervals, shuttling between the terminuses. Yet, amazingly, this one and only train somehow was coping.

The carriages packed to a bursting point and the two principal interchange stations – Khreschatyk and Maidan of Independence – closed down, it was grossly inconvenient. Lots of people would get off at Lev Tolstoy Square station[326] (Blue Line), climb uphill towards Pushkinskaya Street[327] and then walk towards Teatralna station (Red Line). That was the new way for changing to other destinations. My friend explained: 'Sometimes you wait for a train for 40 minutes at Kontraktova Square station, then race along Pushkinskaya towards that Teatralna station, then wait for another 40 minutes. And on the way back, it's the same thing in reverse. Thus, a trivial trip may easily take at least half a day.'

But that was how the cookie crumbled: the principal load now fell on the junction between Lev Tolstoy Square and Palace of Sports stations.

I hadn't used the metro for quite some time – there'd been no need. And then a need appeared – I had to make a delivery to our distant relatives. So, passport at the ready, I entered Kontraktova Square station. Police ran security checks – the passport photo compared with my phiz in real life, contents of both bags emptied on the table, searched and then politely repacked.

I descended to the platform by an escalator, then stood, waiting, in a sea of people, all eager to board the train. So, I, too, got ready for action.

Finally, a rumbling sound came from inside the tunnel, the train whistled, shunted towards the platform, and stopped. I barely managed to squeeze into

---

[326]   In March 2023, the square and the Metro station were renamed to Square of Ukrainian Heroes, commemorating the defenders of Ukraine

[327]   In October 2022, the street was renamed to Yevhen Chykalenko street, the patron of arts and a prominent figure in the Ukrainian national revival in the early 20th century

a carriage, my progress impeded by the two bulky bags. I felt irritated glances of fellow passengers for whom, momentarily, I became worse than a Russian. But I had it tough too, since I could barely breeze in and out. Somehow, I piled my bags one on top of the other and poised myself above.

We finally made it to Tolstoy Square station, I was propelled out of the carriage and pushed to one side. Around me, everyone was rushing forward, swept up in this collective frenzy. Lost for a second, I suddenly realised: 'Our people are nobody's fools! Absolutely! If they bolt off in this way, there must be a reason!' Scooping up my bags, I ran after the crowd towards Palace of Sports station.

Already on the trot, I twigged yet another thing: it wasn't enough just to run, one had to give it one's all. So, what if you wore winter boots, and heavy winter clothes, and were weighed down with those bags…

I was out of breath, but I made it. No sooner did I pop out onto the platform, when the train pulled in. But for this hurdle race, I would've missed it. And would've had to waste another 40 minutes, waiting.

Thus, I learnt how to use the Metro under the conditions of war. If ever I had to do it again, those would be the ground rules: once your train had arrived at a junction, rush forward like a man possessed, since you could never be sure of what and when should be arriving at the station you were headed to.

The Metro personnel put out the train schedule only later, enabling the people to plan their journeys, if only approximately. Why they hadn't done straight away was a mystery…

* * *

OK, the first shock has passed: the government is gradually returning to the usual form of work – what is called 'offline'. Another interesting thing. In early April there appeared rumours calling Zelensky somewhat naïve, because even if fully aware of what had taken place in the occupied suburbs of Kyiv, he still believed that one could reach an understanding with Putin. However, after British Prime Minister Boris Johnson unexpectedly dropped into Kyiv on April 11th, a new round of gossip emerged: there would be no appeasement. Which, allegedly, had already been agreed with Washington. Was it really true? Who could tell?

We had our own news. On April 14th, the 50th day of the war, NSDC secretary Danilov shed some light on the most recent developments. 'We were aware of what was going to happen. Moreover, the planned date for invasion was not the 24th but the 22nd. They had intended to attack our country on the 22nd. The only thing we hadn't expected was the involvement of Belarus in all of this. There had been debates, but eventually we had decided it would happen in a different way. [Why, then, had the Russians been putting together such a spearhead? Building pontoons over the Prypiat six kilometres from the Ukrainian border?] So, what happened happened. But it's completely wrong to blame us for lack of preparations. We couldn't come out and make a public announcement like this: "Dear friends, on February 22nd a war will break out!" From the point of view of state governance, that would have been unacceptable. But we were readying ourselves…'[328]

He also mentioned that Western intelligence services had forecast that at best Ukraine would survive the Russian attack for 21 days.

Well, he did elucidate certain things for the benefit of the country. Yet Taras and I had been aware of all this much earlier – thanks to his chatroom.

* * *

I liked early spring that year, so unhurried and gradual. The temperature kept crawling up but there weren't any hikes. And no cold winter snaps either. Everything green was coming back to life but not instantaneously, as could happen during sudden warming. And thus, it was possible to observe rejuvenation of this sea of green over a certain period of time.

The joy of it all! Buds were swelling on trees and were ready to burst on the bushes. The impatient lilac had already put forth tiny blossoms – small but pert and proud. Flowerbeds and lawns were equally interesting to watch: the grass breaking free from the soil, springing upwards, while the first tiny sprouts of irises must be already up to 10-15 centimetres high!

Everything was waking up from winter hibernation, hungry for a new start. People wanted the same, too: peace, a quiet life… Like the one we'd had before…

But in the first days of April Europe was swept over by some powerful Arctic winds. They had reached us, too. The temperature dropped to a level below that in late March. The city's recent spring rejuvenation that had been a joy to behold now froze, arrested. Of course, everyone was gagging for warmth, hoping it would come soon. As for me, I never liked things developing in a rush, say, when trees end up totally covered with a new foliage within a week. It was so much better when nature followed an unenforced steady course…

....

[328]   UP, 14 April 2022, https://www.pravda.com.ua/news/2022/04/14/7339607/ (accessed 04.07.2025).

A new ritual had emerged with me: every evening, to pull the curtains apart, if only briefly, and look at the house across the road. Not much changed there – still only few windows lit up. Those that had been dark stayed dark. For all that, people started coming back, you could see it in the streets. Except where we lived, hardly anybody had returned. Quite a paradox, really.

Now I was making entries into my pad regularly. I remembered well the days of peace when I had been so keen to write a script properly attuned to our times, or even exclusively about here and now. By now, though, I had too much of a good thing. Way too much…

I made some notes on the forecasts about the end of the war, of which there was a multitude. Everybody tried to promote their own theory but Zelensky warned: 'Russia has entered a second phase of her operational activity in Ukraine's east – the battle of Donbas. It will be a full-scale operation, bigger in its scope than anything we've seen so far. The crucial factor for us is to hold the line.'

Another news of paramount importance, potentially capable to make an impact on the current developments. By about the end of April the West had started altering its attitude. Where previously they had believed that yes, pressure on Russia would be advisable but should not be too painful – so as not to rock the boat, now the Western approach had changed radically. By now the stakes had been placed on the victory by Ukraine. It was no longer acceptable to them to see Ukraine lose, since it would have simultaneously signalled their own failure. So, the new narrative went thus: we want to see Russia *weakened*. So much so that she would *never* be able to do anything similar.

Allegedly, this new Western vector marked a comprehensive rethinking of our strategy in the war with Russia. OK, we would wait and see.

* * *

A proper debate erupted at our defence post today.

'Tell me, what have we achieved with staying on duty at this roadblock?' Denis grimaced sceptically. 'The Russians have rolled back and we haven't detained a single terrorist. And on the whole, we've done nothing spectacular.'

'Come on, what's all this?' the bespectacled Gennady perked up. 'But how's about all those many suspicious types? Only we don't know what happened to them afterwards. We passed them all to the police. It was them checking them out and identifying who was who.'

'OK, I'll give you that. But still, not a single real terrorist!'

'What are on about?' The very thought made me dizzy. 'That we shouldn't have, as they say, even harnessed our horses?'

'Dunno, perhaps not. Anyway, maybe it's time for us to disperse?'

'You in your right mind, guys? Lost your marbles?' The Commander materialised from somewhere – how had we missed him? 'What a miserable way to think! What do you mean – we shouldn't have? If all thought like that there wouldn't have been a single roadblock or defence post in the city! But instead, we've got lots of them! And that's been proof of our might!'

He even wagged his finger forbiddingly.

'Stop this at once. It's an order. And don't even think of dispersing. Don't you read the news? Unaware of the continued threat? Haven't twigged that they are already planning a new attack on Kyiv? So cut this idle chat. Completely!'

The Commander stepped away, but Denis put his finger to his lips and whispered:

'Let me read you something from Arestovych. "Had the Ukrainians been warned that the RF was going to invade, it would've created a mass exodus of refugees. Ten or twelve million people would have completely paralysed the roads, thus blocking access for the army. (It would've been) a very desirable situation for Russia. In such circumstances, we would've lost the war and the Left Bank. The residents on the left bank would've headed towards the Right one, 50 bridges would've been clogged and the only way out would've been ploughing the crowds down with tanks. So, here's the question: what decision should've been taken? To supress the news of war, or to paralyse Ukraine and surrender the Left Bank"?'

Denis cast us all a proud glance:

'Well? What do you say?'

'It might have been correct to not to talk about it, then,' Mykolayovych screwed up his face in a frown, 'but still, they should've been getting ready…'

'So, tell me this, then,' Denis wouldn't calm down, 'I have some people I know in Russia. They write that they are against the war but don't know what to do about it. Should I urge them to join protests?'

'Outside Russia, by all means. Inside Russia – not on your life. It's better to sit inside and keep a very low profile. The risks are disproportionate, no one needs it. They will all end up doing time!' enunciated Andriyovych rapidly, even brusquely.

Meanwhile Platonovych was already waving his mobile in the air:

'Now listen to me! This is what Ukrainians are receiving from their relatives and friends in Russia. They are writing: *"You yourselves are shooting at one another!"; "Life in a basement – it's a lie!"; "These are not photos of your allegedly unbearable life, stop downloading the pictures from the internet!"; "All of this is your endless stage-managed shows! I'm sick and tired of you all! Drama queens"!'*

'There's this one, too!' said Anrdiyovych, springing to his feet. 'Just imagine this new fashionable mantra of theirs: "*Where have you been all those eight years? You did bomb Donbas after all*"!'

'Info for the fools… Our guys were sitting in the trenches and fighting you off!.. Ukraine didn't bomb Donbas but enemy positions in Donbas! If you hadn't been there, those eight years would never have happened!…

'Oh! This one is really priceless. The socials are all abuzz: "*But you were warned, in plain language – go and dig the trenches! Have you dug them?*" And also, this. A journalist is asking one high-ranking military official: "How come that in the South the Russians moved in so fast and practically unhindered? After all, the isthmus of Perekop is like a neck of a bottle that could've been corked and kept closed?" The boss replies: "We didn't expect them to advance through the isthmus"!'

'Goodness gracious, we've got some amazing military officials!' sighed Myk-olayovych.

'That's true. If the Russian troops hadn't moved "practically unhindered" into the continental Ukraine from the side of Crimea, they would've experienced the same treatment as they did near Kyiv. Or worse!'

'There's more. "For the love of God, stop competing on social media! Zelensky has kept the country under such conditions, against such a monster! This is definitely worth something!'

'True enough. Let's stop those discussions,' reasonably suggested Andriyovych.

And we all lapsed into silence.

Commentators in Shchekavytsky Gardens

The initial shock had passed. People became much more positive. The Ruscists had withdrawn, and for some time now the city had been free from encirclement.

The residents started gradually coming back, and with every new day more and more people appeared in the streets. Through late February and for nearly the whole of March, Khreschatyk was absolutely deserted – now it all reminded me of a horrible nightmare. I remembered my rescue mission, when in order to prevent the American vitamin pills from falling into the Russkies' hands, I walked for hours, completely alone… But now, again, our thoroughfare was all bustle and hustle. I was standing aside, all eyes and ears, full of curiosity. Some people walked briskly; their gait resolute – must be attending to some urgent business. Some were just ambling around, perhaps on a walk. Some were even standing still. The little forecourt in front of Khreschatyk Metro station was really crowded. Even if the station itself remained closed, the favourite meeting place was teeming with people. Just like before the war...

I was returning to my Podil, heading towards Shchekavytsky Gardens, when I suddenly spotted there a genuine assembly! Some retirees – most likely, our neighbours, the locals, were seated on benches: one pushed over to face the other – and engrossed in an animated discussion, gesticulating widely.

I came closer, avoiding any eye contact, and lowered myself onto a bench nearby. Fixing my gaze on my mobile screen I pretended to be reading something, while instead, listening attentively.

'So, what then?'

'How d'ye mean – what? Zelensky clearly couldn't have prevented the war but had everything been done in preparation?'

'Yeah... A very good question. But say what you like, we haven't dropped to our knees in front of that fucking country!'

'Yet everyone else did!'

'Being certain that we would, too!'

'The "leader" had been assured that Ukraine was waiting, practically dreaming about his arrival! That it would all be like it was in Crimea – a walk in the park and an easy victory! And in the end? What a powerful blow to Putin's image! It became clear that he, an experienced politician, and a career intelligence officer, proved himself incapable of rejecting the unreliable data!'

'That's true. So now he's getting these reports about the progress of this war. First: it turns out, over there, petty "Nazis" are everywhere. Secondly: in response to this proclaimed demilitarisation Ukraine has become a highly militarised state. Thirdly, instead of subjugating Ukraine we've ended up with an extremely hostile neighbour...'

'And this Putin... He's playing his old political game, passing himself off as someone really insane. It's a very effective method for blackmail...'

'This country there... it's... how shall I put it? Really browbeaten... Yet it wears a disguise of a "superpower"!'

'I'd like to remind you. These very words – "war" and "invasion" – the very words that describe this criminal project, are a strict taboo inside Russia itself! You may be easily sent down, how d'ye like it? They've already put so many people in the nick! And imposed astronomical fines. Here, in Ukraine, it's war. But in Russia one should use the correct phraseology: a "special military operation"!"'

'You're asking what Putin's regime survives on? I'll tell you. On masterly storytelling. On the poppycock about "Russia's greatness" and the "global conspiracies"! And Russia, allegedly, is successfully withstanding it all. Alongside censorship, there's a real conduit for brainwashing people with the info beneficial by the regime! That's how it all works...'

'By the way, for some reason Russia is treated especially kindly in Germany...'

'Must be some persistent blast from the past. Guilt, or what? There's this scientific name for this, escapes me...'

'Germany's buttering up to them, and what do they say in response? Rub their noses in slogans: "To Berlin!" or "We can do it again"!'

'Nah, this is dated, this info. Now, their perception is different. One commentator said this about Germany: "The Germans had lived in a relaxed state for too long. Only now do they come to realise that somehow the real danger comes from the East"!'

'This new generation in Russia – generation Z – that's the real danger!'

'I'd be damned, this letter Z of theirs... Does look like swastika!'

'Aha, I've spotted it too...'

'As for spies in Russia – they're a legion. D'ye remember how they'd been pumping Brandt for information through the Stasi?[329,330] Wriggled every littler secret out of him, till the last morsel. Now they are listening to Scholz with equal enthusiasm...'

'Come on! It can't be true!'

'Oh yes it can. They've installed this super-powerful antenna on their Embassy's roof. It's ideally situated in the governmental quarter. And brought in one hell of a lot of equipment. Can you imagine? Say, Scholz flies into Moscow, or, for example, makes a telephone call, and they're already in the know what he's got to say. And his position has been already analysed in all departments of the Kremlin...'

'Ah well, say what you like but Germans have lent us their shoulder. They've accepted a million refugees. With all their costs!'

'But what about China!'

'Must be observing it all closely. Building a file. They've got their own Taiwan to think about. To them, this war of ours is like a textbook.'

'I'm asking myself, what's the secret of our army? Against this Russian juggernaut? The answer is – 30 years of independence during which there have appeared and matured free people who live in a democratic state!'

....

[329] **Willy Brandt**: a German politician and statesman who was leader of the Social Democratic Party of Germany from 1964 to 1987 and served as the chancellor of West Germany from 1969 to 1974.

[330] **Stasi**: the Ministry for State Security (Staatssicherheit), commonly known as the **Stasi**, was the state security service of East Germany from 1950 to 1990.

'I don't like this word "matured". Our people have always been freedom-loving! Yes, we were oppressed, put upon. But we always remained free in our mentality!'

'To put it concisely – it's a standoff between two worlds: slaves and the people who love and value freedom!'

'What's curious is this: those among us who've preserved at least some of this "Russki spirit" have scraped it out of their souls in the course of these months!'

'This myth about the "mysterious Russian soul" exists only for the benefit of the West. As for Ukrainians, they think it's as primitive as the axe with which Raskolnikov,[331] a character in Dostoyevsky, murdered that old miserable moneylender...'

'Look here, I'll tell you about the "good Russians" I've read it somewhere – some polemics on Facebook. They asked one of our bloggers: *"Why are you at our throat like that? It wasn't Moscow and St Petersburg that have attacked you but the depressed outer sticks. And slitty-eyed minorities. It's shameful to compare those to our famous capital cities, the stars of global calibre! One should never mix Moscow and Peter-city with any of this crap!'*

'So let them shut up, then, about "global stars"! This very Moscow and this very St Petersburg do take part! As if there aren't any Putin supporters there. A little bit fewer in percentage terms, that's all...'

'What about NATO? Has anyone read something new?'

'We all have an axe to grind with this NATO at the moment. This condescending unjustified caution of theirs! They've allowed themselves this attitude from the off, and now are its hostages. Thing is, nowadays any more or less decisive action from their side provokes a squall of fire from the side of Moscow!'

'A pow-wow of windpipes. The way things are structured there, a rapid response is impossible in principle. Nah, the way NATO is now...'

'Come on, guys, don't be like that. NATO do help us. Even if they don't give us everything we need so desperately. That's the real wrinkle.'

'Clearly, they're afraid of providing the modern weapons. What if our military withdraw and leave them behind somewhere? It will then fall into Russian hands! No, none of it is as simple as you think.'

'Bloody hell! If only we could get back everything we had to surrender at the very beginning!'

'That's the crux of the matter. You're only trying to get back what's now in their possession... They've installed their occupying regime on the seized territories!'

....

[331] **Raskolnikov**: the protagonist in *Crime and Punishment* – a novel by Fyodor Dostoyevsky.

'But hardly anyone from among the Ukrainian politicians would change sides and act as a collaborationist. All sorts of lowlife scum would, of course. But anyone from the top – unlikely.'

'Listen to this. The high-placed church officials turned to Putin so that he would prevent the bombing of St Sophia cathedral in Kyiv…'

'And this, too, have you heard? When a Russian colonel was taken prisoner, it turned out he was wearing AFU-issue boxers and socks!'

'God Almighty… If it was a regular private, one could somehow understand it. But a colonel?'

'You see… It's hard to understand the psychology of strangers. There are lots of testimonials that in the houses seized by the Russkis they didn't use the toilets! They would scramble together several bricks to rest their feet on, and then, whatever the room, some place in a corner – they would have a crap.'

'What's that got to do with psychology? It means the toilet in that house had been outside. You would get out at night, and someone would take you out from behind a tree.'

'May well be. Although it's not known how many of our houses would use an outhouse.'

'This, too. Some of us speak Russian – it so happened, it's a separate story. But we are citizens of Ukraine, fully entitled and loyal. They would never get this paradox.'

'Do you know where our "guilt" lies? We don't want to live like them. And we don't want to live with them.'

'This very West made a huge mistake back in 2014. They allowed Putin to go scot-free after he'd grabbed Crimea and Donbas. That's when the war really started. And the West simply closed their eyes.'

'And this eternally irreplaceable leader of theirs… Still, even this period will finally come to an end, it's only logical. And then Russia will have to clear out her wreckage. They have bloody built a mountain of rubble…'

'Hmmm… Dream on. Clear out their rubble… They believe there isn't any!'

'But what are we blabbering like that for? In a word: go fuck yourself, Russian warship!'

Thus, they were leaping from subject to subject and hadn't noticed that a certain individual hobbled along and came close. Not quite a creep but certainly, an 'underground' type. To top it all, across his shoulder he had a guitar.

When already in front of them, he pulled himself up to his full height.

'Wagging your tongues? Well then. Topical stuff? Ah-hmm. I'd rather perform some rock for you, old dears. Very much to the point. By the way, I reckon you'll like it.'

The assembly on benches pulled their faces.

'Nowadays, our home rock has reached such a level as never before!' cried the underground type. 'Le'me dash off this classy number for you.'

The weather outside is horrendous.
Something's ringing out,
Something booms and burns...
So, the time has come
When we should all go to battle,
Get up as one and defend our land!

Yes, it's time to get up. No time to waste.
So, it should be me, but also you.

No way now to hide behind somebody's back.
Either you go forward,
Or no one will.
That's why I yell: we all must rise,
All of us,
Which means me and you.

He finished, mopped the sweat off his forehead with a piece of cloth. From the benches – a total silence, the listeners really stunned.

'Well? Have you liked it?'

He brazenly spat right in front of the benches.

'Ah... What's the point? Seeing as you're so totally out of sync...'

He shot those present a look from under his brow, gave a vexed wave of his hand, and was about to walk off. Instead, he lingered a moment:

'Must be said – all of us here are so relaxed, engaged in discussions. And the frontline is out there, far away. And us, here, we live as though it doesn't involve us. Although, you are, mostly, people of certain age. It's rather addressed to us, the young ones...'

He was about to say something else but turned around and shuffled off.

The Most Important Country in the World

Alla once had told us:

'You know... Somehow, these days I have this acute feeling that I live in the most important country in the world. The country where the most important things happen. Or to be more precise – a battle that will define our times...'

She had stopped momentarily, but then added:

'Recently, I've read this: "Nowadays, Ukraine is the world's trendiest country! Not in the sense of "fashionable". Rather in the sense that it creates powerful reverberations all over, inspiring camaraderie, compassion, sympathy...'

It had hit the mark with me, so much so that after she left, I darted to the post's edge, pulled out my notebook and started scribbling hastily:

'I feel acutely that I live in the most important country in the world where the most important battle of our times is taking place now.

I feel acutely that life is more cruel and powerful than any book, any film, or any script.

I feel acutely that we have become a yardstick to apply to any choice made by many countries. It has become easier to work out what's true and what's false.

I feel acutely that both corruption and honour exist in the world. Thus, can one be friends with a rapist or murderer?

No one will ever be able to brush away the news from Ukraine, even if there are attempts to push this subject under the carpet. All decent people will be proud of my country because every action we take, every step we decide upon today will change the world history for decades to come, perhaps even centuries.

This is because, today, we are upholding the will of tens of million people who have fallen fighting against the Russian, Soviet and Hitler's Empires. Their bequest to us is this: *a new tyranny must be overthrown*!

This is because we have brought face-to-face pure dignity and pure bestiality. And this agglomerated energy will eventually destroy Putin of whom the rest of the world is for now so afraid. Nowhere in life exists a more striking example than the one provided by our multi-million daily feats, accomplished at every step of the way.

We are happy, for we live for each other. We are fighting for a gift of a brighter future for our children.

We feel acutely every minute in life, all farewells we have to bid to our friends while hurting eternally over our bitter losses.

The meaning of our lives is being defined today.

Today is the time to understand who we really are...'

OK, Ukraine today was the trendiest and the most popular country in the world. Perhaps, the word 'trendiest' wasn't all that accurate – let them find a different definition. Yet millions of people the world over did believe us the most important country.

My Ukraine was now the talk of numerous people and nations, and everybody was impressed with our courage. It was a country of free and valorous people. A country where, ubiquitous ruination notwithstanding, people had a future and cast their glances ahead. For our global community, Ukraine had become a symbol.

Zelensky's Transformation

Zelensky was elected president in 2019. What had he really expected from this post? Had he craved domination? Or perhaps he'd been after some radical changes in his life? Looking for a pretext to throw his weight around? We might as well be honest about it: a comic actor had become president largely because the population had grown weary of career politicians. His attraction for his electorate was a promise to stay in power for just one term, his image of a corruption fighter and someone who would ensure a generational revamping of the state apparatus and then step aside and liberate the vacancy for his successor.

Anyway, he came to power with the main slogan of ending the war, for the sake of which he was ready to talk "even with the devil" (that is, with Putin). Dialogue with the Russian president was indeed initiated, although not without problems. They called each other and even met in Paris. Large-scale prisoner exchanges were also held.

His naivety had been overwhelming: he sincerely believed that his charisma and newness of approach would be enough to ensure an understanding with Putin and a stop to the war in Donbas that had been raging since 2014. At the time, in the eyes of many he had been an artless individual about to enter the world of politicians without principles, of oligarchs and cynics of all kinds. And thus, he had been perceived as an easy target. But he had started gradually finding his feet in this new context.

It had taken Volodymyr Zelensky rather a long time to get the measure of Vladimir Putin. In December 2019, following their meeting in Paris within the framework of the Normandy format, he made this statement: 'I'm sure he's understood me. When there is such a rapport – eye to eye – you immediately sense your interlocutor, realise what kind of person he is. Despite all the intelligence data, I think he realises it's time to finish this war (in Donbas) …'[332]

Oleh Sentsov, who served a long sentence in a Russian prison, has commented as follows:[333] 'He's a very dangerous and powerful adversary, extremely

....

[332]   11 February 2020, UP. https://www.pravda.com.ua/news/2020/02/11/7240122/ (accessed 04.07.2025).

[333]   **Oleh Sentsov:** a Ukrainian filmmaker, writer, and activist from Crimea. He was arrested in Crimea in May 2014 and sentenced to 20 years' imprisonment by a Russian court in August 2015 on charges of plotting terrorism. In 2019 he was released in a

cruel too. It's important to realise who you're dealing with. Yet Mr Zelensky doesn't, not really, or believes that he's capable of achieving his goals. Ivan Bakanov [head of the the SSU, the Security Service of Ukraine,] thinks likewise. It's bizarre to hear adult people professing things like this.'[334]

In February 2020, contemplating the terms for ending the war, while at the Security Conference in Munich, Zelensky expressed himself thus: 'In my mentality, in my personal view of the world, in my brain I've finished this war.'[335] In Ukraine he had been accused of practically supporting Putin when the latter had suggested to 'place Crimea outside the brackets', and his speech, essentially, was referred to as a stream of consciousness.

It had all continued pretty much in the same vein until February of 2022, with the authorities sticking to their unchanging narrative – a threat of a Russian attack on Ukraine was 'invented by the West in order to heighten tensions.' Nowadays the president was accused of failing to make the country's defence his priority. Instead of strengthening defence, they'd been building roads and bridges – decimated by now. Instead of creating anti-air defence systems, they'd been building fountains and creating TV channels for their needs. Reportedly, the president hadn't been prepared to listen to any explanations about the error of his ways, or to alternative evaluations of the situation.

And then on February 24th, the situation had turned catastrophic and a panic reigned over the country. Millions had headed westwards and abroad. As for Zelensky himself – there had been offers and invites. The very same Boris Johnson had suggested that he should leave for London and once there, create some sort of a government in exile. Yet despite the extremely difficult circumstances, Zelensky had stayed put in Kyiv, thus providing a powerful boost to the morale of those who'd also stayed on, ready to come to their country's rescue. When your president had stayed with you, displaying no intention of leaving anywhere and constantly going on the air, and not from a bunker of some sort but from the square in front of his Office – that was an eloquent testimonial to the mettle of those who'd stayed. He had thus inspired the army, which then unified the population. Together, they had proved to be equal to the 'second army in the world'. The people's faith in themselves and their country had grown.

In the early days of war, Zelensky had also had it hard because of the sporadic nature of help sent in by Ukraine's Western partners. Arakhamia reminisced:

prison swap between Russia and Ukraine.

[334]   UP, 22 January 2020, https://www.pravda.com.ua/news/2020/01/22/7238130/ (accessed 04.07.2025).

[335]   Priamyi, 17 February 2020, https://prm.ua/u-moyemu-mozku-ya-vzhe-zakinchiv-viynu-zelenskiy/ (accessed 04.07.2025).

'I remember that to start with, you would hardly ever see Zelensky relaxed – he was constantly telephoning somebody, or somebody was telephoning him. You know, a kind of a one-man call centre. He made and received lots of international calls, too. Some world leaders let us down... Nearly all of them. Their grasp of the status quo was extremely weak. Everybody who called was afraid of Putin. I believe one of the war's great achievements is that they've shed this fear, and that's extremely important for the future world order.'[336]

In the wake of the Russian withdrawal from Kyiv the Office staff had returned to their personal offices. Zelensky too. For all that, he had been most often operating out of the 'situation room' – a huge windowless facility. His first morning call would be to the military command, to receive an update on the situation at the fronts. Before going to bed at night, he would also scan the operational digest to assure himself that nothing important had been missed, that all today's priorities had been covered: 'I simply couldn't go peacefully to bed when bombs kept falling on Ukrainian soil.' Another confession: his greatest fear was that he would be buried unidentified... In difficult moments Zelensky called his wife to tell her what clothes he was wearing...

Inspired by this decisive and courageous stance of his, Zelensky's rating had unexpectedly quickly shot up. People invested in him their faith – despite his grievous pre-war miscalculations. In practical terms, within only a few hours Zelensky had become a true leader of the nation. And on February 24th, the country saw a totally different person. Zelensky had realised where his mission now lay. He had seen the writing on the wall and deduced that to withdraw, even by one step, was not an option.

As fate had willed, Volodya Zelensky the actor had now been transformed into the supreme commander of a country at war, and Politician Number One in the whole world. The war had changed him beyond recognition. He'd acquired gravitas in everything: the way he moved, spoke, and acted. The circumstances had changed and he started calling a spade a spade, referring to things the way he saw fit – without his earlier subterfuges. This had registered momentarily. Moreover, he had realised that he was now a role model, and therefore had no right to quake in his boots or shirk troubles, but instead, had to lead by example. A new person had emerged...

For all that, it might be worth remembering the attitudes of Ukrainians towards their hetmans – people didn't feel shy to criticise Zelensky, especially

....

[336]   UP, 11 July 2023, https://www.pravda.com.ua/articles/2023/07/11/7410729/ (accessed 04.07.2025).

in relation to that pre-war period, construction of roads, and underestimating Russia's intentions... Well, anyone could be mistaken, no guarantees had ever existed against it. It could well be that Zelensky had been cursing himself for those 'barbeques', amongst other things. But he had raised above all of this, he had overcome so much... He had outgrown a version of himself as it had existed in 2019...

Unquestionably, the main difference between the Ukrainian and Russian mentalities lay in the fact that Russians would always take off their hats for a tsar. And the Ukrainians? The other way round: if a hetman wasn't to their liking, they would pelt him with their hats! Individualists by nature, we were never in a hurry to trust a government, a president, or a parliament. Perhaps, our Cossack spirit was still racing in our veins. We wanted to see our country in good order, not played by anyone for their benefit. However, talking of our attitudes to powers that be – the trust in the president had gone through the roof. The polls confirmed people's certainty that the country was moving in the right direction – unheard of in a country like Ukraine. It had never happened before... For all that, even now, Zelensky was perceived not so much as a leader but rather as an efficient manager, a person in the right place – a unique one, the only one in the world, extremely difficult, but just right for him. He had managed the impossible: to have kept the country together in conditions of unparalleled danger. And Boris Johnson gave him a character reference: 'But for him, history would've taken a different course...'

So, in March-April 2022 Volodymyr Zelensky didn't know how the war would end and what his place in history would be. He was sure of just one thing: Ukraine needs a war-time president, and he's taken this mission upon himself...

After all of this, the West had transformed, too. When they saw that Zelensky hadn't run away, that Ukraine wasn't just holding the line but fiercely fighting back, their position started to alter. In the end, they had realised that there wasn't any alternative. To reach an agreement with Putin? That would be absurd. Modern Russian diplomacy had long since lost the skills and experience of their Soviet predecessors who had been able to reach an understanding with the West – practically without fail and in extremely dire conditions. Those diplomats of the Soviet era had known how to meet each other half-way, make concessions and agree on compromises. Whereas all that Putin's diplomacy had ever displayed was a wholesale obstinate reluctance to achieve any agreements!

Meeting key leaders of the world Zelensky behaved as their equal, talked in way that was harsh, unequivocal, and free from waffle. At times, at a tipping point... Yet it must have been a fair tactic and a correct approach, for otherwise he might have been unable to reach out to some of them. And the benefits for Ukraine had been considerable.

The war had caused a radical overhaul of the European and global agenda. It had also changed what a leader looked like. In recent decades, the typical European politician had mostly been a bureaucrat, a civil servant. But Ukrainian leaders had made an about-face and initiated a radical overhaul of political standards! It wasn't just a question of clothes and style. Above anything else, it involved a new mentality and responsibility not only for one's own country but also for Europe and the world. Now our politicians had to have a creative streak, possess true courage and the ability to use initiative in their line of duty – qualities of which a Western politician could probably only dream. Zelensky had become a brand. And this had registered in the community. Europe was therefore especially likely to experience this demand for leaders of a new type. Just imagine: since the start of the war some European politicians had started imitating their Ukrainian colleagues in attire and behaviour. Say, before his own presidential elections Macron, too tried this image for size: a T-shirt, a several-days-old stubble... Ah well, such things are not forbidden...

And thus, Russia had probably converted Zelensky into a globally important person. Oh, the paradoxes of modernity... They'd tried to kill him but instead should enjoy their handiwork!

True, Zelensky was now a hero. Even if not to everyone, then definitely for the majority. Not a stand-up comedian from an evening TV entertainment programme anymore, he was now a brave leader of a nation.

His most inspiring traits: whatever the circumstances, he behaved with sangfroid and self-control, but could, if necessary, be forthright. His pronouncements about the West and NATO remained harsh, at times merciless. But there were those who'd deserved it – by their ostrich-like policies, their wobbly attitudes...

And so, contemplating NATO now we definitely had food for thought, and our perceptions started shifting. We had hoped that our courage, heroic behaviour, heavy losses, and the fact that we had been protecting Europe against that onslaught would prompt NATO to be more decisive. Yet even now, NATO helped here, didn't help there, and ignored something else. Wasn't it weird that our defenders, who were defending them too, kept dying – in expectation of a better cooperation?

None of it was rocket science, really: like before, they were wary of Russia and reluctant to become implicated in something unpleasant. Under no circumstances did they want to end up 'dragged into a conflict'...

But Putin, on the other hand, had no fear of being 'dragged in'... Be it a conflict or a genuine full-scale war...

* * *

Retreating from Kyiv in a great hurry, the Russians had abandoned a lot of their equipment marked with that infamous letter Z. The vehicles went to AFU and had all those markings painted over. However, a lot of letter-Z-bearing equipment and battle-worthy manpower had been transferred to Donbas, and the situation over there became extremely tense.

The second half of April saw the beginning of a second phase of Russian invasion into Ukraine: Russians were mounting a new offensive against Donetsk and Luhansk Oblasts. The army had been meticulously regrouped, reinforced, and now presented a new powerful threat to Ukraine's east – Donbas. Their aims, too, became more precise – to seize the territories under Ukrainian control within the oblasts of Donetsk and Luhansk. By that point Russia had outnumbered the AFU in terms of manpower, tanks, armoured vehicles, artillery, missile weapons and military aviation. In return, Ukraine had concentrated over there its best forces. At the same time, the ratio between two artilleries had increased to 12:1 in Russia's favour. Putin's troops daily launched 50-60 thousand shells whereas we, alas, could do nothing of the sort.

But in Kyiv life was little by little getting back to normal. The shops reopened. More public transport now appeared in the streets. And there were visibly many more cars.

Still, the war was all around – for example, all monuments still surrounded with sacks of sand and wooden barriers. And the metro trains lingered at Arsenalnaya station (Levoberezhnaya station on the Left bank) for hours, waiting out air raids. As soon as the sirens started howling, metro communication between the two parts of the city came to a halt. The cars could use the bridges, but the Metro remained paralysed.

Belarus, also, wouldn't let us relax, as ever a constant source of tension. Supposedly, there was a great fear in western Ukraine that the Belarusians would advance in that direction and this would result in a massacre, for our military presence, there, wasn't huge.

A friend had recently been to a railway station. According to him, by now the Lviv-bound trains weren't bursting anymore, and at times were even half-empty. Yet in the reverse direction, towards Kyiv, the crowds had become more numerous.

Spyridon and Bolik had returned from their Berdychiv. Liubchick had reappeared, too. No Arkady, though. Ah well, this was to be expected: if the going got tough, the rich would be the first ones to leg it and the last to come back.

'I'm so impressed!' Bolik cried out on the very first day of his return, grabbing me by my jacket. 'It all looks so different! Roadblocks, defence posts, "hedgehogs"... Not your regular life experience.'

I wasn't sure why Bolik was so impressed with what he saw. After all, nothing around was all that extraordinary anymore, things were getting more or less back to normal. OK, there were roadblocks... And barricades... Or even 'hedgehogs'... We – those who'd stayed – hadn't simply got used to them, we probably even started seeing them as a norm...

Had he been here *then*...

When the sirens screamed from everywhere and your fear-infested body would jerk as if you were a puppet... Unable to work out from where that blasted missile would hit? And then hear it wailing, and following its progress in the sky?

Yet those physical sensations had been possible to describe, even only inadequately. But what to say about the emotional fibre in the days of encirclement – a never-ending anticipation of their 'arrival', aware that life afterwards would be radically different to what it had been before? It was simply impossible to put it in words...

As for Spyridon, from the off he had been full of constructive ideas.

'At last, a long-awaited cordon will be formed! A zone of European civilisation!' He was really animated. 'It will start from the Barents Sea shoreline, on the border between Russia and Norway. It will then go southwards, along the frontier between Russia and Finland, hop over a narrow strait and, bypassing the Baltic states, reach Poland, and go along the Polish-Belarusian border. Then along the Ukrainian-Belarusian and Ukrainian-Russian borders. It will reach the Black Sea and the Sea of Azov and dissolve in their waters.'

'And there will be no arguments, whether its course goes through the east or the west of Ukraine!' Bolik eagerly supported him.

'Ukraine has drawn this line in its blood!' Spyridon chopped the air with his hand, as if cutting it down.

He offered his hand to Taras – chose him for some reason. Taras reciprocated with offering his own palm, they clapped hands and turned to face us, sharply.

And then suddenly, spontaneously, we all burst out, as one:
And we'll make our glorious Ukraine merry,
Hey ho!

April – August 2022. Fierce Fighting – Donbas

Ah well, at last, the real spring had arrived: birdsong coming from everywhere, chestnuts trees newly green and ready to send forth their white 'candles' of blossom.

That day glowed as if washed with some effective detergent, imported from abroad. Not a cloud in the sky. Hmm… All the better to see the rockets coming… I was sure to have a good eyeful in the day to come… By the way, it was time to enter thoughts into my pad.

'As always in spring, the Dnipro has swollen from the influx of meltwater. Long-term residents say: "This ain't much! The way it used to overflow in the past! But now the river's managed within an inch of its life – look at how many reservoirs have appeared along its banks! Hydro-engineers must be having a field day with all this water!'

It had been a month since the Ruscists had pulled back from Kyiv. By now, it was already a diluted memory that huge Russian columns had been looming over Kyiv in the early days of war: 200, 300 or even 400 armoured vehicles each! And it all was rumbling forward in one continuous flow. At times, even we, ourselves, doubted our ability to hold up. Realisation came later – all those masses of military equipment had simply clogged the roads, blocking their offensive. Not to forget that our military had blown up some bridges over smaller rivers near Kyiv. The Russians had come to a complete standstill. And that was when the AFU had started delivering their crushing blows – now in this locality, then – in another…

But now the military communiqués started regularly mentioning Bakhmut. Russians had recently captured Popasna – 30 km away, thus acquiring a vantage point for shelling cities and towns within Donbas Oblast: Lysychansk and Severodonetsk in the north, and Bakhmut in the west.

And so, I started writing:

'Alas, the war continues. Nothing is yet clear. In case of success, they, reportedly, may even break through towards Dnipro-city, cut off the Ukrainian groupings as a result, and conquer nearly half of the Ukrainian territory.

'Meanwhile in Kyiv things carry on very much in a pre-war groove. Yet this calm is deceptive because nothing has been resolved at the level of the country as a whole.

'But Kyivites are turning a blind eye to this danger. Kyiv is jubilant – it has proved able to defend itself! All its sentiments and aspirations now are associated with the coming summer: you bet, the sun is already unceremoniously peeping into every window, sending incredible sparks of light in all directions.

The reflected glow of the sun is everywhere, the whole world is one huge play of light and shadow. The streets are luxurious, adorned with the new foliage of trees and bushes. No, it's impossible to describe – how beautiful the city is now! Still, one can pick up the traces of fatigue, a legacy of the siege that had lasted from February to the end of March. Everybody lives in hope that nothing like this will ever happen again...

'Yet I still can't shake off one of my most vivid impressions –that of a city of four million residents being practically empty: no people on the pavements, no cars on the roads. Even those who'd stayed behind, by the end of February practically stopped going out. That was the way the city was getting ready for its "liberators"... Life in such a dead place isn't something I'll forget in a hurry. What a unique experience – to live when you've no idea what to expect...

'And then – whoops! – everything has changed. And is becoming livelier and livelier with each passing day!

'What a striking contrast!'

I finished writing and walked up to the window to look, yet again, at our closed parking lot.

All cars belonging elsewhere had left, with only one still lingering in a distant corner, under a branchy tree, helpless. A brick under each wheel. No one had even visited it in all this time. What had happened to its owner? Was he still alive?

The neighbours were asking one another:

'What's with that car? Who does it belong to?'

'Must be in the army...'

'Or abroad...'

'Or... Could he have got killed?'

No one knew. But the car wasn't obstructing anyone, and from its secluded corner, wasn't impeding anyone's exit...

So that's it – May in Kyiv was always wonderful. Our famous chestnut trees in blossom, the tapering clusters of their blossom visible from any angle. Large and ostensibly sturdy, they could reach 10 to 15 centimetres in height. Yet their petals were extremely delicate. And should a strong wind raise, or a thunderstorm... Or, God forbid, the explosions would ring out – they would tremble, frightened, and slough. The pavements, then, would be covered with a white veil, as if snow had fallen. Snow – in May?

It felt wistful, perhaps even eerie...

Yet I believed that there would be time when a real spring came to our city, and to our country, too. And the chestnut trees, then, would be in full blossom, proud, unafraid...

That chestnut candle of an inflorescence was the symbol of Kyiv. And we passionately wished that this candle of ours would triumph over their letter Z, a symbol of evil and death…

* * *

The schedule of shifts at the roadblock wasn't so stringent anymore. Who could argue that life was improving, especially in Kyiv? Even American diplomats had started returning slowly, the first of them arriving on May, 8th. Yet poor Kharkiv wasn't so lucky – too close to the border to keep track, properly, of the rocket launches. So, with them, first there'd be a boom of an explosion, with sirens going off afterwards. The entire city bears multiple scars… The worst affected were the northern outskirts, an easy target for Russians and their regular artillery. But in the centre, too, not a single street had survived the consequences of such bombing…

Taras, I, and all ours had slowly returned to our studies, first online, but soon it would be a normal regime. However, our graduation had been delayed by a year – we'd missed too much and therefore had to catch up on all of this.

As for me, I'd assembled a lot of material; my thoughts and observations were now filling a second pad. I wasn't sure, though, if any of this was of value… And would I be able to fit it all into a script of some kind? By now I'd decided not to make too many plans for the future…

As for roadblocks/defence posts… No one knew what was to become of them. For the time being, there'd been no instructions. After all, the traffic was increasing, and those posts at crossroads clearly posed an obstruction. Same about "hedgehogs' and bags of sand. What to do with all of this? Surely, not just get rid of the lot? Perhaps, the best idea would be to push them aside and to clear the path for traffic. Yet it was advisable to be on tenterhooks because the enemy could get a second wind and attack us again – with the same view of liberating us from "Nazism'. In short, the bosses must have been at their wits' end on the subject of the roadblocks.

Taras had finally got under my skin. He'd been following me for a week, whining: 'Show it to me! What's the bother? Let me read it!'

With no fight left in me, I handed over my pad. He retreated into the cellar, to stop people getting in the way. Then he remerged and said:

'Hey, dude… It's more than a script now. It might be closer to a research project. You, Stinger, are a prominent researcher of our times…'

He made a pause, thought it over, and added, searching for more precise words:

'Perhaps, a witness of an entire era…'

His estimation sent my heart aflutter but I kept a firm tab on my emotions, kicked them right back, deep inside.

For all that, I'd been strutting around proud of myself – a 'witness of an era'!

* * *

At our defence post today we first poked fun at the statement made by Lavrov who back in the early May had declared Ukraine completely infested with Nazi ideology because the 'the most ardent anti-Semites are usually Jews.'[337]

'His words have enflamed people. He's also criticized Israel's policy on Ukraine,' commented Andriyovych. 'But let's wait and see if Israel really firms up its position.'

As for Gennady, with relatives in Kharkiv Oblast he was happy with the Ukrainian troops over there, who had already reached the border with Russia.

But that was kinda warming up. The real subject for discussion had come from Denis.

'Who will answer me this: could it be that there aren't any normal people among the Russians?' He sounded genuinely amazed.

'In other words, "good Russians", as we call them today?' responded bespectacled Gennady. 'Of course there are. But here's the wrinkle – the overwhelming majority support Putin wholeheartedly. And it's them who rules the nest, since they form a critical mass. And this war is their project.'

'You're talking about "normal" or "good" ones,' as per usual Mykolaiovych sounded sarcastic. 'How many are they? Three percent? Five? And who could be sure they, too, aren't infected with the same imperial disease? Just ask them who Crimea belongs to, and you'll get the full picture. So how many are "really normal"? A thousand? Two? More? Ask them who Chersonesus – that's where Sevastopol is today – belonged to? It belonged to Kyivan Rus!'

'Perhaps even this isn't the point. Not "whose is Crimea",' Platonovych cast us all an accusing glance. 'After the Second World War Europe reached a consensus, confirmed in 1975 by the Helsinki Final Act: the existing borders, irrespective of when they'd been created, are inviolable. Because if those cornerstone principles get violated everything will go down the drain, yet again. Like in the days of the First and the Second World Wars. Thing is – 'a border's unfair", or "somebody ended up in the wrong country" – but it's like that all over Europe.'

---

[337]   BBC, 3 May 2022, https://www.bbc.com/news/world-middle-east-61296682 (accessed 04.07.2025).

'Well, anything to add to this, Denis?' Andriyovych stood up. 'Of course there are normal people among the Russians. But don't you see the trend that's emerging? Some European countries are denying Russians access, whether they are in opposition or not. Some others introduce quotas, lest they should thus increase the base for Putin's support. Besides, Russia must be planting genuine spies on the quiet...'

'I agree! The "normal" ones – they do exist. In the beginning of the war, they used to be coming out with protests – perhaps, not hundreds of thousand but thousands, definitely. Unlike 1968, when only eight dissidents came out onto Red Square to oppose the invasion into Czechoslovakia!'

'But it's still not enough for a radical change in the situation. Let me emphasise if for the hundredth time – the bulk of them are with Putin. That's why he feels he's in the saddle and does whatever he pleases. He's grinding the "normal" ones down when in custody, penalising them with hefty prison sentences...'

'By the way... I, for one, don't believe all those stories of his ill health!' Denis quickly changed the subject. 'Why is everybody so carried away? Look, a guy is in his seventies, of course there would be some health issues. Perhaps, more than one. But to say that he's about to be carried out feet first? Ha! Moreover, he's obsessed with his health! Daily, twenty laps in a swimming pool, scientifically calibrated nutrition. The whole medical world is fawning on him! They even say they've set up a special R&D facility to research longevity!'

'This blasted longevity!' perked up Mykolayovych, even clapped his hands. 'Do you remember this story with Oleksandr Bogomolets, our academician? Let me remind you; on his initiative, in 1938, in Kyiv convened the world's first-ever conference on aging and longevity. They put out a brochure – 'Extension of Life Expectancy' wherein insisted that it was real to live to be 150!'

'Bah!' the Commander couldn't contain himself.

'Bogomolets did believe that using a particular complex of tools if was possible to reach this age. Stalin immediately took it to heart, after all, like Putin, he'd, in effect, craved immortality. And Bogomolets assured him: 'We'll do everything we can, tovarishch Stalin! You'll live a very long life!' Stalin allocated huge resources to the creation of this Institute of Gerontology. But then Bogomolets somehow unexpectedly died... And Stalin flew into a rage: "You scum! You bastard! Twisted around his finger!"!'

We all burst out laughing.

'True, that's how it happened,' confirmed Andriyovych. 'As regards Putin's complaints... Must admit he doesn't look particularly ill...'

'OK, enough of this. But do you think that those Russian people have a feeling of moral, collective, or historic responsibility?'

'Responsibility, my elbow! Life goes on as usual inside their country, this war doesn't bother them. Also, they live inside themselves. OK, maybe they'll have to surrender those foreign passports[338]... No one will go anywhere, see nothing apart from their country. So what? They'll just go on like this, in this Russkie-land of theirs, stewing in their own juice. And it will all be OK.'

'Ah-ha. But what about those who do want to live in a different way? Should they leave? Should they stay?'

'What sort of a question is that?' Platonovych didn't miss a beat. 'All normal people should leave ASAP. Leg it! So's to preserve their mental and general health, their freedom! Conscience... Thing is – compromises will eventually end in rivers of tears. Use those foreign passports while they still can... Although I'm sure there are people for whom such a definite departure is too expensive, perhaps even impossible. Yet there isn't any other solution for those who want a different life, such are the conditions under which they are forced to live. For the time being it's still feasible to keep an extremely low profile in a bolthole somewhere. But if the war escalates to a new level? Putin will then drive everyone out there. Everyone... And it won't be possible to take refuge in silence. I, personally, am certain that in a medium- to long-term perspective Russia's got no prospects. But in the nearest future, one could still start up, say, a dog-grooming company: to give the pets a wash, and a good brushing, too...

Girls are Trophies Too!

On social media appeared a photo of a dead Russian soldier, his hand wrapped around a trophy – a smartphone. Perhaps he'd wanted to say goodbye to his family before death? Or maybe he'd had no time to do it? Who could tell? Next to him was a semi-open sack out of which an electric kettle had rolled out. Not just any cheap kettle but a well-known European brand. Looked like he hadn't managed to take it to the Belarusian border. And thus, now his family would have to do without, this – and other goodies stuffed into his sack.

Yet there were those who'd successfully taken out their ill-gotten gains and considered themselves lucky: they would send parcels home using the Belarusian or Russian express mail service. But if the need for cash was urgent, they would flog the lot in one of the many markets to be found in Belarusian towns.

....

[338] **Foreign passports:** a vestige of Soviet days. Citizens of post-Soviet republics hold two passports: internal and also external. One can only exit post-Soviet republics if in possession of an external passport.

They must have been dreaming trophies. You'd enter someone's home, have a good look around, and if something was really to your liking, you just took it. And no need to feel guilty or pay for any of this. How tempting…

Those liberated shared stories about occupiers picking over their mobile phones. They hadn't been after any old machine but smartphones only, ignoring those with the buttons completely.

One Ruscist was berating the locals:

'Fancy that – your cars are all foreign-made! Your houses are stuffed full of white goods. You're rolling in bloody clover! Who's allowed you to live in such luxury?'

There were numerous recordings of Russian military calling their relatives. Their mums put in orders for blenders and irons, dads – TVs, fishing rods and angling gear… Their wives, though, were omnivorous: anything would do, down to branded underwear. The main thing – it had to be pretty and manufactured abroad. The order would come laced with an 'absolution': 'You know, this… Shag those Ukes, just don't tell me about it…'

'Dollars? Gold? Diamonds?' the warriors were making rounds of houses. 'Keep quiet, no need to exercise yourself. Just give everything over. Don't forget this basic truth: life is more precious than any of those trinkets.'

They would grab costume jewellery, and adornments, then call their wives and girlfriends and brag. And those, in return, would yell: 'Go on, get what you can!'

But these were lowly soldiers. Costume jewellery and underwear would be beneath the squeamish officers' radar. The officers would be after money and real valuables. There even started a real 'competition over trophies'. After all, the officers were supposed to ensure 'order' – the most expensive stuff went to their own pockets.

There was a story when the residents had been forced to descend from their flats into a cell.

'What for?'

'*We're saving you from the Uke's bombings…*'

And with the homeowners safely out of the way, the time was ripe to burgle their flats.

Later, a Russian POW said that he'd never engaged in looting, all he'd ever taken was a hunter knife found in some flat. He hadn't even treated it as looting, just getting a trophy…

Trophies and spoils alike had been put to good use. The occupiers had set up little bazars in Belarusian cities, putting their loot on offer: washing machines and dishwashers, fridges, air conditioners and kitchen extractors… Also – cars, bikes, cycles… Kitchen wares and rugs, makeup and children's toys, women's adornments. In a word, anything they had managed to lay their hands on.

'I say! This, here, is a well-stocked little bazaar! Get in while stocks last! Buy the lot, citizens! Good bargains guaranteed! A beautiful occasion to remedy your daily troubles! Moreover, we're selling it for peanuts! After all, who's an idiot enough to lug a washing machine from here to home?'

Some locals would grimace in disgust and leave, but the others reached for their wallets.

What was there to add? If even the infamous Chornobyl APS got burgled? They'd nicked the computers through which Belarusians would now read their news. Or perhaps, on those, their children would play computer games about war…

And the 'live' goods – what was wrong with trophies of this kind? Quite the opposite, great stuff. Especially if the girls were young, say, under 14 or 15?

Those would've been locked in a shed or a basement, and then gang-raped by the entire regiment, with industrial efficiency. They'd be kept there for a month or even two… And every day they'd been run through this gauntlet of frenzied soldiers.

'We'll fuck your brains out so that after this you'll never want any of this stuff again. And no little whore would ever give birth to a single tiny Nazi!'

One of the victim's mums narrated:

'He'd followed my girl and then dragged her along. Resistance was useless – he had a submachine-gun, and was doped up to his eyeballs. He then raped her all through the night. In the morning, before letting her go, he tore out a tuft of her hear: *"To remember you by. It might've been the best hours of my life".'*

The sense of laissez-faire and lawlessness must have been intoxicating. The war dogs had realised – not only they wouldn't be held responsible, the other way round, all of this was actively encouraged. One could really push the boat out!

That was life! That was a real spree! Heaven on earth! No need to wait for the other one, in heaven…

And there is a different story.

A valorous Russian soldier called his mum, told her that they were killing civilians and children.

Hid mum replied:

'No, it's not the civilians and children that you kill! You're killing fascists, fuck'em! Do believe me!'

Another one was offering those words of encouragement:

'My son, darling! Don't let your morale slip! If only you knew what they're doing out there! The things they show on TV here! You know – your mission is so lofty!'

While those inspired mothers tried to offer words of lofty wisdom and motivate their sons, it transpired that many Russians employed any subterfuge to avoid being sent down into the Ukrainian meatgrinder. On the other hand, however, the backwater Russia had spotted an excellent opportunity to go looting, not to mention to receive a decent remuneration for joining up. And thus, quite a few volunteers were gagging to go to 'war in order to take trophies'.

And another thing: no recruiters from Moscow or St Petersburg – cities where a 'soft approach' was adopted, whereas most war enthusiasts come from depressed localities with raging unemployment. That was yet another face of the war…

* * *

This time Alla'd tugged Liubchik along, as always providing some simple food. I was making a new entry into my pad. Alla eyed me quizzically:

'There you are, Stinger, scribbling again. Do you know that the lot of us have abandoned our earlier topics? No "Soviet faceted glass" anymore, to say nothing about Lenin or Sverdlov. We've also dropped Mayakovsky and photo models. We're on a lookout now.'

'Why such secrecy?' Liubchik picked up the baton. 'Everything's on the surface. Spyridon and Bolic are collecting materials on a life in the army, the war in trenches, partners' aid. They are even considering going to the frontline, for, like, total immersion. Meanwhile Alla and me will probably write about volunteers and humanitarian aid. Themes are out there. The complexity is to give them artistic treatment…'

'Well, then' that was Alla again. 'Some smartie pants in Russia are trying to work out whether Russian culture had impacted this invasion. They are even trying to find an answer in the work of most prominent writers…'

I snapped my pad shut, got to my feet.

'We should familiarise Stinger with the background, he might've missed it…' Liubchik gave a nod in my direction.

'So,' Alla looked at me askance. 'There's this opinion that responsibility for the aggressive attitude and colonial mentality of Russians lies, up to a point, with many of those writers of the past. The critics assert, literally, this: why do we need all those "wonderful" classical books with which we've grown if they've failed to prevent a war and make people better, make them more humane? Go on, tell me what you think.'

I made an uncertain gesture with my arms.

'Got nothing to say?' Liubchik had no intention of letting me off lightly. 'So there: the time has come to rethink Russian literary standards. Got it?'

'With this I, too, agree.' Taras saved me from having to answer directly. 'Don't you sense it – Russian culture is colonial in its essence? An inherent part of it is this condescending arrogant attitude to other nations. Don't we, Ukrainians, feel it? However...'

A shadow of doubt flashed across his face.

'But is it really colonial through and through? It's used as a tool, that much is true...'

'So, what's your take on it, Stinger?' Liubchik was curious too.

Yet I continued mulling it all over in my head, silently...

I wasn't all that eager to be dragged into a debate and, God forbid, spill the beans over that secret literary brainchild devised by the rector and me. To say nothing about my help towards his monograph on the original sources of *Dead Souls*. The question of who Gogol belonged to – Ukraine or Russia, would then be unavoidable. But really, was it possible to find a straightforward answer to this question?

They'd left and I saw the Commander advancing towards Taras and me, sideways, an unusually gentle smirk on his face.

'Mm-hm. What are your plans for the summer? Go somewhere?'

'We'll stay here. Where could one go in times like this? Besides, our classes have resumed. Online for now but still, best to stay put. What if they switch back to normal?'

'That's great, this. The decision's been already approved – some defence posts are to be axed. Us included. OK, we'll drag the sacks of sand back to the pavement, the "hedgehogs" too. We'll liberate the road completely. Me, personally, I'm being transferred to the training ground. As for you, you're... hmmm... free as a wind. But still...'

His face grew grim again.

'This effing Russia may be only putting out frighteners about a second attack on Kyiv but then again, maybe not. Dunno. So, let's stay in touch. Should anything happen, I'll summon you at once! And the sacks and the "hedgehogs" can go back to the centre of the road. Just like before. Got it, lads?'

The Commander left and I returned to my pad.

'Lots of things in Russia are openly ludicrous. Once Primer Minister, then a President, and then Prime Minister again, D. Medvedev, is untiringly engaging in his anti-West and anti-Ukraine rhetoric. He used to enjoy a reputation of a prominent Russian liberal and insisted that "freedom is better than lack of freedom". By now, however, he's morphed into a die-hard Kremlin "hawk" and started using a different language. He's active on his Telegram channel – threatening the West with nuclear weapons, calling the citizens of Germany "Fritzes" and the USA – "a poof-stan". To him Italians are "Wops", and the Ukrainians – surprise, surprise – "Ukes". He writes: "Our main task is to destroy all enemies – Ukrainian Nazis, the USA, loathsome Poland, and other Western vermin. We must finally regain control over all our lands. To defend our people once and for all."[339]

'Recently, Medvedev has become obsessed with Satan. In answer to the question of what the war was all about he explained that Russia's purpose was to stop Satan and warned that Moscow had the wherewithal to start "the fires of hell". Later he wrote that Russia's mission was to "thwart Hell's Supreme Master, whatever his name is – Satan, Lucifer, or Iblis."

'Nearly a million people subscribed to his Telegram channel. And how many more are reading without subscribing? Even Russians are bewildered at this ferocity. Medvedev responded as follows: "I'm often asked why my posts are so brash. Let me answer: because I hate them! They are bastards and degenerates. They want to see us dead, to see Russia dead. And for as long as I'm alive I'll do what I can to destroy them."

'It's not that difficult to work out the reason behind all this tough-guy behaviour: he would otherwise have been conspicuous as a member of the counter-elite, a counterweight to Putin. And so, he does whatever he can to shed those suspicions, to prove to Putin that he's above any suspicion. Still hoping that he might be useful to the ruler…

'There may be another explanation: they've agreed between themselves that Putin is the "good" cop and Medvedev the "bad" one.

'But is Medvedev aware that the more he foams at the mouth, the more pathetic he looks? Nowadays, in his role as deputy head of the RF Security Council, he is, in essence, unemployed, and he is afraid of remaining alone, without sup-

----

[339] Meduza, 26 June 2023, https://meduza.io/feature/2023/06/26/chto-proizoshlo-s-dmitriem-medvedevym (accessed 04.07.2025).

　　　　　　　　

port or power. He would do whatever he can to stay in the groove, so he's puffing out his chest as much as he can, trying to come across as a tough guy. Yet the main stalwarts of war – like Ramzan Kadyrov and Yevgeniy Prigozhin [340,341] – would hardly be likely to take Medvedev for a "tough 'un".' [342]

* * *

In June, there were considerably more people in the city, and the Kyiv Metro wasn't coping on its previous schedule. So, the intervals between trains were shortened to 4-5 minutes in peak times, and 8-10 minutes in the off-peak periods. The dismal experience of 40 minutes between trains had become a thing of the past. At some stations they even opened second exits from the platforms – like it had been before the war. Yet the trains still made no stops at key junctions. So inconvenient! Yet we were told it was much safer that way.

Most roadblocks and defence posts had been disbanded, including ours. And thus, we had dragged the 'hedgehogs' and the sacks of sand off the roadway onto the pavements, and that was that. The same happened at the other dissolved roadblocks – all they did was pull their gear to one side. No one was going to remove any of it completely. Then again, the District HQ was still operational, and some defence posts, too. Who knew if Putin would take it into his head to launch a new attack? And if Lukashenko would support him? OK, we'll trudge it back and put in place all over again.

As to the news from the front – everything was mostly about the fierce fighting in the East, the situation over there dire. And while the last-ditch battle continued in Donbas Kyiv engaged in debates. The main question was this: 'How has it become possible that Putin has taken such a gamble – this invasion, and gone so far in his brutality?'

One line of reasoning insisted on the Kremlin's total inability to assess the sentiments in Ukrainian society adequately. They had fatally underestimated our capacity to defend ourselves. Carried away with her imperial hauteur, Moscow had overlooked most basic modern realia. And Putin became a most graphic example of this ineptitude. He just couldn't accept that Ukraine had a right to independence. His view of Ukraine was totally delusional.

As for him going so far… There were many theories.

....

[340] **Ramzan Kadyrov:** current head of the Chechen Republic in RF.

[341] **Yevgeny Prigozhin:** a Russian mercenary leader and oligarch. He led the Wagner Group private military company and was for some time a close confidant of the Russian president.

[342] BBC Russian service, 4 November 2022, https://www.bbc.com/russian/news-63506765 (accessed 05.07.2025).

The key problem lay in the fact that such mentality – i.e., negation of Ukrainian statehood and identity – was manifested not only by the current leader of Russia. Attracted to an idea of imperialism, most Russians were incapable of seeing Ukraine as independent. How was it possible – to be separate from Russia? But that was pure nonsense! And thus, Putin was simply reflecting the views in Russia. As simple as that.

Despite logical deductions, I – among the others – kept asking myself: how had it become possible? No, not Putin's transformation but things that had evolved in that nation. Was it a case of collective mental derangement? Obfuscation of vision?

How had it so happened that Russia had nurtured a modern variety of fascism? And that boil that had been growing for 20 years, or perhaps even a hundred – if one counted from the October Revolution – had finally ruptured and all the accumulated pus then gushed at Ukraine? A perforation of the tumour of fascism…

Surely, we weren't the only ones trying to solve this enigma. People would be looking for answers in decades to come. Hundreds of books would appear, dozens of thousand pages would be written – in search of some common denominator, and answer to the question: why a 140-million-strong people, in response to the slogans proposed by their raving Fuhrer, yelled in chorus: 'We are great!', 'Exceptional!', 'We won't allow anyone!', 'If need be, we may arrange a second Berlin!'. And immediately after that they rushed, head over heels, to rip apart and loot their neighbour.

How had dozens of million people allowed to poison them with such cheap rubbish?

While Putin was hiding away in his bunker, encircled by a team of doctors, Russians continued being corrupted by lies and useless references to their 'greatness'. And they continued lapping it all up!

Currently, neither us nor them had any 'medications' to cure this horrible disease.

On the other hand, what 'medications' could be invented if the majority was overcome with blunt animal fear?

Dark Ages… Psychotic delusion… Foul insanity…

Russians had become pariahs of the civilised world. And they would stay this way until they cured themselves. That would be the only way to avoid the nightmare of degradation…

* * *

The war was in its fourth month. President Zelensky announced some horrifying statistics: the Russian troops controlled about 20% of Ukraine, or 125,000 square kilometres. It was worth remembering that prior to the war, the Russians kept over 43 thousand square kilometres in Donbas.

The fierce fighting in the east continued. Our military had been forced to withdraw from main cities in the battle zone. The order to leave Severodonetsk came on June 24th. Lysychansk was surrounded on July 3rd. Those battles had not been strategically significant. Ukraine, too, had sustained serious losses but exhausted the Russian troops, forced them to use up a huge volume of resources and weakened their advance on other segments of the frontline.

Besides, the Russian offensive slackened because the AFU continued systematically annihilating ammunition depots behind the enemy lines. By that time, we had received from our partners HIMARS – long-distance multiple-launch rocket systems. It had become possible to aim at a target from 80 km away, and that made a crucial difference. By about July 18th the situation on the eastern front had stabilised. At the same time the military dispatches started mentioning the city of Bakhmut more and more frequently. However, even if the frontline was approaching, there had been no direct attempts to capture the city itself. The Russians were limiting themselves to bombardments.

Basically, this stabilisation marked an endpoint of the current stage of the Russian attack on Donbas. The war was entering a new phase. Military experts later pointed out that victory in that battle proved to be rather to Russians' disadvantage: having used up their resources on Severodonetsk and Lysychansk, they enabled Ukraine to subsequently proceed with offensives near Kharkiv and Kherson.

OK, we'd sorted this one out. But what about the South? Things started moving there too – in the last ten days of July they started taking out bridges over the Dnipro, eliminating Russian's access to occupied Kherson. And thus, their equipment could not cross over to the right bank. That sent an important message that liberation of the city was imminent.

And on June 30th, our shelling of Serpent Island in the Black Sea forced Russians to pull out. Odesa residents gave a collective sigh of relief since a new disposition didn't allow Russians to threaten the city.

* * *

As for us – it couldn't be helped, the illusion of a life in peace continued. It was high summer now…

Generally, summer always disappeared fast. On the one hand, life was more fun, on the other – time was at a premium. Nowadays we didn't see each other all that often even with Taras. Somehow, we had paired off and drifted apart – he was now with Liubchik, while Alla and me, too, had always been attracted to each other. You could hardly call it love, though… Rather, a sincere affection. Liubchik once said: 'Love – oh, that's so complicated… You always have to figure things out. It gives you a headache and robs of desire to live. Then again, is this what we need now? A normal healthy relationship is the best…' What was there to say? Common sense reigned supreme…

But on July 13th I was really startled. According to the folk calendar that was the highest point of summer! Mid-summer they called it, when the heat was at its peak. On that very day our ancestors would appeal to the Sun to grant them a good crop of grains!

Good God – half of the summer was gone, as if it had never existed.

I called Taras, he was even more appalled:

'Gosh! We've only been to the Dnipro three times! Unbe-effing-lievable!'

I called round everyone in our gang and was firm: 'We're going swimming in the Dnipro! Immediately!'

Nowadays the Hydro Park Metro station was closed, you could only get there on foot, walking from Livoberezhna station – the walk long and boring; hot, too. Thing was, Kyivites couldn't imagine their life in the summer without a bathe in their Dnipro. Everyone wanted to get close to water. And so, the only remaining option was Trukhaniv Island[343], not too difficult to get to – across the Foot Bridge. Despite a roadblock at the entry point, it was still useable.

We all agreed to meet at Post Square. Before the war, it had been a fashionable place, sort of a stamping ground for the young. Allegedly, now it all was coming back.

Taras and me had just emerged out of the Metro station. Wow, everything around looked as if nothing had happened. A throng of people on the pedestrian crossing, you had to elbow your way through. A heaving young crowd at Post Square – indeed, a good place to realise how many people had returned. The impression was – everyone was back! Or at least nearly everyone…

Nearly all of ours had already assembled, stood around waiting. Bolik was the first to spot us, started waving. Even the 'Teutonic beauties' started shouting something but Liubchik seized the initiative – could never stand competition.

....

[343] **Trukhaniv Island**: an island located on the Dnipro River opposite the neighbourhoods of Podil and Pechersk on Kyiv's Right bank. Recreational zone.

'Compared to the East, everything in Kyiv is somewhat different,' she summed it all up. 'If we hear an air raid, everyone's so used to it now that they don't even react.'

'Yet in Kharkiv it's the opposite,' added Alla. 'Our friends called: as soon as it's an air raid, everyone races to a shelter. Out there it's totally different, and they have a different perception of threat.'

'So how are your roadblock buddies?' Spyridon hastened to change the subject.

'Yeah, who's where?' Bolik was curious too. 'What's going on with the bespectacled Gennady? And Denis? And the choir guys?'

'Lots of news, even some to spare!' Taras smirked. 'So much has happened. Gennady and Denis – can you imagine? –enrolled into a course on launching drones!'

'Dear mother and all my relatives!' Liubchik clapped her hands. 'Old Russia, hold fast!'

'The choir guys are keeping busy too,' that was my contribution. 'You can see for yourselves that the city is gradually shifting towards using Ukrainian for preference, so everything Ukrainian is in good demand. Their Capella Choir is now awfully active, and their workload has grown sky-high – if not performing, they are recording...'

And thus, we stood and chattered, non-stop. Even the 'Teutonic beauties' were animated and joined in. Normally, they'd keep their counsel, but today both ran nineteen to the dozen. Alla took it all well but Liubchik... She was understandably vexed but, like a good girl, kept herself in check.

Right... What's the need to stay here? After all, everyone was there, except Arkady. But that was to be expected – the rich ones always proceeded with caution. It couldn't be ruled out that he was sitting tight out there – we didn't even know where – till the 'situation was completely clear'. He called regularly – both Alla and Liubchik, with lots of questions about everyone, asking to pass on his hellos. And still, he never really admitted to where he was. I wasn't at all surprised that he never telephoned me or Taras, neither Bolik or Spyridon, because talking to guys would've been much harder than chatting with girls. That much was clear.

Long story short, we all set off towards the Foot Bridge. The route to it had recently been improved, they'd put in a cycle lane, planted some trees, installed benches. What a beauty it was now! We entered the bridge itself and saw that it was crowded with people, and cyclists speeding along – hither and thither, all like in the days of peace! We stopped at the bridge's edge, right above the Waterfront Avenue.

The avenue was congested, just like in the olden days, its three lanes full of cars in both directions. It was bizarre – the city was still regularly bombarded but all looked exactly like it had been before the war. Yet another paradox of the times of military trouble.

'When they started rebuilding this avenue by the end of the '50s,' Bolik waved in its direction, 'the Council of Ministers of Ukraine had planned to make it a six-lane thoroughfare: three lanes one way, and three for the on-coming traffic. Yet at the time, what effectively was a local issue, couldn't be resolved without Moscow's say so. Not even Moscow's as such, but Comrade Nikita Khrushchev's as he was First Secretary of the CPSU CC.[344] I know be-cause my granddad was on our delegation that went to Moscow to sell the idea to that high-handed despot.'

'Bloody hell!' Liubchik exploded. 'My folk told me, too, that one couldn't erect an effing fence without their approval. That's exactly how they put it – you couldn't drive a nail into a plank under your own steam!'

'So, they'd made an appointment with him.' Bolik pointed his hand at him-self. 'And he told them: "Two lanes one way, two – in reverse. End of discussion. If it were here, in Moscow, yeah, six lanes, no argument. As for you – even four is too much. Be grateful we allow even this.'

'Cretins!' One of the 'Teutons' voiced her indignation.

'Blockheads! If one could set Teutons against them!' The other piped in, too.

'And so?' Taras even poked Bolik on the side of his body. 'Don't spin it out!'

'Well, so. They'd "worked" on this blockhead. They'd brought along several crates of pepper-flavoured horylka, nice cucumbers, lightly marinated tomatoes. A fresh slab of lard. And some Kyivan torts for "afters" which, at the time, was a huge and rare treat even for someone from the Moscow Central Committee. They also included aids and assistants – a hefty share had fallen into their hands, too. Seeing as they had influence. So, they had lured them onto their side. And they did manage to nail the old bastard, he did sign the approval of a six-lane avenue. And that's what we are observing here today…'

Having left the bridge, we turned left towards the island – it was my idea. That was the best place to enjoy the view of Podil. However, had we turned right, we would've had a perfect panorama too – the view of the Kyiv-Pechersk Lavra.[345]

But our choice was better suited for our outing: the beach here was wide and spacious. One could plop down anywhere one liked!

....

[344] **CPSU CC**: the Central Committee of the Communist Party of the Soviet Union.

[345] **Kyiv-Pechersk Lavra** or **Kyievo-Pecherska Lavra**, also known as the Kyiv Monastery of the Caves: a historical Eastern Orthodox Christian monastery which dates to the 11th century and gave its name to one of the city districts where it is located in Kyiv.

The Dnipro here makes a powerful thrust eastward, creating a narrow bottleneck. The current was strong and the water rapid and chilly, even in the summer, because it was never stagnant and there was chance that it would be warmed by the sun.

We bathed, we splashed at each other and then popped out of the water and flopped onto the sand, to get warm.

For some reason Taras and Spyridon started badmouthing France's ex-president Nicola Sarkozi, all because of the latter's shameful stance on Crimea. One could feel the 'Teutonic girls' were dying to say something contemptuous in Sarkozi's address too but couldn't think of anything. To them, Sarkozi was an alien from Mars.

Shortly, however, they lost all interest in the discussion – the waters of the Dnipro had smudged black makeup all over their fresh countenances. Suddenly, the pair of them looked like two unearthly transitory birds. Spyridon and Bolik enjoyed it all immensely. Then the paint started drying up in uncanny designs. More fascination for Spyridon and Bolik! Things being not comme-il-faut, or even ugly never used to trouble either of them. Later, the 'Teutonic girls' would wipe the streaks away, apply fresh makeup and things would go back to wonderful. All that was trifles. As far as Spyridon and Bolik were concerned, the essence lay elsewhere.

'Divine!' Spyridon even smacked his lips. 'Such a blow to the fucking System!'

'A most powerful manifestation of active protest!' Bolik agreed. 'I'd say, quite a graphic one!'

Then we all spread around the island in couples…

* * *

Finally, there was an ideological substantiation of current developments. A genuine scoop! A Russian state-controlled informational site published an article – 'What Russia Must Do to Ukraine'. The author had come to prominence earlier with his suggestion to separate Ukrainians into three categories. This time he went in-depth. The article was completely open about the need to eliminate Ukrainians, their language and culture.

Those who didn't support Russian occupiers were seen as those 'aiding and abetting the Nazis'. They would be 'denazified by way of ideological repressions'. In order to achieve this aim, it was suggested that stringent censorship should be introduced in politics, culture, and education.

'Apart from the top leadership, a considerable proportion of the popular mass is also to blame; they are passive Nazis. This segment of the population should be justly punished by their awakening to the fact that they would have to go through the hardships of war and perceive this experience as a lesson of history. Ukrainians must expiate their guilt before Russia. The way to achieve this is through de-Ukrainization and de-Europisation. Ukrainianism is an artificial anti-Russian construct.'

That was the size of it. Even the name 'Ukraine' had no right to exist. The country had to be split into several parts, all with new names; a new 'people's republic' would be formed and eventually incorporated into Russia.

The Ukrainians – that was to say, us – had to 'part irrevocably with their pro-European and pro-Western illusions'.

The article called Russia the 'last stronghold capable of protecting Europe's historical values'.

'Tragedies and dramas of war benefit peoples who have succumbed to the temptation to become an enemy of Russia.'[346]

Wow, some article, that. It reminded me of something… Possibly, Goebbels' rhetoric – the entire nation would be proclaimed 'wrong' and therefore it would be imperative to wipe it out, along with its country's statehood.

In recent times, the world had really flipped upside down. It had become topsy-turvy. And the common human values had, accordingly, started sliding downwards.

Russian invasion of Ukraine had destroyed all foundations of international security, undermined our faith in organisations we had been associating our hopes with, invalidated international conventions and treaties. For a while it had cast doubts on the world's most powerful alliance – NATO who had appeared to be hypnotised by Russia's aggression. And even now it was lacking self-confidence.

I tore myself away from my computer screen with this nice article and felt a new passage bursting out of me. I grabbed my pad and started writing hastily.

'When their supreme "leader" – the main culprit in what's going on – dies, it cannot be ruled out that Russians would embalm him and place in the mausoleum in Red Square. Why not thrust him inside, seeing how much energy he'd poured into the reinvention of the "Great Empire"? It doesn't sound too eccentric, by the way, since he's supported by the "majority of the population".

'And they would be lying in the mausoleum side by side – Vladimir Lenin and Vladimir Putin. Let's imagine this scenario: Putin will finally get his chance to grab Lenin by the latter's tunic lapel and ask a direct question:

....

[346]   Meduza, 4 April 2022, https://meduza.io/news/2022/04/04/na-sayte-ria-novosti-vyshla-kolonka-o-neobhodimosti-deukrainizatsii-ukrainy (accessed 05.07.2025).

"Why on earth, Vova-dear, have you done it all? I've been dying to ask you this for some time, but somehow it hasn't been possible."

"Wha-t, wha-t are you on about?.. What have I done wrong?"

"Come on, you've created this 'Union member republic', the Ukrainian Soviet and Socialist one… You've carved it out of the territories that had been ours from the time immemorial, and then dreamt up this administrative territorial entity. And even enshrined this principle in the Constitution – think of the ignominy! – that 'republics enjoyed a right to secede from the Union!' What utter insanity!"

"How do you mean, Vova dearest! How else could I have possibly cobbled this union together? It was a union! And everyone had equal rights! Just listen – this right of the nations to self-determination was a corner stone…"

"Why should I listen to you? Here's me, thinking that you, Vladimir Illich, was a real empire person! Like all normal Russians! And now look at you! Rights… Self-determination… And that's why it's all going to the dogs. That was your blunder! A huge geopolitical miscalculation. You've been lying round here for decades, unaware of what double trouble it's turned out to be – since all of them, those here 'republics', popped out of the union at the first available opportunity. And your brainchild has crumbled completely!"

"What's that you're saying? God forbid…"

"So there. As for me, I've been deeply traumatised by the Soviet Union's disintegration. And this ulcer has been eating me away from the inside! For years I've been nurturing plans to rectify it all. My lot has been extremely hard for I had to set it all right, dear Vladimir Illich, everything where you've gone astray…"

'I didn't know if Lenin was going to reply anything to Putin.

'I knew something else. They would hold a Victory Day parade in front of the Mausoleum. Just like before. Following the tanks, howitzers and missile complexes, cheerful excited Muscovites would walk in step. Ostensibly, not the dumbest people in the country, would chant: "Glory! Glory! Glory to Putin!!! Hoorayyyyy!!!!"

'Those people would be sincerely happy. Or, perhaps… braindead? Those representatives of the "great nation"… But no, all those parades that demonstrate rocket launchers and their conceited "might" really would fill them with elation.'

I finished writing. I must've written something more like a pamphlet. A first for me. OK, let it stay this way.

August, too, was drawing to a close. At the moment there was no immediate overland threat to Kyiv. Yet the threat from the air persisted – we continued with regular missile strikes. But in the East... Things were really heating up there.

At this very point Gennady called. Him and Denis were still doing the course – learning all there was to know about drones. None of it could be done in a haste as there were lots of different types of those out there. He said they were often meeting with the Commander.

'What?!' I even sprang up in amazement. 'Denis too? But they didn't see eye to eye at the roadblock!'

'They do now. See, how things change? They've learnt to rub along...'

We switched over to Bakhmut.

'Look,' I told him, 'What's really going on in this Bakhmut? It sounds like the centre of the earth. News non-stop...'

'Well, it's like the Battle of Donbas that Zelensky announced back on April 18th. Now that the Russians have seized Lysychansk and Severodonetsk in Luhansk oblast, their attention has shifted to Sloviansk, Bakhmut and Soledar – that's already Donetsk Oblast. It was quite a thrust – at this segment Russians have a 5 to 1 advantage in manpower. Combat activity there started on August 1st. And gradually they are edging onwards...'

'What sort of a town is this Bakhmut?'

'A relatively small one, 75,000 population. Much smaller than Donetsk or Mariupol. Not a patch even on the next-door Kramatorsk or the occupied Horlivka. Not so important in industrial terms, either. Yet now it's the epicentre of intense hostilities. They now view it as a stronghold in that area.'

For a second there was silence, with only the sound of Gennady clicking his tongue somewhere in the distance. Then he said:

'For all that, by August 21st their offensive capability had been somewhat exhausted, and they went completely off steam. Practically speaking, they haven't managed to seize any important areas. And thus, proved their inability to convert their tactical successes into operational or strategic ones. So, now, by the end of August, most fighting is a dragged-out trench war. There is this issue, though... Now one of the principal strike forces in Bakhmut are the mercenaries from Wagner Private Military Company. So, things will go on a boil soon. Perhaps, even over the top...'

I never knew why but summers always passed at the speed of a bullet. You didn't even have time to register where those days had disappeared.

To top it all, suddenly we students didn't have much free time. Because of horrible lapses in the curriculum, we had to study practically all the second half of July and the whole month of August...

September – November 2022. Ukraine's Wins and Russia's Atrocious Vengeance

Ostensibly, the month of August – during such a precious summer period – should be prime time for active combat. However, nothing of note was happening at the front, despite a commonly shared presentiment that something really important was in the offing. Then, by the end of August new information started seeping through: the AFU were intensifying their activities in Kherson Oblast. And then on August 29th Ukraine announced a new counter-offensive. The folk immersed themselves in their computers and became glued to the TV with doubled zest. What was going to happen now, out in Kherson?

However, in anticipation of a possible Ukrainian attack Russia had redeployed thousands of manpower – some of them elite brigades, thus making their position around Kharkiv considerably weakened and vulnerable. Even if Russian military bloggers had realised that 'something was wrong' and started warning of an inescapable Ukrainian counter-offensive near Izium, Kharkiv oblast, the Russian commandment took no notice and showed no initiative at this segment of the front.

* * *

Out of nowhere, Spyridon and Bolik leapt out from behind some column in the institute corridor, accosting Taras, and me. It felt weird but this time neither had any headphones on.

'People, I've got things to say about our victory,' blurted out Spyridon without bothering to say hello.

Taras and I exchanged a quick glance. Clearly, we were about to hear a mission statement of sorts.

'Ha! Victory! He who lives long enough will be able to enjoy it!' Taras tried to bring Spyridon down to planet Earth.

'Let's consider the type of a country emerging afterwards?' Spyridon wasn't listening, he was agog with a desire to burst out his own coveted thoughts. 'So, will we become an economic miracle? I personally believe that Ukraine is a very promising part of Europe. However, investments will only start coming if the conditions we create are conducive. Which logically leads to a question: what are those basic principles? Supremacy of law, zero corruption, freedom of speech, independent judiciary... I am certain we'll go down this route.'

His face flushed pink with ardour. Taras and I looked at each other yet again: attaboy! The world and his oyster were talking about the same stuff!

'Our civil society was strong but will become stronger: those who took part in the war, volunteers, those who fought and go on fighting – everyone's where they should be. Also, their families. But it's a hell of a lot of people! Immense numbers! Not a single criminal would be able to live like before. I'm certain those who left will return. And we'll rebuild the infrastructure destroyed by the Russian bombs – which was predominantly of the Soviet pedigree – with a new one! Technologically advanced!'

We thought – he belongs on a grandstand!

'Tis all true... However...' ventured Taras.

Yet Bolik was having none of it:

'The future of Ukraine worries everyone! It's in everyone's interests to have a stable country in the middle of Europe. Ukraine must become a "country of dreams"! An example to emulate! The entire Europe will be happy to tell the world: "Look! We can do so much! We've converted Ukraine into a thriving place!" Sure, a lot will depend on us. But the important thing is this... As regards international politics, we are now moving from the status of an object into that of a subject!'

'Hmm... You're painting such a beguiling picture...' Taras miraculously managed to put in a word in edgeways. 'Let's add a drop of common sense. And what should we do with those "used-to-be"-s? Procurators, judges, and investigation officers? Where are you going to stick them, I wonder? And from where will you source scores of thousands of new ones that will be pure as driven snow? Who's gonna train them, educate them – with the old guard all around, acting larger than life? How will the new ones break through this glass ceiling?'

'That's true. Something like a stalemate, God damn it...' Bolik gave a heavy sigh. But as per usual, momentarily made a mental about-face: 'This bit is hard...'

But Taras was pressing on:

'Our partners won't yield Ukraine to Russia, that much is clear. But will they be in any hurry to ensure our victory? A rapid victory creates dangerous repercussions. Our partners would prefer to see Russia bleeding gradually dry... For Russia would never accept a loss in this war. Do we really know what subterranean triggers define the world politics? '

'It's equally possible that the essence is here.' I joined in too. 'They'll try to drag the whole process out and wait till Russia is corroded by the burden of her own internal problems. It does look like their strategy is aiming at exhaustion...'

'Ah well, you're talking about the future...' Taras cast a wistful glance at Spyridon and Bolik. 'Would it be a protracted war, or a frozen conflict... Or, perhaps, victory, after all? Who can really tell how things will pan out in the end?'

* * *

And then, like a bolt from the blue, while continuing our semi-efficient offensive in Kherson Oblast, we launched a concurrent attack in Kharkiv Oblast! Who could've predicted that it would be the biggest disinformation campaign of the entire war conducted with an aim of making Russians pull their forces away from Kharkiv? The Ukrainian military had been actively floating around the idea of strikes in the South, thus successfully misleading Russians as to their real intentions on Slobozhanskyi front in Kharkiv Oblast. Thus, this counter-offensive, successfully planned in secret (even the USA hadn't been put in the picture), turned out to be a complete surprise for the Russians who had been expecting developments near Kherson in the south.

Things started heating up near Slobozhansk on September 3rd, but already on the sixth, the Ukrainian army mounted a full-scale offensive and caught Russians unawares. The very next day our guys broke through the Russian lines and advanced at least 20 km towards Kupiansk and Izium.

On September 8th, they went even further – 50 km to the north of Izium. They entered Balakliya and regained control over one of the biggest ammunition depots nearby. By September 10th, nearly 2,500 square kilometres of our territory had been liberated.

Already on September 10th, having lost the railway hub of Kupiansk, the Russian troops were forced to pull back from Izium – their principal base for material and technical support within the oblast. In a word – the counterattack in Kharkiv Oblast had been carried out with unprecedented speed. The Russian defence collapsed like a house of cards, which stunned the world. Besides, it had been a masterly use of the tactic of surprise – the AFU had been overtly discussing an attack in the South but approached the front from a completely different angle.

The Ukrainian offensive might have been more effective if E. Musk had not turned off Starlink. Reconnaissance drones stopped working, and long-range artillery units experienced difficulties with targeting. Musk's view was that the offensive could provoke a nuclear response from Russia.

Putin lost no time in exacting revenge.

The very next day, September 11th, the enemy sent 12 sea- and air-launched ballistic missiles: Kalibr and X-101. The Ukrainian anti-aircraft defence destroyed nine out of twelve. However, among others, the enemy hit Zmiivska TTP in Kharkiv Oblast – one of Ukraine's biggest Thermal Power Plant, Kharkiv TTP-5 and three high-voltage substations which, in turn, paralysed 40 substations of a smaller size. Hundreds of thousand households in the oblasts of Poltava, Dnipro, Kharkiv, Sumy, and Donetsk were left without electricity.

In response to this dreadful attack President Zelensky made a speech which came to be known as 'Without you'.

'Do you still think we are "one people"?

'Do you still believe that you can frighten us, break us, force to make concessions? Have you really not understood anything? You haven't realised who we are? What we support? What we are all about? Watch my lips: without gas or without you? Without you! Without electricity or without you? Without you! Without water or without you? Without you! Without food or without you? Without you! Cold, hunger, darkness and thirst are nowhere as horrible and lethal as our "friendship" and "brotherhood". History will put all this in its proper place.

'And we shall be – with gas, electricity, water, and food – but without you.'[347]

This speech confirmed yet again Ukraine's determination to fight back against the occupation by Russia.

After the strikes, M. Podolyak, adviser to the head of the President's Office, declared as follows: 'Deliberately targeting direct attacks at key facilities of civilian infrastructure is an unquestionable demonstration of Russia's terrorism and her desire to leave peaceful civilians without light and heating. This is a coward's "response" to his army deserting the battlefield.'[348]

A curious fact: following those strikes at the Ukrainian power stations, pro-Kremlin bloggers and state-controlled media started actively posting photos and videos that showed the rockets launched and the fires caused, praising the actions of the Russian military!

As for Putin himself, he announced: 'Quite recently, the Russian Armed Forces delivered several substantial strikes. Let's consider those to be a warning. If the situation continues in the same vein, our response will be much more serious.'

....

[347]   Meduza, 12 September 2022, https://meduza.io/news/2022/04/04/na-sayte-ria-novosti-vyshla-kolonka-o-neobhodimosti-deukrainizatsii-ukrainy (accessed 05.07.2025).

[348]   X.com, 11 September 2022, https://x.com/Podolyak_M/status/1569034237545684995?mx=2 (accessed 05.07.2025).

On September 12th the AFU entered Sviatohirsk in the north of Donetsk Oblast. By the evening of the same day some 6,000 square kilometres of our territory had been liberated – practically everything that had been occupied within Kharkiv Oblast.

After that, the AFU kept moving further – towards the town of Lyman in Donetsk Oblast. By September 30th Lyman was effectively encircled and then, on October 1st, Ukrainian troops entered the city.

Analysts insisted that dramatic rate of the Ukrainian counter-offensive, and capture of Izium were Ukraine's major military achievements after the victory in the battle of Kyiv. For the first time since the Second World War Russia had lost whole subdivisions. And thus, the prospect of Russia's usurpation of Donetsk Oblast was destroyed.

But that was not all. The loss of Izium and the adjacent territories became a humiliating loss for Putin and Moscow's worst failure since the withdrawal from Kyiv in late March.

Yet the victory tasted bitter, too. Half-a-year of the Russian occupation had exacted a huge toll on the local population. Numerous makeshift prisons had been found in newly liberated Izium and Balakliya where Russians had been torturing and killing Ukrainians.

In a forest on the outskirts of Izium they discovered a burial ground, and in it hundreds of dead civilians killed during the occupation. Another graveyard – this one for the military, where most bodies had their hands tied. For several months the town had lived in horror: rapes, torture, and mass murder, some tower blocks deliberately targeted by air bombs. The houses had been toppling over like toys – the entrances had simply folded up, killing hundreds of people.

In numerous places they organised the exhumation of the dead and obvious evidence of abuse came to light – bodies with hands tied behind them, with clear indication of torture. Investigators had to deal with abundant evidence of brutal sexual crimes, too. The Russian military had practiced it on a broad scale – so that to inflict especially grievous pain and psychological humiliation. Equally wide-spread had been the practice of maiming, severing, or fracturing the limbs – in other words, torture of the most ferocious kind.

Cases of sexual abuse had been so numerous that the General Prosecutor's Office of Ukraine formed a special unit and made it responsible for collating evidence. The range of victims proved nauseating: from four-year-old children to persons of advanced age, sometimes over eighty, both men and women. There were numerous testimonials of sexual crimes committed against our POWs. The conclusion was obvious: a Ukrainian of any age, gender, profession, or faith could become an object of such abuse.

But why had the crimes of this particular nature proved so common? It turned out this had been a 'special strategy' introduced by Russian commanding officers. Soldiers had been supplied with Viagra, to keep them in a state of heightened arousal and incite attacks on women, and children… Russian top brass had been actively provoking an upsurge in rapes, cruel handling, and torture.

On September 17th, Russians launched 13 ballistic missiles – Iskanders, Xs, Kinzhals – at Zelensky home city, Kryvyi Rih. Among the targets were only objects of civilian infrastructure, totally unrelated to anything military. Their purpose was to destroy the dam and thus flood three boroughs with a total population of 150 thousand people. In other words, to shift the brunt of war onto the already exhausted civilians.

* * *

I cycled to my granny's. As soon as I got back, Spyridon called.

'Have you read Zaluzhnyi's article in the American *Time?*'

'Erm… I've heard about it but haven't got round to reading it yet.'

'For crying out loud! Stuff like this should register in mid-flight! He says that on the eve of the February invasion, the AFU had redeployed their military equipment and covered the vehicles with camouflage. They'd moved the aircraft, tanks, armoured vehicles, air-defence units out of their regular bases…'

'But it's been said already!'

'Listen on. Zaluzhnyi was scared that the Russians would see through his manoeuvre: "You can never mistake the smell of war for anything else. And it was already in the air. I was wary lest we should lose the advantage of surprise, lest the Russians catch on. The enemy had to be convinced that we all were sitting around at our normal bases, smoking weed, watching TV, and posting on Facebook".'

'Ah-ha! This is really interesting.'

'So, when the invasion had started the task was to keep control over Kyiv. The plan had been to allow Russians approach the capital, and then proceed to pulverising their convoys at the front, then supply lines that would've stretched over many kilometres. In other words, they had sacrificed some territory for the sake of luring the Russians into a trap. By about the sixth day of the war, that is to say, March 1st, Zaluzhnyi concluded that the plan was working. He said so himself: "Generally speaking, the Russian senior command has committed some mind-boggling mistakes. Meeting with staunch resistance or losing an occasion to replenish resources they just wouldn't withdraw, only drove their soldiers forward to a slaughter. They were choosing a scenario that suited me best." And this other fact is emerging only now... Prior to the invasion, they'd invited the US military attaché to HQ, briefed him on their defence plans, showed him sketches of the AFU deployment and operational diagrams. They'd even allowed him to take notes. However, it later turned out that this was a decoy; Zaluzhnyi had disguised his genuine intentions. Our military source latter commented thus: "At the time we trusted no one. Our plan was the only one tiny chance we had to succeed, and we didn't want anyone to know about any of this." Zaluzhnyi himself summed it all up in the end: "We must be prepared for a long and exhausting struggle. Knowing the Russians, the way I do, this victory of ours won't be final. It will be our chance to have a breather and prepare for a subsequent war".'

I started to work the pedals again, his words pounding in my head: 'We must prepare ourselves for a long and exhausting struggle"... That was the principal message. It came from the AFU Commander-in-Chief, a real specialist! And all the rest of them, experts and analysts competing with each other over the dates for the end of war – 'Before this year is out!'; 'In spring!'; 'In the summer!'; or even 'Two or three months, maximum!' – this stuff was only good for television and the internet, an opportunity to self-promote and self-aggrandise...

* * *

On September 21st, in response to the Ukrainian counter-offensive and in view of extremely high Russian losses at the front, Putin was forced – for the first time since the Second World War! – to declare a 'partial mobilisation'. Although official draft targets were announced as 300,000 men, everyone understood that the real aim might well go over and beyond.

Yet again, Putin introduced the issue of nuclear weapons: 'In case of danger to the territorial integrity of our country, in order to defend Russia and our people we will, unquestionably, employ all resources at our disposal. And it's not a bluff...'

Since it wasn't the first time he had issued a threat of this kind, the internet community wasn't all that surprised. Our resilience was unshakeable, and even this statement of his became an object of mockery. Social media even started contemplating about the best way to spend the final days of your life. Somebody suggested organising a mass orgy on the Shchekavytsia Hill in Kyiv – according to a legend, once upon a time a place for the witches' covens to convene. Allegedly, a semi-hidden Telegram chat forum had already been created whereby Kyivites could make arrangements for racing over there in case of a nuclear strike. Alleging that the Ministry of Digital Transformation was apparently planning a special addition to Diya[349] – to send out automatic notifications about 'orgies next to you' – after the nuclear attack. That was a new type of entertainment.

Taras would tease me from time to time:

'You're in luck, man! Say what you will, but the hill is a stone's throw away from where you live. You'll be the first one to arrive!'

Meanwhile Russians themselves aptly renamed mobilisation 'mogilisation'[350] – mobilisation to your grave. This recruitment campaign caused potential recruits to emigrate from Russia *en masse*: within the following five days over 260 thousand men left the country.

Those who stayed were in for various surprises. Countering a complaint of why people with proper military training were sent into infantry, a certain colonel snapped: 'Why are you being difficult? You are cannon fodder now. What training are you on about? What's it good for?'

Small wonder people started running away. Ah well, in a place where to protest meant subjecting yourself to danger, that was the only way. If you couldn't fight your state – because it was so much more powerful than you – all you could do was to flee as far as you could. Flight became a passive form of resistance. At least some way of saying no. On the other hand, was it possible for dozens of millions to flee? Besides, such a relocation required serious money. In other worlds, it was mostly an option for the middle classes.

The deficit of Russian manpower in Ukraine was filled in various ways. Yevgeniy Prigozhin (a multi-millionaire who had founded Wagner, a private military company) owned a big business. One of his companies provided catering services to top officials in Russia – hence his nickname as Putin's chef. So, he took to personally making rounds of labour camps and prisons, encouraging the inmates to sign up to the war in Ukraine.

The entire prison population would be driven into the inner court, even those in the sick bay. At times as many as fifteen hundred would attend. The inmates would make a circle, with Prigozhin in the centre. He then would explain that after six months' active duty they would all be pardoned. He would continue by insisting that what was going on was the Third World War and one could fight in it on Russia's side, and that he only had use for assault men.

'We are not the armed forces. We are a militarised and organised criminal unit. My boys enter African countries, and within two days they leave nothing alive in their wake. That's exactly how they're annihilating enemies in Ukraine.

....

[349] **Diya**: a mobile app, a web portal, and a brand of e-governance in Ukraine.

[350] **Mogilisation**: a portmanteau of 'mogila' (grave) and 'mobilisation' – a derogatory neologism used in social media.-

Your decision to serve in the PMC is a "contract with the devil". If you follow me out of here, you will either return as a free person or die. You will have a duty to kill enemies and carry out the orders of your superiors. Those who want to turn tail will be executed on the spot. On the plus side: a 100,000 rubles a month plus a bonus of about the same amount. And in the event of your death: five million rubles for your family. I have special powers from the president. I don't give a fuck about anyone. I need to win this damned war at whatever cost. I, myself, did nine years in the north [i.e. in prison], so I know how it all works. So, I think my proposal should suit you. The issues of guarantees and trust go like this. Do you have anyone who would be able to get you out of this camp, given your ten-year sentence? There are only two candidates who are capable of doing this: either Allah or God. Even then, in a wooden box. Whereas me, I am taking you out of here alive! True, I won't return you alive necessarily. So, lads, any questions? Five minutes for thinking it over, while we're here. Those who are interested go with us.'[351]

Prigozhin and his recruitment assistants would step aside. The recruiting agents focused first of all on murderers, those doing time for grievous bodily harm, and recidivists. Drug abusers were taken with caution; the same for rapists.

The prisoners would think it over.

'In general,' witnesses told later, 'he came across as a maniac. However, there was no coercion. He said – you must understand that we need you. True, we went to sign up, quite a few of us. First of all, those who were inside for the first time, or those with long sentences. But quite a few of "idea-driven" ones, too. Those who'd signed up were organised in assault units. Most of them were hoping to get lucky and directly return home. Most of them didn't even understand the danger. Prigozhin's gift for public speech kept them hypnotised. Logic was not part of any of this. They never twigged that only very few would get back from Ukraine.'

That was what it looked like on the surface. It later transpired that nearly all convicts volunteering from the first two camps had been killed.

Yet the authorities realised that partial mobilisation and Prigozhin's appeal had been insufficient. There had been proposals to declare a 'Great Holy War', followed by mobilisation – full or disguised. The economy would have to be shifted onto a war footing. The campaign motto should go thus: 'Even if we lose some territory today, we must win this war! We'll get it all back in time!'

---

[351]   Mediazona, 6 August 2022, https://zona.media/article/2022/08/06/prigozhin (accessed 05.07.2025).

A Kremlin functionary S. Kiriyenko splurged: Russia would win any war if it were declared a 'patriotic' one.

On September 23-27th, the Russian occupiers ran pseudo-referendums on the occupied territories of Ukraine. The question was whether or not the four Ukrainian areas wanted to join Russia. To ensure the right outcome, they started going round the flats. A 'team' like that would appear on your doorstep, policemen in tow, and suggest that you vote – under close supervision. Forget the booths. That was called 'targeted voting'.

On September 30th, referring to the results of those pseudo-referendums, Putin organised in the Kremlin a gala exposition. On live TV, contracts were signed with collaborating leaders, pretty folders changed hands, announcements were solemnly made about the DPR, LPR, Zaporizhzhia and Kherson People's Republics joining the Russian Federation.

And at the same time, slogans were sticking out here and there – all over the occupied territories: 'We've come to stay!'

* * *

By then, in parallel with the Slobozhansk offensive in Kharkiv Oblast, an attack was also gradually taking off the ground on the right bank of Kherson Oblast. By the end of September, the Russian morale was clearly taking a nose-dive – a result of a number of reasons, among those the situation with supply lines. The bridges over the Dnipro had been destroyed. Russian commanders had repeatedly insisted that they should withdraw to more defence-worthy positions but Putin forbade them to leave Kherson.

And thus, in early October things got more intense. Between September 2nd and 4th, the AFU advanced by some 40 kilometres in the north of Boryslav District, step by step liberating right-bank localities in Kherson Oblast.

On top of that, it was extremely important to sever the Russian logistical chain that runs via the Kerch Bridge to Crimea and then on to the left bank in Kherson. So, on the morning of October 8th, something very important happened. With a powerful 'kaboom', an articulated lorry exploded on the bridge. As a result, a section of the auto-road collapsed, while cisterns exploded on the railroad section of the bridge. This was an undertaking so daring that to start with the Kremlin was lost for words. After all, the bridge was Putin's personal 'brainchild'!

Ah well, that triggered Putin's vengeance even further. Following a series of crushing defeats, Russia switched over to terrorism. After October 10th, critical Ukrainian infrastructure became the target of regular missile strikes.

The biggest such attack took place on October, 10th and was aimed at Ukrainian cities. Russia used 84 missiles (43 intercepted), and 24 pilotless drones (13 shot down). Among the targets were cities themselves and various infrastructure facilities. After a long interval, the missiles were falling again on Kyiv's centre. Direct hits at power stations and other facilities interrupted supply of electricity practically all over Ukraine. By the evening there was a complete blackout in about 1,300 communities…

Those attacks continued throughout the night between October 11th and 12th, and all through the day, with ballistic missiles launched, again, from sea and air along with some kamikaze drones. Even if many of them had been intercepted, lots of targets had been hit. All over the country there were reports of glitches in the electricity supplies while, some areas had issues with the supply of water and the internet.

On October 20th and 22nd, more infrastructure facilities were targeted. About 1.5 million households were left in the dark. Trains were delayed, too. Those were the cities whose infrastructure was routinely shelled: Kyiv, Lviv, Zaporizhzhia, Kharkiv, Vinnytsia, Ternopil, Dnipro, Odesa, Kryvyi Rih, Mykolaiv, Voznesensk, Bila Tserkva, Zhytomyr, Khmelnitsky, Rivne, Lutsk, and others. The country's grid was 40% damaged. Eventually, in some areas of the country electricity had to be put on a rota.

In the morning of October 31st came a new massive strike. Out of 55 missiles, 44 were intercepted, while the targets were confirmed as the Ukrainian HEPP: the one in Dnipro-city and the other one in Kremenchuh. Putin announced that targeting civilian infrastructure was a retaliation for a Ukrainian drone attack against the Black Sea fleet in Sevastopol.

According to some creditable researchers, it wasn't only vengeance but an attempt to force our top leadership to enter into negotiations with the Kremlin regime – clearly, on terms advantageous to the latter.

* * *

Whatever the story, but with the Crimean Bridge out of the equation, the AFU could go on the offensive in the northern sector of the Kherson front, every day liberating more and more Right-Bank communities.

And in the beginning of November, despite Putin's personal orders to hold onto Kherson till the last breath, there appeared first signs of the Russian withdrawal. On November 9th the Russian Defence Ministry instructed their troops to pull back from the western (Right) bank of the Dnipro. On November 11th the Russians left the city and the Ukrainian army entered it. On the same day the Russian Defence Ministry officially announced that 'the troops and equipment have been relocated to the left bank of the Dnipro in accordance with our plans and without losses.' A similar statement had been issued earlier, citing 'execution of a manoeuvre to relocate towards pre-prepared positions.'[352]

In view of all of this, the Kremlin Administration circulated a special set of instructions among the mass media, telling them how sell it all to the general public: 'Zelensky wishes to stun the world with a bloodbath that he's preparing. The enemy wants to drag the Russian troops into a trap of Kherson, a battleground that would costs scores of thousands of lives. Yet the main objective of the Russian authorities is to defend the population while saving maximum of the Armed Forces' manpower. The concerned jingoists should calm dawn: Russia will officially consider Kherson a Russian city, a "territory occupied by Ukraine".'

On his Telegram channel Medvedev also hastened to add that the concept of territorial integrity of Russia 'hasn't disappeared. Therefore, all territories occupied by Ukraine will return home. Panic mongers should be reminded more often of the might and boundlessness of the Russian world.'

Prior to veering off from Kherson, they had blown up a TV tower there and pilfered the monuments to Suvorov and Ushakov.[353,354] All that was left were the empty pedestals. They had also nicked Potemkin's relic,[355]along with the valuables from local museums. It was an act of pure burglary.

Well… undoubtfully, that was quite a favourable result but… The military themselves call the liberation of Kherson a 'victory of strategic importance' and only a partial success. 'We failed to destroy the 25,000-strong enemy group located on the Dnipro's right bank. We were short of the artillery shells and time needed to carry out the operation properly… Anticipating the Ukrainian offensive, Russian troops moved to the left bank without losses and entrenched themselves there. This complicates our future actions on the islands and on the left bank…" Unofficially, however, it was rumored that the AFU had not destroyed the Russians during their withdrawal from Kherson due to pressure from the US. Apparently, Biden was afraid that the Russians might use nuclear weapons. In a conversation with Gerasimov, Milli supposedly said that the Russian army would not suffer any catastrophic losses in Ukraine, and there would therefore be no justification for applying the nuclear doctrine.

....

[352] TASS, 11 November 2022, https://tass.ru/armiya-i-opk/16299641 (accessed 05. 07.2025).

[353] **Alexander Suvorov** (1730-1800): a Russian general in the service of the Russian Empire.

[354] **Fyodor Ushakov** (1745-1817): an admiral of the Russian fleet, regarded as one of the greatest naval commanders in history.

[355] **Grigory Potemkin** (1739-1791): a Russian military leader and favourite of Catherine the Great

Today mum and I burst into tears: try not to cry when watching a broadcast where Kherson residents were welcoming our troops in the streets of their liberated city. Celebrations were going ahead in the city centre. A woman wrapped her shoulders with the Ukrainian flag:

'I'm seventy years old. I attended a rally carrying our flag, so they caught me and took me down to a police station. There, they stripped me naked and chained me to a radiator: "Now we gonna cut off yer tits, got it? That'll be a good lesson for ye, you piece of Nazi scum"!'

That was it, their understanding of 'denazification'. Where were they, all those prominent European politicians who had insisted that it was only Putin's war? Was it Putin who had torn off that woman's clothes, and chained her to a radiator threatening her with a knife?

Several days after the city's liberation, President Zelensky came down there on a visit. Russian social media were collectively indignant: '*What cheek! He visits our Russian Kherson that we've temporarily given up!*'

AFU Commander-in-Chief Zaluzhnyi had this to say on the withdrawal of the Russian troops: 'Behind each so-called "goodwill gesture" of our enemy stands a colossal effort on the part of our armed forces. It was the same when the enemy rolled back from Kyiv and Kharkiv and left Serpent Island... Their retreat from Kherson has been brought about by our active input. More specifically, on the Kherson axis, Ukraine's armed forces have destroyed logistical routes and the supply system, thereby thwarting the enemy's ability to manage their troops. And that is how the enemy was left with no other option but to run for it.'[356]

That marked the end of the active engagement – from now on the wide and powerful Dnipro separated the two warring sides.

However, as soon as the Russians had withdrawn to the Dnipro's left bank, they started bombing 'their' Kherson, hitting the city centre, and treacherously concentrating on residential areas. What they were demonstrating was a jackals' rapacity.

They also started erecting some defence structures. Even in the Crimean north they were now renovating the old trenches and digging new ones...

Both fronts – that of Slobozhansk and Kherson – became important stages of war as they had proved the AFU's ability to launch effective offensives and liberate occupied territories.

---

[356] Glavcom, 11 November 2022, https://glavcom.ua/columns/zaluznyi/kozhna-po-razka-voroha-tse-rezultat-nashikh-aktivnikh-dij-888421.html (accessed 05.07.2025).

November – December 2022.
Life in the Dark, Cut Off from the World,
with No Electricity or Running Water…

Late autumn… Daylight was shrinking precipitously. The nights were colder now, and the trees, attuned to changes in nature, embarked on a lengthy preparation for hibernating during the winter. As or our lives, there were some painful changes too. By now the 'fraternal people' hadn't been satisfied with simply bombing our houses. Their strikes were increasingly targeted at our infrastructure. A straightforward bombing meant killing ten, or a hundred, or a thousand, or even ten thousand residents whereas 'infrastructural bombing' would reduce tens of millions to a cave-like existence: with no electricity, water, heating, or communications. This was the real ticket! Eureka!

Within nine months of her invasion of Ukraine (from February to November 2022), Russia had carried out thousands missile strikes, with about 90% of those targeted at civilian facilities. On October 3rd, 2022, the occupiers opened systemic fire against the Ukrainian power industry: HEPPs, TEPPs, CHPPs, distribution substations and gas extraction facilities.

Russian propaganda and pro-Kremlin bloggers never tired of proclaiming that the real purpose should be destruction of civilian infrastructure. However, in the beginning, the Russian authorities refrained from crossing the 'red lines'. All of it changed after the AFU's successful counter-offensive in Kharkiv Oblast. Sources from even within the Russian officialdom admitted those attacks to be a means to terrorising civilians and depriving them of light, water, and heating – all of this on the eve of a winter.

Under international law, such actions amounted to war crimes. At the same time the Ukrainian authorities branded the military strategy applied by Russia as state terrorism, committed with a purpose of sending new waves of Ukrainian refugees out of the country, or forcing Ukraine to enter into peace negotiations with Russia on Russian terms.

In early November Mayor Klitchko warned Kyiv residents of an imminent worst-case scenario, something akin to an apocalypse: 'If Kyiv ends up in a blackout, water will still be distributed in storage tanks, or you will be able to collect water from shelter-protected mineral springs. The worst possible outcome may be the need to leave Kyiv.'[357]

Anyway, with the unexpected transformation of the blitzkrieg into a protracted conflict, information has spread that since the fall of 2022 the policy of the White House has changed: now it is a protracted war aiming at the gradual depletion of Russia. Well, the price is Ukrainian army soldiers' lives – but what can one do?

On the other hand, there was this announcement. Head of the OPU Yermak had put his previous contacts to good use and started regularly bringing into Ukraine pop stars of the international calibre. Now millions could watch Bono performing his hits in the underground foyer of the Metro station on Khreschatyk, or Angelina Jolie rushing towards a bomb shelter within the Lviv Railway Station – to the accompaniment of an air-raid siren, and Sean Penn handing over his Oscar statuette to Zelensky for safekeeping till the end of war.

He told Zelensky just that: 'It will stay in Ukraine till that very day...' [358]

* * *

For the second day running our house had had no electricity. For some reason the house across the road was all lit up. It wasn't all that easy to work out the reasons for this. Mum and I went out of the communal entrance and bumped into our 'tough-guy neighbour'.

'Most likely the guys in that other house are on the same circuit as some vital facility,' was his explanation. 'Although nowadays even professional electricians aren't always sure why some house have it and some simply don't.'

'That's the way it is now,' mum nodded in agreement. 'Very much like living in a cave.'

'Still, there are some elements of modernity, for all that,' our neighbour specified gently. 'A mixture of sorts. But one should view it all philosophically. Once you've accepted this attitude, nothing can really scare you.'

'Hmmm... Some philosophy, this. Have you heard? Over there, in Muscovy, they are jubilant that we are in such a bad place.'

'Tis true,' confirmed the neighbour. 'That's the way they think. What can you do?'

....

[357] New voice, 6 November 2022, https://nv.ua/ukr/kyiv/klichko-rozpoviv-chi-mozhe-v-kiyevi-buti-blekaut-ta-yak-gotuvatisya-novini-kiyeva-50281935.html (accessed 05.07.2025).

[358] TSN, 9 November 2022, https://tsn.ua/youtube/shon-penn-zalishiv-zelenskomu-oskar-do-kincya-viyni.html (accessed 05.07.2025).

'To me that's the most depressing bit,' mum went on. 'The mood over there is practically festive. What kind of a person could celebrate somebody's misfortune?'

'Indeed. They are outdoing each other on TV: *"Serves them right, the Nazi bastards. It's wrong that they still have electricity, even if it's for a pathetic hour… They should have none at all! Keep laying into them, Vova Putin"!*'

'E-e-eh…' mum sighed. 'Are you here for long? Not going back to Ternopil yet?'

'Nope. Got enough stuff to do here.'

Well, had the apocalypse really arrived? The scariest day was November 23rd – as a result of a missile strike, there was a pan-national blackout while half the country was left with no electricity whatsoever. That full-scale blackout tangentially impacted the neighbouring Moldova.

Even if that strike hadn't been the most powerful, it had inflicted the most catastrophic consequences. A temporary de-energising impact had affected all nuclear-power stations, and most of the hydro- and thermal ones. Where the previous attacks had mostly interrupted supplies of electricity, this time the entire generating capacity had been switched off. Most populated areas of Ukrainian cities and villages had been plunged into complete darkness. In many places running water was no more, and there was no heating – all against the background of sub-zero temperatures. The Metro and electric means of transportation had come to a halt in Kyiv and Kharkiv, but the authorities introduced additional bus routes. Public transport had stopped operating in other cities too. Trains would depart with huge delays and diesel locomotives were taken out of reserves and put on the tracks.

Yet again, Kyiv shops were besieged by enormous queues. The most in-demand product now was drinking water – big and small bottles sold out within an hour. Long queues had formed outside enclosed water sources. Both telephones and the internet were playing up. People started queuing for petrol in an attempt to lay in supplies of fuel not only for their cars but also generators. At night now, city was pitch-black – one could only move around with the help of a mobile phone or a flashlight.

No electricity meant not only useless bulbs. It also meant that the elderly and children had to climb up the stairs to the twentieth floor of a high-rise. Also, it meant that one couldn't cook or warm through the meals – most contemporary stoves being electric. And a whole bouquet of other 'inconveniences' into the bargain.

People were murmuring everywhere:

'Shame on this degenerate!'

'It seems that even Hitler didn't go to such lengths… Or perhaps he did, who could tell?'

'Same difference – they're peas out of the same pod…'

NASA satellites registered absence of city lights at night. Images of various regions were quite illustrative: Istanbul, Ankara and Bucharest were seas of light. As for Moscow – it was a real conflagration, and not only in the capital but throughout the entire surrounding area.

In an attempt to put some sort of a tin hat on the situation the authorities started deploying a network of 'Resilience Centres' – properly-heated facilities, supplied with water, electricity, mobile networks, internet, recreational rooms, first-aid points, and assistance to mothers with children.

On the same day came a response from the European Parliament – they had launched a new project, Generators of Hope. The purpose was to collect a maximum number of generators, especially industrial ones, in support of the civilian infrastructure in Ukraine.

Meanwhile the 'brothers' were voraciously nosing about, looking for something else to blow to smithereens, lasciviously narrowing their eyes in anticipation: 'Any minute now! They still have a substation operating? As for that district – weird that we haven't hammered it to pieces at once! Effing Ada! Beat up the Ukes and save Russia! True, a similar slogan existed once, right? OK, it was about Yids back then, so we've had it updated!'

On top of everything else, it was getting bitterly cold and the Russians were getting ready to start bombing our gas supplies, the objective being to make the 'fraternal Ukrainian nation' kick the bucket in the dead of the winter!

At times I felt like popping out, all unkempt, with a bare torso – if only onto socials – and bellow at the top of my lungs: 'Why are they doing this to us? According to you, we are one people! Why are you pummelling "your own" with such ferocity?' But straight away my inner voice would snap back at me: 'Shush! Don't fall for their tricks! You'll spend the winter the best you can. If need be, you'll die from cold, although, God forbid!'

I also wanted to yell into the ears of our allies: 'Hi there, our beloved partners, our source of hope! Esteemed Europe! Why are you still beating about the bush? Why send us those badly needed armaments only drop by drop? And even those aren't too modern, either. Finally, stop oscillating! Drop you fears about triggering something terrible. The terrible is already happening! For now, just to us. But it may well spread towards you as well! Why on earth are you finding it so difficult to take it all on board? Besides, you keep hoping that it will all blow out somehow…'

Already on November 25th, two days after the apocalypse, Kyiv had put in place 400 round-the-clock facilities that provided access to electricity. Mayor Klitchko: 'If your house has been cut off from the supply of electricity for longer than 24 hours, you may use our centres. There you can charge your gadgets and torches, have some tea, receive information on the whereabouts of protected sources of mineral water, find out about the working hours of shops and pharmacies. We are trying to ensure that each such centre provides access to the internet.'[359]

* * *

In the end, autumn yielded its place to winter. Winter meant cold.

Our 'brothers' became even more trigger-happy and increased the intensity of bombing. Now they were realising a new tactical approach: 'smash the effing Ukes' infrastructure with all you've got'. They hoped it would bear fruit – the 'fruit' being Ukraine agreeing to negotiations. No need to explain on what terms…

And that was the situation today – bombardments, bombardments, and more bombardments. At times it felt that neither earth or air would survive those blasts. Yet somehow the people held on.

More often than not, electricity was out, and heating worked at a minimal level. If you wanted tea, you had to drink it immediately, otherwise it would be cold within minutes.

Outside the windows, everything was shrouded in the thick fog of winter. Street lampposts were dead, and in the receding glow of a twilight, the outlines of poorly illuminated buildings loomed like some weird ghosts.

One couldn't go anywhere without a smartphone or a flashlight. Funny but the unevenness of the pavements became particularly obvious in the dark, even if nobody had ever been mindful of it in broad daylight. But now every bump and pockmark meant a real danger of tripping.

On December 5th Russia launched a new series of sea- and air-based ballistic missiles. About 50% of the power infrastructure had already been damaged. Should the present rate of bombing continue, the Ukraine's power system would disintegrate down to a critical level, after which electricity might be unavailable for weeks on end. In such a case, during those four winter months the country's cities would become practically unsuitable for habitation. Just

<hr>

359   RBC Ukraine, 28 November 2022. https://www.rbc.ua/rus/news/vitaliy-klich-ko-maemo-buti-gotovi-shcho-vidklyuchennya-1669591669.html (accessed 05.07.2025).

then arrived a commentary from Putin: 'Russian strikes against the Ukrainian energy-supply system is our "retaliation" for a string of Ukrainian actions"!'

Several days later Mayor Klitchko warned the Kyivites that should the strikes continue, and should a situation of emergency arise during the months of winter, the city residents would have to be ready to leave the city. There was no need for an immediate evacuation but the residents should be prepared. "As of this moment, we've put in about 500 focal points of autonomous supply of heating, another 100 being fitted out to be used in case of an emergency. To meet this target, the city has bought over 400 generators, approximately another 100 have been sourced by volunteers. However, 500 such sources– that's nothing for a city with a population of 3 million.'

At the same time the President's Office explained that should the worst happen, there simply wasn't anywhere to move the Kyiv residents to.

The air raids lasted into the first days in December. As a new development, Russians started using Iran-made kamikaze drones. The tenth mass shelling of Ukraine took place on December 29th. And even on December 31st, Russia still continued sending us her New-Year presents...

* * *

When the horror of this insane war had started, it was also winter. After that, obviously, we'd lived through spring, summer, and autumn. It was winter again, yet no end was in sight.

I was walking down the street; some fresh air had blown into the city. The trees had shed all their leaves and looked sad. Very much like people, they felt cold. Yet there was a definite plus, too – the houses weren't camouflaged anymore, so all the historic features of those old edifices were prominent yet again, for all to see...

And yet, daily news from all over the country left you with a bitter taste in the mouth. The enemy was ramming into our infrastructure practically every day. Because of one monster, millions of people were now forced to sit inside their flats and houses – assuming those were still standing – without light or heating. One could ask – what about battery-empowered bulbs? But those only made sense where electricity was available, at least from time to time, thus providing on opportunity to charge them. But what if you lived in a dugout, a tent, or a hut? Then your only option would be to use an oil lamp of some sort. Also, a candle – if there was a church nearby where you could buy some. How would one cook in a front-line city? On a bonfire built in the courtyard between multi-story residential blocs. To keep the fire going, you needed fire-wood – that is, if any was available. Otherwise, one had to burn whatever came to hand and was inflammable. Just imagine – all around us was the 21ˢᵗ century! Man was preparing to tackle the Universe, and Mars was an object of serious exploration. But we were reduced to the Middle Ages.

After the most recent attack electricity was cut off for over 48 hours – and this on the Kyiv's right bank! In many residential areas on the left bank this had become the norm. Our electricians were doing a super job – putting whatever they could to good use, making at least something out of nothing. To make things worse, days now were short, so there was no time to do anything well while it still was light. By four in the afternoon, it was already dusk…

No electricity made outings into the streets spooky – because of all that din from multiple generators. Nearly all companies and shops had now procured at least one. In front of the house across the street, as many as four were in place. Who lived there? Who knew? The frenzied rumbling carried all over, even to our house.

By mid-December European countries had sent us half-a-million low-intensity generators. Still, we badly needed another 17 thousand high-capacity ones…

Daytime electricity became a rarity. Appliances would be powered up at night, but even then, for two or three hours only. And you just couldn't miss that 'window' – you had to charge battery-powered lamps, your smartphone, the notebook, and every other gadget. So, how to make sure that this precious opportunity wouldn't be missed? Setting the alarm was useless: you'd set it for 2 a.m. but the electricity would be switched on at 3. And then I had a brainwave: all I had to do was to leave my radio tuned into the network. As soon as electricity became available, the radio started blasting. One had to swing out of bed in an instant – not a minute was to be wasted! Sometimes you might only have access for one hour, and you needed to hurry if you wanted to charge anything properly. Our country that had played a role even in the space exploration now found itself as if in the Stone Age.

Only now did I fully appreciate the fact that our life depended on those vital essentials: heating, water, gas, sewerage, and communications, the most important being electricity. None of the above was possible without it. Perhaps it could function briefly but, in the end, would definitely stop. And whatever electricity reserves we still had available were now channelled into functionality of that complex. There was simply none left for regular supplies of the residential dwellings.

Mum was like a hamster in a wheel:

'While there's water we've got so much to do. The most important are laundry and moist mopping. When water's no more, we'll just have to accept living in dust and filth.'

Switching the washing machine on was out of the question, mum washed it all by hand. Smalls and clothes were more or less manageable but bigger items were a problem.

'Tis OK. There were times when people did without. At least we've got water for now.'

'And when it stops, then what?' I asked. 'Shall we go to the Dnipro?'

'If we have to, we will.'

'Imagine! Millions of people rinsing their clothes along the Dnipro banks!' I made a feeble attempt at humour.

'No, I can't even imagine it,' mum sighed in all seriousness.

Communication, too, was wobbly now. If you did manage to reach somebody by phone, you had to speak briefly and quickly. Like everybody else, we switched our mobiles to dark screens and a power-saving mode.

'We must learn to live without telephones, computers, TV and radio,' contemplated mum. 'I used to be asking myself before – which of all these was the most vital? But now I don't even bother thinking about it as none of it is practically available anymore.'

'But we have to live somehow?' I was insistent.

'Probably in the way people used to live before. Still, live they did. For centuries! For how long have all those inventions been around? Several decades, no more. We'll simply get back in time, that's all.'

After that I was ruminating on my own. What would happen if the sewerage stopped working? It would've been easier in the countryside: go outside, dig a hole in the ground and deposit whatever had been 'processed' into it. But in a city – what would you do? Bio-toilets are offered in some places, complete with dissolving chemicals, deodorants, and other useful products, reportedly good to go for an entire week. There was no explanation, though, as to how utilise the final waste. In all likelihood, some new communal service would have to be set up. But naturally, it would mean extra expenditure as such a service was unlikely to come by for free.

Life in the city now was difficult, of course. But staying here might become impossible, should all of it – heating, water, gas, drainage, communications, and electricity – finally collapse. In such a case we would have to move to some village. Life in the country had always been tightly associated with the land. And the land had always been a saviour. One could survive even without electricity: just pop out to a grove nearby and collect some firewood. And lo and behold, you could cook your food and heat yourself. Then, perhaps, buy some produce from the other villagers and live like that for a good while. Mayor Klitchko appeals again and again to the city's residents, urging them to move out of the city: allegedly, the state of emergency could be announced any minute. That was precisely what he said, in plain Ukrainian: 'Countryside will come to our rescue!'

Although it would be easier for those who had family there, or at least owned a dacha, however tiny. Besides, bombardments over there weren't as frequent. Ruscists had no interest in the countryside unless it was located at some vantage point. Anyway, the main thing was to survive… In a word, to hold on till spring when things would become clearer. Besides, by then it would be warm …

By the way, municipal authorities did care for the city people: a lorry had pulled up by the street corner with a sign on its side – 'Drinking Water'! A huge tank fitted out with four little taps. Come along and fill up your bottle! Besides, it was provided free of charge.

So that was how we lived now. At night, for a couple of hours when electricity was available, we all rushed towards our computers, eager to get at least some idea of what was going on in the outer world. As for local news, we knew it all anyway. We were at war.

Military experts pointed out that international pressure had reportedly made Russia abandon the idea of using nuclear weapons in this war with Ukraine. But instead, the RF 'switched over to conceptually different weapons and started targeting the power infrastructure'. The purpose was to create panic among the population and make life intolerable. Now Putin was going to use winter as yet another weapon against Ukraine. Eliminating the Ukraine's power grid was a strategy commonly used by Russia, a way to 'make people suffer' by stripping them of elementary essentials needed for a normal life. It was mentioned that Russia had already applied this tactic during her intervention in Syria: 'to punish people and break their will, thus forcing them to surrender.'

And yet, somewhat later it had become possible to patch up the electric energy system. Besides, rescue came in the form of imports – since Ukraine's grid had been synchronised with the European system. In their turn, the USA allegedly started work on fitting Ukraine out with a new layered system for air defence. This system consisted of units operating at a variety of ranges and altitudes that were all linked up together and shared the data. Also, in order to enhance the Ukrainian anti-missile and anti-drone defence capacity, the Europeans provided a broad range of modern equipment.

There was more news, this time unrelated to the situation with energy. Having completed their course on drones, Gennady and Denis presented themselves at a military commissariat and volunteered for duty in Bakhmut! What a development! What heroes! And now they were in basic training at a camp somewhere…

∗

That day Taras and I had some business to attend to, so we arranged to meet early in the morning in Shchekavytsky Gardens by Zhovten Cinema. The place was still deserted. Suddenly, we both were overcome with joy, and started jumping around, waiving hands, quacking loudly, bellowing at the top of our voices. Completely carried away, we felt like two big birds on a seashore, ready to fly into the future. No, not just any birds – genuine eagles!

We quickly attended to our business, and two hours later ambled back via the same gardens. Christ on a bicycle! As if nothing had changed at all: the same 'commentators of the current affairs' were holding court, perched on the same benches – only now they wore warmer clothes, and had some sort of covers spread underneath for added warmth. It was, after all, winter. Undisturbed, they were deep in conversation, debating something with ardour. Of our 'underground' chum there was neither hide nor hair. Must've taken himself off to somewhere else, and so there was no one to dampen the mood.

Taras and I sat down on a bench nearby, pretending to be buried in our smartphones but in reality listening in.

'So, how goes it, guys, how's life?'

'Fair to middling. Those frequent power cuts... They target the grid now, the motherfuckers.'

'With us, it's two or three times a day. Those "brothers" are a mean lot.'

'Jackals, if you ask me! Putin is a jackal, and Russians are the jackals in his pack. They can't win on the battlefield so they've taken to hammering HPPs and water utilities. Fighting not the army but civilians. And hooting with joy. They're getting a kick, you see, a high from all the excitement, must be leaping about in ecstasy: *'The cold's already arrived, you scum! Let you all freeze to death, Bandera's spawn"!'*

'I've learnt some new stuff about them. So much time has passed since the start of war, so they held this new poll in effing Russia. As per usual, 80% support everything that's going on. In this case, annexation of our territories. Which means, the war itself. So, nothing has changed, nothing!'

'By the way, if you think about this insanely high percentage, a question asks itself – could they all be criminals? After what's happened here, many believe that yes, they all are gangsters. I'll be frank, I'm undecided. Although one thing is clear – most of them do come across as mean and treacherous.'

'That's absolutely true! Clearly, the main problem is Putin. Although in the end he'll get what's coming to him. But that nation is an even bigger problem. And there isn't a medication that could cure them. What's to be done, then?'

'Remember how those bloody Russians were thrown back from Kyiv and the oblast? When all their crimes came to light – in Bucha and other suburbs?

I've heard that there are scores, if not hundreds, of such Buchas around the country. All it takes is time – to liberate those areas and expose it all. Now Izium is under our control, and inside it – hundreds of murdered people. You know? Even children…'

'How they hate us! Won't just execute a person but necessarily torture before death!'

'Why only "before"? What about "after"? Riddling dead bodies with rifle bullets, just for fun. A war, for some, is a rush of adrenalin…'

'They say that those who issued the orders to commit atrocities will be held responsible, that's for sure. And Putin himself won't go scot-free!'

'As a supreme commander in charge of all of this, it's a must. He may well be put on an international trial but how to capture him?'

'Bah, but this bloody Russia hasn't signed the relevant treaty so they won't carry out the court's ruling. They are foresighted like that, the bastards. But even if she did sign it? It won't work. On the whole when did it ever happen that a head of state… It's very doubtful…'

'I wouldn't be so sure. It has happened many times in history that the heads of certain states, even after a long time, did get their comeuppance!'

'And another thing. Air raids are now longer than before.'

'It's because Iranian drones fly slower and can change direction. So, it takes more time…'

'There's this new word now – a "pit". It means a basement in a police station. Some nauseating footage has now appeared, about those "pits" you can hear men and women screaming. People were "processed' there for weeks on end – with no food, teeth knocked out, all internal organs damaged from beatings. Among those arrested – old people, even pregnant women. It looks horrific. A young mother cuddling her baby who's already dead. In another woman's arms – a 7-year-old boy with a bullet wound. He died eventually; she wasn't even related to him. People were crying in their cells for weeks and dying under torture. And before death they were made to undress.'

'I also heard that one 60-year-old woman was taken straight off the street: they threw a plastic bag over the head, and took her away. They then were walking her round the police station with this bag on her head. But if someone was let go, there would be a bag on their head too, must be so that the others were afraid, too. Some young guys had been arrested and no one ever saw them again. There was this lad, Artyom. He'd disappeared at the very beginning, they said they'd found him hiding our flags and insignia. And another two volunteers, they had vanished too. And if someone had belonged to a political party, the Russians treated them all as "Nazis", took all away. Russians didn't mince their words: "We'll shoot your child! Do tell where you keep your Bandera flags, bitch!" You see, they had those lists ready!'

'I, too, saw some footage from Mariupol. In one story they told about Bury-ats. Those stole whatever they could, even electric kettles. They demanded booze, and frequently got legless. Then they would open fire at their own soldiers, the Russians, start such chaotic shootouts. So, the latter would pitch up on the doorsteps of our residents: *If you give them alcohol, we'll pelt you with grenades!* The street scenes were horrible, too: people collecting water from the puddles, dogs lugging around human limbs...'

'I heard Putin is enfeebled now...'

'Still, he doesn't even consider a withdrawal! The other way round, his pressure grows in cruelty. He thinks that the front will stabilise somehow, and then he'll launch a new offensive. Also, he believes that Europe will collapse because they've introduced sanctions and now have to tighten their belts. Their people will start howling and clamouring for gas. Then again, America's far from stable, too. So, he'll stuff the army full of the newly-mobbed and embark on re-capturing the territories he's lost.'

'But the way he's fretting over his health! How he wants to live! One hell of a lot of various super-laboratories been opened along all his routes. Everything's checked for poison, he wouldn't swallow even a mouthful otherwise. A brigade of doctors is always in his wake, wherever he appears. And that case with rea-gents? He's said to have tests done every day.'

'Generally speaking, everything is done to leave Russia the way she is. Some-one has put it adequately: he's fighting the future.'

'The main thing – he's got it all: palaces, dachas, yachts, billions in all sorts of currency! I will never believe that he's prepared to risk it all for the sake of winning a war. He must be eager to continue enjoying what he's assembled and stolen! Take Hitler, for example. He also sat in a bunker but he said: "I'm not afraid of dying. I have nothing!" Stalin could say the same: "I've got nothing apart from my trench coat, a pair of darned long johns and my boots.' Take even Brezhnev. After his death, they found his savings book, and in it – only 60 thousand "wooden" rubles. They weren't destitute, nothing like that, after all the state paid for all their needs, and they could afford whatever they pleased, and the nosh was most refined. But to own billions and then keep them buried in some Central African mines... It's mind-boggling.'

'Wait a minute. Let's get back to our situation. Remember that quite recently we'd been imploring for the modern arms but the West wouldn't oblige. And we kept saying: "If you help us, we'll hold the line!" Had they taken heed then, the situation might have been totally different. Just imagine, what would've happened had we not been holding on? Effing Russians would have now been in Vilnius, Riga, and Tallinn, with their tanks, and the whole shebang. And while NATO continued scratching their heads, they would've reached Warsaw too. Spread like locusts over Poland. And the Polish border is some pithy 100 kilometres away from Berlin. NATO probably wouldn't make it to there in time anyway!'

'Whatever you say, it's still the same enemy!' some sober-minded guy joined the discussion. 'And we've only got one way out: to win. And I'm not talking about some imaginary march on Moscow – this is out of the question. But as for that accursed regime – it has to be replaced. Otherwise, no one will have any peace. After 1991, for some ten years Russians lived in relative freedom. Yet they've opted for their beloved imperial model, a model of conquest. And now it is imperative to make sure – whatever it takes! – that they would be brought to heel. This is the crux of the matter: we should win not over Putin but Russia as she exists. The Russian Federation is just a name. A chimera. There are nearly 200 peoples and various ethnic groups there. Such a conglomerate should be somehow kept in check. It simply cannot be glued together peacefully. From time to time, they need a war.'

'I agree. The territory is so vast that an option of unity simply does not apply. It goes against all recent developments on our planet. How could one keep together such huge imperial territories? Allegedly, they are all united by the Russian language. First thing: allegedly. Second: is just language enough? Also, Russia is simply incapable of bidding farewell to her ideology. And this ideology of theirs is 100% imperial.'

'That's words out of my mouth! Russia had been incorporating new territories through centuries. Being geographically adjacent, and accessible not by ships across the seas or oceans – but by carts on dry land, it was considerably easier to integrate the land and resettle your citizens to over there. Such territories became integral part of the same contiguous mass of land and didn't perceive themselves as colonies. In the days of the Soviet power this subject was taboo. As a matter of fact, the Soviet Union promoted itself as a fighter against colonialism, lending support to national liberation movements in colonies of other empires. But considering the cold facts, could one treat the Caucasus, Central Asia, and the entire Siberia and Far East as colonised territories? And what about us? But even the countries of the East European Soviet bloc could be counted as colonially subjugated entities. So, what does it all mean? It means that disintegration of the Warsaw Pact – that collective defence treaty, and then breakup of the Soviet Union itself spell a beginning of decline and fall of the Russian colonial system. What's happening today is an attempt of the Russian leadership to scramble this empire back together again, whatever the means.'

'Yeah. Phantom pains of a dying monster who's ready to use a full range of methods: hybrid wars, a tug of war over the influence of the Russian language, influence over the army, pressure from the side of organised crime, diplomacy, religion, corruption of elites… A federation of this kind can accordingly survive only under a harshest authoritarian regime. There's no other way. In essence, many ethnic groups have been stripped of their languages, traditions, culture. An alternative would be a civilised confederation of equal members…'

'Uh oh – good grief! What a beautiful analysis… Next, you'll say that it's about to collapse of its own accord. I don't buy it! The various sites and YouTube talk of little else, predicting its disintegration. Yet it's still there…'

'Yet there will be developments. The Russian state will disintegrate, that much is certain, and that will put an end to its imperial ambitions. After all, imperialism is the only efficient rational ideology that does work in Russia. Only it's referred to not as "imperialism" but "nation-building, nation's grandeur, and uniqueness", or any such crap. But in essence it's good old imperialism… In any case, it's all reminiscent of the final stages of the Roman Empire. It's sliding downwards. But whether it'll take years or decades – who can tell?'

'Russia is kept from a collapse only through its military muscle. It's still cemented together by allocation of huge resources of power. It could've lasted for much longer. Yet putting the Russian army through the meat-grinder of the war in Ukraine will only accelerate this inevitable process. If this war ends in a failure, they won't be able to brush it under the carpet. Russia doesn't like her leaders to lose. The myth of Putin as a "macho-conqueror" will dissolve in an instant. Love, even adoration will give way to hatred – the coin always flips quickly. Everything may happen precipitously…'

'Well… I'm sick and tired of the fantasy genre. In the best-case scenario some territories, some outskirts will fall apart, and that will be that. OK, the provinces don't like Moscow… Distrust, even hate it… They might move the capital – tee hee! – to some other place. Perhaps, Yekaterinburg in the Urals, or someplace closer to Siberia. Novosibirsk – that's Siberia 100%. And that will be the whole story. After all, Russia is a bear. And this huge beast is holding fast to what's his! I know just one thing for sure: they are unlikely to go out in the streets in their hundreds and thousands. It's not that kind of a country. It must take some other course out there.'

'Looking at a bigger picture, for as long as the Russian Federation hasn't embarked on a way of democracy, it will remain a threat to the entire world. Take Germany – when occupied, they went through denazification. By the way, it was not smooth and easy… But Russia must go as well through "deputinisation" by self-cleansing because she will never ever be occupied. Unless it will, indeed, fall apart.'

There was a long silence. Then, again:

'What's your view of the future?'

'I'm an optimist. History often repeats itself; every tendency is replayed. The party of the past shall, like always, lose to the party of the future. And so, it's little wonder that the past is firmly grabbing the future with its bony hands. But it is no use. None at all. Still, all of it will cost a lot of blood.'

'OK. Let's think it over… The future of Ukraine is more or less clear. Right now, it's moulding itself anew. It perceives itself as a nation defending its independence, freedom, and democratic values. As for Russia, it all is completely unclear. She's at a crossroads. In the long run, when generational change starts taking place, especially within the elites, there will be scramble for Putin's legacy, both in terms of power and finances. So, then it will be a question of who comes on top.'

'Completely true! Victory can only happen when Russia goes through a change of generations. So that those who are now 30-40-year-old will wipe out those over 50-60. To say nothing about the 70-odd-years oldsters.'

'In a word, we have to hold on for another 10 or 15 years,' the reasonable guy summed it all up. 'That's the prospect… A nice kettle of fish!'

One of the 'commentators' glanced at his watch:

'Look, guys, it's lunchtime already. I'll read you this before we split up. Ursula von Leiden wrote: "The most significant lesson to be learnt from this war is that Europe should have listened to those who know what Putin is all about. Listen to Anna Politkovskaya and other journalists who have uncovered crimes and paid a high price for their activities. Listen to our friends in Ukraine, Moldova, Georgia, and the Belarusian opposition. We should have lent a more attentive ear to the voices from within our Union – those from Poland, the Baltic countries, the entire Central and Eastern Europe.'

* * *

The year was at an end and there was a multitude of events.

Combat activities slowed down in the winter, but the Bakhmut front things were still calamitous. It turned out to be quite a special city.

And then – at long last! – reopened two key stations on the Metro: Maidan of Independence and Khreschatyk. By that point many people had become resentful: *How come that we are whisked through Khreschatyk while world stars are performing there all the time? Day and night – no respite!* Concerts, of course, were well and good but the real point was that two most significant hubs stayed boarded up for a long time now and the ability to change for any other line had been impossible.

Well… but on the whole, life now was not too bad at all. Wonder of wonders, the grid was powered up now not on a whim but in accordance with a schedule that allocated hour-long slots for two weeks in advance. It didn't mean, though, that the schedule was kept to a minute. It could come on half an hour earlier or later. But at least there was a semblance of predictability. So, many things now became possible! But that was life, in our city. After all, a capital city always enjoys a special status. As for the other regions...

My acquaintances told me: they went out of Lviv, at night, by car. And over the whole route they didn't see any light at all, big or small. As if they weren't passing through any built-up areas at all. All around their car, everything was pitch-black.

Now... We were constantly visited by various world leaders. Then on December 21st, President Zelensky, too, left on a visit to the USA, the biggest donor of our military and financial aid. Near the White House he was welcomed by President Biden. Afterwards, he made his triumphant speech at the Congress. It was a true international sensation! Only recently anything of the kind would've been unimaginable.

And this... The news commentators uncovered from somewhere a schedule of movement of a particular Russian unit in the first days of war. The soldiers had been notified about the invasion only several hours prior to its commencement. They had been ordered to approach Kyiv in 18 hours. The first convoy included troops from Special Purpose (OMON) and Special Rapid Deployment Force (SOBR). The progress was delayed from the off: heavy-duty vehicles had become bogged down in mud and it had taken them more than 24 hours only to cross the border. After that, the situation went from bad to worse. And we all knew what happened subsequently...

Mayor Klitchko, too, shared some valuable info. He said that Kyiv now was 'full of people'. Before the war the city population had countered 3.8 million. In March of 2022 – less than a million. In July – already 2-2.5 million. And by the end of December 2022, it was back to 3.6 million, out of which 300 thousand were registered as refugees.

'The times are very hard now. Since Putin is failing on the battlefield, he's eager to ruin the life of common people. He would like to kill off women, children, and the elderly. If the temperature plummets, flats without electricity and heating will become unsuitable for accommodation. Putin's aim is panic, so that everybody would be evacuated abroad. He needs Ukraine as a territory without Ukrainians. And the people are perfectly well aware of this.'

Yet the enemy had another objective in mind. Strikes delivered at the infrastructure was the Kremlin's attempt to disable the Ukrainian air defence. In such a case Ukraine would simply have no capacity to defend its facilities of critical importance – the air defence would have to be distributed all over various cities, thus exposing certain segments of the front. They would be forced to use up precious ammunition.

* * *

True, it wasn't a done thing to praise oneself. Still, I made this entry into my pad:

'The value of my notes is that they will last a lifetime, if only mine. Ten months have passed since the war started, but not only some details, but the overall texture of events is already slipping from memory. Meanwhile this way the invaluable words will be engraved on paper. If ever I have to renew my memory of those events – or maybe someone else wanted to do it? – people will look into this pad, or the book if it comes out, and it will all come back. As for the future generations, thanks to those notes, they will learn some important things. For the written word lives forever.'

Ah well, the insane year was drawing to a close…

True, the year 2022 was very hard to live through. Some could not stand it, for the hardships had been superhuman. And no one would ever have any right to accuse them, for those had been live people and not some robots…

January – May 2023.
Waiting for a Counterattack...

Horrendous and terrifying was the year of Our Lord 2022, when Russia went to war against Ukraine. But now even this year had come to an end. A new one had been ushered in, with only one digit changed – the year now was 2023. What was to come? How would it arrive? Would it be the year when the war finished – just one figure different in the number, but still, it was as many as 365 days within its purview. Or was this war everlasting and would go on, and on, and on?

None of it was comprehensible, at least for now.

All that was left was to follow the news – it wasn't forbidden, follow to your heart's content. Around the clock if such was your wish...

In the later part of the autumn of 2022, the war had reached a certain plateau. Some even asserted that there was a certain degree of stabilisation on all fronts. But stabilisation, in effect, meant freezing, and this spelled nothing good whatsoever.

An expert opinion insisted that this type of stabilisation would thwart the purposes of the war. 'No one wants a break, no one wants to wait for a year or two, or three, or even longer – till Putin puts together a new army and launches a new war. In essence it means this: for as long as the aim of the war has not been reached, the war isn't over. Any cease-fire or truce would only mean an intercession. That is why we and our partners are determined to act resolutely.' To paraphrase: everyone realised that there should be a new offensive.

Walking down Mezhyhirska Street, I heard this:

'This newly elected Brazilian President Luiz Lula says seriously funny things: allegedly, in this war both Russia and Ukraine are to blame, and we should renounce Crimea. Then we'll live practically in paradise. He believes it's just a tiff within a family. He also says that all the West does is fan the embers of war...'

'Atta boy! To put an aggressor and his victim in the same line-up is really cool. He even refused to provide us with ambulances – even refused to sell them! Our guys told him: "Come over here! You'll get a better idea of what's what!"

'No way, not coming. Just general reasoning: "We are against war!" In other words, if one logically extended the argument, we, Ukrainians, are for war!'

'Or take Viktor Orbán in Hungary! Famous Putino-phil. His memory is somewhat vague, though, on how the Soviets, led by their titular nation, in 1956 flattened Hungary with their tanks. Thousands died then...'

'But he's not the only one, millions of Hungarians do not remember this either. And what the leader of the country has to say carries weight. Only 10-15% support Ukraine. The rest are in accordance with Orbán...'

On January 14th, 17 Russian Tu-95 bombers got off the ground and into the air, along with the Russian warship that went out to sea carrying Kalibr cruise missiles. Yet again, they damaged power infrastructure in six oblasts of Ukraine. While flying over Kursk Oblast and the Azov Sea, Tu-22 aircraft launched five ballistic missiles of X-22 class. Unfortunately, Ukraine had no ADS devices to intercept such missiles. Explosions reverberated in many areas of the country. One of those missiles hit a nine-story building in the city of Dnipro. Two public entrances and 72 flats had been completely wiped out; 236 flats damaged. About 50 people had been killed, at least 80 – wounded, out of this number 16 were children. The youngest one was three years old...

But the Russian socials that day were jubilant, overflowing with joy. For all that, in several Russian cities appeared impromptu memorials in honour of those who had died. People were bringing flowers, toys, and the photographs of that building in ruins. Many were apprehended, police brought in their vans for surveillance. On the same night the communal services removed the flowers, yet in the morning they appeared anew, only to be cleaned out again. Quoting some arcane piece of legislation, the police forbade taking pictures of such memorials.

Throughout the months of January and February bombings of the power infrastructure continued. From time to time there were emergency power cuts, and even the Metro services had to be suspended.

However, despite the regular bombings, Ukrainian power system persevered, the staff proving themselves capable of rectifying the damage in the shortest time possible. The power grid of Ukraine, being among the biggest in Europe and consisting of an extensively ramified network of Power Transmission Lines and diversified energy sources – NPSs, HEPPs and stations using traditional and alternative energy sources, had turned this fact to its advantage. At the same time, in order to cut consumption, municipal authorities reduced the volume of street lighting, replaced electric types of public transport with buses, urged the households to save energy during peak hours. As for replenishing and power boosts, priority was given to the systems for heating and water supply. It made sense, since temporary cuts in generating power and heat in the winter could result in the freezing of the mains, and this could lead to breakages. At times, the temperatures plummeting to minus 10 or 20 made the situation really dire.

By about February 11th it had become possible to stabilise the situation and mass-scale rolling power-cuts stopped.

As for the military sphere, the main developments were taking place around Bakhmut that had become a real hotspot of engagement. This name had become known all over the world. After several months of fierce fighting the enemy had managed to advance into several boroughs of the city, and there appeared a realistic danger of Bakhmut's encirclement by the Russian troops.

Events were coming in rapid succession, a real avalanche of developments. Important news overshadowed less significant updates, although it wasn't always possible to tell them apart. And one couldn't always keep track of the goings-on.

This was sending ripples all over the world, involving every person and every household. But even if some believed the war would pass them by, it was a mistake to think so. True, it was only us who found ourselves under direct fire but the whole world was already paying the price for the imaginary 'denazification and demilitarisation' – the goals that allegedly had forced Russia to declare war on Ukraine. As a result, many countries were facing a threat of hunger and cold in the winter, while price hikes and inflation had become a universal phenomenon. Still, we were those who suffered the most.

For example, this horrible story. Starting from April of 2022, the city of Soledar had lived without gas, light, or water. Older women were digging their own graves right underneath the windows of their multi-story apartment blocks – to save everyone the bother in case something did happen. Imagine looking at such a grave out of the window of a building where you'd lived all your life.

Then there was a story of this Russian colonel – the Russians had leaked it themselves. When conducting interrogations, he was invariably drunk – pointing his gun at prisoners' heads, demanding the names of 'nationalists'. He would rip off the detainee's trousers or underwear, and the poor fellow would stand in front of him, his eyes closed.

'*I'll summon a Dagestani now, he'll give you a good seeing to!*'

Addressing another prisoner:

'Got a lass?'

'Yes.'

He dragged down the POW's trousers and guffawed:

'Hey, you out there! Get me a mop. We'll stick its handle up ye asshole, make a video. Then send it to her, she'll see how you've become a girl.'

With their videoclip mentality, many Russians thought in propaganda TV images and pictures from social media. There was this mother, lamenting the death of her son in the war: 'God damn you, Ukraine!' That was exactly what she cried – not 'God damn you, Putin!' In other words, neither Putin nor Shoigu were to blame; her child had been murdered by Ukrainians. Sure we will hear it one day on TV, hysterically reiterated by the propaganda meisters: 'Ukraine is killing your children!'

As for the 'good' and 'liberal' Russians frequently referred to these days, one could see their true colours by using the same simple test, the issue of Crimea: 'Tell us without a stutter – does Crimea belong to Ukraine? Speak from your heart and don't prevaricate!' No one would answer without some beating about the bush at some length. No one had taken on board that fundamental European principle of inviolability of the borders. And another test: 'Is this Putin's war or, when all is said and done, is it Russia's war? Does Putin conduct with his own hands? Does he stay on his throne for so many years without your support? You are the ones who wage this war. With him at the head, of course. And your "We are against war!" means nothing. And "Stop the war!" is even 'better'! To give the occupied territories to Russia and Putin?' All it would reveal would be a double-faced stance supported by many 'good' people in Russia.

But did those 'good' ones even exist – without inverted commas, without irony? Perhaps they did. But we'd been through so many deaths and so much destruction, so much anguish that to us now all Russians were criminals. With rationality not working, it was hard to separate the good from the bad. At the moment hatred reigned supreme.

It made no sense now to read any Russian classics, with their endless chewing over the issue of this 'inscrutable Russian soul'. They had come up with this definition back in the day, as if trying to explain how hard they'd been looking for an answer but failing to find it anywhere. Today this view had changed. In truth, this soul smelled of blood and excrement…

Again and again, we saw images of carefree young people in Moscow and St. Petersburg, enjoying life just like before. And why not? It was spring, and things went according to plan. And the war? But it was far away! Why should it concern them if human losses were running in tens of thousands, while millions had been uprooted and made homeless, but all that was far from them? Nothing like that was happening on the Russian soil, so one couldn't feel any of it. Besides, neither Moscow nor St Petersburg had taken draconian measures when applying recruitment quotas to supply the front. For this purpose, there were Buryats, Dagestanis, other ethnic minorities. One Dagestani put it succinctly: 'The Russians don't have to worry. In a war between Slavs, we'll do it all ourselves...'

Ethnic Russians, of course, were also 'involved in the process'. But most recruits were citizens of Russia that lived in the sticks, in complete hopelessness. One could even formulate it in a different way: for economically depressed Russian regions this war had created an opportunity to earn a living and to achieve upward mobility, a new opportunity to be enjoyed by the lumpen social dregs. The propaganda had successfully filled their micro-brains with febrile hatred and cruelty, and the whole thing had even become fun: something to do, at last, and to be paid decent money for doing it!

These opinions were bandied around too: 'The Russian people are kind and unfortunate; they have never been masters of their own destiny, not even in the Soviet times...' Yeah, right. The real nature of this nation's kindness had been convincingly demonstrated through atrocities committed in Ukraine, none of those performed personally by Putin-the-Tyrant but by these 'kindly and miserable' people. And therefore, today the only way to look at the Russian people and Russia was through the Ukrainian magnifying glass, with Ukrainian eyes. There wasn't any other way.

Those outlanders were content with the way things were. The umbilical cord of a contract uniting the population and the government implied: 'You leave us alone; we leave you alone'. Like before, it was acceptable to all concerned. No one was going to sever it.

Some of them said: 'Of course, Putin isn't a pure-water democrat, but one can live with this.' In other words, Russian democracy was a different nature, a hybrid. They'd invented a new type of 'democracy' to suit their needs and even insisted that there was a degree of evolution. Aiming to find something positive in this bullshit, they were lecturing the whole world.

Or for example the declarations about nuclear weapons. It was like a game of ping-pong: 'I'll use it... I won't... I'll wait a bit...' It was tantamount to an admission that they couldn't win the war in direct combat. And since they couldn't win it any other way, all that was left was to grab a nuclear bludgeon.

At times the news was openly weird. A single father of four was arrested for 15 days in Moscow for listening, in his car... to Ukrainian songs.

* * *

I was walking around the flat extremely vexed with myself. Something was on the tip of my tongue, a curious word – on the strength of it, I could make a good entry. Yet the word was escaping me, even if I felt it would give me a necessary boost.

Uh-huh, there it was – a sweatshirt. More and more frequently Zelensky made his appearance clad in a black sweatshirt with a slogan – 'I'm Ukrainian!' This set the trend and fleeces, sweatshirts, and hoodies with the same message became available from many retailers. That was the boost I'd been looking for. I grabbed the pen and opened my pad:

'Recently another "shaman" appeared in the Russian firmament. This time it's a new pop star by the name of Shaman. To look at him – a nondescript languid guy. Yet when performing, he psyches himself up and transports his audience into a state of rapture. To top it all, he struts around in a hoodie with a slogan "I'm Russian". He did nick the idea from Zelensky, though. In mid-flight, so to speak. And now over there, too, all shops are selling "national" fleeces, hoodies, and sweatshirts with this message. Hit of the season. Such is their ability to intercept anything trendy and make it their own. You may call it stealing, of course. It isn't just impressive, it's fascinating. It's all done so unblinkingly, naturally, without any hint of a sly thought. In this respect they are real virtuosos.'

Everybody was talking about little else but our impending counter-offensive: on the internet, on television and in private chats. There was even a new debate as to how to refer to it: a counter-offensive or just an offensive? Everyone agreed that both were correct.

Long story short, the entire country was waiting for it. And so, in an attempt to countermand this counter-offensive Russia started a mass-scale assault on the eastern front. The main point of engagement was the same city of Bakhmut.

An ominous date was coming close – February 24th, the first anniversary of this infamous war.

A year after invasion, the Kremlin had been forced to shred its principal and most ambitious plan – that of eliminating Ukraine as a state. On the other hand, the Russian society had never realised that this war was the most pointless project in the entire history of their country. On 22 February 2023 another gala took off at Luzhniki Stadium. This time it was held in honour of the first year's anniversary of the 'special military operation'. Compared to the gala concert held in March 2022, there was a difference. That time Putin had spoken for 38 minutes, but now – for only four. Then, the enthusiasm had been palpable whereas now things were much more muted. Some asserted that even this short speech was delivered by Putin's double.

Yet there was a certain spice. Singer Oleg Gazmanov came out wearing a jacket from Prada, the famous logo prudently covered with a sticker. What a bashful crowd, those people!

OK, those were the events over there. But here, too, we expected that something important might happen on February 24th. Many feared the worst – it was a first-year anniversary after all. To add insult to injury, we heard that missile manufacturers in Russia had been operating on a three-shift basis. What if Putin decided to arrange a huge kaboom, targeting us with all his carrying aircraft, submarines, and warships…

The whole country was getting ready in advance – who could rule out Russia delivering new strikes with a doubled or even tripled vehemence. In view of all that, schools and universities had suspended classes for the whole week.

The youngest citizens were in training too. My friends told me how they returned home with their three-year-old son whom they'd picked up at the kindergarten. They took off his outer clothes, but he leapt onto an armchair and started yelling:

'Attension! Air laid! Air laid! All go to a selter!'

During several days leading up to the twenty-fourth, many people had considered it prudent to hide in bomb shelters, basements, or cellars, with a view to stay put until at least the morning of the twenty-fifth. After that, it would hopefully be easier.

Meanwhile President Lukashenko in Belarus stayed true to form. That was, for example, his joke during yet another visit to Moscow: 'Vladimir Vladimirovich and I – [360] we are the two co-aggressors, the most toxic and malign people on this planet… We have only one point of disagreement: who's worse? He says it's me. But I have already started suspecting it's him. Well, in the end we agreed that we are as bad as each other.'

One could only commiserate with the citizens of the country under his leadership. But then again – who could tell? – perhaps they preferred it like that.

By the way, I heard it many times – people contemplating why Lukashenko was so 'active', often rushing forward ahead of the locomotive. Few were aware that from the very beginning of his career in politics he'd cherished a dream – perhaps, still did – to become president of the restored Soviet Union. Even if it was in a slimmed-down version, with only Slavs among its members. Lukashenko was as much a dreamer as his comrade Putin. But would Putin ever allow Lukashenko access to such a helm?

* * *

....

[360] **Vladimir Vladimirovich**: Putin.

Mothers of Buryat soldiers who had died in Ukraine spoke in favour of continuing the 'special military operation'. They admitted that their sons had been taken there by stealth and they hadn't been ready – neither psychologically, nor morally. Yet on they went: *'Russia had to defend herself.' 'It was probably impossible to follow a different course.' 'If we stop now, what has it all been for, then?'*

Either that was the kind of mothers they were, or they had been forced to utter those words. Yet there appeared more revealing statements; *'Putin is conducting this "special operation" through the agency of Buryats, Chechens, and Dagestani, others... In terms of percentages, there are way too many ethnic minorities there...'*

Putin became a pariah in the civilised world, yet in Russia he is an object of worship.

A Western journalist was reporting from the Moscow city centre:

'This personality cult has reached the stage of Putino-mania. The souvenir shops are overflowing with the "artefacts": singlets and T-shirts with his picture on the front, vodka bottles and glasses with his face, letter Z slapped on anything you could think of, straightforward portraits and matryoshka dolls.

"It's all snapped up!" – a happy salesperson shares their impressions. *"Look at those matryoshkas – they are so marvellous: Lenin, Stalin, Putin, Medvedev – the entire family in one!'*

'The buyers shared their views, too: *"I love Russia!"*; *"I adore Putin!"*; *"He's done so much for us!"*; *"Meanwhile you, in the West, are telling lies!"*

'Yet it was impossible to verify any of this. If you didn't toe the line, you could be facing a significant fine, or even a prison sentence.

'But if you leave the souvenir shop and drop into a supermarket, all you will find there, too, will be a brand of vodka called 'Putinka'...'

* * *

The analysts wondered whether, with time, even a model for Russia's future development might become a source of conflict? Would Russia linger within this suffocating imperial paradigm? Would there appear a capacity for change, for evolving into a modern and open country populated not by subjects but citizens? And they will have the right to vote freely and influence their country's destiny?

But for the time being, propaganda watchdogs had been ordered to use the federal TV channels as a platform for presenting the image of the enemy one could hate on a legal basis and with impunity. Evidently, this enemy was the USA. Also, Europe. But ahead of everyone else – Ukraine. To hate them all was everyone's paramount duty, because they were to blame for everything. And for the people of a particular kind, it was much easier to succumb to hatred than to analyse the facts. People would believe what they wanted to believe. What was happening now was the acme of that criminal propaganda campaign – justification of this interventionist war! All of it was pushing the Russian society back into the past, laying waste to the decades of economic, spiritual, and other types of development. However, they didn't view any of this as important.

My troubled thoughts were washing one over another, propelling one another forward, I barely had time to write them down.

'It's been a year since the beginning of the war. From now on the count will be in hundreds of days – four hundred, five, six… More and more… Can it run into thousands?

'The main objectives declared by the enemy – "denazification and demilitarisation" – have not been achieved. The other way round, there are more patriots in our country now than before. Numbers of weapons, too, have grown exponentially. Also, we can hardly say that we are alone – unlike the early days of war when, at times, it seemed that we didn't have any allies at all. Even if we are not accepted into any bloc as a fully-fledged member-country, perhaps they will offer us not just a special status but something super-exceptional? It would be great to have the same protective umbrella currently available to other civilised countries. Can Europe now do without us?

'The civilised world is perceiving this war as an act of unprovoked aggression. There is a consensus in our society: "denazification", "protection of the Russian-speaking people", other blue-sky inventions are nothing more than a con-trick, a chimera. The most important thing was the Kremlin elder's desire to grab some new territories!

'It looks increasingly likely that the West moves towards a shared view that Putin mustn't win and must be held to account for unleashing this war. This will be imperative, in order to teach other dictators a lesson. The future peace-making capacity of the West, and primarily, of the United States, will depend on this. On the other hand, they have trouble imagining the future Russia. It is, after all, too big a country, and this fact causes problems for the entire world.

'The part of Europe geographically closest to this war insists that Russia is unlikely to change. They are convinced that Russia is "genetically inferior", condemned to be an eternal source of danger. By way of an example, they quote the words by Vyacheslav Volodin, the Chairman of the State Duma: "After Putin there will be another Putin." And the atrocities committed by the Russian military serve to emphasise the need to isolate this monster of a country.

'Yet those further away from the theatre of war are undecided: how is it possible, to exclude Russia from the world? On the whole it seems that the West hasn't yet come up with a final answer to the problem of Russia. They aren't sure yet what they should do. Too big a territory. Too large a population. Too powerful her lethal weapons… So, is it possible to do anything about it at all?'

I shut my pad but re-opened it straight away:

'The Russian state – as it exists – is a chimera since it has no genuine institutions. Neither does it have a mechanism in place that could enforce collectively made decisions. There is Putin and this is all it takes. A mafioso structure that runs the country. There may well be people at the top, even in his closest circle, who are dissatisfied with the decisions he makes. But they are afraid… And if suddenly something "big" were to take place – say, a plot – then everything will happen in a flash. For a couple of days, they will be in shock. And then: "But it's all OK! It's clear as day! That was how it had to be. It's all been leading this way…"

'History teaches that systems of this kind may crumble overnight. Then again, they may go on for quite some time. But a question suggests itself: could it be that a recent increase in power enjoyed by Prigozhin and other jingoists is a sign of some process leading to a loss of manageability? If this, indeed, were the case then there's hope that this nauseating Muscovy – that has become a quintessence of Byzantine Orthodoxy and messianism, buttressed by the war machine reminiscent of the Golden Horde[361] – must one day fall…

'The experts assert that the Russian Empire started disintegrating in 1917. The process continued in 1991 but then was frozen. But one way or another, it should be completed. Not everything was achieved then. But when a historic era comes to an end – allegedly, that's what Russia is facing now – there is a need for answers to fundamental questions about how and where the country should go from this point – in order to be transformed from something archaic into something modern and civilised.

'And here's the most principled question: will we – Ukraine – be able to become a herald of such metamorphoses? And not only for Russia – for all nations in the world enslaved by totalitarian and authoritarian regimes? Can one hope that Ukraine's victory will usher in an era an increased collective global self-awareness? After all, Ukraine is chipping away at the myth of the totalitarian and authoritarian systems' indestructibility. It will help many those oppressed to conquer their eternal fear: "They've done it! And we should be able to do it too"!'

That was it. I put a final stop, hoping that my notes – possibly to grow into something more comprehensive – would become at least a tiny brick in the powerful wall of the Ukrainian resistance.

....

[361]   The **Golden Horde:** originally a Mongol and later a Turkic khanate established in the 13th century and originating as the north-western sector of the Mongol Empire.

My notepad had been quite full now, overflowing with notes and various additional cuttings I'd pasted in. It contained a lot of thoughts: contradictory, debatable ones… Obviously, I had to put it all through a finer filter. Previously, short of time, I'd had to jot down anything of interest, anything useful that had occurred to me, almost in short-hand. But now I felt it was time to arrange everything I'd collected in some order. And thus, gradually move over towards writing a script. It would be a story of our daily life at the defence post. But it would be more than that. It would be necessary to find space for a chronology of events, interlace it with my general contemplations on the things around. I had quite a collection now, lots to work with. I also felt that I had to move fast, so that I could submit it to the Script Commission in time and then hope for their approval.

* * *

Recently, many sites posted photos of a 19-year-old girl who had volunteered to the front where she – oh horror! – had lost a leg. She had a face of divine beauty. What would become of her? She dominated my thoughts for quite some time.

Then there was this guy, 23 years of age. He'd lost both legs and his right arm. He, too, was constantly in my mind. But he wasn't the only one, that guy. There were hundreds such boys, thousands…

Snippets of conversations in the street:
'The war turned everything upside down… All our plans… We wanted…'
'We've lost everything too. We thought…'
'And we were about to…'
'That's what I said! We've all been hacked up by it all!'
It wasn't all that important to fill in the blanks. Everyone had been making plans for themselves and their families, envisaging events, looking forward to things… And then it all had been wasted… Never realised…

Uh-huh! Something curious had come through: various members among the country's leadership evaluating and singling out a most difficult period since the start of the war. The opinions differed… Danilov, for example, said this: 'God be praised, it's all OK now. The first three or four days were the most tense. It was how people behaved then that shaped the whole situation…'[362]

<hr>

[362] BBC news Ukraine, 14 April 2022, https://www.bbc.com/ukrainian/news-611 08199 (accessed 05.07.2025).

The majority of those in the military and political hierarchy agreed: 'The most critical were the first three days. After that, it started falling into a sort of a groove. True, it was hard afterwards too, but this sense of a catastrophe wasn't there anymore.'

At the same time, according to Syrsky, the hottest time had been the period in early March when the enemy had captured the springhead around Moshchun. 'That was a very dangerous location: a stone's throw from Kyiv, and a possible point of access all the way to Shevchenko Square [in the northern borough of Obolon], and then into the city. The situation was truly critical. We had used a multitude of measures, stayed at the commander's observation point for nearly 24 hours. We put forward all reserves at our disposal at the time. At the cost of our spine-shattering efforts, the situation was reversed. It changed to our advantage, and the enemy failed to break through...'[363]

S. Nayev was also asked, 'When did our troops breathe a sigh of relief? When you realised that the Russian blitz had gone pear-shaped?' He answered: 'When they failed to capture Kyiv. And then, a second time – when their dreams of heading towards Odesa were thwarted.'[364]

For some unknown reason I couldn't tear myself away from my pad:

'The process of post-Soviet Russia laying claims to somebody else's property started in the early 90', right after the disintegration of the Soviet Union. So, Putin's ideas fell onto a prepared ground – a nostalgia for an "empire that we'd lost."

'Putin and his absolutely unrealistic paranoid worldview, obviously, isn't the entire Russia. It's a large country where there are resourceful, young, active population strata who see the world in a totally different way. Putin does his best to arrest the inevitable appearance of this "new Russia" in which he'll have no place. But this "new Russia", for now, is only a dream. The critical mass is still with Putin. In a word, it's useless to place one's hopes with a median Russian. The elite, however, could've said their word. Perhaps this cowardly community will realise one day (perhaps, they are aware of this even now) that their future doesn't boil down to one individual, and the country will somehow survive without Putin. For as long as Russia and its current leadership (in essence, an autocratic ruler) identify themselves with such a future, there's no

[363]   Ukrinform, 16 February 2023, https://www.ukrinform.ua/rubric-kyiv/3671128-sirskij-nazvav-najkriticnisij-moment-oboroni-kieva-na-pocatku-vtorgnenna.html (accessed 05.07.2025).

[364]   Espreso, 7 October 2022, https://espreso.tv/persha-meta-nastupu-ne-vdalasya-naev-rozpoviv-koli-zrozumiv-shcho-blitskrig-rf-provalivsya (accessed 05.07.2025).

way out of this deadly impasse. They have to be torn apart. But who will be able to do it? Who will have the guts? The courage?'

There was this opinion that Russia, in a common sense of the word, had already stopped existing. And whatever transformations took place, Russia would never survive in her present-day shape and form. Allegedly, Putin had already destroyed her, along with her strategic resources. Fuel dependency of Europe had been created as far back as the Soviet times: it had been a consistent, methodical, sustained policy. Yet Putin, unwittingly, had eliminated it. And it would never be the same again. The Russian culture? What if it was a myth, too – originating back in the days of monarchy? Russia had been sponging on it, and using it to her advantage, flogging the world a frontage of a country possessing the Bolshoi Theatre and other attractive shop windows? Where was all of it now? Putin had thrown it all into a furnace. Would it be reborn to its former glory? Will the oil dollars be enough to ensure a revival? Some of that money had already been frittered away. Some got arrested abroad. Some, God willing, after the war, would go to Ukraine to help restore the damage. Her military might? Russia had been overestimated in terms of her capabilities. And how much time would it take to restore her military potential? With all said and done, the myth of a 'strong and invincible Russia' had been shattered.

Putin complained that the break-up of the Soviet Union had led to a global geo-political catastrophe. But wasn't he now, with his own hands, creating another geo-political catastrophe, this time for Russia?

But then again, was Putin the only one to blame? They all were culpable! Year in, year out, they had been swallowing Putin's cud – ingesting it deeper and deeper, enjoying the process. Even now happily swallowing it whole. Yet the time would come when this cud would get lodged in their throats and choke them…

The civilised world was now trying on for size a life without Russia. No one could have even imagined it earlier. How was it possible – a world where there was no Russia? Yet some had even embarked on a life without Russian energy and had done so quite successfully. Parisian boutiques were still thriving without the dirty Russian money, and the real-estate market in London hadn't collapsed. It was all quite simple, really: the world could survive without Russia whereas Russia was unlikely to survive without the outside world.

Why they were lusting after Kyiv was clear. After all, the main Russian myth had been built on Kyivan Rus, that celebratory façade. Wherever one went three hundred years back – it all led to Kyiv.

If one ever posed a question – 'Who are we?' – this would be answered exhaustively.

Which led to another question: 'What is Russia, then?' Because if Prince Volodymyr the Great and the Christianisation of Kyivan Rus was Ukraine,[365] and Yaroslav the Wise was Ukraine,[366] if the Cossacks and also the Sich were Ukraine,[367,368] if Kyiv was Ukraine, then: what was Russia?

God only knew the answers that would be offered now...

Although in our days the majority didn't give a damn. The clear-cut and beautiful answers to these questions were only needed by powers that be.

And the 'Russian citizens' would, somehow, live without bothering themselves with profound questions like 'Who are we?' They'd just live and generally give a wide berth to any such brain teasers...

What could one say? One could happily live without those "gimmicks"...

* * *

All though the first half of March Bakhmut was at the epicentre of stubborn fighting. By now, ringleader there was PMC Wagner who'd already taken over half of the city. On the whole, Bakhmut was semi-encircled. According to analysts, the full-scale spring Russian offensive was approaching its highest point. It was vital to remember that it had been planned in such a way as to countermand the impending Ukrainian counter-offensive. Hmmm. Interesting...

Well, what else was going on? For example, there was this incident – by now, a norm but still, a wonder. A missile strike at Kharkiv had blown off the door of an empty flat – the owners had gone abroad. The neighbours kept watch and

....

[365] **Vladimir I Sviatoslavich** (c. 958 – 15 July 1015), given the epithet 'the Great', was Grand Prince of Kyiv from 978 until his death in 1015. Under him Rus adopted Christianity (989 A.D.).

[366] **Yaroslav I Vladimirovich**, better known as **Yaroslav the Wise**, was Grand Prince of Kyiv from 1019 until his death in 1054. Before the death of his father (Volodymyr I) he had been Prince of Novgorod and of Rostov. After his return to Kyiv he tried to unite the scattered principalities.

[367] **Cossacks** (from the 15th century): both Ukraine and parts of Russia were inhabited by a predominantly East Slavic Orthodox Christian people who were semi-nomadic and semi-militarised. They were allowed a greater degree of self-governance in exchange for military service and protection of borders. Ukrainian-Cossacks inhabited sparsely populated areas in the Dnipro and Don River basins and in the Kuban region. They played an important part in the historical and cultural development of Ukraine.

[368] The **Sich**: an administrative and military centre of the Zaporozhian Cossacks.

contacted the emergency telephone number. A day or two later, the communal services came round and put the door back in.

But there was an abundance of all types of mind-boggling news. Now, one could buy sweets shaped as artillery shells. I couldn't remember what they were called. Something like 'Hit the Enemy Bull's Eye!' Prior to that, there had been this infamous larger brand – 'Heroes don't Die!' I called Andriyovych for a comment. His take on the issue was that when a great war merged with great entrepreneurship, things like that were inevitable.

New realia had definitely crystallised. The capital city was moving away from the days at the frontline. It wanted to carry on with its own, special life. Explosions boomed all over, so, obviously, in Kyiv, too. But on the whole, life was bearable. Some people started visiting restaurants or clubs or other equally attractive destinations…

At this point Andriyovych offered his corrections to my musings. He said that the historic realia of all great wars proved that a capital city would always teeter between the front line and the home front, between blood on the battlefield and the resounding blast of the restaurant orchestras in the rear. So, Kyiv was no exception.

'Here's an example for you – the battle of Sadowa. After the formidable stand-off near this little Bohemian place, it became the focus of attention of the whole world. It was the greatest battle in the Austro-Prussian war of 1866! That battle had unquestionably defined its outcome in as much as it had brought the Austrian influence over Germany to an end and ensured the Prussian dominance in the region. Even if the manpower had been practically equal, as was the number of cannons, Prussians forced the Austrians to stampede! Their losses exceeded those of the Prussians five to one. The Austrian army miraculously escaped a total wipe-out. By the way, that battle made a significant contribution to the art of war. That experience had been conceptualised, first of all, by Alfred Schlieffen, chief of the Imperial German General Stuff. It then came to be successfully applied at the wars of the 20th century. But I'm talking about something else… On the very day of the battle, and later, following such a crushing defeat, the entire Vienna was abuzz, as if it was a beehive! Restaurants, cafes, and regular joints were all going full blast! It was summer, after all, early July. Life was bubbling over and no bloodbath could stop it…'

* * *

Uh-huh! At last, important news for our year at the Institute. Graduation theses were to be defended in early June. At the same time, we were warned not to expect any deferrals, that was the final deadline.

Alla and I stepped out of the Institute – the spring sun was really powerful. We stopped at a mobile cafeteria for some coffee. Ahead of us, three persons in the queue were discussing the counter-offensive.

'The soil's drying up now, and fast!'

'It's drying up here. On the asphalt. But out there, in the fields…'

'What are you talking about? The roads will only be free from mud in early April…'

'We are between the devil and the deep blue sea now. No one can tell how the attack will go: either the Russian defence collapses or the other way round, we'll be forced to engage in a slow and gradual war of attrition dragged-out all through the year…'

'I don't buy this "collapse". They've built a powerful system of defence, as many as three lines…'

'Horror! What's to come?'

'What, where and with what resources – it must be no more than ten people at the top who are completely in the frame. As for this offensive… Not even those up there know how it will all progress. The recent discussions reveal that the partners are dragging their feet in terms of the weapon deliveries.'

That was the way people talked. The life of our entire country went on in anticipation of that counter-offensive, and people hardly talked of anything else. Besides, so much was still unknown…

By early April of 2023 the Russian army had launched at Ukraine nearly 5,000 missiles, their combined cost being 16 billion Dollars. Thus, Russia had carried out one of the costliest missile campaigns in contemporary history. Yet the Russian plans to eliminate the critical infrastructure of Ukraine had been frustrated – Ukraine had managed to hold out till the warm days of spring. Moreover, it had re-started exporting its electric power to Europe.

Then came the great Christian holiday of Easter.

On 7 April 2023 the annual ceremony of the Stations of the Cross took place in the Roman Coliseum. This year the Pope had selected a prayer entitled 'Voices of Peace in Times of War'.

They tried, yet again, to 'reconcile' the Ukrainians and the Russians, this time engaging teenagers, too. It caused yet another scandal because it was one more attempt to unite a victim with the aggressor. A Ukrainian teenager shared his experiences of fleeing from the Russian-occupied Mariupol. The Russian teenager remembered his elder brother who, several days after turning 18, embarked on a journey (in other words – 'to war'). And then they had been notified of his death. 'The same happened to my dad and my granddad who left (meaning, 'to war") and we have no news of them (in other words – were "killed or are missing in action").'

According to A. Yurash, Ukraine's ambassador to the Holy See: 'The overwhelming majority of the Vatican clergy harbour this view of Russia as a lost sheep, and of the Russian Orthodox church, despite its numerous failings, as a religious institution. The Pope is among those romantics...'[369]

* * *

The socials were bursting with posts about PMC Wagner and Prigozhin. Sometime around the beginning of May he issued a warning that Wagner would draw out of Bakhmut if the RF Defence Ministry failed to supply the ammunition in sufficient quantities. His diatribe grew more forceful, quoting the fleeing Russian troops who thus were exposing the flanks of the Wagner's mercenaries' positions. In Prigozhin's words, Defence Minister Shoigu and Head of the General Staff Gerasimov were criminals. They should be immediately fired and brought to account.

Anyway, Bakhmut continued dominating the news – endless battles, when not inside the city, then around it. This gigantic meatgrinder was still on the go. People were simply ground into smithereens...

Finally, on May 20th, Prigozhin announced their capture of Bakhmut. He added that the operation that had started on 8 October 2022 and lasted 224 days had been necessary 'to give the shabby Russian army a chance to come around.' Then he announced that Wagner was withdrawing from the city. Military experts branded the capture of Bakhmut 'purely symbolic'. [Some people said that the decision to defend Bakhmut for such a long time was taken among the president's circle, not by the military, and that it was a mistake. "Political maneuvering disguised as heroism," was how one of the commanders who took part in these battles described the situation.]

* * *

I was about to make another entry, an important one for me:

'And yet this accursed war of Russia against Ukraine will finish someday. And I imagine waking up one day and there will be nothing in the news about developments at the fronts! There won't be a single item about a downed Ruscist pilot or a destroyed tank! And no one would've bombed us the previous

[369]   Glavcom, 19 May 2023, https://glavcom.ua/interviews/posol-ukrajini-u-vatikani-papa-prodovzhuje-sprijmati-rosiju-jak-zabludlu-vivtsju-928412.html#google_vignette (accessed 6 July 2025).

night! And there wasn't a single missile! And not a single innocent human life would've been lost.

'Will it really happen like that, one day? It's hard to contemplate it, after everything that did happen and continues to happen.

'It's impossible to believe but it's equally impossible to watch. Those whose houses or flats are still standing are in luck. Those who've lost everything are extremely unlucky. And those who died have paid the highest price.

'But for the rest of the world it only now starts in earnest. After all, the global architecture of security has gone to the dogs, nothing works anymore. The world in which we all lived prior to 24 February 2024 doesn't exist. Something else has come to take its place. And its outlines are still nebulous.

When everything is over, questions will be coming from all over, the main one being – how could it have happened at all? Why has the world allowed this insanity to be? I urge anyone to go and answer this question briefly and to the point.

'Isn't it possible to take at least some basic concepts and start putting together – piece by piece – a puzzle of sorts? For a Puzzle like that – let it be spelled with a capital "P" must be put together by somebody, at some point in time.

'There was this stuff in the press, too:

'If the Russian leader suddenly said: "Let's end this war!", the war will stop. But if Ukraine stops the war, it will stop existing. That's the choice we are facing. Therefore, our victory is a must.

'I am also contemplating the phrase – "to win over Russia". Perhaps it's just a figure of speech?

'But how can you win over her? This is one monster of a state, invincible in the classical sense of the word "victory". We simply won't have enough people against those 140 million. We must somehow learn to put our hardware and our brains to a good use.

'So, when all said and done, we must realise what this victory will be like. Considering Russia's size, her potential capabilities and access to nuclear weapons, it's impossible to destroy her completely or put forward a demand for an unconditional surrender. Especially since the war is unfolding outside of her own territory. Yet defeating Russia on the battleground is another story.

'Returning all occupied territories would be victory. Even if somebody insists that it would be desirable to dismantle the Russian Federation and transform her into a number of independent democratic states – no definitive victory would be possible in the absence of a profound transformation of this country. There are various scenarios: a change of regime, democratisation… But all of this had to be achieved through their own efforts and originate from within their own country.

'As regards the disintegration of Russia… I, personally, prefer the term "defragmentation" – it's less categorical and unequivocal. I don't know… For the time being, I'm not that certain. Some perimeter territories may well fall aside but will it mean total disintegration? Goes without saying that we would prefer several friendly, even if neutral, neighbours to a dangerous and powerful one. But even such a process of defragmentation – if it ever took place – would require not two or three years, but decades. What's the point guessing? Only time will tell. In any case, what we have in store are severe days, weeks, and years…

'The most important thing is that Russia should not go on in her current political format because for us it would mean a deferred war.

'And another thing. The issue isn't only fighting and getting back the annexed territories. We would also need guarantees of a life in peace. If such guarantees – and efficient ones at that – are given, that will mean real victory.

'And lastly. I feel that all of us are still on a journey… We are all on the move but no one has reached their destination yet. The picture in front of us now doesn't look like a final point in this undertaking. Equally, it's not clear when are we going to get closer. We – the entire country – now live in a continuous anticipation of some amazing, and yet unforeseen, developments…'

* * *

On mum's birthday Alla gave her a present: opera tickets for Puccini's *Tosca*. Not two tickets, either, but three – how would they cope without me?

'What a lovely idea!' Mum was really pleased. 'I did listen to this opera but it was a lifetime ago. Some memories come back, of course.'

'As for me, I've never heard it. But it's the most popular opera in the world's repertoire!' Alla grinned. 'What about you, Kiril?'

'I haven't heard it either…'

'It's no problem,' mum summed it all up. 'Your lives are only taking off. You'll have a lot of "first times" yet… '

The auditorium was overflowing, not a single free seat. But the two upper tiers were completely vacant.

'As I was buying the tickets, they warned me that in case of an air raid everyone would have to descend into a bomb shelter,' Alla explained. 'It's spacious, true. Still. Not big enough to accommodate all the opera-goers, the orchestra, and the cast. So, the management had been forced to "cordon off" those two tiers…'

The last act, Act III… Sentenced to death and awaiting execution, Mario Cavaradossi sang: 'E lucevan le stele'… It was incredible. And his words, too:

'My time is up, true… And now I have to die. Yet never have I wanted to live so much…' – they just burnt into my heart. It had been written a hundred and twenty years ago but still possessed this incredible power to transport! I felt the same – I really didn't want to die, even less so because of some deranged and insane Russian bombardment… I so wanted to live, today, now!

The audience kept applauding for a good twenty minutes. Finally, they all started to disperse. But we still lingered in our seats.

My hand involuntarily reached in my inside pocket for the pad. The pen was at the ready, too.

'What's this? You gonna…' Alla started saying something but cut herself short.

Meanwhile mum tactfully looked aside.

'One sec… Be with you right away…' was all I could tell them.

'Lots of foreigners in the opera house tonight,' I scribbled hastily. 'A multi-lingual polyphony coming from everywhere. Could it be that they, like own people, are coming back to our city?

'The auditorium was filled to capacity but the two upper tiers remained completely empty. Should a missile approach be announced, everyone would have to descent into a bomb shelter. To accommodate everyone down there – the viewers, the actors, and the orchestra – they had to "cut off" the two upper tiers.

'By the way, one could create a very interesting twist in a story this way. A show is going on but then sirens whine and an air raid alarm is announced. The rockets may well be flying in our direction. Everyone rushes downstairs. And down there, in the shelter, everything gets mixed together: the public and the performers end up cheek by jowl. Some raids may last for quite some time, up to several hours. So, what – was one supposed just to sit around on foldable chairs? That was it? Why not continue the show? OK, the sets have all stayed upstairs, on stage – that's true. But I see that some of the orchestra players have brought their violins along, perhaps they are way too valuable. Enough for an improvised performance.

'And I could clearly visualise how such a show could go on. I could see Mario Cavaradossi singing his celebrated aria here, in the bomb shelter… That would have been the most amazing production in the history of the world opera!'

Ri-i-i-ght, I had to add something else, God help my memory.

Come on, that was just it!

'And then another couple of words about how many foreigners were now in the city. They are here despite frequent air raids and mass-scale destruction.

'I heard that there are many journalists around too. Mass media that haven't yet opened their posts here, are rushing forward to do so. Everyone is getting ready for "something big" that's in the offing. Everyone knows it will be our counter-offensive, yet no one is sure where it will take place and how. But everyone wants to be on the spot!..

'And everyone is waiting…

'We are here, in our own country. And side by side with us are foreign citizens who have come here, and now, just like us, have to seek refuge in bomb shelters.

'It looks as if hundreds of million people all over the world are also waiting…'

'Everyone is waiting for something to happen that will, finally, allow us to live free, and happy, and without fear…

'But for the time being we have to wait and hope. And how much we want to live! Not any other day, but today! Not any other time, but now! As for me – I want to live like never before!'

* * *

And that was how that spring had passed – in expectation of a counter-offensive. Some said it was important to wait till the ground dried up and become free from mud. Something was sure to begin sometime after May 5ᵗʰ or 6ᵗʰ! Then they said that not all the required weaponry had been delivered. After that they said they needed more time to prepare properly… Then there were still other reasons…

And nothing was happening.

Yet everyone was waiting and counting days.

But something did have to start soon, there was no other way…

Summer of 2023.
With Hopes of the Counterattack

As scheduled, graduation theses were to be presented in early June. Yet even before, the 'headhunters' had started prowling the Institute – clearly, various filmmaking studios were hungry for a suitable content. Nothing new about any of this, it had been the same every year.

We didn't pay them much attention because most of the time they hung around the Dean's Office and around various academic departments, going through every graduate's submission. No one could predict what conclusions they would draw. The Dean's Office had been adamant that the 'headhunters' would take no action before the final presentation, and would enter into no negotiations with a single finalist...

My script was approved without any trouble – in effect, it was a mere formality since the Commission members had already spent a month reading it. At the same time, I was handed a two-page list of comments. But that was pure protocol. 'There is a need for some final polishing but on the whole, there are no objections against adapting it into a film' – that was their conclusion.

On the surface, their wording was enough to raise my hopes but nowadays it guaranteed nothing. In other words, no expectations as to having such a film financed. This scrip would have to wait until its time came...

So, what was there to do now? Just like before, I carried on with making notes into my pad. I would've been happy to draw a line under this project, but the war was going on, and the events kept unfolding. And thus, this draft for a script was transforming itself into an on-going project. Christ Almighty, could it be that the infinity of everything happening to us was somehow... directly related to the incompleteness of my script? Pure mysticism... Boundlessness all around...

* * *

Our long-hoped-for counteroffensive finally started in early June. Even if there had been no official bulletins, unofficially everyone realised that things were moving – but was it a real offensive? Things had been building up so gradually that one could hardly be certain. It rather looked like we were probing the enemy's weak points in order to launch, subsequently, a massive attack. So, for the time being our troops were crawling forward. So slowly as to be disappointing at times: a hundred metres a day, two hundred, and on a good day – perhaps half a kilometre…

Yes, the advance progressed at a snail's pace but the reasons for that were obvious: during the intervening time – starting from the previous autumn! – the Russians had had a chance to build and put in place a multi-layer system of defence. From the engineering point of view, the enemy acted rationally: they had built an intricate set of fortifications known as the Surovikin Line.[370] It included an anti-tank ditch, concrete pyramids otherwise known as 'dragon's teeth', fortified strongpoints, a security zone. To top it all, along the entire stretch of the frontline they had put in the minefields. In a word – a properly fortified, heavily defended area. Go and look for any weak points there!

There was something else of importance, too. To be effective, an offensive had to satisfy two conditions: a preparatory artillery barrage and the aircraft, preferably of a more recent generation. At the very least – F16. But instead, we had an ammunition shortage and no such planes. Word was seeping through that the rest of the equipment hadn't yet arrived. Some commentators quoted the NATO attack doctrine, allegedly stipulating that an offensive should be referred to as such only when the aviation was used, too. Yet they were advising us to somehow make do without the aviation…

And another thing: what had decided the outcome in Kharkiv Oblast was the element of surprise. There had been nothing like that around Kherson which impacted the speed of advance accordingly. But now there was no surprise, and a variety of adverse circumstances made it hard…

To walk across a minefield… Reportedly, the first 20 kilometres would be a 'make-or-break' factor. Yet it would be kilometres of hell, nearly impossible to negotiate. Also, there were losses – both in terms of manpower and the equipment. So the top brass decided to change their strategy. Instead of achieving a break-through with the help of the equipment, our troops now moved forward on foot. That was a way to save the personnel – at the expense of a slower rate of de-occupation, but also an attempt to exhaust the enemy.

....

[370]   The Russian general **Sergey Surovikin** had this line of fortifications built during his tenure as the overall theatre commander immediately after Ukraine's 2022 Kharkiv counter-offensive.

Otherwise, nothing had changed: all those missiles, Shahed and Geran drones kept flying like before. Everyday our long-suffering country was subjected to a non-stop ferocious hammering.

Prigozhin – the owner of Wagner – continued hurtling accusations at the Defence Ministry over their disastrous management of the Special Military Operation. He declared that his PMC would sort out the 'scoundrels' who were 'wiping out the Russian soldierly'. His primary target was Defence Minister Shoigu – in Prigozhin's diatribes referred to as an 'old lady' and an 'animal'. Then again, he was laying into the General Staff's Head Gerasimov with remarkable venom, too. And he was allowed to continue like this with complete impunity. It was really weird…

And then all of a sudden, as if in a macabre dance, all was awhirl. On June 6th, something extraordinary happened – the Russians had blown up the Kakhovka HEPP! With hundreds of settlements flooded, it proved to be an ecological catastrophe that sent shockwaves all over the world.

Then there was another poll conducted in Russia, according to which 73% of respondents believed that Russia was heading in the right direction. As for the question of who was to blame for the explosion at the Kakhovka Dam, the answers went thus: 6% blamed Russia, 10% – the USA, and the remaining 84% believed that the perpetrator had been Ukraine. Nothing but a really powerful detergent could cleanse the brains like that. Even accounting for the fault tolerance – clearly, the people over there would be afraid to answer truthfully – the numbers were still shocking.

He Attacked Us, Bit Off a Slice of Our Territory and then Became a Champion for Peace!

For quite some time now, the African leaders had been promoting their own peace plan. On June 16th, they brought it into Kyiv, then continued to St Petersburg.

On June 17th – 11 days after Russia had blown up Kakhovka HEPP, which should have been a warning in its own right – they had a meeting with Putin.

'Dear friends!' started Putin. This form of address alone was enough to cause inebriation. 'Russia has never refused to negotiate. Moreover, the negotiations in March-April of 2022 produced a draft agreement on Ukraine's permanent neutrality and guarantees for its security.'

Putin picked up a piece of paper from the table: 'This is the document initialled by the Ukrainian delegation. Here's the signature…'

Yet he didn't show the signature to his interlocutors. The trusting African leaders didn't insist, they just sat there, nodding in assent.

Independent commentators immediately challenged Putin's words because the delegations taking part in that round of negotiations had only been working on proposals that could be included in the documents. Besides, there would have been signatures of the two presidents – in case an agreement was reached on any point. Yet numerous issues – some of those of key importance – had never been agreed upon. For a simple reason: Russian appetites had been too ambitious.

In the course of subsequent online communication in April, the parties had failed to reach agreement on those key issues. So, even if this 'agreement' of Putin's had been initialled by a member of the Ukrainian delegation, it would have been nothing more than a rough copy of a working draft at the stage of deliberation and coordination, not a binding legal document.

To top it all, what Putin told the African leaders about the situation near Kyiv by the end of March of 2022 was a distorted version of events. In reality his blitzkrieg hadn't worked, the tables had been turned on the Russian army, and, under the threat of losing units to envelopment, it had had to withdraw from Kyiv. Yet the narrative Putin offered to the Africans went as follows: 'We were asked to withdraw [allegedly, to facilitate the negotiations], and we did just that.' As if they hadn't been forced but were 'asked' to retreat and had done so as a gesture of good will. The African leaders, again, were greatly impressed by what they had just heard.[371]

Of interest, though, was something else. This 'document' was made public for the first time, and what's more – to the African leaders. By producing a piece of paper, clearly of no consequence for the current situation, Putin pursued several objectives. It was a good enough informational pitch, effective in the 'Global South'. Yet his main aim was to convince the African leaders of the following: Russia wanted peace but Ukraine was eager to continue fighting. That was the whole story. Showing the respected African politicians a working document that had never been validated was similar to a crooked gambler playing with marked cards…

* * *

Prigozhin was making news yet again! By the end of June – during those two spectacular days of the Russian 'freedom' – all three presidential planes had left from Moscow. Putin was aboard one of them, clearly heading for some-

---

[371] 17 June 2023, https://www.youtube.com/watch?v=HJuVzu2FNZo

where safer. Allegedly he watched the Scarlet Sails Festival from aboard a yacht owned by his friend, businessman Yuriy Kovalchuk. This event had been held in St Petersburg annually to celebrate youth and congratulate secondary school graduates on embarking on an adult life. Rumour had it that it was, indeed, a spectacular affair – why not go and watch it? At least Putin was out of Moscow on the day when Prigozhin's army was marching towards the capital. For all that, Peskov declared: 'The President is in the Kremlin working with the documents.' It was amazing. A heavily armed military column was about to attack the capital – but the President was 'working with the documents'! On the other hand, who would believe Peskov? To lie was his sleazy job description…

The world held its collective breath while following the progress of Prigozhin's revolt. What if things finally came to a head and shifted out of this impasse… Yet nothing moved and nothing shifted.

Shame… Wagner's boss got cold feet. And it would've been really curious to watch such a grand finale. Russians did display a degree of sympathy for his course, and neither the army, nor the common people came out in support of the authorities – most likely eager to wait it all out. On the other hand, as Prigozhin was leaving Rostov there was applause and shouts of approval – but who were those addressed to? Approval of him rising up against the system? Approval of his company's actions in Ukraine? Or could it just be that the uneventful life of a provincial city was thus animated and, finally, there was some fun to be had? No one could be certain about genuine feelings of the Russians…

And still, a certain result had been achieved. The whole world – but primarily the Russians themselves – saw a total impotency of the state system in Russia, of all those Putin's PR-enhanced 'verticals of power'! It was there for all to see: in Russia, verticals of power of any quality were conspicuous by their absence. And as few as 5-10 thousand individuals could topple that praised 'Russian statehood'…

I read an interview that M. Podolyak gave to Meduza:[372] 'Russia has reduced international law to nothing and announced that she does not wish to be bound by it. And it turns out that the international community has no leverage to apply, and no tools to produce an impact. And thus, it follows that if this regime stays, we and you have no rules for resolving issues of contention. The war is being waged by citizens of Russia (in other words, not by Putin single-handedly, as some are trying to allege) who come here in order to cruelly kill our civilians. Unfortunately, the war will go on because there is no evidence of even a semblance of an attempt at internal contrition, of reluctance to act in this manner.

....

[372] **Meduza:** founded in 2014, is a Russian- and English-language independent news website headquartered in Riga, Latvia.

On the contrary, we are witnessing a growing readiness to commit crimes and gloat at their results. These are not bots. It is obvious that this irrational hatred of Ukraine is ubiquitous in Russia. This hatred is off the scale…'[373]

* * *

Once I got a call from an aide to the director of one of our most successful studios. He invited me for a meeting. I tried to glean something out of him, but he was like a partisan under interrogation – betrayed nothing at all. Not even a hint!!!

I was racing to that meeting as if carried by powerful wings.

The aide met me at the gate, took me to the front office, then opened the door and allowed me into the domain of the 'celestial being'.

'I've familiarised myself with your script,' the director raised himself from his desk, led me into the little reception nook made up of several pulled-together sofas. 'Let me say this at once – it's a winner. Shifts at the defence post, events in Kyiv and around it, general reflections – I've been impressed. Let me put it even more forcefully: your script is a real blockbuster. Something incredible may come out of it.'

I perked up.

'For all that, there are some bits there…'

So, I pricked up my ears.

He handed over a list of his comments.

I was about to cast my eye over those, there and then, but he made this gesture with his hand – sort of, you'll look through all of this later.

'That's not the main issue now. These are rather technical points that could be resolved rather quickly. The main issue is something else.'

I grew tense.

'You see, this script of yours… the entire narrative… somehow… has no resolution. In the end, everything with you gets affixed to a specific event and a specific date. But in reality, everything goes on and develops! So, it won't do at all to put a final stop at something concrete…'

'No ending? But you said yourself – the war goes on, and tomorrow will bring new events. So, which ending could I possibly use?'

'That's the whole point – the war goes on and tomorrow will bring some new info. To get stuck at something very specific means to lose. There must be some culmination that would be surprising yet powerful.'

<hr>

[373] Meduza, 8 July 2023, https://amp.meduza.io/feature/2023/07/08/voyna-idet-ne-s-putinym-a-s-grazhdanami-rossii (accessed 05.07.2025).

'But how can I finish it if nothing has been finished yet?'

'That's the crux of the matter. There should be something broader… Deeper… Some universal approach, unrelated to the place, event, or the date. Got it?'

I dropped my head. Of course I'd heard his words. But how could I possibly produce something 'universal'? I didn't have the foggiest…

'Yet that's you who are – the script writer!' the director became animated. 'Which means it's up to you. And the last point. It requires some editing. The material must be "combed through". Accents should be in right places. Logic should be construed, so that the story moves forward naturally. Things that an author, usually, has neither time nor vision for – for he sits on a pile of data and, like a sculpture, carves something out of it. Every classic always has had an editor – are you aware?'

'But of course…'

'So, you've got one of those?'

'Not yet…'

'I see, but after all, you are a rookie. I've got a recommendation… Forty years of experience in literary journals and publishing houses… from Kharkiv. That's the telephone number. So – on we go!'

I left the office flabbergasted. The aide was waiting for me.

'The director's instruction has been to hire you as a trainee scriptwriter. You bring your script to an acceptable level but, already, as our staff member. The starting salary is modest. And then we'll see.'

Then he walked me to the Human Resources.

I was returning home completely elated. So, now I would be working at my script and even be paid for this? Mother of God! It was incredible. Had they really taken me 'on board their ship'? Inconceivable!

Then I slowed down to a crawl. My joy had evaporated. That accursed ending was really troubling me. Not a single thought in my head. My mood, so celebratory only several minutes before, had changed radically. I could shoot myself in sheer despair.

Ha! They have put me on financial support! Double stress this way… It would've been better if they hadn't hired me at all. It would've been easier psychologically. Because now I felt as if I was chained to a lamppost. And not the slightest idea about that ending…

* * *

Although we had flown the nest of our institute, the Dean's Office called us all in advance to announce a debate between our rector and Dmytro Petrovych, our former creative workshop chief, on Ukrainian radio. The subject – 'The Russian Culture and Us'. So, me, like everybody else from our gang, tuned in.

'Dmytro Petrovych, like many our countrymen, you must have noticed that a discussion about the Ukrainians' attitude to the Russian culture has intensified,' the rector threw the floor open. 'Is it possible, after what has taken place, to use the cultural heritage of an aggressor? Or, perhaps, it is yet another instrument of war? Should we curtail it in Ukraine? Should we advocate its boycott all over the world? Lots of questions…'

'Yes, Serhii Olexandrovych, by now it has become clear: the so-called "great Russian culture" is more than often used to disguise goings-on in Russia. It's used as a kind of a shield – to project onto the world the image of Russia as an attractive and civilised country. But in reality – hasn't the same culture been used to cover up arrests of opposition leaders, a campaign of terror against the mass media, an instrument for imposing dictatorships, and preparations for an erosion of the borders of neighbouring countries?'

'In other words, to paraphrase – the Bolshoi ballet receives a thundering ovation in the best houses of the world while backstage… missiles are trained to target Ukraine?'

'That's exactly what I mean. The way it works: this presentable facade – literature, theatres… Moscow and St Petersburg… But there exists another Russia: bestial, die-hard, barbarian, awful…'

'As a result of this revelation, numerous streets and squares in our cities are now being renamed…'

'And what about monuments to Russian cultural luminaries?'

'That's the thing – a great number of people who live with tragedy, who mourn the loss of their relatives, who are forced to leave their homes, are extremely annoyed at those conversations about "respect for the Russian culture". In their minds, the Russian culture is part and parcel of the so-called "Russian world" that has used, and continues using, the culture as a tool of this intrusive – and now, atrocious – force that is trying to enslave Ukraine.'

'Therefore, in our days Ukrainians view the monuments to prominent figures of the Russian culture as an inalienable element of their aggression.'

'Especially since this "culture" is used so graphically. We have all seen that in Mariupol, on the front of the destroyed Drama Theatre onto which the Russian pilots had dropped two 500-kilo bombs thus killing hundreds of innocent women and children, the occupying authorities cynically put up an installation: a huge screen showing classical writers of the Russian literature!'

'Yeah… It should also be pointed out that in Russia culture is an integral part of the propaganda machine, such as the demented pro-Kremlin TV channels and PR. All this logically leads to a question whether Russian culture, in its entirety, even the part of it that is possibly genuine and profound, has become a Kremlin propaganda tool.'

'Therefore, it is advisable to hit a "pause" button in relations with the Russian culture, even with those elements of it that have not been sullied so badly?'

'There is such an opinion. At the very least till the war is over. And it's hardly surprising that Ukrainian theatres have deleted anything Russian from their repertoire. Otherwise, it looks like we are welcoming them into our homes and encourage the propaganda machine to become active on an even greater scale – in Europe and the rest of the world. Yet this culture promotes a disguised image of anything that is real Russia, and of the true essence – not the gift-wrapped stuff – that's taking place in real time.'

'Yet we are left with two complicated questions. Is all Russian culture deformed? And does it all, in its entirety, relate to the contemporary Russian power, in other words, to what is going on today?'

'Yes, these are very good questions. Yet one should settle a couple of points even with this "genuinely great culture". That's point one. Extolling it today is inappropriate. And point two – this war must end. And some time should pass afterwards… It will be easier to sort it all out in a quieter atmosphere. Yet something is already clear: we will never treat it with such deference as before…'

'Unquestionably so. Thank God, attitudes to Russian culture and the dangerous messages it puts forward are now being reconsidered – in Europe and in the rest of the world.'

'Right… After the war, when the dust settles, if only a little, dear Dmytro Petrovych, our understanding will be streamlined. It is febrile at the moment, which is understandable. But the Bible says – "This, too, shall pass…" With God's help this shall pass too, if Russia overreaches herself. Yes, against the background of this horrendous and bloody war and sentiments here, in Ukraine, solidarity with Ukrainian people may take this form, among others – the form of alienation. Certain things in the Russian culture are guaranteed to wither and die, but something will stay. The best, the most humane is sure to survive…'

'Well, Serhii Olexandrovych, the discussion has been opened, and that's already good.'

* * *

As per usual, lots of updates both in the bigger world and here, on our home turf.

For several days now Odesa had been targeted by missiles. They had been directed at the city centre – the quarter protected by UNESCO. Scores of architectural and cultural landmarks had been ruined, including the Cathedral and some museums. Meanwhile at the talk show hosted by Solovyov, one the Kremlin's principal propaganda gurus, the audience cried out demanding that Kyiv, Lviv and Odesa be completely destroyed. *'We won't save Odessa (from missiles). We will rebuild it later from scratch, it will be much simpler that way. What is to be done there? Oh, I remember – perhaps the Opera House should be spared…'*[374] Solovyov summed it all up. *'But the rest should be destroyed!' 'Destroyed! Destroyed!'*, he was echoed by the 'experts' – guests on the show. The broadcast must have been watched by many millions of Russian viewers. And that was the brew that had been served to them daily.

The world's response to our events varied. For example, Hungary's Orbán said that this was 'a dispute between two Slavic nations. And it doesn't have anything to do with us whatsoever.'

Even if the entire civilised world was on our side. What did the others have to say, though?

Looking at the situation from a broader perspective – considering whether to support the USA or China – one realised that there were 127 countries in the world that didn't unequivocally belong to either camp. Yet these countries accounted for nearly 65% of the global population. As for attitudes towards Russia – there were peculiarities there, too. They didn't approve of her politics but were in no hurry to become her enemies. And that was the demarcation line that today ran through the world.

Other countries were polarised: 52 countries (15% of the world's population) made up the West and its friends. Twelve countries were whole-heartedly supporting Russia.

It followed that the 'neutral' ones were more numerous, and despite the West's economic might and influence, they constituted a majority.

A week previously the Belarusian border guards started yelling through their loud-speakers addressing the Ukrainian side: 'When you've got nothing left so's to cook your borsch, come over to our side! Try our recipe, cooked in a Belarusian way, you won't be sorry!'

An answer came from the Ukrainian side: 'We are not slaves and won't eat your Belarusian borsch! Change your ingredients and become a free people, not a forcibly subjugated one!'

But they wouldn't calm down. Today they were hooting about some allegedly 'Columbian flour'. The whole thing must have been 'stage managed' from Minsk…

....

[374]   23 July 2023 https://vk.com/wall-75679763_5709114 (accessed 05.07.2025).

Well, enough. Die-hard putinist Russians were clearly deranged. But why did Belarusians feel they had to behave like this? To stay in good company? Or was their 'potato Fuhrer' issuing those commands?

The most recent poll had now revealed that over two-thirds of our citizens had relatives or friends who'd been killed or wounded in the course of this war.

Even now, driving along the Kyiv-Lviv Motorway – the place molested by the Ruscists – was impossible without getting shivers. Houses without rooves, holes left by the tank fire – as big as half of a wall… A blogger wrote: 'We mustn't forget the prices we've paid for all of this, and continue paying. For, alas, now here appears this nonchalance…'

Results of new polls were coming in, even if they dealt with a different stretch of time – the period prior to the invasion. Sixty-nine percent of Ukrainians had not believed that Russia would start a full-scale invasion. Most of them were older people – 55 to 60 years of age. At the same time 26% of those polled pointed out that they had been completely or fairly certain that Russia would attack. Only 3% of those polled estimated the authorities' preparedness for war as thorough. Another 20% stated that we had been partially prepared. But 73% of those answering the poll asserted that the authorities had not been ready for this eventuality…

As for the counter-offensive in the south. It kept stalling and making practically no progress. Americans were saying: it was imperative to concentrate all forces in one location and deliver one powerful blow! But little heed was paid to this advice – according to some, it was preferable to grope several locations at a time… Also, we were heating things up in the east yet again. The Western partners considered this pulverisation of capacity between the two unrelated fronts a mistake of the Ukrainian headquarters. Besides, the battlefield had practically become transparent, thanks to the extensive use of sensors, and the tools of optic-, electronic-, radio-electronic and radio-technical intelligence. To overlook a build-up of our forces – or theirs – would have been impossible.

Small wonder that an option of switching over to a defence strategy was becoming increasingly popular. At the same time, the military at the front were reporting that combat was shifting to trenches. All of that meant that the war might enter a new stage – that of a dragged-out lengthy conflict. For our side, we were told, it was dangerous…

But what about events in Russia? Those were testimonials of several 'relocatees'[375] who had first fled to avoid mobilisation but then returned:

....

[375] **Relocatees**: this term is often used to refer to Russians who left Russia after the

'Russia that I was leaving behind was abuzz with discussions of what was going on, everyone was on edge. Russia into which I returned calmed down and accepted developments at her core. Now she is simply trying to ignore it. People are afraid of entering into active discussions: while travelling by metro, they would shield their telephones when rifling through the news. Only those responsible for this insanity are not afraid to speak out.'

'The informational field reveals some great tension, as if a new catastrophe is imminent. There are many of those who are in the "internal emigration", and that is why they give the news a very wide berth. The others go on living as before, hoping to sit it all out...'

'... as if the time has stopped. All that's happening is that numerous excesses have become legal norm and people are tired, lost faith and have withdrawn even further into themselves.'

'We have returned to a different Russia...'

'... many of those around me feel insecure and afraid of what might befall them in the future. There is no feeling of safety, people have stopped making long-term plans. I find it hard to imagine now how I should live...'

But those were the people who had relocated back to Russia from abroad. Even if they were a minority, not all of them opposed the war or the regime. Most of them had fled out of fear for their lives.

But on a global level nothing in Russia had changed. It would seem that having seen what had taken place – all that death and destruction – the Russian people should arrive at some conclusions. Yet, sadly, everything just carried on like before. And like earlier, they were whole-heartedly supporting the Special Military Operation.

When asked why the Russians were the way they were, one expert replied:

'There are two components here: a powerful inferiority complex, and, simultaneously, delusions of grandeur. On the one hand – profound dissatisfaction, ferocious umbrage that has grown into a "national religion". Their feelings are hurt on all fronts: for being misunderstood and not properly acknowledged, for an insufficient recognition of the victory in the Second World War and their role in the world's history, for lack of respect. Be it Americans, Ukrainians, erstwhile Soviet Union republics that have become independent states – "nobody loves us, nobody gives us our due." Yet on the other side is this delusion of grandeur, this unshakable certainty that the country – in its contemporary state and shape – should go on indefinitely. This boundless confidence that "we will win over anybody, we live in a great state", "we are Russian, God is

....

outbreak of war in Ukraine, looking for asylum or new opportunities in other countries.

on our side". We are strong and we can do as we please. Say, in 2014 they shot down the Malaysian plane, some three hundred people died. And what? And nothing. Everybody "aahed" and "oohed" for a while, and then everything went calm again. An absolute loss of the sense of times, reluctance to live within a context of modern realia… All of this opens a clear path towards ressentiment: a jaundiced desire to wreak vengeance, to build a new life that would be "not like theirs", to get the better of everybody. This is a country with a chronic complex of its own "exceptionalism". And even if its ambitions often do not match its capabilities, it is masterly placing itself in a winning situation: first, it creates problems, and then involves everybody in resolving them. Russia is drowning in this nightmare; this way lies pure madness.'

There was this eerie news on the subject of 'ethnic replacement'. A commercial video was making rounds over Russia: 'Select a place of your dreams!' – the motto flashed against the background of Ukrainian city names – Kyiv, Kharkiv, Odesa, Mykolaiv, Kherson, etc.

Mariupol was unfolding a massive construction project rebuilding residential houses. One was aware of this picture – houses in ruins on one side of the street, and new multi-story blocs of flats across the road. There popped up new programmes for acquiring accommodation on a beneficial basis. The newcomers were mostly relocating from Siberia. For them, living here felt like paradise: the sea, the spas…

By now some 40 thousand Russians had moved to Mariupol. A local resident said: 'These civilian occupiers will stay – that is, if Ukraine does not liberate the city. Their numbers grow, this is a tendency now. At the current rate, in a year's time some 80-120 thousand RF citizens will have moved here and register their accommodation as their primary place of residence. There are maximum 80 thousand Ukrainians left in the city, with most of them trying to leave for Ukraine. People say: "It's simply impossible to live here if you are Ukrainian. Every trick is applied to force us out. We are simply surviving. But the immigrants have a "green light" everywhere. In other words, we are completely marginalised. Russia has achieved what she set out to do. A normal person has no place here, that is why there is this mass exodus. Whereas the Russians move in in huge numbers.'

There was a reverse movement, too. Thousands of Ukrainian children had been illegally shifted into Russia. Over there, they were forced through filtration and educational camps. After that – enforced 'passportisation' and adoption. Such a heinous international crime…

1991 – 2022. The Puzzle Comes Together

One day the Commander invited the choir guys, Taras, and me for a reunion: 'Just to have a proper chat and swap some thoughts – we haven't seen each other in a while. Just in case we start forgetting what we all look like.'

We met the choir guys on the metro platform and went upstairs. The Commander was waiting for us at the top – clad in a greenish T-shirt displaying this message: 'Jeder Tag ohne Bier ist ein Gesundheitsrisiko!'[376]

He waved towards the Aristocratic Café, for some reason his favourite. The Commander had nothing aristocratic about him whatsoever, but opposites sometimes attract.

Despite its name, the café was quite democratic. Snobs insisted that aristocracy and beer were incompatible. I wouldn't be so sure. As for our 'Aristocratic' joint, the drinks menu was crammed with options – listing anything from the truly refined stuff down to something that wouldn't qualify as aristocratic at all.

'Let's retire to over there,' he pointed towards a remote corner.

We took our seats and set about trading trivia.

Shortly, his face grew sombre.

'That's what I'd like to say,' the Commander said, glancing sidelong at a waiter hovering nearby. 'Yes, for me – two mugs at once. We'll see after that...'

He turned towards the choir guys:

'Seeing as you're well-informed...'

He patted Andriyovych on the sleeve:

'And with your connections...'

We all grew tense, waiting.

'The things I've heard after the invasion! My brain is properly scrambled. I saw a story about Reagan on TV. He used to demand that his advisers' info should fit on maximum a page. Well... I'm not Reagan and won't make any such demands of you. But if you can, do give me an outline of what has just happened – but stay brief, concise, and to the point.'

....

[376] **Jeder Tag ohne Bier ist ein Gesundheitsrisiko:** Any day without beer is a risk to your health! (German)

'I see…' Andriyovych puckered his brow. 'As if we were to send a telegram, or something like that.'

'Something like a brief digest…' piped in Mykolayovych.

'In a word, so that the puzzle interlocked,' specified Platonovych.

'Call it what you will… But the word "puzzle" seems adequate, I like it. I don't know how many years have been squeezed into those several months of war, perhaps it'll look different from a distance of time. So, let's call it putting the puzzle together.'

Silence fell. It felt like no one was even breathing.

'It's been a long time already, and people talk about things – that's true. Yet the information is sporadic, not yet consistent. The whole truth will only be revealed when the war has finished.'

'But still?'

'Well, if you would like to hear us out… We've been discussing it among ourselves many times,' sighed Andriyovych. 'If we were to rewind it all back, the resulting picture would be motley. It is customary with us to refer to the NATO Bucharest summit in 2008. Some remember Putin's speech at the Munich Security Conference in 2007. Allegedly, it had all started from there. There is this opinion, too, that after the Orange Revolution of 2004-2005 Putin had been overcome with fear that it all could spread over to Russia. But I believe that it all started from the very first day when Putin came into power. From the off, he had been fixated on the "global catastrophe brought about by the disintegration of the Soviet Union." He was profoundly shaken by it. And in his mind, he had it worked out a long time ago – it all must be rectified.'

'But if we dig even deeper?' piped up Mykolayovych. 'Everyone is forgetting that it had been only several months after the signing, in December of 1991, of the Belovezha Accords whereby the Union of the Soviet Socialist Republics was declared defunct as "a subject of the international law and geopolitical reality". And supposedly, among other things, Yeltsin, the then president, casually asked Leonid Kravchuk, president of Ukraine: "Leonid Makarovych, do you really believe that you'll be able to keep your independence? Do you really need it?"[377] This is just to confirm that the thought of "unfairness" of what was going on regarding the collapse of the USSR, and the need to "rectify" it all, originated in the times of Yeltsin! Besides, the Ukrainians, "unlawfully", ended up owning Crimea. Last time, in 1999, when Yeltsin was negotiating with Clinton in Istanbul [these materials have recently been declassified], he said: 'Let me have it all,

....

[377] Gordon, 27 January 2023, https://gordonua.com/news/politics/yushchenko-elcin-v-1992-m-kravchuku-govoril-otkryto-leonid-makarovich-ty-schitaesh-chto-vy-uderzhite-nezavisimost-vam-ona-nuzhna-1647542.html (accessed 05.07.2025).

Bill, and I will arrange my own guarantees for them."[378] It was clear. Though, which guarantees he had in mind – Russia would not attack you for as long as you were obedient? That's always been the story with them. Do you remember Krylov's fable:[379] "The stronger always blames the weaker"!'

'There you go, then. Hurt feelings over the things working out so "unfairly". This barely covered up their anguish over a crumbled empire, this ineffable longing – it comes through in everything. And we believed Yeltsin belonged to a cohort of "staunch democrats"!' added Platonovych.

'And thus, from the year 2000 onwards, Putin had been at the helm. It looks like Ukraine was a thorn in his side from day one. But it was too early to do anything about it, he had to work out the lie of the land first. Thing was, the puppet masters had him pegged down as a nice obedient boy. To start with, he was frequenting the retired Yeltsin, as if to get his advice. Then those visits grew less and less frequent. Then they stopped completely. And then, in September 2003, Russia unexpectedly started building a dam in the Kerch Strait (Crimea), linking up their Taman Peninsular and the Tuzla Spit, Ukrainian territory. Kuchma cut short his visit to Latin America, urgently returned to Tuzla and demonstrably organised erection of defence fortifications on the spit. Many researchers and analysts estimate this to be Russia's first attempt to "feel" Ukraine in connection with a possible annexation of Crimea. This attempt was cut short through a rapid and unequivocal reaction from the side of the then president of Ukraine.'

'Another important thing! On April 25, 2005, during his annual address to the Federal Assembly, Putin called the collapse of the Soviet Union in 1991 'the greatest geopolitical catastrophe of the 20th century'. "Because of this, millions of Russians remained outside the borders of new Russia... Russia is committed to protecting the rights of Russian citizens abroad." Here is his future program. That's where it all comes from...'[380]

'But now – let's move on to the Orange Revolution of 2004-2005...' Mykolayovych intercepted. 'That was, after all, a point of crisis. The Kremlin perceived its victory as their humiliating defeat. For the Russian leadership that situation equalled a double challenge: a threat to Russian foreign interests because

....

[378] Gordon, 14 september 2018, https://gordonua.com/publications/ne-pustit-ukrainu-v-nato-otdat-evropu-rossii-i-prizhat-kuchmu-k-stene-glavnoe-iz-rasse-krechennyh-peregovorov-elcina-i-klintona-346572.html (accessed 05.07.2025).

[379] **Ivan Krylov** (1768/9-1844): a Russian writer of innocent-sounding fables that satirised contemporary social types in the guise of beasts.

[380] UP, 25 April 2005, https://www.pravda.com.ua/rus/news/2005/04/25/4387750/ (accessed 05.07.2025).

of Yushchenko's eagerness to bring Ukraine closer to the West,[381] and preservation of the regime in Russia, since the Ukrainian society had presented an example of where a corrupt and repressive authorities had been toppled. That marked an about-face in Russia's foreign policy, moving away from integrating with the West on Russian terms to a desire to "fence the West off" as had been expressed in Putin's speech in Munich in 2007. Russia became firmly convinced that the West had provoked the Orange Revolution in order to install a Western-orientated Yushchenko as president. Disquiet in the couloirs of the Russian power was intensifying: what if the West would try to emulate their success in Russia? By way of undermining "the Kremlin's legitimacy" and "condoning the popular unrest"? The anti-American sentiments in Russia were now spreading much wider, along with strengthening of the authoritarian power. From that point onwards, Moscow's policies had all been targeted towards prevention of 'coloured revolutions". Let's move on. In April of 2008, at the NATO summit in Bucharest, there was an issue on the agenda regarding Ukraine and Georgia acceding to the Membership Action Plan. The press branded it a "summit of great hopes". Putin arrived to take part in the NATO – Russia session. Later, at a closed meeting when Georgia was discussed, he looked calm. But when the conversation turned to Ukraine, he exploded. Turning to George W. Bush he said: "Do you realise, George, that Ukraine isn't even a state? What is Ukraine? One part of its territory is Eastern Europe, and the other part, a significant part, has been gifted by us!"[382] And then he dropped a transparent hint that if they did accept Ukraine into NATO, this state would simply stop to exist. To paraphrase, he practically threatened with annexation of Crimea and Eastern Ukraine. The countries lobbying interests of Ukraine and Georgia, together with President Bush, had spent the night in tense negotiations with Merkel and Sarkozy. But the latter two had been immutable and hadn't supported the NATO Membership Plan.'

A long pause ensued. We all had a sip from out mugs and then the choir guys erupted, interrupting each other:

'Then came 2008 and invasion of Georgia. And in 2014 – annexation of Crimea. The "little green men" – the Russian military without any insignia on their uniforms – came in under somebody else's flag and blocked strategic facilities. False colours are convenient for their deniability – in case of failure

....

[381] **Viktor Yushchenko** (b. 1954): the third president of Ukraine from January 2005 to February 2010. He aimed to orient Ukraine towards the West, the European Union, and NATO.

[382] 7 April 2008, https://www.unian.net/politics/108325-putin-tyi-je-ponimaesh-djordj-chto-ukraina-eto-daje-ne-gosudarstvo.html (accessed 05.07.2025).

it was always possible to declare: "It wasn't us! And we've no idea who it was!" The West then told Ukraine: "What, then? You have put up zero resistance and given up Crimea without a single shot. Who will fight for you, then? Nobody. If you don't fight for yourselves, you'll lose…" And even right after Crimea, when Russians barged into Donbas and we began fighting, the West still preferred to just observe. And that was that. Putin realised that the West was strong when uttering the words of condemnation, and nowhere else…'

'And seizure of the oblast administrations? Have you forgotten? That wave had rolled all over the country. Saboteurs were active… Sleeping agents… But also, they were buying henchmen for peanuts. They had used the weakness of our internal situation at the time. It was horrible. The whole of Ukraine could have gone up in flames!' Happily for us, that attempt failed…

'But then Putin decided to realise his emerging aspirations through a "legal route". He placed huge hopes on the newly-elected President Zelensky. After all, he had come to power on a wave of declarations about the need to stop the war of 2014! And even when elected, he still talked about it. Do you remember? In February 2020, at a Munich lunch: "In my mind, I've already finished this war"!'[383]

'Small wonder Russia was expounding this formula: "We've no need of this Donbas! Keep it if you so wish!" But the elections in the area must go "our way". That is to say, so that this "Trojan horse" – a sizeable portion of the electorate – would create a formidable pro-Russian faction in the Rada. After such a "return of Donbas", no reforms would've been necessary. And no drifting towards Europe. It would've gone like this: "Everything will be Donbas!" and "Everywhere will be Russia!" Yet nothing came out of an attempt to come to terms with Zelensky. Kyiv understood it too well: implementation of the Minsk Accords, the way Russia wanted it, would have converted Donbas into an uncontrollable centre of influence over our foreign and internal policy. And starting from that same 2020, the Ukrainian side took a much tougher stance compared to the times of President Poroshenko.'[384]

'The Russians fail to realise one thing: every responsible Ukrainian politician, even if he harbours some pro-Russian sentiments, once elected president of Ukraine, will follow a pro-Ukrainian course. Even Yanukovych strove to be pro-Ukrainian. Pity he was weak. He immediately had Russian ministers foisted on him, those that would observe and quietly sabotage everything. But he was trying to throw his weight around, true. Could throw a punch in the teeth, or

....

[383] Priamyi, 17 February 2020, https://prm.ua/u-moyemu-mozku-ya-vzhe-zakin-chiv-viynu-zelenskiy/ (accessed 05.07.2025).

[384] **Petro Poroshenko**: the fifth president of Ukraine (2014-2019).

the solar plexus. But as soon as it was something serious, vital to defending his position – he would immediately throw his little hands up. In November 2013 he folded under Putin's pressure, caved in, and didn't sign the association agreement with the EU. And that was the background that sparked a new Maidan. And since then things have been crumbling steadily. At that time Putin intuited that he could afford to be more arrogant…'

'And that's how it happened that Putin – confronted with Zelensky's stubbornness – was left with no other way but a military one. Yeah, starting from around 2020, he increasingly leant towards this very option. And in 2021 he saw that his time had come: the West looked unprecedentedly enfeebled. Then came worrying news from Kyiv – Zelensky had acted on the NSDC's resolution to introduce sanctions against TV channels owned by Viktor Medvedchuk [Putin is godfather to Medvedchuk's daughter]. That made Putin see red, and he decided that the time was ripe to coordinate all efforts and prevent Ukraine from joining the other side. During the winter and spring, under the guise of a joint training exercise with Belarus, Russia continued concentrating her troops along the Ukrainian border. And in June of 2021 Russia started discreet preparations for a change of power in Ukraine. Tension around Ukraine at the time was palpable, but the USA still believed that it could be defused. And so, that same June, Biden and Putin met in Geneva. The result? "The discussion has been constructive." In other words, the result was zero.'

'Putin returned from that meeting but already the next month – in July – appeared his fundamental article whereby his main tenet was put forward, insisting that Russians and Ukrainians were one people. It all had been garnished with his trademark tales about Ukraine having never existed before and having been invented by a Polish magnate, Count Potocki. And then by the beginning of the First World War, its statehood had been mapped out by the Austrian General Staff. Then – lo and behold – Vladimir Lenin had moved from plans to actions, he created Ukraine as a union republic within the Soviet Union. That was the poppycock he presented. Following that, a Kremlin ideologue Vladislav Surkov went on to verbalise even more horrific ideas…'

'And thus, it follows that the main decision to invade Ukraine was taken in the summer of 2021. And while pseudo-historian Putin and ideologue Surkov engaged in verbal exercises, a group of specialists was being put together on Putin's instruction, with a view to plan the invasion…'

'The head of Kremlin identified only general parameters but then the specific content was worked out in detail by this group consisting of V. Gerasimov – the Chief of the General Staff of the Russian Armed Forces and First Deputy Minister of Defence, plus several of his most trusted subordinates, several individuals from the Putin's Administration, and top managers of the FSB Service of

Operational Information and International Relations. The group was basing its conclusions on the data produced by sociological research and maintaining that Ukrainian society was predominantly apathetic, mistrustful of those in power, primarily concerned with economic problems and reluctant to accept a possibility of an escalated war with Russia.'

'But the "preparatory efforts" had started long before that. Just remember the regular demolition of ammunition depots throughout the years of 2003-2019! They burnt all over Ukraine, big and small ones alike. Tens of thousands of tonnes of ammunition, accumulated during the decades of the Soviet power, went up in smoke! All those shells that our army is short of today. The losses ran into billions. Do you see – they'd spent 16 years working on this alone!'

'By the way, it makes sense to name the principal masterminds behind this full-scale invasion. Back in November 2022, leaks revealed who had pushed this plan: Alexander Bortnikov, the director of the FSB, and Nikolai Patrushev, the secretary of the RF Security Council. As Bortnikov and Patrushev saw it, since Putin was already 70, there would not be another chance to talk him into this war. By mid-summer of 2021, a 'critical mass' of thought had formed among Putin's closest circle of friends and advisers. The consensus was that a 'final decisive blow' was inevitable. Supposedly, by the end of summer a 'decision in principle' had been taken. All that remained was to assemble the necessary resources and convince Putin of the need to start the operation. Apart from Bortnikov and Patrushev, a source of influence over Putin regarding the start of a war was his childhood chum billionaire Yuri Kovalchuk who, among other things, was fascinated with the works of the conservative philosopher Ivan Ilyin.'[385]

'Aye, aye! Let me put in a couple of words too!' Mykolayovych sounded caustic. 'There's a quotation from his oeuvre, a real work of beauty. "Russia is the worst country in the world's history, nauseatingly disgusting. By method of selection, they have raised a generation of moral degenerates whose perception of Good and Evil is completely turned inside out. Throughout its entire history, this nation has been wallowing in filth and is desirous to drown the entire world in it." Ah? What d'you say?'

There followed a general excited bustle.

'Well… that's something… But listen on. In spring and summer of the first year of the COVID pandemic, Kovalchuk was spending a lot of time with Putin while the latter was in hiding at his residence in Valdai. And certain tenets put

---

[385] **Ivan Ilyin** (1883-1954): a Russian lawyer, religious and political philosopher, publicist, orator, and conservative monarchist. While he saw Russia's February Revolution (1917) as a 'temporary disorder', the October Revolution, in his view, was a 'national catastrophe'.

forward by Ilyin – not the very same ones, it's true – proved to be very much to Putin's liking…'

'Hmm… Those leaks…' Platonovych joined in. 'According to them, those three are the main culprits. But is it truly so? Of course not. Putin, with his ideological concepts, has been the principal source of this drive. This triumvirate has scattered their "seeds" over an already fertilised soil. Didn't Putin insist, as far back as 2008, that Ukraine wasn't a real country, just an artificial confection? So, it didn't need anyone to "convince" him, he was the yeast in this dough. The triumvirate had only given additional motivation to his insane aspirations.'

'Tis true, no question about it. Further discussions and approvals were carried out by a foursome: Putin, Bortnikov, Patrushev and Shoigu. The latter had some doubts about advisability of such a step. It's worth noting that nobody else – neither more senior officials, nor "oligarchic friends" – knew anything about it. In general, nobody out there could be certain whether the war was on the cards or whether the whole thing was just a bluff. As for such a seemingly key figure as, say, Foreign Minister Lavrov, he most likely had his reasons to believe that Putin's inner circle had firmly set their hearts on war, but no one had even dropped him a hint in this connection. Putin informed him about the attack only at one in the morning of February 24th. And no wonder. Lavrov is only an obedient performer – there had been no point whatsoever to seek his opinion. Yet in order to justify this war, they had come up with some conceptual slogans: "support of the peoples in Donbas", "denazification" and "demilitarisation" of Ukraine. It meant only one thing: a complete destruction of Ukrainian statehood, elimination of the country's top military and political leadership, dilution, and annihilation of the nation…'

'Sure,' the Commander roused himself up. 'What else happened that summer?'

'If we go in bullet points… By the end of July Zelensky had changed our Supreme Commander, having appointed Zaluzhnyi. The same summer, Merkel, together with Macron, had been trying to put together a new European format for negotiating with Putin. The American response had been lukewarm but Merkel had found herself short of power to push this idea through: other leaders had been aware that her authority would expire in the autumn, at the same time they lacked a personal motivation. For all that, by the end of the summer the Americans had accumulated a wealth of new data. In the second half of August, Zelensky was supposed to go on a visit to the USA. The American side asked him to postpone. Officially, it had to do with the withdrawal of the American troops from Afghanistan. But there was an unofficial reason, too – allegedly, Americans had received some important intelligence about Russia versus Ukraine, and needed more time to process it. Eventually, the withdrawal had been completed. Twenty-one years of presence in that country had cost the USA a dear price. But now that burden had been jettisoned and everyone agreed that their attention should concentrate on relevant targets: their main geo-political adversaries – China and Russia.

'OK, most likely the USA received this long-awaited information and on August 30th, Zelensky did fly over. Their conversation with Biden had been planned to take 40 minutes but, in the event, lasted for a whole two mysterious hours. What Biden had said and how Zelensky reacted is unknown. As per usual, the subsequent briefing provided nothing of substance. And then as early as the beginning of September, the USA concluded that Russia was going to attack Ukraine. So, when Yermak and Kuleba arrived in Washington DC, that same month, they were addressed, in plain speak, with a phrase that later became a quote: "Dig trenches, guys! You're about to be attacked"!'[386]

'Let's fast-forward to October. Biden had a conference with top-level officials. The President was presented with satellite images, intercepted communications, agents' reports and other evidence in support of a conclusion that Russia wasn't just pulling the wool but was really going to attack Ukraine. And things were different to April 2021, when Russian troops first gathered by the Ukrainian border but had then partly withdrawn. An additional proof was the fact that Putin had approved of a sharp increase in his military expenditure, in part at the expense of measures to eliminate the aftermath of COVID. And by then, everything in Russia had been ready for a massive strike. Some of those present (perhaps, Biden himself?) found it hard to appreciate the calibre of the Russian leader's ambitions. They couldn't believe that a "reasonable country" may choose such a course. Biden was exerting pressure on those who were making presentations: did they really believe that Putin was about to attack? And they were bringing additional bits of evidence to the table, including the professional analysis of Putin's personality. For example, his understanding of the world and his obsession with Ukraine. He believed it was a forcibly sawn-off part of Russia that had to be brought back in. He was convinced that Ukraine's gravitation towards the West was closing the window of opportunity for slinging it back. He was certain that the West was dissociated – the USA had to cope with an unsuccessful withdrawal of their troops from Afghanistan and were unlikely to be drawn into a new conflict, whereas the situation in Europe was in Putin's favour. Merkel was about to step down from her post, in France, Macron was up to his eyes in the presidential elections, the United Kingdom was facing a slump in the economy as a result of Brexit. Besides, Europe was

....

[386]   Gordon, 15 August 2023, https://gordonua.com/ukr/publications/ekshlava-hurkondratjuk-ukrajinska-vlada-protjahom-32-rokiv-bula-nafarshirovana-rosijskoju-ahenturoju-1676851.html (accessed 05.07.2025).

highly dependent on the Russian fuel supplies, it would be painful for them to scrape together the courage for any serious steps. All of this spoke in favour of Putin's taking a risk. Biden was also informed that Putin's impudent plans presented a direct threat to the NATO's eastern flank. To add insult to injury, it all was threatening the architecture of Europe's security as it had emerged in the wake of the Second World War. As for specifics of that invasions, these boiled down to the following facts. The invasion would start in winter because the tanks would have it easier moving across the frozen terrain. The operation itself would be started from several directions. The main objective would be to surround Kyiv and capture it within three or four days. Russian Special Task operatives were to take out President Zelensky (assassinate him, if need be), and impose a puppet government, friendly towards the Kremlin. The Russian troops were also to start an offensive in the east and reach the city of Dnipro. The units progressing from Crimea would be in charge of occupying the south of Ukraine. The Kremlin envisaged that the whole operation should take several weeks. Having taken a pause for regrouping and re-arming, the Russians were supposed to move westward and reach an imaginary line running from Belarus to Moldova. It had been envisaged that a portion of the Ukrainian state would be left in peace in the west, since according to Putin, that territory was populated by incorrigible neo-Nazi 'Russophobes'.

'And that was exactly the point when it became clear that to defend itself in case of invasion, Ukraine would need sufficient quantities of new armaments. At the same time there emerged quite a few potentially explosive factors that could provoke a conflict between NATO and a nuclear-empowered Russia. Summarising the results of that conference, Biden (who in his presidential campaign manifesto had promised to keep the country out of any wars) decided that Putin should either be deterred or resisted, and that the USA should not act alone. It was thus decided to explore two avenues. The first consisted of sending a highly-placed official to Moscow with a brief to warn Putin of the consequences should he choose to attack. The second one was to inform Ukraine and the allies about the impending conflict, and to convince the allies of the need to take the same firm stance towards Russia, thus enhancing NATO's military capability and aiding Ukraine. That conference in the White House wasn't a one-off event. During that autumn they were held regularly.'

'And then on 1 November 2021 the CIA Director William Burns arrived in Moscow in order to warn of possible repercussions of an invasion. Burns had served as Ambassador to Moscow in 2005-2008 and could read Putin's moods like no one else. He realised one thing: Putin had approved of the decision in principle, all that was left was to identify the date. Supposedly, Burns said that the 'degree of his apprehension intensified… That was a real turning point. The

American administration had seen for themselves what Russia's true intensions were and set about warning their allies and partners about this danger.'

'This is curious, though. Europe listened to those forecasts… with scepticism! Western countries, Germany and France included, believed that Putin was bluffing and doubted that Russia would have guts for a full-scale invasion. Central and Eastern European countries that had only recently joined the bloc assumed an invasion, should it go ahead, would be on a limited scale. But even within Ukraine itself some of its top leaders used to insist: "Don't pay attention! All this is just a hoax! It's Putin and Biden sending us on a wild-goose-chase but in real terms, they are just raising the stakes. There'll be no war!" Only Great Britain, Poland and the Baltic countries believed that a full-scale invasion was possible. Besides, Great Britain had their own intelligence to support of such a possibility.'

'Another important point is this. Just then Putin started complaining about NATO and their military infrastructure getting close to the Russian border, since the Alliance had been accepting more and more new members. And now they were striving to bring Ukraine, too, into their orbit. Russia saw it as an existential threat. And because of it all she simply had to react. Russia started making statements about the "red lines", demanding guarantees on NATO non-expansion eastwards and "finlandisation" of the post-Soviet states, in short, agreements on a new architecture of European security…'

'But then a most amazing thing happened!' exclaimed Andiyovych. 'In an attempt to prevent the invasion, the White House made an unorthodox decision, declassified their intelligence, and took an unprecedented step of leaking it all to mass media. It was a highly unusual solution but the White House was keen to make Putin give up his plans of war, or at least curtail his capacity for disinformation. Simultaneously, Great Britain leaked their info on a puppet government desirable for Russia. And this worked: from that point on the attention of the whole world was focused on the Russian troops along the Ukrainian borders!'

'But what happened on December 17th was absolutely unexpected. Russia's Foreign Ministry published a draft treaty on the "mutual security guarantees"! Russia suggested that the NATO members should commit not to expand and thus renounce their plans in respect of Ukraine and other countries. Moreover, Moscow declared that the published draft wasn't a menu from which one could pick and choose. The West could only approve the Russian proposals in their entirety. And should the West fail to take it seriously, Moscow threatened to turn to a "military-technical alternative". This document was immediately baptised the "Putin's ultimatum". NATO found this approach unacceptable. Their general secretary had turned down similar Russian demands in the past.'

'Analysts were competing with each other in making assumptions. "In view of the West's refusal to accept Russia's demands about NATO's non-expansion to the East and non-acceptance of Ukraine as its member, it is possible to conclude that the official Washington line does not estimate the prospect of the RF invading Ukraine as a threat to themselves (otherwise it would have been necessary to make some concessions and agree on certain compromises with Putin), but rather as a unique chance of dragging Russia into a lengthy period of bloodshed, with themselves remaining above the fray. In other words, the USA discovered a wonderful opportunity to put Russia's military capability to the test. The zest of the situation was that the States would run such a check on Russia but Russia wouldn't be able to reciprocate!'

'For all that, Germany and France tried to find a peaceful way towards an agreement. The White House wasn't against negotiating but believed that Russia wasn't interested. At the same time the USA started building up their military presence in Europe and providing armaments to Ukraine. Even if many actors – in Kyiv and Washington alike – realised that those supplies would be clearly insufficient in case of a proper war. Their allocations had been calculated to last for a few days of defence – let's remind ourselves that after Crimea the USA were not convinced that Ukrainians would fight against Russia. Besides, they didn't have complete confidence in Zelensky whom they saw as a rookie politician.'

'Phew!' cried out Platonovych. 'And that was the way all through the year 2021: the Russian military presence near Ukraine kept augmenting. Was it to be seen as a simple bluff? Rolling the tank armies across the expanse of Russia and keeping them under field conditions was an expensive luxury, and a threat to apply force would have been useless if it was clear in advance that no such force would be applied. By the end of 2021 some Europeans, also, had started warning us of the Russian invasion plans. However, our leaders still urged us not to "fall for those provocations" and maintain equanimity.'

As if on cue, the choir guys fell silent – tired out by this verbal marathon. We all just sat there without a word, each clasping the mug as if holding onto a life saviour…

'So, what now?' Mykolayovych was the first to come round. 'Shall we move over to the glorious 2022? Let me add something. At the extra-ordinary conference of the Foreign Ministers of NATO member-states that was held in Riga on January 7th, they discussed agglomeration of Russian troops along the Ukrainian borders. And that was the beginning of a "big shift" towards the American interpretation of events. The USA produced intelligence that convinced those who up to that point had been sceptical. At the same time Josep Borrell, the leading EU diplomat, paid a visit to Kyiv. During a meeting with Prime Minister Shmyhal, the latter asked: "When they attack us – and they will – will you support us? Will you provide weapons so that we could defend ourselves?' At the time Borrell couldn't give him a clear answer because up till then the European Union had never provided military aid to a warring country…'

'Between January 10th and 13th, there was a succession of talks – in Geneva, Brussels, and Vienna – all on the subject of providing Russia with security guarantees. The whole thing was a resounding fiasco. These were not negotiations as such, rather a podium for Russia to present her "wish list". The whole affair amounted to the diplomats going through the motions – the Russians knew perfectly well that the West would not agree to the proposals they had tabled. They were dead set on "gobbling up" Ukraine and methodically moved towards the implementation of this aim. For them, this diplomatic game was nothing more than a means of distraction from their real intentions.'

'Just then, on January 12th, the CIA director William Burns paid a secret visit to Kyiv. He revealed to Zelensky a key element in the Russian plan: the attack on Kyiv would start with landing an advance party at Antonov Airport in Hostomel, because it had capability to receive large military transport aircraft used for deploying air assault troops. The main objective would be to decapitate the central authorities. The greatest danger hung over the president and his family. Those charged with the mission had already arrived in Kyiv. The plans had been to capture the city within 2-3 days. Burns pointed out that in case of invasion we wouldn't last for more than 72 hours! He offered Zelensky to leave the country. Zelensky replied that he was staying.'

'On January 19th, Blinken flew into Kyiv. He suggested that Zelensky should concentrate on ensuring an uninterrupted operation of the organs of power, and promised to support Zelensky in whatever he would decide. The options were: to stay in Kyiv, to move to the West of Ukraine or to move to Poland. Again, Zelensky answered that he was staying in the capital. "If we sow chaos among the population on the eve of an invasion, they will swallow us whole. Because chaos makes people flee the country"…'[387]

'Now briefly about the well-known facts. On January 21st, in Geneva, Blinken met with Lavrov, warned him, yet again, of the consequences in case of an invasion. In his turn, Lavrov voiced Russia's grievances addressed to NATO. As members of the two delegations started to disperse, Blinken took Lavrov aside and said: "Sergey, what are you trying to achieve?"[388] Lavrov said nothing and

[387] Suspilne noviny, 16 August 2022, https://suspilne.media/271842-zelenskij-rozpoviv-comu-vlada-ne-poperedila-ukrainciv-pro-vtorgnenna-rf/ (accessed 05.07.2025).

[388] Censor.net, 17 August 2022, https://censor.net/ru/news/3361142/the_washington_post_opublikovala_detali_plana_putina_i_rasskazala_kak_ssha_preduprejda-

simply went out of the room. And on February 4th, yet again, two influential publications – *Bild* and *Washington Post* – came out simultaneously carrying pieces on the invasion of Ukraine. Once again, they published maps showing the main thrust of the Russian attack that would be delivered from several directions. The first stage would be to lay siege and capture principal Ukrainian cities. The second involved a convocation of a puppet "Popular Rada" as a replacement for the Supreme Rada. The new element was the third stage. It provided for setting up detention camps for "pro-Ukrainian activists", the lists of names had already been compiled. By way of conclusion, it was announced that Russia's main aim was to create a "new union state" made up of the Russian Federation, Ukraine, and Belarus.'

'And thus, on 4 February 2022 Putin flew into Beijing to attend the opening of the Olympic Games. Goes without saying that such an important decision about Ukraine had to be agreed with China. The cover-up was ideal – a trip to the Olympics. There is no evidence but allegedly President Xi confirmed that China had no objections. Although on one condition – if the victory was quick. Putin assured him on this front. He reportedly announced: "It would be a flask-like victory!" In response, the Chinese leader supposedly gave Putin to understand that in this case he could count not only on the Chinese leadership's understanding but their support, too. Presumably, whatever helped to weaken the USA and their partners would be welcome. Then again, if the issue was resolved quickly, China would find it easier to use it to their advantage. Yet what happened – happened, by now it cannot be unhappened.'

'And then in bullet points. On February 8th, having visited Moscow Macron arrived in Kyiv. He told Zelensky that Putin had assured him – there would be no further escalation. But already on February 10th Biden urged all American citizens to leave Ukraine. Embassies of many countries, the USA among them, reserved premises in Lviv, getting ready to relocate to this city. On the same day – February 10th – the USA warned the leadership of all NATO members: Russia had earmarked the sixteenth as Day X! Specifics were presented at secret briefings: the routes to be used by the invading army and even the tasks set for various units. There was also talk of missile strikes against the Ukrainian military infrastructure…'

'February 10th to 12th… evidence suggests, having returned from China, and considered the whole project, Putin green-lighted the decision to invade. The only question left was the date. Reportedly the option he had chosen was against the advice of the General Staff. Reputedly, they had been in favour of kicking-off with a month of mass-scale missile strikes. But Putin went for a

li_zelenskogo (accessed 06.07.2025).

blitzkrieg. All those years in power Putin had been enjoying the reputation of a "lucky devil". And he was certain that luck, again, would be on his side.'

'February 11th... Ben Wallace, British Secretary of State for Defence, visited Moscow. Leaks revealed that after this meeting Shoigu took Wallace to one side, looked him in the eye, and said, "We have no plans to invade Ukraine...'

'Western intelligence services communicated intelligence about a growing number of Russian saboteurs on Ukrainian soil. Hitmen from various private military companies were arriving in Ukraine in secret, possibly tasked with throwing the population into turmoil, or using special weapons to assassinate designated targets. It was completely possible that Russia masterminded various provocations to use as a pretext for an invasion.'

'This was curious too! On February 12th on Biden's initiative, he spoke with Putin over the phone. They talked for nearly an hour. It was their last personal exchange...'

'On February 14th, Scholz arrived in Kyiv under the umbrella of "Crisis Diplomacy". The following day he flew to Moscow. Putin delivered him a lecture about "Russians, Ukrainians and Belarusians being one people". Answering Scholz about this expected invasion, Putin replied: *Our plans are made as the occasion requires*".'

'One more remarkable fact. Russians kept putting back the date of invasion. In the final two weeks – by a day, or two, or three at a time.'

And again, the narrators made a pause... Before long, though, they picked up from where they'd left it off.

'Bankova Street had mixed feelings about those Western warnings. On the one hand, one couldn't ignore the concentration of the Russian troops. On the other – Putin's war plans were just an assumption. From the Ukrainian leadership's point of view, it all looked insane. They believed that the real plan of action lay elsewhere. Based on various incoming data, they decided that all this commotion had been about Russia making sure that the LPR and DPR were recognised, which would then make it easier to annex those oblasts whole [i.e. to seize territories in Ukrainian-held oblasts]. And that was all there was to it. And no full-scale invasion...'

'In favour of this interpretation was the fact that north of Kyiv the terrain is unsuitable for launching a serious attack while numbers of the Russian troops accumulated out there would be insufficient for capturing the city (even if Kyiv was practically defenceless). So, it made no sense to announce mobilisation in advance – that would've dealt a blow to Ukraine's economy and could be useless, since the date of invasion was as yet unknown. Interceptions of the conversations between the Russian military also confirmed that they were not ready for military action. That was why Kyiv decided that this much talked-about Russian "assault" onto the capital was nothing more than a diversionary tactic. In consequence, the Ukrainian top brass was in no rush to bring in any significant forces capable of defending Kyiv…'

'Based on these conclusions, Bankova acted accordingly: no abrupt gestures or brusque declarations lest they should exacerbate the situation in the East and spread panic among the population. In other words, their decisions were based on a wrong perception of Putin's final aims. According to some sources, the authorities had realised that things would not stop at Donbas only a couple of days before the actual invasion.'

'Bankova had several channels of communication with the Kremlin. Allegedly, bargaining was going on, and not without success. [I wonder: did they suspect that by such "communication" Putin was just playing a game?] This explains why the authorities were keen not to rock the boat and tried to calm the populace. They generally behaved cautiously and in the spirit of "peace". In the end, Ukraine was ready to make some concessions and sign an appropriate agreement. Kozak – in charge of negotiating with the Kremlin – pitched up with this plan in front of Putin. "Ukraine undertakes not to join NATO. The agreement, thus reached, provides for stopping an invasion of Ukraine inasmuch as it is consistent with the Russian demands about our country's neutral status." Kozak recommended that Putin should agree. But the latter retorted: 'This isn't enough anymore. The purposes of the special military operation have been broadened!' [389]'This completely flabbergasted Kozak.

'So, after that – about a week before the invasion – Bankova got really worried and started issuing instructions accordingly. What's more – the military got agitated too, and their orders were hastened downwards. Whether it's true or not, God alone knows. But indirectly… That is what Danilov said already after the invasion: "There had been numerous offers for Zelensky to leave the capital. A whole chain of alternative centres had been prepared from where he could rule the country and make decisions… A week before the war, at a session with Prime Minister Shmyhal they agreed on where the ministries would relocate in a situation of crisis. It was imperative to ensure their continuous operation"…'

'February 18th… A cardinal piece of news! Biden announced to several NATO allies that the USA believed Putin had made his final decision to invade. New American intel predicted the date of February 19th. The Ukrainian upper echelons remained sceptical. Yet by that point nearly all embassies had relocated to Lviv. And practically all air companies had suspended their flights…'

---

[389]   Radio Svoboda, 14 September 2022, https://www.radiosvoboda.org/a/news-putin-viyna-nebazhannia-myr/32033315.html (accessed 06.07.2025).

'Still, nothing happened on February 19th. For all that, President Biden called an urgent briefing: "Putin has already signed off on a decision to invade Ukraine!"[390] Inevitability of the invasion was also confirmed by Boris Johnson. A new invasion date was named – February 22nd…'

'February 20th… Macron still hopeful of a peaceful settlement. He called Putin once more. By the end of their conversation, Macron had suggested a meeting with Biden in Geneva where 'closer attention may be paid to your requests concerning NATO and Ukraine.' Putin answered that he had nothing against that and suggested that they left the details to their assistants. "Frankly speaking, I am about to go play hockey. I'm talking to you from the gym before my training session…'[391]

'Everybody breathed out. Few thought that this, possibly, was a Putin's ruse…'

'February 21st. At 4 p.m. (9 a.m. in Washington D.C.) there was this breaking news. The White House confirmed Biden's willingness to attend a summit with Putin. It became possible as a result of telephone exchanges between Macron, Biden, Putin, Zelensky and Boris Johnson. The agenda for this summit was to be prepared by USA Secretary of State Blinken and Russia's Foreign Minister Lavrov at their meeting, planned for February 24th in Geneva. Overwhelmed with emotions, Macron exclaimed that it was a possible way out of one of the most dangerous crises in Europe in recent decades. And just then (5 p.m. in Moscow, 4 p.m. in Kyiv) the Russian Federal TV channels suspended their normal broadcasts and showed the session of the RF Security Council. You all know what happened there…'

'In his evening telephone conversations with the leaders of France and Germany Putin warned them of a necessity to recognise independence of the DPR and LPR. And not just recognise but accept their territorial integrity within the administrative borders of Luhansk and Donetsk Oblasts, in other words, including the area under Ukrainian control. Putin made a snide comment about Ukraine being a "artificial concoction dating back to the Soviet times and put together at the expense of historic Russian land." His hands trembled, his face grimaced contemptuously. Then they showed Russian President and the leaders of the LPR and DPR signing the relevant documents in the same Kremlin hall that had recently housed the session of the Security Council. It thus became clear that there would be no meeting between Biden and Putin…'

....

[390] TSN , 19 February 2022, https://tsn.ua/politika/vin-uhvaliv-rishennya-bayden-rozpoviv-pro-plani-putina-schodo-ukrayini-1981396.html (accessed 06.07.2025).

[391] New voice, 28 June 2022, https://nv.ua/ukr/world/geopolitics/stenograma-rozmovi-putina-ta-makrona-naperedodni-viyni-rf-proti-ukrajini-novini-ukrajini-50252759.html (accessed 06.07.2025).

'Late in the evening of February 21ˢᵗ the official representative of the USA made an important announcement to NATO members: Biden's assertion about Putin's decision to bring his troops into Ukraine was corroborated by intelligence according to which the Russian advance command had received an order to finalise their preparations for invasion. Apart from Kyiv, other Ukrainian cities were to be targeted, too.'

'Tuesday, February 22ⁿᵈ. All was quiet in the morning. The American date for invasion didn't work yet again. At the same time came the news that in Crimea pontoons were being transported towards Sivash. A vigorous training exercise was in progress, the first of this kind in eight years.'

'Just then Putin appealed to the Federation Council asking for approval to use Russia's armed forces abroad. Approval was granted that same day. Following this development, Putin announced that Russia would provide military aid to the self-proclaimed republics of Luhansk and Donetsk. Just pay attention to the variety of the step he took to distract attention!'

'On the same day, in the White House's Oval Office Biden received D. Kuleba, Ukraine's foreign minister, and warned him that it "It will all happen within the next 48 hours…" Kuleba urgently got in touch with Kyiv and updated the President. Blinken cancelled his meeting with Lavrov as pointless.'

Once more, the narrators took a break, so that everybody could process what they had just heard.

'Now they say that the Kremlin kept the date of invasion a complete secret,' started Platonovych. 'But after February 20ᵗʰ the word started coming through. There were irrefutable facts that the Russian military command – in places of their troop concentration along the Ukrainian border – had received a "go-ahead" from Putin to start the invasion. Reportedly, they had already made specific plans for manoeuvres on the battlefield. Our leaders supposedly knew about this. But the information concerning the march on Kyiv was completely supressed by the Russians. Only a day or two before the events, the General Staff had started issuing certain commands, yet they remained top secret.'

'OK,' the Commander frowned. 'And then?'

'Whether or not our side learnt something, or understood something, but just then, on February 22ⁿᵈ-23ʳᵈ they started evacuating police, security services and procurator's offices from some eastern near-border areas towards localities deeper inside the country. This means that our authorities still believed that things would be happening only in the east…'

'Hmm… On the 22ⁿᵈ…' Platonovych instinctively scratched the back of his head. 'But what about this message that Denis Kireyev sent to our side on the twenty-third? That prominent financier who doubled up as an intelligence officer?'

'The "final decision" on launching the operation – or perhaps just confirmation of an earlier decision – was made by Putin on February 23rd, about 4 p.m. With us, it was 5 p.m. Most likely, that had been Kireyev's intel. Yet no one confirms when exactly our side received it…'

'Meanwhile at 6 p.m., at the President's Office, started a meeting with biggest names in business. President was worried but composed. And, allegedly, nothing indicated that by that time he had already been in the frame…'

'Whether or not he was in the know, some of those present had already been informed. Small wonder… Big business always gets the lowdown ahead of the people on top.'

'Is that true?' the Commander impatiently urged us to carry on with this 'reconstruction'.

'The meeting was over in an hour and a half. Some of the attendees were leaving the building and talking to the press. Allegedly, it had all gone well, everybody was satisfied. Whether or not they were sincere or were just going through the motions, who knows?'

'There you are…' Mykolayovych was overwhelmed. 'At the same time, some of them were deftly sliding through the journalists' cordons heading for their limos. There were those who rushed straight to the airports, for the word had got through that the air space was about to be closed. So, come hell or high water, they had to be able to board their jets!'

'That's probably the gist of it.' Andriyovych sighed. 'It is known that seven hours prior to the invasion the top brass had reportedly received some valuable information, that is to say that information from Kireyev must have reached them. And it became finally clear – it would be an attack from all sides! All directions! And the main thrust would be directed at Kyiv from Belarus. Assault troops would land in Hostomel. The stake would be on a blitzkrieg – elimination of the top people in power, dismantling of Ukraine!'

Andriyovych gasped as if short of air – and wavered.

'And only after this,' he finally recovered, 'they started hastily implementing some preventive measures, for example, moving troops closer to Kyiv.'

'Seven hours,' interrupted Mykolayovych. 'By way of elementary arithmetic, it follows that they started at 9 p.m. In other words, as soon as they received Kireyev's information?'

'It's all just assumptions,' nodded Platonovych. 'But it does look this way. Now our President re-evaluated the situation radically. Only an hour or two earlier, at the meeting with the businessmen, he was in a different mood – simply tense. Now, however, he was extremely alarmed. No one confirmed it but logic suggests that on February 23rd at 9 in the evening, the entire President's Office was in turmoil. Previously there had been hope, however slight, but now there wasn't any. It was abundantly clear, even if the Ukrainian leadership took it on board at the eleventh hour, that the Russian army was concentrating its main troops to attack Kyiv and Chernihiv!'

'Late in the evening of February 23rd, the president was preparing bullet points for his TV address. His appeal went on air at 11:47 p.m. He addressed not only Ukrainians but Russians too: "I am turning to citizens of Russia as a citizen of Ukraine. Today I have approached the president of the Russian Federation with an initiative to hold a telephone conversation. All I heard in response was complete silence. Although silence should reign in Donbas. We and you and are separated by over 2000 kilometres of state border. Along this border are positioned your troops – nearly 200,000 soldiers, thousands of military vehicles. Your leadership gave approval for them to move forward, into the territory of another state. This step may start a big war on the continent of Europe…"[392] But you all know this.'

'And thus, he unequivocally announced that the invasion was imminent!' Platonovych clapped his hands.

'Most people, though, over here and over there, were asleep, unlikely to be listening. But this speech of his was an unambiguous declaration: we know that you are ready to attack us tomorrow!'

'And only few hours separate us from this!' cried out Mykolayovych.

'Yes!' Andriyovych breathed out forcibly. 'The invasion date kept being pushed back. First it was February 16th, then – 19th, then – 22nd. Finally, it was 24th. The enemy was ready, but they were lying in wait. And then the time came. Between 3:30 and 5:00 a.m. – depending on which Ukrainian region you're talking about – the Russian Federation's full-scale invasion of Ukraine began…'

He finished his story and lapsed into silence.

We all sat motionless, as if stupefied, not a word from anyone.

Finally, the Commander broke the silence.

'Well, and what's the bottom line, speaking briefly?'

Andriyovych came back in a flash:

'Bottom line? Chancellor Scholz was hundred times right when he insisted that everything was rather elementary and that the 'threat of NATO's expansion towards the east' was only a pretext used by Moscow to launch this attack. The Kremlin simply used it as a useful excuse for implementing its long-cherished plan of expanding Russia by force.

....

[392] Novynarnia, 24 February 2022, https://novynarnia.com/2022/02/24/hot-yat-ly-russkye-vojn%D1%8B-zelenskyj-zvernuvsya-do-rosiyan/ (accessed 06.07.2025).

'And ours?'

'What's there to say? A strategic miscalculation. They were told – you'd be torn limb from limb. In plain language. Presented with key points… But they are a staunch bunch: "A full-scale something, you say? He-he-he… Ho-ho-ho…" They dismissed it out of hand. And we all see the consequences of belated decisions and how many lives it has cost Ukraine…'

'They could behave differently: "We don't believe it but we are getting ready"!'

'Ah well,' sighed the Commander. 'I've now got a grasp of things. So, what now? Why isn't this counteroffensive going as planned?'

'Hmmm… Hard to say,' Andriyovych answered wistfully. 'The "flash-like" war hasn't happened. Reasons? The Russian army does have some strong characteristics. And now we can't surrender but it's hard to win.'

'The counter-offensive has unravelled. There are reasons for this: minefields… Those defence lines that the Russians have installed… Those lethal kilometres of the first line…'

'To break through this defence, a tank must hoist its body upwards, thus exposing its weakest point, the bottom. And that's exactly where they would aim to deliver a wallop. Also, he who has planes and the artillery rules the nest. Drones, too. It's becoming an increasingly decisive factor.'

'Let me tell you this. This counter-offensive of ours, irrespective of its results, wouldn't have put an end to this war. If it weren't such an endless saga… President himself said: victory would not arrive tomorrow or the day after…'

'Alas, whatever was easy to give away – Crimea and part of Donbas in 2014, now the south of the country – is so hard to win back…'

'Indeed. Which means we must place our hopes on the next season of fighting. Next year…'

'The next one… Or the one after that… I'm telling you – how long is a piece of string?'

'You're right… No end is in sight…' conceded Platonovych.

'So, let's call a spade a spade,' Mykolayovych shielded his face with his hands. 'The war has been going on for quite a few months now. And it's all somehow… It all feels endless… Ye-eh… Endlessness… The infinity of it all…'

After which no one added a word.

As for me, I was so stunned with those words. They made quite an impression: endlessness… infinitude…

* * *

The plane carrying Prigozhin – had crashed! Either it had been downed with a missile, or had a bomb planted… Russia is mourning… A person who'd done nine years in camps, created a private military company – in essence, a criminal sect, made his eerie mark in a string of African countries, recruited into his PMC tens of thousands of career criminals, and then sent them to fight in Ukraine – had become a national hero! Spontaneous memorials to him popped up all over Russia – like mushrooms after a rain. People were coming to those sanctuaries with their children, bending their heads, sobbing. Mountains of flowers…

No, we would never understand these people…

But here is the surprising thing! Prigozhin had been warned! Everybody knew that following his failed march on Moscow he would simply be taken out. And that was what came to be – exactly two months after that 'action'. So, it did look like some morbid symbolism…

I just started thinking it all over when a call came in from the Myrhorod area. Pyvynsky and Yanovsky, of late, had been calling quite frequently.

'Have you noticed?' Pyvynsky was practically yelling into the receiver, clearly agitated. 'Some sly experts in some hidden sites are pushing forward this construct: "Aha, this very invasion! The Kremlin proceeded from a faulty premise which led them pursuing faulty purposes. This war is irrational"!'

'Irrational… Has no point…' that was already Yanovsky speaking. 'But there's no need to reinvent a wheel! It's irrational for us, with neither sense nor purpose. As for Russians – it's rational and makes sense. Their purpose is to eliminate a neighbouring state and annex its land. Europe yells – this philosophy belongs in the previous century! But they don't give a toss. And it's not just Putin who gets off on this philosophy of aggression – it's all their people!'

'That's just it: neither the tenets nor the purposes have been wrong,' Pyvynsky again. 'And the war is rational to a tee – to capture a country and achieve ethnic replacement. Our guys, once out of filtration camps, should go to Siberia and develop northern areas. Let them! But theirs should be brought over here, to where it's warm and nice to live – they've deserved it! Let them have a breather…'

'You see, they have problems with everything of ours… Our history is wrong, and our heroes are wrong,' Yanovsky hastily changed the subject. 'Although it's all clear as noonday. Each country has its own history, and its own heroes. We have ours, so don't you interfere with any of it. And we have our heroes, too. Like in any other country – they're a motley crowd. Some things make you proud, some – considerably less so. They did some good, and some – not so very good. But the most important thing about all of them – they have been thinking and working for the benefit of Ukraine. And that's why they are our heroes…'

'Listen!' Pyvynsky cut in again. 'I've got another sore point to make. Why should we be ashamed of that panic that gripped the country during the first days? The flight of millions of people? Why should we justify ourselves? It was only natural that civilians were scared and ran for dear life!'

'Yeah...' I finally managed to put in a word. 'There are no questions to ask of the civilians, nor can there be. The main point is that those in power behaved as they should – were not afraid and didn't head for the hills. And the army, likewise...'

'That's it!' that was Yanovsky. 'After all that was a situation with no precedent in Europe! It must've been a first in history when out of four million living in a very big city, three upped and left within the space of a day or two! And if we take the entire country, eight million ended up abroad while seven million are now internal refugees. Dreadful stuff. Bombings started, explosions everywhere, and... People were abandoning everything they'd earned over years, grabbing their children and the essentials, rushing to their cars, trying to save their lives by running away. Those without a car crammed themselves into buses and trains, like sardines in a can, standing next to each other, cheek by jowl. All that mattered was to get away! Without the foggiest about their destination, the things in store for them in a new place. That was nothing short of a shattering crisis.'

'Wait!' that was Pyvynsky again. 'Talking about unprecedented incidents, I'd like to delve in history. It's true, nothing like that ever happened in Europe – with the exception of June 1940, when fascists were marching towards Paris. There was incredible panic. At least three million had fled the Parisian conurbation – out of the total of five. It was a real exodus from the capital. Those on the run were horribly scared, dragging their possessions on their backs or attached to bicycles and prams, with children in their arms... Some had nothing to carry, absolutely nothing, travelling completely alone. Shops were closed, shutters locked, blinds down. City streets grew empty, completely deserted. People who tried to escape were heading south or west. The roads were chock-a-block with cars, buses, lorries, barrows, and bicycles. All of this was progressing at a snail's pace because the roads were quickly overwhelmed. And what would you think? The enemy quickly turned this to their advantage: the German aviation started bombing the crowded roads...'

'Enough to drive you insane,' I added quickly. 'The similarity with what happened in Kyiv is striking. Roads as badly dead-locked, city streets as deserted...'

'Yet another similarity was this,' cried Yanovsky 'the Kyiv-Lviv Highway also ended up under fire. The only difference was that the fascists had been shooting from the air, from aboard their planes whereas the ruscists were shooting overground, from their tanks.'

'Just to think of it… Pure horror in those first days…' Pyvynsky was now talking slowly and softly. 'After that there's been a real avalanche of other frightening news, that exodus-episode was somehow… pushed into the background, lost its significance. But that was a human disaster of the huge magnitude! A multi-faceted event. I'm convinced it should be researched in earnest. The time will come when it becomes possible – and necessary! – to talk about it. There will be hundreds of books, various research papers. They'll make films about it!'

'I totally agree,' Yanovsky wasn't bellowing anymore, his voice pensive and wistful. 'In those days the eyes of Europe, of the whole world were on Ukraine, people felt for us. Excepting citizens of Russia who were simultaneously indifferent and hostile. People over there aren't even aware of this nightmarish tragedy, they don't feel it, don't accept it. All they do is cheer and giggle.'

'I wonder…' I did manage to say something during the intervening pause. 'If all of this is over one day, and there will be some peaceful negotiations, how should this event be treated? What was the human cost? How could one even assess it? Could we present a bill like this to the other side? There is another obvious phenomenon: a large European country is drowning in blood, its citizens losing their lives – while the rest of the world is unquestionably sympathetic, providing all kinds of aid, but that's it.'

'You've touched an open nerve, Kiril,' tsked Pyvynsky. 'You see, Europe has been so badly affected by the First and the Second World Wars, lost so many lives, got so immunised, that it would never get itself involved into anything of the kind. That's for starters. And secondly – the idea of the value of an individual human life has gone through a radical transformation. Is it realistic now – to drive hundreds of thousands, or even millions of soldiers into trenches and then force them – as during those wars – to attack the enemy? If we combine those factors…'

'I totally agree!' Yanovsky was bellowing again. 'They may be prepared to engage, put up some resistance, but to carry out a genuine struggle… You'll see, they may finally say that it's better to surrender but stay alive. And the fact that it would be life under the yoke… Take France as we've already discussed today. First, they fled southwards, but then half of them returned – as if nothing had happened – to occupied Paris. If bloody Russkies push their way into Europe, Europe will behave just like that.'

'Wait a minute, buddy! Just wait…'

Pyvynsky was about to convince him of something, his voice slightly annoyed, but Yanovsky cut him short and erupted in real anger:

'That's it! That's the way it will be! And don't you dare argue!'

Ressentiment. The Russian Idea

By the end of the USSR's existence, President Reagan had called it the 'evil empire'. Now it looked as if this empire was here to stay. It remained 'evil' but additionally now held a grudge against the entire world.

Today's Russia had a dominant emotion, and Putin just happened to strike a chord with the overwhelming majority of that society, although he was both a generator and supplier of this emotion. This emotion was a fierce umbrage at the civilized world. Nothing could bring it under control and thus it prevented any sober-minded analysis and attempts to establish some sort of productive relations with other countries.

Perhaps in some remote future the Russians would realise that their hurt feelings worked against themselves. In their eyes, they had been shortchanged by the world order that proved unfair towards them. Responsibility for this disgrace lay with the 'elder'. That is the USA.

True, similar ressentiment was present in other countries too. A considerable portion of the world population had grievances about the existing world order and the USA, in as much as they had assumed the responsibility, achieved hegemony and, to a large degree, became the beneficiary of such a *status quo*. Thus, the countries that supported Putin were: the 'Global South' – that is, countries in Latin America, Africa, Asia, and Oceania that in the recent decades had been affected by a growing gap between the rich and the poor. It applied to the poorest strata in the 'Global North' (also known as the 'countries of the golden billion'), who also perceived themselves as aggrieved and victimised. Practically any country or stratum of the population displaying the phenomenon of ressentiment supported Putin, even if it was never openly demonstrated – after all, Putin hadn't put forward a single new idea.

For all that, compared to other countries, the outrage against the rest of world had struck the most powerful roots in Russia. There it had taken a horrible form, at times bordering on a caricature.

So, what were the reasons for this rancour? Perhaps, the fact that the USA, and partially, Europe, had assumed the role of a 'preacher'? Ideologically, it stemmed from the theory of modernisation. In essence, it boiled down to this: there were countries with their economy in transition (formerly, socialist countries), and the countries with a developing economy (or, those with a centralised economy). There were also countries with a developed economy (market economy). And those successful countries, i.e., the 'golden billion', were the ones who liked to deliver lectures: 'Guys, things are really not right with you! You should arrange things the way we have it here!' When such sermons were coming at you non-stop, who would find it to their liking?

Especially if you were a boundless country nursing the ideas of its imperial grandeur…

Hurt feelings could be contagious. It was a useful emotion since it justified you in feeling right, and often – mistreated.

There were some other important aspects, too. If the prevailing emotion in Russia was umbrage, the derived unifying affect would be fear. Multiplied by hopelessness, because the tyrant was omnipotent. He would get whatever he was after – that had been the way, and that will be the way.

A common-coin explanation according to which they were all duped by their own propaganda was not the whole story. It was linked to this imperial complex and the Russian nationalism. Even those 'decent Europeanised' Russians admitted that they had been affected and tried to somehow cope with the results.

For years, many sensible people had been mocking the Russian imitation of 'democracy', exposing corruption and the nepotic business-capitalism. They poked their fingers: where were the results of searching for the so-called 'Russian idea'? Wasn't it obvious that that 'idea' wasn't based on freedom or integrity but a passionate yearning for an 'imperial might'? Russia had to come across as huge, scary, nuclear-enabled, perpetually capable of delivering a powerful blow to her competitors. So that everything corresponded to the works of the 'Russian classical literature' (Gogol) – everything on Earth receded, casting sidelong glances at that insane 'bird-like troika' and yielding way to it.[393] It was phenomenal!

Foreign researchers pointed out that for a long time this image of a 'bird-like troika' had served as a kind of justification for Russia's 'exceptionalism' and 'moral supremacy' over other nations. As for the 'Russian idea', it was nothing more than a string of concepts in support of the idea of Russia's historical uniqueness, of the special 'mission' and 'calling' of the Russian people and, in the deepest interpretation, the 'mission' and 'calling' of the Russian state.

The 'Russian idea' was that the Russians perceiving themselves as a 'God's chosen people', thus emphasising Russia's cosmic nature, her spiritual communality and universality. Proponents of this idea insisted that Russia would play a pivotal role in the 'global Christian salvation'.

The 'Russian idea' became even more topical following the disintegration of the Soviet Union and the ensuing spiritual vacuum. Some smarty pants went as far as to claim that it gives Russia a special place in the renewed world. According to them, no one but Russia has given the world a new religion, 'common

....

[393]   A reference to the final part of *Dead Souls* by Nikolai Gogol.

for all humanity', to shine down on humankind with the 'Sun of Truth'. Such crazy ravings…

Meanwhile sober-minded researches could see that the 'Russian idea' was just a good smoke screen for geo-political ambitions, or even the ideology of a great-power chauvinism and imperialism.

Summer, Autumn, Winter, Spring… And so on, and so Forth…

Unexpectedly, the summer was over. What a shame – we'd barely had time to enjoy it… And suddenly, it was autumn again…

In September we saw for ourselves that Russia indeed outstripped Ukraine in terms of resources – after all, already the previous year our military leaders had prophetically insisted that the war would grow into a dragged-out conflict! So, the offensive in the South had been aborted completely, and the Ukrainian troops withdrew to their defence positions. What was emerging was a 'dead-end in trenches', a stalemate when neither Russia nor Ukraine were ready to surrender but couldn't fight their way out.

It should be added that our Western partners, likewise, had to decide whose fault it had been – Ukraine's or the West's? In either case, the top brass had only one solution to offer – switch over to defence and try to wear the enemy out.

Ah, well… – we'd lived with this war for so long that sometimes it felt nothing would ever change. We were all extremely tired, but we couldn't just sit around twiddling our thumbs. We had a duty to stay full of strength, energy, and drive, seeing as it now was a war of endurance… Then this again: Donald Trump is pushing through his old idea: give all the Russian-speaking regions back to Russia and everything would be hunky-dory! He either didn't or wouldn't comprehend the obvious: yes, millions of Ukrainian citizens considered Russian to be their mother tongue. But they wanted to live in Ukraine, not in Russia! Ukraine was their motherland…

Taras and I met at Kontraktova square and set off to mine. Suddenly, my mobile started ringing, urgently and insistently. I checked the Caller ID – Pyvynsky; undoubtedly, his deputy and chum Gogol-Yanovsky by his side, but we'd spoken only recently?

'You're right, Kiril,' Pyvinsky's bass reverberated in my ear. 'Of course we are here, both of us. What we want to say is this… Let's assume the world's history has some logic in its footfall. And history shows that in the recent centuries Russia has been shaping up as an empire which always means the same – an empire will expand until it abuts onto the borders of other empires. Nowadays, it could mean all kinds of blocs, unions, communities. So, near-border territories always find themselves in a zone of high-risk. To survive, our state badly needs that Russia should drop this paradigm, shrug off her imperial logic, and stop believing that the 19th century methods were still applicable in today's world...'

'And listen to me, Kiril, as well...' Yanovsky must have snatched the receiver. 'Only such internal transformation will decide if a relapse of hostilities is likely. Otherwise, even if Russia retreats, so many years later she will go back to her old ways. Will she manage to come through with it? I'm not sure. Above all, we don't even know if she wants change. In general, all those debates on the issue bring to mind this proverb about "apportioning the pelt of an as yet alive bear". One has to kill the bear first! To rip out his rapacious fangs and claws, and only then evaluate the resulting options!'

I heard peculiar sounds of a scrabble – that was Pyvynsky snatching the receiver back.

'Do you know, Kiril, what I recall frequently?'

'What's that, Anatoliy Semenovych?'

'Before you left you told us about another subject of yours, the secret one.'

'A-h-h-h...'

'You dropped a hint that you suspected the top person in the neighbouring country, sort of... being... Yuck! It disgusts me to even say it out loud! You know what I mean... Say it yourself...'

Oh no, I thought. *As we had this very conversation in your office in Shyshaky I barely managed to get my tongue round all that foul stuff. Now it's your turn. Go for it!*

So, I kept my dignified silence.

There was nothing else for it but for Pyvynsky to say softly:

'We-e-e-ll... You said then that the most cunning and crafty demons, no matter in which part of the world they get up to their tricks, somehow all take after the Myrhorod demons so vividly brought to life by the genius of our countryman – Mykola Gogol. Allegedly, they are surrounding themselves with his books, scrutinising that accursed "experience" of theirs. Everything that, in his day, Gogol described in minutest detail. I know nothing about literary studies, so cannot speak with absolute confidence. But it does look like Gogol had released a "genie out of the bottle"!'

'Steady on!' having regained the receiver, Yanovsky was adamant. 'I demand respect for my relative!'

Straight away, Pyvynsky was back on the line.

'Let's not, let's not start arguing... no need. And no one's to blame. I'm talking about something else. The day will come – and it will, no doubts about it – when all this horror stops and everybody will try to comprehend what's it all been about. Why and how has it become possible? Europe will be happy, having got away practically scot-free. America will be jubilant too, for their supremacy will've been confirmed and they'd know they have managed to put the snotty nose of a certain person out of joint. And Russia? Duh! Will she even try to work out why she's degraded down to such an ignominy? As for us… Likewise, we'll be blithe and bonny, having rebuffed such an ugly monster. Whether or not demons would've had anything to do with this, is a moot point.'

He lapsed into silence, cleared his throat, then went on:

'Tell me this, Kiril… Do you remember how *The Dead Souls* end?'

'Yeah… On my way to your place, I'd leafed through it. To tell the truth, I never got to the very end…'

'So go and read it. By all means, read it today!'

'But on the whole, I remember rather well what the whole thing had been about.'

'Still, do reread it. I insist.'

Just then the connection suddenly died…

Taras was standing by my side as if on purpose. He'd heard the entire exchange, about the ending, too. A sly grin on his face, he looked ready to get a rise out of me.

'Do you remember, Stinger, how after the lecture we all took ourselves into the corridor where we talked about the evil forces? Made assumptions about the Russian leader? And then rapidly changed the subject. So now, with everything we've learnt during the war – who is he? Have you arrived at any specific conclusion, Sherlock?'

There he was, showing all his fine teeth in a smirk.

Truth be told, I felt reluctant to delve into it, all this 'demonic' stuff. So, I did my best to be brief:

'I don't know… Taking it literally is clearly dubious. We are modern people and the days of Gogol are long past. But there is this tiny detail… Who would argue that he embodies all that's foul about the state of things today? Say what you like but it does look like a genuine connection…'

* * *

So what now, when things had turned out the way they had? I had to refresh my memory about the ending of that novel, after which to depart from Gogol's company, even if he'd been 'accompanying' me for such a long time. It did feel imperative to sharpen my evaluation of *The Dead Souls*, even if it would only be my personal, subjective opinion. So, I had to reread the final paragraphs penned by this prominent Ukrainian, the one who'd become a 'famous Russian author'. Especially after Pyvynsky'd been so insistent – a complex person himself, inextricably connected to Gogol. After all, both originated from the Myrhorod area.

I pulled a volume with *The Dead Souls* off the shelf, unhurriedly turned the pages over and found the final passage. That was how Gogol decided to finish his novel:

'Hey, troika! A bird-like troika! Who has contrived you? You could have only been born amongst the vigorous people, in a land that rebuffs wanton jokes but has spread, smooth and even, over half of the world – so go and count the verst-posts until tiny spots start dancing before your eyes.[394] And the horses, some horses you are! Is it a whirlwind that hides in those manes of yours? They discerned a familiar tune floating downwards from above, strained their copper breasts as one, and at once, and barely touching the land with their hooves, formed a line that flies through the air, inspired by God! Rus! Whither art thou dashing? Do reply! But reply she does not. The horses' bells tinkle wondrously, the shattered air thunders and turns into a tempest, whatever exists on earth flies past and recedes in the distance… And sending an askance glance in their wake, other peoples and nations yield it a right of way and let it pass.'

Wow… Would've been hard to put it more powerfully. In a word, in this poetic passage of his novel, Gogol created a graphic image of Russia as a bird-like troika stampeding in an unknown direction.

Obviously, in the day the Slavophiles had absolutely loved all this exaltation that confirmed exclusivity of the Russian people and Russia's 'special route' in history. Yet Gogol himself hadn't been pleased with this finale. He'd left it in since everybody around him was impressed. Frankly speaking, at times an author would write anything at all to ensure that their words resounded like thunder.

But in reality, based on Gogol's own admission – *The Dead Souls* had scared the readers with their portrayal of the vulgarity and pettiness ubiquitous in Russia at the time. 'Commonness of all and sundry gave the readers a fright. They were put off by a sequence of my characters, one more common than the other – and not a single point of consolation, and no place where the poor reader could relax or catch their breath, and having finished the book, one felt as if emerging from a stuffy cellar into the God's light…'

It was true, some readers and critics had been harassing Gogol for his lack of patriotism, accusing him of slandering Russia. 'My God, his enthusiasm for all that Italian nastiness![395] As soon as he lays his hands on things non-Italian,

....

[394] **Verst**: an obsolete unit of length (slightly more than one kilometre) used in the Russian Empire.

[395] In 1838-1842 Gogol lived in Rome, where he finished his most important novel.

to him, everything becomes false and senseless!' And further on, even more acerbic: 'It's a special world populated by scoundrels, the one that has never existed and cannot exist at all!' So, Gogol decided to stop them running off at the mouth. While his entire novel had portrayed a 'world of scoundrels', by the end he'd successfully sweetened the pill! Who would refuse a candy!

Whatever the real reasons, what we had now was a very powerful ending. The first image was that of a bird-like troika flying God knew where. Another one – the nations stepping aside, yielding passage to this bird-troika. It had been written 200 years ago. It's a good time now to muse on how it fits today's reality.

That Russia is flying in an unknown direction: that much was true.

But nations stepping aside? The weak ones had been forced off the road... As for the others... Either they hadn't made way, or were reluctant to have anything to do with a planetary 'bully', even if considering it wise to shift to one side...

Another eloquent detail. As soon as the full-scale invasion of Ukraine began, Putin took to travelling across Russia predominantly by train, not aboard his plane. Railroad travel, allegedly, had been more difficult in terms of surveillance. Published photos revealed that it was a *de lux* armoured train with no identifying insignia and perpetually shut windows. In places he had visited regularly, they even built secret stations and connecting lines. Witnesses testified that this train 'was hurtling forward as if possessed and all other scheduled services had to yield it passage.'

How apt was that Gogol's description at the end of *The Dead Souls*: everybody shied away into the fringes to give way to this 'bird-like troika'...

In this case, the armoured train – just like two hundred years earlier...

* * *

Not much had changed in my life – I was following the news, dutifully making entries into my pad – yet constantly keeping the main thing at the back of my mind: the need to find a universal ending for my script. How to go about it? When would I finally stumble across any semblance of an idea? For now, it was a complete blank. And so, I bided my time. Along with everyone else in our country, I was waiting for something important to happen.

One more thing, though – I forgot to mention Taras. He was also given a temporary contract – they'd liked his storyboard sketch for my script. He hadn't enlisted a visual artist, or a helpful director but gone and done the whole thing by himself. On the strength of it, he was appointed assistant to a top cameraman. Incredibly, we both had an amazing stroke of luck and ended up employed. My goodness gracious!

Coming to the window, I routinely trained my eyes on that car that, like a piece of flotsam and jetsam, was still parked in our courtyard. By now, here and there green shoots of bramble started appearing. In a short while one wouldn't be able to even approach it. What was the story of its owner? Had something really bad happened? Yet another incomplete narrative. I did say it already – one felt this lack of finality everywhere…

Since the early morning the sirens kept wailing – another blasted raid! Today, though, it sounded different: just like they'd warned us – a really massive strike. And the explosions kept booming all over.

But finally, the all-clear.

Mum let herself into my room.

'Darling, sometimes I think it will never end…'

I wanted to reply but then realised – whatever I said would be just words, just a verbal reaction. I wouldn't be able to give her a proper answer since I didn't have it myself.

Mum, meanwhile, pushed a magazine into my hands:

'Here, read it. I've circled bits in it with in red felt pen.'

It was a report from the front. Reportedly, some military sources believed that the situation had reached a point of strategic balance. 'No one has sufficient resources for the rapid breakthrough needed to crush the enemy. The war is incrementally becoming a protracted affair. Now, two options are equally possible: either we go down the route of strategic defence and running the enemy into the ground, or we agree to freeze the conflict…'

Just then Taras called:

'How are things with you? They say something's been shot down, right where you live. You OK?'

'Looks like it…'

'Has something flopped down nearby?'

'Not that I know of.'

'Did you keep your windows open?'

'From the off, so they're in one piece.'

'Same here – everyone's safe and sound, nothing fell, nothing shattered. So, it must've been elsewhere. I don't know where it happened but hope everyone's OK. We'll learn in good time.'

We stayed silent for a bit.

'Look here, do you think it will ever be over?'

'How d'ye mean "ever"? It will be over after our victory.'

After which nothing was left to add.

So, he said nothing, and after a long beat:

'Alright then. Let's talk again later.'

Right after him, Alla called:

'Here, the wreckage has just showered down onto the road!'

'Christ Almighty!'

'Thank God, nothing too big, though. And practically no damage – just one car was slightly grazed. What about your windows? This time it really roared...'

'Indeed. It was a first.'

'Sure thing. Muscovy says it's their vengeance for what the AFU's doing! Do tell me this: will any of it ever...'

I could've finished her sentence for her, so I cut her short, rather abruptly:

'I'm sorry, the kettle's whistling in the kitchen, about to explode. I'll call you back...'

Of course there was no kettle. It was the question – when would all of it end? While there existed a country populated by 140 million people, 80-odd percent of whom ardently wished us dead... Clamoured aloud even, demanding our annihilation... The people who had attacked us first but now, when drones started flying back in retaliation, developed a furious umbrage – what was going on? Horror of horrors, they became targets too! Were those people intellectually challenged? This war, though, wasn't a computer game. And thus, what would it matter if a person in power was Putin or somebody else? Today it was Putin. Tomorrow –not. But they would always elect somebody similar anyway. And the whole world was powerless to do anything about it. But perhaps, it wasn't that world wasn't all that whole? Seeing that it had irrevocably split into a 'provisional North' and a 'provisional South'?

I was rootling through my papers when a call came in. The Commander.

'How are things with you?'

This time it was me who voiced this burning question. After all, he was a military man, with a lot of experience gained during his eight years in the ATO.

'What's your take, Commander, will this ever end?..'

He said nothing in response, just grew silent. I was about to apologise and hang up.

But that was when he started speaking:

'When at the defence post, you, Kiril, mostly kept your counsel. Somehow it so happened that all the talking was done by somebody else. You, on the other hand, rather concentrated on entering stuff into your pad. Still, at times you'd make an input too. Mostly, questions. Some of those questions were really difficult to answer. That's just how you are.'

Another pause.

'Dear me. Another one of your questions. Let me be frank – I'm not happy to have to answer it. I've got things to arrange, and missions to perform. You, meanwhile, put forward a question like this. I'm not happy because now I'll spend the entire day pondering it over. Tomorrow, too. And the day after tomorrow. And all the days after that. Days, months… perhaps even years. Because even if we win… Even if we turn the tables on them… Will it ever end, you asked me. We live under a cloud of some insidious incompleteness…'

He rang off without saying goodbye.

It's Finally Clear What Denazification Was All About…

Finally, there was clarity about the meaning of that damned denazification. One could work out the idea of demilitarisation from the off. It meant that we shouldn't have anything to defend ourselves with, but at the same time they should be armed to their eyeballs and capable of pouncing on us any time at their convenience. But the abracadabra of that denazification had been something that nobody could explain coherently.

And then came an explanation. Recently, Russia had introduced a new history textbook for secondary schools. It turned out that Ukrainian Nazism was different to the one that had existed in Germany. This bastard of a phenomenon had modernised itself but had remained just that – Nazism. The first step in fighting it would be to cancel all the new names introduced by the criminal Ukrainian authorities. There shouldn't be Mazepa and Hrushevsky Prospects, Petliura and Sahaidachny streets,[396,397] but instead it was imperative to reinstate all names originating from the Soviet era. Monuments to the abovementioned persons should be destroyed and replaced with the monuments that had been in their place beforehand.

....

[396]   **Symon Petliura** (1878-1926): the Supreme Commander of the Ukrainian People's Army. He led the Ukrainian People's Republic during the Ukrainian War of Independence. Note Lenin's words in 1922: 'No Denikins, Yudenichs [leaders of the White Army] are a danger to us, their programs are outdated. We, the Bolsheviks, are frightened of only one leader – Petliura, whose program is dangerous for us. So long as he lives, so long as the uprising movement is against us, we cannot expect peace in the South [Ukraine]. Therefore, Petliura must be killed. I instruct Stalin, Dzerzhinsky and Trilisser on the part of the Cheka [the forerunner of the KGB] to accomplish this task'. Simon Petliura was killed on May 25, 1926 in Paris by a Cheka agent.

[397]   **Petro Konashevych-Sahaidachny** (1582-1622): a Ukrainian political and civic leader, hetman of the Ukrainian Zaporozhian Cossacks from 1616 to 1622, a brilliant military leader of the Polish–Lithuanian Commonwealth both on land and sea.

I tried to dig deeper. After all, if the first step was renaming, there would never be a final act. They would eliminate our blue-and-yellow flag, the trident, our state as such…

Just as I thought – the executive summary emphasised that it was important to ban all political parties of the past, vet all officials, set up filtration facilities, and resort to extradition in case of a failure to go through the process of 'de-nazification'. What was envisaged eventually was creation of new 'democratic republics', and establishment of a new 'correct' society. Also, control over mass media, the internet, the socials; applying *'soft force of the Russian world'* – including dissemination of its linguistic and cultural achievements, 'restoration of historical memory'.

The whole thing was rather light-hearted in tonality, seeing that the target audience were students. And thus, thank God, we got our degree of clarity too.

All day yesterday and today I had been watching YouTube – playing and re-playing the story about the Kyiv-Zhytomyr Motorway. This road continued towards the Ukrainian western border. As was already said on the 24th, and afterwards, that had been the road used by everyone trying to escape. It was nicknamed the 'Road of Death' later – after our 'brothers' had killed countless members of their 'fraternal' nation.

Yet some had proved 'lucky'. A local villager had not been killed but shoved into a bunker. That had been a standard practice – drive the owners into a cellar and then move into their houses and flats. It had been done to enable the occupiers to sleep at night, otherwise the situation was fraught with 'incidents'.

Same story here: they'd rounded up 130 people from the surrounding houses – men, and women. Then they'd brought in six buckets: *'Sleep and shit here, you cavemen. To yer hearts' content!*

Several days later the women asked the guards to allow the men take out what had accumulated.

'Like hell! Live with it! Maybe sometime later…'

From time to time, they'd thrown them some remains of food. And that had been their lives till they were liberated.

* * *

Each new day was bringing news. I had come across a piece about the 'evolution of Putin's worldview'.

In 2016, at a Russian Geographical Society awards ceremony to honour the best secondary-school students, Putin asked one of them: how far do Russia's borders stretch? 'Her borders,' started the student, 'come to an end at the Bering Strait that separates Russia from the USA…' Putin corrected him: 'Russia's borders never end.'[398]

In 2017 Putin declared: 'Inside our people, inside each Russian individual, is something like a nuclear reactor. This passionarity is what propels our country forward…'[399]

In 2021 Putin turned to this subject again: 'I believe in the theory of passionarity. Russia hasn't reached her peak. We are on a march, a march of development. Problems abound. However, unlike other older or aging nations, we are on the way up! We are younger by 600 years, and our younger ethnos is yet to come into its own. Russia is still in with a chance. The disintegration of the USSR isn't the whole story, it isn't the fall of our civilisation…'[400]

Whatever the narrative, residents in modern Russia had a very dim view of Gumilyov's theories, only ever viewed as new and exciting against the background of the Communist dogma as it existed in 1980-1990. Eventually, works by international authors became available in translation and Gumilyov had been superseded. However, representatives of the 'Russian elites', those on the wrong side of 70 whose youth had coincided with the peak of Gumilyov's popularity, were still receiving their sense of direction from his oeuvre.

At a regular meeting of the Valdai Discussion Club held in October of 2023, Putin was at it again: 'The war unleashed by the regime in Kyiv and directly encouraged by the West has been going on for ten years. And the aim of the special military operation is to put an end to it. The Ukrainian crisis is not a territorial conflict. The issue is much broader and more fundamental: it's about the principles on which to predicate a new world order. The West always needs an enemy. Russia is a favourite subject for Western politicos. Western elites are tirelessly creating an 'enemy image' out of anybody who behaves independently: be it China, or India, or the Arab countries. The USA forces Europe to accept its decisions on security and economy… not bothering to disguise its loutish manner; it lectures everybody on how they should behave. Who do they think

---

[398]   BBC Russian Service, 24 November 2016, https://www.bbc.com/russian/news-38093222 (accessed 06.07.2025).

[399]   Meduza, 14 November 2022, https://meduza.io/feature/2022/11/14/kazhetsya-putin-i-pravda-dumaet-chto-mozhet-pobedit-zapad-pochemu (accessed 06.07.2025). **Passionarity**: a reference to the theory of the pseudo-historian Lev Gumilyov, a consistent anti-Western Eurasian supporter who insisted that Russia's destiny was to follow her own 'special way', which would lead her to victory over the 'disintegrating West'; to attain this aim, however, members of the Russian ethnos had to demonstrate 'their preparedness to sacrifice themselves' for the sake of this shared objective…

[400]   Meduza, 14 November 2022, https://meduza.io/feature/2022/11/14/kazhetsya-putin-i-pravda-dumaet-chto-mozhet-pobedit-zapad-pochemu (accessed 06.07.2025).

they are? One feels like saying: look around yourselves, the era of colonial power is over…'[401]

That was Putin's 'world view' in a nutshell.

Recently, he had reportedly advised the Europeans to replace lettuce and tomatoes in their diets with… turnips.[402] The war, started by Europe together with their Ukrainian lickspittles, had created a temporary shortage of vegetables while the prices had skyrocketed. Putin had expressed his confidence that Europeans would switch to turnip in the nearest future. At the same time, they'd have nowhere to buy it from – except Russia. And this would create a stampede. Go and try to work out whether it was an arrogant trolling attempt or just pure drivel.

Meanwhile the International Criminal Court had issued a warrant for his arrest over the deportation of Ukrainian children to Russia – no drivel at all.

News and comments continued gushing in…

In September 2023 Zelensky made a visit to the USA. His welcome was much lower key than in the first year of the war. He himself admitted that he felt tired because of the constant need to convince our allies that Ukraine could only win with their support. No one, he said, believed in Ukraine's victory as he did… American politicians asked him about Ukraine's prospects if the USA cut off help. Zelensky replied that Ukraine would lose. And that the worst of it was that a certain part of the world was becoming used to what was happening. War fatigue was advancing like a wave. One could see it in the USA, in Europe… Zelensky grumbled that for residents of Western countries it was like a soap opera: "I don't want to watch it for the umpteenth time"…

The main conclusion in Ukraine, after 20 months of exhausting war, was profound disappointment with the Western allies – specifically with the USA, which had reduced its aid to Ukraine. To top it all, doubts had emerged inside the president's own circle, where there were supposedly people who claimed that he was turning down ideas for a more pragmatic approach to the future.

Then there was Taras's chatroom: 'The president's entourage mention Zelensky's temper. He has concluded that the Western allies have betrayed him, unable even to agree on the scope of new aid packages. One can observe a watering down of the intensity of political and moral support, hear allegations of the collective West's fatigue and the need to finish the war ASAP… We, here,

[401]   Website of the RF embassy in Poland, 5 October 2023, https://poland.mid.ru/ru/press-centre/news/vystuplenie_prezidenta_rossiyskoy_federatsii_v_v_putina_v_khode_xx_zasedaniya_mezhdunarodnogo_diskus/ (accessed 06.07.2025).

[402]   **Turnip**: a traditional Russian root vegetable.

read news like this with disappointment and resentment: the degree of the allies' involvement in our war is not so significant that they could get so tired of it... The truth is that the Western world isn't so much tired by the war as used to it.'

Zelensky also complained of people outside Ukraine that they see this war on socials and, when they get bored with it, just turn over the page. He was worried by the world's response to this war and by how this response was growing weaker. His mission, he said, was to impel the free world to perceive the war as Ukraine does: as a matter of their own survival. It could well be that in 2023 Ukraine was failing to live up to the world's expectations. But not everything gets done as quickly as some may imagine...

It's true that at the very beginning of the Russian invasion of Ukraine, it was the most powerful emotional shock for the West. The world was profoundly appalled. Missiles sent to hit peaceful cities! Mass murder of civilians... Large-scale battles unheard-of in Europe since 1945! None of it could have left a rank-and-file European viewer indifferent. But by now they had become accustomed to the fact that Ukraine was a space where people die regularly and en masse by violent death. Tragedy started morphing into statistics. What had ripped your heart apart in February of 2022 had become routine by the end of December 2023. What once disturbed the Western picture of the world had become commonplace. Unfortunately, Russian aggression against Ukraine had stopped invoking the same emotional response. Instead, the truth lay elsewhere: irrespective of the West's possible tiredness, wars of this magnitude could never be waged and won by an individual effort. The 'crisis in Ukraine' was augmenting with each passing day. And no end was in sight...

But no matter what, Zelensky remained unswerving in his belief in complete victory for Ukraine. If Ukraine failed to put a meaningful stop to Russia's attempt at hegemony, the situation, he thought, would only evolve in a downward spiral. The Third World War could then start anywhere: in Ukraine, continue in Israel, and spread to Asia. After which it would erupt elsewhere. And he didn't see any alternative but to carry on with the war. He didn't believe that Ukraine could afford to become tired of it...

* * *

Everyday realia just grab you by the throat – more and more with each day... It was confirmed even officially that the war had entered a new stage. Opinions over the sore point of the war ending, diverged: from rosy prospects of liberating the occupied territories and reinstating ourselves within the borders of 1991, to the most pessimistic ones – there would be no negotiations but instead, a "Korean option' whereby the frontline would be frozen...

In early November of 2023 Zaluzhnyi put forward some new important ideas in an article published in *The Economist*. He claimed that, just as happened in the First World War, a higher technological level has been achieved that has forced us into a dead-end. Most likely, there will be no comprehensive and successful breakthrough. The truth of the matter is that we see everything the enemy does, and, likewise, they see everything we do. He concluded, stunningly, that Ukraine is now trapped in a lasting war in which Russia has an advantage. The highest risk of an exhausting trench war is that it may well last for years, exsanguinating the Ukrainian state. At this point Zaluzhnyi made a proposal: to extricate ourselves from this impasse, we need a radically new approach. Exactly like the Chinese, who had once invented gunpowder. Finally, he concluded that we would need a powerful technological thrust.

All that meant that the stand-off was going to continue. Even if the option of demarcation – desirable for some – was accepted. In this case, we would be given guarantees, but should a new war erupt, we would fight it on our own. We did know Russia's attitude to any negotiations. She would treat their results as no more than an ordinary piece of paper. Besides, Russia would never seriously favour any freeze or negotiations. They'd grown stronger by now – why would they need this? And so, the thought of this infinitude hovering above all of us continued to hover over me…

But all that was plans and assumptions. The reality today was that a new picture was emerging. Given Russia's abundance of resources, our win over her was questionable. More and more people were talking about victory being conceivable only after changes within Russia herself. But Russia wasn't ready for any such changes. The bloody war had been going on for a long time now, with the cost being paid only by the population of one of the warring parties. People living in the other one had never even registered it properly. Worse than that – they'd been jolly and supportive of the whole thing. Which meant it would be advisable to make them take notice and pay the price. Perhaps, at least this could be a nudge in the right direction? So, what, then? Transfer the warfare onto Russia's own soil? Many spoke in favour…

As for a possibility of things in Russia unravelling any minute…There had been similar examples in Russian history: in 1917, the great empire had collapsed within a couple of days. On the other hand, the Soviet Union had taken a long time to split asunder. And when in 1991 it had finally come to pieces, for some bizarre reason no one from among its 20-million-strong body of Communists and hundreds of thousands of KGB personnel had come forward to defend it. Or yet another example, a recent one: in June of 2023 – that notorious Prigozhin's putsch! He was marching on Moscow and nobody tried to arrest his progress. In other words, it was credible – the Kremlin regime wasn't invincible. Yet, this archaic structure could survive for years to come. For all that, disintegration of the Russian Federation was impossible in the absence of preliminary liberalisation. To see Russia's break-up, we had to live long enough to hear talks of freedom and democracy within Moscow itself. Would we last that long?

Such news and comments were overwhelming us daily.

But I had something else to say, something really important for me, personally.

I had a dream, perhaps just a pie in the sky. And that was what I entered into my pad:

'I'd like to erect a monument to the "fraternal" Russian people. I know it sounds weird.

'Coming from the lips of a Ukrainian it sounds almost insane. Especially if one remembers that a monument signifies something extremely positive, a recognition of achievements…

'Yet it would be a particular type of a "monument". It would expose Russians as they've finally revealed themselves to be. It would be a monument to revulsion. A "monument of shame" addressed to this nation, a symbol of what they've done.

'Even now, some esteemed world leaders go out of their way to convince us that we and the Russians were "fraternal nations". For some reason they are turning a very blind eye to the obvious reality. For so many years now, we've been at cross purposes, at times – with weapons in our arms. And even if this war ever stops it would never mean that the arms should be thrown away.

'To those political – and not only political – leaders, too bright by half, those who keep pestering us with advice on absolutely everything, one could only reply with an invitation to come and visit us. Preferably, in a place closer to the frontline. See for yourselves what it feels like living under a daily fire from your "fraternal" people. Also, surviving winter in a flat where windows have no windowpanes. Or, perhaps, in a wooden shed, if your private house has burnt down. Go and live without electricity, or light, for at least a few days. To make it more convincing, make sure that food is scarce, or not available at all. Only then will you have the moral right to bang on about "fraternity"…'

But I got distracted, should I go back to that 'monument'?

'It would be amazing if a proper Master, a really good sculptor came forward! And could design such a "monument": an enormous beast-like brutal Russian soldier resting his foot on a pile of our children's dead bodies. Also, this figure should be on a pediment, a very tall one, inscribed with this letter Z of theirs – as the real essence of our "fraternal" nation.

'This monument should be erected in Kyiv. And beyond Kharkiv, in a barren field of some kind, there should be another one. It should consist of piled up remnants and fragments of the damaged and burnt Russian vehicles. At the bottom – heavy howitzers, with their lengthy barrels, row upon row. Then – in turn – the heavy tanks, medium ones, and the light ones on top. Infantry fighting vehicles must be lined up closer to the pinnacle. Then – something lighter still. And at the very top – the missiles poking at the sky: XXs, Iskanders, Kalibrs… The very same with which they've been killing us and still carry on killing.

'One more thing – this monument should be huge, perhaps even 100 metres high! A genuine article too, not some installation that could be taken to pieces later. A proper monument, for centuries to come!

'Also, a gigantic inscription should be etched on its base "R-U-U-U-S-S-I-I-A"!!!!'

* * *

The world, meanwhile, carried on as before. Hundreds of millions of people continued attending to their daily business.

Smaller numbers, whose affairs were more important, at times, significant, carried on too. Politicians were all where they should be, building variegated constructs. Their thoughts were concentrated on saving the world from an even scarier catastrophe.

Pope Francis, as appropriate, stayed in the Vatican and – who'd argue? – kept lobbying for peace. Recently he'd spoken online at a meeting of the All-Russian Catholic Youth in St Petersburg:

'Never forget your heritage. You are heirs to great Russia – the Russia of saints, rulers, the great Russia of Peter the First, Catherine the Great, of that empire – a great one, an enlightened one, an empire of great culture and humanity. Never renounce your great heritage as you inherit the sublime Mother Russia. Go forward with this. And thank you. Thank you for your way of life and the ability to be Russian…'[403]

Peskov, Putin's loudspeaker, emphasized that the 'pontiff knows his Russian history, and that's very good. It really is a comprehensive history, with strong roots…'[404]

....

[403] Radio Svoboda (Russian service), 29 August 2023, https://www.svoboda.org/a/kiev-vozmuschyon-slovami-papy-rimskogo-o-velikoy-rossii-/32569480.html (accessed 06.07.2025).

[404] Glavcom, 29 August 2023, https://glavcom.ua/country/society/papa-rimskij-pidihruje-putinu-chomu-oburilisja-ukrajintsi-952730.html (accessed 06.07.2025).

At the same time Ukraine's Foreign Ministry found a more precise definition for the Pope's words, calling them 'imperialist propaganda'.

Generally speaking, Pope Francis had chosen the wrong time for his address. The day before, there had been a powerful missile attack launched by the 'heirs', targeted at the cities of Ukraine. On the other hand, it would've been hard to find a good time, seeing as the attacks were taking place practically every night.

The 'stray sheep' (according to the Pope) was also in his place, in the Kremlin, attending to his daily business of bombing the neighbouring country and wiping out its population. At times, he would come up with something extraordinary – say, put explosives under a HEEP...

Ukraine was in its place too, as before, fighting for survival...

A new poll among the Russians. Even if the results might have differed from the previous surveys on some isolated scores, where it mattered, they remained stable. The same 80% were supporting the war: some 30% aggressively, some 50% passively. Another 10% found it hard to tell. Russia still hadn't grasped the land-grabbing, unfair and aggressive nature of this war.

An expert was approached: 'Do you have a global picture of things happening in Russia?'

'In a way I do. The people have been confused and browbeaten by years of propaganda. In a society where social disintegration is vast, TV has become a shortest route to comfort. By now it's dearer than your family, friends, or mates. This is the most essential element of their lives...'

Answering a question about probability of new SMOs against, say, Kazakhstan, the Baltics or Georgia, only 14-17% responded that they would never support any of it. The rest would accept the same arguments used by the Russian power today as a way to justify the current goings-on: supposedly, the 'Nazis are in power, those countries pose a threat and put the Russian-speaking population in danger.'

In today's Russia, the prevailing view dictated that neighbouring countries, Ukraine above all, were there to be subjugated and dominated, never to co-exist and cooperate with. Most Russians had no idea that Russia was physically annihilating Ukraine. They do believe in the existence of 'Nazis' on that side of the border, the official target of Russian war efforts. And the Ukrainian population is neither here nor there.

Remarkably, the Kremlin propaganda was now pushing forward a motto declaring that a loss in this war would spell the end of Russia. That was why some people said: 'I, personally, am against war and we probably were wrong to go down this route, but we cannot be against our own state... Even if our truth runs against some moral principles, still, it belongs to us.' At the same time, for the majority it was an open-and-shut case: 'It is our country, and our prestige, and we won't tolerate anyone showing us disrespect. It's impossible that we could ever lose. This war will only improve Russia's authority in the world. We are proud of our Motherland!'; 'We are Russian, which means we are right!'

So that was how it all went. Russian military units now had… political commissars, just like in the Red Army! Their brief was to indoctrinate the newly mobilised intake with these home truths: 'There were plans of an attack against Russia. NATO try to use Ukraine as their stepping stone. That is why we've started this preventive military operation. Besides, Nazis have long since entrenched themselves in Kyiv and it's our duty to liberate those put-upon people…' And of course, people were lapping it up. With genuine enthusiasm…

Another interesting thing. Today's Russian leaders had all been born in the '50s. By the time the USSR had gone to pieces, they had been about 40 years of age and had developed traits unique to this generation. They had lived through the final years of Communist rule – had lampooned it as an idea and of course, had never believed in it. They had grown to be rational and cynical. They'd become hypocrites who found it difficult to tell right from wrong. And therefore, those of about 40 now who'd ended up within the System, had no other option but to adapt to the mindset of those raggedy old men, aged 70 or more, who had ensconced themselves in power.

It should be mentioned that one of the profound differences between Russia and Ukraine was precisely that: we'd various generations represented in power. Rulers in Russia were mostly seventy-odd whereas in Ukraine, the average age was forty. They looked at the world through different lenses.

Also, there are no fanatics at the Russian top. They were people with a straightforward MO – to steal in Russia but to legalise the loot in the West. For them, severance of Western ties must have been intolerable. A curious detail: legally, Putin was trying to cover his tracks – even if he'd been quite clumsy about it. The fact had been clearly demonstrated during the public castigation of the Russian top management at the session of the Security Council on the eve of the full-scale war. Clearly, if it ever came to this, Putin had no intention of facing the music alone. And they all knew exactly what he'd been doing.

The only fanatic in the Kremlin was Putin himself. At some point that was what he'd become – a person for whom his ideas came first, ahead of his personal interests and the interests of those around him. This behaviour was not without considerable risks. When Mussolini's near circle had realised, one beautiful day, that their roads had diverged, they went and overthrew him. He then was arrested and transported from one secret location to another until liberated by Otto Skorzeny's special task force.

Putin now was over 70. Anything could happen, and nothing could be ruled out. When he had weakened and his attention lost focus, his entourage would receive a certain impetus and try to improve their future chances. If such was their wish, of course. To tell you the truth, most of those ruminations came from my imagination. The old bastard was still going strong.'

Meanwhile Prigozhin had been buried. The funeral service was announced as taking place in a particular cathedral but in reality, had been held elsewhere. The burial had been planned at this cemetery, and they had even brought in extra security. But in reality, he had been buried in a different location. As per usual, Peskov had done his best to muddy the waters, explaining that the place, time, and format of the service would've been chosen by the family. But unofficially, it was believed that going for such secrecy, the Russian authorities had tried to prevent any undesirable outbursts from the side of Prigozhin's henchmen. They've showed themselves reluctant to see a dearly departed Yevgeniy cast as a national hero. They did their best to avoid mentioning that revolt of his: give it time and he'll simply be forgotten…

* * *

Once, I was walking Taras to the metro station.

'So, now we have to fight on our own,' he was reflecting. 'And if anyone encroaches on us in the future, we'll have to withstand it under own steam, too. There'll be aid, of course. Just like there is now. It goes without saying that the stand-off – in one form or another – will not just go away. A kind of infinitude… We keep consoling ourselves like that, over and over, but the only hope is on some positive shifts within Russia herself, something that will urge them towards democracy.'

'If those shifts happen or even start…' I echoed his sentiments.

I was returning from the Metro station, deep in thought.

Just then bespectacled Gennady called from somewhere in the vicinity of Avdiivka.

'You see, if we talk in general terms, everything around us starts coming though as some infinite process.'

Exactly what Taras had just said, as if they had colluded.

'Moscow has been putting forward a litany of claims, starting from 1169 – when Andriy Bogoliubsky, Prince of Vladimir-Suzdal, expressed a desire to transfer the centre of Russia from Kyiv to his principality. His coalition stormed Kyiv. The town was ruined and pillaged, its many residents killed. In 1708, Peter the Great burned down the Hetman's capital of Baturyn, killing most of the locals. In 1775, Catherine the Great signed the manifesto "On the Liquidation of the Zaporozhian Sich..." – the mainstay of Ukrainian Cossacks. Under Alexandre II, in 1863 and 1876, appeared the circulars on curtailing the use of Ukrainian language...'

'Listen, you've mentioned infinitude. Can it really mean...'

'Just look at the Eastern front where I'm stationed now. Infinitude here is obvious. Do you even know for how long things have been going on down here?'

'From some point last year...'

'Let me be more precise – starting from April of 2022. All of it is basically concentrated around this small site...'

I heard some rumbling and explosions.

'Can you hear them hitting us? I'll tell you more – we've been trying to contain this northern neighbour of ours for four hundred years now. And who could tell how many more years we've got left. It's a form of infinity...'

The roaring was growing in volume.

'That's it!' he cried. 'They really mean it this time! Must dash, hole up some-where...'

The line went dead, he must have run for cover.

I was left in the middle of the street, unable to move. Those words – be it end-lessness or infinity – had really made an impression. Now I could hear them uttered by all and sundry.

They stuck in my head for the remainder of that day, stamped on my mind.

And only closer to the evening it occurred to me: what if those words – 'in-finity' and 'endlessness'– were the key words for the ending of my script, or at least a nudge in the right direction?

So, I opened my pad and sank into reverie.

Still So Much to Overcome...

The literary editor from Kharkiv reached me by phone.

'I'm not calling about work now, just to share some observations. Where we live, the houses are set at a distance from one another, the size of a football field between them. Recently they've cleared the rubbish left after Russia's bomb attacks, taken it all away. Then they started paving walkways, putting in flowerbeds. And today a communal service has pitched up. They unloaded the boxes, and it's turned out that inside those were planters with flowers! They set about putting it all into soil, and not just in any usual way, but arranged artistically. There are all sorts of flowers there – some already in bloom, and some that will come into flower later. It's nothing short of a miracle. The war is on, we're constantly bombed but here they were, planting the flowers! They also said: "This is to make your life a bit more beautiful. So that you could enjoy your walks. So that the kids were taken for walks around the flowerbeds that line the pathways. Your courtyard is spacious; it can take many more flowers...'

We said our goodbyes and I thought that perhaps this was another case of infinity – the endless process of planting the wonderful flowers...

* * *

To start with, it had been a hundred days of war... Then two hundred, three hundred... six hundred... It did feel rather convenient to go by hundreds. Would we really have to move into thousands?

International organisations were toting up the official lists of the dead. The figures they'd come up were 'ridiculous' – some ten or twenty thousand. Concurrently, an unofficial count had arrived at the totals that left one speechless with figures running into hundreds of thousands...

The stand-off was developing new characteristics. The option of engaging in negotiations had only really been considered at the very beginning. Yet before long it became clear that negotiating on the enemy's 'terms' was as good as agreeing to surrender. So now what? Continue fighting even if the price would be annihilation of the country and people?

At the front, there was a stalemate, the overall situation reminiscent of the First World War. Back then, trench warfare had led to a deadlock, rendering any desperate attempts to advance futile and resulting in thousands of fatal casualties. Today, likewise, any direct frontal attack was claiming lots of soldiers' lives.

Coming back to that idea of infinitude...

Their elderly ruler would live and reign from inside his bunker for another 10 or perhaps even 15 years. After all, their entire medical science was at his disposal. More to the point: who could tell what would happen after he was no more? Remember Volodin's notorious assertion: 'After Putin there'll be Putin!'?[405] Hence the question – for how much longer would things continue

---

[405] Website of the Russian State Duma, 18 June 2020, http://duma.gov.ru/news/48844/ (accessed 06.07.2025).

in the same vein? This evil could be only prevailed upon by a united world. Just like Professor Dashkevych had predicted in his lecture. The world was helping us, no argument there. But half-heartedly, indecisively. The world was coming across as wary and scared of its own shadow. The world shied away from actual fighting but, instead, was parsimonious and often late with supplies of weaponry: 'You can't do this! Nor can you do that! As for this, perhaps, someday… As to that, we yet have to decide…' To paraphrase, their reading of the situation went like this: 'You should take attacks against your infrastructure lying down, but there's no way you could use our arms for levelling your attacks at their territory!'

Then again, not the whole world was rushing forward, ready to help. 'Neutral' countries were keeping mum, and that was another source of encouragement for Putin. Yet another reason for this endlessness …

In trying to keep pace with my thoughts, I was writing as fast as I could:

'Forecasts for future developments and options come from everywhere. What else is up the Kremlin leader's sleeve?

'"Putin is a bad loser," wrote one observer. 'He's even less capable of admitting a possibility of defeat. To lose now, after everything that's taken place, would be like issuing a death sentence to himself. Following his logic, it would be better to die. He's talking tongue in cheek, of course, because "to die" is meant for those hastily mobilised, not for himself. In 2018, at a meeting of the Valdai Discussion Club, Putin made a venomous reference to an increased risk of nuclear war: "We'll go to heaven like martyrs. As for them, they'll just drop dead."[406]

'Following this incident, some even hinted that Putin was practically out of his mind. Nothing of the kind, he's sane. That was just a dig. He's a type – a petty embittered individual, ranting against everyone and everything. The one who's no idea of empathy, who's prepared to commit any crime, and is, therefore, dangerous. This is a graphic example – or an apt illustration – of ressentiment.

'Some insist that his complexes originate in his childhood. No one is completely sure about who his father was. The whole story was complicated, brushed under the carpet and shrouded in mystery. There exist two varying biographies of his, with two disparate accounts of his early years. One thing is certain, though – he's a product of St Petersburg's back streets. As a boy, he was scrawny – skin and bones, so there was nothing for it but to make as if he was a tough thug. And he strictly adhered to a rule that one should always strike first.

....

[406] BBC Russian service, 18 October 2018, https://www.bbc.com/russian/media-45903216 (accessed 06.07.2025).

'And thus, today we are saddled with a situation that's quite comfortable for the Russian liberals and their Western "colleagues": "All this trouble has been fomented by just one person! Worse, he's inveigled his compatriots into all this violence!"

'"One person has started it all?" Yeah, right. But wasn't a subsoil there rich in nutrients? Wasn't that humus fertile? Even if somebody believes that there's no such thing as collective guilt.

'Moreover, those very compatriots go weak at the knees, and act as backing vocalists, singing in many millions of voices. All of it – free from coercion, one could even say – willingly! Hooting and making wolf whistles! Bellowing "tally-ho"! Getting off on this obscurantism of theirs…

'Nowadays the world is in an absurd situation inasmuch as international institutions simply do not function. The main one among them, the UN, has the aggressor sitting on its Security Council, for all its bestial policy of anni-hilating its neighbour. And this constitutes a lethal danger not only for the victimised country but for the whole world. To add insult to injury, they've got the right to veto any relevant proposal. No, something has to be done about all of this…'

After which I was simply recording whatever came to mind. Perhaps it was a bit chaotic, my thoughts turbulently overtaking one another. My head was already bursting. But no matter, the important thing was to jot it all down, however sketchily, and then edit my own records.

'The war has been going on for so long that by now it feels endless. We have defended ourselves and stopped the enemy, that's true. But there's so much more that needs doing. We must somehow progress to victory, even if with each new day it looks more and more complicated. Eventually, we should be able to start a process of such negotiations where the results were satisfacto-ry for our side. We must, somehow, secure reparations. Start rebuilding our country. All the while we must be able to prevent another war in the future, and yet another standoff. Because that other country and its people believe in their mission, or, perhaps, have a desire – to conquer. We should… we must… there's so much of what we should and must. There's yet so much we have to overcome. We must overcome the infinity of this endless agglomeration of problems.

'Zelensky, when taking a tough stand in dealing with the global leaders, frequently heard: 'Come on! This way you'll scare the whole Europe away! The whole world!"

'So how was he supposed to have behaved as his country was drawn and quartered? Sparkle with diplomacy? Come across as a minor player?

'Well, that's how it has been until now: "We're partners, aren't we? Oh, but we are. We sure are. Would you mind waiting in reception while we agree on certain things among ourselves…"

'This, too, comes to mind. One day approximately six months before the war Zelensky quipped: "I don't want to be erased by history."[407] Most likely, he won't be, now.

'Only recently we were a sort of a periphery state. Yet now it's a question of equality – OK, let's be frank, of almost equal relations. And we are seated at the high table, not somewhere in the wings.

'May well be that we are centre-stage now for yet another reason – because we are an ancient people. But our nation is young. While our backbone is eternal, our blood is fresh and new. If only we didn't have to see too much of it spilled, lest we ended up exsanguinated.

'Our partners, reportedly, are showing signs of fatigue. So, what, then – a truce? There are those who nudge us in this direction. Or some kind of a freeze? But surely if the demarcation lines were drawn, not long afterwards there'll be another war? Any portion of our territory that remains under occupation will simply serve as a springboard for a new attack. And us? Wouldn't we want to return what's ours?

'I'm coming back to the fact that our partners are way too cautious – it may well be to their own disadvantage. They know full well that Russia is a danger to the world. Simultaneously, they are afraid of some abrupt developments on Russia's own territory. For all that, what's happening now is not a local European conflict, the problem goes much deeper. The threat hangs not only over Ukraine but over the whole world. Given the current events it's imperative to prove – even by force – that international rules do exist! As a reliable foundation for co-existence of all countries!

'This is a quote from Speaker of Parliament Stefanchuk: "After victory, Ukraine will have to identify its future philosophy. Russia won't disappear from the vicinity of our geographic borders. So, it is imperative for us to open a discussion about Ukraine's doctrine, about what shape it will take tomorrow. I believe that Ukraine tomorrow should become the eastern fortress of the civilised world. This should be reflected in rules for building cities, where each new school, each kindergarten, should be fitted out with adequate security tools and each community should comply with certain standards of defence. I don't like comparisons with Israel; the situation here is different. We are just that – the eastern outpost of civilisation…"[408]

[407]   Glavred, 25 June 2021, https://glavred.net/ukraine/hochu-chtoby-menya-istoriya-ne-sterla-zelenskiy-raskryl-svoe-glavnoe-zhelanie-10282746.html (accessed 06.07.2025).

[408]   UP, 19 June 2023, https://www.pravda.com.ua/rus/articles/2023/06/19/7407411/ (accessed 06.07.2025).

'Nowadays, the whole world has finally seen that the person described as a "successful world leader", a "lucky player in the sphere of global politics" is, in fact, an embodiment of ramshackle archaic views, an individual ready to drag in senseless constructs for hastily justifying his actions.

'And what is to be done under the circumstances?

'The only option from which everyone will benefit means ensuring that Russia has lost. For us, it's the only option. The guarantee that it will never happen again.

'But even if we win on the battlefield, it will not mean a victory on Russian soil. Russia possesses an enormous territory and bottomless resources, also, people who are prepared to put up with whatever difficulties. Therefore, the only way to win over this monster – how many times has it been said? – is through transformations within Russia herself. But how to make it happen? Not clear at all. There is this popular belief – she is unlikely to ever become a democracy. Nothing can be done to remove her founding core – whether it's authoritarianism or totalitarianism. The scenario that emerges looks rather pessimistic…'

My thoughts were somewhat jumbled… But I left it all as was, for now.

Yesterday as we'd been chatting with Taras, I casually mentioned a key words: infinitude. I'd referred to our struggle, for by now those blasted words had stuck in my head.

Today he called me back.

'Look here, don't you remember Zaluzhnyi's article in *Time*, the American one, back in September 2022?'

"Well… Give me a hint…'

'I saved it in translation on my comp and have now accidentally come across it. Zaluzhnyi was winding down his narrative with the thought that we should prepare for a long and exhausting fight. Knowing Russians the way he did, he continued, our victory would not be final. It would be a breather that would give us time to get ready for a new war.'

I was flabbergasted – it coincided precisely with my thoughts on things not being final!

'It wasn't just anyone saying this but the AFU's Commander-in-Chief! He uses different words but it's all about this very infinitude. To paraphrase – this war isn't a local conflict whereby a piece of land is snatched, then the parties sit down, talk to each other and one of them ends up the owner of that territory. No, this is a world war, existential in nature. Somebody must lose and withdraw. Better still if somebody is transformed. But when will it happen? Such questions take more than a year or two to be resolved. Or, more likely, decades.

Or even… Long story short – for now, it's fighting and infinitude. Those with access to the inside info are certain it will take at least several decades… So, you, man, are heading in the right direction, with those assessments of yours. We live under infinitude. And that's what you should write about!'

* * *

True enough, many had abandoned their optimistic hopes for a counter-offensive in the South and thus, felt disappointed – what with no breakthroughs at the front. In the autumn of 2023, the atmosphere in the Ukrainian society was very different to what it had been by the end of 2022. Back then, following the AFU's successes in Kharkiv and Kherson oblasts, Ukraine and its allies had been brimming with hopes that the Russian army would be crushed in the nearest future. However, the situation had now changed radically. Russia had managed to rebuff that offensive and launched her own attacks, advancing from several directions. Taking into account that the war had started turning into a stalemate some time earlier, the failure to launch a successful counter-offensive was another confirmation of the fact. To resolve the situation, would take some advantage which neither side could achieve. By now, both armies had an approximate parity in terms of material resources and manpower, various types of intelligence and availability of remotely piloted vehicles – the latter being a source of transparency whereby both parties knew everything about each other's positions…

Zaluzhnyi admitted recently: 'One of my principal mistakes was this. I believed that the level of losses inflicted by us on the enemy could stop them. Any other country would've been stopped in its tracks. But not the Russian Federation. Regrettably, that's the way they treat their own people. It's hard to predict how much and how many they have to lose before they stop…' [409]

The situation was changing, though. Russia tried to increase her armaments production – certain factories even worked around the clock. Also, they managed to bolster up the army with new recruits, even in the absence of a general mobilisation. The state system, too, proved quite effective in switching the economy onto a war footing. After heavy losses in 2022, the army had successfully restructured itself and launched attacks on several fronts. Overall, the society remained stable and continued demonstrating a high level of support for the authorities. The authorities, too, were 'taking pains' to keep things

----

[409] Ukrinform, 26 December 2023, https://www.ukrinform.ua/rubric-ato/3805128-zaluznij-nazvav-pomilkou-svou-viru-v-te-so-velika-kilkist-vtrat-moze-zupiniti-rf.html (accessed 06.07.2025).

under control: losses at the front, strikes at the Crimean Bridge and at Russian territory were presented as something 'normal'. Those in power were doing their best to maintain the perception of this war as something happening far away, while Russia lived her 'normal life'. There could be no doubts that the society would reconcile itself to a prospect of a dragged-out war. More than likely, they hadn't even registered the strain, not yet.

And thus, since the original concept based on Russia's quick defeat had not worked, and no one was eager to finish the war in a truce on all fronts, the concept of Ukraine's actions had to be dramatically overhauled. Ukraine now would have to move over to a situation of strategic defence and a lasting war – in a hope that the balance of forces at the front would change. And thus, we would be rebuilding our strength, replenishing our losses and also, expecting new supplies from the West – aircraft, and long-range rockets. The troops on the battlefield were tasked to take out as many hostile manpower and equipment as possible. On the home front, we had to rebuild the economy and develop our own base for military production.

It all was true. Yet life was always a sum of whopping paradoxes. After all the cataclysms, in 2023, for the majority of our citizen's daily life followed a more or less predictable pattern. People became used to regular air raids and enemy sorties over towns and cities behind the lines. The air defence system had been reinforced; businesses and offices fitted generators to help cope with the blackouts.

The country had become used to the uncertainty of its future and gradually returned to a project of rejuvenating its economy, step-by-step, and viewing donations to the military as a sufficient sign of support and solidarity with those at the frontline. Our hope depends on how we talk about this war with each other. We need to move away from heroic-optimistic stories that we will necessarily and quickly win. Such narrative forms inflated expectations, after which the frustration inevitably comes.

Yet by the end of the year, it had become clear that 'adapting to war' wasn't enough. The ongoing battle against a powerful and ruthless adversary required a higher level of support from the entire population. The problem point is that the new epoch in the war action has begun – now it's not an easy task to make people go to the fight. Thus, a new item on the agenda now was a large-scale mobilisation, in other words, hundreds of thousands of civilians. And if we take into account the families of the future mobilized, then the count would probably run into millions. Starting from 2024, the lives of all those people had changed, become more difficult. Would Ukraine cope with this new challenge? Would the middle class and big cities' residents be prepared to go to war? Would the Ukrainian authorities be able to find adequate arguments, incitements, and words of motivation for the majority of their countrymen? So much depended on this...

* * *

By 2024-25 it had become obvious that the country needed change, and quite a few things now were viewed in a new light. The sense of disappointment in our society was palpable. People had felt depressed that a quick victory hadn't happened and was unlikely to happen. To top it all, a lack of the AFU's successes and a new war that had erupted in the Gaza Strip made our allies more and more sceptical of Ukraine's war prospects. Much is still unclear in this situation. The only certainty was that the conflict would be extended, and that there would be new bloodshed – because no one could predict when either of the two sides would run out of resources: within a year, or two, or five, or more... On the other hand, if this war had taught us one thing it was that no forecasts ever played out. No one could predict the run of the wheel of fortune even if talking of the nearest months...

Taras and I were walking to my place along the Shchekavytsky Gardens.

"It's some time since I've been here last!' he exclaimed. 'Have a look! Everything's in its place, good as ever!'

True, everything was where it should be: the fountain inside, Zhovten Cinema nearby, the house topped with a spire and those huge windows – across the road. Similarly, Shchekavytska Hill and the TV tower on its hilltop were where they'd always been. Even Prince Oleh's grave hadn't moved or disappeared, still there, underneath the old observatory.

'Only our defence post is no more. Not every local would even remember now where exactly it had stood. But look here! The same "commentators" still sit on their benches, as with it as ever...'

There were no seats available nearby, so we'd plopped down a bit further away and thus could only overhear snatches of the conversation. The 'commentators' themselves looked a bit distracted, interrupting each other, never letting one another finish, hopping from one subject to another.

'Look! This war's been going on for so long, hard to even credit it!'

'D'ye remember forecasts in the beginning? All those experts, political analysts, officials – it felt like they were vying for position, competing with one another! "Two weeks – tops!" "No, three weeks – and that will be it!" To start with, they talked in weeks. Then slid into months: "In April!" "In May"!'

'But then they went directly into seasons: "In the summer!" "No, in autumn!" "Next winter's a cinch"!'

'Small wonder. They applied their technologies since it was such horror! Panic and chaos! Before anything else, people had to be calmed down with those promises. They needed at least some hope! So that the population would little-by-little get used to the new realia. And secondly, few believed that "this rain is forever"! After all the war was mostly seen as something irrational, absurd that cannot but finish fast…'

'Turned out, this view was wrong. For many people said it was rational! And it had a point to it – that of grabbing the territories! Concordantly to erase the unloved Ukraine!'

'But for how long will it go on? Stoltenberg, the former General Secretary of NATO, said: "We must be ready for a lengthy war in Ukraine. Most wars last far longer than expected when they first started. A peace accord championed by some parties should not become a reprieve for Russia enabling her to launch yet another attack. We cannot allow Russia to continue challenging security in Europe…'

'Look, guys, we've got a new team upstairs in Ukraine: a new prime minister, defence minister, National Security Council secretary, AFU commander-in-chief, head of the General Staff…'

'And? Still the same song – no sufficient shipments… The adversary holds the initiative and all we do is fight back and gradually retreat, no scope for edging forward…'

'With nice allies like this, all we can do is lose. So, who's to blame? Remember how it was in the beginning – "We're with you to the end"!'

'So right! As far as the real end goes, it's just us, the miserable wretches…'

They stayed silent, briefly, and then one of them changed the subject:

'Listen here, I'm not inventing any of this. They write about it everywhere. Intended for those who don't believe that Putin's got doubles. There was this piece on TV: he was chairing the Security Council session. And at the same time, another one on a different channel: he's laying a wreath by the monument and receiving some foreign leader! And all of it happening in parallel and live!..'

'By Jove! If only Putin… He could, when he'd first acceded to power, lead the country along a normal route! Russia would have belonged to a civilised world today! Nothing like this would've happened, and everyone would've been happy!'

'"Happy"? Don't make me laugh. A KGB creature[410] – and a "civilised trajectory"?'

....

[410]   A reference to the fact that Putin served as a KGB agent.

'Have you listened to Zelensky? He said that the Russians have allowed the evil to go on a spree – with their taciturn silence, their aloofness…'

'Hmm… It's nothing about being taciturn or aloof. The support for him is insane! For deeply traditional Russian people, Putin embodies sentiments, aspirations, and ideals as they exist in the collective consciousness. The fact that he's managed to stay in power for 25 years isn't random. In essence, Putin is a leader that is to the Russian people's liking. Judging from what they like about him, that says something about the people. Each country has the leader it deserves. What Russia deserves is Putin.'

'I don't agree with that 'deeply traditional' bit. Neither Moscow nor St Petersburg have singled themselves out all that much. Over there it's even worse than in the country! Want to know the reason? Half a million of those who are against the war left. Another half a million – military and from the deepest provinces – moved in.'

'Ah well. In the beginning, one of the most important claims that the Ukrainians laid in front of the Russians was that they hadn't come out and topple that power. Failed to change Russia through their protests… What happened was the opposite: whooping and hooting, they've expressed their approval of that power. Moreover, they've egged it on to go further…'

'And those who were against… All that much-extolled Russian military might is, in reality, based on fear and coercion. The power signalled to the population that they should sit tight and keep low. The same way as their parents and grandparents had done before them. And that's what they are doing, for when a regime gets so fossilised as to shed any fear of applying brutal force – any resistance is useless…'

'I used to think that when such cataclysms occur, presidents, tsars, and dictators are to blame. Today, I have the complete opposite opinion. The people of any country who elect a dictator, keep him in power, and who allow him to do what Putin is doing today are to blame. Russians are guilty of killing Ukrainians. Guilty of genocide. They are guilty of bringing Putin to power and that he is still sitting in the Kremlin.'

'God in Heavens. Will this jingoism ever end? How could one make sure that there were more of those "normal Russians? So that at least in several decades' time they would outnumber and oust this Putin's majority?'

'This 'rag tag'? But there's no way anyone could help! No matter what they're like and where those Russians live – be it England, Germany, or the USA. They can't be helped in principle…'

'Another interesting thing. That's what Putin says today – sort of, yeah, we've been proved not ready for a large-scale action like this but it's good we've learnt about it this way and not while being conquered by NATO. What lunacy…'

'I'm about something else entirely. It's about Bulgakov's museum on Andrew's Descent.[411] It shouldn't be closed down, whatever anyone can say. It needs a different angle, though: "Museum of Imperialist Discrimination in Ukraine as Illustrated by Mikhail Bulgakov's Heritage". People will queue to get in...'

'An interesting idea! But the name is somewhat longish...'

'And me – I was thinking – where's our singer with his guitar?'

'That one, with the shaggy hair? Haven't seen him recently... Might've headed to the front... with a guitar and all...'

'It would be wrong if he were sent to the front. I'm not sure he's fighting material. Should better be touring the troops with his songs. Would've been at least some entertainment for our lads. He did sing rather well, though, a gifted kid. Also, such a patriotic programme...'

'By the way, what's the chat with the Europeans now, concerning all this "fraternal peoples" stuff? Have you seen – Macron's done a complete about-face!'

'While Pope Francis was calling on Ukraine to put out a white flag. "The word 'negotiations' is a word of courage. When you see you're losing and things go wrong, you should have the courage to enter into negotiations."[412] Bravo! As per usual, no appeals ever get addressed to the aggressor, only to his victim.'

'I've read somewhere that, allegedly, what the Commander-in-Chief wanted in the summer of 2022 was not to liberate Kharkiv but to head towards Crimea – to get there before the Russians had put in their fortifications. But the upstairs had killed the plan...'

'Our upstairs? Or Biden's America? With his ever-frightened Sulliwan... they'd got such a scare from the Russians' nuclear threats. Do you think Medvedev is clowning around for no good reason? It was Putin who'd cast him in this role of a "nuclear fruitcake". They are unparalleled masters of the bluff... Americans should really take a leaf out of their book...'

'Who can tell what's really happened? Better say something about those reportedly all-out sanctions.'

'Pseudo-sanctions. An adequate measure would be a total ban on oil and gas supplies, blockade of the banking system, efficacious controls. But that would backfire against the global economy. What's better – to have a war going on, or to have the world's economy going to the dogs? So there...'

....

[411] **Mikhail Bulgakov** (1891-1940): a Soviet writer, playwright active in the first half of the 20th century. His *White Guard* portrayed an extremely complicated period in Ukrainian history during a couple of years after the Revolution of 1917, as witnessed by the author. A highly controversial figure in contemporary Ukraine.

[412] Maydan, 13 March 2024, http://maydan.drohobych.net/?p=146212 (accessed 06.07.2025).

They lapsed into silence. Taras and I locked our gazes: *Wow, what a performance! To waltz like that across a total range of subjects!* But the 'commentators' got back to business.

'When things are fine, or at least OK, no one asks any questions. But when trouble strikes, it's questions galore. So, now it's about this mobilisation...'

'It should've been announced at least two years earlier! We won't manage without a new wave. The enemy will never go back on their intentions, a threat that our state's gonna be wiped out is still very much there...'

'Eww... All those faults in strategic planning... If Russia, a country with a much bigger potential – that's including human resources – has been carrying out a disguised mobilisation for quite some time now and putting the country on a war footing, we should have an even stronger motivation to put it all in place ourselves!'

'And here comes the moment of truth: the problems have piled up and must be attended to urgently. That requires tough decisions. Remember what Zelensky said? "The West has lost a sense of urgency regarding military aid to Ukraine, and many Ukrainians have lost a sense of existential threat. Both must be revived. Perhaps we haven't been as successful [with the counteroffensive in 2023] as the world would've wanted us to be. Perhaps things take much longer than somebody imagined. Giving us money or weapons, you are supporting yourselves! You are protecting your children, not ours. If Russia is ready to infringe upon the rights of Ukrainians, she is ready to break the law all over the world! Putin senses weakness like a predator. But he is a predator! He picks up the smell of blood and is conscious of his own might. If he wins, he'll eat you all for afters – with all your NATOs, EUs, freedom, and democracy..."[413]

'Well, for the time being, though, it's our country that's being decimated. Intentionally, maliciously... My granddad is now ninety, he was eight when fascists had invaded. He says destructions at the time were nowhere near as extensive. Yet now it's total ruination...'

'And another thing. What's going on now is the true disintegration of the USSR! Back in 1991, it all had happened relatively peacefully. Yet then there was this wide-spread feeling that things had been too good and pain-free to be true. So, now's the time to pay this "Union" bill...'

Another pause ensued, everyone suddenly depressed.

'What's with NATO these days?'

....

[413]   Rubryka, 2 January 2024, https://rubryka.com/2024/01/02/zelenskyj-dav-interv-yu-the-economist-govoryv-pro-putina-mobilizatsiyu-ta-bytvu-za-krym/ (accessed 06. 07.2025).

'They've come up with a "wonderful" formula: "We will be able to invite Ukraine to join the alliance when the allies are all in agreement and the conditions have been met."[414] Cautious to a tee. The list of conditions may be endless. Besides, any "third-rate" puny country of no defence or military value may jump in near the end and, pardon my language, play silly buggers. Even with everyone else in favour, some tiny Putin's chum would scream: "No! I don't want them here! And that's that"!'

'Nothing doing. Countries who'd jumped aboard this gravy train in good time have been in luck. They'd read the lay of the land correctly. But we'd missed our chance, kept admiring dear Russia for too long, some even salivating in excitement. And now we have to stand against them on our own. That's our lot.'

'Why are you making all this fuss about NATO? You may be overstating its importance. It doesn't have an army. The armies of separate countries – apart from France? OK, Poland, too. The UK? It's a naval power after all. And that's the whole story. NATO can assemble an army of 300 thousand, no more. Europe is not ready for a war of attrition with Russia… And that Article 5 of theirs… Nothing about everybody coming to the rescue of an underdog and defending them till a bitter end. Each country decides for itself the shape of its involvement and the type of its assistance. Say, one of them decides to limit their aid with 5,000 helmets – and that's that. The partners are a motley crew: on the one hand, the Baltic countries who may be swallowed whole tomorrow. On the other end of the spectrum – the countries referred to as Russia's Trojan horses.'

'You know what the most interesting thing is? They don't allow shooting down missiles and drones over their territory! They say the threat is not so great as to justify irritating Russia! A gathering of impotents…

'NATO is yesterday's news! It is held back by inflated membership, endless approvals… While they are busy with this chatter, Putin will easily devour them! Before they can so much as blink! What's needed is a new organization: five to six really powerful countries without the burden of those who give nothing but only put a spoke in the wheel. And when things get hot, these countries will urgently call each other and immediately adopt a decision!'

'Look here,' that reasonable one piped up again, 'why talk like this? You feel you're entitled to all of it: the aid, the military involvement. The way it happened in the Second World War Great Britain and France interceded on behalf of Poland, if not very adequately. But nowadays it's impossible.'

....

[414]   Slovo i dilo, 11 July 2024, https://www.slovoidilo.ua/2024/07/11/novyna/polityka/pidsumkova-deklaracziya-samitu-nato-hovorytsya-pro-chlenstvo-ukrayiny (accessed 06.07.2025).

'Unfortunately, our country is a frontier between the past and the future. Between our people, and those who've ended up in the grip of one of the biggest and most absurd empires of the past. Until this empire falls irrevocably, peace along its borders is impossible in principle. You see, for as long as their current System goes on, things over here will never take a final shape. It's this phenomenon of endlessness …'

'The scariest thing would be to find ourselves completely alone. The European Union is sending 155-mm rounds not to Ukraine but to Christ only knows whom. Certain countries are openly pro-Russian… Poland is blocking our border. The American aid – that was our main source of support – has stopped altogether.'

'Rats… The West might've already wasted its best chance to help Ukraine liberate its territory completely…'

'The reason for the lack of our victory is the fact that partners were always late with the necessary weapons transfer. If Ukraine had been provided with F-16s, ATACMS, HIMARS, tanks, missiles and other things at the beginning, and not drop by drop over the course of these years, then everything would have been different. We… how should I put it… for these last few years we've been taking a master's program in international geopolitics, the price of which has been Ukrainian blood. I think this is worthy of condemnation. This is beneficial for Russia and specifically for Putin, who is getting closer to calling this war a success. Although an hour ago it looked like a failure…

'Absolutely! If all this is given now, then why was it not correct to do it two years ago?

'Democracies and European bureaucracies tend to debate decisions at length, or to make them only partially, passing the problems on to next generations. This style of decision-making encourages Russia – and not only it – to continue its expansion wishes.'

'Correct. The entire Western establishment misjudged and mishandled Vladimir Putin. As a result, he got away with so many terrible things. He invaded Georgia – there were no consequences. He seized Crimea – no consequences either. He carpet-bombed Syria – no consequences. And all this indifference and appeasement that came from the West gave Putin confidence that there would be no consequences for a full-scale invasion to Ukraine. Which he did. And if the West had been more persistent, more aggressive, and had responded to his illegal, outrageous actions earlier – the war could have been prevented. The full-scale invasion of Ukraine might not have happened. Yes, it is a heartbreaking reality – the West could have stopped this but did not.'

'Come on, guys! 'Remember what Zaluzhnyi said before his dismissal? "Our military experience, especially from 2022 – is unique. However, to secure victory, we must be constantly finding new ways and new possibilities that would make us stronger than our enemy. This victory will require a unique strategy for creating an absolutely new state system that enables technological rearmament.'[415]

'Things one hears about technology today! I've heard that if we hold out for another two years, we'll live in an era of roboticized operations! Can you imagine? Robots will replace people on a battlefield! Then there'll be no need for a mobilisation, or the rotation of manpower!'

'Ahem... robots... It won't happen tomorrow. And the people, by now, can't even imagine a world with no war. Fighting till the Russian empire falls to bits? But this isn't gonna happen tomorrow either. And so, we must live with complete uncertainty...'

'Also, the war has become mundane. In the beginning the country was whole, but now atomisation has started, everybody is out for themselves. War is a complicated thing, not everyone can endure it. Ah, 'tis true, Ukraine has it so hard. The situation is so dire...'

'Looks like it. I am 70. I may not even live long enough to see our victory – when will it ever come...? For we've got a long way yet to go, step by step...'

"Tis all true. But who will answer this main question, for now overlooked by everyone? Who's to blame that we weren't properly prepared?'

'Who do you expect to answer this?..'

They stopped their verbal thrust-and-parry for a brief moment but then resumed.

'It's clear now that this 'conflict' will never end... So, what's needed is a revision of some basic concepts. After the invasion we were learning to live with war. Now we must move on to a new reading of the situation. We need new skills: learning to live under conditions of enduring war. Perhaps, a long-lasting one. For this is a war of attrition.'

'Coming back to this frontier. Why, for example, they do want to accept Ukraine into the European Union? Perhaps they expect that it will play a fundamental role in ensuring its security? Since it looks like NATO is not on top of the situation... After all, not a single European country will ever have an army comparable to ours.'

'He-he... So, we'll become a sort of a zone where resources accumulate for a possible confrontation? It's a rather sad picture, really... In this case Ukraine won't be able to become a normal democratic state because it'll forever linger

---

[415] Mukachevo.net, 1 February 2024, https://mukachevo.net/news/zaluznyy-pered-zsu-stoyit-vyklyk-stvoryty-systemu-tekhnolohichnoho-pereozbroyennia_6021349.html (accessed 06.07.2025).

in the area of constant threats and conflicts. Democracy doesn't go hand in hand with any of this, so various limitations will be inevitable. Autocracies have it easier – they tighten the screws, empower security services, step up repressions…'

'Ah well… Let's rather concentrate on here and now. We must be patient and drop the language of victory: "Defeat Russia, dispose of Putin!" Putin or not, that's their vector. The most important point is for Ukraine to survive, and continue existing independently. And that will be our victory!'

'Let me add just one more thing. Nowadays we must position ourselves as experienced people. Thing is, as a victim you aren't terribly attractive for your partners. We must be seen, globally, as a country with an experience of survival! Partners' help is all well and good, but these things we can only achieve ourselves!'

'Righty-oh! Especially since the partners are tired. They're giving us precisely as much as it takes to survive. But have got tired even of this…'

'Oh guys, you're at it again. The West is tired…' – The 'sensible' one tried to offer his words of wisdom, yet again. – 'They, perhaps, have a right to be tired. But Ukraine has no such right. Let me tell you about one brilliant option that we could take…'

Just then a tram made a sharp turn emerging out of Shchekavytska street into Kostiantynivska, screeching loudly with all its wheels, and neither Taras nor I had heard anything else, and thus we never learned what brilliant option had been offered to everyone's attention.

* * *

For some reason Taras and I badly wanted to pay our choir guys a visit. It didn't hurt to remind them of our existence, and also, to listen to some wise talk. And why not? We'd taken a trolleybus and made it to their recording studio just in time for their lunch break. Nothing much had changed: Platonovych was as judgemental, Mykolayovych as sarcastic while Andriyovych shuttled between the two, calming them both down and trying to make them see sense.

'I'll cut straight to the chase, no point beating about the bush,' Platonovych announced bluntly. 'What's happened was a cardinal strategic miscalculation. They were told: "You're about to be torn asunder! Get ready! Do at least something!" All this in plain language, while indicating key points on the map. Banging on about a list of dates, one after another. As if one couldn't work out that Putin was changing dates to play with them, to pull even more wool over their eyes? Yet our lads proved to be such a "tough crew"! "A full-scale invasion, you say? Ha-ha! We're bursting our sides!" They were so stubbornly convinced that it was a no go!'

'They could've acted differently… 'Yes, we don't believe it's gonna happen but doing our best to get ready!' Mykolayovych added fuel to his fire.

'Argh… what's left to say?' even Andriyovych didn't argue.

'Do you remember? When the situation started approaching a gridlock, leaders of the "Global South" countries tried to get their act together…' Mykolayovych was warming up to his subject. 'There was constantly someone popping up with a new peace plan. But not a single one among them – be it the guys from Brazil, or South Africa, or Indonesia, or somebody else, ever said: "Let's end this war fairly. We have an aggressor, and we have a victim. We also have international law. And there shouldn't be any alternative interpretations about who must withdraw." But no, it was the other way round! All of them, with certain variations, were saying: "It may all be resolved very quickly! You are a victim, so you must yield. Give them this, and that, or perhaps everything they wish… And that will put an end to the conflict!" In other words: "Let's support the bigger one at the expense of the smaller one… He who's bigger and stronger has messed up a bit, that's true, but what's to be done? Nothing would work otherwise, but it must all be put to bed… The whole world is paying the price…" Such an easy and convenient solution. A tongue-in-cheek attitude. And all of this without as much as blinking an eye!'

'Just to listen to the lot of them,' by now, Platonovych was properly fired up, '"Peace! Peace! Peace! Peace and nothing else! Stop hostilities, remain at everyone's current positions, and restore an ever-lasting peace!" If one reads between the lines: "You, darling victim, should stop putting on airs and hold the whole world by the short and curlies. Can't you see how hard it is to overcome brutal force? Perhaps even impossible. So, crawl back and it will be your present to the whole world!'

'Indeed. Everybody knows how to put an end to all of this within 24 hours,' Mykolayovych picked up the thread. 'Everyone's got a plan of genius, the only one that'll work: "You see, it just so happens that Russia is an *enfant terrible* in Europe and in the world. To top it all, the "baby" is powerful and rich in resources. And now everything has reached a level beyond any joke. So, we've got to resolve it somehow. Give them those strips of your territory and be overwhelmed with happiness!" As I said – trample the victim underfoot and everything will be settled to everyone's satisfaction. Such experienced "fixers", my elbow. Whereas it should've been the opposite. If all of them got together at some bloody powwow and cried in one voice – d'ye hear? One voice! – "Putin! You've set the ball rolling, so stop it at once! You! You! Nobody else but you! In saying this to you, we've got the support of billions of those who live on our planet. The very same ones who have to suffer so much because of you. Perishing from hunger!!!" That would've been the ticket.'

'That's what I think,' by now Mykolayovych was properly wound up. 'In his fundamental conclusion, your Professor Dashkevych – you told us about his lecture more than once – was right a thousand times over: to triumph over this evil, we should all stand shoulder to shoulder. EVERYBODY!!! So that not only the civilised world came to the victim's rescue, but everyone. That's when things start changing. Otherwise, this cat-and-mouse game will go on forever. Because…'

'OK, this is now clear,' Platyonovych cut right across him. 'Better tell us about your defence post buddies in the East. Thing is, while we, here, are singing, and you're dreaming up your film, the guys out there go into battle. Are you at least in touch?'

'But of course! Looks like for now they're…'

'Just think about it!' – today keeping up wasn't easy as they all kept interrupting each other. 'Thousands of houses destroyed in Kharkiv! Tens of thousands are without a roof over their heads. Can they go on like this?'

'By the way, d'ye know how much this war is costing us? Around 150 million Dollars a day…'

'And the cereal crops? They're stealing our grain and flog it off as theirs! And what they can't nick they bomb: ports, silos, and granaries. Bomb and torch…'

'And the overall situation?' Taras could hardly put in a word in edgeways.

'Our partners have opted for a totally wrong strategy: their aid comes slowly, drop-by-drop, with long delays. Had they given all we need in one go, the situation would've been radically different. Also – they saw Russia switching over to a wartime economy and stepping up her arms production but all that time they did nothing. For us to win now requires an *effort* on their part. Perhaps a great effort. But nothing like this is in the pipeline. So, the prospects are sorrowful.' Andriyovych gave a heavy sigh. 'Neither America nor Europe are fighting this war directly. The West is fighting with their resources and at the cost of Ukrainian lives. And resources are provided in moderation. So, we must hold the line under the conditions of a metered-dose support…'

'At the same time the intensity of Russian air strikes is on the up. Russians are now using their strategic aviation, so the missile strikes against Ukraine are widescale. In Kyiv and other targeted cities, that means civilian deaths, devastation, and fires. There are days when the stench of burning hangs in the air from early in the morning till late at night,' added Platonovych. 'The country is bleeding to death…'

'It's all so horrible…' Mykolayovych sighed too.

'For so long it goes on… Will we manage to win over the most resource-rich country in the world? We won't have enough Ukrainians to do it,' it was Andriyovych's turn to sigh. 'The principal question now is what's gonna happen to the country?'

'Yeah… It will be all decided at the front. So much is still unknown. We don't know what our lives will be like in half a year, in a year or two… Russia won't give up her plans to conquer at least the Left Bank…'

Briefly, we all stayed silent.

'Oh dear…' the three of them exhaled in unison.

'Oh dear…' Taras and I echoed the sentiment.

* * *

Today was a funny day. For some reason, I felt fit for absolutely nothing – whatever I turn myself to, I was all thumbs. Then again, it was nearly evening and no one had called me! Gosh! Probably, no one needed me anymore…

Hmm… The Denis's name lit up on my mobile.

But the conversation was strange – he kept asking me about everyone, wouldn't let me put a word in. Asked me to tell him about this one, and that one – eager to know every titbit of news.

Once he'd got all those updates from me, he grew silent. I finally could ask him some of my own questions.

'How are things with you?'

'Well… sort of… better now, worse a minute later…'

'And you, you personally, how goes it?'

'I've lost two fingers on my left hand. So, now I'm… uhm… basically… a bit disabled… But this is nothing…'

'And Gennady?'

He fell quiet.

'Did you hear this? Gennady?'

Still, not a word.

I suddenly felt weird, little chills running up and down my spine.

'I am asking…'

'Gennady…' Denis cut me short. 'Gennady… it's over…'

'How d'ye mean – over? What's that you say…'

'Gennady is no more. He's in a better world now…'

God Almighty!

'Killed? What? How?'

'A shell fragment. Next to his heart. If it went straight into the heart, it would've been instantaneous. But this way… Me and guys from our division were taking him to the hospital. He could barely breathe… Unconscious… I yelled at those paramedics: "Is there hope?" They probably only answered because I yelled so much: "There's always hope… The surgeons will work it all out. Our task is to bring him there." But then they added: "... Hope... Of course... there's always hope. But if a wound is fatal"...'

I was listening to him and felt like I'd been flattened with a heavy club.

'It happened two weeks ago. I haven't called, 'cause it's hard to talk about it. Also, how could you help, you and Taras? But his family – those I called at once. Thing is, apart from giving them the news, there's also a lot of other stuff. The family must urgently come over and collect the body from the mortuary. If they take their time, that's it, they may never be able to find it. I had his details; we'd swapped those back when they sent us to Bakhmut... I got his relatives' telephone numbers, and he had mine... I now have to find somebody and leave my data with this person. The HQ have all those records, of course, but it's a different story. They have their own headaches. It's always better to have a backup...'

I was lost for words, couldn't find a thing to say.

'Well, Kiril, take care. I can't talk for long.'

True enough, his voice was trembling.

'Don't call me for a bit. It's too hard. Maybe later... We'll get in touch...'

* * *

I made another entry into my pad:

'The fate has decreed that we should have such a "neighbour". Geography can't be altered. Perhaps this neighbour will forever remain aggressive and rapacious. For centuries now, we've been following this endless road that leads towards our right to survival.

'An original Russian idea of a lightening-like war has been frustrated. So, nowadays we are fighting against a totally new set of realia. It is a war of attrition...

'We must hold on, hold our ground, and survive. And if we've achieved just this, it will be our victory.

'But for now so much is yet unknown. The picture on the battlefield changes practically daily. There will be a new attack from their side, and our counter-offensive...

'One can't rule out that the war will gravitate towards a conflict of a variable, possibly, lower intensity that would last for an indefinite term. What's certain is drone and missile attacks against the Ukrainian oblasts, constant fighting along the borders, attempts to crush our defence at certain segments of the front. This, too, will become mundane. Bombings, sporadic battles, an impossibility to develop our economy, numerous deaths. A war of this type equals infinity...'

Every now and then I would show up at the studio, for even though I was freelance, I was still a team member, no less. I had no personal desk, so simply wandered round getting a better look – it was all so interesting.

Today, in the corridor, I bumped into the boss.

'So, how are things? Is this ending taking any shape?'

I nearly jumped out of my skin.

'I'm … working out some details… Something is coming through…'

And then, against myself, blurted out:

'No luck, for now.'

I scared myself with this. The boss was sure to give me a proper dressing-down, there and then!

To my surprise, he only patted me on the shoulder.

'Keep groping around. Wrack your brain…'

He turned round and was about to walk away but then suddenly said:

'Things like that always pop out of nowhere. You are not even expecting it anymore but then – bingo! – it just drops on you from heaven. It'll be the same for you – the life will choose its moment and all will be revealed.'

* * *

Many things from before the war would never reappear. Those who'd died and were killed. We'd never realise our plans for the future, the ones we'd had then. That pure intense joy of simply being alive would not be with us either. All we had left was faith and hope.

How would it all pan out? What would happen to me, personally? To some ten people who made up my greater family? To some 100-200 people I knew – mates, friends, fellow students, acquaintances? Several millions of Kyivites? Tens of million Ukrainians? Eight billion inhabitants of our globe?

No one knew and no one could know. The world's architecture had become wobbly and no one knew how to fix it. The principal world's entity – the UN – was powerless to perform its functions. What and how would happen to this planet? Will there ever emerge at least some semblance of a world order? All that was around was this total obscurity… Infinitude…

People lived with no idea of what was to befall them the following day. Perhaps deep inside they were already getting ready to accept a world where all of this was here to stay. What was going on wasn't a sprint. It was a marathon – we would have to bear with it for a long time, so it was imperative to pace oneself.'

* * *

Lots of things were disappearing from memory. And not just details, at times it was something of essence. At a certain point in future people would like to return to their origins. 'To wind the film back' and remind themselves – what had it been like? Where had it all started? How had the events unfolded? There would be so many questions…

Which all meant that I really needed to bring this project to completion. So that all of it were recorded in 'lines of iron' – such that would never go bad or burn…

I remembered how before the war – in January and the first half of February of 2022 – I had been upset that a contemporary subject for my graduation script had been proving elusive. I had been so, so hungry for something modern, I'd worked myself into a right lather. I'd wanted something that would've been not about a 'Soviet faceted vodka glass', or the potty General Secretary Brezhnev in his declining years of rule. And not even about an 'ethnographic paradise' in the God-blessed Myrhorod area. Neither had I been swept off my feet after imaginary collisions with unique characters of Gogol's…

And that was what I'd ended up with – THIS TYPE OF MODERNITY. Was I to blame that this modernity had taken such a shape? When everything around me was boiling over and going haywire?

At times it felt that there was too much of modernity of this kind. And yet there was nothing I could do…

After all, those chronicles reflected our *lives at this point.*

It was Chronicles of Peace and War.

And that was how it had all appeared from under my pen…

Still, I wanted to believe that those notes… entries… my script – whatever one called it all – would be of value, perhaps, something to last. The memory faded, things became forgotten, they lost prominence and receded into the past – it was only human, after all. But those Chronicles, once put to paper – every little bit, were akin to a sculptor's engraving of the words on marble. Those were here to stay and to keep the memories going. Even many years later, they would be a testimonial and a reminder for the descendants.

An endless number of other things were yet to happen. 'Endless' reminded me of the infinitude of our struggle…

By now we'd been fighting for our independence for over 400 years.

But what if we started counting from the days of Kyivan Rus? The total would be much longer. Endlessness…

The war had been going on for quite some time now.

How long could it possibly go on for? How long would we have to follow this arduous route? Could it be indefinitely?

It did look likely, though, for now. Because even if we did win, ahead of us was an endless road leading into the future and so, into future battles.

Yet one couldn't live without faith. So, we believed in the promise of a future, even if we weren't sure when it would arrive.

All we knew was that it would take years, a lot of effort and painful losses until this infinity would finally come to a resolution.

* * *

Zhovten Cinema was today showing an arthouse programme. It all looked promising, had been announced a month before, and our gang had had the foresight to buy the tickets in advance. We all met by the exit from the metro station. We leisurely ambled to the boulevard separating the Upper and the Lower Vals and just sat there waiting for the show to start.

Suddenly, out of nowhere, came a weird thought which got stuck in my mind. It was ringing very distant bells, so was difficult to capture….

What if it were the scenario ending working its way into my consciousness. What if?

And so, I took myself to one side, found a bench nearby, perched myself on it and started scribbling.

All of a sudden, our crew were all around me.

'Stinger!' Spyridon and Bolik cried in unison. 'Put your bloody pad aside! Let's get into Zhovten, it'll be more comfortable to wait inside.'

'D'ye hear?' Liubchik gave her fringe a whirl. 'Don't turn your back on your own!'

'Are you coming? Or I'm not even sure what's going on.' Alla sounded hurt too.

I promptly slid the pad into my inside pocket and raced after them.

We'd nearly made it to the crossing when who did we meet, coming towards us? I could hardly believe my eyes! Professor Dashkevych! A huge package in his hand, most likely, groceries.

'By Jove!' he put his package down on the ground. 'I do remember you. You were the most active ones then. At that lecture of mine…'

We'd all made serious faces – he was, after all, a professor.

Taras gave me a wink: 'We're in luck! Who better to answer this question that's haunting us all – when will it all be over, but most importantly – how?'

'Good afternoon, dear Professor! It's so great that you recognise us. We often turn back to that lecture of yours. Especially your parting words…' Bolik beat the lot of us to it.

'You said then – that a war, or putting it milder, an attack or invasion, or even a stand-off was inevitable!' Spyridon quickly caught up with him. 'You must have had a crystal ball!'

'So, now, when this war has been going on for so long…' Taras picked up the thread. 'Which scenario, to you, looks the most likely? Or perhaps, like it often happened in the past, all analysts are wrong and life will come up with something totally unexpected, something that no one's even thinking of now?'

'True…', the professor sighed. 'History never repeats itself, and life always turns out in an unpredictable way. What's unavoidable, somehow, is that what happens in the future is unknown and unimaginable for us now.'

'Excuse us for keeping you like this,' Alla joined in. 'But your intuition, your ability to make sense of the future are extremely important to us…'

'Well…' Professor looked embarrassed. 'Such a complex question…'

'If only briefly…' I piped up too. 'What's in store for us?'

'Please, do us a favour…' we all cried in chorus.

Professor clapped his hands together, thought it over for a moment or two.

'We realise it's hard to make forecasts… But perhaps in broad-brush strokes?' He said:

'Well, then, shall we take a seat? Over there, on one of those benches.'

He didn't start talking straight away. First, out of his pocket he pulled a handkerchief, took off his glasses and unhurriedly cleaned them. Then he put the glasses back on his nose again.

'Alas, my friends… What's in store? No one can tell. I have no image of the future — everything is in such a state of limbo now. We live in times of unpredictability and chaos. And it's not my place to predict military developments or forecasts answer to questions of "when" and "how". But I'd ask something else – "what" and "in which way". Our country has been through such a rough patch. Tectonic shifts! Similar to an earthquake. During this time everything has changed and got upended. And not only in Ukraine – everywhere else in the world. In the end there is this growing understanding that humankind must radically reconsider the paradigm of their existence…'

'Yeah, everything has changed and everything is upside down…' Taras was enunciating clearly, most likely to keep the dialogue going.

'And when the change is so profound, it becomes a powerful trigger. Something that mustn't be wasted or overlooked. It should be used to advantage. The main question is – what will Ukraine be like after war? So that it finally could become a normal democracy…'

'Aren't we a democracy already?

'Of a kind. Political parties in Ukraine are always one-off leadership projects. There is always a latest "messiah" who promises to lead the nation into a happy tomorrow. Such parties shower voters with beautiful slogans and promise to do their best, even achieving the impossible. But once in the Parliament, everyone realises that those projects have had rich sponsors with specific agendas. And this is how it's done here all the time. Unfortunately, in the course of those thirty years, our citizens have learnt nothing. We must move from "messiahs" and sponsors to parties promoting ideas: liberals, social democrats, conservatives… Everything should be arranged in a new way and we must build the country on a new foundation. The state of Ukraine needs a restart! Ukraine is to be reformed in the course of war!'

The Professor grew silent and we were quiet too, digesting what we'd just heard.

A thought flashed in my mind: my gut feeling was telling me that possibly that was a longed-for ending for my script. And I, too, had to put it to good use: to say that we had to build a new country, a different country!

'These ideas are already crystallising…' the Professor went on. 'The ideas about a new state that would be based on genuinely democratic principles. We've already had one built on this quasi-basis. But we cannot return into the past.'

'A new country… Of course there's no going back!' Alla cried out. 'Only how to build it, this new one? Doesn't it require new people?'

'Where can we find them? 'Spyridon threw up his hands. 'New and honest MPs, procurators, judges, customs officers, and others… Where?'

'That's precisely the challenge. The complexity of the task. Its immensity. There are lots of questions. But not so many answers. One thing is clear, though, we've still so much to overcome! So, so much. But first of all, we must tough it out and survive.'

He took to his feet and picked up his package.

'I've told you so much. Just one last thing: we believe that we are right, and that our nation has spirituality; we have a clear understanding of which basic ideas must be translated into reality. And this is already a lot. We'll have it hard. But to cope with this task, we must all come together. Everyone! Everybody in this country!'

'Everybody…' one could barely hear Taras saying the words. 'But how difficult it will be…'

'Difficult. But for the sake of our victory, it's absolutely necessary that the whole world comes together, too. Do you remember the main conclusion of that lecture?'

'To triumph over evil, the world should stand united? Yeah, we do.'

'So there, this conclusion holds. We need unity. That's what we all need. The whole world: Europe, America, Australia, Japan… That very 'Global South', too. Working out the only true attitude. The only one that will enable a harsh and convincing response, the only response possible to those who have knocked a previously stable structure over.'

He made a brief pause.

'And another thing. It's important that you, the new generation, realise your strength and abilities. You should be aware that you'll have to step up to the plate.'

Package in hand, he lingered for a second.

'Everyone must do their duty in their place. Everyone follows their own path to Fuji. I follow mine. And you should follow yours…'

We all stood around him, thanking him for his explanation – so concise yet graphic.

'Well, you did ask for broad-brush strokes. Good day to you now.'

And with this he left.

We all were quiet for a while.

Alla was the first to come round:

'As for me, I lose my power of speech when the TV shows our dead. Especially children. The children of our country – killed like this. We did nothing to deserve such crimes. For the sake of some "borders". Because somebody is living in territory which is "not his"…'

Her eyes welled up.

'Listen up, now!' Liubchick perked up. 'It's so wrong! So's not to lose all our marbles, we should… It's imperative to find an optimistic one-liner!'

'Right!' Bolik clapped his hands. 'It's been done before. Say, this American song – 'We Shall Overcome!' It's become an unofficial anthem of everyone who's fighting for freedom and independence. The Library of Congress called it "the most powerful song of the 20th century!" It was performed by the best names in business – Pete Seeger, Joan Baez, Bruce Springsteen! They sang it at rallies, festivals, concerts!'

'"Tis true!' Spyridon was also excited. 'That's it, a magic formula for every day of war: "We shall overcome"!'

'I've recalled something too!' exclaimed Taras. 'In Prague, in 1989, in the memorable days of the "Velvet Revolution", hundreds of thousand people were singing it unison in Wenceslas Square! Laying a special emphasis on the words "I believe"!'

'In America,' Bolik picked it up, 'they even haggled over copyright. Although it's not that important, it's about something else. The court restored justice and used this wording in their verdict: "We would like to gift this song to everyone who's not indifferent to the fate of our Motherland"…'

Such weighty words! We all stopped in our tracks, looking forward to hear something existential, something carrying a lot of weight…

'Come on, now!' For a moment, Alla looked pensive. 'Can't we find something along these lines in Ukrainian?'

That was when I erupted:

'Sure, we can! It's right here!'

They all stopped, stunned, and looked at me in amazement. And I struck up:

Oh, but in a meadow a red viburnum is bending low…
Why is our glorious Ukraine now saddened so?

I paused for an instant, curious – would they pick up on it?

Spyridon and Bolik did.

But we'll go and raise this viburnum,
And we'll go and cheer up our Ukraine!
Hey-hey!

And then all of us: Liubchik, Alla, Taras, me – thundered together:

Hey-hey, we'll cheer her up!

Hooray, we did find it – something optimistic and adequate.

We trailed off and just stood there, dumfounded, looking at one another.

And – oh, miracle! – everybody's eyes shone in a heart-felt resonance with this last line of the 'Ukrainian Riflemen's Anthem'.

As for me, I'd been visited by my own miracle. That was it – the ending to my script.

All I had left was to write it down.

The city of Kyiv, Ukraine.
Planet Earth.
No date or month.
No year.
No nothing.

Instead of an Epilogue

It had been a year since our group had left our *alma mater,* the Institute. Everyone – Alla, Liubchik, Spyridon and Bolik – had found some employment, even if not in a job they'd been trained for. But that was the way things now went – there was a lot of work to go round since our country continued haemorrhaging its workforce. Arkady was still abroad. For quite some time it had been clear that he would return only when peace had been re-established. Perhaps not ever, who could tell?

Only Taras and myself worked in our specialist area, even if only in a junior capacity on somebody else's projects. Thing was, our own script, even if properly completed, was for the time being in limbo. In other words, even if we had a suitable ending for as long as this war was going on, it felt like there was still a kind of endlessness to it. Or was it rather an infinity of events? I still couldn't properly decide which word was more apt: endlessness or infinitude? Perhaps, they were synonymous?

In 2022 President Zelensky, together with the AFU and the nation, kept the country from falling. And they're still doing so. But for how long – Christ only knows. One couldn't envy the president his job – it was getting more and more complicated with each passing day, with new challenges popping up all over. Say, tonight several TU-95 strategic bombers had left, again, towards Ukraine. A couple of hours later they reached their strategic positions and launched rockets at the long-suffering Ukrainian cities. An additional aggravation was that these rockets could initially head westwards, then alter their trajectory and aim at a different target area. When we are shelled, flocks of birds rush like crazy... They don't understand what is happening and do not know in which direction they should fly to hide... But the city that has it the toughest has been Kharkiv. Its proximity to the border placed it within reach of even strikes delivered by regular artillery.

With us, everybody talked of little else but those Patriot batteries that we'd been asking for from Europe. In response we heard this: 'And what if we ourselves become a target, then what? First of all, we've got to protect ourselves...' Such a weighty argument. But they were amazed that Ukraine wouldn't understand their logic.

While the partners remained amazed, our 'brothers', in good cheer, tripled their efforts in delivering missile strikes directed at residential quarters, defence facilities, and power infrastructure. In addition, compared to a year before, their rockets had become much more precise. They'd already destroyed most power plants, and there were constant blackouts.

There was a painful shortage of artillery shells, so if our defence had crumbled, the Russians would have been able to attack big cities like Dnipro, Zaporizhzhia, and yet again, Kharkiv. The AFU were actively looking for ways that would enable them to continue holding the front.

The Commander – every time we'd bump into him – continued mulling over the issue of mobilisation: 'I'm telling you we've run out of heroes. We are left with common folk. And the normal people, they are… what's it?… afraid…' Although a minute later he would correct himself: 'What's that – no more heroes? They do exist! The ones at the frontline are heroes. But the problems are piling up. The world is not falling over itself to help us: financial aid is fitful; sanctions, or rather pseudo-sanctions, are not that effective; armaments arrive only now and then. How can one defeat Russia?'

He would then sigh heavily and add:

'In the beginning we thought: now we'll be victorious over Russia and receive reparations. Their people will very nearly repent… But what do we have now? We are nowhere near winning. Reparations? They're now debateable. Repentance is conspicuous by its absence. Why would they repent if they hardly realise that a war is going on? And against the background of their successes, they are beating their chests, they are proud of their country: "*We are fighting against the entire NATO and coming out on top*"!'

As before, the Commander didn't have a minute to spare. At this point he had to transfer the shooting range into somebody's reliable hands and then attend to some other important business. 'They've now opened some underground schools in Kharkiv. And I've been assigned a new task: I have to find a location that could house an underground repair hub. Looks like we'll have to descend below the surface of the earth. Because there's no place for us here, on the surface. Such is our destiny.'

Denis, like before, fought at the frontline. Thank God, all was good with him, although he was complaining of a certain 'misunderstanding' between those in the trenches and those on the home front. On the other hand, he was aware that now there couldn't be as many people eager to join up:

'It's the same story whatever the country. In any society people who are prepared to volunteer are a minority. It's one of the contemporary realia, although perhaps not the most glorious one…' acknowledged he. 'By the way, the nucleus of our force, those who are 40-45 years of age, aren't all that fascinated with NATO. They say its role is exaggerated. This Alliance looks increasingly like an artificial construct. Too many participants – a proper crowd. Take the coalitions before the two World wars – that was the real thing. Only a few countries were involved and even when there'd been problems, they did put their shoulder to the wheel in earnest.'

The choir guys kept holding their musical frontline – as important as any other.

The caustic Mykolayovych contemplated:

'It's possible to draw up some conclusions, even if they give little comfort. A question suggests itself to be put before the allies: in front of your very eyes a country is being mercilessly crucified. Your reaction? An inclination to observe. I don't know what an adequate response on their part may look like. But I do know that somehow it should not be like that…'

And then he continued to jeer:

'With of their over-cautious approach to supplies of arms and a fear of Russia each time she decides to rip a fart, they've landed us all in it. Russia has recovered and grown stronger, so now it would take ten times the effort to bring things to a head.'

'Well-well-well… Yet again you're looking for someone else to blame.'

'Christ! I really can't stand this soothing tone of yours, Andriyovych!'

'Right now, this America of yours – to call a spade a spade – has betrayed us!' Platonovych added oil to the flames, and in order to better drive the point home, squeezed poor Andriyovych's shoulder. 'And this shuffling they initiated with Russia… The US has turned its three-year policy towards Ukraine upside down, and now Ukraine is paying even a higher price… Everything is being arranged at its expense. It feels like this is a deal between Putin and Trump… If you're embarrassed to admit this, just keep mum!'

'Hm… A deal?' Mykolayovych grimaced. 'It looks pretty gloomy – something like a reward for Russia for the lands it has seized and the damage it has caused. And it makes Ukraine vulnerable to another attack. Quite possibly in the next few years…'

And thus, Andriyovych took their words on board and stayed silent.

Last time, as expected, Putin was re-elected yet again. Over 86% of those who had turned up gave him their vote. Pyvynsky was genuinely amazed:

'It's pretty obvious that he enjoys support of over eighty percent. But given the difficult times, why hasn't the old fart, if only for the sake of national unity, scrawled a figure of say, just over ninety? To make it look "nice and neat"? Another thing… as for Putin's health, whatever they say, he's in a pretty good nick. Quite fit to discharge his presidential duties – willingly granted to him by his subordinate Russians. Hells be there for a long time yet, perhaps in perpetuity – till the point where he experiences "absolute cessation of all vital functions". Oh dear… Where's a modern Gogol who'd describe it all?'

In his turn Yanovsky was more concerned about international affairs. He was greatly taken with Macron's about-face.

'What a trajectory! After all those sermons about "fraternal peoples" he now proposes sending troops that would defend us from those very "brothers"! He sees many moves ahead. Nowadays he's a brave leader full of innovative ideas! Suggesting a leap from the tranquil obsolete certainty of yesterday into the stringent realia of the new times. Sure thing, the allies aren't too enthusiastic about any of this. Small wonder, too… Because tomorrow is so scary that it's best to just push it out of your thoughts. If Ukraine loses it will be Europe's defeat too. Who knows – maybe America's also. Their image will be blown sky-high'.-

But Pyvynsky had snatched the phone back and started advancing his narrative: 'The "Global South" means latent ressentiment, something like a disguised rancour. Their thinking goes like this: "You've lived this 'Golden billion's' life for so long! All this luxury and numerous kicks. You've been putting on airs, looking at us down your noses and constantly lecturing us on what we should do to find a comfortable niche in the world. Like hell! Now you'll be the ones who'll get proper slaps in your well-fed mugs! And we'll sit on the fence for now, we'll watch and wait – where it's all gonna end and how it's gonna look in the future. He-he…'

But Yanovsky was not one to put up with a mobile unceremoniously snatched from his grip. He was on the line again, bellowing so loud as if he was standing next to me:

'What's your take on the Russians as an ethnic group? Are they all bad? All scum? Or worse?'

I uttered an initial sound in reply but he wasn't listening.

'Let me tell you this! There isn't such a thing as bad ethnicity. It's just that these people have found themselves living on a certain territory under a certain regime. The very same that fills their heads with all that crap, brainwashes them through television with its malicious propaganda, implants imperial narratives. They had all sorts of foul stuff there before, but now they'd been showered with much, much more! If they lived in a normal context, perhaps things might've been more sensible. I know you'll say that they've spread all over the world and remained unchanged but…'

That was when the sound disappeared. Nowadays, lines were regularly down.

But the connection was restored and I overheard him addressing Pyvynsky:
'Step to one side, will you? I need a word with Kiril.'
He spoke to me, all sotto voce:
'You know, I've got a lot of stuff to attend to… But I've put everything aside to concentrate on the most important. I've got to pick up speed.'
'Why is that?'
'You see, we live in such an unstable place, there's an airbase nearby… I don't know about you, but here the air raids are getting more and more frequent… Everything may be over in an instant. Especially for me. Say, at night you're still alive, asleep, tossing around in your bed. You get up in the morning: you've got to do this and that, chores, and all. And then – kaboom! Something has flown over and you're no more. That's why I say it's imperative to finish the most important things. Just not to leave any debts behind …'
I said nothing in response. But I felt my flesh crawl…

Walking out of the front entrance I bumped into Fedor, our own resident toughie, and a businessman.
'Hi! Long time no see! There's a couple of things to say but I'm in a bit of a rush: some important final talks. Looks like I'll get the tender to supply eggs to our glorious armed forces!..'-
'My congratulations…' The only thing I could manage to utter…
'Chronically starved for time! So, in bullet points. The question: who's to blame for that fact that we find ourselves up this particular shit creek? Was it this self-enamoured Europe, which nurtured a new variety of fascism smack under their noses? Was it our side, who simply couldn't wean themselves off the Russian teat and, when there was clarity, just wouldn't face up to it? Or America because of its super-cautious approach and later complete turn around? Thanks to all of this we've been sucked into this infinity… Yet, in 1922 it all could've been dealt with quickly! But now try and find a way out of all of this mess…'
He took a breath.
'As for the current situation… I'm not too optimistic here. Russia with Putin at her head that's started wars against us twice – in 2014 and in 2022 – will remain a threat, and not only to us. Such an enormous territory is a threat in its own right. Now it has increased its territory, and the new bit are not just strips of permafrost but most fertile land. To win over this insane country, with its resources, manpower and a people capable of eternal patience – is it even conceivable? Besides, the West has no leader who could confront Putin. And so, the threat will persist for as long as this helmsman stays in power in the Kremlin. And there is nobody in today's Russia who would dare tell him it's time to depart from the political arena. He can only be forced out by the security services or

the military. Which is doubtful. Another scenario is if the situation over there started unravelling from within. That too is hard to imagine. So, the most likely scenario is: the way your mates Pyvynsky and Yanovsky put it – to wait until this prominent "pseudo-historian" reaches the point of "natural cessation of all vital functions". Which means another 10-15 years. Enough time to blow up the entire world!'

He rushed to his car and sped off.

Every morning mum would swing herself out of bed and immediately turn on the TV, the computer, and the radio – to find out if we were still alive. Also, what if a miraculous development had taken place in Russia? What if a 'black swan' had paid them a visit – to gladden our hearts and the hearts of so many people in the world? And if it did, perhaps the clouds would have parted in an instant?

Taras once crossed paths with the Professor and grabbed his chance to share his thoughts:

'My impression is that the West is in a passive role: they're listening and burbling incomprehensibly in response to the Kremlin. And the Kremlin mean-while is enforcing its own priorities. Its tactic is as simple as the unpolished tall boot of a Russian soldier: to keep scaring NATO and carry on playing the same tune on the same fiddle ad nauseum. And so, I think: democracies get scared and yield. And what about autocracies? They are going from strength to strength… step-by step… Where will it end?'

'Well, you do know, Taras, of this axiom whereby democracies are weak by definition while autocracies are strong. Yes, democratic values are a huge asset. But as regards management… For as long as things are good, the system looks effective. But in situations of crisis, it starts coughing, backfiring, and is all but ready to die…'

'So it looks as if it's not just a question of Russia waging war against Ukraine. From a global perspective, this is a war between autocracy and democracy. What are the results? Will democracy lose?'

'There's this nuance too. Russia has no love of democracy. A few of those Russians that do, a mere handful, have done a runner, chosen survival. But Putin has got more than enough admirers among the democracies. Marines and Lucs in one country, Viktors and Sarahs elsewhere. And this is just the tip of the iceberg. Millions are supporting him without realising the true nature of this danger…

He gave a dejected wave with his hand and went on: 'I'll tell you another thing… My colleagues are now saying: "Your plan that everyone, absolutely everyone, would at once and in a friendly manner unite against the evil and defeat it was wonderful, no objections! But – you must admit – this is nothing other than an idyll... It doesn't happen in this world that everything is beautiful, is in order and is perfectly adjusted. The world is arranged in such a way that there is no justice in it by definition... In short, respected professor, your plan did not work...".'

His hands were shaking; his eyes were watering with disappointment.

'So... it didn't work... And what do we have now? A painfully familiar, ordinary thing... Appeasement – in one form or another – of the aggressor... Here you go: take it! Sew new territories to your own with coarse shoe threads, tack them onto yours with roofing nails! Everything – for you: everything! Just calm down at least for a while...'

As for my old friends from Podil, they proved to be real mates. Walking down my native Shchekavytska Street, I heard the TV tower always trying to say something supportive.

Kontraktova Ploscha was also where it should be, in its traditional place.

'Tell me, Kiril... Don't think long about it, just say as it comes into your head – which three squares in Kyiv are the fairest of them all?'

'Erm...' I could certainly guess what they were but still tried to come up with a convincing sequence.

'Sophia, Mykhailivska and Kontraktova...' But it didn't want to wait till I compiled my list. 'Watch out! If a foreign tourist asks you – well, after the war there will be herds of them – you should have your answer ready without any 'erms'. Got it?'

The Ferris wheel had overheard this conversation and gave me a toothy grin but still, considered it prudent to keep its silence. It really didn't mind it one way or the other – as long as Kyivites kept paying promptly for their rides. Because war or no war, the life went on, with all its attractions.

The same old story with the socials – they were consumed with their own passions. A certain Russian wrote this: 'To hope that Russia would be normal in the nearest future is not only naïve but DANGEROUS. The darkness intensifies. We are dealing with a malignant process that won't be arrested overnight. If only because Russia is a gigantic country, and her resources are gigantic too. It's imperative to realise that things will be bad. Not only in Russia but everywhere, the war will be spiralling upwards. And there's no one to stop it. Ukraine is incapable and the whole world behaves as if they don't know how to countermand Putin's lunacy. War seeps through every crack, and it's very easy to disappear, die in this "process". These days, to hope for the future is a most harmful thing. We must tell the truth: against this evil we are too weak. So, it's really important to realise: our situation is really shitty, and honestly we've no idea what to do…'

* * *

Oh, Christ, how time flies unleashed: soon we'll be nearing the end of 2025… Ukraine is struggling desperately to keep up with the situation. These are difficult conditions. American support – the main support we used to have – fluctuates widely: from the initial "we will be with you to the end" to the complete termination of all assistance. As for Europe, new ideas are born there. But whether beautiful and powerful words will be implemented in actions, only time will show…

Pyvynsky and Yanovsky call quite regularly, and each time they try to summarize what's happening.

'Listen… I have a few words to say on the role of personality in history…' Pyvynsky mused. 'One person umm… in America… he… that person climbed to the top – just one out of eight billion in the whole world! – and everything has started dancing off its legs! The world order is collapsing before our eyes!'

'Absolutely!' picked up Yanovsky. 'The old is already dying… But the new cannot yet be born. Be that as it may, the era of neoliberal globalization is coming to an end. The leading powers, instead of concluding new agreements for the purpose of universal economic integration, are now trying to protect their own national strategic interests…'

'That's it: everything changes rapidly… But here as far as concerns us… Whatever happens – suspension of hostilities, truce, peace agreement… and in whatever format it may take place – this is all temporary. The main words we had – infinitude and endlessness – they didn't go anywhere…'

'Uh… it used to be infinitude and endlessness, but now another word has been added: unpredictability…'

'Correct. After all, the story will not end with the departure of the current Russian leader. The break in the clouds will become possible only after the destruction of this awful empire state… God, it's even scary to think how much time it may take…'

* * *

Well… Nothing is a big change to me personally apart from one peculiar thing that happened recently. As usual, today I tried to avoid direct contact with the studio boss. It's hard to say what's the reason for all that. But this morning he spotted me from afar and came towards me like a battering ram.

'My God, how much more work is in store for you!' he balled his fists till they crackled.

I raised my eyebrows questioningly.

'You think you've put a full stop at the end of your script and that's that? Take a broader look! Search deeper!'

'What? What are ye talking about?' I still was in the dark.

'You forgot that apart from the script you've got a chronicle of events? You've been keeping it all this time. And that's what you'll now have to do – carry on with this project. For as long as the war goes on, you'll have to keep updating your chronicle!'

I just stood there, dumbstruck, lost for words.

'Who knows, perhaps you'll have to continue with it all your life… And you know what? It has to be presented not just as a chronicle. All those questions, nuances – it won't hurt to explore it all in more depth. Hear me? Explore! Investigate!'

'Me? Explore?' I knew I was shaking. 'But will I be good enough? Aren't I too young for such a task? Not experienced enough?'

'The task?' It looked like a jolt went through him too. 'Is it all only about tasks? I think, this is your… mission… now…'

'Mission? For me?..'

'No one else. That's the way it's all turned out.'

The boss gripped my hand and held it tight.

'What can you do against fate? It a mission, no less. So go on. Explore!'

He gave me a strong push and quickly walked away.

I just stood there, for a while, overwhelmed with everything that had just happened. Then my hand reached inside my jacket. The pad was already at the ready.

I opened it and wrote:

'Certain things – say, my script – may last for a long time, or even a very long time. But eventually, it all comes to an end and is completed… But other things – for example my Chronicles – cannot be finished. It's impossible to bring them to a completion for as long as the subject-matter goes on…

'The endlessness of something like this Chronicle of mine…'

'The infinitude of this Chronicle…'

Acknowledgements

I would like to express my heartfelt gratitude to all those who, in one way or another, played a crucial role in bringing this book to life.

First and foremost, I owe my deepest thanks to Peter Knip, former Director General of VNG International and a longstanding friend, whose vision and unwavering support were the driving forces behind this monumental project. Without Peter's initiative and dedication, this book would not have been possible.

A special note of appreciation goes to Marc Janssen, whose generous sponsorship and immense support were indispensable throughout this journey.

I am also profoundly grateful to Corien Pels Rijken, a masterful event organizer whose expertise in Ukrainian literature grew over time. Her efforts and insight into the intricacies of this field have greatly enriched this project.

I would like to extend my sincerest thanks to all those who contributed to the crowdfunding campaign, no matter the size of their donation. Your support means more than words can express, and it has been invaluable in ensuring the recognition of my work.

My gratitude also goes to Svetlana Payne, whose brilliant translation of this text went far beyond the linguistic; her insightful comments on the historical, political, and social contexts—rooted in her deep knowledge of Ukrainian, Russian, and Soviet realities—were indispensable. Furthermore, her expertise in translating the specific songs and verses into poetic, flowing English was nothing short of virtuosity.

Many thanks to Volodymyr Dibrova, the Harvard University lecturer, media specialist at Harvard Ukrainian Research Institute and a distinguished writer himself for his advice during the book's writing, as well as for his valuable consultations on Ukrainian literature for crowdfunding events.

A special mention must go to two exceptional editors: John Nikolson and Jack Monro. Their meticulous work and expert editing have been essential to the refinement of this text, and their contributions have added immeasurable value to the final product.

Lastly, my heartfelt thanks to the team at Glagoslav Publications, particularly Maxim Hodak, Managing Director. Their tireless management and supervision transformed this complex, multifaceted manuscript into a beautifully crafted work. I also extend my deep appreciation for their patience and understanding throughout the process.

Many thanks to the Emile Foundation, which focuses on the return of the illegally deported children of Ukraine by Russia, and the support of their families, for the logistical support rendered for the preparation of this book.

Thank you all for your invaluable contributions.

About the Author

Oleksandr Sambrus is a distinguished Ukrainian author who writes both in Ukrainian and Russian. Having graduated from Kyiv State University, he worked for some time abroad.

Upon his return to Ukraine, he played an active role in European projects aimed at transforming Ukrainian society and improving local governance. His insight into these topics found a platform in several most influential media outlets. He was also a columnist there often focusing on American subjects. He furthered his experience with studies in the USA under the program "Print press in the USA".

Sambrus began his literary journey by contributing "small form" literary pieces to various media outlets. His debut novel *The Summer Heat. Extravaganza* was quickly followed by *The Partially Consumed Marriage. A Collection of Irreconcilable Stories* – a compilation of short stories and a novelette. His subsequent novels were, *Uar-Marr. The Drama of Modern Life* and *Our Times Hero*, along with short story collection *Tsigel-tsigel…*

A steadfast observer of his nation's heartbeat, Sambrus chose to remain in Kyiv after the Russian military invasion of Ukraine on February 24, 2022. His experience during the turbulent period inspired him to write *Letter Z*, a poignant response to the war. His recent endeavours also include the theatrical play *Verbatim vs Devil*, a metaphorical representation of Ukraine's resistance.

Oleksandr Sambrus's works, characterized by a deep understanding of cultural and social dynamics, contribute to resonate with readers in Ukraine and beyond.

About the Translator

Svetlana Payne (AKA Svetlana Dubovitskaya) was born in Ternopil on the western rim of the Soviet Union in 1961 and graduated with honors in philology, foreign language teaching, and translation from Lviv University.

The illustrated compilation of poetry by Daniel Kharms in Sveta's translation, *The Charms of Harms*, appeared in 2011 and is still selling today. In a reversal of the cultural tide, in 1997 she produced a Russian translation of T. S. Eliot's *Old Possum's Book of Practical Cats*, which has now achieved gold edition status for numerous reprints. In 2012, her translation of Carol Ann Duffy's *The World's Wife* appeared, along with the libretto for *Jesus Christ Superstar* to enable a performance of this popular musical in Russian.

Sveta has translated a biography of Boris Yeltsin (*Boris Yeltsin: The Decade that Shook the World*, Glagoslav), a novel by Arseny Revazov (*Loneliness-12*, A&NN), and collaborated on two novels by the prize-winning Russian author Victor Pelevin (*S.N.U.F.F.* and *Empire V*, Gollancz).

Her most recent works, all published by Glagoslav, include a translation of Mikhail Osorgin's *Sivtsev Vrazhek* (*The Riven Heart of Moscow*), a poignant book written in the aftermath of the Revolution and the First World War; the bilingual edition *The World of Koliada*, which she translated and edited; and Oleksandr Sambrus's *Letter Z*.

Kyiv & Kyiv Region Map

Kyiv satellite towns/settlements distance to Kyiv centre:

Boryspil – 60 thousand inhabitants, 35 km.
Boryspil International Airport – 29 km.
Borodyanka – 13 thousand, 58 km.
Brovary – 110 thousand, 26 km.
Bucha – 40 thousand, 33 km.
Vasilkov – 37 thousand, 33 km.
Vasylkiv Air Base – 26 km.
Vyshgorod – (Kiev hydroelectric power station), 33 thousand, 21 km
Hostomel (Antonov) airfield – 27 km. and 10 km. to the Kyiv City Strip
Zhulyany – Kyiv International Airport, within the administrative boundaries of the city
Ivankiv – 10 thousand, 70 km.
Irpin – 70 thousand, 27 km.
Makariv – 16 thousand, 50 km.
Moshchun – 800 inhabitants, 4 km. to the Kyiv City Strip
Stoyanka – 400 inhabitants, 5 km. to the Kyiv City Strip
Chornobyl - after the 1986 accident at the Chernobyl NPP – a partially abandoned town within 30 km non-residential exclusion zone; 110 km.

Bilorus
Prypiat
Chornobyl
Maksymovychi
Krasiatychi
Ivankiv
Kukhary
Dymer
Chernihiv oblast
Novi Petrivtsi
Kalyta
Borodianka
Hostomel
Moshchun
Velyka Dymerka
Kodra
Bucha
Vorzel
Vyshhorod
Kalynivka
Irpin
Brovary
Zhurivka
Stoyanka
Kyiv
Makariv
Vyshneve
Baryshivka
Boiarka
Chabany
Boryspil
Berezan
Zhytomyr oblast
Yahotyn
Borova
Vasylkiv
Ukraynka
Pereyaslav
Fastiv
Obukhiv
Hrebinky
Rzhyschiv
Terezyne
Uzyn
Kaharlyk
Bila Tserkva
Myronivka
Skvyra
Rokytne
Bohuslav
Cherkasy oblast
Volodarka
Tarascha
Tetiiv
Stavysche
Dnipro River

Kyiv city plan

1 Podil city district

2 Obolon city district

3 Petchersk city district

4 Troyeshchina city district

5 St Sophia Cathedral

6 Kreshchatyk street/ Maidan Nezalezhnosti (Independence Square)

7 Mezhyhorska street/ Zhovten Cinema

8 Kontraktova Square

9 Kyiv-Petchersk Lavra

10 Governmental quarter [Office of the President of Ukraine, Verkhovna Rada (parliament), Cabinet of Ministers]

11 Peremohy (Victory) Avenue

12 Zhuliany (Kyiv Int. airport)

13 Trukhaniv island

14 Hydropark island

15 The Dnipro river

16 Right bank of the city

17 Left bank of the city

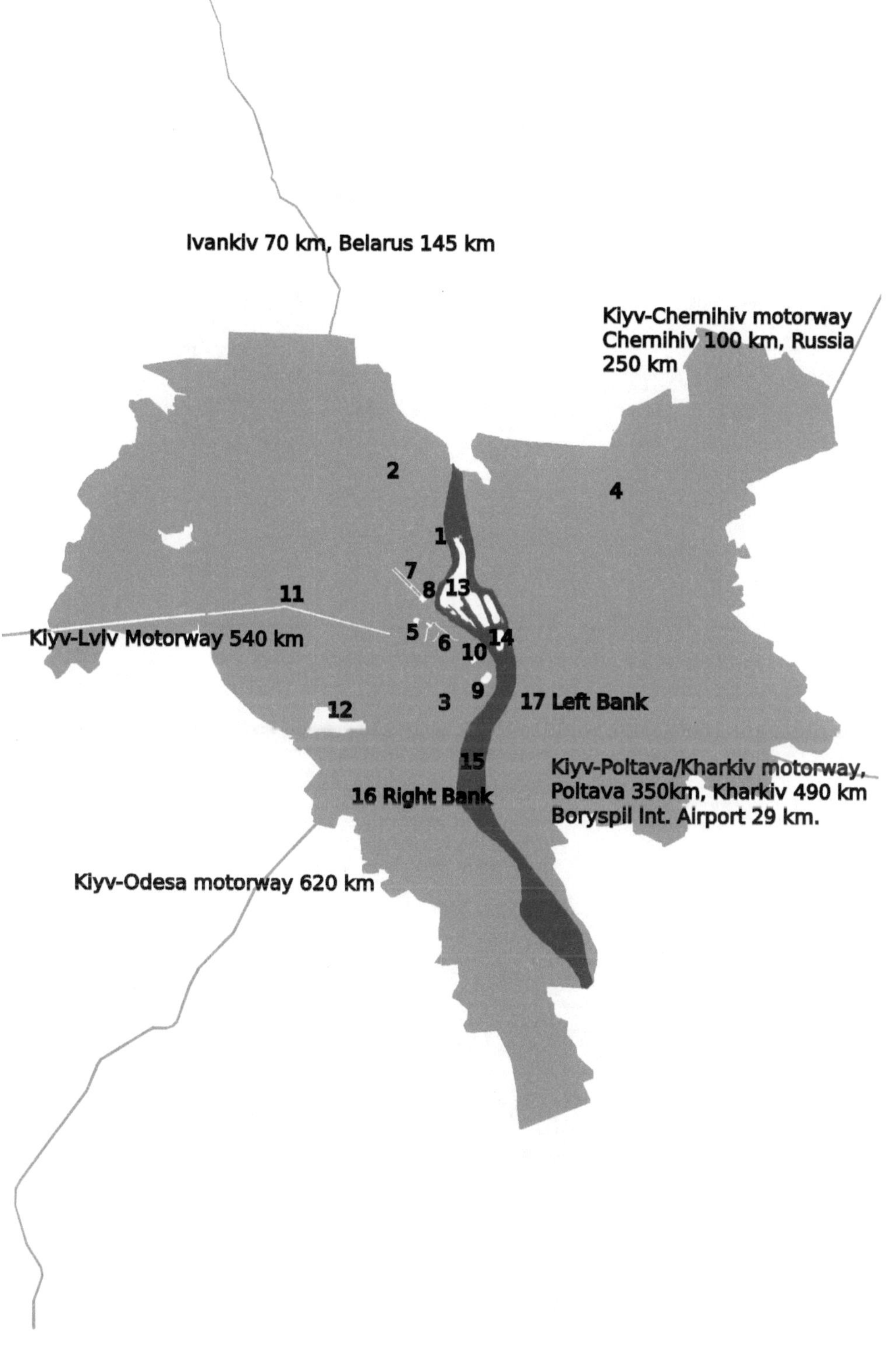

Ivankiv 70 km, Belarus 145 km
Kiyv-Chernihiv motorway
Chernihiv 100 km, Russia 250 km
2
4
1
7
8 13
11
Kiyv-Lviv Motorway 540 km
5
6
10
14
3
9
17 Left Bank
12
15
16 Right Bank
Kiyv-Poltava/Kharkiv motorway,
Poltava 350km, Kharkiv 490 km
Boryspil Int. Airport 29 km.
Kiyv-Odesa motorway 620 km